Great Short Works
of
Fyodor Dostoevsky

Great Short Works
of
Fyodor Dostoevsky

With an Introduction by
Ronald Hingley

A Perennial Classic
Harper & Row, Publishers
New York

GREAT SHORT WORKS OF FYODOR DOSTOEVSKY

Introduction, chronology, and bibliography copyright © 1968 by Ronald Hingley.

Printed in the United States of America.

The translation of *The Double* by George Bird is reprinted by permission of Indiana University Press, copyright © 1958 by Indiana University Press. The translations of "White Nights," *Notes from the Underground,* "A Gentle Creature," and "The Dream of a Ridiculous Man" by David Magarshack are reprinted by his permission. The translation of "A Disgraceful Affair" by Nora Gottlieb is reprinted by permission of The Merlin Press, Ltd., London.

First PERENNIAL CLASSIC edition published 1968 by Harper & Row, Publishers, Inc., 10 East 53rd Street, New York, N.Y. 10022.

6—74

Contents

Introduction

by Ronald Hingley

Dostoevsky, like Tolstoy, is chiefly known for his long novels—in particular for the five masterpieces which appeared in the years 1866-80, beginning with the publication of *Crime and Punishment* and continuing with *The Idiot, The Devils* (also known in English as *The Possessed*), *The Raw Youth*, and *The Brothers Karamazov*. These great fictional monuments have come to dwarf his numerous smaller-scale writings, with the result that his shorter works have either been neglected or valued too exclusively for the light which they shed on the quintet of the long novels. But though it is admittedly impossible to evaluate or understand Dostoevsky's major work properly without taking into account his less voluminous writings, it is also true that many of his shorter works are masterpieces in their own right—as it is hoped readers of the present volume may remind themselves or discover for the first time.

Among the eight stories or short novels in this collection, one item in particular has exercised a fascination over Dostoevsky's critics greater than that of all the rest combined. This is his *Memoirs from a Dark Cellar* (1864), usually known as *Notes from the Underground*, which has been called the prelude to the five-act tragedy of the long novels. But *Notes from the Underground* is a double-hinged work which opens on Dostoevsky's past as well as on his future. It sums up or brings to final shape many of the ideas and images which he had been evolving during the previous two decades, ever since he had first startled the Russian reading public with the short novel *Poor Folk* (1846). In particular, *Notes from the Underground* shows the finished portrait of a downtrodden and humiliated male figure for which the hero—or perhaps "anti-hero" would be a more accurate term—of almost every earlier work of Dostoevsky's fiction can be regarded as a preliminary sketch. Previous samples of the type represented in this

vii

book include the protagonists of *The Double* (1846) and "White Nights" (1848). These despised, feeble, usually poverty-stricken personages are all introspective in inspiration and may be considered as self-portraits of the author as seen in the distorting mirror of his imagination—portraits, that is, of the Dostoevsky who was the butt of his fellow cadets in the army engineering school where he received his main education, and who later provoked the sneers of Turgenev and other members of his literary set in St. Petersburg shortly after achieving notoriety with the publication of his first fiction. Brooding and hypersensitive by nature, Dostoevsky bitterly resented contemporaries who were richer, better-looking and more elegantly dressed than himself, that is, almost everyone he knew. Yet, while detesting the humiliations which his daily life heaped upon him, he also appears to have courted such experiences with a certain masochistic gusto, and the point is repeated again and again in his fiction (not least in *Notes from the Underground*) that pain, even toothache, can be a source of enjoyment.

Another feature of Dostoevsky's early underdog-heroes is the ease with which some of them change from the role of victim to that of dispenser of humiliation; "a mean spirit, emerging from oppression, itself becomes an oppressor," as is said of one of these victim-tyrants, the odious Foma Fomich Opiskin in *The Village of Stepanchikovo* (also known as *The Friend of the Family*) which appeared in 1859. Such a mean spirit is the unnamed "Underground Man"—the narrator of *Notes from the Underground*. He is characterized in three superb anecdotes, of which the first two depict him at the receiving end: the story of the officer who insults him at the billiard table, and the episode where he intrudes so ineptly on the farewell party of his old school friends. These incidents show Dostoevsky's gift for painful comedy to great advantage, but it is in the third episode, that describing the humiliated hero's humiliation of the prostitute Liza, which rounds the story off, showing the former victim now in the opposite role of tyrant; which in Dostoevsky's representation was merely the other side of the same coin. Many of his other heroes also oscillate up and down what has been called the "humiliation slot," alternating as recipients and purveyors of embarrassment and anguish.

Whereas the "Underground Man" is portrayed as a victim who can become an oppressor, the confrontation of victim-oppressor is presented in a more original and ingenious form in *The Double*. Here the central character is, as it were, split in two. Golyadkin senior takes the part of the helpless victim, his persecutor being his own double: Golyadkin junior, who treats him with increasing contempt and cruelty as the story proceeds to its harrowing finale. This, Dostoevsky's second published work, is by far the most significant item in the writings of his first period—the four years from his debut as an author up to his arrest as a political conspirator in 1849, which was followed by the celebrated occasion when he was led out to suffer the ordeal of a mock execution on the orders of the Emperor Nicholas I.

Though many contemporaries preferred Dostoevsky's earlier and more sentimental *Poor Folk* to *The Double*, and some modern critics have shared that view, the author himself was surely fairer to the virtues of his second work when he wrote that "the idea of it [*The Double*] was . . . more serious than anything else which I have ever carried out in literature. But [he went on] I utterly failed with the form of the story. . . . If I were to take up this idea now and to expound it anew, I should choose quite a different form." The faults of the story are sufficiently obvious, for it is long-winded, repetitive, and in parts obscure; above all, it suffers from the tendency to parody Gogol's Russian, for which reason it is perhaps better read in an excellent translation such as Mr. Bird's than in the original. With all its defects, however, *The Double* remains a considerable work of art—not least because of the successful "deadpan" treatment of a fantastic theme. This technique had already been pioneered by Gogol, for example, in his story "The Nose," which describes how a government official wakes up one morning to find that his nose is absent, and after making enquiries of the police later discovers the missing member walking about disguised as a senior civil servant. In similar manner the appearance of the second Golyadkin—a personage identical in almost every detail with the first—is treated entirely as a matter of course in the office where both Golyadkins work; no one is inclined to regard this astonishing and impossible phenomenon as in any way out of the ordinary. Here Dostoevsky again uses a Gogolian technique, but contrives to improve on his master. Particularly successful as a sample of Dostoevsky's grotesque sense of humour is the scene in the café where Golyadkin senior, having consumed a single pie, finds himself presented with a bill for eleven pies, the extra ten having been eaten by his double, who has slipped away without paying.

As this episode illustrates, *The Double* also shows Dostoevsky pioneering a theme which was to become of abiding importance in his work—that of the Scandal. "A Russian [he writes in *The Devils*, that great novel of Scandals] takes incredible delight in every kind of scandalous public upheaval." The key Scandal in *The Double* is the occasion on which Golyadkin Senior intrudes uninvited into a reception given by a high official with whose daughter he imagines himself in love. Three features are especially typical of this unhappy occasion. The first is the way in which Dostoevsky seeks to work up suspense by informing the reader that instructions have already been given not to admit the victim to the house. The second is that one of Golyadkin's humiliators at the reception is a tall, handsome officer before whom our hero feels like a complete insect; it is notable that Dostoevsky, himself the somewhat unconventional product of a military school, regularly chooses officers as purveyors of fictional humiliation—as the Underground Man also experiences, among many other underdog-heroes. Finally, it is particularly characteristic that the gate-crashing episode in *The Double* should end with the victim being thrown downstairs. An obsession with staircases, winding, narrow, dirty, and sticky is—as no reader of *Crime and Punishment* will easily forget—a staple feature of Dostoevsky's writings, whether or not one regards this (like so much else in the Russian master's work) as an anticipation of the Freudian system of symbols.

By comparison with certain improprieties in Dostoevsky's later work, the reception in *The Double* is a somewhat tame affair, but connoisseurs of the Scandal will find themselves richly catered for elsewhere in the present volume. Apart from the various outrages provoked by the Underground Man, to which reference has already been made, "A Disgraceful Affair" relates the adventures of a progressive General who intrudes uninvited on a subordinate's wedding reception and becomes so drunk that he falls face forward into a plate of blancmange and has to be put to bed in the only available place—the nuptial couch. Another vintage Scandal included in this collection occurs in *The Gambler*, where the supposedly dying Granny (thought to be safely expiring in Russia) suddenly turns up in the German spa which is the scene of the story to confront the preposterous General Zagoryansky who is counting on inheriting her fortune—which she then proceeds ostentatiously to hazard at the local gambling tables. The General's protest that she is "bringing shame on the name of Russia" by such conduct is, in its context, one of the great comic lines in literature. It may be noted in passing that all of Dostoevsky's numerous Generals are more or less comic figures; it is the junior officers who are used as purveyors of humiliation, while the senior ranks are usually its recipients.

As a work of art *The Gambler* is probably superior to any other story in the present collection, though it has naturally attracted less attention than *Notes from the Underground* because it is a less "philosophical" work and one with less cogent implications affecting Dostoevsky's longer masterpieces. It is, however, a characteristic product in that it depicts humanity under strain, as does every other item here in a greater or lesser degree—humanity in a state of tranquillity appears to have held no interest whatever for Dostoevsky. He himself could only tolerate existence provided that no element of serenity was permitted to invade his personal life. He showed great persistence (at least until his later years) in shunning peace and quiet by courting arrest, cultivating anguished love affairs, and also by frenetic gambling—his *Gambler* being an autobiographical study by an addict of his own fixation (from which he eventually recovered). As his gambling period illustrates, Dostoevsky was a seeker of strong mental sensations or, to put it differently, he usually preferred to be violently unhappy rather than to be mildly happy. As a source of such violent mental anguish, gambling and love went hand in hand in his fiction as in his life, for the heroine of *The Gambler* is modelled on the tempestuous Apollinaria Suslov who became Dostoevsky's mistress for a time and tormented him in various satisfying ways. It was, however, a less flamboyant figure—the stenographer, Anna Grigoryevna Snitkin—whom Dostoevsky married as his second wife after she had helped him to finish *The*

Gambler in time to meet a deadline, and who eventually supplied him with a secure haven against anguish both erotic and financial.

Whereas the underdog theme is more or less abandoned after *Notes from the Underground*, the Scandal remains an abiding obsession of Dostoevsky's, pullulating almost as freely in *The Brothers Karamazov* as in the writings of his youth. A third preoccupation in *Notes from the Underground* is one which does not figure at all in his earliest works: an obsessive loathing of left-wing political attitudes, whether labelled as progressive, socialist or nihilist. It was a peculiar feature of Dostoevsky's thought that he came to lump Roman Catholics with socialists as the supreme ideological heretics whom he held guilty of the grievous sin of attempting to organize humanity for its own good, and of attempting to base all human activity on the dictates of reason. Though it may seem surprising to some that either Catholics or socialists should be accused of this "crime," Dostoevsky certainly considered them culpable. The important point is that this curious fixation gave him the stimulus to write his greatest work. His violent antagonism toward socialism and reason powers the philosophical discussion with which *Notes from the Underground* begins. This section is of extreme interest as an introduction to the long novels of Dostoevsky's maturity, and it is principally because of these theoretical disquisitions that it is possible to speak of this short work as a prelude to the five-act tragedy of the mature novels. Among other works contained in this volume, *A Disgraceful Affair* (1862) and that fascinating allegory *The Dream of a Ridiculous Man* (1877) were also inspired by his irritation with "progressives."

Finally, these stories also richly illustrate Dostoevsky's attitude toward love, which is portrayed with uncanny subtlety in *The Eternal Husband* (1870) and "A Gentle Creature" (1876), besides figuring also in the earlier "White Nights" and elsewhere. As the later stories show with particular vividness, Dostoevsky saw sexual love as inextricably interwoven with a power situation in which one partner seeks to gain ascendancy over another—with especially tragic results in the case of "A Gentle Creature." Like so much else in Dostoevsky's fiction, this story was originally suggested to him by a real incident reported in the press: the suicide of a young girl who had thrown herself from a window clutching an icon. This remarkable story therefore illustrates something which is further borne out to some extent by most of Dostoevsky's other works: that the world's supreme novelist of ideas had his feet firmly on the ground of observed fact. He also wielded a formidable technique worked out over many years of persistent experiment. Of both his experiments and his achievements the present volume provides rewarding examples.

Great Short Works
of
Fyodor Dostoevsky

The Double

A Poem of St. Petersburg

TRANSLATED BY GEORGE BIRD

NOTE BY TRANSLATOR

FROM DOSTOEVSKY'S time until our own, *The Double* has been neglected by all save scholars and critics, and no translator has offered an English version in which the merits of the original are apparent. This new translation has been made in the hope that it may win for *The Double* the recognition that Dostoevsky thought it to deserve.

The present translation is from the generally published revised text of *The Double*, prepared by Dostoevsky for a new edition of his works in 1866. This revision, which consisted mainly in pruning the work as first published, was executed in haste. As a result, an improved form has been achieved at the price of creating a few obscurities, particularly towards the end of the book, and notably in Klara Olsufyevna's letter, and in details connected with the elopement. The translator has rejected the idea of collating the text with the original. These faults, if such they can be called, do not arrest the reader in mid-sentence, and far from marring the author's intention, often reinforce it, by adding slightly to the already frightening inconsequence of Mr. Golyadkin's later arguments. The manner of Mr. Golyadkin's entry into Olsufy Ivanovich's courtyard at the beginning of Chapter 13 is somewhat abrupt, though not unduly so. Several puns on the name Golyadkin are lost in English, but their loss seems preferable to renaming the hero "Mr. Poorfellow."

Chapter 1

IT WAS a little before eight when Yakov Petrovich Golyadkin, a minor civil servant, came to, yawned, stretched, and finally opened his eyes wide after a long night's rest. For two minutes or so he lay motionless in bed, like a man as yet uncertain whether he is awake or still asleep, whether all at present going on about him is reality or a continuation of his disordered dreams. But in a short while Mr. Golyadkin's senses began recording their usual everyday impressions more clearly. Everything looked back at him familiarly: the messy green walls of his little room, begrimed with soot and dust, his mahogany chest of drawers, his imitation mahogany chairs, the red painted table, the reddish oilcloth-covered ottoman patterned with sickly green flowers, and lastly the clothing he had hastily discarded the night before and thrown in a heap onto the ottoman. And then the foul, murky, grey autumnal day peered in at him through the dirty panes in such a sour, ill-humoured way, that Mr. Golyadkin had no longer any possible ground for doubting that he lay, not in some distant fairy realm, but in his own rooms on the fourth floor of a large tenement house in Shestilavochnaya Street, in the capital city of St. Petersburg. Having made a discovery of such importance, Mr. Golyadkin twitched his eyes shut again, as though regretting his recently-ended slumbers and wishing to recall them for a moment. But an instant later, having in all likelihood at last stumbled upon the one idea about which his scattered and inconsequent thoughts had been revolving, he bounded out of bed, and ran to a small round mirror standing on the chest of drawers. Although the sleepy, weak-sighted and rather bald image reflected was of so insignificant a character as to be certain of commanding no great attention at a first glance, its possessor remained well pleased with all that he beheld in the mirror.

"A fine thing it would be if there was something wrong with me today," said Mr. Golyadkin under his breath.

"A fine thing if something untoward had happened,

and a strange pimple had come up, or something equally unpleasant. Still, I don't look too bad. So far all's well."

Taking a great pleasure in the fact that all was well, Mr. Golyadkin replaced the mirror, and though barefoot and still dressed in the manner in which he was accustomed to retire to bed, ran to the window and began looking intently for something in the courtyard below. What he saw was evidently also to his satisfaction, for his face lit with a self-contented smile. Then, after first peeping behind the partition into the closet occupied by his servant Petrushka, and assuring himself of his absence, he tiptoed to the table, unlocked one of the drawers, and rummaging in a far corner, finally produced from beneath some old yellow-stained papers and other rubbish a worn green note-case, carefully opened it, and looked cautiously and with manifest enjoyment into the most remote of its secret pockets. And probably the bundle of nice green, grey, blue, red and particoloured notes it contained looked up at Mr. Golyadkin with equal approval and affability, for, with face beaming, he placed the open note-case in front of him on the table, and rubbed his hands energetically in a manner betokening extreme pleasure. At last he drew out his comforting bundle of banknotes, and for the hundredth time since the day before, began counting them, rubbing each carefully between finger and thumb.

"Seven hundred and fifty roubles in notes!" he breathed finally in a half-whisper. 'Seven hundred and fifty roubles. A good sum! A pleasant sum,' he continued, his voice trembling and somewhat weakened by the emotion of his gratification, the wad of notes clenched in his hands, and his face wreathed in smiles. "A very pleasant sum indeed! A pleasant enough sum for anyone! I'd like to see the man now who'd think it wasn't. A man can go a long way on a sum like this!"

"But what's this, where's Petrushka got to?" thought Mr. Golyadkin, and clad as he was, took another look behind the partition. Petrushka was still nowhere to be seen, but on the floor where it had been set, quite beside itself, fuming, working itself into a passion, and threatening the whole while to boil over, was the samovar; and what it was probably saying as it burred and lisped away furiously at Mr. Golyadkin in its own strange tongue was:

"Come along and fetch me, good people, I'm quite ready, you see."

"To hell with him!" thought Mr. Golyadkin. "That lazy lump is enough to drive a man out of his wits. Where's he disappeared to?"

Seething with righteous indignation, he went out into the hall, which consisted of a small corridor terminated by the door of the entrance, and caught sight of his servant surrounded by a whole crowd of menials and riff-raff. Petrushka was busy recounting something, the others were all attention. Clearly neither the subject of conversation nor the conversation itself were to Mr. Golyadkin's liking, for he immediately called to Petrushka, and went back into the room looking thoroughly displeased, and even disturbed.

"That wretch would betray anyone for a song, his master especially," he thought. "And he's betrayed me, I'm certain of that—for a miserable farthing, I wouldn't mind betting . . . Well?"

"They've brought the livery, sir."

"Put it on, and come here."

Having done so, Petrushka came into his master's room grinning foolishly. His costume was odd in the extreme. He was attired in green footman's livery, trimmed with gold braid and very much worn, that had obviously been intended for someone a good two feet taller. He held a hat decorated with green feathers and also trimmed with gold braid, and wore at his side a footman's sword in a leather scabbard. To complete the picture he had, following his favourite practice of going about in a homely state of undress, nothing on his feet.

Mr. Golyadkin inspected Petrushka thoroughly and seemed well pleased. Evidently the livery had been hired for some special occasion. And it was noticeable that Petrushka throughout the inspection watched his master with a strange air of expectancy, and followed his every move with unusual curiosity, much to Mr. Golyadkin's embarrassment.

"What about the carriage?"

"That's come too."

"For the whole day?"

"Yes. Twenty-five roubles."

"Have they brought the boots?"

"They've brought them as well."

"Blockhead! Can't you say 'Yes, they have, *sir*'?"

Having expressed his gratification at the manner in which the boots fitted, he ordered his tea and washing and shaving water to be brought. He shaved and washed with extreme care, hurriedly sipping his tea between whiles; then, setting about his final and major toilet, donned an almost new pair of trousers, a shirt front with little bronze buttons, and a waistcoat brightly adorned with nice little flowers; about his neck he tied a speckled silk cravat, and lastly pulled on a uniform jacket, carefully brushed and also nearly new. Several times while thus engaged he looked lovingly at his boots, raising first one foot then the other to admire the style, all the while muttering something to himself, and occasionally winking and making an expressive grimace as a thought occurred to him. On this particular morning however, Mr. Golyadkin was extremely preoccupied, for he scarcely noticed the grins and grimaces that Petrushka directed at him while assisting in his toilet. Finally, when he had arranged everything as it should be and was completely dressed, Mr. Golyadkin put his note-case into his pocket, took a last admiring look at Petrushka—who, having put on his boots was also quite ready—remarked that everything was done and that there was nothing to wait for, and went bustling down the stairs, his heart throbbing slightly.

A sky-blue hired carriage emblazoned with some sort of coat of arms came thundering up to the door. Petrushka, exchanging winks with the driver and some lounging bystanders, saw his master seated, and in a strange voice, being scarcely able to contain his idiotic laughter, shouted "Drive off!" sprang onto the rear footboard, and the whole equipage thundered away with a crashing and jingling in the direction of the Nevsky Prospect.

No sooner had the sky-blue carriage passed through the gateway, than Mr. Golyadkin rubbed his hands convulsively and shook with silent mirth, like a merry fellow who has managed to pull off some splendid joke, and is as pleased as Punch about it. But immediately after this gleeful outburst, the laughter on Mr. Golyadkin's face yielded to an expression that was curiously apprehensive. In spite of the damp dismal weather, he lowered both windows of the carriage and began looking anxiously to left and right at the people in the street, assuming a studied air of decorum and sobriety immediately he noticed anyone looking at him. At the junction of Liteynaya Street and the Nevsky Prospect he shuddered, having suddenly experienced a most unpleasant sensation, and screwing up his face like some unfortunate whose corn has been trodden on, pressed himself hastily, and fearfully even, into the darkest corner of his carriage. The reason for this was that he had encountered two of his colleagues, two young officials from the very department in which he himself was employed. It seemed to Mr. Golyadkin that they for their part were utterly confounded at encountering him thus, and that one of them even pointed at him. It seemed that the other called him loudly by name, which was, of course, very unbecoming in the street. Our hero concealed himself, and did not respond.

"What uncouth young men!" he thought. "What's so unusual about being in a carriage? If you need a carriage, you take one. Uncouth lot! I know them, the young hooligans. A good drubbing is what they need! Playing heads or tails with their salary and roaming the streets, that's all they're good for. I'd tell them all a thing or two . . ."

Suddenly petrified, Mr. Golyadkin left his sentence unfinished. An elegant droshky, drawn by a pair of mettlesome Kazan horses well known to Mr. Golyadkin, was rapidly overhauling his carriage on the right. The gentleman seated in the droshky, chancing to catch sight of Mr. Golyadkin's face, which the latter had rather rashly thrust out of the carriage window, seemed quite amazed at such an unlooked-for encounter, and, leaning out as far as he could, peered most interestedly and inquisitively into the very corner of the carriage in which our hero was with all haste concealing himself. The gentleman in the droshky was Andrey Filippovich, the departmental head under whom Mr. Golyadkin held the position of assistant to the chief clerk. Seeing that concealment was quite out of the question since Andrey Filippovich, having recognised him, was now staring hard at him, his eyes nearly popping out of his head, Mr. Golyadkin coloured up to the ears.

"Shall I bow? Shall I make some response? Shall I admit it's me, or shan't I?" thought our hero in indescribable anguish. "Or shall I pretend it's not me, but someone extraordinarily like me, and just look as if nothing had happened? It really isn't me, it *isn't* me, and that's all there is to it," said Mr. Golyadkin, raising his hat to Andrey Filippovich and not taking his eyes off him. Soon, however, the droshky overtook the carriage, bringing to an end the magnetic influence exerted by the gaze of the departmental head, but leaving Mr. Golyadkin blushing, smiling and muttering to himself.

"I was a fool not to respond," he thought finally. "I ought simply to have spoken up boldly, been frank and open about it. 'There it is, Andrey Filippovich, I've been asked to dinner as well!' "

Then suddenly remembering that he had made a fool of himself, our hero flushed like fire, scowled and directed at the opposite corner of the carriage a look both terrible and defiant, that was intended to reduce all his enemies instantaneously to ashes. Finally, impelled by some sudden flash of inspiration, he tugged at the cord attached to the driver's elbow, stopped the carriage, and ordered the driver to turn back to Liteynaya Street. The truth was that Mr. Golyadkin had felt an immediate need, probably for his own peace of mind, to communicate something of the greatest importance to his doctor, Krestyan Ivanovich Rutenspitz. His acquaintance with the latter was admittedly of short standing, for it had been only the week before that he had visited him for the first time, on account of certain ailments. But after all, a doctor was supposed to be like a confessor, and to hide away from him would be foolish, since it was his job to know his patient.

"Will it be all right, I wonder?" pondered our hero, alighting at the entrance of a five-storeyed house in Liteynaya Street, before which he had ordered the carriage to stop.

"Is it a right and proper time to call? Well, what does it matter?" he continued, trying as he mounted the stairs to get his breath and stop his heart from throbbing, as it invariably did on other people's staircases.

"Well, what does it matter? After all, I've come on my own account. There's nothing wrong in that. It would be stupid to go hiding away. I'll just make out I didn't come for anything special, but was just passing . . . He'll see that's as it should be."

While busy with these thoughts, Mr. Golyadkin had

reached the second floor, and stopped outside Flat No. 5 which had affixed to the door a fine copper plate with the inscription:

KRESTYAN IVANOVICH RUTENSPITZ

Physician and Surgeon

Standing before the door, our hero lost no time in assuming a countenance of due ease and affability, and prepared to pull the bell. Thus poised, he came to an immediate and rather opportune decision that it might perhaps be better to leave his visit till next day, since there was no great necessity for it at the moment. But suddenly hearing footsteps on the stairs, Mr. Golyadkin promptly reversed his new decision, and at the same time rang resolutely at Dr. Rutenspitz' bell.

Chapter 2

Dr. Rutenspitz, Physician and Surgeon, was an exceptionally healthy, albeit elderly gentleman, with bushy, greying eyebrows and side-whiskers, an expressive twinkling gaze that seemed by itself to scare away all maladies, and a high decoration upon his breast. On this particular morning, he was sitting in a comfortable armchair in his consulting room, smoking a cigar, drinking coffee brought to him by his wife herself, and now and then writing prescriptions for his patients. The last draught prescribed by him had been for an old man with haemorrhoids, and now, having seen this worthy out of a side door, he was sitting awaiting the next patient.

In walked Mr. Golyadkin.

Evidently the doctor neither expected nor wished to see Mr. Golyadkin, for he was for the moment suddenly bewildered, and unwittingly allowed a strange look, one might almost say a look of annoyance, to cross his face.

As, for his part, Mr. Golyadkin somehow almost invariably turned up at the wrong time, and lost his head the moment he had occasion to approach someone on a personal matter, so now, having failed to prepare the opening sentence which was the real stumbling-block for him at such times, he grew dreadfully confused, muttered something that might have been an apology, then, being at a loss what to do next, took a chair and sat down. Suddenly recollecting that he had not been invited to do so, and sensing the impropriety of his action, he made haste to rectify this breach of social etiquette and *bon ton* by rising from the seat he had so unceremoniously taken. Gathering his wits and realising vaguely that he had committed two blunders at once, he then resolved without delay upon committing a third, that is, he attempted an apology, muttered something with a smile, grew flushed and confused, relapsed into an expressive silence, sat down again, this time for good, and protected himself against every eventuality by means of that defiant look which possessed the singular power of enabling him to reduce all his enemies to ashes and utter destruction. It was, moreover, a look that gave full expression to Mr. Golyadkin's independence, making it clear that he had nothing to worry about, that he went his own way like anyone else, and had in any case nothing to do with what concerned other people.

Dr. Rutenspitz coughed and cleared his throat, evidently as a sign that all this met with his agreement and approval, and fixed a searching inquisitorial gaze upon Mr. Golyadkin.

"Dr. Rutenspitz," began Mr. Golyadkin, smiling, "I have come to bother you a second time, and for a second time I venture to ask your indulgence."

Mr. Golyadkin was obviously finding difficulty in selecting the right words.

"M-m yes," said Dr. Rutenspitz, allowing a stream of smoke to escape from his mouth, and placing his cigar on the table. "But you must follow my instructions, you know. I told you your treatment must take the form of a change of habits. Amuse yourself, visit your friends and acquaintances, don't grudge yourself a bottle occasionally, and keep gay company."

Still smiling, Mr. Golyadkin was quick to remark that as he saw it he was just like anyone else; he was his own master, had his amusements just like anyone else, and naturally could go to the theatre, for like other people he had the means; he was at his post in the office during the day, but was at home in the evening; he was all right, and was, as he saw fit to observe here in passing, as well off as the next man; he had his own place, and finally he had his man Petrushka. At this point Mr. Golyadkin faltered.

"M-m-m no, that's not the sort of life at all, I wasn't meaning to ask you about that," said the doctor. "What I want to know is whether you are fond of gay company, whether you have a good time. Now then, are you leading a melancholy sort of life, or a gay one?"

"Dr. Rutenspitz, I . . ."

"H-m, what I'm saying," interrupted the doctor, "is that you must radically reform your whole life, and in a sense change your character completely." Dr. Rutenspitz strongly emphasised the word 'change', and paused for a moment with a highly significant look.

"Don't fight shy of gay life," he continued. "Go to theatres, go to a club, and in any case don't be afraid of an occasional glass. It's no use staying at home. You simply mustn't."

"I like peace and quiet," said Mr. Golyadkin, throwing a meaning glance at the doctor, and obviously seeking the words that would best render his thoughts. "There's no one at my place except myself and Petrushka—I mean my man, Doctor. What I mean is, Doctor, I go my own way, my own peculiar way, Doctor. I keep to myself, and so far as I can see am not dependent on anyone. Also I go for walks, Doctor."

"What's that? . . . Yes. But there's not much pleasure in that at the moment. The weather is terrible."

"Yes, Doctor. But as I believe I have already had the honour of explaining, although I am a quiet sort of person, my path is separate from other people's. The road of life is a broad one, Doctor . . . What I mean, what I mean to say is . . . Forgive me, Doctor, I have no gift for fine phrases."

"M-m-m, you were saying . . ."

"I say you must forgive me, Doctor, for having so far as I can see no gift for fine phrases," said Mr. Golyadkin in a half-offended tone, now a little lost and perplexed. "In this respect, Doctor, I am not as other people," he added with a peculiar sort of smile. "I'm no great talker. I haven't learnt to embellish what I say. But to make up for it, I'm a man of action, a man of action, Doctor."

"M-m-m . . . What's that? . . . So you're a man of action," responded the doctor. Then for a moment there was silence, while the doctor stared in a strange and in-credulous way at Mr. Golyadkin, and the latter, in turn, looked incredulously askance at the doctor.

"Peace is what I like, Doctor, not the tumult of so-ciety," continued Mr. Golyadkin, still in his former tone, a little exasperated and bewildered by the doctor's stub-born silence. "With most people—in society, I mean—you have to know how to bow and scrape." (Here Mr. Golyadkin did a bow.) "That's expected of you in society. You're asked to make puns, too, if you please, pay scented compliments, that's what's expected of you. But I haven't learnt to do this, Doctor—I haven't learnt all these cun-ning ways, I've had no time for them. I'm a plain simple man. There's no outward show about me. On this point, Doctor, I lay down my arms—or to continue the meta-phor, I surrender."

All this, of course, was delivered in a manner that made it quite clear that our hero had no regrets about his metaphorical surrender and his inability to acquire cunning ways, but entirely the reverse. While listening to him, the doctor, his face unpleasantly grimaced, kept his eyes upon the floor, as if preoccupied with a presenti-ment of some sort.

Mr. Golyadkin's tirade was followed by a rather long and significant silence. At length, in a low voice, the doc-tor said:

"You seem to have wandered a little off the subject. I confess I have not quite followed you."

"I'm not one for fine phrases, Doctor," said Mr. Golyad-kin, this time in an abrupt incisive tone. "I am not, as I have already had the honour of informing you, Doctor, one for fine phrases."

"H-m-m!"

"Dr. Rutenspitz, when I came in, I began by apologiz-ing. Now I repeat what I said before, and again ask your indulgence for a time." Mr. Golyadkin began once more in a low taut expressive voice, that dwelt upon every point, and had a solemn ring about it. "Dr. Rutenspitz, I have nothing to conceal from you. I am a little man, you know that yourself. But fortunately I have no regrets about be-ing a little man. Quite the contrary, Doctor, and to be completely frank, I'm even proud of being a little man and not a big one. Not being an intriguer—that's some-thing else I'm proud of. I don't do things on the quiet, but openly, without a lot of artifice, and though I could do my share of harm, and do it very well too, and though I even know whom to harm and how to do it, I don't sully myself with these things, I wash my hands of them, Doctor. I wash my hands of them, Doctor!" For a moment Mr. Golyadkin relapsed into an expressive silence. He had been speaking with mild enthusiasm.

"I go about straight and openly," he continued suddenly. "I don't go beating about the bush, because that's a way of doing things I scorn, and leave to others. I don't go trying to humiliate those who maybe are better than you or I . . . That is, better than I, I didn't mean to say 'better than you,' Doctor. I don't like odd words here and there, miserable double-dealing I can't stand, slander and gossip I abominate. The only time I put on a mask is when I go to a masquerade, I don't go about in front of people in one every day. I will merely ask, Doctor, how *you* would take revenge on your worst enemy, or him you regarded as such?" concluded Mr. Golyadkin, glancing defiantly at Dr. Rutenspitz.

But though Mr. Golyadkin had spoken throughout with the utmost clarity, precision and assurance, weighing his words and relying on those calculated to produce the best effect, he was now looking at the doctor with ever-growing uneasiness. He was all attention, timidly awaiting the doctor's reply with a sick uneasy feeling of impatience. But Dr. Rutenspitz, to Mr. Golyadkin's surprise and utter consternation, muttered something under his breath, pulled his chair up to the table, observed dryly, but none the less politely, something to the effect that his time was of value to him, and that somehow he did not quite follow; he was prepared to be of assistance so far as lay in his power, and to the extent of his abilities, but beyond that, into matters of no concern to him, he would not venture. At this point he took his pen, drew towards him a sheet of paper from which he cut a strip the size of a doctor's prescription, and announced that he would prescribe what was appropriate.

"No, Dr. Rutenspitz, it's not appropriate! It's not appropriate at all!" said Mr. Golyadkin rising from his seat and seizing the doctor's right hand. "There's no need for that at all in this case!"

While he was speaking, a peculiar change came over Mr. Golyadkin. His grey eyes flashed with strange fire, his lips trembled, all his muscles and features twitched and disarranged themselves. His whole body shook violently. Having followed his first impulse in arresting the doctor's hand, Mr. Golyadkin now stood stock-still as though lacking self-assurance, and awaiting inspiration for further action.

A rather peculiar scene followed.

For the moment somewhat at a loss, Dr. Rutenspitz remained glued to his seat, and stared at Mr. Golyadkin in open-eyed amazement, while the latter stared back in the same fashion. At length the doctor rose, supporting himself to some extent by one of the lapels of Mr. Golyadkin's jacket. Thus for a few seconds they stood, motionless, not taking their eyes off one another. Then, however, followed in a most extraordinary manner Mr. Golyadkin's second impulsive action. His lips trembled, his chin quivered, and quite unexpectedly, he burst into tears. Sobbing, bobbing his head up and down, beating his breast with one hand and clutching at the lapel of Dr. Rutenspitz' coat with the other, he tried to speak, tried to offer some sort of explanation, but no words came.

Dr. Rutenspitz recovered at last from his amazement.

"That's enough of this. Calm yourself. Sit down," he said, attempting to seat Mr. Golyadkin in the arm-chair.

"I have enemies, Doctor, I have enemies. I have deadly enemies who have sworn to ruin me . . ." replied Mr. Golyadkin in a fearful whisper.

"Enough about your enemies! No need to bring them in. No need at all. Sit down, sit down," continued the doctor, finally getting him into the chair.

Mr. Golyadkin settled himself in the chair, not taking his eyes off the doctor, who began striding from one corner of his consulting room to the other, looking extremely displeased.

A long silence ensued.

"I'm grateful to you, Doctor, extremely grateful, and am most sensible of all that you have done for me. I shall not forget your kindness till the day I die," said Mr. Golyadkin at length, rising from the chair with a hurt expression.

"Enough, enough, I tell you!" retorted the doctor at this sally, again forcing Mr. Golyadkin into his seat. "What's the matter? Tell me what's upsetting you now, and who these enemies are you speak of. What's it all about?" he continued.

"No, Doctor, let's leave it at this," answered Mr. Golyadkin, looking at the floor. "It's best left till another time, Doctor . . . Till a more convenient time when all will be made clear, when the masks will fall from certain faces, and this and that will come to light. But meanwhile, after what has passed between us . . . You yourself will agree, Doctor . . . Allow me to wish you good morning," said Mr. Golyadkin, rising from his seat gravely and deliberately, and reaching for his hat.

"Well, as you wish . . . H-m-m . . ." (A momentary silence.) "For my part, you know . . . Anything I can do . . . And, er . . . I sincerely wish you all the best."

"I understand, I understand, Doctor. I take your meaning perfectly . . . At any rate, forgive my bothering you, Doctor."

"M-m-m no, I didn't mean that. Still, as you wish. Carry on with the medicine as before."

"I'll carry on with the medicine as you say, Doctor. I'll carry on with it, and get it at the same chemist's . . . It's a grand thing being a chemist nowadays, Doctor . . . A grand thing."

"Eh? In what sense?"

"In the most usual sense, Doctor. I mean that's how the world is nowadays . . ."

"H-m-m."

"And that every little whipper-snapper—and not only in chemists' shops—looks down his nose at a gentleman."

"H-m. How do you mean?"

"I'm speaking of someone well known, Doctor . . . A mutual friend of ours . . . Shall we say Vladimir Semyonovich, for instance?"

"Ah!"

"Yes, Doctor. And some I could name aren't so bound by what people think that they can't occasionally come out with the truth."

"How do you mean?"

"Well, like this. It's neither here nor there, but still . . . They know how to spring the odd surprise."

"How to what?"

"Spring a surprise, Doctor. It's a saying we've got. They sometimes know how to pay someone a compliment that's very much to the point for instance. There are such people, Doctor."

"Pay someone a compliment?"

"Yes, Doctor, as an intimate acquaintance of mine did the other day."

"An intimate acquaintance of yours, eh? How was that, then?" said Dr. Rutenspitz, regarding Mr. Golyadkin attentively.

"Yes, a certain intimate acquaintance of mine was congratulating another very intimate acquaintance, who was, moreover, a close friend of mine, 'a bosom friend' as the saying is, on his promotion to the rank of Assessor. The way he chanced to put it was: 'I'm heartily glad of this opportunity of offering you my congratulations, my *sincere* congratulations, Vladimir Semyonovich, on your promotion—the more so since nowadays, as all the world knows, those who push their favourites are no more.' " Here Mr. Golyadkin wagged his head roguishly and squinted at Dr. Rutenspitz.

"H-m. He said that, did he?"

"That's what he said, Doctor, and he looked at Andrey Filippovich, the uncle of our dear Vladimir Semyonovich. But what does it matter to me his being made an assessor? Is that any business of mine? And there he is wanting to get married and his mother's milk still wet on his lips, if you'll pardon the expression. I said as much. 'There it is Vladimir Semyonovich,' I said. Now I've told you all there is, and with your permission I'll be getting along."

"H-m-m."

"Yes, Doctor, you must allow me to be getting along, I say. But to kill two birds with one stone, after I'd given the young man a start with that bit about pushing favourites, I turned to Klara Olsufyevna, who'd just been singing a tender ballad—all this was the day before yesterday, at her father's—and I said: 'Your singing is full of tenderness, but those who listen haven't got pure hearts.' I gave a clear hint there, you see Doctor, a clear hint, so that they didn't take it as referring to her, but looked further afield."

"And what about him?"

"He looked as if he'd bitten a lemon, as the saying is."

"H-m-m . . ."

"Yes, Doctor, I spoke to the old man also, and I said:

'Olsufy Ivanovich,' I said, 'I know I am indebted to you, and I deeply appreciate the benefits you have lavished upon me since I was almost a child. But open your eyes, Olsufy Ivanovich,' I said. 'Take a good look around. I myself deal frankly and openly, Olsufy Ivanovich.' "

"Quite so."

"Yes, Doctor, there it is."

"And what did he say?"

"What did he say? He hummed and ha-ed, said this and that, about knowing me and about his Excellency's beneficence—and went all round the mulberry bush . . . But what can you expect? He's shaky with age, as they say."

"So that's how it is now!"

"Yes, Doctor. That's how it is with all of us! Poor old chap! Already one foot in the grave and smelling of incense, as the saying is, but the moment they start some old wives' gossip, he's there to listen; they can't get on without him . . ."

"Gossip, you say?"

"Yes, Doctor, they've made up some gossip. Our friend the Bear and his dear little nephew had a hand in it. They got together with the old women, and cooked it up. And what do you think? They've thought up a plan to destroy someone."

"Destroy someone?"

"Yes, Doctor, to destroy someone morally. They put out a rumour . . . I'm still speaking of my close friend . . ."

Dr. Rutenspitz nodded.

"They put out a rumour about him . . . I must confess, Doctor, I feel ashamed to speak of it."

"H-m-m . . ."

"They put out a rumour saying he'd made a written promise of marriage when he was married already. And who do you think it was to, Doctor?"

"No idea."

"A cook, a disreputable German woman who used to give him his dinner. He offered her his hand instead of payment."

"Is that what they say?"

"Can you believe it, Doctor? A German, a vile beastly brazen German woman, Karolina Ivanovna, if you know . . ."

"For my part, I confess . . ."

"I understand you, Doctor, I quite understand, and feel it myself . . . ."

"Tell me, please, where you're living now."

"Where I'm living now, Doctor?"

"Yes . . . I wanted . . . I seem to remember you used to live . . ."

"I did, Doctor, I did, I did use to. How could I help doing so?" replied Mr. Golyadkin, accompanying his words with a short laugh.

The doctor was somewhat nonplussed by this reply.

"No, you missed my meaning. I wanted to . . ."

"So did I, Doctor, so did I . . ." continued Mr. Golyadkin with a laugh. "But I've sat taking up too much of your time, Doctor. Pray allow me to wish you good morning."

"H-m-m . . ."

"Yes, Doctor, I understand you. I now understand you perfectly," said our hero, assuming a rather theatrical pose. "And so allow me to wish you good morning."

With this our hero bowed, and walked from the room, leaving Dr. Rutenspitz utterly amazed.

On his way down the doctor's staircase, he smiled and rubbed his hands with glee. Once on the front steps and breathing the fresh air, he felt free, and was even ready to admit himself the happiest of mortals and go straight to the office. Then suddenly his carriage came rumbling in at the gate. One look, and it all came back to him. Petrushka was already opening the carriage door. A strange, extremely unpleasant sensation seized Mr. Golyadkin's whole body. His face seemed to flush for a moment. He had a stabbing pain in his side. Just as he was about to set foot on the step of the carriage, he turned to look at Dr. Rutenspitz' windows. It was as he thought! The doctor was standing at one of them, smoothing his side-whiskers with his right hand, and gazing rather curiously at our hero.

"That doctor is stupid," thought Mr. Golyadkin as he concealed himself in his carriage. "Terribly stupid. He may be able to cure his patients, but he's as soft as they make them, all the same."

Mr. Golyadkin sat back, Petrushka cried "Drive on!" and the carriage moved out again into the Nevsky Prospect.

Chapter 3

This whole morning was one of frightful activity for Mr. Golyadkin. Once in the Nevsky Prospect, our hero ordered the carriage to stop at the Arcade. Jumping down, he ran in accompanied by Petrushka, and made a bee-line for a shop displaying gold and silver ware. From his very appearance it was plain that Mr. Golyadkin was a man with his hands full and a terrible amount to get through. After settling for the purchase of a complete tea and dinner service for one thousand five hundred roubles, together with a fantastically-shaped cigar-case and a complete shaving outfit in silver for a similar sum, after finally inquiring the price of other trifles, pleasing and useful in their way, Mr. Golyadkin concluded by promising to return on the morrow without fail, or even to send for his purchases that same day, noted the number of the shop, listened attentively while the shopkeeper solicited a small deposit, and promised that there should indeed be a small deposit in due course. Thereupon he bade the stupefied shopkeeper a hurried good-day, and pursued by a whole swarm of assistants, made his way along the row of shops carefully searching for somewhere new, and turning every minute to look at Petrushka. On the way he darted into a money changer's, and changed his big notes into notes of smaller denominations, losing on the transaction, but acquiring nevertheless a great number of small notes to swell his pocket-book, which evidently afforded him the keenest satisfaction. At length he stopped at a shop dealing in various ladies' materials. Here again, after bargaining over the purchase of goods worth a considerable sum, Mr. Golyadkin promised the shopkeeper to return without fail, took the number of the shop, and the question of a small deposit being raised, repeated that there would in due course be a small deposit. He then visited several other shops, and in each bargained for goods and inquired prices, sometimes having long arguments with the shopkeepers and walking out only to come back three times afterwards—in short, he showed unusual activity. From the Arcade our hero betook himself to a well-known furnisher's, where he ordered furniture for six rooms, and admired an intricately designed ladies' dressing-table in the latest style. After assuring the shopkeeper that he would send for it all without fail, he left the shop with his customary promise of a small deposit, and drove off to order something else. To put it briefly, there seemed no end to his activity.

At last Mr. Golyadkin seemed to grow sick and tired of it all, and even began, heaven knows why, to be troubled by twinges of conscience. Nothing on earth would have induced him to meet Andrey Filippovich or Dr. Rutenspitz for instance.

Finally the city clocks struck three, and as Mr. Golyadkin got back into his carriage, a pair of gloves and a bottle of perfume for one and a half roubles represented all that he had actually purchased.

As he was still rather early, Mr. Golyadkin ordered the driver to stop at a well-known restaurant in the Nevsky Prospect which so far he had known only by repute. He jumped down and hurried in to have a bite to eat and take his ease till the appointed time.

After eating as befits a man with the prospect of a sumptuous dinner-party before him—that is, having snatched the odd something to stay the pangs as the saying is, and swallowed a glass of vodka—Mr. Golyadkin settled himself in an arm-chair, and after a discreet look round, quietly attached himself to a certain meagre national newspaper. After reading a few lines he rose, looked at himself in the mirror, righted his dress and smoothed his hair; after which he went to the window to see if his carriage was there, then resumed his seat and took up the newspaper. Our hero was clearly in a state of extreme agitation. Glancing at the clock, and seeing that as it was only a quarter past three there was still some time to wait, Mr. Golyadkin decided that it was not proper just to sit there, and ordered a chocolate that he did not particularly want. After drinking the chocolate and noting that the time had got on a bit, Mr. Golyadkin went to pay his bill. Suddenly someone clapped him on the shoulder.

He turned and saw before him his two office colleagues, the two fellows young in years and junior in rank, whom he had met that morning in Liteynaya Street. Our hero was on no particular footing with them, was neither friendly nor openly hostile towards them. Correctness, of course, was observed on both sides, but nothing further. Indeed, there could be nothing further. The present encounter was disagreeable to Mr. Golyadkin in the extreme. He frowned slightly and was for the moment embarrassed.

"Yakov Petrovich, Yakov Petrovich!" twittered the two clerks. "You here? What brings you . . . ?"

"Oh, it's you, gentlemen," interposed Mr. Golyadkin hurriedly, somewhat disconcerted and scandalized by the clerks' surprise at seeing him, and by their familiarity, but pretending despite himself to be a free and easy sort of fellow. "So you've deserted the office, eh? Ha-ha-ha!" And here, to preserve his dignity and patronize the office juniors, from whom he always kept his proper distance, he tried to tap one of the young men on the shoulder. But on this occasion the popular approach failed Mr. Golyadkin, and instead of his making a seemly, intimate gesture, something quite different happened.

"Well, is our old Bear still sitting there?" he blurted out.

"Who do you mean, Yakov Petrovich?"

"Come, come. As if you didn't know!"

Mr. Golyadkin gave a laugh, and turned to collect his change. "I'm speaking of Andrey Filippovich, gentlemen," he continued, when he had finished with the cashier, now addressing the clerks with a very earnest expression. The two clerks exchanged knowing winks.

"He's still there, Yakov Petrovich, and he was asking for you."

"He is, eh? Well, let him stay there, gentlemen. And so he was asking for me, was he?"

"Yes, he was, Yakov Petrovich. But what's all this perfume and pomade? You're the real dandy."

"Yes, that's how it is gentlemen. But enough——" replied Mr. Golyadkin looking away with a forced smile. Seeing him smiling, the clerks burst out laughing. Mr. Golyadkin pouted.

"I'll tell you something as a friend, gentlemen," he said after a short silence, as if he had made a momentous decision to confide in the clerks. "You all know me, gentlemen, but up to now you have only known one side of me. No one can be reproached for this, and I confess I am partly to blame." Mr. Golyadkin pursed his lips and looked at the clerks significantly. The clerks again winked at each other.

"Up to the present you have not really known me, gentlemen. To explain here and now would not be at all appropriate. I'll merely give you a hint in passing. There are people, gentlemen, who don't like beating about the bush, and mask themselves only to go to a masquerade. There are people who don't see that man's one purpose in life is to be adept at bowing and scraping. There are people who don't say they're happy and enjoying life to the full just because their trousers fit well, for instance. And finally there are people who don't like leaping and whirling around when there's no need, fawning, making eyes, and, what's most important of all, gentlemen, poking their noses in where they're not asked. I have said practically all there is, gentlemen. Now, if you will allow me, I must be off." He paused, and the clerks, having had their money's worth, burst suddenly and in a most discourteous manner into a great roar of laughter. Mr. Golyadkin flushed red with anger.

"Go on, laugh, gentlemen, laugh for the time being. You'll see when you're a bit older," he said with injured pride, taking his hat and retiring towards the door. "But I'll tell you something else, gentlemen," he added, turning to the clerks for the last time. "I'll tell you something else now we're all here face to face. My rule, gentlemen, is, if at first I don't succeed, I take courage. If I do succeed, I hold on, and in any case I don't try undermining anyone. I'm not one for intrigue, and I'm proud of it. As a diplomat I'd be no good at all. 'The bird flies to the huntsman,' they say, gentlemen. That's true, I'm ready to admit. But who's the huntsman here, and who the bird? That's another question, gentlemen."

Mr. Golyadkin lapsed into an eloquent silence, and making a most expressive face, that is, raising his eyebrows and pursing his lips as tightly as possible, he raised his hat to the clerks and walked out, leaving them dumbfounded.

"Where to?" asked Petrushka rather grimly, having probably grown fed up with hanging about in the cold. "Where to?" he asked Mr. Golyadkin, and met that fearful all-annihilating glare with which our hero had already protected himself on two occasions that morning, and to which he now had recourse a third time while descending the steps.

"The Izmaylovsky Bridge."

"The Izmaylovsky Bridge!" ordered Petrushka.

"They don't begin dinner till after four, or perhaps not

till five," thought Mr. Golyadkin. "Isn't it a bit too early now? Still, I can arrive a bit early. After all, it's a family dinner. I can just go along *sans façon*, as the saying is in the best circles. The Bear said it would all be *sans façon*, so that goes for me too."

Such were Mr. Golyadkin's thoughts, but meanwhile his agitation was increasing every minute. He was evidently preparing himself for something extremely troublesome, to say the least. He was whispering to himself, gesticulating with his right hand, and gazing incessantly out of the carriage window, so that no one seeing him then would have said that he was on his way to dine informally as one of the family, or *sans façon* as the saying is in the best circles.

At last, just by the Izmaylovsky Bridge, Mr. Golyadkin indicated a house, and the carriage thundered in at a gate to stop by some steps on the right. Noticing the figure of a woman in one of the second-floor windows, Mr. Golyadkin blew her a kiss. But he had no idea what he was doing, for at that moment he was neither dead nor alive, but somewhere in between. He emerged from the carriage, pale and distracted, climbed the steps to the entrance, removed his hat, straightened his clothes mechanically, and with a slight trembling at the knees made his way up the stairs.

"Is Olsufy Ivanovich at home?" he inquired of the servant who opened to him.

"Yes sir—that is, no sir. He's not at home, sir."

"Eh? What do you mean, my dear chap? I've come to dinner, my friend. You know me, don't you?"

"Of course, sir. But my orders are not to admit you."

"Y-y-you must be making some mistake, my friend. It's me. I've been invited. I've come to dinner," said Mr. Golyadkin, discarding his overcoat, and showing every intention of going in.

"I'm sorry, it's no good, sir. Orders are to refuse you admittance. That's how it is."

Mr. Golyadkin turned pale. At that moment the door of one of the inner rooms opened, and Gerasimych, Olsufy Ivanovich's old butler, appeared.

"There's a gentleman here trying to get in, and I . . ." said the servant.

"You're a fool, Alexeich. Go along and fetch that scoundrel Semyonovich here." Then turning to Mr. Golyadkin he said politely but firmly: "It's impossible, sir. Out of the question. The master begs you to excuse him. He cannot receive you."

"Did he say he couldn't receive me?" asked Mr. Golyadkin with a note of uncertainty. "Excuse my asking, Gerasimych, but why is it impossible?"

"Quite impossible, sir. I announced you, and he said: 'Ask him to excuse me. I cannot receive him,' he said."

"But why?"

"I'm sorry, sir."

"But what's the reason? It's impossible! Go and announce me . . . How's it happened like this? I've come to dinner."

"I'm sorry, sir, I'm sorry . . ."

"Ah well, if he begs to be excused, it's a different matter. But tell me, Gerasimych, why is it?"

"Excuse me, excuse me, sir!" exclaimed Gerasimych, firmly pushing Mr. Golyadkin to one side to make room for two gentlemen who were at that moment entering the hall. It was Andrey Filippovich and his nephew Vladimir Semyonovich. Both looked in a puzzled way at Mr. Golyadkin. Andrey Filippovich was on the point of saying something, but Mr. Golyadkin's mind was made up, and with eyes lowered, scarlet-faced, smiling, and looking thoroughly confused, he was already on his way out.

"I'll come back later, Gerasimych. I'll explain. I hope all this won't cause any delay in clearing things up in good time," he said, beginning in the doorway and finishing on the stairs.

"Yakov Petrovich, Yakov Petrovich . . ." came the voice of Andrey Filippovich hard behind him.

Mr. Golyadkin was then already on the first landing. He turned quickly to face Andrey Filippovich.

"What can I do for you, Andrey Filippovich?" he said in a fairly resolute tone.

"What's the matter with you, Yakov Petrovich? How is it that . . ."

"Nothing, Andrey Filippovich. I'm here on my own account. This is my private life, Andrey Filippovich."

"What's all that?"

"I say that this is my private life, and that regarding my official relationships, nothing reprehensible is, so far as I can see, to be found in my presence here."

"How do you mean, 'Regarding your official . . .' What's the matter with you, sir?"

"Nothing, Andrey Filippovich, nothing at all. A miserable cheeky girl, nothing else . . ."

"What! What!" Andrey Filippovich was utterly perplexed.

Mr. Golyadkin, who so far had carried on the conversation from the foot of the stairs, looked as if he were about to fly at Andrey Filippovich's face, and now, seeing the confusion of his departmental head, he almost unconsciously took a step forward. Andrey Filippovich drew back. Mr. Golyadkin moved up one stair, then another . . . Andrey Filippovich looked round uneasily. Suddenly and with great rapidity Mr. Golyadkin bounded to the head of the stairs. With even greater rapidity Andrey Filippovich sprang back into the room, slamming the door after him.

Mr. Golyadkin was alone. There was a mist before his eyes. He was completely bewildered, and stood vacant and hesitant, as though calling to mind some very stupid event that had recently occurred. "Ah well," he murmured, forcing a smile. In the meantime footsteps and voices had become audible on the stairs below, heralding in all probability the arrival of other of Olsufy Ivanovich's invited guests. Mr. Golyadkin came partially to his senses, and quickly turning up the raccoon collar of his overcoat and concealing as much of himself as possible behind it, stumbled awkwardly downstairs as fast as his legs would carry him. He felt weak and numb inside, and his confusion was such, that on emerging from the door, he made his way straight across the muddy courtyard to his carriage, instead of waiting for it to draw up. As he prepared to climb in, Mr. Golyadkin felt as if every living soul in Olsufy Ivanovich's house was staring at him from every window, and wished inwardly that he might sink through the ground or disappear into a mousehole, carriage and all. If he turned round he knew he would fall dead on the spot.

"What are you laughing at, blockhead?" he fired at Petrushka.

"I'm not. What have I got to laugh about? Where to now?"

"Home."

"Home, driver!" yelled Petrushka, perching himself on the backboard.

"He's got a voice like a crow," thought Mr. Golyadkin.

The carriage was already some way beyond the Izmaylovsky Bridge, when suddenly our hero pulled the cord with all his might and shouted to the driver to turn back immediately. The driver turned the horses, and two minutes later they were again driving into Olsufy Ivanovich's courtyard.

"No, you fool, back again!" screamed Mr. Golyadkin, and it was as if the driver had been expecting such an order, for without either stopping or offering a word of protest, he drove the whole way round the courtyard and out again into the street.

But Mr. Golyadkin did not drive home. As soon as they had passed the Semyonovsky Bridge, he ordered the driver to turn into a side street and stop outside a rather unpretentious-looking restaurant. Once our hero had alighted he paid off the driver, and so was finally rid of his carriage. Telling Petrushka to walk home and await his return, he went into the restaurant, took a private room, and ordered dinner to be served. He felt extremely unwell, and his head seemed in a state of chaos. For a long while he paced the room in agitation. Then at last he sat down, propped his forehead on his hands, and began striving with all his might to think things out and get something settled with regard to his present position.

Chapter 4

The day—that festal day whereon occurred the anniversary of the birth of Klara Olsufyevna, only daughter of Civil Counsellor Berendeyev, sometime benefactor of Mr. Golyadkin—was marked by a dinner, splendid, magnificent, and such as has not been witnessed within the walls of any civil servant's apartment in or about the neighbourhood of the Izmaylovsky Bridge for many a day; a dinner that was more like Belshazzar's Feast, there being something Babylonian about its effulgence, sumptuosity and sense of the occasion; a dinner with Veuve Clicquot, with oysters, with the fruits of Yeliseyev's and Malyutins',* with every kind of fatted calf, and an official programme setting forth the rank of each diner. The festal day signalized by so fine a dinner ended with a bril-

* Fashionable St. Petersburg stores.—*Translator.*

liant ball—a small, intimate, family ball, but brilliant none the less for its good taste, polish and seemliness. Such balls do, I concede, take place, but they are a rare phenomenon. Resembling as they do more joyful family occasions than anything else, they can only be given in a house such as Civil Counsellor Berendeyev's. I will go even further and say that not every civil counsellor could give such balls.

Would I were a poet! A Homer or a Pushkin, of course, for with a lesser talent one would not attempt it—and then I would boldly and vividly depict for my readers the whole of that supremely festal day. Or rather, my poem would open with the dinner, and I should lay particular emphasis on that striking and triumphant moment of the raising of the first goblet to the health of the Queen of Festivities. I should depict the guests plunged in reverentially expectant silence—a silence of almost Demosthenian eloquence. I should then describe Andrey Filippovich, as most senior among the guests, having with his venerable grey hairs and the orders appropriate to them upon his breast some claim to precedence, rising from his seat, and holding aloft a goblet of a sparkling vintage—no common wine, but nectar—conveyed hither from a distant realm expressly to be tasted at moments such as these. I should depict for you the happy parents of the Queen of Festivities, and the guests, raising their goblets after Andrey Filippovich, and gazing at him, filled with expectancy. Then I should depict for you that same Andrey Filippovich, of whom frequent mention is made, shedding a tear into his champagne glass, delivering a speech of felicitation, and proposing and drinking the health of Klara Olsufyevna. But I must confess, and confess freely, that it would be beyond my powers to depict the full pageantry of the moment in which the Queen of Festivities, flushed like a rose of spring with the bloom of blissful modesty, sinks for excess of joy into the arms of her loving mother; how her loving mother lets fall a tear; and how at this, that venerable old man, her father Olsufy Ivanovich, who has lost the use of his legs in long service, and has for his zeal been rewarded by fate with a little capital, a small house, some small estates and a beautiful daughter, begins sobbing like a child and proclaims through his tears the beneficence of his Excellency. I should be quite unable to depict for you the general heartfelt enthusiasm which promptly ensues, and which finds eloquent expression in the behaviour of a junior clerk who in listening to Andrey Filippovich sheds a few tears of his own—looking for the moment more like a civil counsellor than a humble junior. Andrey Filippovich at this moment of triumph does not look at all like a collegiate counsellor and head of a section in a certain department. No, indeed . . . In some way he is different. I do not quite know in what way he is different, but certainly he is unlike a collegiate counsellor. He is more exalted! And finally . . . Oh, why do I not possess the secret of elevated, forceful style—of an exultant style, to depict all these beautiful and edifying moments of mortal existence, contrived as it were expressly in evidence of the fact that virtue will sometimes triumph over vice, envy, free-thinking and evil intent! I will say nothing, but will point out to you in silence—for this will be better than eloquence—that fortunate young man entering upon his twenty-sixth year, Vladimir Semyonovich, nephew of Andrey Filippovich, who has in turn risen, and is in turn proposing a toast, while upon him rest the tearful eyes of the parents of the Queen of Festivities, the proud eyes of Andrey Filippovich, the modest eyes of the Queen herself, the rapturous eyes of the guests, and the decorously envious eyes of certain colleagues of this brilliant young man. I will say nothing, although I cannot help observing that everything about this young man—who, let it be said in his favour, is more like an old man than a young one—everything, from his rosy cheeks to the rank of Assessor with which he is invested, speaks at this triumphant moment of the lofty heights to which one may be elevated by good manners! I shall not describe how finally Anton Antonovich Setochkin, the chief clerk of a certain department, a colleague of Andrey Filippovich, and a former colleague of Olsufy Ivanovich, as well as being an old friend of the family and godfather to Klara Olsufyevna, an old man as grey as a badger, while proposing a toast, crows like a cock and speaks some jolly verses; and how by this decorous breach of decorum, if one may use such a phrase, he sets the whole company laughing till the tears run, and Klara Olsufyevna, on instructions from her parents, rewards his mirth and amiability with a kiss.

I shall merely state that the guests, feeling as guests

naturally must after such a dinner, rose at last from the
table, brothers and bosom friends. The older and more
staid gentlemen, after a short while spent in friendly conversation and the exchange of eminently decorous and
amiable confidences, proceeded sedately to another room,
where, breaking up into parties, they lost no time in seat-
ing themselves with proper dignity at the green baize-
covered tables. The ladies, once seated in the drawing-
room, suddenly became unusually amiable, and started
chatting about various materials. The esteemed master of
the house, who had lost the use of his legs in true and
faithful service, and been recompensed for this by all that
I have mentioned above, hobbled amongst his guests on
crutches, supported by his daughter and Vladimir Semyonovich—when suddenly, also waxing unusually amiable, he resolved upon improvising a modest little ball,
regardless of expense. To this end a bright young man—
the one who at dinner looked more like a civil counsellor
—was dispatched to summon musicians. The musicians
arrived, eleven strong, and at last, at half past eight precisely, came the inviting strains of a French quadrille.
Various other dances followed . . .

I need hardly mention that a fitting description of this
ball improvised by the singular amiability of the grey-
haired host is beyond the powers of my feeble pen. How
can I, the humble chronicler of the adventures of Mr.
Golyadkin, which are, however, very curious in their way,
depict this singular and seemly medley of beauty, bril-
liance, decorum, gaiety, amiable sobriety and sober
amiability, sprightliness and joy; depict all the playfulness and laughter of the functionaries' daughters and
wives, who, and I mean this as a compliment, are more
like fairies than ladies, with their pink and lily-white
shoulders and faces, their slender waists, their lively,
twinkling, and—to use a grand word—*homoeopathic*
feet? How, finally, can I depict for you the brilliant civil
service cavaliers, both stolid and gay—level-headed young
men, both merry and decorously melancholy—some
smoking pipes in intervals between dances in a remote
small green room, others not smoking; cavaliers of proper
rank and good family to a man; cavaliers deeply imbued
with a sense of elegance and of their own worth; who
converse with the ladies for the most part in French, but
who, when speaking Russian, employ only the very best

expressions, pay compliments, and voice profundities; cavaliers who only in the smoking-room permit themselves an occasional amiable departure from language of the highest tone, in phrases of amicable, good-natured intimacy after the style of: "You stepped a pretty fine polka, Petka my boy!" or "Vasya, you old so-and-so, you gave your little lady a jolly rough time of it!"

All this, as I have informed the reader earlier, is beyond the power of my pen, and therefore I remain silent. Let us rather return to Mr. Golyadkin, the true hero of my veracious tale.

His present position was curious to say the least. He also was there, ladies and gentlemen—not *at* the ball, that is, but very nearly. He was quite all right, and going his own way—although for the moment he had chosen anything but a direct route. He was standing—it's a funny thing to have to say—on a landing on the back stairs of Olsufy Ivanovich's apartment. But there was nothing wrong with his standing there. He was quite all right. He was pressed into a corner where, if it was not particularly warm, it was at least as dark as possible, and he was partially hidden, amidst all kinds of lumber and rubbish, by an enormous cupboard and some old screens. Here he was concealing himself until the appointed hour, and meanwhile merely following the general course of things as an outside observer. He was just watching . . . He could go in if he wanted . . . After all, why shouldn't he? A few steps, and in he'd go, with all the ease in the world. It was only after he had been standing between the cupboard and screens amidst all kinds of lumber and rubbish for over two hours in the cold, that to justify himself he quoted a phrase of the late lamented French Minister Villèle, to the effect that all comes in due season to him who wisely waits. It was a phrase he'd seen some time before in a book on some quite extraneous subject, but to have recalled it at that moment was particularly appropriate. In the first place it was a phrase well-suited to his position, and, secondly, why shouldn't it have occurred to someone who had spent nearly three hours on a cold dark landing, waiting for a happy ending to his troubles? Immediately following this appropriate quotation, Mr. Golyadkin for some unknown reason called to mind the late Turkish Vizier Martsimiris and the lovely Margravine Luise, both of whom he had read about at

some time or other in a book. He then called to mind
that the Jesuits had a maxim that all means were justified, provided the end was attained. A little encouraged
by this historical fact, he asked himself what the Jesuits
were. Numskulls, every one of them! He'd outshine the
lot. And if only the buffet—a door of which opened onto
the back stairs and Mr. Golyadkin's landing—were clear
of people for a minute, Jesuits or no Jesuits, he'd march
straight through—through the tea *salon*, through the
room where they were playing cards, and into the ball-
room where at that moment they were dancing a polka.
He'd march straight through, in spite of everything . . .
Just slip past. No one would notice. And once there he
would know what to do.

Such, ladies and gentlemen, is the position in which
we discover the hero of our very true story. Although to
explain exactly what had been happening to him is difficult.

He had been able to get as far as the stairs and landing, for the simple reason that everyone else had, and he
didn't see why he shouldn't too. But go farther, he dare
not—that was clear. Not because he wouldn't, but because he didn't want to, because he preferred to stay quiet.
And there he was, staying quiet just as he had been for
the past two and a half hours. But why shouldn't he?
Villèle waited.

"But what's Villèle got to do with it?" thought Mr.
Golyadkin. "Why drag him in? Supposing . . . Supposing I marched in now?"

"A walking-on part—that's all you've got!" said Mr.
Golyadkin, pinching his numbed cheek with his numbed
fingers. "What a poor stupid fool you are!"

These blandishments were merely by the way, and
served no apparent purpose. Mr. Golyadkin was about to
intrude, and had already started forward. The time had
come. The buffet was clear. He could see that through a
tiny window. Two steps, and he was at the door and already opening it.

"Shall I, or shan't I? Shall I? . . . Yes, I will—why
shouldn't I? The brave go where they please!" Thus reassuring himself, our hero suddenly and quite unexpectedly withdrew behind the screen.

"No," he thought. "Suppose someone comes in? There
you are—now someone has. Why did I stand gaping when

no one was there? Gone straight in—that's what I ought
to have done! But what's the good of saying that when
you're made like me? It's a vile tendency I've got! I simply
went into a blue funk. That's me all over! Always making a hash of it—no question of that. And here I am
standing round like a blinking idiot! I could be at home
now drinking a cup of tea . . . A cup of tea would be
jolly nice. Petrushka will grumble if I'm late. Why not go
home? To hell with all this! Come on, I'm off!"

Having settled things thus, Mr. Golyadkin shot forward
as if a spring had been touched off inside him. Two
strides, and he was in the buffet. Flinging off his hat and
coat and stuffing them hurriedly into a corner, he
straightened his jacket, smoothed his hair, and proceeded
to the tea *salon*. From there he whisked on into the next
room, slipped unobserved between the card-players absorbed in the excitement of their game, and then . . .
At this point Mr. Golyadkin became oblivious of all that
was going on around, and suddenly, like a bolt from the
blue, he entered the ball-room.

As if to spite him, no one was dancing. The ladies
were promenading in picturesque groups. The men were
gathering in little knots, or darting about engaging part-
ners. Mr. Golyadkin noticed none of this. All he saw was
Klara Olsufyevna, and standing near her, Andrey Filippovich, Vladimir Semyonovich, two or three officers, and
two or three other very interesting young men who, as
one could judge at first sight, were also the subject or the
embodiment of great hopes. He saw one or two other
people as well. Or rather—he didn't. He was no longer
aware of anybody. Propelled by the same spring that had
brought him bounding into a ball to which he had not
been invited, he continued to advance steadily. He collided with a counsellor and trod heavily on his foot; he
stepped on the dress of a certain venerable old lady and
tore it slightly; he jostled a man with a tray; he elbowed
somebody else, but still forged on, noticing none of this,
or, more accurately, *noticing* it, but not looking at anyone, until suddenly he found himself face to face with
Klara Olsufyevna. At that moment there's not a shadow
of doubt he would have dropped through the floor with
the greatest pleasure in the world, and without so much
as blinking. But what's done can't be undone—it's quite
impossible. What *could* be done?

"If at first you don't succeed, hold on. If you do succeed, take courage," thought Mr. Golyadkin. He was, of course, not one for intrigue—no adept at bowing and scraping . . . It had happened now. Added to which the Jesuits were mixed up in it somehow . . . But Mr. Golyadkin had no time for them! Suddenly, as though at the wave of a hand, all noise, movement, conversation and laughter ceased, and gradually a crowd formed around him. But he seemed to hear and see nothing. He couldn't look . . . He merely stood there, keeping his eyes glued to the ground, but secretly vowing on his word of honour that somehow or other he'd blow his brains out that very night.

"Here goes!" thought Mr. Golyadkin after this, and suddenly, to his own infinite astonishment, he began to speak.

Mr. Golyadkin opened with felicitations and seemly good wishes. The former went well, but over the latter he stumbled. He had sensed that if he once stumbled everything would immediately go to the devil. And so it did. Having stumbled, he got stuck. Having got stuck, he blushed. Having blushed, he became confused. Becoming confused he raised his eyes, looked about him—and froze with horror. They were all standing, speechless and expectant. A little way off someone began to whisper. Nearer at hand there was a sudden boisterous laugh. Mr. Golyadkin glanced, humbly embarrassed, at Andrey Filippovich. Andrey Filippovich retaliated with a look which would have crushed our hero completely, had he not been completely crushed already.

"This concerns more my private life and my personal affairs, Andrey Filippovich," said Mr. Golyadkin, more dead than alive, in a voice that was barely audible. "It's not an official matter."

"You ought to be ashamed, sir!" said Andrey Filippovich in a half-whisper, with a look of indescribable indignation on his face, taking Klara Olsufyevna by the arm and turning away from Mr. Golyadkin.

"I've nothing to be ashamed about, Andrey Filippovich," replied Mr. Golyadkin, also in a half-whisper, confused, and looking unhappily around in an attempt to find his milieu and proper sphere in that bewildered crowd.

"It's nothing, nothing, gentlemen. Why, it could happen to anyone," whispered Mr. Golyadkin, shifting his position slightly in an attempt to extricate himself from the encircling throng. Way was made for him, and with difficulty our hero passed between the two rows of puzzled and curious spectators. Fate was drawing him on —he could feel it. Certainly he'd have given a great deal if without any breach of decorum, he could at that moment have found himself back on the landing. Since, however, this was quite impossible, he tried to slip into some corner where he could just stand, modest, decorous, and independent, annoying no one, calling no particular attention to himself, but at the same time finding favour with both host and guests. But Mr. Golyadkin felt as if the ground were being washed away beneath him—felt as though he were swaying and falling. He reached a corner at last, and stood there in the manner of a rather indifferent outside observer, resting his hands on the backs of two chairs to assert full possession of them, and attempting as far as possible to give those of Olsufy Ivanovich's guests who had grouped themselves around him a jaunty look. Standing closest to him was an officer, a fine tall figure of a man beside whom Mr. Golyadkin felt like something out of a cheese.

"Both these chairs are taken, Lieutenant. One is for Klara Olsufyevna, the other is for the Princess Chevchekhanova, who is dancing here. I'm keeping them for them," said Mr. Golyadkin breathlessly, looking beseechingly at the lieutenant. The lieutenant gave him a withering smile and turned away without a word. Having suffered a rebuff in one quarter, our hero set about trying his luck elsewhere, and straightway addressed a certain pompous-looking counsellor wearing about his neck the cross of an important decoration. But the counsellor measured him with a stare that was like a sudden drenching tubful of icy water. Mr. Golyadkin fell silent. He decided it was better not to start up conversation, but to hold his peace and show that he was all right, that he was like anyone else, and that his position, as far as he could see, was at all events a proper one. To this end he glued his eyes to the cuffs of his jacket, then raised and fixed them upon a certain gentleman of extremely venerable appearance.

"This gentleman is wearing a wig," thought Mr. Golyadkin. "And if it's taken off, his head will be just like a billiard ball."

After making this important discovery, Mr. Golyadkin thought of Arab emirs, and the green turbans they wear to symbolize their kinship with the prophet Mohammed. Remove the turbans and there'll also be nothing but bare, hairless heads. Then, probably by a peculiar association of ideas, Mr. Golyadkin got on to Turkish slippers, apropos of which he at once remembered that the boots Andrey Filippovich was wearing were more like slippers than boots. Clearly he was to some extent familiar with his situation.

"That chandelier up there," flashed through Mr. Golyadkin's mind—"supposing it broke from its fittings and fell on the company—I'd rush and save Klara Olsufyevna at once. When I'd saved her I'd say: 'Don't worry, young lady—it's nothing. I'm your rescuer.' Then . . ." Here Mr. Golyadkin gave a sidelong glance to see where Klara Olsufyevna was, and caught sight of Gerasimych, Olsufy Ivanovich's old butler, making straight for him, with an imposingly official look of concern on his face. An unaccountable and at the same time most unpleasant sensation made Mr. Golyadkin shudder and pucker up his face. Mechanically he looked around. He had thoughts of quietly edging himself out of harm's way, and merging in with the background, that is, of acting as if nothing whatever was the matter, and he wasn't concerned in it at all. Before he could reach any decision, however, there was Gerasimych, standing in front of him.

"Can you see that candle in the candelabra, Gerasimych?" said our hero, smiling slightly. "It's going to fall in a minute. Just go and tell someone to put it right. I'm sure it'll fall . . ."

"The candle, sir? Oh no, sir, that's all right. But there's someone asking for you, sir."

"Who's asking for me, Gerasimych?"

"I don't know exactly, sir. It's someone with a message. 'Is Yakov Petrovich here?' he said. 'Then call him,' he said—'it's something very vital and urgent . . .' "

"No, Gerasimych, you're mistaken, quite mistaken."

"Hardly, sir."

"There's no 'hardly' about it! No one is asking for me, there's no one to ask. And I'm quite at home here—that is, I'm where I belong."

Mr. Golyadkin paused for breath, and looked around. It was as he thought! Every living soul in the room was watching, listening and solemnly waiting. The men were crowding closer, all ears. Further off, the ladies were exchanging alarmed whispers. The host himself was no great distance from Mr. Golyadkin, and though he gave no indication of the direct and immediate interest he too was taking in the latter's affairs—for the whole thing was being conducted with delicacy—Mr. Golyadkin distinctly felt that the decisive moment had come. He clearly perceived that the hour for a bold stroke and the humiliation of his enemies was at hand. He was agitated. He felt a kind of sudden inspiration, and in a quavering but solemn voice he again addressed the waiting Gerasimych.

"No, my friend, no one is asking for me. You are mistaken. I will go further—you were mistaken this afternoon in giving me to understand—in *daring* to give me to understand, I say," (Mr. Golyadkin raised his voice) "that Olsufy Ivanovich, who has been my benefactor for as long as I can remember, and who, in a certain sense, has been a father to me, had forbidden me his house at a time when his paternal heart was filled with family exultation." (Well satisfied with himself, but deeply moved, Mr. Golyadkin looked about him. Tears started to his eyes.) "I repeat, my friend," concluded our hero, "you were mistaken—cruelly and unpardonably mistaken."

It was a moment of triumph. Mr. Golyadkin felt he had produced exactly the right effect, and stood, eyes modestly averted, awaiting Olsufy Ivanovich's embrace. There were clear signs of excitement and bewilderment amongst the guests. Even the formidable and unshakable Gerasimych stuttered over his "Hardly, sir . . ." Then suddenly, for no apparent reason, the unpitying orchestra struck up a polka. All was lost—thrown to the winds. Mr. Golyadkin shuddered. Gerasimych took a step back. The whole ball-room surged like the sea, and there was Vladimir Semyonovich sweeping off Klara Olsufyevna in the first couple, followed by the splendid lieutenant and the Princess Chevchekhanova in the second. Onlookers, filled with curiosity and delight, thronged to take a peep at the dancers—the polka being a fashionable new dance that was all the rage. Mr. Golyadkin was temporarily forgotten. But suddenly there was general alarm and perturbation. The music stopped . . . Something odd had happened.

Fatigued by the dance and almost breathless, Klara

Olsufyevna, her cheeks glowing and her breast heaving, had sunk exhausted into an arm-chair. All hearts had gone out to that delightful enchantress. Everyone was vying with everyone else to salute her and thank her for the pleasure she had afforded them, when suddenly—there was Mr. Golyadkin. He was pale, extremely ill at ease, and he too seemed to be in a state of exhaustion, for he could hardly walk. For some reason or other he was smiling and extending an inviting hand. Failing in her amazement to withdraw her hand in time, Klara Olsufyevna rose mechanically to Mr. Golyadkin's invitation. Mr. Golyadkin took one tottering step forward, then a second. He raised one foot, did a sort of bow, gave a sort of stamp, and stumbled. He too wanted to dance with Klara Olsufyevna.

Klara Olsufyevna screamed. Everyone rushed to free her hand from Mr. Golyadkin's, and in a flash our hero was pushed almost a dozen yards away by the crowd. A small group formed around him. There were cries and shrieks from two old ladies whom Mr. Golyadkin had nearly bowled over in his retreat. The confusion was appalling. Everyone was shouting, arguing and questioning his neighbour. The orchestra had fallen silent. Turning round inside the small circle of people, and half smiling, Mr. Golyadkin was mechanically muttering under his breath something about: why shouldn't he? The polka was, as far as he could see, a novel and extremely interesting dance, contrived to delight the ladies . . . But if this was how it had turned out, he was prepared to acquiesce.

But Mr. Golyadkin's acquiescence was, it seemed, not asked for. A hand fell on his arm, another descended lightly on his back, and he felt himself being steered with especial care in a certain direction.

He noticed at last that he was heading straight for the door. He thought of trying to do or say something . . . But no. He didn't want to any more. He just laughed it off. He felt himself being put into his overcoat, and his hat being rammed down over his eyes. He became aware of the cold dark landing and the stairs. Finally he tripped, and seemed to be falling into an abyss. He tried to cry out, and all of a sudden found he was in the courtyard. A chill blast of air struck him, and he stopped. Just at that moment he caught the sound of the orchestra strik-

ing up again. It all came back to him. His energy seemed
suddenly restored. He had been standing rooted to the
spot, but now he broke away, and rushed headlong out
of the courtyard into the open, to freedom and wherever
his legs might carry him.

Chapter 5

Every tower in St. Petersburg that was wont to tell and
strike the hour sounded midnight as Mr. Golyadkin
rushed out, demented, onto the Fontanka Embankment
near the Izmaylovsky Bridge, seeking safety from enemies and persecution, a shower of insults, the alarmed
shrieks of the old ladies, the sobbing and sighing of the
other women, and the murderous glances of Andrey
Filippovich. He had no more life in him. He was finished
in the full sense of the word, and if at that moment he
was still able to run, it was only by some incredible miracle.

It was a dreadful night, a real November night, dank,
misty, rainy and snowy, a night pregnant with colds,
agues, quinsies, gumboils, and fevers of every conceivable
shape and size—put in a nutshell, a night bestowing all
the bounties of a St. Petersburg November. The wind
howled through the streets, lashing the black waters of
the Fontanka high above the mooring rings, and vigorously rattling the feeble lanterns along the embankment,
which responded with those thin, ear-piercing squeaks,
that compose the unceasing concert of jarring sound so
familiar to every inhabitant of St. Petersburg. It was raining and snowing all in one. The sheeting rain was broken
up by the wind and sprayed almost horizontally, as if
from a fireman's hose, stabbing and stinging the face of
the unhappy Mr. Golyadkin like so many pins and
needles. In the night stillness, disturbed only by the distant rumble of carriages, the howl of the wind and the
squeak of the lanterns, was heard the dismal sound of
water gushing and gurgling from every roof, porch, gut-
ter and cornice, onto the granite pavement. There was
not a soul anywhere, nor could there be it seemed, at such
an hour in such weather. And so, alone with his despair,
Mr. Golyadkin jogged along the Fontanka, taking his
usual short quick steps, and hastening to reach as soon as

possible his Shestilavochnaya Street, his fourth floor and his own rooms.

Although snow, rain and all the nameless afflictions of a wet and windy St. Petersburg November night were suddenly and with one accord assailing Mr. Golyadkin— weighed down as he was with enough misfortune already —giving no quarter or respite, gumming up his eyes, cutting into him from all sides, chilling him to the bone, and driving him off his path and out of his mind; although all this had fallen upon him at once as if by express agreement with his enemies to give him a day and a night he would not forget in a hurry, Mr. Golyadkin remained almost unaware of this final evidence of a persecuting fate, so stunned and shaken was he by all that had befallen him a few minutes earlier at Civil Counsellor Berendeyev's. Any detached and impartial observer who at that moment merely glanced at Mr. Golyadkin and saw his anguished step, would immediately have been imbued with a sense of the appalling horror of his misfortunes, and would certainly have said he had the look of a man wishing to hide and escape from himself. And that is exactly how it was. We will say more: at that moment Mr. Golyadkin wanted not only to escape from himself, but to annihilate himself completely, to return to dust and cease to be. He was oblivious of all around, and looked as if the vexations of that vile night—the long walk, the wind and the rain—no longer existed for him. A galosh parting company with Mr. Golyadkin's right boot, remained where it was in the slush and snow of the Fontanka pavement. Mr. Golyadkin had no thought of going back for it, for he had not noticed its loss. So great was his perplexity that every now and then, regardless of everything around, he would stop short and stand stockstill in the middle of the pavement, completely absorbed by the awfulness of his downfall. At such moments he would depart this life and cease to exist. Then suddenly, off he would go like a madman, and run and run without looking back, as though being pursued and fleeing some still more dreadful calamity. His was indeed an awful predicament. At last, his strength exhausted, Mr. Golyadkin stopped, and leaning over the railings like someone with a sudden nose-bleed, stared fixedly at the troubled black waters of the Fontanka. How long he spent thus engaged it is impossible to say. All one can say is that Mr.

Golyadkin had then reached such depths of despair, had been so wearied, tormented and dispirited, that he had forgotten everything—the Izmaylovsky Bridge, Shesti-lavochnaya Street, and the position he was in. What did it matter? He didn't care. The thing was over and done with—signed, sealed and delivered. Why should he worry? . . . Suddenly he shuddered all over and instinctively leapt sideways a couple of yards. Filled with unspeakable uneasiness, he peered about him. But there was no one. Nothing out of the ordinary had happened, and yet . . . And yet he thought someone had just been standing right there beside him, also with elbows on the railings, and, strange to relate, had even spoken to him —had spoken quickly, jerkily and not altogether intelligibly, but had said something of intimate concern to him.

"Did I dream it?" said Mr. Golyadkin, again peering around. "But where am I? Ugh!" he concluded, shaking his head, and began uneasily and fearfully to stare into the wet murky distance, straining his short-sighted eyes to the uttermost in an effort to penetrate the sodden darkness that lay before him. But there was nothing new. Nothing peculiar struck Mr. Golyadkin's eye. Everything seemed to be as it should—the snow falling harder and thicker, not a thing visible over twenty yards, the lanterns squeaking even more shrilly than before, and the wind taking up its mournful song on an even more piteous and plaintive note, like an importunate beggar pleading for a copper for food.

"What's wrong with me?" thought Mr. Golyadkin, setting off on his way again, and still looking round occasionally. He felt a strange new sensation coming over him—a mixture of fear and anguish. . . . A feverish shudder ran through every nerve. It was an unbearably dreadful moment.

"Well, it doesn't matter," he said to cheer himself up. "Perhaps it's nothing, and not a disgrace to anyone's honour. Perhaps it had to be so," he continued, not understanding himself what he was saying. "Perhaps in due course this will all turn out for the best. There won't be anything to complain of, and everyone will be vindicated."

So saying, and putting his mind at ease with words, Mr. Golyadkin shook himself off a bit and dislodged the snow with which his hat, collar, overcoat, scarf and boots were thickly encrusted. But he was still unable to shake off and rid himself of that strange vague feeling of anguish. Somewhere in the distance a cannon was fired.

"Fine weather this is," thought our hero. "Hark! Won't that be for a flood? You can see the water's up too high."

No sooner had Mr. Golyadkin said or thought this than he saw someone coming towards him—someone who probably like himself had been delayed on some matter or other. A meaningless, quite fortuitous thing it seemed, but for some unknown reason Mr. Golyadkin was disturbed, scared even, and rather unsure of himself. Not that he was afraid of it being anyone unpleasant, but . . .

"Who knows who this belated fellow may be?" flashed through Mr. Golyadkin's mind. "Perhaps he's the same as the rest . . . Perhaps *he's* the most important part of it, and isn't just out for his health but with the express purpose of crossing my path and provoking me."

But Mr. Golyadkin may not exactly have thought this; he may momentarily have sensed something very disagreeable that was much the same. Still, there was no time for thoughts or sensations. The man was a couple of yards away. Mr. Golyadkin lost no time in assuming as was his wont a very special expression that said clearly that he, Golyadkin, was going his own way and was all right, that the road was wide enough for everyone, and that he, Golyadkin, was obviously doing no harm to anybody. Suddenly, as though struck by a thunderbolt, he stopped dead in his tracks, and spun round like a weathercock in the wind to stare after the man who had passed and was disappearing rapidly into the whirl of snow. He also was in a hurry. He was dressed and muffled exactly like Mr. Golyadkin from head to foot, and was scuttling along the Fontanka at almost a run, with the same short rapid step.

"What's this?" whispered Mr. Golyadkin—there was a smile of incredulity on his face, but his whole body was trembling. A cold shiver ran down his spine. The man had meanwhile disappeared completely, and the sound of his footsteps could no longer be heard. But Mr. Golyadkin still stood gazing after him. Gradually he recovered his senses.

"What is it?" he thought irritably. "Have I gone mad or something?"

He turned and went his way, walking steadily faster and doing his best not to think. With this object he even closed his eyes. Suddenly above the howling wind and the noise of the storm he again heard footsteps very close. He shuddered and opened his eyes. Twenty yards away was again the dark figure of a man drawing rapidly nearer. He was hustling along at a brisk trot, and the distance between them was diminishing rapidly. Mr. Golyadkin could now see his new late-night companion quite distinctly, and uttered a cry of horror and amazement. His legs buckled beneath him. It was the same man he had passed ten minutes before! This and something else so astounded Mr. Golyadkin that he stopped, gave a cry, tried to say something, then rushed to overtake the stranger, shouting in an attempt to halt him as quickly as possible. The stranger halted some ten yards from Mr. Golyadkin, where his whole figure was illuminated by a nearby lantern. He turned, and looking puzzled and impatient, waited for what Mr. Golyadkin had to say.

"Excuse me. Perhaps I'm mistaken," quavered our hero.

The stranger turned away with a gesture of annoyance, and walked quickly on without a word, as if in a hurry to make up the two seconds wasted over Mr. Golyadkin. As for the latter, he was trembling all over. His knees turned to jelly, and with a groan he sat down on a tall kerbstone. There was indeed cause for alarm, for he thought there was something familiar about the stranger. This by itself would have been nothing. But he was now almost sure it was someone he knew. He'd seen him often. He'd seen him somewhere quite recently even. But where? Was it yesterday? But the fact that he'd seen him often wasn't of primary importance, there was nothing very special about him, nothing certainly that would have made anyone look twice at him. He was just like anyone else, of course, respectable, and perhaps even had certain quite good points; he was, in short, a man going his own way. Mr. Golyadkin felt no hatred, enmity or even the slightest unfriendliness towards him—quite the reverse it would seem. And yet—and this was the main thing—he would not have wished to meet him for all the tea in China, and particularly under circumstances such as the present. Mr. Golyadkin, we must add, knew this man perfectly well, knew his name even. But again, not for all the tea in China would he have spoken his name, or been willing to admit that that over there was so-and-so whose father was so-and-so. How long Mr. Golyadkin's mental confusion lasted, or how long he remained seated on the kerbstone, we cannot say. But at last recovering somewhat, he took to his heels and ran as hard as he could without looking back. His lungs felt as if they would burst. Twice he tripped and nearly fell, and on one of these occasions his other boot parted company with its galosh. Finally he slackened his pace a little to get breath. A rapid glance round showed that he had without noticing it run the whole of his usual route along the Fontanka, crossed the Anichkov Bridge, and was now at the corner of Liteynaya Street, some way along the Nevsky Prospect. He turned into Liteynaya Street. At that moment he was in the position of a man standing on the brink of a fearful precipice when the ground gives way beneath him . . . A tremor—the ground moves, a last shudder—and it's falling with him into the abyss . . . The hapless man has neither the strength nor the willpower to leap back or to take his eyes from the yawning chasm . . . He is drawn towards it, and finally jumps to hasten his end. Mr. Golyadkin knew, felt and was quite convinced, that some new evil would befall him on the way, and that some fresh unpleasantness would burst upon him; that there would be, for instance, another meeting with the stranger. Oddly enough he even wanted this to happen, considering it inevitable and only asking that the whole thing might be got over as quickly as possible, and that he might know where he stood. Only let it be soon! Meanwhile he ran on and on as though propelled by some external force, for he felt numb and weak all over. He was incapable of thought, but his mind clutched brier-like at everything. A miserable little stray dog, wet and shivering with cold, attached itself to Mr. Golyadkin and trotted along beside him, ears down and tail between its legs, every now and then looking up at him, timidly and intelligently. A long-forgotten idea, a recollection of something that had happened in the distant past now came into his head and hammered away there, irritating him and refusing to let him be.

"Ugh! Wretched little dog!" muttered Mr. Golyadkin, not understanding what he was saying.

At last he caught sight of his stranger at the corner of Italyanskaya Street. But now instead of coming towards him, he was going in the same direction. He was several yards in front, and also running. They turned into Shesti-lavochnaya Street. Mr. Golyadkin caught his breath. The stranger had stopped right outside the house in which he lived. The bell rang, and the iron bolt grated back almost simultaneously. The wicket opened, the stranger stooped, remained visible for a second, then disappeared. Mr. Golyadkin got there at almost the same moment, and went through the wicket like a shot out of a gun. Ignoring the grumbling porter, he rushed breathlessly into the courtyard and for a moment regained sight of his interesting companion at the foot of the staircase leading to his rooms. He hurled himself in pursuit. The staircase was dark, dank and dirty, and mountains of junk belonging to tenants blocked every landing. Any stranger journeying up it after dark would run the risk of breaking a leg, and would be forced to spend about half an hour over it, cursing the staircase together with his friends for having settled in such a place. But Mr. Golyadkin's companion was darting lightly up the stairs, encountering no difficulties, and showing perfect knowledge of the ground. Mr. Golyadkin nearly caught him up. Several times the hem of the stranger's coat brushed his nose. Suddenly his heart sank. The mysterious man had stopped and knocked at the door of Mr. Golyadkin's flat. Petrushka answered at once as if he had been waiting up (at any other time this would have surprised Mr. Golyadkin), and lighted the stranger in with a candle. Half out of his wits our hero followed, and without removing hat or overcoat, dashed down the short corridor. On the threshold of his room he stopped as though struck by a thunderbolt. His worst fears were realised . . . Everything he had dreaded and foreseen was now fact. Sitting on *his* bed, also wearing a hat and coat, smiling slightly, puckering up his eyes and tipping him a friendly nod, was the stranger. Mr. Golyadkin wanted to scream, but could not—wanted to make some form of protest, but lacked the power. His hair stood on end, and he collapsed senseless with horror on the spot. And small wonder. He had fully recognized his friend of the night. It was none other than himself—Mr. Golyadkin . . . Another Mr. Golyadkin, but exactly the same as him . . . It was, in short, his double . . .

Chapter 6

Next morning at eight precisely, Mr. Golyadkin came to, lying in bed. Immediately he remembered and saw in his mind's eye the full horror of all the extraordinary events of the preceding day, and the almost impossible adventures of the whole incredibly strange night. Such fierce diabolical malice on the part of his enemies, particularly as last demonstrated, made Mr. Golyadkin's blood run cold. But at the same time it was all so peculiar, incomprehensible and absurd, it all seemed so impossible even, that really one could hardly credit it. Mr. Golyadkin would have been only too ready to regard the whole thing as a delirious fancy, a momentary derangement of the imagination or a clouding of the mind, had he not fortunately known from bitter experience of life the lengths to which a man may sometimes be driven by malice, and the furious extremes to which an enemy avenging pride and honour may sometimes go. The reality of last night's walk and to some extent of what had occurred during that walk, was, moreover, confirmed and supported by his weary limbs, his muzzy head, his breaking back and hacking cough. And finally he had known for ages that they were cooking something up, and that there was someone else in with them. But what of it? On mature consideration Mr. Golyadkin decided to keep quiet, to yield, and not protest until a certain time.

"Perhaps their idea was just to give me a fright, and when they see me not minding or protesting, but submitting and humbly putting up with it, they'll give way first."

Such were the thoughts that ran through the mind of Mr. Golyadkin, as, stretching himself in bed and easing his aching limbs, he lay waiting for Petrushka to make his usual appearance. He had already been waiting for about a quarter of an hour, listening to the lazy fellow fussing about with the samovar behind the partition, but unable to make up his mind to call him. One might go further and say that Mr. Golyadkin was a little scared of facing Petrushka.

"Heaven knows what he thinks about it all, the scoundrel," he thought. "Doesn't say a word, but he's crafty."

At last the door creaked and Petrushka appeared, bearing a tray. Mr. Golyadkin watched him timidly out of the corner of his eye, waiting impatiently for something to happen, waiting to see whether he'd say anything on a certain matter. Petrushka said not a word, and was somehow even more sullen and uncommunicative than usual. He squinted darkly around, and was quite clearly extremely displeased about something. He did not so much as glance at his master, and this we may observe somewhat irritated the latter. He put everything he had brought on the table, turned, and disappeared behind his partition without a word.

"He knows! He knows all about it, the good-for-nothing!" muttered Mr. Golyadkin as he set to to drink his tea. But although Petrushka came in several times for various things, he put no questions to him.

Mr. Golyadkin was most agitated. The thought of going to the office terrified him. He had a strong presentiment of something being not quite right there.

"If you go, you'll run slap into it," he thought. "Isn't the best thing now to be patient for a bit? Wouldn't it be better to wait, and let them get on as they like? I could wait here today, getting my strength back, recuperating and thinking it all out. Then I could pick a moment, and give them the surprise of their lives, and pretend nothing whatever was wrong."

Pondering thus, Mr. Golyadkin smoked one pipe after another. Time flew, and soon it was almost half past nine.

"Well, it's half past nine," thought Mr. Golyadkin. "It's late to go now. Apart from that I'm ill. Of course I'm ill. Who's to say I'm not? And if they send anyone to see —let the administrative officer come if he likes—what do I care? I've got a backache. I've got a cough. I've got a cold in the head, and I can't go. I can't possibly in this weather. I might be taken ill, and die. There's a heavy death-rate nowadays . . ."

At last, by means of such arguments, Mr. Golyadkin salved his conscience completely, and justified himself in advance against the reprimand he might expect from Andrey Filippovich for neglecting his work. In all such situations our hero was very fond of justifying himself in his own eyes by various irrefutable arguments, and so salving his conscience completely. And so, his conscience salved, he picked up his pipe, filled it, and had no sooner got it drawing nicely, than he sprang up from the sofa, tossed it away, quickly washed, shaved and combed his hair, dragged on his uniform jacket and other things, and grabbing some papers, shot off to the office.

Timidly Mr. Golyadkin entered his section, trembling in anticipation of something extremely nasty, trembling with an expectancy which, if unconscious and vague, was at the same time unpleasant. Timidly he seated himself at his usual place next to Anton Antonovich Setochkin, the chief clerk. Without looking round or allowing himself to be distracted, he buried himself in the papers before him. He had decided and promised himself to keep as far aloof as possible from anything provocative, anything that could in any way compromise him, such as indelicate questions, unseemly insinuations, and pleasantries about the events of the preceding night; he had even made up his mind to forgo the usual courtesies with his colleagues—inquiries as to their health etc. But to keep this up was obviously an impossibility. Uneasiness and uncertainty about something that touched him intimately always tormented him more than the thing itself. And that is why, despite his promise not to become involved whatever happened, and to keep aloof from everything, no matter what it was, Mr. Golyadkin kept raising his head, furtively and ever so slightly, to take a sly peep at the faces of his colleagues to left and right, in an attempt to decide whether anything new or special concerning him was for some improper reason being concealed. He supposed there to be a direct connexion between everything at that moment around him and what had happened the day before. At last he began to wish in his anguish that it might all end as speedily as possible, though heaven alone knew how—in some disaster if need be—it didn't matter! Fate took him at his word. No sooner had he made the wish, than his doubts were resolved, albeit in a most peculiar and unexpected manner.

The door of the next room opened with a timid little squeak as if to announce a person of no great consequence, and a figure, well known to Mr. Golyadkin, came and stood diffidently before the desk at which he was sitting. Our hero did not raise his head. No. One fleeting glance at this figure, and he knew, he understood it all to the last detail. He flushed with shame, and just as the ostrich pursued by a hunter hides its head in the burning sand, so Mr. Golyadkin buried his wretched head in his papers. The newcomer bowed to Andrey Filippovich, and then could be heard those silkily formal tones in which the heads of all government departments are wont to address newly-arrived subordinates.

"Sit here," said Andrey Filippovich, indicating Anton Antonovich's desk to the new recruit. "Sit here opposite

Mr. Golyadkin, and we'll give you some work right away."
He ended with a rapid and decorous admonitory wave of
the hand, and was lost in the perusal of various documents from the great pile in front of him.

At last Mr. Golyadkin raised his eyes, and if he did not
faint away, it was solely because he had had from the first
a presentiment of the whole thing, had been forewarned,
and had already known in his heart who the newcomer
was. His first move was to take a rapid glance around to
see whether there was any whispering, whether any office
witticisms were taking shape on the subject, whether anyone's face expressed surprise, and finally whether anyone
had collapsed beneath his desk with fright. But to his great
astonishment he could detect nothing of the sort. He was
amazed by his friends' and colleagues' behaviour. It
seemed beyond the bounds of common sense. He was even
frightened by such unusual silence. The reality of the thing
spoke for itself. It was strange, hideous, absurd. It *was*
something to make a stir about. All this of course, merely
flashed through Mr. Golyadkin's mind. He felt as if he
was being slowly roasted alive, and not without reason.
Sitting opposite, was the terror of Mr. Golyadkin, the
shame of Mr. Golyadkin, his nightmare of the day before,
in short, Mr. Golyadkin himself; not the one who was now
sitting on his chair with mouth agape and a dry pen in
his hand; not the one who was assistant to the chief clerk;
not the one who liked to efface and hide himself in the
crowd; not the one who said plainly by the way he walked,
"Don't touch me, and I won't touch you," or "Don't touch
me, I'm not hurting you." No. This was a different Mr.
Golyadkin, quite different but at the same time identical
with the first—the same height, same build, dressed the
same, bald in the same place; in short, the resemblance
was perfect; nothing, absolutely nothing had been omit-
ted, so that had they been stood side by side, not a soul
would have undertaken to say who was the real Mr. Golyadkin, and who the counterfeit, who the old, and who
the new, who the original and who the copy.

Our hero, if comparison is possible, was like a man
on whom some wag has secretly focussed a burning-glass
by way of a joke.

"Is it a dream, or isn't it?" wondered Mr. Golyadkin.
"Is it real, or is it yesterday's business continued? But how
can it be? What right has this to happen? Who admitted this

clerk? Who authorized it? Am I asleep? Am I dreaming?"

Mr. Golyadkin tried pinching himself, and even thought of pinching somebody else . . . No, it wasn't a dream, so that was that. He felt the sweat pouring from him. What was happening to him was, he sensed, unprecedented, unheard-of, and therefore, to crown his misfortune, unseemly, for he perceived and understood the full disadvantage of being the first example of such lampoonery. He began finally even to doubt his own existence, and although he had been prepared for everything in advance, and had himself wished for his doubts to be resolved in some way, what had happened was, of course, in the nature of a surprise. He was wrung with anguish. Now and then he would lose all power of reasoning and lapse into unconsciousness. After one such moment he recovered to find himself automatically and unconsciously guiding his pen over the paper. Not trusting himself, he began checking what he had written, but could make nothing of it.

At last, the other Mr. Golyadkin, who all this while had been sitting quietly and decorously at his place, got up, and disappeared into the other section on some matter. Mr. Golyadkin took a look around, but there was nothing. All was still. Nothing could be heard but the scratching of pens, the rustle of turning pages, and a murmur of conversation from corners a little further removed from the seat of Andrey Filippovich. Mr. Golyadkin glanced at Anton Antonovich, and seeing our hero's expression, which in all likelihood reflected his mood at that moment, and was in keeping with the whole drift of the affair, the good Anton Antonovich laid aside his pen, and with unusual concern inquired after Mr. Golyadkin's health.

"I-I-I'm all right, Anton Antonovich. I'm perfectly well, Anton Antonovich," stammered Mr. Golyadkin. "I've nothing at the moment to complain of, Anton Antonovich," he added uncertainly, not yet fully trusting this Anton Antonovich whose name he was using so freely.

"There. I thought you were poorly. It wouldn't have been surprising, I'm afraid. All sorts of epidemics about, especially at present, you know."

"Yes, Anton Antonovich, I know there are . . . But Anton Antonovich, that's not the reason for which I . . ." continued Mr. Golyadkin, staring hard at him. "You see, Anton Antonovich—I don't know how to put it to you—that is, I mean, from what angle to tackle this matter . . ."

"What was that? I confess I don't quite follow you, you know. You . . . um . . . You tell me a bit more fully what the trouble is," said Anton Antonovich who, seeing the tears start to Mr. Golyadkin's eyes, was becoming a little troubled himself.

"I really . . . There's a clerk here, Anton Antonovich . . ."

"Well? I still don't follow."

"What I mean, Anton Antonovich, is that there's a newly-arrived clerk here."

"Yes. A namesake of yours."

"Wh-a-t?" cried Mr. Golyadkin.

"A namesake of yours. He's Golyadkin, too. Your brother, perhaps?"

"No, Anton Antonovich, I . . ."

"H-m. You don't say. I thought he must be a near relation. There's a certain family resemblance, you know."

Mr. Golyadkin was stunned with amazement, and for a while, speechless. How *could* he treat so lightly a thing so unparalleled and monstrous—a thing so rare in its way as to astound the most uninterested observer! How *could* anyone speak of a family resemblance, when here was a mirror image!

"Do you know what I advise you to do, Yakov Petrovich?" continued Anton Antonovich—"go and see a doctor and ask his advice. Somehow you don't *look* at all well, you know. Your eyes have got a funny look about them."

"No, Anton Antonovich, naturally I feel . . . That is, what sort of a person is he, this clerk? That's what I want to know."

"Yes?"

"That is, haven't you noticed something peculiar about him, Anton Antonovich—something very significant?"

"What exactly?"

"I mean a striking resemblance to someone—to me for instance. Just now you said something, just a casual remark, about a family resemblance . . . Do you know twins are sometimes as alike as two peas in a pod, so that you can't tell one from the other? Well, that's what I'm talking about . . ."

"Yes," said Anton Antonovich, after pondering for a

moment, as though this had never struck him before.
"Yes. Quite right. Really, the resemblance is amazing,
and you're perfectly correct—you could be taken for one
another," he continued, with a look of ever-increasing
astonishment. "Do you know, it's a wonderful—it's a fantastic likeness, as they sometimes say. He's you exactly
. . . Have you noticed, Yakov Petrovich? I meant to ask
you about it myself. I must confess, I wasn't paying proper
attention at first. It's a wonder, it really is! And tell me,
Yakov Petrovich, you weren't born here, were you?"

"No."

"Neither was he. Perhaps you're from the same parts.
Where did your mother spend most of her life, if you don't
mind my asking?"

"Did you say . . . Did you say he wasn't born here,
Anton Antonovich?"

"No, he's not from these parts. It's an absolute marvel,"
continued the loquacious Anton Antonovich, for whom it
was a real treat to have something to prattle about.

"It really does make you curious. The number of times
you pass him, brush up against him or knock into him,
and don't notice. But don't you worry. It's a thing that
does happen. Do you know, I must tell you this, the very
same thing occurred to an aunt of mine on my mother's
side. She saw her own spit and image before she
died . . ."

"No, I . . . Forgive my interrupting you, Anton
Antonovich, but what I should like to know is how this
clerk—that is, how does he stand here?"

"He's got the vacancy left by Semyon Ivanovich who
died. A place fell vacant, so they put him in. A good-
hearted fellow, poor Semyon Ivanovich. Left three little
kiddies, so they say. His widow came, and went down on
her knees to his Excellency. But they say she hides it
away. She's got a bit of money, but she hides it . . ."

"No, I'm still on about the other thing, Anton Antonovich."

"What's that? Ah, yes. But why are you so concerned
about it? Don't worry, that's what I say. It'll all pass.
What does it matter? It's no affair of yours. It's God's doing, it's His will, and to grumble at that is a sin. *His* infinite wisdom is apparent in this, and you, Yakov Petrovich, so far as I can gather, are in no way to blame. The
world is full of wonders! Mother Nature is generous.

And by way of example, while we're on the subject, you've heard, I take it, about—what d'you call 'em—the Siamese twins, being joined back to back, and living, eating and sleeping together like it. They earn good money, people say."

"Anton Antonovich, allow me . . ."

"I take your meaning. Well, what of it? It doesn't matter. I tell you, to my mind there's nothing to get upset about. He's a clerk just like anyone else—seems a capable chap. Says he's called Golyadkin. Isn't from hereabouts, he says, and he's a clerk. He's had a personal talk with his Excellency."

"What about?"

"Oh, nothing. Gave an adequate account of himself, they say. Stated his case: "Such and such, and such and such, your Excellency. I've no fortune, I'd like to serve, and would be especially proud to do so under you . . ." Well, everything as it should be, you know. Put it all very nicely. Must be a clever fellow. Came with a recommendation, of course. Can't do much without one, you know."

"Who was it from? What I mean is, who exactly is mixed up in this scandalous business?"

"Oh, yes. It was a good recommendation, so they say. They say his Excellency had a laugh with Andrey Filippovich over it."

"Had a laugh with Andrey Filippovich?"

"Yes. He just smiled, and said it was all right, and he had no objections, provided he did his job properly . . ."

"Well, what happened next? You're cheering me up quite a bit, Anton Antonovich. Tell me what happened next, I beg you."

"Forgive me. Again I don't quite . . . Ah well, it's no matter. It's quite simple. Don't you go worrying, that's what I say. There's nothing fishy about it . . ."

"No, what I want to ask you, Anton Antonovich, is didn't his Excellency add anything to that, about me for instance?"

"Oh, certainly! Or rather, no, not a thing. You can be quite easy in your mind. Do you know—it's striking enough, of course, yet at first . . . Well, take me for instance. I almost missed it at first. Why I didn't notice till you mentioned it, I don't know, I'm sure. But still, you can be easy in your mind. He said nothing special, nothing whatever," added the good Anton Antonovich, rising from his seat.

"Well, Anton Antonovich, I . . ."

"Er, look, excuse me, will you? Here I've been, babbling away, and I've got something urgent and important to do. I must get it finished."

"Anton Antonovich," came a polite summons from Andrey Filippovich, "his Excellency has been asking for you."

"Coming, Andrey Filippovich, coming at once."

And grabbing a pile of papers, Anton Antonovich sped first to Andrey Fillipovich, and then into his Excellency's room.

"So that's how we stand," thought Mr. Golyadkin to himself. "So that's the way things are. Not bad. Things have taken a much pleasanter turn," he said to himself, rubbing his hands, and in his joy, oblivious of everything.

"So it's quite ordinary, this business of ours. It's all come to nothing. It's all blowing over. No one's noticed in fact. Not a squeak out of them, the cut-throats—they're sitting and getting on with their work. Splendid! Splendid!

"I like the man, always have done, and respect him . . . But now I come to think of it, I'd be afraid to trust him with anything. He's very grey and doddery is Anton Antonovich. Still, the main and most important thing is his Excellency's not saying anything, but just letting it pass. That's good. I approve of that. Only why's Andrey Filippovich got to butt in with his sneers? What's it got to do with him? Crafty old devil! He's always in your way, always trying to mess things up, always crossing and spiting, spiting and crossing you!"

Mr. Golyadkin took another look round, and was again encouraged. But a vague and unpleasant idea that he had, nevertheless troubled him. The thought crossed his mind of somehow enlisting the support of the clerks, of somehow stealing a march on them, and, approaching them ostensibly on business, or as they were all leaving, of making in the course of conversation some reference to the subject such as "Such and such, and such and such, gentlemen—a striking resemblance—very strange—sailing under false colours, that's what it is." Thus, by treating it as a joke, he would gauge the extent of the danger. For still waters ran deep, he concluded. But his thought remained nothing more than a thought. He changed his mind in time. He realized that would be going too far.

"That's you all over!" he said, tapping his forehead. "Now you'll be full of fun. You're happy! Honest soul that you are. No. We'd better have patience, Yakov Petrovich. We'll have patience and wait."

None the less Mr. Golyadkin was, as we have mentioned, filled with renewed hope, and felt like someone risen from the dead.

"It's all right," he thought. "It's like having a ton-weight off your chest. 'To open it you simply raised the lid.' * It's as simple as that. Krylov's right. He knows all about it. He's an artful one, Krylov, and a great fable-writer!

"And as far as this other fellow is concerned, let him work here. Let him, and good luck to him, provided he doesn't hinder or interfere with anyone. Let him—he's got my consent and approval!"

All this time the hours had been slipping by, and four struck before Mr. Golyadkin noticed it. Office hours were over. Andrey Filippovich went for his hat, and as usual everyone followed his example. Mr. Golyadkin hung about for a bit, deliberately leaving last, after everyone had gone their separate ways. Once out in the street, he felt as if he was in paradise, so much so that he conceived a desire to make a detour and go along the Nevsky Prospect.

"It's fate—everything taking this unexpected turn," said our hero. "And the weather's better. There's a nice frost, and sledges are out. Frost's good for a Russian. I like Russians. And there's a bit of snow—*fresh-fallen* snow as a hunter would say. That's the time to go after hares, when there's fresh-fallen snow. Ah well! It doesn't matter."

Thus did Mr. Golyadkin express his delight, but all the while there was a sort of anxiety at the back of his mind, and at times a gnawing pain at his heart for which he could find no relief.

"Still, we'll wait a day before we start rejoicing. But what's wrong? We'll think it all out, and see. Well, come on my young friend, let's think it out then. First of all,

---

* Last line of a fable by I. A. Krylov describing the clever attempts made to open a certain box in every way but the obvious, and suggesting that difficulties should not be seen where they do not exist.—*Translator.*

there's someone like you, exactly like you. Well, what is there in that? Supposing there is—any need for me to cry over it? What's it matter to me? I'm out of it all. I don't care, and that's that. I accept it, and there you are. Let him work in the office! It's strange and wonderful, they say, about the Siamese twins . . . Well, why drag them in? Suppose they are twins—even great men have looked silly at times. History even tells us the great Suvorov used to crow like a cock . . . Still, all that was for political reasons. And even the great generals . . . But what are generals? I go my own way. I don't bother about anyone else, and being innocent, I scorn my enemies. I'm no intriguer, and proud of the fact. Frank, upright, mild, agreeable, orderly . . ."

Mr. Golyadkin broke off suddenly, began trembling like a leaf, and shut his eyes for a moment. Trusting what had frightened him to have been an illusion, however, he opened them again, and glanced timidly to the right out of the corner of his eye. It was no illusion! Trotting along beside him, smiling, looking straight at him, and waiting, it seemed, for a chance to start a conversation, was the person whose acquaintance he had made that morning. But conversation was not started. They continued thus for about fifty yards. All Mr. Golyadkin's efforts were directed towards muffling himself up as much as possible, burying himself in his overcoat, and pulling his hat as far as it would go down over his eyes. To add insult to injury, even the other's hat and coat were identical with Mr. Golyadkin's—they might have been taken from his own back.

"We go different ways, it seems, sir . . ." said Mr. Golyadkin finally, not looking at his friend and trying to keep his voice to a whisper. "I'm quite sure we do," he said after a short pause. "I'm sure you at last take my meaning," he threw in rather stiffly.

"I should like . . ." said Mr. Golyadkin's friend at last. "I should like . . . You'll kindly forgive me, I hope . . . I don't know who to turn to here . . . Placed as I am . . . I trust you'll excuse my making so bold, but I thought you were so sympathetic as to take some interest in me this morning. Speaking for myself, I felt drawn to you from the first. I . . ."

At this point Mr. Golyadkin silently wished that his new colleague might disappear through the ground.

"If I might venture to hope that you would condescend to hear me out, Yakov Petrovich . . ."

"Here we're, er . . . We'd better go to my place," replied Mr. Golyadkin. "'Let's cross the Nevsky now. It's more convenient for us on the other side. Then there's a little side street we can take . . . Yes, we'd better do that."

"Yes, certainly, we'll take the little side street," said Mr. Golyadkin's submissive companion, seeming to intimate by his diffident tone that he could not pick and choose, and that, situated as he was, he was prepared to be satisfied with the little side street.

As for Mr. Golyadkin, he had no idea what was happening to him. He could not trust his own senses. He had not yet recovered from his astonishment.

Chapter 7

On the stairs and at the door of his rooms he recovered a little.

"What a dim-wit I am!" he chided himself. "Where am I taking him? I'm putting a rope around my own neck. What will Petrushka think, seeing us together? What won't the wretch think now! He's suspicious as it is . . ."

But it was too late for any regrets. Mr. Golyadkin knocked, the door opened and Petrushka began helping guest and master out of their coats. Mr. Golyadkin stole a quick look, just a glance at Petrushka, in an attempt to read his thoughts from his face. But to his great astonishment his servant showed no surprise—quite the reverse, as if he had been expecting something of the sort. Of course, he was far from friendly. He wouldn't look you in the eye, and seemed all set to bite someone's head off.

"What's wrong today? Is everyone under a spell?" thought our hero. "Some demon must have been around. Certainly something has got into them. What a damned worry it is!"

Such were Mr. Golyadkin's reflections as he conducted his guest into his room, and humbly invited him to take a seat. The guest showed every sign of being acutely embarrassed and overcome with shyness, dutifully watched his host's every move and caught his every glance, striving, it seemed, to divine what he was thinking. There was something abject, downtrodden and fearful about every gesture he made, so that at this moment he was, if one may use the simile, rather like a man who, having no clothes of his own, has donned someone else's, and can feel the sleeves riding up and the waist nearly round the back of his neck, and is all the time pulling down the miserably short waistcoat; he edges away, tries hard to hide, looks at every face to see if people are ashamed on his account or laughing at him, strains his ears to find out if they're discussing his affairs; he goes red, and gets confused; his pride suffers. Mr. Golyadkin had put his hat on the window ledge. A sudden careless movement knocked it to the floor. At once his guest shot forward, picked it up, dusted it off, and carefully replaced it, putting his own on the floor beside a chair on the very edge of which he meekly perched himself. This trivial incident was something of an eye-opener to Mr. Golyadkin. Realising that his guest was in sore straits, he no longer felt at a loss how to begin, but very properly left it all to him. But he would not begin either, and waited for his host to make the opening—whether this was out of shyness, embarrassment or politeness, would be difficult to say. At this moment Petrushka appeared, and stood in the doorway, his eyes fixed on the opposite corner of the room to that in which his master and the guest were sitting.

"Shall I bring dinner for two?" he asked casually, in his rather husky ioice.

"I—I don't know . . . Er, yes—dinner for two."

Mr. Golyadkin glanced at his guest, and saw that he had gone as red as a beetroot. Being a kind-hearted person, he formed a theory accordingly.

"Poor fellow," he thought, "only been at the office a day. Probably been through it in his time. Only got what he stands up in, perhaps, and can't afford dinner. What a downtrodden specimen he is! Well, it doesn't matter. It's better like that in some ways . . ."

"Forgive my asking," began Mr. Golyadkin, "but what are your Christian names?"

"I'm—I'm Yakov Petrovich," said the guest almost in a whisper, as though ashamed, embarrassed and apologetic that this should be so.

"Yakov Petrovich!" echoed our hero, unable to hide his confusion.

"Yes, that's right. . . . We're namesakes," replied

Mr. Golyadkin's lowly visitor, making so bold as to smile and say something jocular. But seeing his host was in no mood for jocularity, he immediately stopped short and assumed a most serious but rather embarrassed look.

"Er . . . May I ask to what I can attribute the honour . . ."

"Knowing you to be upright and generous," interposed his guest quickly but timidly, half rising from his seat, "I have ventured to appeal to you for your friendship and protection," he concluded, finding obvious difficulty in expressing himself, and selecting words that were not too adulatory and not too self-abasing, to avoid hurting his pride, nor yet too bold and savouring of an equality that was not proper. Mr. Golyadkin's guest was, as one might put it, behaving like a beggar of gentle birth who, with darns in his coat and the papers appropriate to his true status in his pocket, has not yet learnt how to stretch out his palm.

"You embarrass me," replied Mr. Golyadkin, looking down at himself, at the walls of his room, and then at his guest. "How can I . . . what I mean is, in what respect can I be of service to you?"

"I felt drawn to you at first sight, Yakov Petrovich, and—be so generous as to forgive me—I dared to put my trust in you. I . . . I'm all at sea here, Yakov Petrovich. I'm poor. I've suffered much, Yakov Petrovich, and I'm still new here. Discovering that you, with all the innate good qualities of a noble spirit, were of the same name as myself . . ."

Mr. Golyadkin frowned.

". . . And were from the same parts, I resolved to come and acquaint you with my difficult position."

"Quite so, quite so. I don't know what to say, I'm sure," replied Mr. Golyadkin disconcertedly. "Look, we'll have a talk after dinner."

The guest bowed. Dinner was brought in. Petrushka placed everything on the table, and guest and host set about satisfying their appetites. The meal did not last long for both ate hurriedly—the host because he was not his usual self and felt ashamed that the dinner was bad when he would have liked to do his guest well, and show that he did not live like a pauper—the guest because he was extremely shy and embarrassed. Having once helped himself to a slice of bread and eaten it, he was afraid to reach out a second time. He scrupulously avoided taking the best of anything, and every minute assured his host that he wasn't hungry, that the meal was excellent, and that he was completely satisfied and would remember it till the day he died. The meal over, Mr. Golyadkin lit his pipe, and offered another that he had acquired for friends, to his guest. They seated themselves facing each other, and the guest began his tale.

The tale of Golyadkin junior lasted three or four hours, and was composed of the most trivial, one might almost say the most footling, incidents. It spoke of service in some provincial law-courts, of presidents and prosecutors, of office intrigues, of the rottenness of one of the chief clerks, of an inspector, of a sudden change of departmental head, and of how Golyadkin II had suffered entirely through no fault of his own; it spoke of his aged aunt Pelageya Semyonova, of how through the various machinations of his enemies he had lost his post and walked to St. Petersburg; it spoke of his wretched and painful existence in that city, of his long, fruitless search for a job, of how he exhausted his funds, spent his last penny on food, practically lived in the street, ate stale bread moistened by his own tears, and slept on bare boards; it spoke finally of how some kind person had taken trouble on his behalf, had given him introductions and magnanimously found him a new position. In the telling of this Mr. Golyadkin's guest wept and dabbed away his tears with a blue check handkerchief that looked very much like a piece of oilcloth. In conclusion he opened his heart to Mr. Golyadkin, and confessed that he was for the moment not only without means to support himself and settle in somewhere, but also quite unable to fit himself out properly. He had not even been able to raise the price of an old pair of boots, and his uniform he had borowed for a short while.

Mr. Golyadkin was moved, was genuinely touched. Trivial as his guest's story had been, he had received every word of it like manna from heaven. Forgetting his recent misgivings, he allowed himself to feel joyously free, and mentally wrote himself down as a fool. It was all so natural! What a thing to get distressed and alarmed about! Actually there was one thorny point, but it didn't matter. It couldn't disgrace you, damage your pride and ruin your career when you were innocent—when Nature herself was involved. Moreover the guest had begged his protection, had wept and accused fate; he seemed so simple, so completely without malice or artifice, so pathetic and insignificant; and now, although it might have been for other reasons, he too appeared embarrassed by the strange resemblance he bore to his host. His behaviour was completely dependable. His very expression was intended to please his host, and was that of a man tormented by pangs of conscience and a feeling of guilt. If, for instance, conversation touched on any doubtful point, the guest at once agreed with Mr. Golyadkin. If, by an oversight, he somehow advanced an opinion that was contrary to Mr. Golyadkin's, and then noticed his slip, he would immediately correct himself, explain, and give his host to understand that he thought exactly the same and viewed the whole thing in precisely the same light as he. In short, he did his level best to win Mr. Golyadkin over, and the latter finally decided he must be a most likable fellow in every way.

Tea was served. It was now after eight. Mr. Golyadkin felt in excellent spirits. He livened up, began to enjoy himself and get into his stride a bit, and finally launched out into a most lively and entertaining conversation with his guest. Sometimes, in merry mood, Mr. Golyadkin was fond of recounting odd items of interest. So it was now. He told his guest a great deal about the capital, its entertainments and its beauties; he told of the theatre, the clubs and of Brülow's latest picture; of the two Englishmen who travelled from England to St. Petersburg expressly to see the railings outside The Summer Gardens, and then went straight home again; of his work at the office, of Olsufy Ivanovich and Andrey Filippovich; he told how Russia was hourly approaching perfection, and literature and learning were thriving; he told of an anecdote he had read lately in *The Northern Bee;* he told of an extraordinarily powerful boa constrictor in India; and lastly he spoke of Baron Brambeus. In brief, Mr. Golyadkin was perfectly happy. His mind was completely at ease; far from fearing his enemies, he was now ready to challenge the lot of them to a decisive battle; and he was acting as someone's protector, and at last doing good. But in his heart of hearts he confessed that he was still not quite happy, and that even now another tiny little worry was gnawing away inside him. He was much tormented

by the memory of the previous evening at Olsufy Ivanovich's. At that moment he would have given a lot to wipe
out some of the events of the day before.

"Still, it doesn't matter," decided our hero finally, firmly
resolving that he would henceforth behave himself, and
not perpetrate such blunders.

Now that he had let himself go and was happy, Mr.
Golyadkin had a mind to enjoy life a bit. Rum was
brought in by Petrushka, and punch made. Guest and
host drank one glass, then a second. The guest became
more likable than ever, and more than once gave evidence
of having a happy forthright nature. He entered whole-
heartedly into Mr. Golyadkin's joyous mood, seemed to
rejoice at his rejoicing, and to look upon him as his one
true benefactor. Taking a pen and a small sheet of paper, he begged Mr. Golyadkin not to watch, and then
when he had finished showed him what he had written.
It was a quatrain, rather sentimental but elegantly
phrased, beautifully penned, and evidently of the amiable
guest's own composition. It ran thus:

> If me thou ever shouldst forget,
>   I'll remember thee;
> Much in life may happen yet,
>   But remember me!

With tears in his eyes, Mr. Golyadkin embraced his
guest, and finally, overcome with emotion, let him into
some of his secrets, with particular reference to Andrey
Filippovich and Klara Olsufyevna.

"Yes Yakov Petrovich, we'll be friends, you and I," said
our hero. "We were made for each other. We're like twin
brothers. We'll fox 'em, my dear fellow. We'll fox 'em together. We'll start an intrigue of our own to spite them,
that's what we'll do. Don't you trust any of them. I know
you, and understand you, Yakov Petrovich. You're an
honest soul. You'd go and tell them everything. You keep
away from them all, my dear chap."

The guest agreed to everything, thanked Mr. Golyadkin, and shed a few tears of his own.

"I tell you what, Yasha," continued Mr. Golyadkin, his
voice weak and quivering, "you come and move in here
for a time, or come for good. We'll get on all right. How
does that appeal to you, eh? It's no good worrying
or grumbling about this strange thing between us. It's a

sin to grumble, my friend. It's Nature! And Mother Nature is generous, Yasha! I'm saying this because of my affection, my brotherly affection for you. We'll fox 'em, Yasha, you and I. We'll do some underhand work of our own, and make 'em laugh on the other side of their faces."

They had had a third and a fourth glass of punch, and Mr. Golyadkin was becoming aware of two things: an extraordinary feeling of happiness, and an inability to stand. The guest was naturally invited to spend the night, and somehow a bed was made by placing together two rows of chairs. Mr. Golyadkin junior declared that under a friendly roof bare boards would make a soft couch, and that he would sleep anywhere, humbly and gratefully; he was now in Paradise; he had been through a great deal in his time, had known tears and sorrow, and had endured much; and might, for who knew what the future held, have more to endure. Mr. Golyadkin senior protested at this, and began to argue that one should put full trust in God. The guest entirely agreed, remarking that there was, of course, no one like God. Mr. Golyadkin senior observed that the Turks were in some respects right to invoke the name of God even in sleep. Then, while disagreeing with the aspersions cast by some scholars upon the Turkish prophet Mohammed, and recognising him as a great politician in his way, Mr. Golyadkin proceeded to an extremely interesting account of an Algerian barber's shop that he had read in some miscellany. Guest and host laughed heartily at the artlessness of the Turks, but could not help marvelling at their opium-engendered fanaticism . . .

At last the guest began undressing, and Mr. Golyadkin, imagining in his goodness of heart that he might not have a proper shirt, disappeared behind the partition, partly to avoid embarrassing his guest, who had suffered quite enough already, and partly to reassure himself as far as possible about Petrushka, to sound him, cheer him up if possible and be nice to him, so that everyone should be happy, and that there should be no ill feeling. Petrushka, it must be observed, still made Mr. Golyadkin feel a bit uncomfortable.

"You get along to bed now, Petrushka," said Mr. Golyadkin gently, walking into his servant's room. "Go to bed now, Pyotr, and wake me tomorrow at eight, will you?"

Mr. Golyadkin's voice had been unusually soft and tender. But Petrushka remained silent. He was fussing about by his bed, and didn't even turn to face his master, as he should have done merely out of respect.

"Do you hear what I say, Pyotr?" continued Mr. Golyadkin. "Go to bed now, and tomorrow wake me at eight. Is that clear?"

"I've got a memory, haven't I?" muttered Petrushka under his breath.

"Now now, Petrushka. I'm only telling you so that you can be happy and easy in your mind. We're all happy now, and you should be happy and contented too. And now I wish you good night. Get some sleep Petrushka, get some sleep. We all have our work to do. And don't you go thinking anything . . ."

Mr. Golyadkin left his sentence unfinished.

"Haven't I said a bit too much?" he thought. "Haven't I gone too far? It's always the same. I always overdo it."

Feeling very dissatisfied with himself, our hero left Petrushka. Apart from anything else, he had been rather hurt by the latter's rudeness and intractability.

"You're nice to him—you show him some respect, and the scoundrel doesn't appreciate it. Still, they've all got the same nasty way, that sort!" thought Mr. Golyadkin.

Rather unsteadily he made his way back to his room, and seeing that his guest had turned in, sat down beside his bed for a minute.

"Come on, own up, Yasha," he began in a whisper, wagging his head. "You're the one who's in the wrong, aren't you, you rascal? You've got my name, you know . . ." he went on, bantering his guest in a rather familiar manner.

At last, bidding him a friendly good night, Mr. Golyadkin retired to bed. The guest began to snore. As Mr. Golyadkin climbed between the sheets, he chuckled and whispered to himself: "You're drunk tonight, Yakov Petrovich, old boy. What a rascal you are. Poor old Golyadkin! And what's it you've been so pleased about? Tomorrow it'll be all tears—you're a proper one for snivelling. What's to be done with you?"

At this moment a rather peculiar sensation of something approaching doubt or remorse pervaded his whole being.

"I let myself go," he thought, "and now my brain's fuddled, and I'm drunk. I didn't keep a grip on myself. What a fool I am! I talked a string of nonsense when I meant to be cunning. To forgive and forget is the first of all virtues, of course, but it's bad all the same! It is!"

Here Mr. Golyadkin got up, and taking a candle, tiptoed to have another look at his sleeping guest. For a long time he stood over him, deep in thought.

"Not a very pleasant picture! Sheer lampoonery—and that's all you can say about it!"

Finally Mr. Golyadkin went to bed. His brain was fuddled. His head was splitting. Gradually he began to doze . . . There was something he was trying hard to think of and remember, some very important and extremely ticklish matter he was trying to decide, but could not. Sleep descended upon his poor unfortunate head, and, as is customary with those who, being unused to it, suddenly consume five glasses of punch in a friendly evening, he was dead to the world.

Chapter 8

Next day Mr. Golyadkin woke as usual at eight, instantly remembered all that had happened the night before, and frowned.

"I let myself go like a proper fool yesterday, he thought," raising himself a little to take a look at his guest's bed. But imagine his amazement to find not only the guest but also the bed on which he had slept, gone from the room!

"What's this?" he almost shrieked. "What's happened? What does this new thing mean?"

While Mr. Golyadkin was staring perplexed and openmouthed at the empty space, the door creaked and in came Petrushka, bearing the tea-tray.

"Where is he? Where is he?" said our hero in a barely audible voice, pointing at the place that had been given over to the guest the previous night. Petrushka did not reply or even look at his master at first, but directed his gaze at the right-hand corner of the room, obliging Mr. Golyadkin to do likewise. Then, after a silence, he replied rather gruffly that his master was not at home.

"I'm your master, Petrushka, you fool!" faltered Mr. Golyadkin, staring open-eyed at his servant.

Petrushka made no answer, but cast an offensively reproachful look at Mr. Golyadkin that was tantamount to a piece of downright abuse, and made him go as red as a beetroot. Mr. Golyadkin gave up, as the saying is. At length Petrushka announced that *the other* had left about an hour and a half ago, not wishing to wait. This of course was both probable and plausible. Clearly Petrushka was not lying, and his offensive look and use of the words "the other" were merely a result of the whole odious occurrence of which we have heard. All the same Mr. Golyadkin realized, albeit vaguely, that there was something not quite right about it, and that fate had something else in store for him.

"Very well, we'll see," he thought. "We'll see, and in due course we'll get to the bottom of it all."

"Oh God," he moaned, his voice now quite different. "Why did I invite him here? What was the point? I'm sticking my neck right into their noose, and pulling the rope tight myself. Oh, what a fool I am. I've got no restraint. I go blabbing away like a kid, like some miserable clerk, like someone with no position to think of, like some gutless, weak-willed creature! What a gossip, what an old woman I am! Saints above! He wrote verses, the rascal, and said how he liked me! What's the best way of showing him the door if he comes back, I wonder? There are lots of ways of putting it, of course. I could say that with my limited salary and so forth . . . Or frighten him up a bit and say that taking such and such into consideration, I'm obliged to ask him to pay half the rent and half the cost of food in advance. Oh damn it! That's no good. That's giving myself a bad name. It's not quite the thing. Perhaps I could tip off Petrushka to be nasty to him or slight him in some way, or be rude to him, and get him out like that? Set one off against the other. No, blast it! That's risky, and looked at from another point of view, it's not very nice. Not nice at all. And supposing he *doesn't* come? That'll be bad too. I let my tongue run away with me yesterday. It's a bad state of things. Very bad indeed. What a damned fool I am! I just can't hammer any sense into my head. What if he comes and won't agree? I hope to God he does come. I'd be jolly glad—I'd give a lot if he would."

Such were Mr. Golyadkin's thoughts as he gulped his tea, keeping an eye on the clock.

"Quarter to nine. Time to be off. Something's going to

happen, but what? I'd like to know what's behind all this—the aim and object, and what the various snags are. It would be nice to know what these people are trying to get at, and what their first step is going to be . . ."

Mr. Golyadkin could bear it no longer, and leaving his pipe half smoked, he dressed and set off for the office, desiring, if possible, to take the source of danger by surprise, and to satisfy himself about everything at first hand. There *was* danger. He knew it.

"Now we'll find out all about it," he said, removing his coat and galoshes in the entrance hall. "Now we'll go into it."

Having thus decided on a course of action, our hero straightened his jacket, and, assuming a correct and official air, was about to pass into the next room, when suddenly, right in the doorway, he came face to face with his friend and acquaintance of the day before. Golyadkin junior seemed not to notice him, even though they practically bumped noses. He was, it seemed, busy. He was dashing off somewhere, and was out of breath. His expression was official and business-like: "On a special errand," it said for all to see.

"Oh, it's you, Yakov Petrovich," said our hero, seizing him by the hand.

"Not now, not now. Excuse me. You can tell me later," cried Golyadkin junior, bursting forward.

"But excuse me, Yakov Petrovich. I believe you, er . . ."

"What's that? Hurry up. What's it about?" Here Mr. Golyadkin's guest halted as though it were an effort and against his will to do so, and stuck an ear right in front of Mr. Golyadkin's face.

"I'm surprised at your behaviour, Yakov Petrovich, I must say. It's not what I should have expected at all."

"There's a proper form for doing everything. Apply to his Excellency through his Excellency's secretary in the proper way. Got a petition?"

"Really, Yakov Petrovich! You astound me! Perhaps you don't recognise me, or perhaps in your usual jolly way you are joking."

"Oh, it's you!" said Golyadkin junior, as if only now seeing and recognising Golyadkin senior. "So it's you. Well, did you have a good night?"

Here Golyadkin junior gave a little smile, a formal

official smile, not at all like the one he should have given, since at all events he owed Golyadkin senior a debt of gratitude, and added that he was extremely glad the latter had had a good night. Then he bowed slightly, took a few quick steps, looked left, right, and then at the floor, made for the door at his side, and with a muttered "special business," slipped into the next room, and was gone.

"There's a nice thing for you!" whispered our hero, momentarily stunned. "There's a nice thing! So that's how it is." He felt his flesh creep.

"Still, I've been saying that for a long time," he continued as he made his way to his section. "I had a presentiment ages ago about his being on special business. I said as much only yesterday."

"Have you finished that document you were doing yesterday? Have you got it here?" asked Anton Antonovich Setochkin as Mr. Golyadkin took his seat beside him.

"It's here," whispered Mr. Golyadkin, regarding his chief clerk with a rather lost expression.

"Ah yes. I only mention it because his Excellency has asked for it twice already. I'm afraid he'll ask again any minute."

"It's all right. It's ready."

"Oh well, that's all right then."

"I have, I believe, always performed my duties properly, Anton Antonovich, taken care over the tasks entrusted to me by my superiors, and dealt with them assiduously."

"Yes. But what do you mean by that?"

"Nothing, Anton Antonovich. I only want to explain that I . . . That is, I was trying to say that sometimes no one is spared, as ill-will and envy seek their noisome daily bread . . ."

"Forgive me, I don't quite follow you. Who are you getting at now?"

"All I mean, Anton Antonovich, is that I keep to the straight path and scorn beating about the bush. I'm not one for intrigue, and that, if you'll allow me to say so, is something I can very justly be proud of."

"Yes. Quite so. And as I understand it, I concede the full justice of what you say. But allow me to point out to you, Yakov Petrovich, that remarks about other people are not allowed in good society; and that I, for example, can put up with what goes on behind my back, but will permit no one to be impertinent to my face, sir. I, sir, have grown grey in the service, and will allow no one to be impertinent to me in my old age!"

"No, Anton Antonovich, you see . . . You don't seem to have quite taken my meaning. Good gracious, Anton Antonovich, I personally can only account it an honour . . ."

"In that case I beg your pardon too. I've been brought up in the old school. It's a bit late for me to go learning your new ways. I've had enough wit to serve my country up to now. I hold, as you are aware, sir, a medal for twenty-five years' unblemished service . . ."

"I know, Anton Antonovich, I fully realize all that. But that's not what I was getting at. I was talking about a mask, Anton Antonovich."

"A mask?"

"That is, you again . . . I'm afraid you'll take it the wrong way—the sense of what I say, that is—as you yourself put it. I'm merely developing the theme, putting forward the idea that people who wear masks are no longer uncommon, and that it's difficult nowadays to recognise the man underneath."

"It's not so hard as all that, you know. Sometimes it's fairly easy. Sometimes you don't have to go far to find him."

"No, Anton Antonovich. Speaking of myself for instance, I only put on a mask in the literal sense when there's some call to—when there's a carnival or a merry gathering; I don't, in a more cryptic sense, go about in one every day."

"Oh well, let's leave it at that for now. I haven't got time . . ." said Anton Antonovich, rising from his seat, and gathering up some papers he was to report on to his Excellency. "I don't suppose it'll be long before this affair of yours is cleared up. You'll see yourself who to blame and who to accuse, and I must ask you to spare me any further explanations and discussions to the detriment of the work."

"No, Anton Antonovich. That's not what I was thinking . . ." began Mr. Golyadkin, paling slightly. But Anton Antonovich was walking away.

"What is it?" he continued, now to himself. "Which way is the wind blowing now? What does it mean, this new piece of pettifoggery?"

Just as our dazed, half-annihilated hero was preparing to solve this new question, there was a sudden noise and burst of activity in the next room. The door opened, and there, quite out of breath, stood Andrey Filippovich, who a short time before had betaken himself to his Excellency on some matter. He called Mr. Golyadkin, and the latter, realising what it was about and not wishing to keep him waiting, sprang up, and as was fitting, made a great fuss about getting the required papers tidy and in order preparatory to following both them and Andrey Filippovich to his Excellency's room. Suddenly, and from practically under the arm of Andrey Filippovich, who was standing right in the doorway, in shot Golyadkin junior. He was breathless, he appeared exhausted by his official labours, and he had an earnest and decidedly formal air about him. He came bustling into the room, and marched straight up to Golyadkin senior—the very last thing the latter had expected.

"The papers, Yakov Petrovich, the papers, his Excellency has been pleased to inquire if you've got them ready," gabbled Mr. Golyadkin's friend under his breath. "Andrey Filippovich is waiting."

"I know without your telling me," shot back Golyadkin senior, also in a low voice.

"No, I didn't mean that. I didn't mean that at all, Yakov Petrovich. I feel for you, and I'm prompted by genuine concern."

"Spare me your concern, I beg you. Now, excuse me."

"Of course, you'll put them in a folder, Yakov Petrovich, and insert a page as a marker. Allow me, Yakov Petrovich . . ."

"No. Allow me, please . . ."

"But there's a blot here, Yakov Petrovich. Did you notice it?"

At that moment Andrey Filippovich called Mr. Golyadkin for the second time.

"Coming, Andrey Filippovich. I've just got to . . ." Then to Golyadkin junior: "Can't you understand plain language, sir?"

"The best thing is to get it out with a pen-knife, Yakov Petrovich. You'd better leave it to me. Best not touch it yourself, Yakov Petrovich. Leave it to me. I'll get it out."

Andrey Filippovich called Mr. Golyadkin for the third time.

"Where is it, for goodness' sake? I can't see any blot."

"It's an enormous one. Look, here's where I saw it. Just allow me, Yakov Petrovich. I'll do it with a pen-knife. I'll do it out of friendship and pure goodness of heart. . . . There! That's done it."

Getting the better of Golyadkin senior in the momentary struggle that had arisen between them, Golyadkin junior at this point suddenly, quite unexpectedly, for no apparent reason, and quite against the other's will, seized the document required by their chief, and instead of attending to it with a pen-knife, "out of pure goodness of heart" as he had perfidiously assured Golyadkin senior, he quickly rolled it up, thrust it under his arm, and in two bounds was at the side of Andrey Filippovich; the latter having noticed none of his pranks, shot off with him to the Director's room. Mr. Golyadkin stood glued to the spot, a pen-knife in his hand, looking as if he was getting ready to scratch something out with it.

He had not yet grasped what had happened to him, or gathered his senses. He had felt a sudden blow, but thought it was nothing serious. Filled with indescribable anguish, he at last tore himself away, and rushed straight off to the Director's room, praying to heaven as he went that the whole thing might somehow turn out for the best, and be all right. With one room still to go, he came face to face with Andrey Filippovich and Golyadkin junior, who were both on their way back. Andrey Filippovich was smiling and talking gaily. Mr. Golyadkin's namesake was also smiling. He was trotting along, keeping a respectful distance from Andrey Filippovich, but playing up to him and whispering delightedly into his ear, while the latter affably nodded assent. Our hero saw the whole situation in a flash. His work, as he discovered later, had exceeded his Excellency's expectations, and had, in fact, been delivered by the time appointed. His Excellency had been most gratified, and had, it was even rumoured, thanked Golyadkin junior, thanked him warmly and said he would bear it in mind when the time came, and wouldn't forget. The first thing for Mr. Golyadkin to do, of course, was to protest with the utmost possible vigour. Pale as death and almost out of his mind, he rushed up to Andrey Filippovich. But the latter, hearing that Mr. Golyadkin's business was of a personal nature, refused to listen, remarking bluntly that he hadn't a minute to spare for his own requirements. His flat refusal and matter-of-fact tone left Mr. Golyadkin dumbfounded.

"I'd better go about it a different way. I'd better go to Anton Antonovich," he thought.

Unfortunately for Mr. Golyadkin Anton Antonovich was not available. He was also busy somewhere.

"So there was some purpose in his asking to be spared discussions and explanations," thought our hero. "So that's what he was getting at, the cunning old devil! In that case I'll simply be bold and petition his Excellency."

Still pale, feeling his head to be in a state of complete chaos, and at an utter loss what to decide on next, Mr. Golyadkin sat down on his chair.

"It would have been much better if it had all been a mere nothing," he kept thinking to himself. "Anything as black as this was really quite inconceivable. It's nonsense. It can't happen. It's probably been some sort of an illusion—either something different happened from what actually did—or it was me who went, and somehow I took myself for someone else. To put it briefly, the whole thing is impossible."

No sooner had Mr. Golyadkin decided that the whole thing was impossible, than all of a sudden Golyadkin junior came flying into the room, with papers in both hands and under both arms. Saying a few needful words to Andrey Filippovich as he passed, exchanging a remark or two with one, civilities with another and banter with a third, Golyadkin junior, having apparently not a moment to waste, seemed just on the point of going out again, when, fortunately for Golyadkin senior, he stopped by the door to have a word in passing with two or three young clerks who happened to be standing there. Golyadkin senior hurled himself forward. Noticing this, Golyadkin junior began looking round uneasily to see how to make good his escape. But Mr. Golyadkin had already got him by the sleeve. The clerks surrounding the two officials stepped back to give them room, and stood inquisitively awaiting events. Golyadkin senior realized only too well that opinion was not now disposed in his favour, and that he was the victim of intrigue. This made it all the more necessary that he should now stand up for himself. It was a decisive moment.

"Well?" inquired Golyadkin junior, looking rather impudently at him.

Golyadkin senior was barely breathing.

"I don't know how you can explain your strange behaviour to me now, sir," he began.

"Well, go on." Here Golyadkin junior looked around and winked at the surrounding clerks as if giving them to understand that the comedy would now begin.

"The impertinent and shameless manner in which you have treated me in the present instance, exposes your true nature better than any words of mine could do. I shouldn't rely on the game you're playing. It's not a very good one."

"Tell me, what sort of a night did you spend, Yakov Petrovich?" asked Golyadkin junior, looking him straight in the eye.

"You're forgetting yourself, sir!" said our hero, utterly flabbergasted, hardly knowing whether he was on his head or his heels. "I trust you will change your tone."

"There, my dear chap!" said Golyadkin junior, making a rather improper grimace at Golyadkin senior, and all of a sudden, moving as if to caress him, he pinched his chubby cheek. Our hero flushed scarlet. As soon as he saw that his adversary, now speechless with rage, red as a lobster, and shaking in every limb, had been driven to breaking point and might attempt an assault, Golyadkin junior at once forestalled him in a most shameless manner. After playing with him a few seconds more, patting his cheeks and tickling him in the ribs while he stood motionless and out of his mind with rage, Golyadkin junior, to the huge delight of the young men standing around, and with an effrontery that was nothing short of disgusting, finished by giving Golyadkin senior a prod in his rather prominent stomach, and saying with an insinuating and positively malicious leer:

"You're a tricky one you are, Yakov Petrovich, old chap. We'll fox 'em, you and I."

Then, before our hero had time to make even a partial recovery, Golyadkin junior, after a preliminary grin at his audience, assumed a most brisk, business-like and official air, drew himself in, and with a rapid "on a special errand", jerked his stumpy little legs into life, and darted off into the next room. Our hero could not believe his eyes. He was still in no state to regain his senses.

At last he recovered. Realising in a flash that he was done for, that he had in a manner of speaking destroyed himself, that he had been disgraced, that his reputation was ruined, and that he had been scorned and ridiculed in front of others—realising that he had been perfidiously abused by him he had considered his greatest and most trusty friend, and finally, realising that he had been utterly shamed, Mr. Golyadkin charged in pursuit of his enemy. He tried not to think of those who had witnessed the outrage.

"They're all hand in glove together," he said to himself. "They all back each other up, and one sets the other against me."

Seeing after a dozen steps, however, that pursuit was in vain, he turned back.

"You won't get away!" he thought. "I'll beat you in good time. You'll pay for all the misery you've caused!"

Filled with cold fury and violent determination, he went to his chair and sat down.

"You won't get away," he repeated.

Any form of passive defence was now out of the question. There was something decisive, something of an offensive in the air, and anyone who at that moment saw Mr. Golyadkin, flushed and hardly able to control his agitation, jab his pen into the inkstand, and saw the fury with which he started scribbling on the paper, could have told that the matter would not be allowed to pass and end in some old-womanish way. In his heart of hearts he had formed a resolution which in his heart of hearts he had sworn to carry out. To be truthful, he still did not quite know or rather, he had no idea what steps to take. But it didn't matter.

"Imposture and effrontery, sir, get you nowhere today. Imposture and effrontery, sir, lead to no good. They lead to destruction. The False Demetrius was the only one to gain by imposture, sir—after deceiving a blind people—but not for long."

In spite of this Mr. Golyadkin thought he would wait for the masks to fall from certain faces, and one or two things to come to light. The first requisite was that office hours should end as quickly as possible, and until they did, he proposed to do nothing. When office hours were over, he would take a certain step. After that he would know how to act, and how to plan his whole campaign to shatter the horn of arrogance and crush the serpent, as in impotent rage it gnawed the dust. He could not allow any-

one to wipe their dirty boots with him. He could not agree
to that, particularly in the present case. But for the last
humiliation, our hero might have swallowed his feelings,
said nothing, and given in without too stubborn a protest;
he would have argued a bit, taken slight offence, aired a
few grievances, proved himself in the right, and then
would have climbed down a little; he might perhaps have
climbed down a little further, and then agreed entirely;
then, and especially then, when the other party solemnly
acknowledged him to be in the right, he might even have
made peace and displayed a little emotion; and who
knows, a new friendship might have been born—a firm,
warm friendship on a broader basis than that of the
preceding evening—a friendship that might finally have
so eclipsed the unpleasantness of the rather improper resemblance between them, that both would have known
unbounded delight and lived to be a hundred, and so on.

To tell all, Mr. Golyadkin was beginning rather to regret that he had stuck up for himself and his rights when
disagreeableness had been his immediate reward.

"If he'd give in, and say it was a joke, I'd forgive him,"
thought Mr. Golyadkin. "I'd forgive him all the more if
he'd only admit it out loud. But I won't be used as a boot-
rag. I haven't allowed others to wipe their boots with me,
and that's all the more reason for not letting some depraved fellow try to do so. I'm not a boot-rag, sir. I'm
not!"

Our hero had in short made up his mind:

"You yourself are the guilty one, sir!"

He had made up his mind to protest with all his power
and to the uttermost. That was the sort of man he was!
He could not permit himself to be insulted, still less to be
used as a boot-rag by someone depraved.

But let there be no argument about it. Perhaps if
anyone had wanted—had suddenly felt a desire to turn
Mr. Golyadkin into a boot-rag, they could have done so
with impunity, encountering no resistance—Mr. Golyadkin had occasionally sensed that himself—and a boot-
rag there would have been, and not a Golyadkin; a nasty
dirty boot-rag, it's true, but still no ordinary one; this boot-
rag would have had pride, would have been alive and
had feelings; pride and feelings might have remained concealed deep in its filthy folds and been unable to speak for

themselves, but all the same they would have been there.

The hours seemed incredibly long, but at last it struck four. A few minutes later everyone got up, and following out their departmental head, made for home. Mr. Golyadkin mingled with the crowd, keeping his quarry in sight. He saw him dash up to the porters who were handing out the overcoats, and stand ingratiating himself with them in his usual blackguardly way while waiting for his. The moment had come. Somehow Mr. Golyadkin pushed his way through the crowd and tried to get his overcoat, not wishing to be left behind. But the first to be served was Mr. Golyadkin's friend, for here too he had managed in his own inimitable fashion to wheedle and whisper his way round people.

Flinging on his coat, Golyadkin junior glanced ironically at Golyadkin senior, spiting him boldly and openly. Then, surveying all around with an impudence peculiarly his own, he made a last rapid round of the clerks—probably so as to leave them with a good impression—having a word with one and a whisper with another, oozing respect to a third, smiling at a fourth, giving his hand to a fifth—and finally darted gaily down the steps. Golyadkin senior followed. To his indescribable delight he overtook Golyadkin junior on the last step, and seized him by the coat-collar. Golyadkin junior seemed a little scared and looked round with a bewildered expression.

"What do you mean by this?" he said in a half-whisper.

"If, sir, you are a gentleman, I trust you will recollect our cordial relationship of yesterday," said our hero.

"Ah, yes. Well, did you have a good night?"

For the moment Golyadkin senior was speechless with rage.

"Yes, I did. But let me tell you, it's a complicated game you're playing"

"Who says so?—My enemies!" retorted the self-styled Mr. Golyadkin, breaking away from the feeble grasp of the real one. Once free, he dashed away, and catching sight of a cab, rushed up to it, climbed in, and a moment later was out of sight.

Abandoned by all and filled with despair, our minor civil servant gazed around, but there was no other cab. He tried to run, but his legs bent beneath him. Looking utterly downcast, his mouth sagging open, he leant against a lamp-post, feeling shrivelled up and finished. And thus for several minutes he remained, in the middle of the pavement. For Mr. Golyadkin all seemed lost . . .

Chapter 9

Everything, even Nature herself, seemed to be up in arms against Mr. Golyadkin. But he was still on his feet and unbeaten. He was ready to do battle. He would not give in—so much was plain from the spirit and vigour with which he rubbed his hands on recovering from the first of his amazement. But danger, obvious danger was upon him. He sensed it. Yet how to tackle it?—that was the question.

"Why not leave it like this? Why not just break with him without any formality?" flashed across his mind.

"Why not? There's nothing to it. I'll keep to myself as if it isn't me. I'll let it all pass. It isn't me, and that's all there is to it. He'll also keep to himself. Maybe he'll break with me. He'll be all over me for a bit, the wretch, then he'll turn round and break with me. That's how it will be. I'll triumph through meekness. Where's the danger in that? What danger is there? I'd just like someone to show me. It's a mere nothing. The sort of thing that happens every day!" Here Mr. Golyadkin stopped short. The words died on his lips. He cursed himself for thinking such thoughts, and accused himself of being mean and cowardly. However, his cause was still no further advanced. To make some sort of decision at this moment was, he felt, a matter of absolute necessity. But he would have given a lot to anyone who could have told him what exactly the decision should be. How was he to find out? Still, there was no time for that now. To avoid wasting any more time he took a cab and hastened homewards.

"Well? How are you feeling now?" he thought to himself. "How are you feeling now, Yakov Petrovich? What will you do? What will you do now, you abject wretch? You brought yourself to this, and now you're snivelling and crying!" Thus did Mr. Golyadkin taunt himself as he jogged up and down in his rickety cab. He derived considerable pleasure from turning the knife in his wound in this fashion—there was something almost voluptuous about it.

"If some magician were to come along now," he thought, "or if it were put to me in some official sort of way: 'You give a finger of your right hand, Golyadkin, and we'll be quits. There won't be any *other Golyadkin*, and you'll be happy but minus a finger'—I'd give it willingly, without a murmur."

"Damn and blast it all!" he cried at last in despair. "What's it all for? Why did this of all things have to happen? As if nothing else were possible! And it was all all right at first. Everyone was happy and content. But no, this had to happen! Still, talking won't get me anywhere. Action is what's needed."

With this much decided, Mr. Golyadkin, once back in his rooms, grabbed his pipe without a moment's delay, and sucking away at it as hard as he could and emitting clouds of smoke to left and right, began pacing to and fro in extreme agitation. Meanwhile Petrushka started laying the table. Suddenly, his mind at last made up, Mr. Golyadkin threw down his pipe, dragged on his overcoat, and announcing that he would not be in for dinner, charged out. On the stairs, he was caught up by Petrushka, panting for breath and holding the hat he had forgotten. Mr. Golyadkin took it, and meant to say something about "There! I forgot my hat" by way of justifying himself, and to stop Petrushka thinking anything out of the ordinary; but as the latter did not so much as look at him and immediately went back, he put on his hat without more ado, and ran downstairs, repeating to himself that everything might be for the best and that the business would be settled somehow, although he was conscious amongst other things of a nasty chill sensation all over him. He went into the street, took a cab, and shot off to Andrey Filippovich's.

"Wouldn't tomorrow be better?" he wondered, reaching for the bell-pull at the door of Andrey Filippovich's flat. "Besides, have I got anything special to say? There's nothing special about it. It's such a paltry business—it really is. It's paltry, piffling—or almost—the whole thing . . ."

Suddenly Mr. Golyadkin pulled the bell; it tinkled, and footsteps were heard within. At this juncture Mr. Golyadkin cursed himself for his boldness and precipitance. Cer-

tain recent distressing incidents, which he had almost forgotten while at work, and his misunderstanding with
Andrey Filippovich, immediately recurred to him. But it
was too late for flight. The door opened. As good luck
would have it, Mr. Golyadkin was informed that Andrey
Filippovich had not returned from the office, and was
dining out.

"I know where—by the Izmaylovsky Bridge—that's
where he dines," thought our hero, overjoyed. On the
footman inquiring what message he would leave, he replied, "Oh, that's all right. I'll pop back later, my man,"
and ran down the stairs with an almost jaunty air. In the
street he decided to dismiss the cab, and settled with
the driver. When the latter solicited a tip, pleading that
he had a long wait and hadn't spared his horse for the
gentleman, he gave him an extra five kopeks quite cheerfully, and then set off on foot.

"Really it's the sort of business you can't just leave like
that," thought Mr. Golyadkin. "But if you think about it
—if you really think about it sensibly, what actually is
the point of fussing about here?—No. I still repeat what
I've said—why should *I* have all the bother? Why should
I kill myself, toiling, worrying and making all the effort?
What's done can't be undone, for a start. It can't! We'll
argue it this way: along comes a man with adequate ref-
erences, a capable clerk, well-behaved, but badly-off—
had an unpleasant time of it one way and other—been
some trouble. Well, poverty's no crime. It's nothing to
do with me. What's all the nonsense about then? It so
happens that Nature has made someone the spit and image, the exact replica, of someone else. Can you refuse to
employ him because of that? If it's fate—if it's only fate
or blind fortune that's to blame, how can you treat him
like dirt and refuse him a job? What justice would there
be after that? There he is, penniless, brow-beaten, forlorn. . . . Your heart aches for him. Fellow-feeling demands you should look after him. Fine people departmental heads would be if they argued the same way as a
ruffian like me! What a brain I've got! Sometimes I'm as
stupid as a dozen fools put together! No. They did well,
and I say thank you to them for taking care of the poor
wretch . . .

"Well, suppose for the sake of example that we are
twins—twin brothers. What of it? Nothing! All the clerks

can be got used to it. And no one coming in from outside would think there was anything unseemly or outrageous about it. It's rather touching even; divine Providence creates two identical beings, the beneficent authorities behold the divine handiwork, and here they are giving them a place of refuge. It would of course have been better," went on Mr. Golyadkin, taking breath and lowering his voice, "if there'd been none of this touching business, and no twins either . . . Why did it have to be, blast it! What particular and urgent necessity was there for it? God! What a damned mess! Look at the sort of person he is! He's frivolous and beastly. He's a blackguard. He's here and here and everywhere. He's a toady and a lick-spittle. That's the sort of Golyadkin he is! He'll misbehave some more, I shouldn't wonder, and drag my name in the mud, the scoundrel. And now I've got to look after him and humour him, if you please! What a punishment! Still, what of it? It doesn't matter. He's a blackguard. Well, suppose he is—the other Mr. Golyadkin's straight. He'll be the blackguard, and I'll be the honest one, and people will say, "That Golyadkin's a blackguard. Don't you take any notice of him, and don't mix him up with the other one who's honest, virtuous, gentle and forgiving, who's very reliable at work and deserves promotion." That's it! All right, then . . . But . . . But what if they do get us mixed? He's capable of anything. Oh God! He's the sort of blackguard who'll deliberately take your place as though you were just dirt. He won't stop to think that you're not. Oh God! What horrible luck!"

Reasoning and complaining thus, Mr. Golyadkin scuttled along, heedless and almost unaware of where he was going. He came to in the Nevsky Prospect, and then only by virtue of a head-on collision with someone, that made him see stars. He muttered an apology, keeping his head lowered, and only when the other, after growling something uncomplimentary was well on his way again, did he raise it to see where he was and how he had got there. Finding himself to be right by the restaurant in which he had taken his ease prior to the dinner-party at Olsufy Ivanovich's, he became suddenly conscious of a rumbling and rattling in his stomach, and remembered he had not dined. There was no prospect of a dinner-party anywhere, and so, without losing precious time, he darted up the stairs and into the restaurant, to snatch a quick bite of something to avoid delay. The restaurant was rather on the expensive side, but that did not stop Mr. Golyadkin. There was no time to stop over trifles like that now. In the brightly illuminated room, quite a crowd of customers was standing at a counter heaped with an assortment of all the good things that respectable people might consume by way of light refreshment. The waiter was hard put to it, filling glasses, serving, taking money and giving change. Mr. Golyadkin waited, and as soon as his turn came, reached modestly for a fish pasty. Retiring to a corner and turning his back on the company, he ate with relish. When he had finished he went and returned his plate, and knowing the price, left a ten-kopek piece on the counter, catching the waiter's eye to let him know he'd had one fish pasty and had left the money, etc.

"That'll be one rouble ten kopeks," said the waiter contemptuously.

Mr. Golyadkin was amazed.

"What's that you say? I-I've only had one, I think."

"You've had eleven," retorted the waiter with conviction.

"I think you're making a mistake. I took one, I assure you."

"Eleven you took. I counted. You must pay for what you've had. We don't give stuff away."

Mr. Golyadkin was stupefied. "What's happening to me? Is it some piece of wizardry?" he thought. The man stood waiting for him to make up his mind. A crowd had gathered. Mr. Golyadkin slipped his hand into his pocket for a rouble, meaning to square up at once and avoid further trouble.

"If he says eleven, eleven it is," he thought, turning a lobster red. "Well, what's wrong with eating eleven pasties? If a chap's hungry and eats eleven pasties, well, let him, and good luck to him. There's nothing funny or wonderful about that . . ."

Feeling a sudden stabbing pain in his side, he looked up. The mystery, the wizardry became suddenly clear. He was perplexed no longer . . . Standing in the doorway of the next room, almost directly behind the waiter and facing Mr. Golyadkin—standing in the doorway, which till then he had taken to be a mirror—was a little man. It was Mr. Golyadkin, not Golyadkin the elder, the hero of our tale, but the other, the new Golyadkin, and evidently in the best of spirits. He kept smiling, nodding and winking at Golyadkin I, shifting restlessly from one foot to the other, and looking as though he might at the least provocation disappear into the next room and slip out by a back way, foiling all attempts at pursuit. He held in his hand the last morsel of his tenth pasty, and this, before Mr. Golyadkin's very eyes, he consigned to his mouth, smacking his lips with enjoyment.

"He's passed himself off as me, the blackguard!" thought Mr. Golyadkin, flushing red with shame. "He's got no qualms about other people being present! Can they see him? I don't think so."

Mr. Golyadkin threw down the rouble as though it burnt his fingers, and without noticing the waiter's insolent smile of triumph and cool mastery, broke out of the crowd, and dashed off, not daring to look back.

"Thank goodness he at least didn't compromise anyone completely," he thought. "Thanks are due to him, the villain, and to fate that it still got settled all right. There was just the cheekiness of the waiter. Still, he was within his rights. It should have been one rouble ten kopeks, so he was within his rights. "We don't give stuff away," he said. He could have been a bit more polite about it though—the horrible man!"

All this Mr. Golyadkin said to himself as he made his way downstairs to the street-door. On the last step, however, he stopped dead in his tracks, his face grew suddenly red and tears started to his eyes as he suffered a paroxysm of injured pride. After standing motionless for half a minute, he gave a determined stamp, bounded out into the street, and panting for breath and unconscious of his weariness, he headed for Shestilavochnaya Street and home without once looking back. As soon as he was indoors he seated himself on the ottoman, still wearing his overcoat—which was quite contrary to his custom of making himself comfortable in his own house—and without even observing the preliminary of reaching for a pipe, drew the inkstand toward him, took a pen and a sheet of notepaper, and began, his hand trembling with suppressed excitement, to scribble the following missive.

Dear Yakov Petrovich,

I should never have taken up my pen, had not circumstances, and you yourself, sir, compelled me to do so. Believe me when I say that necessity alone has obliged me to embark upon explanations with you, and I beg above all, sir, that you will regard this not as a deliberate attempt to insult you, but as an inevitable consequence of those things which are now a link between us.

"I think that's all right—polite and proper—although at the same time, firm and forceful. . . . I don't think there's anything for him to take exception to there. Besides, I'm within my rights," thought Mr. Golyadkin, reading over what he had written.

Your appearance, sir, singular and unheralded on a tempestuous night, following upon coarse and unseemly conduct towards me on the part of my enemies, whose names I shall not mention for the contempt I bear them, was the genesis of all those misapprehensions which at present exist between us. Your persistence in forcing an entry into the circle of my existence, and into all my relationships in practical life, exceeds the bounds dictated by common courtesy and social custom. There is, I think, little need to remind you here of your appropriation of papers of mine, together with my own good name, for the purpose of currying favour with those in authority—a favour you have not merited. I need hardly make mention here of the offensive and calculating manner in which you have avoided tendering those explanations which these acts have rendered indispensable. Finally, to withhold nothing from you, I do not allude to your recent peculiar—one might almost say incomprehensible—behaviour towards me in the coffee house. Far be it from me to complain of what proved the needless expenditure of one rouble. Nevertheless I cannot but vent my indignation at the recollection of your flagrant attempt to prejudice my honour, and what is more, to do so in the presence of several persons of breeding, albeit not personal acquaintances of mine . . .

"Am I going too far?" wondered Mr. Golyadkin. "Isn't it a bit strong? Isn't it being too touchy—that hint about breeding for instance? No, it doesn't matter! Firmness is the thing with him. Still, to soften the blow, I can butter him up a bit at the end. We'll see."

I should not however be wearying you with this letter, were I not firmly persuaded that your nobility of heart and forthrightness will suggest to you the means of rectifying all omissions and restoring the status quo ante.

I venture to hope and trust that you will not take this

letter as offensive to yourself, and that at the same time you will not decline to write explaining yourself—sending your reply by my servant.

In anticipation, I remain, Sir,

Your obedient servant,

Y. Golyadkin.

"There, that's all right. It's done now. It's got to the stage of letter-writing. But who's to thank for that? He is. He's the one who reduces you to the necessity of having something in writing. I'm within my rights."

After reading over the letter for the last time, Mr. Golyadkin folded it, sealed it up, and summoned Petrushka, who appeared as usual looking bleary-eyed and extremely put out about something.

"I want you to take this letter. You understand?"

Petrushka remained silent.

"I want you to take it to the office, and find Vakhrameyev—he's duty secretary today. You understand?"

"Yes."

"'Yes!' Can't you say, 'Yes, sir'? Ask for Vakhrameyev, and tell him your master sends his compliments, and wonders if he would be so good as to look up the office address book and find where Golyadkin the clerk is living."

Petrushka made no reply, and Mr. Golyadkin thought he detected him smiling.

"Well, that's it, then. Ask the address, and find out where Golyadkin the new clerk is living."

"Right."

"Ask the address, and then take this letter there, got it?"

"Yes."

"If, when you get there, this gentleman you're taking the letter to—this Golyadkin . . . What are you laughing at, dolt?"

"Me? What have I got to laugh about? It's not for the likes of me to laugh."

"Very well then . . . If this gentleman should ask how your master is, or how he's getting on or anything like that, you just keep your tongue to yourself, and say 'My master's all right, and asks for a written reply.' You understand?"

"Yes, sir."

"Very well then. 'My master's all right,' you'll say. 'He's quite fit and is just going visiting,' you'll say. 'And he asked for a written answer.' Got that?"

"Yes."

"Well, off you go."

"What a job it is with this blockhead too! He just laughs. And what at? Things have come to a pretty pass! Still, perhaps it will all turn out for the best . . . The wretch will probably loiter about for a couple of hours now, then disappear somewhere. You can't send him anywhere. What a mess it is. What a mess!"

Being thus sensible of how full was the cup of his affliction, Mr. Golyadkin resolved to adopt a passive rôle for the two hours during which he should await Petrushka. For one of them he paced the room, smoking. Discarding his pipe, he sat down to a book. He had a short lie-down on the ottoman. He resumed his pipe. He began coursing about the room again. He tried to thrash things out, but found himself quite unable to do so. Finally, as the agony of remaining passive reached its peak, he made up his mind to do something.

"Petrushka will be back in an hour," he thought. "I can give the key to the porter, and go and, um . . . investigate on my own meanwhile."

Losing no time in his haste to investigate, he took his hat and went out, locking up behind him. He handed the key to the porter together with a ten-kopek tip—he had become unusually liberal of late—and set off.

He headed first for the Izmaylovsky Bridge, a walk of half an hour or so. On arriving at his goal, he went straight into the courtyard of the house with which he was familiar, and glanced up at the windows of Civil Counsellor Berendeyev's apartments. All save three hung with red curtains were in darkness.

"I don't suppose Olsufy Ivanovich has got any visitors today," thought Mr. Golyadkin. "They're all at home on their own."

He stood in the courtyard quite a while, trying to make a decision. But the decision was evidently fated to remain unmade, for suddenly he thought better of it, and with a wave of the hand returned to the street.

"No, I shouldn't have come here. What is there for me to do here? I'd better go now, and, um, investigate in person."

With that Mr. Golyadkin set off for the office. He had a long walk ahead of him, added to which it was dreadfully slushy underfoot, and great soggy flakes of snow were falling fast. But difficulties seemed not to exist for him. True, he was drenched to the skin and not a little bespattered with mud, but that was just by the way, provided his object were attained. And he was indeed nearing his goal. He could see the huge government building looming dark in the distance.

"Hold on!" he thought suddenly. "Where am I going? And what am I going to do when I get there? Suppose I find out where he lives—Petrushka will have got back meanwhile with the answer. I shall just be wasting my valuable time for nothing, as I've done already. It doesn't matter, though. The whole thing can still be put right. But oughtn't I to go and see Vakhrameyev? No! I can do that afterwards. Confound it! I needn't have come out at all. But that's what I'm like. I've got a knack of trying to rush ahead whether there's any need to or not. H-m . . . What time is it? Nine, I suppose. Petrushka may get back and find me gone. I was a fool to come out. Oh, what a fuss and bother it is!"

After frankly admitting himself to have been a fool, our hero dashed back to Shestilavochnaya Street, and got there tired and exhausted. From the porter he learnt that Petrushka had not yet appeared. "There! Just as I foresaw," he thought. "And it's nine already. What a useless thing he is. Always boozing somewhere. Oh, God! What a miserable day it's been for me!"

Reflecting and lamenting thus, Mr. Golyadkin let himself into his rooms. He got a candle, undressed, lit a pipe, and weak, weary, worn and hungry, lay down on the ottoman to await Petrushka. The candle burnt dimly. Its light flickered on the walls. He gazed thoughtfully into space, and finally fell dead asleep.

Late at night he awoke. The candle, which had burnt right down, was smoking and on the point of going out altogether. Mr. Golyadkin sprang to his feet, jerked himself into life, and remembered everything. Through the partition came the resonant snores of Petrushka. He rushed to the window—not a light anywhere. He opened the vent—not a sound. The city slept. It must therefore have been two or three in the morning. And indeed it was, for with a sudden effort the clock behind the partition struck two. Mr. Golyadkin charged into the next room.

Somehow after prolonged effort he roused Petrushka and succeeded in getting him to sit up in bed. At that precise moment the candle went out for good. It was about ten minutes before he found and lit another, and during that time Petrushka managed to drop off again.

"Blackguard! Villain!" shouted Mr. Golyadkin, rousing him once more. "Get up! Wake up, will you!"

After half an hour's solid effort Mr. Golyadkin succeeded in stirring his servant into life, and dragging him into his own room. Only then did he see that Petrushka was, as the saying is, as drunk as a lord, and hardly able to stand.

"Lounger! Rogue!" cried Mr. Golyadkin. "Shamed me, that's what you've done!

"Oh God! Where has he got rid of the letter? What's happened to it? And why did I write it? Was there any need? Like a damned fool I let myself get carried away by my pride. And this is where it's got me. So much for your pride!

"What have you done with the letter, you thief? Who did you give it to?"

"I didn't give any letter to anybody. I didn't have any letter. So there!"

Mr. Golyadkin wrung his hands in despair.

"Listen Pyotr, listen to me."

"I'm listening."

"Where've you been? Tell me."

"To see nice people, that's where I've been. What do I care!"

"God help me! Where did you go first? The office? Listen Pyotr—perhaps you had a drop too much."

"Me? Strike me dead on the spot—n-n-not a d-d-drop. So there!"

"It doesn't matter your being drunk, I was only asking. It's all right your being drunk. I don't mind, Petrushka, I don't mind. Perhaps you've just forgotten for a bit, but you'll remember. Now come on, try. Did you see the clerk Vakhrameyev, or not?"

"No. There wasn't any clerk. Strike me dead."

"No, no, no, Petrushka. I don't mind, you know. You can see I don't. Well, then. It was cold out, and wet, so you had a quick one. I don't mind. I'm not angry. I had one today myself, old chap. Now come on, and try to remember, old fellow. Did you see Vakhrameyev?"

"Well, it was like this. Honest truth—I did go, straight I did . . ."

"That's fine, Petrushka. Fine. I'm not angry, you see," continued our hero, coaxing his servant still more, patting him on the shoulder and smiling at him. "So you had a quick one, you rogue? Ten kopeks' worth, eh? You bad man! Well, it doesn't matter. You can see I'm not angry. I'm not, old chap. I'm not at all."

"I'm not a bad man. You can say what you like . . . Just because I went to see some nice people. I'm not a bad man, and I never have been."

"No, Petrushka, of course not. Listen, Petrushka, I'm not scolding you, you know, when I call you a bad man. I mean it in a nice sense, to cheer you up. You know Petrushka, it's a compliment to some men, if you call them rogues or sly ones. It means they're no fools and don't let themselves get taken in. Some people like that. Well, never mind. Now, come on Petrushka. No beating about the bush. Tell me straight—like you would a friend. Did you go to Vakhrameyev and did he give you an address?"

"Yes, he did. He gave me that too. He's a nice official. 'And your master's a nice man too,' he said, 'a very nice man.' 'And give your master my compliments,' he said, 'and thank him, and tell him how much I like and esteem him,' he said. 'For your master's a good man, Petrushka, and you're a good man too.' "

"God give me strength! The address, the address, you Judas!" These last words he almost whispered.

"Yes, he gave me that."

"He did? Well, where does he live, this Golyadkin?"

" 'You'll find Golyadkin in Shestilavochnaya Street,' he said. 'As you walk down it, you'll see a staircase on the right, and it's the fourth floor. That's where you'll find Golyadkin,' he said."

"Swindler, cutthroat!" shouted our hero, finally losing all patience. "That's me you're talking about. There's another Golyadkin, and I mean *him,* you twister!"

"Just as you like. I don't care. Have it your own way."

"But the letter! The letter!"

"What letter? There wasn't any letter. I didn't see any letter."

"What did you do with it, you crook?"

"Delivered it. 'My compliments and thanks to him,' he said. 'He's a good man, your master. Give him my compliments,' he said."

"*Who* said? Golyadkin?"

For a moment Petrushka remained silent, then, staring his master straight in the face, he gave a broad smile.

"Listen, you villain!" began Mr. Golyadkin, breathless and losing his head in his fury. "What have you done to me? Come on, tell me! Played me a filthy trick—landed me in the cart! You horrible wretch! You—Judas!"

"Have it your own way. What do I care?" said Petrushka firmly, retiring behind the partition.

"Come here! Come here, you idle fool!"

"Shan't now! Shan't! I don't care! I'm going to nice people. Nice people live honestly. Nice people don't live falsely and don't have doubles."

Mr. Golyadkin's hands and feet turned to ice. He couldn't breathe.

"Yes," continued Petrushka, "they don't have doubles —ever. They aren't an insult to God and honest men."

"You're drunk, you lazy lump! Sleep now, you miserable thing, and tomorrow you'll get what's coming to you!" said Mr. Golyadkin, his voice almost a whisper. Petrushka muttered something else, and then could be heard making the bed creak as he lay down. He gave a prolonged yawn, stretched himself out, and finally began snoring away in what is called the sleep of the just.

Mr. Golyadkin felt more dead than alive. Petrushka's behaviour, his strange albeit vague insinuations—which were nothing to get annoyed about, especially as he had been drunk—and the whole ugly turn of things had shaken him to the core.

"Whatever possessed me to go for him in the middle of the night?" said our hero. A morbid sensation was causing him to tremble all over. "Something egged me into getting tied up with him when he was drunk! What sense can you get out of anyone in that state! It's a lie every time he opens his mouth. What was he getting at, though? Good God! And why did I go writing all those letters? My own executioner—that's what I am! I can't keep quiet. I *must blab!* And that of all things! I'm heading for destruction, I'm like a boot-rag, and yet I've got to bring my pride into it. 'My pride's hurt, I must save it!' I'm my own executioner!"

Thus spoke Mr. Golyadkin, sitting on his ottoman and too frightened to stir. Suddenly his eyes lighted upon an object that excited all his attention. Dreading that it might prove an illusion or figment of his imagination, he reached out his hand timidly, hopefully and with unutterable curiosity towards it. No! It was no illusion, no figment of the imagination. It was without a single shadow of doubt a letter, and it was addressed to him. He picked it up from the table. His heart was pounding within him.

"That scoundrel must have brought it, put it down here, and forgotten about it," he thought. "That's probably what happened. That's it."

The letter was from Vakhrameyev, a young colleague who at one time had been a friend of his.

"Still, I anticipated all this," thought our hero. "And I've anticipated what it'll say."

The letter was as follows:

Dear Yakov Petrovich,

Your man is drunk, and as no sense is to be got from him I prefer to reply by letter. I hasten to inform you that I shall carry out faithfully and exactly the commission you have laid upon me, namely of handing a letter to you know who. This person, who has taken the place of a friend to me—I refrain from mentioning his name, not wishing to sully needlessly the reputation of one who is completely innocent—lodges with us at Karolina Ivanovna's in the room which, when you were staying here, was occupied by an infantry officer from Tambov. He is, however, always to be seen in the company of sincere and honest folk, which is more than I can say for some. I intend to sever my connexions with you as from today, it being impossible for us to preserve the same friendly spirit and unanimity of our former association. And therefore I request, sir, that you forward me on receipt of this candid epistle, the two roubles owing for razors of foreign manufacture which, if you remember, I sold to you on credit seven months ago when you were living with us under the roof of Karolina Ivanovna, a lady for whom I have a most profound respect. I am acting thus because according to accounts I have received from people of intelligence, you have lost your reputation and sense of honour, and become a moral menace to the innocent and uncontaminated. For there are some who abide not by the truth; their words are a lie, and their air of good intent is suspect.

As to standing up for Karolina Ivanovna—who has always been an honourable lady, decorous in demeanour, and who, albeit a spinster no longer in the bloom of youth, is the daughter of a good foreign house—people capable of so doing can always be found everywhere. This I have been asked by several persons to mention to you here in passing, and I do so also on my own behalf. In any case you will learn all in good time, if you have not done so already, for you have by all accounts been making yourself notorious from one end of the capital to the other, and may consequently have heard what you should hear about yourself in many quarters. In conclusion, sir, I must tell you that the person you know, whose name I do not for certain honourable reasons mention—is highly esteemed by right-minded people, and is moreover of a pleasant and cheerful disposition, as successful at his work as he is in intelligent society, and true to his word and to his friends, not insulting them behind their backs while being nice to their faces.

> At all events I remain,
>> Your obedient servant,
>>> N. Vakhrameyev.

PS. Get rid of your man—he is a drunkard and probably causes you a lot of trouble—and take on Yevstafy, who used to be in service here and is now without a place. Your present servant is not only a drunkard but a thief as well. Only last week he sold Karolina Ivanovna a pound of lump sugar on the cheap, which in my opinion he could only have done by steadily stealing small quantities from you over a period. I tell you this as a well-wisher, although all some individuals can do is to insult and deceive everybody, preferably those who are honest and good-natured, slandering them behind their backs, and making them out to be the opposite of what they are, out of pure envy and because they're not as good themselves.

V.

After reading Vakhrameyev's letter, our hero remained motionless on the ottoman for a long while. Some new light was breaking through the vague mysterious mist that had been surrounding him for the past two days. He was beginning to understand a little . . . He was about to try and get to his feet and take a turn or two up and down to refresh himself, collect his scattered thoughts, focus them on a certain subject, and then, having got himself straight a bit, to give the position his mature consideration. But no sooner did he attempt to stand, than he at once fell back again, weak and feeble.

"I anticipated all this, of course. But how did he come to write that, and what do those words really mean? Suppose I do know their sense, where does that lead? He should have told me straight, 'Such and such, and such and such, and this and that is required,' and I'd have done it. The thing has taken such an unpleasant turn! I wish tomorrow would hurry up and come, and then I could get down to it! I know what to do. 'Such and such a thing,' I'll say. 'I agree to argue it, but I won't sell my honour, etc.' But how's this person we know of . . . How's this beastly individual come to get mixed up in it? Why, exactly? Oh, I wish it would soon be tomorrow! Till then they'll slander me! They're intriguing, they're working to spite me! The main thing is not to waste any time, and to write a letter now simply mentioning this and that, and just saying I agree to such and such. And tomorrow at the crack of dawn I'll send it off, then get to the office as early as possible myself, before they do, and forestall these pleasant gentlemen . . . They'll slander me, they will!"

Mr. Golyadkin drew some paper towards him, took pen, and wrote the following reply to Vakhrameyev's letter:

Dear Nestor Ignatyevich,
   I have read your obnoxious letter with sorrow and amazement, for I clearly perceive that in speaking of certain indelicate persons and others of false good intent, you are referring to myself. With genuine distress I perceive with what rapidity and success and to what great depths has calumny spread its roots to the detriment of my prosperity, honour and good name. And what is all the more deplorable and outrageous, is that even decent men, genuinely high-minded, and, what is most important, endowed with open, forthright natures, should abandon the interests of honourable folk and attach themselves and all their best qualities to that pernicious putridity which has, unfortunately, been so widely and so very insidiously propagated in our own difficult and unprincipled time. Let me say in conclusion that I shall consider it my sacred duty to repay in full the debt of two roubles that you mention.

Your allusions to a certain female, as also to the intentions, speculations, and various designs of same, I do not, let me tell you, sir, clearly or fully apprehend. I must beg you, sir, to allow me to preserve my high thoughts and good name unsullied. At all events I shall be pleased to enter into explanations with you in person, preferring personal contact to correspondence as being more trustworthy, and am moreover ready to make various peaceable agreements, on mutual terms of course. To this end, sir, I beg that you will intimate to this person my readiness to come to a personal understanding, and request her furthermore to name time and place for the interview. Your insinuations about my having offended you, betrayed our original friendship and spoken slightingly of you, made bitter reading. The whole of this I attribute to misunderstanding, base calumny, and the envy and malevolence of those whom I may justly call my bitterest enemies. They are probably unaware, however, that innocence is the strength of innocence, that their brazen impudence and infuriating familiarity will sooner or later earn them common contempt, and that they will come to destruction solely through their own impropriety and depravity. In conclusion, I beg that you will convey to these persons that their strange pretensions, and their ignoble and chimerical desire to oust others from the places that they occupy by their very existence in the world, and to supplant them, are deserving of consternation, contempt and pity, and what is more, qualify them for the madhouse. Moreover, attitudes such as these are strictly forbidden by law, and in my opinion, quite justly so. There are limits to everything, and if this is a joke, it is a pretty poor one. I will say more—it is utterly immoral, for I venture to assure you, sir, that my own ideas about keeping *one's place*, and these I have amplified above, are purely moral.

I have the honour to remain, Sir
Your obedient servant,
Y. Golyadkin.

Chapter 10

Mr. Golyadkin had been shaken to the core by the events of the preceding day. He passed an extremely bad night, being unable to get a full five minutes' sleep. It was as if some mischievous person had sprinkled his bed with bristles. He spent the whole time in a semi-somnolent condition, tossing from one side to another, sighing and groaning, dropping off one moment and waking the next; and all this was attended by a strange feeling of anguish, vague memories, hideous visions—in short, by every conceivable unpleasantness.

Sometimes he saw the figure of Andrey Filippovich in a weird mysterious twilight, a gaunt angry figure, with a cold harsh look on its face and some stonily polite word of reprimand on its lips; he would be on the point of going up to Andrey Filippovich to justify himself in some way, and prove that he was not as his enemies made him out to be, but like this and like that, with such and such, and such and such in his favour, over and above his usual innate qualities; but the moment he did so, a certain notoriously beastly person appeared, ruined everything at a single blow and by the most infuriating means, blackened Mr. Golyadkin's reputation there and then, practically to his face, trampled his pride in the mire, and immediately supplanted him, both at the office and in society.

Sometimes he felt his head tingling from a blow that he had recently received and meekly accepted, either in the society of his fellow men or while performing his duties, when remonstration would have been difficult. As he racked his brains to discover *why* it should have been difficult, his thoughts on this subject would without his noticing it run over into others concerning a certain small but also rather important act of meanness that he had recently witnessed, heard about, or had himself committed, and committed often not for any mean motive or through any mean impulses; sometimes, for instance, it had just been by chance—for reasons of delicacy; another time—because he was completely defenceless; and lastly because . . . But Mr. Golyadkin knew perfectly well *what* it was because of. At this point he would blush in his sleep, and as he tried to hide his blushes, would mutter that there, for instance, one might have shown resolution, a great deal of resolution; and then concluded by asking what that was, and why he need mention it then. But what enraged and exasperated him most of all was that a certain person notorious for his revolting behaviour and scurrilous tendencies would at that moment, whether bidden or not, unfailingly appear, and with a nasty little smile mutter quite gratuitously, "Resolution? What's that got to do with it? What resolution could you and I show Yakov Petrovich?"

Sometimes he would dream that he was in the splendid company of people celebrated for their breeding and wit. He, too, distinguished himself by his amiability and wit, and everyone took a liking to him—even certain of his enemies who were present—and this pleased him greatly. Everyone gave him precedence, and at last he had the agreeable experience of overhearing the host speak flatteringly of him to one of the guests whom he had drawn aside. And all of a sudden, for no apparent reason, a person notorious for his evil intentions and brutish impulses in the shape of Golyadkin junior appeared, and by so doing demolished at one fell swoop all the glory and triumph of Golyadkin senior, eclipsing him, dragging him into the mire and clearly demonstrating that Golyadkin senior, the real Mr. Golyadkin, was not real at all but a fraud; *he* was the real one, and Golyadkin senior was not what he seemed, but this and that, and consequently had no right to the society of well-intentioned, well-bred people. And all this happened so quickly that Golyadkin senior did not even have time to open his mouth, before everyone was heart and soul with the revolting and false Golyadkin junior, disowning Golyadkin senior, real and innocent as he was, in a most profoundly contemptuous manner. There was no one whose opinion had not in a twinkling been changed by the revolting Golyadkin to suit his own. There was no one, even amongst the lowliest of the company, on whom the spurious and good-for-nothing Golyadkin had not fawned in his most sugary manner—no one with whom he had not ingratiated himself, and over whom he had not poured sweet unction that brought tears of delight to their eyes. And the main thing was that it all happened in a matter of seconds. The speed with which the suspect and worthless Golyadkin moved was astonishing. No sooner had he got one well-disposed towards him, than before you could blink, he was quietly making up to another. The moment he had drawn a benevolent smile from this one, he jerked his rather dumpy little legs into life, and was off wooing a third. Before you had time to register surprise, he was at the same game with a fourth. It was horrible. It was sheer wizardry. Everyone was pleased with him, everyone liked him, everyone praised him to the skies and proclaimed in chorus that for amiability and satirical humour he was far and away above the real Golyadkin, so putting the latter to shame. They disowned and pushed out the upright and well-intentioned Golyadkin, and showered insults upon him who was well-known for the love he bore his neighbour.

Anguished, terrified and enraged, the Mr. Golyadkin who had suffered so much, rushed out into the street, and tried to hire a cab to take him straight to his Excellency's, or failing that, at least to Andrey Filippovich's. But horror of horrors! The drivers flatly refused him, saying, "We can't take two people exactly alike, sir. A good man tries hard to live honourably, not just anyhow, and never has a double."

Looking about him, distracted with shame, the entirely honourable Mr. Golyadkin saw that the cabmen and Petrushka, who had thrown in his lot with them, were right. The depraved Golyadkin was actually standing close beside him, and in his usual blackguardly fashion was at that critical moment preparing to do something very improper that would in no way display the nobility of character required by breeding that he, the abominable Golyadkin II, was so fond of vaunting on every suitable occasion.

Out of his mind with shame and despair, the ruined but rightful Mr. Golyadkin fled blindly wherever fate might lead. But as often as his footfalls rang upon the granite pavement, an exact image of Golyadkin the depraved and abominable, would spring up out of the ground. And each of these exact images would come waddling along behind the next, in a long procession like a gaggle of geese, after Golyadkin senior. Escape was impossible. The pitiable Golyadkin grew breathless with terror. In the end there sprang up so fearful a multitude of exact images that the whole capital was blocked with them, and a police officer, perceiving this breach of decorum, was obliged to grab the lot by the scruff of the neck and fling them into a police-box that happened to be near at hand . . .

Our hero awoke, stark frozen with horror. And stark frozen with horror, he realized that his waking hours were hardly any better. He felt tormented and oppressed. His anguish was such that his heart felt as if it were being gnawed from his breast.

Finally he could bear it no longer. "It shall not be!" he cried, boldly sitting up in bed, and at once came to.

Evidently it had been day for some time. The room was unusually light. Rich sunlight was filtering through the frost-encrusted panes and flooding the walls, which surprised him not a little for this normally happened only at noon, and there had been, to the best of his recollection, no such anomaly in the course of the heavenly luminary before. No sooner had he registered surprise at this, than the wall-clock behind the partition began to make a whirring sound preparatory to striking.

"There!" thought Mr. Golyadkin, and listened anxiously . . .

But the clock, to his final and utter consternation, summoned all its energy, and struck once.

"What's this?" cried our hero, leaping out of bed. Clad as he was, he dashed round the partition, unable to believe his ears. The clock really did say one. He looked at Petrushka's bed, but there was no sign of Petrushka there or anywhere else. The bed had clearly been made for some time and left, and Petrushka's boots were nowhere to be seen—a sure indication that he really was out. Mr. Golyadkin rushed to the door. It was shut.

"Where is he?" he whispered, strangely agitated and feeling his whole body trembling violently. Struck by a sudden thought, he charged to his table, and searched and rummaged about. But Vakhrameyev's letter was gone. Petrushka was gone, the clock said one, and several new points about Vakhrameyev's letter which had been obscure the day before, now became quite clear. At last it was obvious—even Petrushka had been bought! Yes, that was it!

"So that's where the main plot has been hatched!" cried Mr. Golyadkin, striking his forehead, with a look of growing amazement on his face. "In the den of that odious German woman—that's where the whole evil genius is hidden now! Telling me to go to the Izmaylovsky Bridge was only a strategic diversion. She was putting me off the scent, throwing dust in my eyes—the wicked old hag! That's how she's been undermining me! That's it! If you look at it that way, that's the whole thing exactly— and it accounts for that scoundrel turning up. It all boils down to the same thing. They've been keeping him for a long time, preparing him and saving him up for the fatal day. And see now how it's all turned out—what it's all come to! Ah well, it doesn't matter. No time has been lost!"

Here Mr. Golyadkin remembered with horror that it was now after one.

"What if they've now had time . . ." He uttered a groan. "No. They won't have. They're telling lies. We'll see . . ."

He flung on some clothes, and seizing pen and paper scribbled the following:

Dear Yakov Petrovich,
It's either you or me. There isn't room for both of us. And therefore I tell you plainly that your strange, ridiculous and unattainable desire to appear my twin and to pass yourself off as such, will serve to achieve nothing more than your complete disgrace and discomfiture. Thus for your own good I must ask you to step down, and make way for those who are genuinely noble and well-intentioned. Failing this, I am prepared to decide in favour of most extreme measures. I lay down my pen, and wait . . .
I remain ready to oblige—even with pistols.
                                        Y. Golyadkin.

When he had finished this note, our hero rubbed his hands vigorously. Then, donning his hat and overcoat, he unlocked the door with a spare key, and set off for the office. But when he got there, he could not make up his mind to go in. It was too late. His watch showed half past two. Suddenly an apparently trivial thing occurred to relieve him of some of his doubts. Around the corner of the office building popped a small, breathless, red-faced figure of a man, who scuttled in a furtive rat-like manner up the steps and into the vestibule. It was Ostafyev, a clerk, who was quite well known to Mr. Golyadkin. He was a useful fellow who would do anything for ten kopeks. Knowing Ostafyev's weakness, and suspecting that after absenting himself from the office "on some most urgent business", he would be more avid for kopeks than before, our hero made up his mind to be lavish, and slipping up the steps after him, called to him, and with an air of mystery, motioned him into a secluded corner behind an enormous iron stove. Here he began interrogating him.

"Well, my friend, how are things—if you take my meaning?"

"How do you do, sir. At your service, I'm sure."

"All right, all right, my friend. I'll make it worth your while. Look—how is it?"

"What's that you want to know?" For a moment Ostafyev held his hand up to his mouth which had unexpectedly dropped open.

"Look my friend, I, er . . . Don't go thinking anything— Is Andrey Filippovich here?"

"He is."

"And the clerks?"

"Here as they should be."

"And his Excellency as well?"

"And his Excellency as well." Here the clerk again held his hand up to his gaping mouth, and gave Mr. Golyadkin, or so it seemed, a strangely inquisitive look.

"And there's nothing special, my friend?"

"No, nothing."

"About me, I mean . . . Isn't there anything . . . You take my meaning?"

"No, nothing at the moment." The clerk again covered his mouth and looked strangely at Mr. Golyadkin. The latter was now trying to fathom Ostafyev's expression, and discover whether he was keeping anything back. It seemed in fact that he was. He had grown more and more discourteous and unfriendly, and was no longer showing the same sympathetic interest in Mr. Golyadkin's affairs as at the beginning of the conversation.

"He's partly within his rights," thought Mr. Golyadkin. "What am I to him? Perhaps the other side has given him something, and that's why he was off 'on urgent business'. Ah well, I'll um . . ." He realised the time for disbursing kopeks had come.

"Here you are, my dear chap."

"Very much obliged, sir."

"I'll give you more."

"Yes sir?"

"I'll give you more in a minute, and as much again when we're finished, understand?"

The clerk said nothing, but stood stiff as a ramrod, staring fixedly at him.

"Tell me now, have you heard anything about me?"

"I don't think so . . . Not so far . . ." replied Ostafyev, pausing as he spoke, and maintaining, like Mr. Golyadkin, an air of mystery, wrinkling his brow a little and staring at the floor—in short, doing his utmost to earn what he had been promised. The money he had been given he regarded as earned already.

"Isn't there anything?"

"Not so far."

"But listen—there may be something, eh?"

"Yes, there may of course."

"Not so good!" thought our hero.

"Listen, here's something else for you, old fellow."

"Much obliged, sir, I'm sure."

"Was Vakhrameyev here yesterday?"

"He was, sir."

"And anyone else? See if you can remember, old chap."

The clerk searched his memory for a minute, but could find nothing suitable.

"No sir, no one."

"H-m!"

A silence followed.

"Look, here's something else for you, my friend. Now tell me all the ins and outs of it."

"Very good, sir."

Ostafyev was now as meek as a lamb, which was just what Mr. Golyadkin wanted.

"Tell me old chap, how does he stand now?"

"All right, quite well," answered the clerk, staring hard at him.

"How well?"

"Well, um . . ." Ostafyev twitched his brows significantly. But he had finally come to a dead end and didn't know what to say.

"It's bad," thought Mr. Golyadkin.

"Wasn't there some further development with Vakhrameyev?"

"Everything's as it was."

"Try to think."

"They say . . ."

"Well?"

Ostafyev put his hand in front of his mouth for a moment.

"Wasn't there a letter for me from there?"

"Mikheyev the caretaker has been to Vakhrameyev's lodgings today—to that German lady there—so I'll go and ask if you like."

"If you would, my dear chap. Please do, for God's sake. I'm just . . . Don't go thinking anything—I'm just—you know. You inquire and find out whether they're cooking up anything to do with me—what action *he's* taking—that's what I want. You find that out my friend, and I'll make it worth your while."

"I will sir—and Ivan Semyonovich sat in your place today."

"Ah! He did, did he?"

"Andrey Filippovich told him to."

"He did? What for? Find that out, my friend. For God's sake find that out! You do all that, and I'll make it up to you, my dear chap. That's what I want to know. And don't you go thinking anything."

"Very good sir. I'll go at once. Won't you be coming in today?"

"No. I, er . . . I just, um . . . I just came to have a look—but I'll make it worth your while after."

"All right."

The clerk ran quickly and eagerly up the stairs, and Mr. Golyadkin was left to himself.

"It's bad," he thought. "Bad, bad! Things don't look too good for me. What was the meaning of it all? What did that drunkard mean by some of his hints? Who's at the back of this? Ah! Now I know. They probably found out, and then put him there . . . but did they? It was Andrey Filippovich put Ivan Semyonovich there. But why did he do that? What was the point? Very likely they found out . . . This is Vakhrameyev's work —no, not Vakhrameyev—he's as stupid as they make 'em. They're all doing the work for him. They put that other scoundrel up to coming here for the same thing. And that one-eyed German woman made her complaint! I always suspected all this intrigue had more in it than met the eye, and that there was bound to be something in all that old wives' gossip. I said as much to Dr. Rutenspitz. "They've sworn to cut someone's throat, in the moral sense," I said "—and they've got hold of Karolina Ivanovna." No. This is the work of master hands, you can see that. It's not Vakhrameyev. No sir, this is the work of a master! Vakhrameyev's stupid, as I said . . . But I know now who's doing their work for them—it's that impostor! That's the foundation of his career, and that explains why he's successful in better society. But really I'd like to know how he stands with them now. Only *why* have they taken on Ivan Semyonovich? What damned use is *he* to them? It's as if they couldn't find anyone else. Still, whoever they put there it would have been the same. All I know is, this Ivan Semyonovich has been on my list of suspects for a long time. I remarked what a nasty horrible old man he was ages ago. Lends out money on interest, they say—like a Jew. All this is the Bear's handiwork. He's been mixed up in the whole thing. At the Izmaylovsky Bridge—that's where it all started . . ."

Here Mr. Golyadkin screwed up his face as if he had bitten a lemon. Evidently he had remembered something very unpleasant.

"Still, it doesn't matter," he thought. "It's just that I keep coming back to my own troubles. Why doesn't Ostafyev come? He's probably sat down to something, or been detained somehow. It's good to have this intrigue afoot and be doing some undermining of my own. I only have to give Ostafyev ten kopeks and he's on my side. But is he? That's the thing! Maybe they've got at him too, and he's agreed to be part of *their* plot. He looks a thorough crook! He's keeping something back, the scoundrel! 'No, nothing,' he says. 'Very much obliged to you sir, I'm sure,' he says. Cutthroat that he is!"

Hearing a sudden noise, Mr. Golyadkin cowered back behind the stove. Someone came down the stairs, and passed out into the street.

"Who could that have been now?" thought our hero to himself. A minute later other footsteps were heard. Unable to bear the suspense, he popped just the tip of his nose out of cover, and instantly drew it back as if it had been jabbed with a pin. This time it was someone he knew. It was the scoundrel, the intriguer, the pervert —flouncing past with his usual quick horrible little steps, and throwing out his feet as if he was getting ready to give someone a kick.

"Blackguard," muttered our hero to himself, but he could not help noticing that the blackguard had under his arm an enormous green dispatch-case belonging to his Excellency.

"Another special errand," he thought, flushing with

vexation and shrinking back still further. No sooner had Golyadkin junior flashed past, unaware of the presence of Golyadkin senior, than a third lot of footsteps were heard, which the latter guessed to be those of the returning clerk. And a clerk it was, a sleek-haired clerk—not Ostafyev, but one Pisarenko—who peered round the stove at Mr. Golyadkin. The latter was amazed.

"Why has he let others into the secret?" he thought. "Nothing is sacred to this barbarous lot!"

"Well?" he said, turning to Pisarenko. "Who sent you, my friend?"

"I've come about your business. There's nothing from anyone so far. But if there is, we'll let you know."

"What about Ostafyev?"

"Couldn't get away. His Excellency's walked through the section twice already, and I can't stay now."

"Thanks, old man. But tell me . . ."

"Really, I can't stay . . . He's asking for us every minute . . . You just stand here for a bit, and if there's anything about your business we'll let you know."

"No, tell me, my friend . . ."

"Please! I can't stay," said Pisarenko breaking away from Mr. Golyadkin, who had seized him by a lapel. "Truly, I haven't time. You stand here for a bit and we'll let you know."

"Just a minute! Just a minute! Look, here's a letter. I'll make it worth your while."

"All right."

"Try and give it to Mr. Golyadkin."

"Golyadkin?"

"Yes, Mr. Golyadkin."

"All right. As soon as I get off, I'll take it. You stay here meanwhile. No one will see you here."

"No. Don't go thinking I'm standing here so as not to be seen. I won't be here, I'll be in the side street. There's a coffee-house—that's where I'll be waiting. If anything happens, you'll let me know everything—is that understood?"

"All right. But let me go. I understand."

"And I'll make it worth your while, old man!" he shouted after Pisarenko, who had at last succeeded in freeing himself.

"That rogue seemed to get ruder towards the end," thought our hero, creeping out from behind the stove.

"He's another twister—that's clear. First it was this and that . . . Still, he really was in a hurry. There may be a lot of work. And his Excellency walked through the section twice . . . What was that for? Ah well, it doesn't matter! It may be nothing. We'll see."

He was about to open the door and go, when at that very moment his Excellency's carriage came thundering up to the entrance. Before he could recover, the occupant had opened the door, and jumped down. It was none other than Golyadkin junior, who had gone out ten minutes before. Golyadkin senior suddenly remembered that the Director's apartments were only a step or two away.

"He's on his special errand," he thought.

After removing the fat green dispatch-case and some papers from the carriage, and giving some orders to the driver, Golyadkin junior flung open the door, nearly hitting our Mr. Golyadkin, and cutting him dead to spite him, shot up the office stairs.

"It's awful," thought our hero. "This is what we've come to now. Heavens above, just look at him!"

For about half a minute our hero stood motionless. At last he made up his mind. Without waiting to think, his heart pounding, and trembling all over, he charged upstairs after his friend.

"Here goes, and I don't care what happens. I'm out of it all," he thought, as he removed his hat, overcoat and galoshes in the ante-room.

It was nearly dark as Mr. Golyadkin walked into his section. Neither Andrey Filippovich nor Anton Antonovich was there. Both were with the Director handing in their reports, and the Director, as could be plainly heard, was in a hurry to report to a still more exalted person. Because of this, and also because darkness was falling and office hours were drawing to a close, certain clerks, the senior ones mainly, were, at the moment of Mr. Golyadkin's entry, engaged in whiling away the time. They were gathered together talking and laughing, while some of the most junior, the lowest of the low among the clerks, were taking advantage of the general hubbub to have a quiet game of pitch and toss in a corner by the window. Knowing what was proper, and feeling at that moment a particular need to find and win favour, Mr. Golyadkin went up to some of those he knew best to pass the time of day and so forth. But his colleagues reacted somewhat strangely to his greetings. He was unpleasantly struck by a certain iciness, abruptness, and one might almost say sternness, in the way they received him. No one held out a hand. Some simply said hello and walked away; some merely nodded; one turned his back, pretending not to have noticed him; while others—and this is what was more offensive to Mr. Golyadkin than anything else— others, that is to say some of the most junior ungraded clerks, mere lads, who, as he had rightly said, were only good for playing pitch and toss and roaming the streets, gradually surrounded him in such a way as to make escape almost impossible. They all looked at him with a sort of impudent curiosity.

It was an ill omen. He sensed that, and wisely prepared to ignore it. Then all of a sudden something quite unexpected happened, that finished—that completely sank him, as the saying is.

Suddenly, almost as if on purpose, at what was his most anxious moment, Golyadkin junior appeared among the encircling clerks. Gay, smiling, full of beans as ever, nimble-footed, nimble-tongued, he frolicked, toadied, gambolled and guffawed. He was, in short, his usual self—exactly as he had been the day before, when he had also turned up at a most unpleasant moment for Mr. Golyadkin.

Skipping, simpering and whirling around with a smile that wished "Good evening" to all assembled, he burst in on the little crowd of clerks. One he shook by the hand, another he clapped on the shoulder, a third he lightly embraced, to a fourth he explained the business on which he had been employed by his Excellency—where he had been, what he had done, and what he had taken with him —and a fifth, who was probably his best friend, he kissed resoundingly on the lips . . . To put it briefly, everything was happening just as in Golyadkin senior's dream.

When he had capered about to his heart's content, when he had dealt with them all in his own inimitable way, disposing each and every one of them favourably towards himself, whether there was any need or not, suddenly and probably in error, having so far failed to notice his oldest friend, Golyadkin junior even stretched out his hand to Golyadkin senior. The latter, probably also in error, although he had had ample time to observe the ignoble Golyadkin junior, eagerly seized the unexpectedly proffered hand, and impelled by some sudden strange inner urge, tearfully grasped it in the firmest and friendliest manner. Whether he had been deceived by his enemy's first move, whether he had lost his presence of mind or sensed and realised in his heart of hearts how completely defenceless he was, is difficult to say. The fact remains that Golyadkin senior, in full possession of his faculties, of his own free will and before witnesses, solemnly shook the hand of him he called his mortal foe. But how great his amazement and fury, horror and shame, when his foe and mortal enemy, perceiving the error of the innocent man he had persecuted and perfidiously deceived, suddenly, with insufferable effrontery and grossness, brazenly, callously, and showing neither conscience nor compassion, snatched his hand away! Not satisfied with that, he shook it as if it had been contaminated. Even worse, he spat, and made a most offensive gesture! And worst of all, taking out his handkerchief, he wiped each finger that had momentarily rested in the hand of Golyadkin senior. All the while he looked about him deliberately, in his usual blackguardly way, so that all should see what he was doing, and looked everyone in the face in an obvious attempt to convey to them most unpleasant things about Golyadkin senior. The behaviour of the odious Golyadkin junior seemed to arouse general indignation amongst the encircling clerks. Even the empty-headed juniors indicated their disapproval. There were murmurs on all sides. The general stir did not fail to impress itself on Golyadkin senior, but a sudden well-timed sally from Golyadkin junior shattered and destroyed our hero's last hopes, and restored the balance in favour of his deadly foe.

"Our Russian Faublas, gentlemen! Allow me to present the young Faublas," squeaked Golyadkin junior with his customary insolence, rapidly weaving his way through the clerks and pointing at the petrified but genuine Mr. Golyadkin.

"Let us embrace, my dear fellow!" he continued with unbearable familiarity, making towards the man he had treacherously insulted. The worthless Golyadkin junior's sally found a ready response, containing as it did a cunning allusion with which all were evidently familiar. Our hero felt the hand of his enemies heavy upon him. But his mind was finally made up. With eyes ablaze and a rigid smile upon his pallid face, he somehow broke out of the crowd, and with uneven hurried steps made straight for his Excellency's sanctum. With one room to go, he met Andrey Filippovich just returning from his Excellency's presence, and although there were quite a number of people about who were at that moment strangers to Mr. Golyadkin, he tried not to pay any attention to them. Boldly, openly and resolutely, amazed by his own temerity and yet inwardly praising himself for it, he accosted Andrey Filippovich on the spot. The latter was very much taken aback by this unexpected assault.

"Ah! What do you, er . . . What do you want?" asked the departmental head, not listening to what Mr. Golyadkin was trying to stutter.

"Andrey Filippovich . . . Andrey Filippovich, can I talk to his Excellency confidentially?" asked our hero clearly and distinctly, giving Andrey Filippovich one of his most determined looks.

"What? Of course not." Andrey Filippovich looked Mr. Golyadkin up and down.

"I say all this, Andrey Filippovich, because I am amazed that no one here should have unmasked this rogue and impostor."

"Wha-at?"

"This impostor . . ."

"Who are you calling that?"

"A certain person, Andrey Filippovich—it's a certain person I'm getting at. I'm within my rights. I think our superior ought to encourage such action," added Mr. Golyadkin, obviously beside himself. "You can probably see yourself, Andrey Filippovich, that it's acting honourably and that it shows every kind of good intention on my part to regard our superior as a father. I look upon our benevolent superior as a father, and blindly trust him with my fate. That's how it is . . ."

His voice began to tremble, his face grew red, and two tears ran down his eyelashes.

So amazed was Andrey Filippovich by what Mr. Golyadkin had said, that he involuntarily started back a couple of paces. He looked around uneasily. How things would have ended it is difficult to say. But all of a sudden the door of his Excellency's sanctum opened, and his Excellency himself emerged, accompanied by several officials.

Everyone in the room followed on after them. His Excellency beckoned Andrey Filippovich and walked beside him, opening conversation on some matter of business. When they had all moved off, Mr. Golyadkin recovered. Now in a quieter state, he took refuge beneath the wing of Anton Antonovich, who came hobbling along last of all, with what seemed a stern and apprehensive look on his face.

"I've let my tongue run away with me, and I've made a mess of it this time too," he thought to himself. "Well, it doesn't matter."

"I hope that you at least will consent to hear me, Anton Antonovich and consider my case," he said softly, his voice still trembling a little with emotion.

"Spurned by all, I appeal to you. I'm still wondering what Andrey Filippovich meant by what he said. Please explain to me if you can."

"It will all be explained in good time," replied Anton Antonovich severely, and paused with a look that seemed to make it quite clear that he had no desire to continue, the conversation. "You'll soon know all about it. You'll be informed officially today."

"What do you mean by 'officially', Anton Antonovich? Why 'officially'?" he inquired timidly.

"It's not for us to discuss what our superiors are deciding, Yakov Petrovich."

"Our superiors?" said Mr. Golyadkin, growing still more timid. "Why our superiors? I see no reason for bothering them, Anton Antonovich. Perhaps you mean something about yesterday."

"No. It's nothing to do with yesterday. This is something else that's wrong with you."

" 'Wrong', Anton Antonovich? I don't think there is."

"Weren't you going to 'fox' somebody?" asked Anton Antonovich, sharply cutting short the perplexed Mr. Golyadkin.

The latter shuddered and went as white as a sheet.

"Of course, Anton Antonovich, if you pay attention to slander, and listen to people's enemies without hearing what the other side has to say, then of course one just has to suffer, innocently and for nothing," he said in a voice that was barely audible.

"Precisely. And how about your improper behaviour

that prejudiced the good name of a noble young lady, of a highly moral, respected and well-known family that had done you a lot of good?"

"What behaviour, Anton Antonovich?"

"Precisely. And the laudable way you've acted towards another lady who, although poorly-off, is of honourable foreign extraction—you don't know anything about that either?"

"Listen, Anton Antonovich—listen to me, please!"

"And your treachery, and slandering of someone else—accusing him of something you're guilty of yourself—what d'you call that, eh?"

"I didn't drive him out, Anton Antonovich," said our hero, beginning to quake. "And I didn't put Petrushka—my man that is—up to anything like that either . . . He ate my bread, Anton Antonovich. He enjoyed my hospitality," added our hero with such expression and deep feeling that his chin began to tremble slightly, and tears were all ready to start to his eyes.

"That's what you say, Yakov Petrovich," smirked Anton Antonovich, and there was a note of slyness in his voice that clawed at Mr. Golyadkin's heart.

"Let me humbly ask you one more thing, Anton Antonovich. Does his Excellency know about all this?"

"Of course! But you must let me go now. I haven't got time to spend with you. You'll hear all you should today."

"Please, Anton Antonovich, just one minute more, for God's sake!"

"You can tell me afterwards."

"No, Anton Antonovich, you see I . . . Please just listen . . . I'm no advocate of free-thinking. I keep away from it. I'm quite prepared myself—and have on the contrary been known to say . . ."

"All right, all right. I've heard that."

"No, Anton Antonovich, you haven't—not this. This is different, Anton Antonovich. This is good—really it is. It makes pleasant listening . . . I have, as I've said before, made it known as my view that these two identical beings were created by Providence, and that our beneficent superiors, seeing the hand of Providence, gave the twins refuge. That's good, Anton Antonovich—very good, you can see it is, and you can see I'm far from being a free-thinker. I look upon our beneficent superior as a father. 'Such and such,' says our beneficent superior, 'and you, er . . . A young man must have employment,' he says . . .

"Back me up, Anton Antonovich. Take my part. I don't mean anything . . . For God's sake, Anton Antonovich, just one more word . . . Anton Antonovich!"

But Anton Antonovich was already some distance away. So shaken and bewildered was our hero by all that he had heard and experienced, that he had no idea where he was, what he had been told, or what he had done. He had no idea of what had happened to him, or of what was going to happen.

With an imploring gaze he searched the throng of clerks for Anton Antonovich, intending to justify himself still further in the latter's eyes, and make some extremely reasonable, generous and agreeable remark about himself. But gradually new light was beginning to penetrate his troubled mind, a new and terrible light that suddenly revealed a whole vista of things hitherto quite unknown and totally unsuspected. At that moment our disconcerted hero felt a nudge in his ribs, and looking round saw Pisarenko.

"A letter, sir."

"Ah! You've been round then, old chap?"

"No. It came here this morning at ten o'clock. Sergey Mikheyevich, the porter brought it from Vakhrameyev's place."

"All right, all right old chap. I'll make it up to you."

So saying, Mr. Golyadkin concealed the letter in a side-pocket, and buttoned his jacket right up. He then took a look round, and noted to his astonishment that he was in the vestibule, and standing amidst a crowd of clerks who, since office hours were over, had been making for the door. Nor was this last fact the only thing that had escaped his notice, for he had no memory of recollection of how he came suddenly to be wearing his overcoat and galoshes, and holding his hat.

The clerks were all standing stock-still, waiting respectfully. His Excellency had stopped at the bottom of the steps, and while awaiting his carriage, which for some reason was delayed, was having a very interesting conversation with Andrey Filippovich and a couple of counsellors. Somewhat removed from these three, stood

Anton Antonovich Setochkin and some other clerks, who, seeing his Excellency laughing and joking, were themselves all smiles. The clerks gathered at the top of the steps were also smiling as they waited for another laugh from his Excellency. The only one who was not smiling was Fedoseich, the corpulent commissionaire who stood, stiff as a ramrod, grasping the handle and waiting impatiently for his diurnal portion of pleasure, which consisted in flinging open one of the doors with a single sweep of his arm, bowing to the ground, and ceremoniously allowing his Excellency to pass. But the one whose pleasure and happiness seemed greatest of all, was Mr. Golyadkin's unworthy and ignoble enemy. He was for the moment oblivious of all his colleagues, had even left off fussing and trotting round them in his usual odious way, and was even neglecting a suitable opportunity for making up to someone. He was all eyes and ears, his gaze did not shift from his Excellency, and he seemed in some strange fashion to have shrunk—probably in the effort to hear better. Only an occasional and barely perceptible twitch of arm, leg or head betrayed his secret impulses.

"He's quite giddy with it!" thought our hero. "He looks the favourite, the scoundrel! I'd like to know just how he manages to succeed in good society—no brains, no character, no refinement, no feeling! He's got luck, the villain. Good God! When you think of it, how quickly one can get on, and make friends with everybody. And he'll get on! He'll go a long way, I swear he will! He'll get there, he's got luck! Another thing I'd like to know is what he keeps whispering in everyone's ear all the time, what mysteries they're starting between them, and what secrets they talk about. Oh God! How could I just . . . How could I get in with them as well? 'Such and such,' I'd say—perhaps I should ask him . . . 'Such and such,' I'd tell him, 'and I won't do it again. It was all my fault,' I'd say, 'but a young man can't live without work nowadays, your Excellency. My obscure position doesn't trouble me at all.' That's it! I won't protest in any way. I'll put up with it all humbly and patiently—that's what I'll do. But is that really the way to act? No. You'll never get the scoundrel to see reason—he's too thick-skinned. You can't hammer any sense into him—he doesn't give a damn for anything. Still, we'll have a try. If I happen to hit on a good moment, I'll try . . ."

Sensing in his anguish, agitation and bewilderment that things could not be left like that, that the decisive moment was at hand, and that there was someone he must come to an understanding with, our hero was just moving a little closer to where his unworthy and enigmatic friend was standing, when his Excellency's long-awaited carriage came thundering up to the entrance. Fedoseich flung open the door, and bowing low, let his Excellency out. All those who had been waiting at once rushed for the door, and Golyadkin senior was for the moment thrust away from Golyadkin junior.

"You won't get away!" thought our hero, forcing his way forward, and keeping his quarry in sight. The crowd opened out at last, and suddenly feeling himself free, he charged in pursuit of his enemy.

Chapter 11

His lungs bursting, Mr. Golyadkin sped after his rapidly retiring adversary as if on wings. He felt tremendous energy inside him. But for all his energy he had no doubt that a mere mosquito, had such a creature been able to exist in St. Petersburg at such a time, could easily have knocked him down with one wing. He felt that he had grown utterly weak and feeble, and that he was being borne along not by his own legs—for these were buckling beneath him and no longer obedient—but by some quite peculiar external force. Still, all that might turn out for the best.

"It might, and it might not," thought our hero, almost stifled for lack of breath after running so hard. "But the game's up—there isn't a shadow of doubt. I'm sunk—that's certain. The whole thing is signed sealed and delivered."

All the same, he felt suddenly resurrected—felt as if he had lasted out the battle and snatched a victory, as he succeeded in seizing his enemy's overcoat, just as the latter had one foot on the step of a cab.

"Sir! Sir!" he cried to the ignoble Golyadkin junior— "I trust that you will . . ."

"Please don't then," replied his callous enemy evasively, one foot on the step, the other waving uselessly in the air, as he strove to get it into the cab, maintain his balance, and at the same time to wrench his coat away from Goly-adkin senior, who was clutcing it with all the strength nature had bestowed upon him.

"Yakov Petrovich—just ten minutes . . ."

"Excuse me, I haven't time."

"You must agree, Yakov Petrovich . . . Please, Yakov Petrovich . . . For God's sake, Yakov Petrovich. Let's have it out . . . Man to man . . . One second, Yakov Petrovich!"

"My dear good fellow, I must dash," replied the other with discourteous familiarity disguised as sincere *bonhomie,* "Some other time . . . With the best will in the world, believe me . . . I really can't now."

"Blackguard!" thought our hero. "Yakov Petrovich!" he cried, filled with anguish, "I have never been your enemy. Spiteful people have given an unfair picture of me. For my part I'm prepared . . . If you like, let's go somewhere this minute—you and I—shall we, Yakov Petrovich? Let's go into this coffee-house, and with the best will in the world, as you rightly said just now, let's talk it over, nobly, man to man. Everything will explain itself, Yakov Petrovich. It's bound to."

"This coffee-house? All right, I don't mind. But on one condition, old chap, and on one condition only, that everything *does* explain itself," said Golyadkin junior, getting down from the cab and brazenly clapping our hero on the shoulder. "You're a dear good friend, and for you I'm ready 'to take a little side street', as you once put it. You really are a rascal, you do just what you like with a man," he continued with a smile, coaxing and cajoling him.

The coffee-house into which the two Mr. Golyadkins went, stood secluded from the main streets, and was at that moment quite deserted. No sooner had they sounded the bell, than a plumpish German woman appeared behind the counter. Mr. Golyadkin and his unworthy enemy passed through into a second room, where a pasty-faced urchin with close-cropped hair was fiddling around by the stove with a bundle of firewood, making an effort to bring some life back into a dead fire. At Golyadkin junior's request, chocolate was served.

"There's a nice full-bodied woman," said Golyadkin junior, with a roguish wink at Golyadkin senior.

Our hero blushed and said nothing.

"But forgive me, I forgot. I know what you fancy. We're sweet on *slim* little Fräuleins, you and I, aren't we, Yakov Petrovich? Not-unattractive, slim little Fräuleins? We lodge with them, we lead them astray, we give them our hearts for their *Biersuppe* and their *Milchsuppe*, we give them various written undertakings—that's what we do, isn't it—you Faublas, you serpent!"

While making these utterly futile albeit fiendishly subtle allusions to a certain person of the female sex, Golyadkin junior had been fawning on Golyadkin senior, and affecting an amiable smile in a false show of affability and pleasure at their meeting. But noticing that Golyadkin senior was by no means so stupid or lacking in education and breeding as immediately to take him at his word, the ignoble man decided to change his tactics and come into the open. With infuriating effrontery and familiarity, the spurious Golyadkin followed up his odious speech by slapping the trustworthy Golyadkin on the back—not content with which, he began to frolic in a manner quite unbecoming in good society, and suddenly took it into his head to repeat his former heinous trick of pinching—regardless of his resistance and subdued cries—the indignant Mr. Golyadkin's cheek. Confronted with such depravity, our hero seethed with rage, and remained silent —but only for a while.

"That is what my enemies say," he replied finally, prudently keeping himself in check. His voice trembled. Golyadkin junior was evidently in excellent spirits, and ready to indulge in all sorts of pranks inadmissible in a public place, and, generally speaking, in good society.

"Just as you please," answered Golyadkin junior gravely, draining his cup in a shamefully greedy fashion, and placing it on the table.

"Well, I haven't much time to spend with you. How are you getting on now, Yakov Petrovich?"

"There's only one thing I can say to you, Yakov Petrovich," replied our hero coolly and with dignity, "I have never been your enemy."

"H-m-m . . . Well, how's Petrushka? I think that's his name, isn't it? How is he—all right? Same as ever?"

"The same as ever," answered Golyadkin senior, a little taken aback. "I don't know, Yakov Petrovich, but for my part—from a candid and honourable point of view— you'll agree yourself . . ."

"Yes. But you know yourself, Yakov Petrovich, these are hard times we live in," replied Golyadkin junior quietly and expressively, making himself out to be sorrowful, repentant, and worthy of pity. "I appeal to you, Yakov Petrovich—you're a clever man and will judge fairly," he threw in as an abject piece of flattery. "Life isn't a game—you know yourself," he concluded, making himself out to be the wise and learned man able to discourse on lofty subjects.

"For my part, Yakov Petrovich," answered our hero animatedly, "scorning beating about the bush, speaking honourably, openly, man to man and straight from the shoulder, and putting the whole thing on an honourable level, I tell you, Yakov Petrovich—I can assert frankly and honourably that I am perfectly blameless, and that, as you know yourself . . . an error on both sides . . . anything is possible . . . the world's judgment, the opinion of the servile throng . . . I tell you frankly, Yakov Petrovich, anything is possible. I'll say more, if one considers the matter thus, if one regards it from a noble and lofty point of view, then I will say boldly, without any false shame, that it will be a pleasure to find I've been mistaken, and a pleasure to admit it. You know yourself —you're intelligent and generous . . . Without shame, without any false shame, I'm ready to admit it . . ." he concluded, nobly and with dignity.

"It's fate, Yakov Petrovich. But let's leave all this," sighed Golyadkin junior. "Let us rather employ these brief minutes together in pleasant and profitable conversation, as two colleagues should. Really, all this time I don't seem to have said two words to you. I'm not to blame for that."

"Nor I!" interrupted our hero eagerly. "My heart tells me that. Let's blame it all on fate," he added in a thoroughly conciliatory tone. His voice was gradually beginning to weaken and quaver.

"Well, how are you keeping?" inquired the erring one agreeably.

"Coughing a bit," answered our hero still more agreeably.

"Look after yourself. With all the epidemics that are going about, you can easily get throat trouble. I don't mind telling you, I'm starting to wear flannel."

"Yes. You can easily get throat trouble," said our hero

after a short silence. "Yakov Petrovich, I see I've been wrong! I'm touched by the memory of those happy moments we passed together beneath my humble, but I venture to say hospitable roof."

"That's not what you said in your letter," rejoined Golyadkin junior somewhat reproachfully. And for once he was perfectly right.

"I was wrong, Yakov Petrovich! I now see clearly I was wrong in that unfortunate letter of mine. I feel ashamed to look at you. You can't believe . . . Give me that letter so that I can tear it up in front of your eyes. And if that's not possible, then I beseech you, read it the other way round in a deliberately friendly way, giving each word its reverse meaning. I was wrong. Forgive me, Yakov Petrovich—I've been utterly, grievously wrong."

"What's that?" inquired Mr. Golyadkin's perfidious friend in an indifferent, absent-minded sort of way.

"I say I've been utterly wrong, Yakov Petrovich, and for my part, I'm completely without false shame . . ."

"Ah well, that's all right then," retorted Golyadkin junior rudely.

"I even had the idea," added our hero nobly, completely unaware of the dreadful perfidy of his false friend, "I even had the idea of two identical beings being created . . ."

"You did?"

At this point the notoriously worthless Golyadkin junior rose, and reached for his hat. Still blind to the hoax, Golyadkin senior rose also, smiling generously and good-naturedly at his false friend, and endeavouring in his innocence to be nice to him, to reassure him, and so to strike up a new friendship.

"Farewell, your Excellency!" cried Golyadkin junior suddenly.

Our hero shuddered, noticing something almost Bacchanalian in his enemy's face, and with the sole object of getting rid of him, thrust two fingers into the reprobate's outstretched hand. But the brazenness of Golyadkin junior exceeded all limits. After first gripping his two fingers, the worthless man decided to repeat before his very eyes the shameless trick he had performed that afternoon. It was more than flesh and blood could stand . . .

He was just pocketing the handkerchief with which he

had wiped his fingers, when Mr. Golyadkin recovered his senses, and rushed after him into the next room, whither in his usual noxious way he had hastened to effect his escape. There he was, standing by the counter as if it were the most natural thing in the world, eating pastries and making polite conversation to the German confectioneress—jut like any decent moral person.

"Not in front of ladies," thought our hero, and went up to the counter, almost beside himself in his agitation.

"She's not bad. What do you think?" said Golyadkin junior, up to his smutty pranks again, counting no doubt on Mr. Golyadkin's infinite patience.

The plump German woman looked at both customers with her dull stupid eyes, and smiled affably, obviously not understanding a word of Russian. Our hero flushed fiery red, and unable to control himself, sprang at the shameless man, evidently intending to tear him limb from limb, and finish him for good. But Golyadkin junior was as usual far away—he had taken to his heels and was already out of the door. Needless to say, Golyadkin senior, as soon as he had recovered from the first momentary feeling of bewilderment that had naturally beset him, charged as fast as his legs would carry him in pursuit of his abuser, who was getting into the cab which had obviously been waiting for him by agreement. At that moment however, the plump German, seeing the flight of her two customers, gave a shriek and rang her little bell as hard as she could. Turning almost in mid-air, our hero threw her some money to cover himself and the shameless man who had left without paying, and without waiting for change, succeeded, in spite of this delay and again almost in mid-air, in catching up with his enemy. He seized hold of the splashboard by every means in his power, and was carried some way along the street, struggling to clamber onto the carriage, while Golyadkin junior did his utmost to fight him off. The driver urged on his sorry horse, using words, whip, reins and feet, until quite unexpectedly it burst into a gallop, taking the bit between its teeth and kicking up its hind legs in a peculiarly nasty fashion. At last our hero managed to hoist himself up into a position where he sat back to back with the driver, and face to face and knee to knee with his brazen, depraved and most obdurate foe, gripping the moth-eaten fur collar of the latter's overcoat in his right hand.

The enemies were carried some way in silence. Our hero could scarcely recover his breath. The road was terrible, and he was continually being thrown into the air and in danger of having his neck broken, added to which his enemy, still refusing to admit defeat, strove to topple him into the mud. To crown everything, the weather was as bad as it could possibly be. Snow fell in huge flakes which did their best in every way to creep inside the unbuttoned overcoat of the real Mr. Golyadkin. All around not a thing could be seen. It was difficult to tell through what streets and in which direction they were going. It seemed to Mr. Golyadkin that there was something familiar about what was happening to him. For a moment he tried hard to remember whether he had not had some presentiment or other the day before—in a dream for instance. His anguish at last became acute agony. He pressed himself against his pitiless foe, and was about to utter a cry, but it died on his lips.

It was at this moment that Mr. Golyadkin forgot everything and decided the whole thing didn't matter; it was all just happening in some inexplicable way, and it would be vain and so much wasted effort to protest. But suddenly, almost as he was deciding this, an inconsiderate jolt altered the whole complexion of the matter. He fell from the carriage like a sack of potatoes and rolled over and over, confessing as he did so, and quite rightly, that his fit of temper had really been most inopportune. Jumping to his feet, he saw that the cab had stopped in the middle of a courtyard which he recognised at a glance as that belonging to the house wherein resided Olsufy Ivanovich. The same instant he noticed his enemy mounting the steps, probably on his way to visit Olsufy Ivanovich. In indescribable anguish he was about to rush and catch him up, but fortunately and sensibly thought better of it. Not forgetting first to settle up with the cab-driver, he dashed out into the street and ran on blindly as fast as his legs would carry him.

It was wet, dark and snowing hard, just as before. Our hero did not run, he flew, bouncing off and bowling over men, women and children as he went. From all quarters came shrieks, shouts and a fearful hubbub of voices, but

Mr. Golyadkin seemed barely conscious, and heeded none of it. He came to by the Semyonovsky Bridge, and then only because he had collided awkwardly with two peasant women, knocking them over together with the goods they were hawking, and falling down himself.

"It doesn't matter," he thought, "it can all be settled for the best," and immediately slipped his hand into his pocket for a rouble to make good the gingerbreads, apples, peas and various other things he had upset. Suddenly new light dawned upon him; in his pocket he felt the letter he had been handed that afternoon. Remembering there was an inn he knew close by, he ran off to it, and once inside, lost no time in establishing himself at a small table lit by a tallow candle. Heedless of all around, and ignoring the waiter who appeared for his order, he broke the seal, and began to read the following, which utterly amazed him:

To the noble one who suffers for my sake and is eternally dear to my heart.

I am in distress, I perish, save me! A slanderer, intriguer and notoriously worthless man has ensnared me and I am undone, lost! Him I abominate, while you . . . We have been kept apart, my letters to you have been intercepted, and all this has been done by an immoral man availing himself of his one and only good quality —his likeness to you. One can however be ugly, but still fascinate by one's wit, strong sensibilities and good manners . . .

I perish! I am being forcibly married, and the one who has schemed most in this, desiring probably to secure my place and connexions in good society, is my father, my benefactor, the Civil Counsellor Olsufy Ivanovich. But my mind is made up, and I protest by every means in my power. Await me in your carriage outside Olsufy Ivanovich's windows tonight at nine exactly. We are having another ball, and the handsome lieutenant is coming. I shall leave, and we shall fly.

Besides, there are other official posts where one may still be of service to one's country. Remember at all events, my friend, that innocence is the strength of innocence.

Farewell. Be waiting with the carriage at the entrance. I shall rush to your protecting embrace at 2 a.m. precisely.

Yours till the grave,
Klara Olsufyevna.

For some minutes he remained thunderstruck. Then, in a fearful state of anguish and agitation, and with his face as white as a sheet, he paced several times up and down the room, holding the letter in his hand. To complete the awfulness of his situation, although he was not at that moment aware of it, every eye in the place was upon him. His disordered clothes, his lack of control, his walking, or rather dashing up and down the room, his two-handed gesticulations and the few enigmatic words he addressed absent-mindedly to the world at large, all this can have done little to commend him to the other customers. Even the waiter began to look at him suspiciously. Recovering his senses, our hero found himself standing in the middle of the room, and staring in a rude and almost shameless way at a very respectable-looking old man who, having finished dinner and offered thanks before an ikon, had resumed his seat, and was staring back. Our hero looked about him uneasily, and saw everyone looking at him in a most ominous and suspicious fashion. Suddenly a retired army man with a red collar to his tunic called loudly for *The Police Gazette.* Mr. Golyadkin shuddered, blushed, and chancing to look down suddenly, noticed that his attire was unseemly to a degree that would have been inadmissible in his own home, let alone in a public place. His boots, trousers and the whole of his left side were plastered in mud. His left trouser-strap had been ripped off, and his coat was torn in many places. In sore distress, he went over to the table at which he had been reading, and saw the waiter approaching with a strange, impudently insistent look on his face. Bewildered and utterly dejected, Mr. Golyadkin began to examine the table at which he was standing. There were plates left from somebody's dinner, a dirty serviette, and a recently-discarded knife, fork and spoon.

"Who's been eating here?" he wondered. "Could it have been me? Anything is possible."

Looking up, he again saw the waiter standing beside him, and on the point of saying something.

"What do I owe you, old chap?" inquired our hero in a voice that quavered.

There was loud laughter all around. The waiter smiled. Mr. Golyadkin realised he had put his foot in it, and committed some awful blunder. He was so overcome with confusion, that he was constrained to feel for his handkerchief, just for the sake of something to do, instead of simply standing there. But to his indescribable amazement as well as to that of all around, in place of his handkerchief he pulled out the bottle of medicine prescribed by Dr. Rutenspitz four days earlier. "Get it at the same chemist's," flashed through his mind. Suddenly he shuddered and almost screamed with terror. New light was dawning. The dark loathsome reddish fluid gleamed ominously before his eyes. The bottle slipped from his grasp and was instantly smashed. With a cry he leapt back to avoid the spilled liquid. He was trembling in every limb. Sweat was breaking out upon his brow and temples.

"So my life is in danger!"

The room was filled with uproar and excitement. They were all surrounding him, they were all saying things to him, some were even laying hold of him. But our hero was speechless, motionless, unseeing, unhearing and unfeeling. At last, tearing himself away, he rushed from the inn, shaking off all and sundry who sought to detain him. He collapsed almost unconscious into the first cab that came along, and hurtled back to his rooms.

On his way in he met Mikheyev the office porter, holding an official envelope in his hand.

"I know, my friend. I know it all, it's official," said our exhausted hero, weakly and miserably.

The envelope did in fact contain an order signed by Andrey Filippovich to the effect that he should hand over to Ivan Semyonovich. Taking it and giving the porter ten kopeks, Mr. Golyadkin entered his rooms to find Petrushka piling all his belongings and odds and ends together, obviously intending to leave him and go to Karolina Ivanovna, who had enticed him into replacing Yevstafy.

Chapter 12

Petrushka came swinging into Mr. Golyadkin's room. His manner was singularly casual, and he had the menial's look of triumph on his face. He had evidently got some idea into his head, and was feeling quite within his rights. He looked a complete stranger, that is, like someone else's servant, and nothing like the former servant of Mr. Golyadkin.

"I say old fellow," began our hero, still short of breath, "what's the time now?"

Without a word Petrushka went behind the partition, and coming back, announced in a rather independent tone of voice that it was nearly seven-thirty.

"Oh, that's fine. Well, if I may say so, my dear fellow, everything seems over between us."

Petrushka said nothing.

"Since it is, tell me frankly now, as you would a friend, where it is you've been."

"Me?—With nice people."

"I know, my friend, I know. You've always given me satisfaction, and I'll give you a reference. So you're with them now, are you?"

"Well sir, you know yourself, a good man won't teach you any bad ways, of course."

"I know, I know, old fellow. Good people are rare nowadays. Treasure them, my friend. And how are they?"

"You know how they are, sir. Only I can't work for you any more now, you can see that."

"I do, I do, my dear chap. I know how keen and hardworking you are. I've seen it all, I've noticed. I respect you, my friend. I respect a good honest man, even if he's a servant."

"Yes, I know. Our sort, of course, as you know yourself, must go where things are best. That's how it is. And what can I do about it? It's well known, sir—without a good man, it's impossible."

"Yes, yes. I appreciate that. Well, here's your money and your reference. Now let's shake hands and say goodbye. There's just one last thing I'd like to ask you to do," said Mr. Golyadkin solemnly. "You see, my dear chap, anything can happen. Sorrow lurks e'en in gilded halls, my friend, and you can't get away from it. I think I've always been kind to you, you know . . ."

Petrushka said nothing.

"I think I've always been kind to you . . . How am I off for linen, my dear fellow?"

"It's all there. Six shirts linen, three pairs socks, four shirt-fronts, one vest flannel, two sets underwear. You know all that yourself. I've got nothing of yours. I look after my master's things. You know me, sir. That's never been one of my weaknesses. You know that."

"I believe you, my friend. I believe you. That's not what I mean. You see . . ."

"I know. We all know that, sir. Why, when I was with General Stolbnyakov—he let me go when he went to Saratov—he had an estate there . . ."

"No, my friend. I don't mean that. I don't mean anything like that. Don't go thinking anything, my dear fellow . . ."

"I know. The likes of us can be slandered any minute, as you're well aware. But I've given satisfaction everywhere. Ministers, generals, senators, counts, I've been with them all. Prince Svinchatkin, Colonel Pereborkin, General Nedobarov—he also went away to his estate . . ."

"Yes my friend, yes. Very good. And now *I'm* going away. We all have different roads to travel, my dear fellow, and no one knows on which he may find himself. Now give me a hand to get dressed. Lay out my uniform jacket, my other trousers, sheets, blankets, pillows . . ."

"Shall I make a bundle of it all?"

"Yes please, my dear fellow. A bundle. Who knows what may happen to us? And now you go and find me a carriage."

"A carriage?"

"Yes my friend, a big roomy one, and for a definite time. And don't go getting any ideas . . ."

"Do you wish to go far?"

"I don't know, my friend. That's also something I don't know. My feather-bed had better go in too, I think. What do you think, my dear chap? I'm relying on you."

"Are you actually thinking of going now, sir?"

"I am, my friend. I am. That's how things have turned out. So there it is."

"I know, sir. Same thing happened to a lieutenant in our regiment. He carried off the daughter of the local landowner."

"Carried her off? How do you mean, my dear good fellow?"

"Yes. He carried her off, and they got married from another house. Everything had been got ready beforehand. There was a pursuit. But the late prince stuck up for them, and it was all settled."

"They got married, did they? But how is it—how did you get to know?"

"We know, sir. The world's full of rumours. We know

it all. It could happen to anyone. Only let me tell you, sir, in plain servants' talk, if it's come to that, you've got a rival, sir, a strong one."

"I know, my friend, I know. So I'm relying on you. What are we to do now? What do you advise?"

"Well sir, if roughly speaking that's the style of thing you're going in for, there are things you'll have to get, sheets, pillows, another feather-bed—a double one, a good blanket . . . There's a woman underneath here, sir, a common woman, she's got a fine fox cloak. You might have a look at that, and buy it. You could pop down and see it now. It's just what you need now, sir, a fine fox cloak lined with satin . . ."

"All right my friend, I agree. I rely on you entirely. Let's have that then. But be quick about it. For God's sake be quick! It'll soon be eight. For God's sake be quick!"

Dropping the linen, pillows, blankets and various oddments he had been about to bundle up, Petrushka rushed headlong from the room. Mr. Golyadkin dragged out the letter again, but was unable to read it. Clutching his poor head in his hands, he leant against the wall, dazed and incapable of thought or action. He didn't know what was happening to him. At last, seeing the time getting on, and still no sign of Petrushka or the cloak, he decided to go himself. Opening the door into the hall, he heard a hubbub and clamour of voices down below. A number of women living in the same block were jabbering, shouting and arguing. He knew exactly what about. Petrushka's voice could be heard for a moment, then there was the sound of footsteps.

"Good God! They're bringing the whole world into it!" groaned Mr. Golyadkin, wringing his hands in despair. Diving back into his room, he fell almost senseless onto the ottoman, face downwards on the cushion. After lying there for about a minute, he leapt to his feet, and deciding not to wait for Petrushka, put on his hat, overcoat and galoshes, snatched up his note-case and charged blindly down the stairs.

"Don't bother! It doesn't matter. I'll see to it all myself. I shan't need you for the time being, and everything will probably be settled for the best meanwhile," muttered Mr. Golyadkin, meeting Petrushka on the stairs. Then he dashed out into the courtyard, and away. He felt sick at heart, and was still unable to make up his mind what to do, and how to act at this critical juncture.

"What in heaven's name am I to do, that's the question," he cried in despair, as he hobbled blindly and aimlessly along the street. "Why did all this have to happen? But for *this,* everything would have been settled. One stroke, one deft, resolute, vigorous stroke, would have put the whole thing right at once. I'd give a finger to do that. I even know how it could be done—like this. 'Such and such,' I'd say, 'it's neither here nor there, sir, if you'll allow me to say so. Things aren't done that way—no, sir. Impersonation won't get you anywhere here. An impostor, sir, is good for nothing, and no use to his country. Do you understand, sir?' That's how it would be. But no. That's not how it is, not at all. I'm talking through my hat like a fool—my own executioner, that's what I am. You're your own executioner! But you can see how it's happening now, you depraved man! Still, where am I to go, what am I going to do with myself now? What am I fit for? Just what, for instance, poor unworthy fellow that I am!

"Well, what now? We must get a carriage. 'Have a carriage here,' she says, 'we'll get our little feet wet if you don't . . .' And who would have thought it? Well well, my virtuous young miss, who everyone thinks the world of, you've surpassed yourself and no mistake. And it all comes of an immoral upbringing. Now I've gone into it a bit and got the hang of it, I can see it's nothing more nor less than that. Instead of taking the stick to her now and then when she was young, they stuffed her with sweets and confectionery, and the old man slobbered all over her with his 'You're my daddy's this and that, and we'll marry you to a count!' And this is what they get for it. She's shown us her hand now. 'This is what we're up to,' she says. Instead of keeping her at home, they send her to a boarding-school—to some French emigrée, Madame Falbala, or something of the sort. And a lot of good she's learnt there! Now she turns out like this. 'Come and be happy,' she says! 'Be outside the windows at such and such a time in a carriage,' she says, 'and sing a tender Spanish ballad. I'll be waiting. I know you love me, and we'll fly together and live in a cottage.' But it won't work, young lady. If that's what it's come to, it won't work, because it's against the law to take an honest, innocent young lady from her parents' house without their consent. Why do it? What need is there? She should marry who she's supposed to, as fate intended, and that's that. I'm in the service. I could lose my job through it. I might finish up in court, young lady! So that's how it is, if you didn't know. It's the work of that German woman. It all goes back to her, the witch. She's the one who started all the rumpus. Slandering a man, making up some old wives' gossip and a cock-and-bull story about him on the advice of Andrey Filippovich. It all goes back to her. How would Petrushka have got into it otherwise? What's he want here? Is it any of that scoundrel's business? No, young lady, I can't. I can't possibly. This once you must excuse me somehow. You're the source of the whole thing, young lady, not the German, not the old witch, it doesn't come from her at all, but simply and solely from you. She's a good woman, she's not to blame for anything, but you are, young lady. You're getting me accused of something I'm not guilty of . . . Look, here's a man losing control of himself, losing sight of himself, on the point of vanishing for ever—and you're talking about a wedding! And what will be the end of it all? And how will it turn out? I'd give a lot to know."

Thus reasoned our hero in his despair. Returning suddenly to his immediate surroundings, he noticed that he was standing somewhere in Liteynaya Street. The weather was terrible. A thaw had set in, and it was snowing and raining just as it had been at that dreadful and never-to-be-forgotten midnight hour when all his misfortunes had begun.

"How can you go on a journey in this?" he thought. "It's certain death. Oh God! Where am I to find a cab here, for instance? There seems to be some dark object on the corner there. Let's go and investigate. Oh God!" continued our hero as he tottered feebly in the direction of what looked like a cab. "No. This is what I'll do. I'll go and throw myself at his feet, if I can, and make humble entreaties. 'Such and such,' I'll say, 'I put my fate into your hands, into the hands of my superiors. Protect me, your Excellency, show me your support. This and that and such and such a thing is an unlawful act,' I'll say. 'Don't ruin me. I look upon you as a father. Don't forsake me. Rescue my dignity, name and honour . . . Deliver me from a depraved villain. He's one man, your Excellency, and I am another. He goes his way, and I go mine. I do, your Excellency, indeed I do. I can't resemble him,' I'll say. 'Replace him, your Excellency. Order him to be replaced, I beg you, and put an end to an ungodly and unwarranted impersonation, that it may not serve as a precedent for others. I look upon you as a father.' A benevolent superior having the welfare of his subordinates at heart must surely encourage such action. There's a touch of chivalry about it. 'You, my benevolent superior, I regard as a father,' I'll say. 'I put my fate in your hands. I'll make no objections. I trust in you. I myself withdraw from the affair.' That's it!"

"Are you a cabman?"

"I am."

"I want a cab for the evening."

"Going far, sir?"

"For the evening, I want it, and to go wherever may be necessary."

"You don't mean out of town?"

"Maybe, my friend. I don't know myself yet, and can't tell you. The point is, it may all turn out for the best, you see. You know how it is."

"Yes, of course, sir. God grant as much to everyone."

"Yes, my friend. Yes. Thank you. Well, how much will it be?"

"Do you want to go now?"

"Yes, that is—no. You'll have to wait a little at a certain spot . . . Just a little, not long . . ."

"Well, if you hire me for the whole time, I couldn't do it for less than six roubles in weather like this."

"All right, all right. I'll make it worth your while, old chap. You'll take me now then, will you?"

"In you get. Excuse me, I'll just put it right a second. That's it. Now in you get. Where to?"

"Izmaylovsky Bridge, my friend."

The driver clambered onto the box, and with some difficulty dragged his two miserably-thin horses away from the hay-trough, and roused them to move in the direction of the Izmaylovsky Bridge. But all of a sudden Mr. Golyadkin tugged the cord, stopped the cab, and implored the driver to turn and go to another street instead. The driver did so, and ten minutes later Mr. Golyadkin and his newly-acquired carriage drew up before the house in which were his Excellency's apartments. He jumped down, urged the driver to wait, and with his heart in his boots, charged up to the second floor and pulled the bell. The door opened, and he found himself in his Excellency's hall.

"Is his Excellency at home?" he inquired of the servant who had opened to him.

"What do you want?" asked the servant, looking him up and down.

"I-I'm Golyadkin, the clerk, my friend. I've come to explain, tell him."

"Wait, you can't . . ."

"I can't wait, my friend. My business is important, and doesn't admit of any delay."

"Who are you from? Have you brought papers?"

"No. I've come on my own account. Announce me, my friend, and say I've come to explain."

"I can't. Orders are to receive no one. He has visitors. Come at ten in the morning."

"Announce me. I can't wait—it's impossible. You'll answer for this . . ."

"Go on, announce him. What's the matter, saving shoe-leather or something?" said another lackey, who till then had merely been lolling on a seat in the hall.

"Shoe-leather be damned! Orders were not to receive anyone, see? Their turn is mornings."

"Go on. Afraid your tongue will come off?"

"All right, I will. I'm not afraid of my tongue coming off, but orders were as I said.—Come in here."

Mr. Golyadkin went into the first room. There was a clock on the table. He glanced at it. It was eight-thirty. He felt torn with anguish. He was about to turn back, but at that very moment a lanky footman stationed at the door of the next room, loudly announced Mr. Golyadkin's name.

"What a voice!" he thought, in indescribable agony. " 'Such and such a thing,' he ought to have said, 'he has most dutifully and humbly come to explain. Will you kindly see him?' Now it's ruined. All I've done has been thrown away. Still, it doesn't matter."

There was no time for reflection however. The lackey returned, and with a "come on", took Mr. Golyadkin into the study.

The moment he walked in, he felt as if he had been suddenly blinded, for he could see nothing. He had, however, caught a glimpse of two or three figures.

"Ah yes, those are the visitors," flashed through his mind.

At last he was able to make out the star upon his Excellency's frock-coat; then by a gradual process he proceeded to an awareness of the black frock-coat itself, and finally received the faculty of complete vision.

"What is it?" asked a familiar voice above his head.

"Titular Counsellor Golyadkin, your Excellency."

"Well?"

"I've come to explain."

"What's that?"

"Yes, it's like this. I said I've come to explain, your Excellency, sir."

"Who are you?"

"M-M-Mister Golyadkin, your Excellency, a titular counsellor."

"Well, what do you want?"

"I'll tell him this and that," he thought. "I look upon him as a father. 'I'm withdrawing from the matter, and protect me from my enemies,' that's what I'll say."

"What's that?"

"Of course . . ."

"Of course what?"

Mr. Golyadkin said nothing. His chin was beginning to twitch slightly.

"Well?"

"I thought it chivalrous, your Excellency. There's chivalry about it, I thought. And I look upon my departmental head as I would a father . . . Protect me, I b-b-beg you with t-t-tears in my eyes . . . s-s-such action m-m-must b-b-be encouraged . . ."

His Excellency turned away. For some minutes our hero's eyes could distinguish nothing. There was a great weight upon his chest. His lungs were bursting. He did not know where he was. He felt ashamed. He felt sad. What happened next, he had no idea.

When he recovered, he saw that his Excellency was talking to his visitors; he seemed to be debating something with them in an abrupt and forceful manner. One of the visitors our hero recognised at once. It was Andrey Filippovich. Another he did not recognise, although his face seemed familiar. He was tall, thick-set, elderly, with very bushy side-whiskers, and a keen and expressive gaze.

About his neck he wore a decoration, and in his mouth was a cigar. He smoked steadily, keeping the cigar in his mouth, and every now and then glanced towards Mr. Golyadkin and nodded meaningly. Mr. Golyadkin began to feel uneasy. Shifting his gaze, he caught sight of yet another strange visitor. In a doorway, which till then our hero had as on a previous occasion taken for a mirror, *he* appeared, the *he* who is already familiar to the reader, Mr. Golyadkin's very intimate friend and acquaintance! Golyadkin junior had until this moment been in another small room, writing something in a hurry. Now, because it had evidently become necessary to do so, he emerged carrying the papers under his arm, went up to his Excellency, and while awaiting the latter's undivided attention, succeeded very cleverly in worming his way into the general counsel and confabulation, taking up a position behind Andrey Filippovich's back, and partly hidden by the cigar-smoking stranger. Golyadkin junior was clearly acutely interested in the conversation, to which he was listening in a genteel fashion, nodding assent, shifting from one foot to the other, and smiling and glancing every other minute at his Excellency, as if imploring to be allowed to put his word in.

"Wretch!" thought Mr. Golyadkin, and involuntarily took a step forward. Just then his Excellency turned, and came rather uncertainly towards Mr. Golyadkin.

"Well, that's all right. Off you go then. I'll look into your case, and I'll get someone to show you out." The general glanced at the stranger with the bushy side-whiskers. The latter nodded.

Mr. Golyadkin sensed and realised quite clearly that they were taking him for something that he wasn't, and not at all as they ought.

"I must explain somehow or other," he thought. " 'Such and such a thing, your Excellency,' I'll say."

In his perplexity he looked down at the floor, and was amazed to observe large white patches on his Excellency's boots.

"Surely they haven't split?" he thought. He soon discovered they had not, but were merely acting as powerful reflectors, a phenomenon fully explained by their being of shining patent leather.

"Those are what they call 'high-lights'," he thought. "That's the name that's reserved for them, especially in artists' studios. Elsewhere they're known as 'bright spots'."

At this point he looked up, and saw it was time to speak, as things might easily take a turn for the worse and end badly. He took a step forward.

"'Such and such a thing,' I said, your Excellency, 'but impersonation will get you nowhere.'"

The general made no answer, but tugged hard at the bell-pull. Our hero took another step forward.

"He's vile and perverted, your Excellency," he said, highly agitated and sick with fear, but still pointing boldly and resolutely at his unworthy twin, who was at that moment fidgeting about near his Excellency. "That's what I say, and I'm alluding to someone we all know."

These words were followed by general commotion. Andrey Filippovich and the stranger nodded their heads. His Excellency, in his impatience, tugged the bell-pull with all his might to summon servants. At this juncture Golyadkin junior stepped forward.

"Your Excellency," he said, "I crave your permission to speak." There was a decisive ring in his voice. Everything about him showed that he felt completely within his rights.

"May I ask," he began, anticipating his Excellency's reply in his eagerness, and now addressing Mr. Golyadkin, "may I ask if you know in whose presence you are thus expressing yourself, before whom you are standing, and in whose study you are?"

Golyadkin junior was unusually agitated, his face was completely red, and he was burning with anger and indignation. There were even tears in his eyes.

"The Bassavryukovs!" roared a footman at the top of his voice, appearing suddenly at the door.

"A fine noble name—they're from the Ukraine," thought Mr. Golyadkin, and immediately felt a friendly hand rest upon his back. This was followed by another. He saw clearly that he was being steered towards the study door, while his vile twin fussed about in front, showing the way.

"It's just as it was at Olsufy Ivanovich's," he thought, and found himself in the hall. Looking round he saw two of his Excellency's footmen and his twin.

"My friend's coat! My friend's coat! My best friend's coat!" babbled the perverted man, snatching the overcoat from one of the servants, and throwing it right over Mr.

Golyadkin's head to put him to ridicule in a most black-guardly and outrageous manner. As he fought his way out from under the coat, Mr. Golyadkin could clearly hear the two footmen laughing. But paying no heed to the sounds around him, he marched out of the hall and found himself on a lighted stairway. Golyadkin junior followed.

"Good-bye, your Excellency," he shouted after Golyadkin senior.

"Villain!" said our hero, beside himself.

"I don't mind . . ."

"Pervert!"

"Just as you like . . ." answered the worthy Golyadkin's unworthy foe from the top of the stairs, looking the former unblinkingly straight in the eye, in that peculiarly vile way of his, begging him to go on, as it were. Our hero made an indignant gesture, and ran down and out into the street. Such was his state of despair that he had no recollection at all of how or by whose agency he got into the carriage. On regaining his senses, he found that he was being driven along the Fontanka.

"We must be going to the Izmaylovsky Bridge," he thought. There was something else he was trying to think of, but could not. It was so terrible as to defy explanation.

"Well, it doesn't matter," he concluded, and proceeded to the Izmaylovsky Bridge.

Chapter 13

The weather, it seemed, was trying to change for the better. The wet snow which till then had been falling in prodigious quantities, began gradually to ease, and finally stopped altogether. The sky appeared, and here and there a tiny star began to twinkle. But it was wet and muddy underfoot, and it was muggy; Mr. Golyadkin, who had difficulty in catching his breath as it was, found it particularly so. His overcoat, which had become sodden and heavy, made him feel disagreeably warm and wet all over, while his enfeebled legs buckled beneath its weight. Sharp feverish shivers ran through his whole body. He broke into a cold sickly sweat from sheer exhaustion. Appropriate as the moment was, he quite forgot to reiterate with his customary resolution and determination his favourite phrase that it would all perhaps, somehow, in all probability, certainly turn out for the best.

"Still, none of this matters for the time being," said our sturdy hero, still undismayed, wiping from his face the cold drops of water which were trickling from all round the brim of his saturated hat. Adding that that didn't matter either, he tried sitting down for a while on a fair-sized log lying near a stack of firewood in Olsufy Ivanovich's courtyard. Spanish serenades and silken ladders were, of course, past thinking about. What he must try to think of, was some quiet little corner which, if not altogether warm, would at least be convenient and concealed. He was, it may be observed in passing, strongly tempted by that particular corner on Olsufy Ivanovich's landing where, on an earlier occasion, almost at the beginning of this true story, he had spent over two hours of his time standing between a cupboard and some old screens amidst all sorts of lumber and rubbish. He had now stood waiting two hours in Olsufy Ivanovich's courtyard. As far as his former quiet and convenient little spot was concerned, there were certain disadvantages that had not existed before. Firstly, it had probably been marked since the to-do at Osufy Ivanovich's last ball, and safety precautions had probably been taken; and secondly, he had to await the agreed signal from Klara Olsufyevna, for there was bound to be something of the sort. There always was, and as he said, "We aren't the first, and we won't be the last." He immediately remembered quite opportunely and by the way a novel he had read long ago, in which the heroine had given an agreed signal to her Alfred under exactly similar circumstances by tying up a pink ribbon at her window. But now, after dark, with a St. Petersburg climate notorious for its wetness and unreliability, a pink ribbon was out of the question; to put it briefly, it was impossible.

"No. This is no time for silken ladders," thought our hero. "I'd better stay quietly where I am, out of sight. That's what I'd better do." And he selected a position facing the windows, and near the wood-stack. There were, of course, postilions and coachmen, and a number of other people walking about the courtyard, added to which there was the rattle of wheels, the snorting of horses and so forth. But for all that it was a convenient position, whether anyone saw him or not, having at least the advantage of being to some extent in shadow, so that he could observe positively everything without being himself observed. The windows were all lit up. Some sort of gala reunion was taking place at Olsufy Ivanovich's, but no music could be heard as yet.

"So it's not a ball. They're gathered for some other occasion," thought our hero with a sinking heart. "But was it today?" flashed through his mind. "Maybe there's a mistake in the date. Anything is possible. Or perhaps the letter was written yesterday, and didn't reach me because that scoundrel Petrushka got mixed up in the business. Or perhaps it said tomorrow. Perhaps that's when I'm supposed to do everything and be waiting with the carriage."

With a sudden thrill of horror, he felt in his pocket for the letter to check the point. But to his amazement the letter was not there.

"How's this?" whispered Mr. Golyadkin, feeling more dead than alive. "Where've I left it? Have I lost it? That's all I needed!" he concluded with a groan. "What if it gets into the wrong hands? Perhaps it has already! Oh God! What will come of this? What will happen if . . . Oh, what hideous luck!"

He began trembling like a leaf, as it occurred to him that his shameful twin might have thrown the overcoat over him for the express purpose or purloining the letter, having got wind of it from his enemies.

"And what's more, he's seized it as evidence!" thought Mr. Golyadkin. "But why?"

After the first numbing blow of horror, the blood rushed back to his head. Groaning, gnashing his teeth and clutching his heated brow, he sank down on the log, and tried to think. But his thoughts would not connect themselves to anything. Faces, and various long-forgotten events flashed through his mind, some vague, some vivid; silly song-tunes crept into his head. His anguish was such as it had never been before.

"Oh God," he thought, recovering a little and suppressing his dull sobs, "oh God, grant me firmness of spirit in the unfathomable depths of my misfortune! That I am ruined, that I have ceased to exist, there is no longer any doubt at all. And this is in the nature of things, for it could not be otherwise. In the first place, I've lost my job—I've certainly done that. It was inevitable.

"Now let's suppose it all comes right somehow. We'll

assume I've got enough money to begin with. I'll need a new place to live, and some sort of furniture. I won't have Petrushka for a start. I can manage without the scoundrel—get help from the people in the house. Splendid! I can come and go when I like, and there won't be any Petrushka to grumble because I'm late. That's a good way of doing it. Well, let's suppose it is, but how is it I'm talking about completely the wrong thing?"

His predicament again dawned upon him. He looked around.

"Oh God! What on earth have I just been talking about?" he wondered, clutching his burning head in utter bewilderment.

"You'll be going soon, won't you, sir?" said a voice above him. He shuddered. Standing before him, also wet through and chilled to the bone, was the driver, who, growing impatient at having nothing to do, had conceived the idea of coming to take a look at Mr. Golyadkin behind the firewood.

"I'm all right, my friend. I won't be long. You wait . . ."

The driver went away, muttering to himself.

"What's he grumbling about?" thought Mr. Golyadkin tearfully. "I hired him for the evening, didn't I? I'm within my rights! I've taken him for the evening, and that's all there is to it. He can stand there the whole time—it's all the same. It's as I please. I go if I want to—if I don't, I don't. My standing here behind the firewood doesn't matter at all, and no one dare say anything to the contrary. If a gentleman wants to stand behind the firewood, he stands behind the firewood. He's not spoiling anyone's reputation doing that. So there it is, young lady, if you really want to know. As to living in a cottage, as you say, no one does nowadays, no one. And in our industrial age, young lady, you won't get anywhere without good behaviour. You're a dreadful example of that. 'Work as a chief clerk, and live in a cottage by the sea,' you say. In the first place, young lady, there are no chief clerks by the sea; and in the second, the post of chief clerk is something you and I won't get. Suppose, for the sake of example, I put in a petition, and go along and say this and that, 'make me chief clerk and protect me from my enemies.' 'We've plenty of chief clerks,' they'll tell you. 'You're not at Madame Falbala's learning good behaviour now,' they'll say, 'and a pretty poor example you give of that.' Good behaviour means staying at home, honouring your father, and not thinking of suitors before you should, young lady. There'll be suitors at the proper time. You must, of course, exhibit talent in various ways, by playing the piano a bit sometimes, speaking French, and knowing your history, geography, scripture and arithmetic, but nothing more. And then there's cooking. Cooking must be included in every nicely-behaved girl's store of knowledge. But what's the position? To begin with, my fine young lady, they won't let you go. They'll pursue you, then they'll play their trump card, and into a nunnery with you. Then what, young lady? What will you have me do then? Come to a nearby hill as they do in certain silly novels, and pine away in tears, watching the cold walls that shut you in, and finally die as habitually described by some horrid German poets and novelists? Is that it? Firstly, let me tell you in a friendly way, things aren't done like that; and secondly, you ought to have been given a sound beating, and your parents as well, for giving you French books to read. You learn no good from them. They're poison, deadly poison, young lady! Or do you think we'll get away with it, may I ask, and find a cottage by the sea, and bill and coo, and discuss our various feelings, and live happily ever afterwards? And then when there's a little one, shall we go to our father, the Civil Counsellor, and say, 'Look, Olsufy Ivanovich, there's a little one. Will you take this as a suitable occasion to remove your curse and bless us both?' No, young lady, it's not done like that. And the main thing is there won't be any billing and cooing, so don't hope for it. Nowadays, young lady, the husband is master, and a good well-brought-up wife must humour him in every way. Tender words aren't popular any more, in our industrial age. Jean-Jacques Rousseau's times are past. Nowadays the husband comes home from the office hungry, and says, 'Can't I have a little something before dinner, darling, just a mouthful of herring and a nip of vodka?' And you must have it ready, young lady. Your husband will tuck in with relish, and won't so much as give you a glance. 'Run into the kitchen, poppet, and keep an eye on the dinner,' he'll say. And just once a week perhaps, he'll give you a kiss, and a cold peck at that. That's what it will be like, young lady—just a cold peck. And what

have I got to do with it? Why have you got me mixed up
in your fancies? 'To the beneficent one who suffers for
my sake, and is in every way dear to my heart, etc.,'
that's what you said. To start with, I'm no good for you,
young lady. I'm no adept at compliments, as you know
yourself. I'm not fond of talking sweet-scented nonsense
for the ladies. I don't like gay deceivers, and I must confess, I've never got anywhere on my looks. You'll find no
bounce or false shame about me, and I tell you that now
in all sincerity. An open forthright nature and common
sense are the two things I possess. I have nothing to do
with intrigues. I'm no intriguer, and proud of it. I don't
go about in front of good people wearing a mask, and to
say all there is to be said . . ."

He gave a sudden start. The dripping-wet red beard of
the cabman was again peeping over the firewood at him.

"I'm coming now, my friend. I'm coming directly, you
know," he quavered feebly.

The cabman scratched the back of his head, ran his
hand over his beard, stepped back a pace, stopped, and
looked at him mistrustfully.

"I'm coming now, my friend. I must just wait a teeny
second, you see."

"Don't you want to drive anywhere at all?" asked the
cabman, making a direct and determined approach.

"Yes, I'm coming. I'm waiting, you see."

"I see."

"You see, I . . . What village are you from, my
friend?"

"I'm a serf."

"Got a good master?"

"Not bad."

"Stay here for a bit, my friend. Have you been in St.
Petersburg long?"

"A year I've been driving."

"And are you all right?"

"Not bad."

"Well, you should thank Providence, my friend. You
look for a good man. They're rare nowadays. A good man
will see to your comfort, will give you meat and drink.
But sometimes, my friend, you see even rich men weeping . . . You see a pitiful example—that's how it is, my
dear fellow . . ."

The cabman suddenly seemed to feel sorry for him.

"I'll hang on, sir. Will you be waiting long?"

"No, my dear chap, I—er—you know what it is . . . I won't wait any more. What do you think? I rely on you. I won't wait any more."

"Don't you want to drive anywhere?"

"No, my friend, no. But I'll make it worth your while. What's the damage, my dear fellow?"

"What we agreed, sir. I've had a long wait, and you wouldn't do a chap down, sir."

"Well, here you are then." He gave the cabman the full six roubles, and having seriously made up his mind to waste no more time, but to clear off before something unpleasant happened—particularly, as with the matter settled and the cabman dismissed, there was nothing else to wait for—he walked out of the courtyard, turned left through the gate, and breathless but rejoicing, set off as fast as his legs would carry him.

"It may all turn out for the best," he thought. "And this way I've avoided trouble." His mind suddenly felt unusually at ease.

"If it only would turn out for the best!" he thought, but did not believe that it would.

"I know what . . . No. I'd better try a different approach. Or wouldn't it be better for me to . . ."

While searching to relieve the doubts that were thus assailing him, he ran as far as the Semyonovsky Bridge, where he cautiously decided to go back.

"That's the best thing," he thought. "I'd better try a different approach. This is what I'll do—I'll just be an outside observer, and nothing more. 'I'm an onlooker, an outsider, that's all,' I'll say. And whatever happens it won't be me who's to blame. That's it. That's how it will be now."

Our hero did indeed do as he had decided and went back, and went all the more readily for having, thanks to a happy thought, become an outsider.

"It's the best thing. You're not answerable for anything, and you'll see what you should."

His calculations were perfectly correct, and there was nothing more to it. Reassured, he stole back into the peaceful and soothingly protective shadow of the woodstack. This time he did not have to watch and wait for long. All of a sudden there was a strange commotion at every window; figures appeared and disappeared; the curtains were drawn back, and Olsufy Ivanovich's windows were crammed with people peering out and looking for something in the courtyard. Our hero followed the general commotion with interest and curiosity from the security of his wood-stack, craning his head just as far out to left and right as the short shadow afforded by his cover would allow. Suddenly he was filled with panic, he shuddered, he almost collapsed with the horror of it. He realised at once. They were not just looking for anything or anybody, but for *him*. They were all gazing and pointing in his direction. Escape was impossible—they'd see! Panic-stricken, he pressed himself to the wood-stack as tightly as he could. Only then did he observe that the treacherous shadow had played him false by failing to cover him completely. Had it only been possible, he would at that moment with the greatest pleasure in the world have crawled into any mouse-hole the wood-stack might offer, and sat quiet. But it was out of the question. In his agony he stared at all the windows at once, boldly and openly. It was the best thing to do. Suddenly he blushed with fiery shame. They had all seen him at the same time. They were all beckoning, nodding, calling. Several of the windows clicked open. Several voices began shouting something at him simultaneously.

"I'm surprised they don't whip these wretched girls when they're children," he muttered, completely disconcerted.

All of a sudden, tripping, whirling and prancing down the steps, breathless, hatless and wearing just his uniform, came *he*—someone we know—with an air that treacherously expressed how most frightfully glad he was to see Mr. Golyadkin.

"You here, Yakov Petrovich?" warbled the notoriously worthless man. "You'll catch a cold. It's chilly. Come along in."

"No. I'm all right, Yakov Petrovich," mumbled our hero submissively.

"You *must*, Yakov Petrovich. They most humbly beg you—they're waiting for us. 'Do us the pleasure of bringing in Yakov Petrovich,' they said.

"No, Yakov Petrovich, you see, I'd better . . . I'd better be off home," said our hero, so horrified and abashed that he felt he was being frozen to death and roasted alive at the same time.

"Not at all, not at all!" twittered the odious man. "Nothing of the sort! Come on!" he said firmly, dragging Golyadkin senior towards the steps. The latter did not want to go in the least, but went, because to kick and struggle with everyone watching would have been stupid. To say that he went is not, however, strictly accurate, for he had little idea what was happening to him.

Before he had time to tidy himself or recover his senses, he was in the reception-room. Pale, ruffled and dishevelled, he gazed dully around, and saw a multitude of people. It was horrible! The reception-room and everywhere else was filled to overflowing. There were people without number, there were galaxies of lovely ladies, and they were all milling and pressing around him, and bearing him, as he clearly perceived, in a definite direction.

"This isn't the way to the door," flashed through his mind, and indeed it was not. He was heading straight for the comfortable arm-chair of Olsufy Ivanovich. On one side of this, pale, languid and melancholy, but sumptuously arrayed, stood Klara Olsufyevna. Mr. Golyadkin was particularly struck by the wonderfully effective tiny white flowers adorning her raven hair. On the other side, in a black morning coat, and wearing his new decoration in his buttonhole, stood Vladimir Semyonovich. Mr. Golyadkin was, as we have already intimated, being conducted straight towards Olsufy Ivanovich; steering him by one arm was Golyadkin junior, who had now assumed an extraordinarily decorous and well-intentioned air—which was a source of some gratification to our hero—and at the other, looking very grave, was Andrey Filippovich.

"What's this?" wondered Mr. Golyadkin.

The moment he saw before whom he was being taken, his brain cleared with lightning rapidity. He thought in a flash of the purloined letter . . . With a feeling of immeasurable anguish, he stood before Olsufy Ivanovich's chair.

"What am I to do now?" he thought. "Be bold, speak out, of course—but with a certain nobleness of manner. This and that, I'll say, and so on."

But what our hero had apparently been fearing, did not happen. Olsufy Ivanovich seemed to receive him quite well, and although he did not proffer his hand, he did at least gaze at him, and shake his awe-inspiring grey head in a sad, solemn, but at the same time affable manner. So at least it seemed to Mr. Golyadkin. In those lustreless eyes he seemed even to detect a glistening tear. Looking up, he saw what appeared to be a tiny tear sparkling upon the lashes of Klara Olsufyevna. Vladimir Semyonovich seemed also to have something of the sort in his eyes. No less eloquent of sympathy than the general lachrymation, was the calm, inviolable dignity of Andrey Filippovich; while the young man who at one time had looked very much the important counsellor was at this moment sobbing bitterly. Or perhaps it all merely seemed so to Mr. Golyadkin because he was himself overcome with powerful emotion, and could distinctly feel the hot tears coursing down his frozen cheeks. Reconciled with man and destiny, filled at that moment with affection not only for Olsufy Ivanovich, but for all the guests put together—even for his pernicious twin, who was now apparently not pernicious at all and not even his twin, but a stranger and a perfectly amiable person in his own right—Mr. Golyadkin was about to pour forth his soul to Olsufy Ivanovich in a moving speech, his voice choked with sobs. But his feelings were too much for him. His voice failed him, and he could only point eloquently at his heart. At last, wishing no doubt to spare the grey-haired old man, Andrey Filippovich drew Mr. Golyadkin a little to one side, and left him, completely at liberty it seemed. Smiling, muttering to himself, a little perplexed but at all events almost reconciled with man and destiny, our hero began to move through the dense throng of guests. Everyone made way and regarded him with strange curiosity, and a concern that was puzzling and unaccountable. Our hero passed into the next room, and received the same attention. He was dimly aware of the whole crowd following him, watching his every step, discoursing quietly on something of extreme interest, shaking their heads, debating and whispering. He would have liked to know what it was all about. Looking round, he noticed Golyadkin junior beside him. Feeling obliged to catch hold of his arm and take him aside, Mr. Golyadkin earnestly begged him to support him in all future undertakings, and not to abandon him at a critical moment. Golyadkin junior nodded gravely, and gave him a firm squeeze of the hand. So overwhelming was our hero's emotion, that his heart trembled within him. But then he gasped for breath. He felt a terrible weight upon his chest. He felt oppressed and stifled beneath the stare of so many eyes . . . He caught a glimpse of the counsellor wearing a wig. He was eyeing him in a stern, searching manner, that showed he had been quite unmollified by the general aura of sympathy. Our hero was on the point of marching over to him, giving him a smile, and clearing things up immediately, but somehow did not manage to do this. For a moment he almost lost consciousness; memory and senses forsook him. When he came to, he noticed that the guests had formed a large circle around him. His name was suddenly shouted from the next room, and the shout was immediately taken up by the whole crowd. Uproar and excitement ensued. Everyone rushed for the door, almost carrying him along with them. Close beside him was the stony-hearted counsellor in the wig. The latter finally took him by the arm, and sat him on a chair next to his, directly opposite but some distance away from where Olsufy Ivanovich was sitting. Everyone else in the place sat down on several rows of chairs arranged around Mr. Golyadkin and Olsufy Ivanovich. All grew hushed and still. Everyone was observing a solemn silence and gazing towards Olsufy Ivanovich, obviously expecting something rather out of the ordinary. Mr. Golyadkin noticed the other Mr. Golyadkin and Andrey Filippovich sitting next to Olsufy Ivanovich, and facing the counsellor. The silence lasted a long time. They were, in fact, waiting for something.

"Just as it is in any family when someone's going on a long journey," thought our hero. "It only wants us to get up, and say a prayer."

All Mr. Golyadkin's reflections were interrupted by a sudden strange commotion. The long-expected was happening.

"He's coming! He's coming!" ran through the crowd.

"Who's coming?" ran through Mr. Golyadkin's head. A peculiar sensation caused him to shudder.

"Now!" said the counsellor, looking intently at Andrey Filippovich. The latter shot a glance at Olsufy Ivanovich, who nodded gravely and solemnly.

"Up we get," said the counsellor, hoisting Mr. Golyadkin to his feet. Everyone rose. The counsellor then took Golyadkin senior by the arm, Andrey Filippovich did the same to Golyadkin junior, and surrounded by the eagerly expectant crowd, they solemnly brought these two completely identical beings together. Our hero, perplexed, began to look about him, but was immediately checked, and shown Golyadkin junior, who was offering him his hand.

"They want to reconcile us," thought our hero suddenly, and greatly touched, he held out his hand to Golyadkin junior, then offered his cheek. The other did likewise. At this juncture Golyadkin senior thought he saw his treacherous friend smile, and give a quick mischievous wink to all around; he thought he detected something sinister in his face, and thought he even grimaced as he gave his Judas kiss. His head rang. Darkness swam before his eyes. A whole procession of identical Golyadkins seemed to be bursting loudly in at every door. But it was too late. The resounding treacherous kiss had been given.

At this point something quite unexpected occurred. The door flew open with a bang, and on the threshold stood a man whose very appearance made Mr. Golyadkin's blood run cold. He stood rooted to the spot. His cry died away unuttered. His chest felt constricted. But he had known it all beforehand, and had long anticipated something of the sort. Gravely and solemnly, the stranger advanced towards him. It was a figure he knew very well, and had seen often, very often—that same day even. It was a thick-set man in a black morning coat; about his neck he wore the cross of an important decoration; he had very black bushy side-whiskers; all that was missing was the cigar. His eyes froze Mr. Golyadkin with horror. With a grave, solemn visage, this terrible man approached the sorry hero of our tale. Our hero stretched out his hand. The stranger took it, and pulled him along after him . . . Our hero gazed around, crushed and bewildered.

"It's Krestyan Ivanovich Rutenspitz, doctor of medicine and surgery, an old friend of yours, Yakov Petrovich," twittered a repulsive voice right in Mr. Golyadkin's ear. He glanced round. It was his abominable blackguardly twin. His face was shining with an unseemly glee that boded ill. He was rubbing his hands in ecstasy, rapturously rolling his head, and fussing delightedly around all and sundry. He looked ready to dance with joy on the spot. Finally he leapt forward, and seizing a candle from one of the servants, lighted the way for Dr. Rutenspitz and Mr. Golyadkin. The latter clearly heard everyone in the room rushing after them, crowding and squashing each other, and all repeating with one accord: "It's all right. Don't be afraid, Yakov Petrovich. It's an old friend and acquaintance of yours—Dr. Rutenspitz."

They came at last to the brightly-illuminated main staircase, and this too was crowded with people. The front door was thrown open with a crash, and Mr. Golyadkin found himself on the steps with Dr. Rutenspitz. Drawn up at the bottom was a carriage and four. The horses were snorting impatiently. Three bounds, and the maliciously gloating Golyadkin junior was down the steps and opening the carriage-door. Dr. Rutenspitz motioned Mr. Golyadkin to get in. There was no need for that at all, however, for there were quite enough people to help him up. Sick with horror, he looked back. The whole of the brightly-lit staircase was thick with people. Inquisitive eyes were watching him from all sides. On the topmost landing in his comfortable armchair, presided Olsufy Ivanovich, watching with attentive interest all that was taking place below. They were all waiting. A murmur of impatience ran through the crowd as Mr. Golyadkin looked back.

"I trust there is nothing reprehensible . . . concerning my official relationships . . . that could provoke any severe measure . . . and excite public attention," said our hero in his confusion. There was general hubbub. Everyone shook their heads. Tears gushed from Mr. Golyadkin's eyes.

"In that case I am ready . . . I have complete faith in Dr. Rutenspitz, and give my fate into his hands . . ."

No sooner had he said this, than there burst from those around a shout of joy, ear-splitting and terrible, that was echoed ominously by the whole waiting throng. Then Dr. Rutenspitz and Andrey Filippovich each took one of Mr. Golyadkin's arms and started putting him into the carriage—the double, in his usual blackguardly way, assisting from behind. The unhappy Golyadkin senior took one last look at everything and everybody, and trembling like a drenched kitten—if one may use the simile—he climbed into the carriage. Dr. Rutenspitz got in immediately after. The door slammed. The whip cracked. And the horses drew the carriage away . . . Everyone dashed in pursuit. The shrill, frantic cries of all his enemies rang after him like so many farewells. For a while he caught glimpses of people around the carriage as it bore him away, but gradually they were left behind, and

finally they were lost to sight completely. Mr. Golyadkin's
unseemly twin stayed longer than all the rest. Hands
thrust into the pockets of his green uniform trousers and
with a satisfied look on his face, he kept pace with the
carriage, jumping up first on one side, then on the other,
and sometimes, seizing and hanging from the window
frame, he would pop his head in and blow farewell kisses
at Mr. Golyadkin. But he, too, began at last to tire. His
appearances became fewer and fewer, and finally he vanished for good. Mr. Golyadkin's heart ached dully within
him. Fiery blood was rushing to his head. He was suffocating. He wanted to unbutton coat and shirt, bare his
breast, and fling snow and cold water upon it. At last
he fell unconscious . . .

When he came to, he saw the horses were taking him
along a road he did not know. Dark forest loomed to
left and right. It was lonely and desolate. Suddenly he
grew stark with horror. Two burning eyes were staring out
of the darkness at him, two eyes burning with evil and
infernal glee. This wasn't Dr. Rutenspitz! Who was it?
Or was it him? It was! Not the earlier Dr. Rutenspitz, but
another, a terrible Dr. Rutenspitz!

"I-I'm all right, I think, Dr. Rutenspitz," began our
hero, timid and trembling, and wishing to propitiate the
terrible Dr. Rutenspitz by a show of meekness and obedience.

"You vill haf lodging, viz firevood, light and service,
vich is more zan you deserf," came Dr. Rutenspitz' reply, stern and dreadful as a judge's sentence.

Our hero gave a scream, and clutched his head. Alas!
He had felt this coming for a long time!

White Nights

A Sentimental Love Story
(From the Memoirs of a Dreamer)

TRANSLATED BY DAVID MAGARSHACK

And was it his destined part
Only one moment in his life
To be close to your heart? . . .

Ivan Turgenev

First Night

IT WAS A lovely night, one of those nights, dear reader, which can only happen when you are young. The sky was so bright and starry that when you looked at it the first question that came into your mind was whether it was really possible that all sorts of bad-tempered and unstable people could live under such a glorious sky. It is a question, dear reader, that would occur only to a young man, but may the good Lord put it into your head as often as possible! . . . The mention of bad-tempered and unstable people reminds me that during the whole of this day my behaviour has been above reproach. When I woke up in the morning I felt strangely depressed, a feeling I could not shake off for the better part of the day. All of a sudden it seemed to me as though I, the solitary one, had been forsaken by the whole world, and that the whole world would have nothing to do with me. You may ask who "the whole world" is. For, I am afraid, I have not been lucky in acquiring a single acquaintance in Petersburg during the eight years I have been living there. But what do I want acquaintances for? I know the whole of Petersburg without them, and that, indeed, was the reason why it seemed to me that the whole world had forsaken me when the whole town suddenly arose and left for the country. I was terrified to be left alone, and for three days I wandered about the town plunged into gloom and absolutely at a loss to understand what was the matter with me. Neither on Nevsky Avenue, nor in the park, nor on the embankment did I meet the old familiar faces that I used to meet in the same place and at the same time all through the year. It is true I am a complete stranger to these people, but they are not strangers to me. I know them rather intimately, in fact; I have made a very thor-

147

ough study of their faces; I am happy when they are happy, and I am sad when they are overcast with care. Why, there is an old gentleman I see every day on the Fontanka Embankment with whom I have practically struck up a friendship. He looks so thoughtful and dignified, and he always mutters under his breath, waving his left hand and holding a big knotty walking-stick with a gold top in his right. I have, I believe, attracted his attention, and I should not be surprised if he took a most friendly interest in me. In fact, I am sure that if he did not meet me at a certain hour on the Fontanka Embankment he would be terribly upset. That is why we sometimes almost bow to one another, especially when we are both in a good humour. Recently we had not seen each other for two days, and on the third day, when we met, we were just about to raise our hats in salute, but fortunately we recollected ourselves in time and, dropping our hands, passed one another in complete understanding and amity. The houses, too, are familiar to me. When I walk along the street, each of them seems to run before me, gazing at me out of all its windows, and practically saying to me, "Good morning, sir! How are you? I'm very well, thank you. They're going to add another storey to me in May"; or, "How do you do, sir? I'm going to be repaired tomorrow"; or, "Dear me, I nearly got burnt down, and, goodness, how I was scared!" and so on and so on. Some of them are great favourites of mine, while others are my good friends. One of them is thinking of undergoing a cure with an architect this summer. I shall certainly make a point of coming to see it every day to make sure that its cure does not prove fatal (which God forbid!). And I shall never forget the incident with a pretty little house of a pale pink hue. It was such a dear little house; it always welcomed me with such a friendly smile, and it looked on its clumsy neighbours with such an air of condescension, that my heart leapt with joy every time I passed it. But when I happened to walk along the street only a week ago and looked up at my friend, I was welcomed with a most plaintive cry, "They are going to paint me yellow!" Fiends! Savages! They spared nothing, neither cornices, nor columns, and my poor friend turned as yellow as a canary. I nearly had an attack of jaundice myself, and even to this day I have not been able to screw

up my courage to go and see my mutilated friend,
painted in the national colour of the Celestial Empire!

· So now you see, dear reader, how it is that I know the
whole of Petersburg.

I have already said that until I realised what was the
trouble with me, I had been very worried and upset for
three whole days. In the street I felt out of sorts (this one
had gone, that one had gone, and where on earth had the
other one got to?), and at home I was not my old self,
either. For two evenings I had been racking my brains
trying hard to discover what was wrong with my room.
What was it made me so peevish when I stayed there?
And, greatly perplexed, I began examining my grimy
green walls and the ceiling covered with cobwebs which
Matryona was such a genius at cultivating. I went over
my furniture and looked at each chair in turn, wondering
whether the trouble lay there (for it upsets me to see even
one chair not in its usual place); I looked at the window—
but all to no purpose: it did not make me feel a bit better! I even went so far as to call in Matryona and rebuke
her in a fatherly sort of way about the cobwebs and her
untidiness in general. But she just gave me a surprised look
and stalked out of the room without saying a word, so
that the cobwebs still remain cheerfully in their old places.
It was only this morning that at last I discovered the real
cause of my unhappiness. Oh, so they are all running
away from me to the country, are they? I'm afraid I
must apologise for the use of this rather homely word, but
I'm not in the mood now for the more exquisite refine-
ments of style, for everybody in Petersburg has either left
or is about to leave for the country; for every worthy gentleman of a solidly-prosperous and dignified position who
hails a cab in the street is at once transformed in my
mind into a worthy parent of a family who, after his usual office duties, immediately leaves town and, unencum-
bered by luggage, hastens to the bosom of his family—to
the country; for every passer-by now wears quite a different look, a look which almost seems to say to every person he meets, "As a matter of fact, sir, I'm here by sheer
chance, just passing through, you understand, and in a
few hours I shall be on the way to the country." If a window is thrown open and a most ravishing young girl, who
at a moment ago had been drumming on it with her lovely

white fingers, pokes out her pretty head and calls to the man selling pots of plants in the street, I immediately jump to the conclusion that the flowers are bought not for the purpose of enjoying the spring and the flowers in a stuffy old flat in town, for very soon everybody will anyway be leaving for the country and will take even the flowers with them. Why, I've got so far in my new discovery (quite a unique discovery, you must admit) that I can tell at once, just by looking at a man, in what sort of a cottage he lives in the country. The residents of the Stone and Apothecary Islands can be recognised by their studied exquisiteness of manners, their smart summer clothes, and their wonderful carriages in which they come to town. The inhabitants of Pargolov and places beyond "inspire" your confidence at the first glance by their solidly prosperous position and their general air of sobriety and common sense; while the householder of Krestovsky Island is distinguished by his imperturbably cheerful look. Whether I happen to come across a long procession of carters, each walking leisurely, reins in hand, beside his cart, laden with whole mountains of furniture of every description—tables, chairs, Turkish and non-Turkish divans, and other household chattels—and, moreover, often presided over by a frail-looking cook who, perched on the very top of the cart, guards the property of her master as though it were the apple of her eye; or whether I look at the barges, heavily laden with all sorts of domestic junk, sailing on the Neva or the Fontanka, as far as the Black River or the Islands—both carts and barges multiply tenfold, nay, a hundredfold in my eyes. It really seems as though everything had arisen and set off on a journey as though everything were moving off in caravan after caravan into the country; it seems as though the whole of Petersburg were about to turn into a desert, and it is hardly surprising that in the end I am overwhelmed with shame, humiliation, and sadness. For I have no possible excuse for going to the country; neither have I any country cottage I can go to. I am willing to leave with every cart or every gentleman of respectable appearance who hails a cab; but no one, absolutely no one, invites me to go with him, as though they had all forgotten me, as though I were no more than a stranger to them!

I walked for hours and hours, and, as usual, had for some time been completely oblivious of my surroundings, when I suddenly found myself near the toll-gate. I felt cheerful at once, and, stepping beyond the bar, walked along the road between fields of corn and meadows of lush grass, unconscious of any fatigue, and feeling with every breath I drew that a heavy weight was being lifted from my heart. All the travellers I met looked so genially at me that it seemed that in another moment they would most assuredly bow to me. All of them seemed to be happy about something, and every one of them without exception smoked a cigar. And I, too, was happy as never before in my life. As though I had suddenly found myself in Italy—so strong was the impact of nature upon me, a semi-invalid townsman who had all but been stifled within the walls of the city.

There is something indescribably moving in the way nature in Petersburg, suddenly with the coming of spring, reveals herself in all her might and glory, in all the splendour with which heaven has endowed her, in the way she blossoms out, dresses up, decks herself out with flowers. . . . She reminds me somehow rather forcibly of that girl, ailing and faded, upon whom you sometimes look with pity or with a certain compassionate affection, or whom you simply do not notice at all, but who in the twinkling of an eye and only for one fleeting moment becomes by some magic freak of chance indescribably fair and beautiful; and, stunned and fascinated, you ask yourself what power it was that made those sad and wistful eyes blaze forth with such a fire? What caused the rush of blood to her pale and hollow cheeks? What brought passion to that sweet face? Why did her bosom heave so wildly? What was it that so instantaneously suffused the face of the poor girl with life, vigour, and beauty? What forced it to light up with so brilliant a smile? What animated it with so warm, so infectious a laugh? You look round; you wonder who it could have been; you begin to suspect the truth. But the brief moment passes, and tomorrow perhaps you will again encounter the same wistful and forlorn gaze, the same wan face, the same resignation and diffidence in her movements, and, yes, even remorse, even traces of some benumbing vexation and despondency for that brief outburst of passion. And you feel sorry that the beauty, so momentarily evoked, should have faded so quickly and so irrevocably, that she should have burst upon your sight so deceptively and to so little purpose—

that she should not have given you time even to fall in love with her. . . .

But all the same my night was much better than the day! This is how it happened:

I came back to town very late, and, as I was approaching the street where I lived, it struck ten. My way lay along a canal embankment where not a single living soul could be seen at that hour. It is true, I live in a very remote part of the town. I was walking along and singing, for when I am happy I always hum some tune to myself like every happy man who has neither friends nor good acquaintances, and who has no one to share his joy with in a moment of happiness. Suddenly I became involved in a most unexpected adventure.

A little distance away, leaning against the railing of the canal, a woman was standing with her elbows on the rail; she seemed to be engrossed in looking at the muddy water of the canal. She wore a most enchanting yellow hat and a very charming black cloak. "She's young," I thought, "and I'm sure she is dark." She did not seem to hear my footsteps, for she did not stir when I walked past her with bated breath and a thumping heart. "Funny!" I thought, "she must be thinking about something very important." Suddenly I stopped dead, rooted to the spot. The sound of suppressed weeping reached me. No, I was not mistaken. The girl was crying, for a minute later I distinctly heard her sobbing again. Good gracious! My heart contracted with pity. And timid though I am with women, this was too good a chance to be missed! . . . I retraced my steps, walked up to her, and in another moment would have certainly said "Madam!" if I had not known that that exclamation had been made a thousand times before in all Russian novels of high life. It was that alone that stopped me. But while I was searching for the right word with which to address the girl, she had recovered her composure, recollected himself, lowered her eyes, and darted past me along the embankment. I immediately set off in pursuit of her, but she must have guessed my intention, for she left the embankment and, crossing the road, walked along the pavement. I did not dare to cross the road. My heart was fluttering like the heart of a captured bird. But quite an unexpected incident came to my assistance.

A gentleman in evening dress suddenly appeared a few

yards away from the girl on the other side of the street. He had reached the age of discretion, but there was no discretion in his unsteady gait. He was walking along, swaying from side to side, and leaning cautiously against a wall. The girl, on the other hand, walked as straight as an arrow, quickly and apprehensively, as girls usually walk at night when they do not want any man to offer to accompany them home. And the reeling gentleman would most certainly not have caught up with her, if my good luck had not prompted him to resort to a stratagem. Without uttering a word, he suddenly set off in pursuit of the girl at an amazing speed. She was running away from him as fast as her legs would carry her, but the staggering gentleman was getting nearer and nearer, and then caught up with her. The girl uttered a shriek and—I have to thank my good genius for the excellent knobbly walking-stick which, as it happened, I was at the time clutching in my right hand. In less than no time I found myself on the other side of the street, and in less than no time the unwelcome gentleman took in the situation, took into account the undeniable fact of my superior weapons, grew quiet, dropped behind, and it was only when we were far away that he bethought himself of protesting against my action in rather forceful terms. But his words hardly reached us.

"Give me your arm," I said to the girl, "and he won't dare to molest you any more."

She silently gave me her arm, which was still trembling with excitement and terror. Oh, unwelcome stranger! How I blessed you at that moment! I stole a glance at her—I was right! She was a most charming girl and dark, too. On her black eyelashes there still glistened the tears of her recent fright or her recent unhappiness—I did not know which. But there was already a gleam of a smile on her lips. She, too, stole a glance at me, blushed a little, and dropped her eyes.

"Well, you see, you shouldn't have driven me away before, should you? If I'd been here, nothing would have happened."

"But I didn't know you. I thought that you too . . ."

"But what makes you think you know me now?"

"Well, I know you a little. Now why, for instance, are you trembling?"

"So you've guessed at once the sort of man I am," I

replied, overjoyed that the girl was so intelligent (this is never a fault in a beautiful girl). "Yes, you've guessed at once the sort of man I am. It's quite true, I'm afraid, I'm awfully shy with women, and I don't want to deny that I'm a little excited now, no less than you were a moment ago when that fellow scared you. Yes, I seem to be scared now. It's as though it were all happening to me in a dream, except that even in a dream I did not expect ever to be talking to any woman."

"How do you mean? Not really?"

"Yes, really. You see, if my arm is trembling now, it's because it has never before been clasped by such a pretty little hand as yours. I've entirely lost the habit of talking to women. I mean, I never really was in the habit of talking to them. You see, I'm such a lonely creature. Come to think of it, I don't believe I know how to talk to women. Even now I haven't the faintest idea whether I've said anything to you that I shouldn't. Please tell me frankly if I ever do. I promise you I shan't take offence."

"No, I don't think you've said anything you shouldn't. And if you really want me to be frank with you, I don't mind telling you that women rather like shy men like you. And if you want me to speak more frankly, I like it too, and I promise not to send you away till we reach my home."

"I'm afraid," I began, breathless with excitement, "you'll make me lose my shyness at once, and then good-bye to all my schemes!"

"Devices? What schemes, and what for? I must say that isn't nice at all."

"I beg your pardon. I'm awfully sorry. It was a slip of the tongue. But how can you expect me at this moment not to wish. . . ."

"To make a good impression, you mean?"

"Well, yes. And do, for goodness' sake, be fair. Just think—who am I? At twenty-six—yes, I'm twenty-six—I've never really known anyone. So how can you expect me to speak well, cleverly, and to the point? You, too, I think, would prefer us to be straightforward and honest with each other, wouldn't you? I just can't be silent when my heart is moved to speak. Well, anyway . . . I know you'll hardly believe me, but I've never spoken to any woman, never! Never known one, either! I only dream that some day I shall meet someone at last. Oh, if only you know how many times I've fallen in love like that!"

"But how? Who with?"

"With no one, of course. Just with my ideal, with the woman I see in my dreams. I make up all sorts of romantic love stories in my dreams. Oh, you don't know the sort of man I am! It's true I have known two or three women—you can't help that, can you?—but what sort of women were they? They were all so mercenary that . . . But let me tell you something really funny, let me tell you how several times I longed to talk to a society lady in the street, I mean, talk to her when she was alone, and without any formality. Very humbly, of course, very respectfully, very passionately. Tell her how horribly depressed I am by my lonely life; ask her not to send me away; explain to her that I have no other way of knowing what a woman is like; suggest to her that it is really her duty as a woman not to reject the humble entreaty of an unhappy man like me; finally, explain to her that all I want of her is that she should say a few friendly words to me, say them with sympathy and understanding, that she should not send me away at once, that she should believe my protestations, that she should listen to what I had to tell her, laugh at me by all means, if she wanted to, but also hold out some hope to me, just say two words to me, and then we need not see each other again! But you're laughing. . . . Well, as a matter of fact, I only said that to make you laugh. . . ."

"Don't be cross with me. I'm laughing because you are your own enemy, and if you had tried you would, I'm sure, have perhaps succeeded, even though it all happened in the street. The simpler, the better. Not one kind-hearted woman, provided, of course, she was not a fool, or angry at something at the time, would have the heart to send you away without saying the two words you were so humbly asking for. But I may be wrong. She would most likely have taken you for a madman. I'm afraid I was judging by myself. I know very well, I assure you, how people live in the world!"

"Thank you," I cried, "thank you a thousand times! you don't know how much I appreciate what you've just done for me!"

"All right, all right! Only tell me how did you guess I'm one of those women with whom . . . well, whom you thought worthy . . . of your attention and friendship. I mean, not a mercenary one, as you call it. What made you decide to come up to me?"

"What made me do that? Why, you were alone, and that fellow was much too insolent. It all happened at night, too, and you must admit it was my duty. . . ."

"No, no! I mean before. On the other side of the street. You wanted to come up to me, didn't you?"

"On the other side of the street? Well, I really don't know what to say. I'm afraid I . . . You see, I was so happy today. I was walking along and singing. I had spent the day in the country. I don't remember ever having experienced such happy moments before. You were . . . However, I may have been mistaken. Please, forgive me, if I remind you of it, but I thought you were crying, and I—I couldn't bear to hear it—I felt miserable about it. But, goodness, had I no right to feel anxious about you? Was it wrong of me to feel a brotherly compassion for you? I'm sorry, I said compassion . . . Well, what I meant was that I couldn't possibly have offended you because I had an impulse to go up to you, could I?"

"Don't say anything more, please," said the girl pressing my hand and lowering her head. "I'm to blame for having started talking about it. But I'm glad I was not mistaken in you. Well, I'm home now. I live in that lane, only two steps from here. Goodbye and thank you."

"But shall we never see each other again? Surely, surely, you can't mean it. Surely, this can't be our last meeting?"

"Well, you see," the girl said, laughing, "at first you only asked for two words, and now. . . . However, I don't think I'd better make any promises. Perhaps we'll meet again."

"I'll be here tomorrow," I said. "Oh, I'm sorry, I seem to be already making demands. . . ."

"Yes, you are rather impatient, aren't you? You're almost making demands. . . ."

"Listen to me, please, listen to me!" I interrupted. "You won't mind if I say something to you again, something of the same kind, will you? It's this: I can't help coming here tomorrow. I am a dreamer. I know so little of real life that I just can't help re-living such moments as these in my dreams, for such moments are something I have very rarely experienced. I am going to dream about you the whole night, the whole week, the whole year. I'll most certainly come here tomorrow. Yes, here, at this place and at this hour. And I shall be happy to remember what happened to me today. Already this place is dear to me. I've two or three places like this in Petersburg. Once I even wept because I remembered something, just as you—I mean, I don't know of course, but perhaps you too were crying ten minutes ago because of some memory. I'm awfully sorry, I seem to have forgotten myself again. Perhaps you were particularly happy here once. . . ."

"Very well," said the girl, "I think I will come here tomorrow, also at ten o'clock. And I can see that I can't possibly forbid you to come, can I? You see, I have to be here. Please don't imagine that I am making an appointment with you. I hope you'll believe me when I say that I have got to be here on some business of my own. Oh, very well, I'll be frank with you: I shan't mind at all if you come here too. To begin with, something unpleasant may happen again as it did today, but never mind that . . . I mean, I'd really like to see you again to—to say two words to you. But, mind, don't think ill of me now, will you? Don't imagine I'm making appointments with men so easily. I wouldn't have made it with you, if. . . . But let that be my secret. Only first you must promise. . . ."

"I promise anything you like!" I cried, delighted. "Only say it. Tell me anything beforehand. I agree to everything. I'll do anything you like. I can answer for myself. I'll be obedient, respectful. . . . You know me, don't you?"

"Well, it's because I know you that I'm asking you to come tomorrow," said the girl, laughing. "I know you awfully well. But, mind, if you come it's on condition that, first (only you will do what I ask you, won't you?—You see, I'm speaking frankly to you), don't fall in love with me. That's impossible, I assure you. I'm quite ready to be your friend. I am, indeed. But you mustn't fall in love with me. So please, don't."

"I swear to you . . ." I cried, seizing her hand.

"No, no. I don't want any solemn promises. I know you're quite capable of flaring up like gunpowder. Don't be angry with me for speaking to you like this. If you knew. . . . You see, I haven't got anyone, either, to whom to say a word, or whom to ask for advice. Of course, it's silly to expect advice from people one meets in the street, but you are different. I feel I know you so well that I couldn't have known you better if we'd been friends for twenty years. You won't fail me, will you?"

"You can depend on me! The only thing is I don't know how I shall be able to survive for the next twenty-four hours."

"Have a good sleep. Good night, and remember I've already confided in you. But, as you expressed it so well a few minutes ago, one hasn't really to account for every feeling, even for brotherly sympathy, has one? You put it so nicely that I felt at once that you're the sort of person I could confide in."

"For goodness' sake, tell me what it is. Please do."

"No, I think you'd better wait till tomorrow. Let it remain a secret for the time being. So much the better for you: at least from a distance it will seem more like a romance. Perhaps I'll tell you tomorrow, perhaps I won't. I'd like to have a good talk to you first, get to know you better. . . ."

"All right, I'll tell you all about myself tomorrow. But, good Lord, the whole thing is just like a miracle! Where am I? Tell me, aren't you glad you weren't angry with me, as some other women might well have been? Only two minutes, and you've made me happy for ever. Yes, happy. Who knows, perhaps you've reconciled me with myself, resolved all my doubts. Perhaps there are moments when I . . . But I'll tell you all about it tomorrow. You shall know everything, everything. . . ."

"All right, I agree. I think you'd better start first."

"Very well."

"Goodbye!"

"Goodbye!"

And we parted. I walked about all night. I couldn't bring myself to go home. I was so happy! Till tomorrow!

Second Night

"Well, so you have survived, haven't you?" she said to me, laughing and pressing both my hands.

"I've been here for the last two hours. You don't know what I've been through today!"

"I know, I know—but to business. Do you know why I've come? Not to talk a lot of nonsense as we did yesterday. You see, we must be more sensible in future. I thought about it a lot yesterday."

"But how? How are we to be more sensible? Not that I have anything against it. But, really, I don't believe anything more sensible has ever happened to me than what's happening to me at this moment."

"Oh? Well, first of all, please don't squeeze my hands like that. Secondly, let me tell you I've given a lot of thought to you today."

"Have you? Well, and what decision have you come to?"

"What decision? Why, that we ought to start all over again. For today I've come to the conclusion that I don't know you at all, that I've behaved like a child, like a silly girl, and of course in the end I blamed my own good heart for everything. I mean, I finished up, as everybody always does when they start examining their own motives, by passing a vote of thanks to myself. And so, to correct my mistake, I've made up my mind to find out all about you to the last detail. But as there's no one I can ask about you, you'll have to tell me everything yourself. Everything, absolutely everything! To begin with, what sort of man are you? Come on, start, please! Tell me the story of your life."

"The story of my life?" I cried, thoroughly alarmed. "But who told you there was such a story? I'm afraid there isn't any."

"But how did you manage to live, if there is no story?" she interrupted me, laughing.

"Without any stories whatsoever! I have lived, as they say, entirely independently. I mean by myself. Do you know what it means to live by oneself?"

"How do you mean by yourself? Do you never see anyone at all?"

"Why, no. I see all sorts of people, but I'm alone all the same."

"Don't you ever talk to anyone?"

"Strictly speaking, never."

"But who are you? Please explain. But wait: I think I can guess. You've probably got a grandmother like me. She's blind, my granny is, and she never lets me go out anywhere, so that I've almost forgotten how to talk to people. And when I behaved badly about two years ago and she saw that there was no holding me, she called me in and pinned my dress to hers—and since then we've sat pinned to one another like that for days and days. She knits a stocking, blind though she is, and I have to sit beside her sewing or reading a book to her. It's a funny sort of situation to be in—pinned to a person for two years or more."

"Good gracious, what bad luck! No, I haven't got such a grandmother."

"If you haven't, why do you sit at home all the time?"

"Look here, do you want to know who I am?"

"Yes, of course!"

"In the strict meaning of the word?"

"Yes, in the strictest meaning of the word!"

"Very well, I'm a character."

"A character? What kind of a character?" the girl cried, laughing merrily, as though she had not laughed for a whole year. "I must say, you're certainly great fun! Look, here's a seat. Let's sit down. No one ever comes this way, so no one will overhear us. Well, start your story, please! For you'll never convince me that you haven't got one. You're just trying to conceal it. Now, first of all, what is a character?"

"A character? Well, it's an original, a queer chap," I said, and, infected by her childish laughter, I burst out laughing myself. "It's a kind of freak. Listen, do you know what a dreamer is?"

"A dreamer? Of course I know. I'm a dreamer myself! Sometimes when I'm sitting by Granny I get all sorts of queer ideas into my head. I mean, once you start dreaming, you let your imagination run away with you, so that in the end I even marry a prince of royal blood! I don't know, it's very nice sometimes—dreaming, I mean. But, on the whole, perhaps it isn't. Especially if you have lots of other things to think of," the girl added, this time rather seriously.

"Fine! Once you're married to an emperor, you will, I think, understand me perfectly. Well, listen—but don't you think I ought to know your name before starting on the story of my life?"

"At last! It took you a long time to think of it, didn't it?"

"Good lord! I never thought of it. You see, I was so happy anyway."

"My name's Nastenka."

"Nastenka! Is that all?"

"Yes, that's all. Isn't it enough for you, you insatiable person?"

"Not enough? Why, not at all. It's more than I expected, much more than I expected, Nastenka, my dear, dear girl, if I may call you by your pet name, if from the very first you—you become Nastenka to me!"

"I'm glad you're satisfied at last! Well?"

"Well, Nastenka, just listen what an absurd story it all is."

I sat down beside her, assumed a pedantically serious pose, and began as though reading from a book:

"There are, if you don't happen to know it already, Nastenka, some very strange places in Petersburg. It is not the same sun which shines upon all the other people of the city that looks in there, but quite a different sun, a new sun, one specially ordered for those places, and the light it sheds on everything is also a different, peculiar sort of light. In those places, dear Nastenka, the people also seem to live quite a different life, unlike that which surges all round us, a life which could only be imagined to exist in some faraway foreign country beyond the seven seas, and not at all in our country and in these much too serious times. Well, it is that life which is a mixture of something purely fantastic, something fervently ideal, and, at the same time (alas, Nastenka!), something frightfully prosaic and ordinary, not to say incredibly vulgar."

"My goodness, what an awful introduction! What shall I be hearing next, I wonder?"

"What you will be hearing next, Nastenka (I don't think I shall ever get tired of calling you Nastenka), is that these places are inhabited by strange people—by dreamers. A dreamer—if you must know its exact definition—is not a man, but a sort of creature of the neuter gender. He settles mostly in some inaccessible place, as though anxious to hide in it even from the light of day; and once he gets inside his room, he'll stick to it like a snail, or, at all events, he is in this respect very like that amusing animal which is an animal and a house both at one and the same time and bears the name of tortoise. Why, do you think, is he so fond of his four walls, invariably painted green, grimy, dismal and reeking unpardonably of tobacco smoke? Why does this funny fellow, when one of his new friends comes to visit him (he usually ends up by losing all his friends one by one), why does this absurd person meet him with such an embarrassed look? Why is he so put out of countenance? Why is he thrown into such confusion, as though he had just committed some terrible crime within his four walls? As though he had been forging paper money? Or writing some atrocious poetry to be sent to a journal with an anonymous letter, in which he will explain that, the poet having recently died, he, his friend, deems it his sacred duty to publish his verses? Can you tell me, Nastenka, why the conversation between the two friends never really gets going? Why doesn't laughter or some witty remark escape the lips of the perplexed caller, who had so inopportunely dropped out of the blue, and who at other times is so fond of laughter and all sorts of quips and cranks? And conversations about the fair sex. And other cheerful subjects. And why does the visitor, who is most probably a recent acquaintance and on his first visit—for in this case there will never be a second, and his visitor will never call again—why, I say, does this visitor feel so embarrassed himself? Why, in spite of his wit (if, that is, he has any), is he so tongue-tied as he looks at the disconcerted face of his host, who is, in turn, utterly at a loss and bewildered after his herculean efforts to smooth things over, and fumbles desperately for a subject to enliven the conversation, to convince his host that he, too, is a man of the world, that he too can talk of the fair sex? The host does everything in fact to please the poor man, who seems to have come to the wrong place and called on him by mistake, by at least showing how anxious he is to entertain him. And why does the visitor, having most conveniently remembered a most urgent business appointment which never existed, all of a sudden grab his hat and take his leave, snatching away his hand from the clammy grasp of his host, who, in a vain attempt to recover what is irretrievably lost, is doing his best to show how sorry he is? Why does his friend burst out laughing the moment he finds himself on the other side of the door? Why does he vow never-to call on this queer fellow again, excellent fellow though he undoubtedly is? Why at the same time can't he resist the temptation of indulging in the amusing, if rather farfetched, fancy of comparing the face of his friend during his visit with the expression of an unhappy kitten, roughly handled, frightened, and subjected to all sorts of indignities, by children who had treacherously captured and humiliated it? A kitten that hides itself away from its tormentors under a chair, in the dark, where, left in peace at last, it cannot help bristling up, spitting, and washing its insulted face with both paws for a whole hour, and long afterwards looking coldly at life and nature and even the bits saved up for it from the master's table by a sympathetic housekeeper?"

"Now, look," interrupted Nastenka, who had listened to me all the time in amazement, opening her eyes and pretty mouth, "look, I haven't the faintest idea why it all happened and why you should ask me such absurd questions. All I know is that all these adventures have most certainly happened to you, and exactly as you told me."

"Indubitably," I replied, keeping a very straight face.

"Well," said Nastenka, "if it's indubitably, then please go on, for I'm dying to hear how it will all end."

"You want to know, Nastenka, what our hero did in his room, or rather what I did in my room, since the hero of this story is none other than my own humble self? You want to know why I was so alarmed and upset for a whole day by the unexpected visit of a friend? You want to know why I was in such a flurry of excitement, why I blushed to the roots of my hair, when the door of my room opened? Why I was not able to entertain my visitor, and why I perished so ignominiously, crushed by the weight of my own hospitality?"

"Yes, yes, of course I do," answered Nastenka. "That's the whole point. And, please, I do appreciate the beautiful way in which you're telling your story, but don't you think perhaps you ought to tell it a little less beautifully? You see, you talk as if you were reading from a book."

"Nastenka," I said in a very grave and solemn voice, scarcely able to keep myself from laughing, "dear Nastenka, I know I'm telling my story very beautifully, but I'm afraid I can't tell it any other way. For at this moment, Nastenka, at this moment, I am like the spirit of King Solomon when, after being imprisoned for a thousand years in a jar under seven seals, all the seven seals have at last been removed. At this moment, dear Nastenka, when we've met again after so long a separation—for I've known you for ages, dear Nastenka, for I've been looking for someone for ages and that's a sure sign that it was you I was looking for and, moreover, that it was ordained that we two should meet now—just at this very moment, Nastenka, a thousand floodgates have opened up in my head and I must overflow in a cataract of words, or I shall burst. So I beg you to listen to me like a good and obedient girl and not to interrupt me, Nastenka, or I shan't say another word."

"No, no, no! Please go on. You mustn't stop. I shan't say another word, I promise."

"Well, to continue. There is, Nastenka, my dear, dear friend, one hour in my day which I love exceedingly. It is the hour when practically all business, office hours and duties are at an end, and everyone is hurrying home to dinner, to lie down, to have a rest, and as they walk along they think of other pleasant ways of spending the evening, the night, and the rest of their leisure time. At that hour our hero—for I must ask your permission, Nastenka, to tell my story in the third person, for one feels awfully ashamed to tell it in the first—and so at that hour our hero, who has not been wasting his time, either, is walking along with the others. But a strange expression of pleasure plays on his pale and slightly crumpled-looking face. It is not with indifference that he looks at the sunset which is slowly fading on the cold Petersburg sky. When I say he looks, I'm telling a lie: he does not look at it, but is contemplating it without, as it were, being aware of it himself, as though he were tired or preoccupied at the same time with some other more interesting subject, being able to spare only a passing and almost unintentional glance at what is taking place around him. He is glad to have finished till next day with all tiresome *business*. He is happy as a schoolboy who has been let out of the classroom and is free to devote all his time to his favourite games and forbidden pastimes. Take a good look at him, Nastenka: you will at once perceive that his feeling of joy has had a pleasant effect on his weak nerves and his morbidly excited imagination. Look! he is thinking of something. Of dinner perhaps? Or how he's going to spend the evening? what is he looking at like that? At the gentleman of the solidly prosperous exterior who is bowing so picturesquely to the lady who drives past in a splendid carriage drawn by a pair of mettlesome horses? No, Nastenka, what do all those trivial things matter to him now? He is rich beyond compare with his *own individual* life; he has become rich in the twinkling of an

eye, as it were, and it was not for nothing that the farewell ray of the setting sun flashed so gaily across his vision and called forth a whole swarm of impressions from
his glowing heart. Now he hardly notices the road on
which at any other time every trivial detail would have
attracted his attention. Now 'the Goddess of Fancy' (if
you have read your Zhukovsky, dear Nastenka) has already spun the golden warp with her wanton hand and
is at this very moment weaving patterns of a wondrous,
fantastic life before his mind's eye—and, who knows,
maybe has transported him with her wanton hand to the
seventh crystalline sphere from the excellent granite pavement on which he is now wending his way home. Try
stopping him now, ask him suddenly where he is standing
now, through what streets he has been walking, and it is
certain he will not be able to remember anything, neither
where he has been, nor where he is standing now, and,
flushing with vexation, he will most certainly tell some lie
to save appearances. That is why he starts violently, almost crying out, and looks round in horror when a dear
old lady stops him in the middle of the pavement and
politely asks him the way. Frowning with vexation, he
walks on, scarcely aware of the passers-by who smile as
they look at him and turn round to follow him with their
eyes. He does not notice the little girl who, after timidly
making way for him, bursts out laughing as she gazes at
his broad, contemplative smile and wild gesticulations.
And still the same fancy in her frolicsome flight catches
up the old lady, the passers-by, the laughing little girl,
and the bargees who have settled down to their evening
meal on the barges which dam up the Fontanka (our
hero, let us suppose, is walking along the Fontanka Embankment at that moment), and playfully weaves everybody and everything into her canvas, like a fly in a
spider's web. And so, with fresh food for his fancy to feed
on, the queer fellow at last comes home to his comfortable little den and sits down to his dinner. It is long after
he has finished his meal, however, when, after clearing
the table, Matryona, the preoccupied and everlastingly
melancholy old woman who waits on him, gives him his
pipe, that he recovers from his reverie and is shocked to
find that he has had his dinner, although he has no recollection whatever how it has all happened. It has grown
dark in the little room; he feels empty and forlorn;

his castle in the air comes crumbling noiselessly around him, without a sound, and it vanishes like a dream, without leaving a trace behind, and he cannot remember himself what he was dreaming of. But a vague sensation faintly stirs his blood and a perturbation such as he has known many times before agitates his breast. A new longing temptingly tickles and excites his fancy, and imperceptibly conjures up a whole swarm of fresh phantoms. Silence reigns in the little room; solitude and a feeling of indolence enfold his imagination in a sweet embrace; it catches fire, burning gently at first, simmering like the water in the coffee-pot of old Matryona, who is moving placidly about her kitchen, making her execrable coffee. Very soon it begins flaring up fitfully, and the book, picked up aimlessly and at random, drops out of the hand of my dreamer, before he has reached the third page. His imagination is once more ready for action, excited, and in a flash a new world, a new fascinating life, once more opens up enchanting vistas before him. A new dream—new happiness! A new dose of subtle, voluptuous poison! Oh, what is there in our humdrum existence to interest him? To his corrupted mind, our life, Nastenka, yours and mine, is so dull, so slow, so insipid! To his mind we are all so dissatisfied with our fate, so tired of our life! And, to be sure, Nastenka, how cold, gloomy, and, as it were, out of humour everything about us is at the first glance! 'Poor things!' my dreamer thinks. And it is not surprising that he should think so! Look at those magical phantoms which so enchantingly, so capriciously, so vastly, and so boundlessly, are conjured up before his mind's eye in so magical and thrilling a picture, a picture in which, needless to say, he himself, our dreamer, in his own precious person, occupies the most prominent place! Look what an amazing sea of adventures, what a never-ending paradise of ecstatic dreams! You will perhaps ask me what is he dreaming of? But why ask? He is dreaming of everything—of the mission of the poet, first unrecognised, then crowned with laurels, of St. Bartholomew's Night, of Diana Vernon, the heroine of 'Rob Roy', of what a heroic role he would have played at the taking of Kazan by Ivan Vassilyevich, of Walter Scott's other heroines—Clara Mowbray and Effie Deans, of the Council of the Prelates and Huss before them, of the rising of the dead in 'Robert the Devil' (remember the music? It smells of the churchyard!), of the Battle of Berezina, of the poetry reading at Countess Vorontsova-Dashkova's, of Danton, of Cleopatra *i suoi amanti*, of Pushkin's 'Little House in Kolomna', of his own little home and a sweet creature beside him, who is listening to him, with her pretty mouth and eyes open, as you are listening to me now, my dear little angel. . . . No, Nastenka, what can he, voluptuous sluggard that he is, what can he find so attractive in the life which you and I desire so much? He thinks it a poor, miserable sort of life, and little does he know that some day perhaps the unhappy hour will strike for him too, when he will gladly give up all his fantastical years for one day of that miserable life, and give them up not in exchange for joy or happiness, but without caring what befalls him in that hour of affliction, remorse, and unconstrained grief. But so long as that perilous time is not yet—he desires nothing, for he is above all desire, for he is sated, for he is the artist of his own life, which he re-creates in himself to suit whatever new fancy he pleases. And how easily, how naturally, is this imaginary, fantastic world created! As though it were not a dream at all! Indeed, he is sometimes ready to believe that all this life is not a vision conjured up by his overwrought mind, not a mirage, nor a figment of the imagination, but something real, something that actually exists! Why, Nastenka, why, tell me, does one feel so out of breath at such moments? Why—through what magic? through what strange whim?—is the pulse quickened, do tears gush out of the eyes of the dreamer? Why do his pale, moist cheeks burn? Why is all his being filled with such indescribable delight? Why is it that long, sleepless nights pass, as though they were an infinitesimal fraction of time, in unending joy and happiness? And why, when the rising sun casts a rosy gleam through the window and fills the gloomy room with its uncertain, fantastic light, as it so often does in Petersburg, does our dreamer, worn out and exhausted, fling himself on the bed and fall asleep, faint with the raptures of his morbidly overwrought spirit, and with such a weary, languorously sweet ache in his heart? No, Nastenka, you can't help deceiving yourself, you can't help persuading yourself that his soul is stirred by some true, some genuine passion, you can't help believing that there is something alive and palpable in his vain and empty dreams! And what a delusion it all is! Now, for instance, love pierces his heart with all its boundless rapture, with all its pains and agonies. Only look at him and you will be convinced. Can you, looking at him, Nastenka, believe that he really never knew her whom he loved so dearly in his frenzied dream? Can it be that he has only seen her in ravishing visions, and that his passion has been nothing but an illusion? Can it be that they have never really spent so many years of their lives together, hand in hand, alone, just the two of them renouncing the rest of the world, and each of them entirely preoccupied with their own world, their own life? Surely it is she who at the hour of their parting, late at night, lies grieving and sobbing on his bosom, unmindful of the raging storm beneath the relentless sky, unmindful of the wind that snatches and carries away the tears from her dark eyelashes! Surely all this is not a dream—this garden, gloomy, deserted, run wild, with its paths overgrown with weeds, dark and secluded, where they used to walk so often together, where they used to hope, grieve, love, love each other so well, so tenderly and so well! And this queer ancestral mansion, where she has spent so many years in solitude and sadness with her morose old husband, always silent and ill-tempered, who frightened them, who were as timid as children, and who in their fear and anguish hid their love from each other. What misery they suffered, what pangs of terror! How innocent, how pure their love was, and (I need hardly tell you, Nastenka) how malicious people were! And why, of course, he meets her afterwards, far from his native shores, beneath the scorching southern sky of an alien land, in the wonderful Eternal City, amid the dazzling splendours of a ball, to the thunder of music, in a *palazzo* (yes, most certainly in a *palazzo* flooded with light, on the balcony wreathed in myrtle and roses, where, recognising him, she hastily removes her mask, and whispering, 'I'm free!' breaks into sobs and flings herself trembling in his arms. And with a cry of rapture, clinging to each other, they at once forget their unhappiness, their parting, all their sufferings, the dismal house, the old man, the gloomy garden in their faraway country, and the seat on which, with a last passionate kiss, she tore herself away from his arms, numbed with anguish and despair. . . . Oh, you must agree, Nastenka, that anyone would start, feel embarrassed, and blush like a schoolboy who has just stuffed in his pocket an apple stolen from a neighbour's garden, if some stalwart, lanky fellow, a fellow fond of a joke and merry company, opened your door and shouted, 'Hullo, old chap, I've just come from Pavlovsk!' Good Lord! The old count is dying, ineffable bliss is close at hand—and here people come from Pavlovsk!"

Having finished my pathetic speech, I lapsed into no less pathetic a silence. I remember I wished terribly that I could, somehow, in spite of myself, burst out laughing, for I was already feeling that a wicked little devil was stirring within me, that my throat was beginning to tighten, my chin to twitch, and my eyes to fill with tears. I expected Nastenka, who listened to me with wide-open, intelligent eyes, to break into her childish and irresistibly gay laughter. I was already regretting that I had gone too far, that I had been wasting my time in telling her what had been accumulating for so long a time in my heart, and about which I could speak as though I had it all written down—because I had long ago passed judgment on myself, and could not resist the temptation to read it out loud, though I admit I never expected to be understood. But to my surprise she said nothing, and, after a pause, pressed my hand gently and asked with timid sympathy:

"Surely you haven't lived like that all your life, have you?"

"Yes, Nastenka, all my life," I replied, "all my life, and I'm afraid I shall go on like that to the very end."

"No, you mustn't do that," she said, "that must not be, for if it were so, I too might spend all my life beside my granny. Don't you think it's just too awful to live like that?"

"I know, Nastenka, I know," I cried, unable to restrain my feelings any longer. "More than ever do I realise now that I've been wasting the best years of my life. I know that, and the realisation of it is all the more painful to me now that God has sent me you, my good angel, to tell me that and to prove it to me. Sitting beside you and talking to you now, I feel terrified to think of the future, for in my future I can discern nothing but more loneliness, more of this stale and unprofitable life. And what is there left for me to dream of now that I've been so happy beside you in real life and not in a dream? Oh, bless you, bless you a thousand times, my dear, for not having turned away from me at first, for making it possible for me to say that for at least two evenings in my life I have really lived!"

"Oh, no, no," Nastenka cried, and tears glistened in her eyes, "it can't go on like that! We shan't part like that! What are two evenings in a man's life?"

"Oh, Nastenka, Nastenka, do you realise that you've reconciled me to myself for a long, long time? Do you know that I shall never again think so ill of myself as I have sometimes done in the past? Do you know that I shall never again accuse myself of committing a crime and a sin in the way I live, for such a life is a crime and a sin? And for goodness' sake don't imagine I've exaggerated anything. Please, don't imagine that, Nastenka, for there are moments when I'm plunged into such gloom, such a black gloom! Because at such moments I'm almost ready to believe that I shall never be able to start living in earnest; because the thought has already occurred to me often that I have lost all touch with life, all understanding of what is real and actual; because, finally, I have cursed myself; because already after my fantastic nights I have moments of returning sanity, moments which fill me with horror and dismay! You see, I can't help being aware of the crowd being whirled with a roaring noise in the vortex of life, I can't help hearing and seeing people living real lives. I realise that their life is not made to order, that their life will not vanish like a dream, like a vision; that their life is eternally renewing itself, that it is eternally young, that not one hour of it is like another! No! Timid fancy is dreary and monotonous to the point of drabness. It is the slave of every shadow, of every idea. The slave of the first cloud that of a sudden drifts across the sun and reduces every Petersburg heart, which values the sun so highly, to a state of morbid melancholy—and what is the use of fancy when one is plunged into melancholy! You feel that this *inexhaustible* fancy grows weary at last and exhausts itself from the never-ending strain. For, after all, you do grow up, you do outgrow your ideals, which turn to dust and ashes, which are shattered into fragments; and if you have no other life, you just have to build one up out of these fragments. And meanwhile your soul is all the time craving and longing for something else. And in vain does the dreamer rum-

mage about in his old dreams, raking them over as though
they were a heap of cinders, looking in these cinders for
some spark, however tiny, to fan it into a flame so as to
warm his chilled blood by it and revive in it all that he
held so dear before, all that touched his heart, that made
his blood course through his veins, that drew tears from
his eyes, and that so splendidly deceived him! Do you
realise, Nastenka, how far things have gone with me?
Do you know that I'm forced now to celebrate the anniversary of my own sensations, the anniversary of that
which was once so dear to me, but which never really
existed? For I keep this anniversary in memory of those
empty, foolish dreams! I keep it because even those foolish dreams are no longer there, because I have nothing
left with which to replace them, for even dreams, Nastenka, have to be replaced by something! Do you know
that I love to call to mind and revisit at certain dates the
places where in my own fashion I was once so happy? I
love to build up my present in harmony with my irrevocably lost past; and I often wander about like a shadow,
aimlessly and without purpose, sad and dejected,
through the alleys and streets of Petersburg. What memories they conjure up! For instance, I remember that exactly a year ago, at exactly this hour, on this very pavement, I wandered about cheerlessly and alone just as I
did today. And I can't help remembering that at the time,
too, my dreams were sad and dreary, and though I did
not feel better then I somehow can't help feeling that it
was better, that life was more peaceful, that at least I
was not then obsessed by the black thoughts that haunt
me now, that I did not suffer from these gloomy and miserable qualms of conscience which now give me no rest
either by day or by night. And you ask yourself—where
are your dreams? And you shake your head and murmur:
how quickly time flies! And you ask yourself again—what
have you done with your time, where have you buried the
best years of your life? Have you lived or not? Look, you
say to yourself, look how everything in the world is growing cold. Some more years will pass, and they will be
followed by cheerless solitude, and then will come tottering old age, with its crutch, and after it despair and deso-
lation. Your fantastic world will fade away, your dreams
will wilt and die, scattering like yellow leaves from the
trees. Oh, Nastenka, what can be more heartbreaking

than to be left alone, all alone, and not have anything to regret even—nothing, absolutely nothing, because all you've lost was nothing, nothing but a silly round zero, nothing but an empty dream!"

"Don't," said Nastenka, wiping a tear which rolled down her cheek, "please don't! You'll make me cry if you go on like that. All that is finished! From now on we shall be together. We'll never part, whatever happens to me now. You know, I'm quite an ordinary girl, I'm not well educated, though Granny did engage a teacher for me, but I do understand you, for I went through all that you've described when Granny pinned me to her dress. Of course, I could never have described it as well as you," she added diffidently, for she was still feeling a sort of respect for my pathetic speech and my high-flown style, "because I'm not educated; but I'm very glad you've told me everything about yourself. Now I know you properly. And—do you know what? I'd like to tell you the story of my life too, all of it, without concealing anything, and after that you must give me some good advice. You're so clever, and I'd like to ask your advice. Do you promise to give it me?"

"Oh, Nastenka," I replied, "though I've never given any advice to anyone before, and though I'm certainly not clever enough to give good advice, I can see now that if we always lived like this, it would be very clever of us, and we should give each other a lot of good advice! Well, my sweet Nastenka, what sort of advice do you want? I'm now so gay, happy, bold, and clever that I'm sure I shan't have any difficulty in giving you the best advice in the world!"

"No, no," Nastenka interrupted, laughing, "it isn't only good advice that I want. I also want warm, brotherly advice, just as though you'd been fond of me for ages!"

"Agreed, Nastenka, agreed!" I cried with enthusiasm. "And if I'd been fond of you for twenty years, I couldn't have been fonder of you than I am now!"

"Your hand!" said Nastenka.

"Here it is!" I replied, giving her my hand.

"Very well, let's begin my story!"

Nastenka's Story

"Half my story you know already, I mean, you know that I have an old grandmother."

"If the other half is as short as this one——" I interrupted, laughing.

"Be quiet and listen. First of all you must promise not to interrupt me, or I shall get confused. Well, please listen quietly.

"I have an old grandmother. I've lived with her ever since I was a little girl, for my mother and father are dead. I suppose my grandmother must have been rich once, for she likes to talk of the good old days. It was she who taught me French and afterwards engaged a teacher for me. When I was fifteen (I'm seventeen now) my lessons stopped. It was at that time that I misbehaved rather badly. I shan't tell you what I did. It's sufficient to say that my offence was not very great. Only Granny called me in one morning and saying that she couldn't look after me properly because she was blind, she took a safety-pin and pinned my dress to hers. She told me that if I didn't mend my ways, we should remain pinned to each other for the rest of our lives. In short, at first, I found it quite impossible to get away from her: my work, my reading, and my lessons had all to be done beside my grandmother. I did try to trick her once by persuading Fyokla to sit in my place. Fyokla is our maid. She is very deaf. Well, so Fyokla took my place. Granny happened to fall asleep in her arm-chair at the time, and I ran off to see a friend of mine who lives close by. But, I'm afraid, it all ended most disastrously. Granny woke up while I was out and asked for something, thinking that I was still sitting quietly in my place. Fyokla saw of course that Granny wanted something, but could not tell what it was. She wondered and wondered what to do and in the end undid the pin and ran out of the room. . . ."

Here Nastenka stopped and began laughing. I, too, burst out laughing with her, which made her stop at once.

"Look, you mustn't laugh at Granny. I'm laughing because it was so funny. . . . Well, anyway, I'm afraid it can't be helped. Granny is like that, but I do love the poor old dear a little for all that. Well, I did catch it properly that time. I was at once told to sit down in my old place, and after that I couldn't make a move without her noticing it.

"Oh, I forgot to tell you that we live in our own house, I mean, of course, in Granny's house. It's a little wooden house, with only three windows, and it's as old as Granny herself. It has an attic, and one day a new lodger came to live in the attic. . . ."

"There was an old lodger then?" I remarked, by the way.

"Yes, of course, there was an old lodger," replied Nastenka, "and let me tell you, he knew how to hold his tongue better than you. As a matter of fact, he hardly ever used it at all. He was a very dried up old man, dumb, blind and lame, so that in the end he just could not go on living and died. Well, of course, we had to get a new lodger, for we can't live without one: the rent we get from our attic together with Granny's pension is almost all the income we have. Our new lodger, as it happened, was a young man, a stranger who had some business in Petersburg. As he did not haggle over the rent, Granny let the attic to him, and then asked me, 'Tell me, Nastenka, what is our lodger like—is he young or old?' I didn't want to tell her a lie, so I said, 'He isn't very young, Granny, but he isn't very old, either.'

" 'Is he good-looking?' Granny asked.

"Again I didn't want to tell her a lie. 'He isn't bad-looking, Granny,' I said. Well, so Granny said, 'Oh dear, that's bad, that's very bad! I tell you this because I don't want you to make a fool of yourself over him. Oh, what terrible times we're living in! A poor lodger and he would be good-looking too! Not like the old days!'

"Granny would have liked everything to be like the old days! She was younger in the old days, the sun was much warmer in the old days, the milk didn't turn so quickly in the old days—everything was so much better in the old days! Well, I just sat there and said nothing, but all the time I was thinking, Why is Granny warning me? Why did she ask whether our lodger was young and good-looking? Well, anyway, the thought only crossed my mind, and soon I was counting my stitches again (I was knitting a stocking at the time), and forgot all about it.

"Well, one morning our lodger came down to remind us that we had promised to paper his room for him. One thing led to another, for Granny likes talking to people and then she told me to go to her bedroom and fetch her accounts. I jumped up, blushed all over—I don't know why—and forgot that I was pinned to Granny. I never thought of undoing the pin quietly, so that our lodger shouldn't notice, but dashed off so quickly that I pulled Granny's armchair after me. When I saw that our lodger knew all about me now, I got red in the face, stopped dead as though rooted to the floor, and suddenly burst into tears. I felt so ashamed and miserable at that moment that I wished I was dead! Granny shouted at me, 'What are you standing there like that for?' But that made me cry worse than ever. When our lodger saw that I was ashamed on account of him, he took his leave and went away at once!

"Ever since that morning I've nearly fainted very time I've heard a noise in the passage. It must be the lodger, I'd think, and I'd undo the pin very quietly just in case it was he. But it never was our lodger. He never came. After a fortnight our lodger sent word with Fyokla that he had a lot of French books, and that they were all good books which he knew we would enjoy reading, and that he would be glad to know whether Granny would like me to choose a book to read to her because he was sure she must be bored. Granny accepted our lodger's kind offer gratefully, but she kept asking me whether the books were *good* books, for if the books were bad, she wouldn't let me read them because she didn't want me to get wrong ideas into my head."

" 'What wrong ideas, Granny? What's wrong with those books?'

" 'Oh,' she said, 'it's all about how young men seduce decent girls, and how on the excuse that they want to marry them, they elope with them and then leave them to their own fate, and how the poor creatures all come to a bad end. I've read a great many such books,' said Granny, 'and everything is described so beautifully in them that I used to keep awake all night, reading them on the quiet. So mind you don't read them, Nastenka,' she said. "What books has he sent?"

" 'They're all novels by Walter Scott, Granny.'

" 'Walter Scott's novels? Are you certain, Nastenka, there isn't some trickery there? Make sure, dear, he hasn't put a love letter in one of them.'

" 'No, Granny,' I said, 'there's no love letter.'

" 'Oh, dear,' said Granny, 'look in the binding, there's a good girl. Sometimes they stuff it in the binding, the scoundrels.'

" 'No, Granny, there's nothing in the binding.'

" 'Well, that's all right then!'

"So we started reading Walter Scott, and in a month or so we had read through almost half of his novels. Then he sent us some more books. He sent us Pushkin. And in the end I didn't know what to do if I had no book to read and I gave up dreaming of marrying a prince of royal blood.

"So it went on till one day I happened to meet our lodger on the stairs. Granny had sent me to fetch something. He stopped. I blushed and he blushed. However, he laughed, said good morning to me, asked me how Granny was, and then said, 'Well, have you read the books?' I said, 'Yes, we have.' 'Which did you like best?' I said, 'I liked *Ivanhoe* and Pushkin best of all.' That was all that happened that time.

"A week later I again happened to meet him on the stairs. That time Granny had not sent me for anything, but I had gone up to fetch something myself. It was past two in the afternoon, when our lodger usually came home. 'Good afternoon,' he said. 'Good afternoon,' I said.

" 'Don't you feel awfully bored sitting with your Granny all day?' he said.

"The moment he asked me that, I blushed—I don't know why. I felt awfully ashamed, and hurt, too, because I suppose it was clear that even strangers were beginning to wonder how I could sit all day long pinned to my Granny. I wanted to go away without answering, but I just couldn't summon enough strength to do that.

" 'Look here,' he said, 'you're a nice girl, and I hope you don't mind my telling you that I'm more anxious even than your Granny that you should be happy. Have you no girl friends at all whom you'd like to visit?'

"I told him I hadn't any. I had only one, Mashenka, but she had gone away to Pskov.

" 'Would you like to go to the theatre with me?' he asked.

" 'To the theatre? But what about Granny?'

" 'Couldn't you come without her knowing anything about it?'

" 'No, sir,' I said. 'I don't want to deceive my Granny. Goodbye.'

" 'Goodbye,' he said, and went upstairs without another word.

"After dinner, however, he came down to see us. He sat down and had a long talk with Granny. He asked her whether she ever went out, whether she had any friends, and then suddenly he said, 'I've taken a box for the opera for this evening. They're giving *The Barber of Seville*. Some friends of mine wanted to come, but they couldn't manage it, and now the tickets are left on my hands.'

" '*The Barber of Seville*!' cried my Granny. 'Why, is it the same barber they used to act in the old days?'

" 'Yes,' he replied, 'it's the same barber,' and he glanced at me.

"Of course I understood everything. I blushed and my heart began thumping in anticipation.

" 'Oh,' said Granny, 'I know all about him! I used to play Rosina myself in the old days at private theatricals.'

" 'Would you like to go today?' said the lodger. 'My ticket will be wasted if nobody comes.'

" 'Yes, I suppose we could go,' said Granny. 'Why shouldn't we? My Nastenka has never been to a theatre before.'

"My goodness, wasn't I glad! We started getting ready at once, put on our best clothes, and went off. Granny couldn't see anything, of course, because she is blind, but she wanted to hear the music, and, besides, she's really very kind-hearted, the old dear. She wanted me to go and enjoy myself, for we would never have gone by ourselves. Well, I won't tell you what my impression of *The Barber of Seville* was. I'll merely mention that our lodger looked at me so nicely the whole evening, and he spoke so nicely to me that I guessed at once that he had only meant to try me out in the afternoon, to see whether I would have gone with him alone. Oh, I was so happy! I went to bed feeling so proud, so gay, and my heart was beating so fast that I felt a little feverish and raved all night about *The Barber of Seville*.

"I thought he'd come and see us more and more often after that, but it turned out quite differently. He almost stopped coming altogether. He'd come down once a month, perhaps, and even then only to invite us to the theatre. We went twice to the theatre with him. Only I wasn't a bit happy about it. I could see that he was simply sorry for me because I was treated so abominably by my grandmother, and that otherwise he wasn't interested in me at all. So it went on till I couldn't bear it any longer: I couldn't sit still for a minute, I couldn't read anything, I couldn't work. Sometimes I'd burst out laughing and do something just to annoy Granny, and sometimes I'd just burst into tears. In the end I got terribly thin and was nearly ill. The opera season was over, and our lodger stopped coming down to see us altogether, and when we did meet—always on the stairs, of course—he'd just bow to me silently, and look very serious as though he did not want to talk to me, and he'd be out on the front steps while I'd still be standing halfway up the stairs, red as a cherry, for every time I met him all my blood rushed to my head.

"Well, I've almost finished. Just a year ago, in May, our lodger came down to our drawing-room and told Granny that he had finished his business in Petersburg and was leaving for Moscow where he would have to stay a whole year. When I heard that I went pale and sank back in my chair as though in a faint. Granny did not notice anything, and he, having told us that he was giving up his room, took his leave and went away.

"What was I to do? I thought and thought, worried and worried, and at last I made up my mind. As he was leaving tomorrow, I decided to make an end to it all after Granny had gone to bed. I tied up all my clothes in a bundle and, more dead than alive, went upstairs with my bundle to see our lodger. I suppose it must have taken me a whole hour to walk up the stairs to the attic. When I opened the door of his room, he cried out as he looked at me. He thought I was a ghost. He quickly fetched a glass of water for me, for I could hardly stand on my feet. My heart was beating very fast, my head ached terribly, and I felt all in a daze. When I recovered a little, I just put my bundle on his bed, sat down beside it, buried my face in my hands, and burst into a flood of tears. He seemed to have understood everything at once, and he stood before me looking so pale and gazing at me so sadly that my heart nearly broke.

" 'Listen, Nastenka,' he said, 'I can't do anything now. I'm a poor man. I haven't got anything at present, not even a decent job. How would we live, if I were to marry you?'

"We talked for a long time, and in the end I worked myself up into a real frenzy and told him that I couldn't go on living with my grandmother any more, that I'd run away from her, that I didn't want to be fastened by a pin all my life, and that, if he liked, I'd go to Moscow with him because I couldn't live without him. Shame, love, pride seemed to speak in me all at once, and I fell on the bed almost in convulsions. I was so afraid that he might refuse to take me!

"He sat in silence for a few minutes, then he got up, went to me, and took me by the hand.

" 'Listen to me, darling Nastenka,' he began, also speaking through his tears, 'I promise you solemnly that if at any time I am in a position to marry, you are the only girl in the world I would marry. I assure you that now you are the only one who could make me happy. Now, listen. I'm leaving for Moscow and I shall be away exactly one year. I hope to settle my affairs by that time. When I come back, and if you still love me, I swear to you that we shall be married. I can't possibly marry you now. It is out of the question. And I have no right to make any promises to you. But I repeat that if I can't marry you after one year, I shall certainly marry you sometime. Provided of course you still want to marry me and don't prefer someone else, for I cannot and I dare not bind you by any sort of promise.'

"That was what he told me, and the next day he left. We agreed not to say anything about it to Granny. He insisted on that. Well, that's almost the end of my story. A year has now passed, exactly one year. He is in Petersburg now, he's been here three days, and—and——"

"And what?" I cried, impatient to hear the end.

"And he hasn't turned up so far," said Nastenka, making a great effort to keep calm. "I haven't heard a word from him."

Here she stopped, paused a little, lowered her pretty head, and, burying her face in her hands, suddenly burst out sobbing so bitterly that my heart bled to hear it.

I had never expected such an ending.

"Nastenka," I began timidly, in an imploring voice,

"for goodness sake, Nastenka, don't cry! How can you tell? Perhaps he hasn't arrived yet. . . ."

"He has, he has!" Nastenka exclaimed. "I know he's here. We made an arrangement the night before he left. After our talk we went for a walk here on the embankment. It was ten o'clock. We sat on this seat. I was no longer crying then. I felt so happy listening to him! He said that immediately on his return he would come to see us, and if I still wanted to marry him, we'd tell Granny everything. Well, he's back now, I know he is, but he hasn't come, he hasn't come!"

And once more she burst into tears.

"Good heavens, isn't there anything we can do?" I cried, jumping up from the seat in utter despair. "Tell me, Nastenka, couldn't I go and see him?"

"You think you could?" she said, raising her head.

"No, of course not," I replied, checking myself. "But, look here, why not write him a letter?"

"No, no, that's impossible!" she replied firmly, but lowering her head and not looking at me.

"Why is it impossible? What's wrong with it?" I went on pleading with her, the idea having rather appealed to me. "It all depends what sort of a letter it is, Nastenka. There are letters and letters, and—oh, Nastenka, believe me it's true. Trust me, Nastenka, please! I wouldn't give you bad advice. It can all be arranged. It was you who took the first step, wasn't it? Well, why not now——?"

"No; it's quite impossible! It would look as if I was thrusting myself on him. . . ."

"But, darling Nastenka," I interrupted her, and I couldn't help smiling, "believe me, you're wrong, quite wrong. You're absolutely justified in writing to him, for he made a promise to you. Besides, I can see from what you've told me that he is a nice man, that he has behaved decently," I went on, carried away by the logic of my own reasoning and my own convictions. "For what did he do? He bound himself by a promise. He said that he wouldn't marry anyone but you, if, that is, he ever married at all. But he left you free to decide whether or not you want to marry him, to refuse him at any moment. This being so, there's no reason on earth why you shouldn't make the first move. You're entitled to do so, and you have an advantage over him, if, for instance, you should choose to release him from his promise. . . ."

"Look, how would you have written——?"

"What?"

"Such a letter."

"Well, I'd have started, 'Dear Sir. . . .' "

"Must it begin with 'Dear Sir?' "

"Of course! I mean, not necessarily. . . . You could. . . ."

"Never mind. How would you go on?"

" 'Dear Sir, you will pardon me for . . .' No, I don't think you should apologise for writing to him. The circumstances themselves fully justify your letter. Write simply: 'I am writing to you. Forgive me for my impatience, but all the year I have lived in such happy anticipation of your return that it is hardly surprising that I cannot bear the suspense even one day longer. Now that you are back, I cannot help wondering whether you have not after all changed your mind. If that is so, then my letter will tell you that I quite understand and that I am not blaming you for anything. I do not blame you that I have no power over your heart: such seems to be my fate. You are an honourable man. I know you will not be angry with me or smile at my impatience. Remember that it is a poor girl who is writing to you, that she is all alone in the world, that she has no one to tell her what to do or give her any advice, and that she herself never did know how to control her heart. But forgive me that doubt should have stolen even for one moment into my heart. I know that even in your thoughts you are quite incapable of hurting her who loved you so much and who still loves you.' "

"Yes, yes, that's exactly what I was thinking!" Nastenka cried, her eyes beaming with joy. "Oh, you've put an end to all my doubts. I'm sure God must have sent you to me. Thank you, thank you!"

"What are you thanking me for? Because God has sent me to you?" I replied, gazing delighted at her sweet, happy face.

"Yes, for that too."

"Oh, Nastenka, aren't we sometimes grateful to people only because they live with us? Well, I'm grateful to you for having met you. I'm grateful to you because I shall remember you all my life!"

"All right, all right! Now listen to me carefully: I arranged with him that he'd let me know as soon as he came back by leaving a letter for me at the house of some people I know—they are very nice, simple people who know nothing about the whole thing; and that if he couldn't write me a letter because one can't say all one wants in a letter, he'd come here, where we had arranged to meet, at exactly ten o'clock on the very first day of his arrival. Now, I know he has arrived, but for two days he hasn't turned up, nor have I had a letter from him. I can't possibly get away from Granny in the morning. So please take my letter tomorrow to the kind people I told you of, and they'll see that it reaches him. And if there is a reply, you could bring it yourself tomorrow evening at ten o'clock."

"But the letter! What about the letter? You must write the letter first, which means that I couldn't take it before the day after tomorrow."

"The letter . . . ?" said Nastenka, looking a little confused. "Oh, the letter! . . . Well——"

But she didn't finish. At first she turned her pretty face away from me, then she blushed like a rose, and then all of a sudden I felt that the letter which she must have written long before was in my hand. It was in a sealed envelope. A strangely familiar, sweet, lovely memory flashed through my mind.

"Ro-o-si-i-na-a!" I began.

"Rosina!" both of us burst out singing. I almost embraced her with delight, and she blushed as only she could blush and laughed through the tears which trembled on her dark eyelashes like pearls.

"Well, that's enough," she said, speaking rapidly. "Goodbye now. Here's the letter and here's the address where you have to take it. Goodbye! Till tomorrow!"

She pressed both my hands warmly, nodded her head, and darted away down her side-street. I remained standing in the same place for a long time, following her with my eyes.

"Till tomorrow! Till tomorrow!" flashed through my mind as she disappeared from sight.

Third Night

It was a sad and dismal day today, rainy, without a ray of hope, just like the long days of my old age which I know will be as sad and dismal. Strange thoughts are crowding into my head, my heart is full of gloomy forebodings, questions too vague to be grasped clearly fill my mind, and somehow I've neither the power nor the will to resolve them. No, I shall never be able to solve it all!

We are not going to meet today. Last night, when we said goodbye, the sky was beginning to be overcast, and a mist was rising. I observed that the weather did not look too promising for tomorrow, but she made no answer. She did not wish to say anything to cloud her own happy expectations. For her this day is bright and full of sunshine, and not one cloud will obscure her happiness.

"If it rains," she said, "we shan't meet! I shan't come!"

I thought she would not pay any attention to the rain today, but she never came.

Yesterday we had met for the third time. It was our third white night. . . .

But how beautiful people are when they are gay and happy! How brimful of love their hearts are! It is as though they wanted to pour their hearts into the heart of another human being, as though they wanted the whole world to be gay and laugh with them. And how infectious that gaiety is! There was so much joy in her words yesterday, so much goodness in her heart towards me. How sweet she was to me, how hard she tried to be nice to me, how she comforted and soothed my heart! Oh, how sweet a woman can be to you when she is happy! And I? Why, I was completely taken in. I thought she——

But how on earth could I have thought it? How could I have been so blind, when everything had already been taken by another, when nothing belonged to me? Why, even that tenderness of hers, that anxiety, that love—yes, that love for me was nothing more than the outward manifestation of her happiness at the thought of her meeting with someone else, her desire to force her happiness upon me too. When he did not turn up, when we waited in vain, she frowned, she lost heart, she was filled with alarm. All her movements, all her words, seemed to have lost their liveliness, their playfulness, their gaiety. And the strange thing was that she seemed doubly anxious to please me, as though out of an instinctive desire to lavish upon me what she so dearly desired for herself, but what she feared would never be hers. My Nastenka was so nervous and in such an agonising dread that at last she seemed to have realised that I loved her and took pity upon my unhappy love. It is always so: when we are unhappy we feel more strongly the unhappiness of others; our feeling is not shattered, but becomes concentrated. . . .

I came to her with a full heart; I could scarcely wait for our meeting. I had no presentiment of how I would be feeling now. I little dreamt that it would all end quite differently. She was beaming with happiness. She was expecting an answer to her letter. The answer was he himself. He was bound to come; he had to come running in answer to her call. She arrived a whole hour before me. At first she kept on laughing at everything; every word of mine provoked a peal of laughter from her. I began talking, but lapsed into silence.

"Do you know why I'm so happy?" she said. "Do you know why I'm so glad when I look at you? Do you know why I love you so today?"

"Well?" I asked, and my heart trembled.

"I love you so, because you haven't fallen in love with me. Another man in your place would, I'm sure, have begun to pester me, to worry me. He would have been sighing, he would have looked so pathetic, but you're so sweet!"

Here she clasped my hand with such force that I almost cried out. She laughed.

"Oh, what a good friend you are!" she began a minute later, speaking very seriously. "You're a real godsend to me. What would I have done if you'd not been with me now? How unselfish you are! How truly you love me! When I am married, we shall be such good friends. You'll be more than a brother to me. I shall love you almost as I love him! . . ."

Somehow I couldn't help feeling terribly sad at that moment. However, something resembling laughter stirred in my soul.

"Your nerves are on edge," I said. "You're afraid. You don't think he'll come."

"Goodness, what nonsense you talk!" she said. "If I hadn't been so happy, I do believe I'd have burst out crying to hear you express such doubts, to hear you reproaching me like that. You've given me an idea, though. And I admit you've given me a lot to think about, but I shall think about it later. I don't mind telling you frankly that you're quite right. Yes, I'm not quite myself tonight. I'm in awful suspense, and every little thing jars on me, excites me, but please don't let us discuss my feelings! . . ."

At that moment we heard footsteps, and a man loomed out of the darkness. He was coming in our direction. She almost cried out. I released her hand and made a movement as though I were beginning to back away. But we were both wrong: it was not he.

"What are you so afraid of? Why did you let go of my hand?" she said, giving me her hand again. "What does it matter? We'll meet him together. I want him to see how we love one another."

"How we love one another?" I cried.

"Oh, Nastenka, Nastenka," I thought, "how much you've said in that word! Such love, Nastenka, at certain moments makes one's heart ache and plunges one's spirit into gloom. Your hand is cold, but mine burns like fire. How blind you are, Nastenka! How unbearable a happy person sometimes is! But I'm afraid I could not be angry with you, Nastenka!"

At last my heart overflowed.

"Do you know, Nastenka," I cried, "do you know what I've gone through all day?"

"Why? What is it? Tell me quickly! Why haven't you said anything about it before?"

"Well, first of all, Nastenka, after I had carried out all your commissions, taken the letter, seen your good friends, I—I went home and—and went to bed."

"Is that all?" she interrupted, laughing.

"Yes, almost all," I replied, making an effort to keep calm, for I already felt foolish tears starting to my eyes. "I woke an hour before we were due to meet. But I don't seem to have really slept at all. I don't know how to describe the curious sensation I had. I seemed to be on my way here. I was going to tell you everything. I had an odd feeling as though time had suddenly stopped, as though one feeling, one sensation, would from that moment go on and on for all eternity, as though my whole life had come to a standstill. . . . When I woke up it seemed to me that some snatch of a tune I had known for a long time, I had heard somewhere before but had forgotten, a melody of great sweetness, was coming back to me now.

It seemed to me that it had been trying to emerge from my soul all my life, and only now——"

"Goodness," Nastenka interrupted, "what's all this about? I don't understand a word of it."

"Oh, Nastenka, I wanted somehow to convey that strange sensation to you," I began in a plaintive voice, in which there still lurked some hope, though I'm afraid a very faint one.

"Don't, please don't!" she said, and in a trice she guessed everything, the little rogue.

She became on a sudden somehow extraordinarily talkative, gay, playful. She took my arm, laughed, insisted that I should laugh too, and every halting word I uttered evoked a long loud peal of laughter from her. I was beginning to feel angry; she suddenly began flirting.

"Listen," she said, "I'm really beginning to be a little annoyed with you for not being in love with me. What am I to think of you after that? But, sir, if you insist on being so strong-minded, you should at least show your appreciation of me for being such a simple girl. I tell you everything, absolutely everything. Any silly old thing that comes into my head."

"Listen, I think it's striking eleven!" I said, as the clock from some distant city tower began slowly to strike the hour.

She stopped suddenly, left off laughing, and began to count.

"Yes," she said at last in a hesitating, unsteady voice, "its eleven."

I regretted at once that I had frightened her. It was brutal of me to make her count the strokes. I cursed myself for my uncontrolled fit of malice. I felt sorry for her, and I did not know how to atone for my inexcusable behaviour. I did my best to comfort her. I tried hard to think of some excuse for his failure to come. I argued. I reasoned with her. It was the easiest thing in the world to deceive her at that moment! Indeed, who would not be glad of any word of comfort at such a moment? Who would not be overjoyed at the faintest glimmer of an excuse?

"The whole thing's absurd!" I began, feeling more and more carried away by my own enthusiasm and full of admiration for the extraordinary clarity of my own arguments. "He couldn't possibly have come today. You've got me so muddled and confused, Nastenka, that I've lost count of the time. Why, don't you see? He's scarcely had time to receive your letter. Now, suppose that for some reason he can't come today. Suppose he's going to write to you. Well, in that case you couldn't possibly get his letter till tomorrow. I'll go and fetch it for you early tomorrow morning and let you know at once. Don't you see? A thousand things may have happened: he may have been out when your letter arrived, and for all we know he may not have read it even yet. Anything may have happened."

"Yes, yes!" said Nastenka. "I never thought of that. Of course anything may have happened," she went on in a most acquiescent voice, but in which, like some jarring note, another faintly perceptible thought was hidden away. "Yes, please do that. Go there as soon as possible tomorrow morning, and if you get anything let me know at once. You know where I live, don't you?"

And she began repeating her address to me.

Then she became suddenly so sweet, so shy with me. She seemed to listen attentively to what I was saying to her; but when I asked her some question, she made no reply, grew confused, and turned her head away. I peered into her eyes. Why, of course! She was crying.

"How can you? How can you? Oh, what a child you are! What childishness! There, there, stop crying please!"

She tried to smile, to compose herself, but her chin was still trembling, and her bosom still rising and falling.

"I'm thinking of you," she said to me after a minute's silence. "You're so good that I'd have to have a heart of stone not to feel it. Do you know what has just occurred to me? I was comparing the two of you in my mind. Why isn't he you? Why isn't he like you? He's not as good as you, though I love him more than you."

I said nothing in reply. She seemed to be waiting for me to say something.

"Of course it's probably quite true that I don't know him very well. No, I don't understand him very well. You see, I seemed always a little afraid of him. He was always so serious, and I couldn't help thinking proud as well. I realise of course that he merely looked like that. I know there's more tenderness in his heart than in mine. I can't forget the way he looked at me when—you remember?—

I came to him with my bundle. But all the same I seem to look up to him a little too much, and that doesn't seem as if we were quite equals, does it?"

"No, Nastenka, no," I replied. "It does not mean that you are not equals. It merely means that you love him more than anything in the world, far more than yourself even."

"Yes, I suppose that is so," said Nastenka. "But do you know what I think? Only I'm not speaking of him now, but just in general. I've been thinking for a long time, why aren't we all just like brothers to one another. Why does even the best of us seem to hide something from other people and keep something back from them? Why don't we say straight out what's in our hearts, if we know that our words will not be spoken in vain? As it is, everyone seems to look as though he were much harder than he really is. It is as though we were all afraid our feelings would be hurt if we revealed them too soon."

"Oh, Nastenka, you're quite right, but there are many reasons for that," I interrupted, for I knew that I myself was suppressing my feelings at that moment more than ever before.

"No, no!" she replied with great feeling. "You, for instance, are not like that. I really don't know how to tell you what I feel. But it seems to me, for instance—I mean I can't help feeling that you—that just at this moment you're making some sacrifice for me," she added shyly, with a quick glance at me. "Please forgive me for telling you that. You know I am such a simple girl. I haven't had much experience of the world and I really don't know sometimes how to express myself," she added in a voice that trembled from some hidden emotion, trying to smile at the same time. "But I just wanted to tell you that I'm grateful, that I'm aware of it too. . . . Oh, may God grant you happiness for that! I feel that what you told me about your dreamer is not true, I mean it has nothing to do with you. You are recovering, you're quite different from the man you described yourself to be. If you ever fall in love, may you be happy with her. I don't need to wish her anything, for she'll be happy with you. I know because I'm a woman myself, so you must believe me when I tell you so."

She fell silent and pressed my hand warmly. I was too moved to say anything. A few minutes passed.

"Yes, it seems he won't come tonight," she said at last, raising her head. "It's late."

"He'll come tomorrow," I said in a very firm, confident voice.

"Yes," she added, looking cheerful again, "I realise myself now that he couldn't possibly come till tomorrow. Well, goodbye! Till tomorrow! I may not come, if it rains. But the day after tomorrow I shall come whatever happens. You'll be here for certain, won't you? I want to see you. I'll tell you everything."

And later, when we said goodbye to each other, she gave me her hand and said, looking serenely at me—

"Now we shall always be together, shan't we?"

Oh, Nastenka, Nastenka, if only you knew how terribly lonely I am now!

When the clock struck nine, I could remain in my room no longer. I dressed and went out in spite of the bad weather. I was there. I sat on our seat. I went to her street, but I felt ashamed and went back when I was only a few yards from her house without even looking at her windows. What a day! Damp and dreary. If it had been fine, I should have walked about all night.

But—till tomorrow, till tomorrow! Tomorrow she'll tell me everything.

There was no letter for her today, though. However, there's nothing surprising in that. They must be together by now. . . .

Fourth Night

Good Lord, how strangely the whole thing has ended! What a frightful ending!

I arrived at nine o'clock. She was already there. I noticed her a long way off. She was standing, leaning with her elbows on the railing of the embankment, just as she had been standing the first time I saw her, and she did not hear me when I came up to her.

"Nastenka!" I called her, restraining my agitation with difficulty.

She turned round to me quickly.

"Well?" she said. "Well? Tell me quickly!"

I looked at her utterly bewildered.

"Well, where's the letter? Haven't you brought the letter?" she repeated, gripping the railing with her hand.

"No, I haven't got any letter," I said at last. "Hasn't he come?"

She turned terribly pale and stared at me for a long time without moving. I had shattered her last hope.

"Well, it doesn't matter," she said at last in a strangled voice. "If he leaves me like that, then perhaps it's best to forget him!"

She dropped her eyes, then tried to look at me, but couldn't do it. For a few more minutes she tried to pull herself together, then she turned away from me suddenly, leaned on the railing with her elbows, and burst into tears.

"Come, come," I began, but as I looked at her I hadn't the heart to go on. And, besides, what could I have said to her?

"Don't try to comfort me," she said, weeping. "Don't tell me he'll come—that he hasn't deserted me so cruelly and so inhumanly as he has. Why? Why did he do it? Surely there was nothing in my letter, in that unhappy letter of mine, was there?"

Here her voice was broken by sobs. My heart bled as I looked at her.

"Oh, how horribly cruel it is!" she began again. "And not a line, not a line! If he'd just written to say that he didn't want me, that he rejected me, but not to write a single line in three days! How easy it is for him to slight and insult a poor defenceless girl whose only fault is that she loves him! Oh, what I've been through these three days! Lord, when I think that it was I who went to him the first time, when I think how I humiliated myself before him, how I cried, how I implored him for a little love! And after that! . . . But, look here," she said, turning to me, and her black eyes flashed, "there's something wrong! There must be something wrong! It's not natural! Either you are mistaken or I am. Perhaps he didn't get my letter. Perhaps he still doesn't know anything. Tell me, for heaven's sake, explain it to me—I can't understand it—how could he have behaved so atrociously to me. Not one word! Why, people show more pity to the lowest creature on earth! Perhaps he has heard something, perhaps someone has told him something about me," she cried, turning to me for an answer: "What do you think?"

"Listen, Nastenka, I'll go and see him tomorrow on your behalf."

"Well?"

"I'll try and find out from him what the position is. I'll tell him everything."

"Well? Well?"

"You write a letter. Don't refuse, Nastenka, don't refuse! I'll make him respect your action. He'll learn everything, and if——"

"No, my friend, no," she interrupted. "Enough! Not another word, not another word from me, not a line—I've had enough! I don't know him any more, I don't love him any more, I'll f-f-forget him."

She did not finish.

"Calm yourself, calm yourself, my dear! Sit here, Nastenka," I said, making her sit down on the seat.

"But I am calm. I tell you this is nothing. It's only tears —they'll soon dry. You don't really think I'm going to do away with myself, drown myself, do you?"

My heart was full: I tried to speak, but I couldn't.

"Listen," she said, taking my hand, "you wouldn't have behaved like this, would you? You wouldn't have abandoned a girl who had come to you of her own free will, you wouldn't have made a cruel mockery of her weak foolish heart, would you? You would have taken care of her. You would have reminded yourself that she had nobody in the whole world, that she was so inexperienced, that she could not prevent herself from falling in love with you, that she couldn't help it, that it wasn't her fault —no, it wasn't her fault!—that she had not done anything wrong. Oh, dear God, dear God. . . ."

"Nastenka," I cried, unable to restrain myself any longer, "this is more than I can endure! It's sheer torture to me! You wound me to the heart, Nastenka! I can't be silent! I must speak! I must tell you of all the anguish in my heart!"

Saying this, I raised myself from the seat. She took my hand and looked at me in surprise.

"What's the matter?" she said at last.

"Listen to me, Nastenka," I said firmly, "listen to me, please! What I'm going to say to you now is all nonsense. It is foolish. It cannot be. I know it will never happen, but I cannot remain silent. In the name of all that you're suffering now, I beseech you beforehand to forgive me!"

"Well, what is it? What is it?" she demanded, and she stopped crying and looked intently at me, a strange gleam of curiosity in her startled eyes. "What is the matter with you?"

"It's out of the question, I know, but—I love you, Nastenka! That is what's the matter with me. Now you know everything!" I said, with a despairing wave of my hand. "Now you can judge for yourself whether you ought to go on talking to me as you did just now, and—what is perhaps even more important—whether you ought to listen to what I'm going to say to you."

"Well, what about it?" Nastenka interrupted. "Of course I knew long ago that you loved me, only I always thought that—well, that you loved me in the ordinary way, I mean that you were just fond of me. Oh dear, oh dear! . . ."

"At first it was in the ordinary way, Nastenka, but now—now I'm in the same position as you were when you went to him with your bundle that night. I'm in a worse position Nastenka, because he wasn't in love with anyone at the time, and you—you are."

"Goodness, what are you saying to me! I really can't understand you. But, look, what has made you—I mean, why did you—and so suddenly too! Oh dear, I'm talking such nonsense! But you——"

And Nastenka got completely confused. Her cheeks were flushed. She dropped her eyes.

"What's to be done, Nastenka? What can I do about it? It's entirely my fault, of course. I've taken an unfair advantage of—But no—no, Nastenka, it isn't my fault. I know it isn't. I feel it isn't because my heart tells me I'm right, because I could never do anything to hurt you, because I could do nothing that you would ever take offence at. I was your friend? Well, I still am your friend. I have not been unfaithful to anyone. You see, I'm crying, Nastenka. But never mind. What if tears do run down my cheeks? Let them. They don't hurt anyone. They'll soon dry, Nastenka."

"But sit down, do sit down, please," she said, making me sit down on the seat. "Oh dear, oh dear!"

"No, Nastenka, I shan't sit down. I can't stay here any longer. You'll never see me again. I'll say what I have to say and go away. I only want to say that you'd never have found out that I loved you. I'd never have told my secret to a living soul. I'd never have tormented you with my egosim at such a moment. Never! But I could not bear to be silent now. It was you who began talking about it. It's your fault, not mine. You just can't drive me away from you."

"But I'm not—I'm not driving you away from me!" Nastenka said, doing her best, poor child, not to show how embarrassed she was.

"You are not driving me away? No—but I meant to run away from you myself. And I will go away. I will. Only first let me tell you everything, for, you see, when you were talking to me here, I couldn't sit still; when you cried here, when you tormented yourself because—well, because (I'd better say it, Nastenka)—because you were jilted, because your love was slighted and disregarded, I felt that in my heart there was so much love for you, Nastenka, so much love! And I so bitterly resented not being able to do anything to help you with my love that—that my heart was bursting and I—I couldn't be silent any longer, Nastenka. I had to speak!"

"Yes, yes, tell me everything, do speak to me like that!" said Nastenka with a gesture that touched me deeply. "It may seem strange to you that I should be speaking to you like this, but—do say what you have to say! I will tell you afterwards. I'll tell you everything!"

"You are sorry for me, Nastenka. You're just sorry for me, my dear, dear friend! Well, what's done is done. No use crying over spilt milk, is it? Well, so you know everything now. At any rate, that's something to start with. All right. Everything's fine now. Only, please, listen. When you were sitting here, when you were crying, I thought to myself (Oh, do let me tell you what I was thinking!), I thought that (I know of course how utterly impossible it is, Nastenka)—I thought that you—that you somehow —I mean quite apart from anything else—that you no longer cared for him. If that is so, then—I already thought of that yesterday, Nastenka, and the day before yesterday—then I would—I most certainly would have done my best to make you care for me. You said yourself, Nastenka—you did say it several times, didn't you?—that you almost loved me. Well, what more is there to tell you? That's really all I wanted to say. All that remains to be said is what would happen if you fell in love with me—that's all—nothing more! Now listen to me, my friend—for you are my friend, aren't you?—I am of course an ordinary sort of fellow, poor and insignificant, but that doesn't matter (I'm afraid I don't seem to be putting it very well, Nastenka, because I'm so confused), what matters is that I'd love you so well, so well, Nastenka, that even if you still loved him and went on loving the man I don't know, my love would never be a burden to you. All you'd feel, all you'd be conscious of every minute, is that a very grateful heart was beating at your side, Nastenka, an ardent heart which for your sake—Oh, Nastenka, Nastenka, what have you done to me?"

"Don't cry, I don't want you to cry," said Nastenka, rising quickly from the seat. "Come along, get up, come with me. Don't cry, don't cry," she said, drying my tears with her handkerchief. "There, come along now. Perhaps I'll tell you something. Well, if he has really given me up, if he has forgotten me, then though I still love him (and I don't want to deceive you)—But, listen, answer me! If, for instance, I were to fall in love with you—I mean, if only I—Oh, my friend, my friend, when I think, when I only think how I must have offended you when I laughed at your love, when I praised you for not falling in love with me! Oh dear, why didn't I foresee it? Why didn't I foresee it? How could I have been so stupid? But never mind, I've made up my mind now. I'm going to tell you everything."

"Look here, Nastenka, do you know what? I'll go away. Yes, I'll go away! I can see that I'm simply tormenting you. Now you're sorry you've been making fun of me, and I hate to think—yes, I simply hate to think that in addition to your own sorrow—Of course, it's all my fault, Nastenka, it's all my fault, but—goodbye!"

"Stop! Listen to me first, please. You can wait, can't you?"

"Wait? What should I wait for? What do you mean?"

"You see, I love him, but that will pass. It must pass. It's quite impossible for it not to pass. As a matter of fact, it's already passing. I can feel it. Who knows, maybe it'll be over today, for I hate him! Yes, I hate him because he has slighted me, while you were weeping with me. I hate him because you haven't let me down as he has, because you love me, while he has never really loved me, because—well, because I love you too. Yes, I love you! I love you as you love me. I've told you so before, haven't

I? You heard me say it yourself. I love you because you're better than he is, because you're more honourable than he is, because he——"

She stopped crying at last, dried her eyes, and we continued our walk. I wanted to say something, but she kept asking me to wait. We were silent. At last she plucked up courage and began to speak.

'Look," she said, in a weak and trembling voice, in which, however, there was a strange note which pierced my heart and filled it with a sweet sensation of joy, "don't think I'm so fickle, so inconstant. Don't think that I can forget him so easily and so quickly, that I can be untrue to him. I have loved him for a whole year, and I swear I have never, never for a moment, been untrue to him even in thought. He has thought little of that, he has scorned me—well, I don't mind that. But he has also hurt my feelings and wrung my heart. I don't love him because I can only love what is generous, what is understanding, what is honourable, for I'm like that myself, and he's not worthy of me. Well, let's forget about him. I'd rather he behaved to me like that now than that I was disappointed later in my expectations and found out the sort of man he really was. Anyway, it's all over now. And, besides, my dear friend," she went on, pressing my hand, "who knows, perhaps my love for him was nothing but self-deception, nothing but imagination. Perhaps it started just as a joke, just as a bit of silly nonsense because I was constantly under Granny's supervision. Perhaps I ought to love another man and not him, quite a different man, a man who'd have pity on me, and—and—anyway," Nastenka broke off, overcome with emotion, "don't let's speak of it. Don't let's speak of it. I only wanted to tell you—I wanted to tell you that even if I do love him (no, did love him), even if in spite of this you still say—or rather feel that your love is so great that it could in time replace my love for him in my heart—if you really and truly have pity on me, if you won't leave me alone to my fate, without consolation, without hope, if you promise to love me always as you love me now, then I swear that my gratitude—that my love will in time be worthy of your love. Will you take my hand now?"

"Nastenka," I cried, my voice broken with sobs, "Nastenka! Oh, Nastenka!"

"All right, all right!" she said, making a great effort to

speak calmly. "All right! That's enough! Now everything's been said, hasn't it? Hasn't it? Well, you are happy
now, aren't you? And I too am happy. So don't let's talk
about it any more. Just wait a little—have patience—
spare me! Talk of something else, for God's sake!"

"Yes, Nastenka, yes! Of course don't let's talk about it.
Now I'm happy. Well, Nastenka, do let's talk of something else. Come on, let's. I don't mind."

But we did not know what to talk about. We laughed,
we cried, we said a thousand things without caring
whether they made sense or not. One moment we walked
along the pavement, and the next we suddenly turned back
and crossed the road, then we stopped and crossed over
to the embankment again. We were like children. . . .

"I'm living alone, now, Nastenka," I began, "but tomorrow——You know, of course, Nastenka, that I'm poor,
don't you? I've only got twelve hundred roubles, but that
doesn't matter."

"Of course not, and Granny has her pension, so that
she won't be a burden to us. We'll have to take Granny,
of course."

"Of course we'll take Granny! Only—there's Matryona——"

"Goodness, I never thought of that! And we've got
Fyokla!"

"Matryona is a good soul, only she has one fault: she
has no imagination, Nastenka, none whatever! But I don't
suppose that matters!"

"It makes no difference. They can live together. You'll
move to our house tomorrow, won't you?"

"How do you mean? To your house? Oh, very well, I
don't mind."

"I mean, you'll take our attic. I told you we have an
attic, didn't I? It's empty now. We had a woman lodger,
an old gentlewoman, but she's left, and I know Granny
would like to let it to a young man. I said to her, 'Why a
young man, Granny?' But she said, 'Why not? I'm old and
I like young people about. You don't think I'm trying to
get a husband for you, do you?' Well, I saw at once of
course that that was what she had in mind."

"Good Lord, Nastenka!"

And we both laughed.

"Oh, well, never mind. But where do you live? I've forgotten."

I told her I lived near a certain bridge in Barannikov's house.

"It's a very big house, isn't it?"

"Yes, it's a very big house."

"Oh, yes, I know it. It's a nice house, but I still think you ought to move out of it and come and live with us as soon as possible."

"I'll do so tomorrow, Nastenka, tomorrow. I'm afraid I'm a little behindhand with my rent, but that doesn't matter. I shall be getting my salary soon and——"

"And you know I could be giving lessons. Yes, why not? I'll learn everything myself first and then give lessons."

"That's an excellent idea, Nastenka, an excellent idea! And I'll be getting a bonus soon. . . ."

"So tomorrow you'll be my lodger. . . ."

"Yes, and we'll go to *The Barber of Seville*, for I believe they're going to put it on again soon."

"Oh yes, I'd love to," said Nastenka, laughing. "Perhaps not *The Barber*, though. We'd better see something else."

"Oh, all right, something else then. I don't mind. I suppose something else would be better. You see, I didn't think——"

Talking like this, we walked along in a sort of a daze, in a mist, as though we did not know ourselves what was happening to us. One moment we would stop and go on talking in one place for a long time, and the next we would be walking again till we would find ourselves goodness knows where—and more laughter, more tears. Then Nastenka would suddenly decide that she ought to be going back home, and I would not dare to detain her, but would insist on accompanying her to her house. We would start on our way back, and in about a quarter of an hour would find ourselves on the embankment by our seat. Then she would sigh, and tears would come into her eyes again, and I would be plunged into despair and a chilly premonition of disaster would steal into my heart. But she would at once press my hand and drag me off again to walk, talk, chatter. . . .

"It's time—time I went home now," Nastenka said at last. "I think it must be awfully late. We've been behaving like children long enough!"

"Yes, of course, Nastenka. Only I don't suppose I shall be able to sleep now. No, I won't go home."

"I don't think I shall sleep, either. Only see me home, will you?"

"Of course, I'll see you home. . . ."

"On your word of honour? Because, you see, I must get back home some time, mustn't I?"

"On my word of honour!" I replied, laughing.

"All right, let's go."

"Let's go. Look at the sky, Nastenka, look! It'll be a lovely day tomorrow! What a blue sky! What a moon! Look, a yellow cloud is drifting over it. Look! Look! No, it has passed by. Look, Nastenka, look!"

But Nastenka did not look. She stood speechless, motionless. A minute later she clung somewhat timidly close to me. Her hand trembled in mine. I looked at her. She clung to me more closely.

At that moment a young man passed by us. He suddenly stopped, looked at us intently for a moment, and then again took a few steps towards us. My heart missed a beat.

"Nastenka," I said in an undertone, "who is it, Nastenka?"

"It's him!" she replied in a whisper, clinging to me still more closely, still more tremulously.

I could hardly stand up.

"Nastenka! Nastenka! It's you!" we heard a voice behind us, and at the same time the young man took a few steps towards us.

Lord, how she cried out! How she started! How she tore herself out of my hands and rushed to meet him! I stood and looked at them, utterly crushed. But no sooner had she given him her hand, no sooner had she thrown herself into his arms, than she suddenly turned to me again, and was at my side in a flash, faster than lightning, faster than the wind, and before I could recover from my surprise, flung her arms round my neck and kissed me ardently. Then, without uttering a word, she rushed back to him again, clasped his hands, and drew him after her.

I stood a long time, watching them walking away. At last both of them vanished from my sight.

Morning

My nights came to an end with a morning. The weather was dreadful. It was pouring, and the rain kept beating dismally against my windowpanes. It was dark in the room; it was dull and dreary outside. My head ached. I felt giddy. I was beginning to feel feverish.

"A letter for you, sir," said Matryona, bending over me. "Came by the city post, it did, sir. The postman brought it."

"A letter? Who from?" I cried, jumping up from my chair.

"I don't know, sir, I'm sure. I suppose whoever sent it must have signed his name."

I broke the seal: the letter was from her!

"Oh, forgive me, forgive me!" Nastenka wrote to me. "I beg you on my knees to forgive me! I deceived you and myself. It was all a dream, a delusion. I nearly died today thinking of you. Please, please forgive me!

"Don't blame me, for I haven't changed a bit towards you. I said I would love you, and I do love you now, I more than love you. Oh, if only I could love both of you at once! Oh, if only you were he!"

"Oh, if only he were you!" it flashed through my mind. "Those were your own words, Nastenka!"

"God knows what I would do for you now. I know how sad and unhappy you must be. I've treated you abominably, but when one loves, you know, an injury is soon forgotten. And you do love me!

"Thank you, yes! thank you for that love. For it remains imprinted in my memory like a sweet dream one remembers a long time after awakening. I shall never forget the moment when you opened your heart to me like a real friend, when you accepted the gift of my broken heart to take care of it, to cherish it, to heal it. If you forgive me, I promise you that the memory of you will always remain with me, that I shall be everlastingly grateful to you, and that my feeling of gratitude will never be erased from my heart. I shall treasure this memory, I'll be true to it. I shall never be unfaithful to it, I shall never be unfaithful to my heart. It is too constant for that. It returned so quickly yesterday to him to whom it has always belonged.

"We shall meet. You will come and see us. You will not leave us, will you? You'll always be my friend, my brother. And when you see me, you'll give me your hand, won't you? You will give it to me because you've forgiven me. You have, haven't you? You love me *as before,* don't you?

"Oh, yes, do love me! Don't ever forsake me, because I love you so at this moment, because I am worthy of your love, because I promise to deserve it—oh, my dear, dear friend! Next week I'm to be married to him. He has come back as much in love with me as ever. He has never forgotten me. You will not be angry with me because I have written about him, will you? I would like to come and see you with him. You will like him, won't you?

"Forgive me, remember and love your
                    Nastenka."

I read this letter over and over again. There were tears in my eyes. At last it dropped out of my hands, and I buried my face.

"Look, love, look!" Matryona called me.

"What is it, Matryona?"

"Why, I've swept all the cobwebs off the ceiling. Looks so lovely and clean, you could be wed, love, and have your wedding party here. You might just as well do it now as wait till it gets dirty again!"

I looked at Matryona. She was still hale and hearty, quite a *young-looking* old woman, in fact. But I don't know why all of a sudden she looked old and decrepit to me, with a wrinkled face and lustreless eyes. I don't know why, but all of a sudden my room, too, seemed to have grown as old as Matryona. The walls and floors looked discoloured, everything was dark and grimy, and the cobwebs were thicker than ever. I don't know why, but when I looked out of the window the house opposite, too, looked dilapidated and dingy, the plaster on its columns peeling and crumbling, its cornices blackened and full of cracks, and its bright brown walls disfigured by large white and yellow patches. Either the sun, appearing suddenly from behind the dark rain-clouds, had hidden itself so quickly that everything had grown dark before my eyes again, or perhaps the whole sombre and melancholy perspective of my future flashed before my mind's eye at that moment, and I saw myself just as I was now fifteen years hence, only grown older, in the same room, living the same sort of solitary life, with the same Matryona, who had not grown a bit wiser in all those years.

But that I should feel any resentment against you, Nastenka! That I should cast a dark shadow over your bright, serene happiness! That I should chill and darken your heart with bitter reproaches, wound it with secret remorse, cause it to beat anxiously at the moment of bliss! That I should crush a single one of those delicate blooms which you will wear in your dark hair when you walk up the aisle to the altar with him! Oh no—never, never! May your sky be always clear, may your dear smile be always bright and happy, and may you be for ever blessed for that moment of bliss and happiness which you gave to another lonely and grateful heart!

Good Lord, only a *moment* of bliss? Isn't such a moment sufficient for the whole of a man's life?

A Disgraceful Affair

TRANSLATED BY NORA GOTTLIEB

Our beloved motherland was experiencing a renais-
sance; her brave sons, fired with impulses at once
touching and naïve, were seeking with an uncontrol-
lable yearning for new destinies and hopes. It was
at this time that the following disgraceful affair
took place.

ONE CLEAR and frosty winter's night—incidentally, it was
already past eleven o'clock—three highly reputable personages were sitting in a comfortable, even luxuriously
furnished room in a certain fine two-storied house on the
Petersburg Side. They were engaged in a measured and
lofty discussion on a most curious topic. All three were
worthies of the rank of General in the Civil Service. They
sat around a small table, each in a fine, soft arm-chair,
in the course of their conversation now and again sipping champagne with quiet enjoyment. The bottle was
ready at hand on the little table, in a silver wine-cooler.
The fact was that the host, Privy Councillor Stepan Nikiforovitch Nikiforov, an old bachelor of about sixty-five,
was simultaneously celebrating a house-warming in his
newly acquired house and incidentally his birthday as
well, which just happened to fall on the very same day,
and which he had never celebrated up to now. The cele-
bration was nothing very much; as we have already seen,
there were only two guests, both former colleagues and
subordinates of Mr. Nikiforov's, namely: one, Actual
State Councillor Semyon Ivanovitch Shipulenko; and the
other, also Actual State Councillor, Ivan Ilyitch Pralinski. They had come to take tea around nine o'clock and
had afterwards tackled some wine, and they knew that
they would have to leave promptly at half past eleven.
Their host had all his life had a liking for regular habits.
Let me say two words about him: he had begun his career
as an impecunious petty Government official, gently spinning it out for forty-five years, knowing too well how far
he could hope to rise. He could not bear to snatch at the
stars above (although he already wore two of them on
his tunic) and in particular he disliked expressing his own
personal views on any matter whatever. He was honest,

too; or rather, he had never had occasion to be particularly dishonest; an egoist, he was single; he was no fool, but disliked parading his intellect. He could not stand disorder and enthusiasm, which he considered a sort of moral untidiness, and by the end of his life he was submerged in a kind of sweet, indolent comfort and well-ordered solitariness. Although he himself had sometimes visited his superiors, even as a young man he had been unable to endure receiving guests, and lately, when he was not playing Grand Patience, he had contented himself with the company of his dining-room clock. Drowsing in an arm-chair, he would listen placidly for whole evenings to it ticking on the mantelpiece beneath its glass case. In appearance he was very respectable; clean-shaven, he looked younger than his years; he was well preserved, showed signs of living for a long while yet, and conformed to the highest standards of gentlemanly behaviour. The position he held was comfortable enough: he sat on a Board and signed something or other.

In brief, he was considered a most worthy person.

He had only one passion, or better, one ardent desire: that was to possess his own house, and in particular a house built in the style of a gentleman's residence, not a tenement for letting at a profit. At last this wish had been realized. He had looked round and bought a house on the Petersburg Side; true, it was rather far out, but it was an elegant residence, and, moreover, it had a garden. The new owner maintained it was even better for being farther out; he did not like entertaining at home, and for visiting anyone or driving to the office, he had a fine chocolate-coloured two-seater carriage, a coachman called Mikhei and a pair of small but strong, handsome horses. All this was the fruit of forty years' painstaking economy, and his heart rejoiced in it.

Hence, when he had bought the house and moved in, Stepan Nikiforovitch was overcome by such contentment that in the serenity of his heart he actually invited guests on his birthday, which formerly he had carefully kept from even his closest friends.

. . .

He had, however, an ulterior motive in inviting one of his guests. He himself occupied the upper floor of his house, while the ground floor, which was set out in exactly the same way, required a tenant. And so Stepan Nikiforovitch looked to Semyon Ivanovitch Shipulenko, and in the course of the evening had twice steered the conversation towards this objective. But Semyon Ivanovitch was non-committal. Here was a man who had also made his way painstakingly and over a long period; he had black hair and whiskers and a jaundiced countenance. Married, a surly stay-at-home, he tyrannized his household; he performed his duties with self-confidence, and he, too, was well aware of his capabilities and, better still, of what he would never achieve; he was sitting pretty in a comfortable job, and sitting tight. He looked on the new order of things not entirely without rancour, yet was not unduly concerned. He was very sure of himself and it was not without malicious scorn that he listened to the ramblings of Ivan Ilyitch Pralinski on topics of the day. As a matter of fact, they had all had a little too much to drink, so that even Stepan Nikiforovitch condescended to launch forth in a slight argument with Mr. Pralinski on the subject of the new reforms. But a few words must be mentioned about His Excellency Mr. Pralinski, particularly as he is, in fact, the chief hero of our story.

* * *

Only four months had passed since State Councillor Ivan Ilyitch Pralinski had begun to be addressed as "Your Excellency"; in fact he was a newly created General. And he was still young in years, about forty-three, certainly not more and looked, and liked to look, younger. He was a handsome man, tall, and clothes-conscious; he had the proper knack of wearing a distinguished order round his neck. From childhood he had learned to adopt some habits of the fashionable world, and, as a bachelor, he dreamed of a rich bride, even a bride from high society. There were many other things he dreamed of, though he was far from stupid. At times he was a great talker, and even liked to adopt the airs of a parliamentarian. He was of good family, the pampered son of a General, and at a tender age was clothed in velvet and fine linen; he had been educated in an aristocratic establishment, and although he had gained little learning therein he had succeeded in office and managed to rise to the rank of General. His superiors regarded him as a gifted person and had great hopes for him. Stepan Nikiforovitch, under whom he had begun and continued his office career almost up to the time when he rose to the rank of a General, had never considered him very businesslike and had no hope whatsoever for him. But it pleased him that he was of good family, had private means—that is, he owned a large and profitable house, with its own caretaker—was related to folk of good standing and, above all, had a certain air of distinction about him. Stepan Nikiforovitch secretly reproached him for his excess of imagination and frivolity. Ivan Ilyitch himself sometimes felt that he was too vain and even over-sensitive. It was a queer thing: at times he had attacks of morbid conscience and even a slight feeling of remorse. With bitterness and secret heartache he admitted to himself that he did not really fly as high as he liked to think. At these moments he felt dejected, especially when his attack of piles was at its worst, and called his life *"une existence manquée"*, lost faith (privately, of course) even in his debating abilities, referring to himself as an empty talker and a phrase-monger. Although all this was certainly much to his credit, it did not in the least impede his spirits from rising half an hour later, when he would more obstinately and more presumptuously than ever reassure and convince himself that he still had time to prove his worth and would not only reach a high rank but would moreover become a great statesman, long to be remembered in Russia. At times he even visualized monuments raised in his honour. From all this one can gather that Ivan Ilyitch aimed high, though he concealed, with certain misgivings, the vague dreams and hopes that lay beneath the surface. In short, he was a kind man and even a poet at heart. In recent years he had more frequently been overcome by painful moments of disillusionment; he had become in fact especially irritable and suspicious, ready to consider any contradiction an insult. However, the regeneration of Russia suddenly raised great hopes in him. Attainment of the rank of General only confirmed them. He blossomed forth and held up his head once more. He suddenly began to speak eloquently and profusely: he spoke on the most topical subjects, which he felt very strongly about and which he had absorbed with unexpected rapidity. He sought out occasions to speak; he went about town and in many places succeeded in becoming known as a desperate liberal, which flattered him greatly.

. . .

On the evening in question, having consumed about four glasses of champagne, he was particularly talkative. He wanted to make a total convert of Stepan Nikiforovitch, whom he had not seen for a long time and whom he had until now always respected and even obeyed. For some reason he regarded him as a reactionary and attacked him with unusual ardour. Stepan Nikiforovitch hardly bothered to object, although the subject interested him, but merely listened slyly. Ivan Ilyitch became agitated and in the heat of an imaginary dispute had recourse to the glass more often than he should. Whereupon Stepan Nikiforovitch took up the bottle and at once refilled the glass; this, for no reason at all, began to offend Ivan Ilyitch; more especially as Semyon Ivanovitch Shipulenko, whom he particuarly despised and feared for his cynicism and spitefulness, sat beside him in crafty silence, smiling more often than was necessary. "They appear to me taking me for a puppy!" the thought flashed through Ivan Ilyitch's mind.

"No, sir it's time, it was time long ago," he continued hotly. "We have talked too long and it is my opinion that the chief thing is to be humane, to be considerate towards one's inferiors, bearing in mind that they too are human beings. Idealism will save all, will be the universal panacea. . . ."

"He-he-he!" chuckled Semyon Ivanovitch from his corner.

"But why are you reproaching us?" finally objected Stepan Nikiforovitch with an amiable smile. "I must confess, Ivan Ilyitch, I have not yet been able to grasp what you are so kindly explaining to us. You are extolling idealism. That means love of mankind, doesn't it?"

"Yes, perhaps, granted, call it love of mankind. I . . ."

"Permit me, sir! As far as I can judge, that is not the whole point. There was always a need for love of mankind; the Reform Act does not stop at that. Various problems have arisen relating to the peasantry, the law, agriculture, the payment of compensation, morals and . . . there is no end to these problems, and all in all, united, they could cause, so to speak, great upheavals. That was what we feared, not merely some sort of idealism . . ."

"Yes, sir, the matter is rather more involved," remarked Semyon Ivanovitch.

"I understand very well, sir, and permit me to remark, Semyon Ivanovitch, that I am in no way ready to lag behind you in comprehending the depths of the problem," remarked Ivan Ilyitch caustically, "but, nevertheless, I'll venture to remark to you, Stepan Nikoforovitch as well, that you too have not understood me at all. . . ."

"Indeed, I have not."

"Yes, I expressly continue to uphold and I attempt to spread the idea that idealism, consideration, particularly towards one's inferiors, from official to clerk, clerk to house-servant, house-servant to peasant—idealism, I say, could serve as the keystone to the impending reforms and, on the whole, to the regeneration of every facet of life. Why? This is why: take the following syllogism: I am humane, consequently I am loved. They love me, then presumably they trust me. They put their trust in me, consequently they believe in me, therefore love me . . . that is, no, I mean to say, if they believe, they will also believe in reform, they will understand, so to speak, the very heart of the matter. They will, so to speak, morally embrace one another, and will settle everything fundamentally in a friendly spirit. What are you giggling about, Semyon Ivanovitch? Don't you follow?"

Stepan Nikiforovitch raised his brows in silence; he was astonished.

"It seems to me I've had a drop too much," remarked Semyon Ivanovitch maliciously, "and therefore I am a little slow on the uptake. A kind of mental blackout, sir."

Ivan Ilyitch winced.

"We shan't live up to it," Stepan Nikiforovitch suddenly pronounced on brief reflection.

"What's that? We shan't live up to it?" asked Ivan Ilyitch, surprised at this sudden and abrupt remark coming from Stepan Nikiforovitch.

"Just that: we shan't live up to it." Stepan Nikiforovitch evidently did not want to enlarge on his remark.

"Are you referring to 'new wine in old bottles'?" retorted Ivan Ilyitch, not without irony. "Oh no, sir, I am sure I can vouch for myself."

At that moment the clock struck half past eleven.

"Here we sit like birds in a desert," said Semyon Ivanovitch, preparing to rise. But Ivan Ilyitch forestalled him, immediately getting up and taking his sable hat from the mantelpiece. He looked hurt.

"What about it, Semyon Ivanovitch, will you think it over?" said Stepan Nikiforovitch, seeing his guests off.

"About the flat? I'll think it over. Yes, I'll think it over."

"And let me have your decision quickly?"

"Still talking business?" remarked Mr. Pralinski ingratiatingly, playing with his hat. It seemed to him as though he was being left out.

Stepan Nikiforovitch raised his eyebrows and remained silent, as a sign that he was not detaining his guests. Semyon Ivanovitch hurriedly took his leave.

"Ah . . . well . . . have it your own way! If you don't understand common courtesy," decided Mr. Pralinski, and with a particularly conscious air of independence he held out his hand to Stepan Nikiforovitch.

In the hall Ivan Ilyitch wrapped himself in his light and expensive fur coat, trying not to notice Semyon Ivanovitch's well-worn raccoon and they both began to descend the stairs.

"It seems our old man is offended," said Ivan Ilyitch to the silent Semyon Ivanovitch.

"Not in the least," answered the other calmly and coldly.

"Serf mentality!" thought Ivan Ilyitch.

When they had stepped down from the porch, Semyon Ivanovitch's sledge was brought up, with its plain grey nag.

"What the devil! What has Trifon done with my carriage?" cried Ivan Ilyitch, not seeing it.

He glanced hither and thither, but there was no carriage in sight. Stepan Nikiforovitch's servant had no idea of its whereabouts. They inquired of Varlam, Semyon Ivanovitch's coachman and were told Trifon had been around the whole time, the carriage as well, but now they were gone.

"Disgraceful!" put in Mr. Shipulenko. "Would you like a lift?"

"What wretches these people are!" cried Mr. Pralinski in a rage. "He asked me, the scoundrel, to let him off for a wedding somewhere here on the Petersburg Side, some sort of relative was to be married, the devil take her. I strictly forbade him to abandon his post. And now I'll bet he has gone there."

"That's actually what he has done," remarked Varlam. "He went there, but promised to be back in a jiffy; that is, to be back just in time."

"So that's it! I somehow felt this would happen. You wait; he'll catch it."

"You'd better have him thrashed twice at the police station; that will make him carry out your orders better," said Semyon Ivanovitch, drawing the fur cover of the sledge over himself.

"Please don't worry, Semyon Ivanovitch."

"So you don't want a lift home?"

"No, *merci*. A pleasant journey."

Semyon Ivanovitch drove away, while Ivan Ilyitch, feeling intensely irritated, set off walking along the wooden causeway.

.   .   .

"I'll show you now, you rogue! I'll walk home on purpose, just to make you realize, just to frighten you! You'll return and find out that the master has had to go off on foot . . . good-for-nothing!"

Never before had Ivan Ilyitch sworn so at anyone, but he was in an excessive rage, and on top of this his head was humming. He was unaccustomed to drink, which is why some five or six glasses of champagne quickly affected him. However, the night was enchanting. It was frosty but unusually silent and still. The sky was clear and full of stars. The full moon shed her pale silvery light over the earth. It was so lovely that having gone about fifty paces Ivan Ilyitch almost forgot his misfortune. He began feeling particularly contented. People in a state of intoxication are prone, in any case, to quick changes of mood. He even began to like the unsightly little wooden houses of the empty street.

"It's a good thing, after all, that I've had to walk," he thought. "It's a lesson to Trifon and a pleasure for me. I really ought to take walks more often. It won't do me any harm. I shall find a cab at once on the Bolshoi Prospect. What a lovely night! What odd little houses these are! Probably small folk live here—petty officials . . .

shopkeepers maybe. . . . That queer Stepan Nikiforovitch! What reactionaries they all are! Wet blankets. Wet
blankets, that's precisely what they are, *c'est le mot*. . . .
He is a clever man, though: he has this *bon sens*, a sober,
practical understanding of things. But in spite of this they
are real old men! They lack the—what could one call it?
Well, they lack something. . . . We shan't live up to it!
What did he mean by that? He even became thoughtful
when he said it. . . . Incidentally, he never understood
me at all. And how could he fail to understand? It was
more difficult not to understand than to understand. The
main thing is that I am convinced, convinced in my innermost heart. Idealism—love for mankind! To restore
man to himself. . . . To restore him his self-respect and
then—with such material in hand, set to work. It seems
clear enough! Yes, sir. Just permit me this, Your Excellency; take the following syllogism: we meet, for instance,
a petty clerk, a poor, downtrodden clerk. Well . . . and
who are you? The answer is: a clerk. Very well, a clerk;
more: what kind of clerk? The answer is: such and such
a clerk, he says. Are you working? Yes, I am working!
Do you want to be happy? I do. What do you need to
make you happy? This and that. Why? Because . . . And
here you have a man who understands me at once, the
man is mine, caught, so to speak, in my nets, and I can
do anything I like with him. That is, for his own good.
Disgraceful man, that Semyon Ivanovitch! and what a
nasty mug he has. To have Trifon whipped at the police
station—he said that deliberately. No, you're wrong,
whip him yourself; I am not in favour of whipping, I'll
put Trifon in his place with words, with a rebuke, that
will make him realize. As for using the whip, h'm . . .
that question is as yet unsolved, h'm. . . . Shall I look in
at Emerance's? Ugh! The devil take these damned pave-
ments!" he cried out as he tripped up on something. "And
this is the capital. This is supposed to be civilization! You
might break your leg. H'm. . . . I cannot stand that
Semyon Ivanovitch, a most unpleasant mug. He was sniggering at me when I talked about 'moral embrace'. Well,
and if they embrace, what's that got to do with you?
Don't worry, I won't embrace you; rather embrace a peasant. . . . If I come across a peasant, well, I'll talk to him.
However, I was drunk and perhaps did not express myself quite clearly. Even now, perhaps, I'm not expressing

myself properly. . . . H'm. . . . I'll never get drunk again. In the evening you talk freely and next day you regret it. I am not swaying on my feet, am I? Ah well, they are all scoundrels, just the same!"

·   ·   ·

So, at random, Ivan Ilyitch, conducted an incoherent discussion with himself as he continued to walk along the pavement. The fresh air was having its effect on him and had, you might say, sobered him. Five minutes later he would have calmed down and felt sleepy. But suddenly, within a couple of paces of the Bolshoi Prospect, he thought he heard the sound of music. He looked round. On the other side of the street, in a very ramshackle wooden house, one-storied but long, a party seemed to be in full swing; the fiddles hooted, the double-bass creaked and the flute sang shrilly to the tempo of a gay quadrille. A crowd had gathered below the windows, mostly of women in quilted coats and shawls over their heads; they were trying their best to see between the chinks of the shutters what was going on. Apparently all was gaiety within. The thump of the dancers' feet could be heard across the street. Ivan Ilyitch noticed a policeman near by and approached him.

"Whose house is it, old fellow?" he asked, throwing open his expensive fur-lined coat a little, just enough to let the policeman see the important decoration he was wearing.

"It is Pseldonymov's; he is a clerk, a registrar," answered the policeman, straightening himself as he caught a glimpse of the medal.

"Pseldonymov's! I never! What about him! Is he getting married?"

"He is, Your Honour, to the daughter of a Titular Councillor. Mlekopitayev, Titular Councillor he is . . . the one who used to work in the City Council. This house goes with the bride."

"So that is now Pseldonymov's and not Mlekopitayev's house?"

"It is Pseldonymov's, Your Honour. It used to be Mlekopitayev's before, but now it is Pseldonymov's."

"H'm. I am asking you this, my good man, because I

am his chief. I am the General in charge of the very office in which Pseldonymov works."

"Quite so, Your Excellency," said the policeman, finally drawing himself up to his full height, while Ivan Ilyitch appeared to grow pensive. He stood there, thinking. . . .

Yes, indeed, Pseldonymov was in his department, even in his own office; he did remember that. He was a very junior official with a salary of some ten roubles a month. As Mr. Pralinski had only very recently taken over his department, he did not remember all his underlings too well, but Pseldonymov he did remember, just because of his name. It had immediately caught his eye, so that he had been curious enough to look more closely at the owner of so strange a name. He now remembered a very young man with a long hooked nose and colourless bristly hair; he was anaemic and underfed, and wore an impossible uniform and impossible, even indecent, nether garments. He remembered that at the time the thought had crossed his mind: ought he not to give the poor devil a bonus of ten roubles for the New Year to rig himself out? But because the poor fellow wore an over-hypocritical expression on his face and because his appearance was extremely unattractive, even to the point of repulsion, the kind thought had somehow evaporated, so that in the end Pseldonymov had remained without bonus. He was all the more surprised when, a week earlier, this same Pseldonymov had approached him with the request to get married. Ivan Ilyitch remembered that at the time he had been too busy to take the matter up properly, so that the question of the marriage was decided casually and hurriedly. Nevertheless, he distinctly remembered that his bride was bringing Pseldonymov a wooden house and a clear four hundred roubles; this fact had astonished him at the time; he remembered he had even made a pun about the combination of the surnames Pseldonymov and Mlekopitayev. All this he clearly recalled.

As he remembered he became more and more lost in reflection. It is well known that a whole train of thought can pass through one's mind in a flash in the form of some kind of feeling, without being translated into human language, let alone into writing. However, we shall try to convey all the feelings of our hero and bring before the reader at least something of their substance, so to speak, everything that was most essential and most plausible in them. Because many of our feelings, put into ordinary words, would appear quite implausible, would they not? That is why they are never revealed, but remain locked up within us. Of course, Ivan Ilyitch's feelings and thoughts were a little incoherent. But then you know the reason for this.

. . . .

"Now, why," passed through his mind, "is it that we all indulge in talk, but when it comes to action nothing comes of it but a mockery? For instance, take that self-same Pseldonymov: he came back from the wedding ceremony a short while ago, all excited, full of hope, ready to taste joy . . . this is one of the most blissful days of his life. Now he is fussing around with his guests, giving a party—a modest, meagre party, but all the same a happy and genuine one. . . . What would happen if he realized that at this very moment I—I—his most exalted director, am standing by his house and listening to his music? Indeed, what would he do? But really! what would he do, if I suddenly took it into my head to go in? H'm . . . naturally, he would at first take fright, struck dumb with confusion. I should disturb him, spoil everything, perhaps . . . yes, this would happen, if any other General intruded, but not with me. . . . That's the point, with any other, but assuredly not with me. . . .

"Yes, Stepan Nikiforovitch! You refused to understand me a short while ago, but here you have a living example. Yes, sir. We are all shouting about humanitarianism, but are incapable of herosim, of a heroic act.

"What heroism? Why, this! Just consider: despite the way all members of society feel about each other, here I myself shall turn up at one o'clock in the morning at the wedding of my underling, a registrar, earning ten roubles a month; but this is madness, this would create havoc, wouldn't it turn things upside down, the last day of Pompeii, utter chaos? Nobody would understand it. Stepan Nikiforovitch wouldn't understand it to his dying day. Didn't he say: we shan't live up to it? But that refers to you old men, paralyzed and stagnating, whereas I shall! I'll transform the last day of Pompeii into the sweetest day for my clerk, and an eccentric act into a normal, patriarchal, lofty and moral gesture. How? Like this. Kindly listen:

"Well . . . let's suppose that I go in: they are astonished, break off dancing, draw back, overawed. Yes, but it is here that I reveal my quality: I march straight up to the frightened Pseldonymov and say with the most affectionate smile, in the simplest words: 'It's like this,' I say. I have been visiting His Excellency Stepan Nikiforovitch. I expect you know him, a neighbour of yours. . . . ." And then, in a slightly comic tone, I recount the incident with Trifon. From Trifon I pass on to the fact that I had to walk. . . . Well, then—that I heard music, asked of the policeman what the noise was and learned that you, my friend, had just got married. I'll go to my underling's house, think I; I'll see how my clerks enjoy themselves and how they get married. I don't suppose you'd show me the door, would you? Turn me out! What an expression in the mouth of one's underling. What the devil—turn me out indeed; I think he would more likely lose his head, rush to settle me in an arm-chair, tremble with delight, at first quite distracted.

"Now what could be simpler, more gracious than such an action? Why did I go in? That is another question. That is, so to speak, the moral aspect of the matter. That is the core of the matter.

"H'm . . . oh dear me, what was I thinking about? Oh yes.

"And naturally they will put me next to the most important guest, some sort of Titular Councillor or relative, a retired staff-captain with a red nose . . . how well Gogol described these characters! And, of course, I am introduced to the bride. I compliment her, I encourage the guests. I ask them to be at their ease, to go on enjoying themselves, continue dancing; I play the wit, I laugh—in short, I am amiable and charming. After all, I always am amiable and charming when I am pleased with myself. . . . H'm . . . the truth is, I'm still, it seems, not exactly drunk, but somewhat . . .

". . . Of course, being a gentleman I shall treat them as equals and on no account demand any special attention. . . . But from the moral point of view . . . this is another matter: they will understand and appreciate me properly . . . my action will revive in them a sense of their own dignity. . . . Well, I stay there, for half an

hour . . . maybe even a whole hour. It is obvious that I
leave just before supper. They will start bustling, start bak-
ing and roasting, they will bow low before me, but I shall
just drink to the health of the newly-weds and decline to
take supper. I shall say: 'I have some business to attend
to', and as soon as I say the word 'business' everyone's
face will assume a respectful and serious expression. In
this way I shall tactfully remind them that between myself and them there is a difference. . . . Like heaven and
earth. Not that I mean to suggest that, but one has got to
. . . even from the moral point of view it is necessary,
whatever one may say. Incidentally, I shall promptly
smile, perhaps even laugh a little, then everyone will feel
reassured. . . . I may joke once more with the bride, h'm.
. . . I can even do this: I can hint that I'll return again
exactly in nine months in the capacity of godfather. Ha-
ha! She is sure to give birth by that time. After all, these
people breed like rabbits. Well, they'll all break into laughter, the bride will blush; I shall kiss her forehead with
genuine affection, I may even give her my blessing and
. . . tomorrow in the office everyone will know of my
exploit. Tomorrow I shall be stern once more, exacting,
even obdurate, but at the same time they will all know
who I really am. They will know my soul, they will
know my innermost self: 'As a chief he is strict, but as a
man—he is a perfect angel!' That is how I shall win them
over; I shall catch them by some small action which you
will never imagine. They are sure to be won over; I am
their father, they my children. . . . Come now, Your
Excellency Stepan Nikiforovitch, go thou and do likewise. . . .

"Do you realize, do you understand that Pseldonymov
will tell his children about how the General himself
feasted and even drank at his wedding? And these children will tell their children, and they in their turn their
grandchildren, as their most treasured recollection, how
the high dignitary, the statesmen (I shall be all this by
then) had done them the honour, and so on, and so on.
I shall raise the spirits of the downtrodden. I shall restore
him to himself. . . . To think that he gets ten roubles
salary a month! . . . If I were to repeat this, or
something of the kind, five or ten times, I should achieve
universal popularity. My action will be imprinted upon

all hearts, and the devil only knows what may be the outcome of all this, of all this popularity, I mean . . ."

* * *

It is in this or a similar manner that Ivan Ilyitch talked the question over with himself. (Well, my friends, what can a man not say to himself, especially when he is in a somewhat odd state?) It took perhaps one minute for all these arguments to flash through his mind, and undoubtedly he would have contented himself with these reveries, and imagining Stepan Nikiforovitch brought to shame, would have quietly set off for home and retired to bed. And that would have been a good thing, too. But the trouble was that that particular moment was no ordinary one. As if on purpose at that same moment the self-satisfied faces of Stepan Nikiforovitch and Semyon Ivanovitch formed in his imagination.

"We shan't live up to it," Stepan Nikiforovitch had repeated with an artful glance.

"Ha-ha-ha!" chimed in Semyon Ivanovitch with his nastiest smile.

"Just let's see, whether we shan't live up to it," said Ivan Ilyitch so resolutely that his face actually flushed. He walked off the wooden pavement and directed his steps firmly across the road towards the house of his subordinate, the registrar Pseldonymov.

* * *

He was being led astray by his evil star. Passing briskly through the open gate, he kicked away contemptuously the long-haired mongrel which had long lost its voice and which, more from a sense of duty than ferocity, threw itself at his feet with a hoarse bark. He went along the path raised above the ground leading to the little covered porch which jutted out into the courtyard and, climbing three very rickety wooden steps, found himself in a tiny passage. Although a tallow candle end or some sort of nightlight was burning somewhere in the corner, Ivan Ilyitch was not saved from stepping with his left foot, clad in a galosh, into a dish of brawn which had been put out to set. Ivan Ilyitch bent down and, glancing round with curiosity, saw that there were two other similar dishes with aspic, as well as two moulds evidently full of blancmange. The squashed brawn rather disconcerted him and for one fleeting moment he considered the idea of slipping away immediately. But he decided this would be unworthy of him. Maintaining that nobody had seen him and that he would surely not be suspected, he hastily wiped his galosh to eradicate all traces, felt for the padded door, opened it, and found himself in a very small hall. One half of the hall was literally choked with various coats, fur jackets, cloaks, hoods, scarves and galoshes. In the other half the musicians had spread out: two violins, a flute and a double-bass, four men in all who, doubtless, had been picked up off the streets. They sat at a small plain wooden table and by the light of one tallow candle were scraping away with all their might at the last figure of the quadrille. Through the open door to the adjoining room the dancers could be seen in a haze of dust, tobacco smoke and kitchen vapours. An atmosphere of frantic merriment enveloped the whole company. Bursts of laughter, shouts and piercing shrieks were heard from the ladies. The men stamped like a squadron of horse. The commands of the Master of Ceremonies could be heard above the uproar, his collar unbuttoned and coat-tails flying. "Gentlemen, forward, *chain de dames*, balance!" and so on. Ivan Ilyitch, in a state of some excitement, flung off his fur coat and his galoshes and, with his sable hat in his hand, entered the room. By now he had given up reasoning.

For the first instant no one noticed him; they were all busy finishing the dance. Ivan Ilyitch stood as if stunned and could not make out a thing in this hotchpotch of ladies' dresses, men with cigarettes between their lips, which flitted by . . . one lady's pale-blue scarf floated by, catching his nose. She was followed by a medical student, his hair all dishevelled as if swept by a whirlwind, who rushing by him in frenzied rapture gave him a hard push. An officer of some regiment, who was as tall as a barge-pole, also flashed past him. Someone who flew past, stamping with the rest, cried out in an unnaturally shrill voice: 'Eh-eh-ekh Pseldonymushka!" Beneath Ivan Ilyitch's feet the floor felt sticky: they had evidently waxed it. There must have been about thirty guests in the room, which was quite sizeable.

However, in another minute the quadrille was over, and almost immediately everything happened exactly as Ivan Ilyitch had imagined as he stood dreaming on the wooden pavement. The guests and dancers had not time to regain their breath and wipe their faces when a murmur ran through the room, an extraordinary whisper. All eyes, all faces turned quickly in the direction of the guest who had just entered. Then followed a general shuffling back as everyone gently retreated. They tugged at the clothes of those who had not noticed the visitor to attract their attention; these now looked round and immediately fell back with the rest. Ivan Ilyitch still stood in the doorway without advancing, while between him and the guests the gap, strewn with countless sweet-papers, tickets and cigarette ends, widened. Suddenly a young man stepped timorously forward; he wore the uniform of a civil servant and had bristly, light-coloured hair and a hooked nose. He stepped forward all hunched up, and looked at the guest in exactly the same way as a dog looks at his master when summoned to receive a beating.

"How do you do, Pseldonymov? Recognize me?" said Ivan Ilyitch, and instantly felt that he had said it extremely awkwardly; he also felt that at that moment he was perhaps committing the most dreadful piece of stupidity.

"Your E-e-excellency!" muttered Pseldonymov.

"Well, now! I have dropped in quite by chance, my friend; dropped in on my way home, as you have probably guessed."

But Pseldonymov obviously had guessed nothing. He stood there, his eyes wide open, terribly perplexed.

"I suppose you won't turn me out . . . Glad or not glad, we have to welcome our guests . . ." continued Ivan Ilyitch, continuing to feel embarrassed to the point of weakness. He wanted to smile but no longer could; he felt that to tell his humorous story about Stepan Nikiforovitch and Trifon was becoming progressively less and less possible. Yet Pseldonymov, as if purposely, would not emerge from his stupor, and continued foolishly gazing at him. Ivan Ilyitch winced, he felt that it wanted only a moment more for the whole situation to become grotesque.

"Perhaps I have disturbed you . . . I'll be going!" he

muttered, and a certain nerve began to twitch in the right corner of his mouth. But Pseldonymov had recovered.

"Your Excellency, for goodness' sake . . . an honour . . ." he mumbled, bowing hastily. "Do us the honour of being seated . . ." and recovering still more he pointed with both hands to the sofa, from which the table had been pushed back to make room for the dancing.

Ivan Ilyitch felt easier in his mind and sank down on the sofa; immediately someone rushed forward to move the table towards it. He cast a glance round and noticed that he alone was seated, while all the others, even the ladies, were standing. This was a bad omen. But the moment had not yet come to reassure and encourage them. The guests were still backing away and before him Pseldonymov alone stood, hunched up, still comprehending nothing and no flicker of a smile on his face. It was an unpleasant situation; in fact, our hero at that moment experienced so much anguish that this invasion *à la* Haroun al Raschid, in accordance with his principles of behaviour towards inferiors, might really have been regarded as a heroic deed.

But suddenly another small bowing figure appeared beside Pseldonymov. To his unspeakable pleasure, not to say relief, Ivan Ilyitch at once recognized the chief clerk of his department, Akim Petrovitch Zubikov. He was not, of course, acquainted with him personally, but knew of him as a capable official and a man of few words. He rose immediately and held out his hand, his whole hand, not merely two fingers. Akim Petrovitch received it in the palms of both his with the greatest reverence. The General had triumphed; the situation was saved.

And, in fact, Pseldonymov had now become, so to speak, not the second but the third person. He could now tell the story directly to the head clerk, in an hour of necessity driven to accept him as a friend, even as a crony. While all Pseldonymov could do was to merely remain silent, trembling with awe. Consequently, the rules of propriety were observed. But it was essential to tell the story; Ivan Ilyitch felt this; he saw that all the guests expected something, that all the members of the household, crowded in the two doorways, were almost scrambling over each other to get a look and hear him speak. However, it was aggravating that the chief clerk, out of sheer stupidity, still would not sit down.

"What about you?" said Ivan Ilyitch, awkwardly pointing to the place on the sofa by his side.

"If you please, sir . . . I am fine here, sir. . . ." And Akim Petrovitch quickly sat down on a chair which was swiftly offered to him by Pseldonymov, who still persisted in standing.

"Just imagine . . ." began Ivan Ilyitch, addressing Akim Petrovitch only, at first a little shakily but then in a voice tinged with familiarity. He even drawled slightly, stressing each word, emphasizing syllables, mispronouncing letters; in short, he was conscious of his affectation, but was no longer able to regain control of himself: some external force directed him. At that moment he was painfully becoming aware of a great many things.

"Just think, I have come straight from Stepan Nikiforovitch—you may perhaps have heard of him, the Privy Councillor—the one—you know . . . on that commission . . ."

Akim Petrovitch respectfully bent his whole body forward, conveying that he could hardly not know of him.

"He is now your neighbour," continued Ivan Ilyitch, for a moment turning to Pseldonymov in order to be correct and polished; but he soon looked away as he saw at once by Pseldonymov's eyes that he was quite indifferent to what he heard.

"The old man, as you know, has dreamed all his life of buying a house. . . . Well, he has bought one. A most attractive house. Yes . . . and it also happened to be his birthday. He has never celebrated it before. You know, he even used to conceal the date from us, ignored it out of meanness." He chuckled. "And now he is so delighted with his new house that he invited me and Semyon Ivanovitch. Do you know him—Shipulenko?"

Akim Petrovitch bowed again. He bowed eagerly. Ivan Ilyitch felt a little more relieved. Otherwise it had already occurred to him that the head clerk might perhaps guess that he was at that moment a necessary prop for His Excellency. That would be the worst that could happen.

"Well, the three of us sat down together; he treated

us to champagne; we talked about business, one thing and another . . . about various subjects . . . we even had an argument . . . ha-ha!"

Akim Petrovitch raised his eyebrows respectfully.

"But that's not the point. At last I took my leave of him—he's an old man of regular habits, goes to bed early in his old age, you know. I left the house. My coachman, Trifon, was nowhere to be seen. I got worried and made inquiries: 'What has Trifon done with my carriage?' It transpired that, in the hope that I should be late, he'd gone off to the wedding of his sister . . . God knows who, somewhere here on the Petersburg Side, and, as it happens, had taken the carriage with him!"

Once again, for courtesy's sake, the General glanced at Pseldonymov. The latter bowed immediately, but not at all in the way one would bow to a General. "He's unsympathetic and hard," flashed through Ivan Ilyitch's mind.

"You don't say!" said Akim Petrovitch in great astonishment, and a low murmur of surprise ran through the assembled company.

"You can imagine my position . . ." Ivan Ilyitch glanced round the room. "There was nothing left for me to do but to begin walking. I thought that if I reached the Bolshoi Prospect I should be sure to find some Vanka or other. Ha! ha! ha!"

"Ha! ha! ha!" echoed Akim Petrovich respectfully. Once more a murmur, this time of amusement, ran through the assembly. At that moment the glass of one of the lamps hanging on the wall splintered and broke. Someone rushed forward to deal with it. Pseldonymov gave a start and stared sternly at the lamp, but the General paid no attention whatsoever to it, and once again all was calm.

"There I was, walking along—the night was so lovely, so still. Suddenly I heard music, the stamping of feet, the sound of dancing. I inquired of the policeman what was going on. I was told it was Pseldonymov's wedding. Well, my friend, you *are* throwing a party on a grand scale, aren't you? Ha! ha!" he said suddenly, addressing Pseldonymov again.

"Ha! ha! ha! Yes, sir . . ." echoed Akim Petrovitch; the guests stirred, but the most absurd part of it was that, even now, though he bowed again, Pseldonymov still did not smile. He looked as though he was made of wood. "He must be a fool," thought Ivan Ilyitch. "Why, the old ass should smile and everything would go off smoothly." His heart throbbed with impatience.

"I'll drop in on my subordinate, I thought. After all, he won't kick me out . . . welcome or unwelcome, guests must be received. Forgive me, my friend, if I have inconvenienced you in any way. I shall leave. . . . I only dropped in for a moment."

But by this time the assembled company was gradually becoming restless. Akim Petrovitch assumed a sweet expression: "As if Your Excellency could possibly disturb us!" The guests stirred and at last began to show signs of being at their ease. Nearly all the ladies were now seated, which was a good and positive sign. The boldest of them were fanning themselves with their handkerchiefs. One lady, in a worn velvet dress, said something in a deliberately loud voice. The officer to whom she had addressed herself wanted to reply in a loud voice too, but as no one else was speaking loudly thought better of it.

The men, mostly Government clerks with one or two students among them, exchanged glances, as if encouraging one another to relax, began coughing and actually moving a step or two in either direction. As a matter of fact, no one was particularly embarrassed; it was simply that they were awkward and regarded the man who had barged in on them and interrupted their merrymaking with something verging on hostility. The officer, ashamed of his feebleness, gradually began to sidle up to the table.

"Look, my friend, may I ask your name and patronymic?" Ivan Ilyitch inquired of Pseldonymov.

"Porfiry Petrov, Your Excellency," he answered, staring ahead as if he were on parade.

"Introduce me, Porfiry Petrov, to your young wife. . . . Take me to her. . . . I . . ."

And he made as if to rise. But Pseldonymov threw himself as fast as he could towards the drawing-room. As it happened, the bride was already standing at the door, but hearing her name mentioned she quickly hid herself. In a second Pseldonymov was leading her in by the hand. Everyone stepped aside, making way for them. Ivan Ilyitch rose solemnly and turned to her with his most amiable smile.

"I am very very pleased to meet you," he said with a slight bow, in the manner of a grand seigneur, "especially on such a day. . . ."

He gave a significant smile. The ladies became pleasantly agitated.

"*Charmée,*" said the lady in the velvet dress, under her breath.

The bride was worthy of Pseldonymov. She was a slim young lady of barely seventeen, with a very tiny pale face, and sharp little nose. Her small, swivelling eyes did not in the least suggest shyness, but, on the contrary, stared fixedly and indeed a shade maliciously. Clearly Pseldonymov had chosen her for her beauty. She wore a white muslin dress over a pink slip. Her neck was scraggy, her body like that of a pullet, with protruding bones. She found simply nothing to say in reply to the General's greeting.

"That's a sugar plum you have there," he continued in a low voice, as if addressing Pseldonymov alone, but purposely in such a way that the bride would hear him also. But again Pseldonymov had absolutely nothing to say, and this time he did not even make as if to bow. By his eyes it seemed to Ivan Ilyitch almost as though there were something cold and secret hidden within him, even something sly, peculiar and sinister. Yet at all costs he must provoke an emotional response from him. That, after all, was why he was here.

"Not a bad pair," he thought. "However . . ." and he turned again to the bride, who had seated herself on the sofa beside him. But he only got "no" or "yes" in answer to the one or two questions he addressed to her, and to tell the truth he could hardly even make these words out.

"If only she were slightly less embarrassed," he went on to reflect, "then I could start joking. As it is, I am in a hopeless fix." Akim Petrovitch also remained silent, as if on purpose; it was unpardonable, even though it was out of stupidity.

"Ladies and gentlemen, are you sure I have not interrupted your fun?" he was saying to the whole party. He even felt the palms of his hands sweating.

"No, sir . . . don't worry about that, Your Excellency, we shall begin again in a minute; just now . . . we are taking a breather, sir . . ." answered the officer.

The bride gave the officer a look of appreciation; he was still young and wore the uniform of some obscure regiment. Pseldonymov had remained standing on the same spot, his head inclined slightly forward, his hooked nose seeming to jut out farther than ever. He listened, with the look of a footman holding his master's coat, waiting for the end of the latter's leave-taking. Ivan Ilyitch thought up this comparison himself; he felt bewildered and awkward, dreadfully awkward, as if the ground were giving way under his feet, as though he had entered some place of no return, as if he were in the dark.

All at once the guests made way for a short, stocky, middle-aged woman; she was dressed simply—though smartened up—with a large shawl round her shoulders, pinned at the throat, and a cap, which she was obviously unaccustomed to wearing. In her hands she held a small round tray on which stood an untouched, uncorked bottle of champagne and two glasses—no more and no less. The bottle was evidently intended for only two of the guests.

The elderly woman approached the General.

"Accept us for what we are, Your Excellency," she said, bowing, "and since you have deigned to honour my son's wedding with your presence, out of the goodness of your heart drink a toast to the young couple. Don't offend us by refusing."

Ivan Ilyitch clutched at her as if at salvation. She was by no means an old woman, not more than forty-five or -six. But she had such a kind, rosy face, an open, round Russian face—she smiled so good-naturedly, bowed so simply, that Ivan Ilyitch was almost comforted and was again filled with hope.

"So you, you are the . . . mother of your son," he said, rising from the sofa.

"My mother, Your Excellency," mumbled Pseldonymov, stretching his long neck and again thrusting his nose forward.

"Ah, very pleased . . . ve-ry pleased to meet you."

"Your Excellency won't refuse . . ."

"Not at all. I'd be delighted."

The tray was placed on the table. Pseldonymov jumped forward to pour out the wine, and, still standing, Ivan Ilyitch took a glass.

"I am particularly glad of this opportunity to be

able—" he began—"to be able . . . to witness this . . .
In short, as your chief, I wish you, madam," he turned
to the bride, "and you, my friend Porfiry—I wish you all
prosperity and lifelong happiness."

With feeling, he emptied his glass; it was the seventh
that evening. Pseldonymov looked on seriously, even
gloomily. The General began to detest him with all his
might.

"And this blockhead here" (he glanced at the officer)
"is still hanging around her. Couldn't he give a cheer?
Then things would go like a house on fire. . . ."

"And you too, Akim Petrovitch, drink a glass and congratulate them," added the elderly woman, turning to
the head clerk. "You are his chief, he is your subordinate.
Look after my son's interests, my dear; I ask you as his
mother. And don't forget us in times to come, love, Akim
Petrovitch, kind man that you are."

"What excellent people these old Russian women are!"
thought Ivan Ilyitch. "She has put new life into us all.
I've always loved the common people. . . ."

Just then another tray was brought to the table. It
was carried by a maidservant in a rustling new cotton dress and crinoline. The tray was so large that she
could hardly hold it in her two hands. On it stood any
number of small dishes with apples, bonbons, glacé fruits,
jellied sweets, walnuts and many other things. Until then
the tray had been standing in the drawing-room as refreshments for all the guests in particular for the ladies.
But now it was brought in for the General alone.

"Don't refuse our refreshments, Your Excellency;
what's ours is yours," said the elderly woman, bowing.

"Indeed, no, it's a pleasure," said Ivan Ilyitch; and he
gladly took a walnut and cracked it between his fingers.
After all, had he not decided to be as agreeable as possible.

Meanwhile, the bride burst into giggles.

"What's the joke?" asked Ivan Ilyitch, smiling, pleased
to see any sign of animation.

"It is just Ivan Kostenkinytch who is making me laugh,"
she answered, lowering her eyes.

The General noticed a fair-haired, rather good-looking
young man, hiding himself on a chair behind the sofa,
whispering something to Mrs. Pseldonymov. The young
man half rose; he was evidently very young and shy.

"I was telling her about the 'Book of Dreams', a book which interprets dreams, Your Excellency," he murmured almost apologetically.

"What sort of Book of Dreams?" asked Ivan Ilyitch indulgently.

"It's a new Book of Dreams, sir, quite a reputable one! I told her, sir, that if one dreamt of Mr. Panayev, that meant spilling coffee on one's shirt-front, sir."

"There's Innocence for you!" thought Ivan Ilyitch, with a feeling of irritation. Though the young man blushed as he spoke, he was nevertheless very pleased with himself for telling this story about Mr. Panayev.

"Yes, yes, I have heard of it," responded His Excellency.

"No, but there's an even better one," put in another voice quite close to Ivan Ilyitch. "A new encyclopaedia is being published, Mr. Krayevski is to write for it, they say, and Alferaki will be a contributor too . . . and there will be scarrilous pieces . . ."

This was said by a young man who, far from being timid, was rather bold in manner. He wore a white waistcoat and gloves and held a hat in his hands. He did not dance and, since he was on the staff of the satirical magazine *The Firebrand,* he behaved with an air of superiority that he lent to the company in which he found that he was by chance an honoured guest. He and Pseldonymov were on intimate terms with each other, having a year previously lived together in some obscure *quartier.* However, he did not say no to a glass of vodka and had already retired repeatedly for that purpose to a secluded back room which everyone was acquainted with. The General took a violent dislike to him.

"And what is so funny, sir," joyfully put in the fair-haired young man who had told the story of the shirt-front, and whom the journalist in the white waistcoat consequently regarded with hate, "what is so funny, Your Excellency, is that the speaker assumed that Mr. Krayevski does not know how to spell and thinks that 'scurrilous' is written with an 'a'."

But the poor young man hardly had time to finish. He could see by the General's eyes that he had long been acquainted with this fact and that, as a result, he felt embarrassed. The young man felt abashed; he rapidly managed to make himself inconspicuous and remained dejected for the rest of the evening. However, the bold journalist on *The Firebrand* approached nearer, as though he intended to sit down somewhere in the vicinity of the General. This kind of familiarity seemed to Ivan Ilyitch a little presumptuous.

"Come, Porfiry, tell me—" began the General, for something to say, "I have always wanted to ask you personally—why are you called Pseldonymov and not Pseudonymov? Surely you ought to be called Pseudonymov?"

"I can give no precise reason, Your Excellency," answered Pseldonymov.

"Perhaps it was his father, sir, when he entered the service; there may have been some mistake in the papers, and he has remained Pseldonymov," suggested Akim Petrovitch. "It can happen."

"Un-doubt-ed-ly," took up the General eagerly, "un-doubt-ed-ly, you can judge for yourself—Pseudonymov has its origin in the literary word 'pseudonym', but Pseldonymov doesn't mean anything."

"Out of ignorance, sir," added Akim Petrovitch.

"How do you mean, out of ignorance?"

"Sometimes the common people change the letters out of ignorance, sir, and pronounce them in their own way. For example, they say 'nevalid' when they should say 'invalid', sir."

"Oh, yes, 'nevalid' . . . Ha! ha! ha! . . ."

"They also say 'mumber,' Your Excellency," blurted out the tall officer, who had long been itching to say something himself.

"What do you mean by 'mumber'?"

"'Mumber' instead of 'number', Your Excellency."

"Oh, yes, quite, 'mumber' instead of 'number' . . . Oh, yes, yes . . . ha! ha! ha!"

Ivan Ilyitch felt also obliged to give a little laugh for the officer's sake.

The officer adjusted his tie.

"And they also say 'bast'," broke in the contributor to *The Firebrand*. But His Excellency tried not to listen to him. After all, he was not obliged to laugh for everybody's sake.

"'Bast' instead of 'past'," badgered the journalist with obvious annoyance.

Ivan Ilyitch looked at him severely.

"What are you bothering him for?" whispered Pseldonymov to the journalist.

"What do you mean? I am just making conversation.
Can't a man even talk?" he was on the point of continuing the argument in a whisper, but instead he held his
tongue and left the room with concealed anger.

He went straight to the back room, which had been
made attractive to the gentlemen by a small table covered with a Yaroslav tablecloth on which were two sorts of
vodka, herrings, small pieces of bread with caviar, and a
bottle of extremely strong Russian sherry, which had been
placed there for their benefit at the beginning of the evening. Still fuming, he had just finished pouring himself a
glass of vodka when the medical student with the dishevelled hair suddenly rushed in. He was the chief dancer
and can-can expert at Pseldonymov's ball. In hasty greed
he attacked the decanter.

"They are going to begin directly," he muttered quickly
in a dictatorial manner. "Come and have a look. I shall
give them a solo performance standing on my head, and
after supper I shall risk a can-can. It will be quite the
thing for a wedding. A kind of friendly hint to Pseldonymov . . . she's a poppet that Cleopatra Semyonovna;
you can risk anything you like with her."

"He's a reactionary," answered the journalist gloomily, emptying his glass.

"Who is a reactionary?"

"That individual who was treated to jellied sweets.
He's a reactionary, I tell you."

"Go on with you," muttered the student, and hearing
the *ritornella* of the quadrille, rushed out of the room.

Left alone, the journalist poured himself another glass
to support his courage and independence, drained it
and helped himself to the savouries; never has His Excellency State Councillor Ivan Ilyitch had a more bitter
enemy or a more implacable avenger than the slighted
contributor to *The Firebrand*, especially after two glasses
of vodka. Alas! Ivan Ilyitch was totally unsuspecting. Furthermore, he was oblivious of another very important
fact, which was to affect the attitude of the guests towards His Excellency. The fact was that though he, for his
part, had given a proper and even detailed explanation of
his presence at the wedding of a subordinate, this expla-

nation had not really satisfied anybody and the guests continued to feel ill at ease. But suddenly, as if by magic, everything changed; they seemed reassured and ready to enjoy themselves, laugh, scream and dance, just as if the unexpected guest were not present in the room. The reason for this was that suddenly, by some mysterious means, a whispered rumour spread the news that the guest seemed "just a little bit . . . too merry on account of . . ." And although on the surface this rumour seemed dreadful slander, it became more and more evident that it was true and explained everything. The company relaxed. And it was at that very moment that the quadrille, the last before supper to which the medical student had hurried back, began.

Ivan Ilyitch was just on the point of addressing the bride again, trying this time to overcome her shyness with a joke, when the tall officer ran up and with a flourish sank down on one knee before her. She immediately jumped up from the sofa and flitted off with him to take her place in the quadrille. The officer did not even apologize, nor did she glance at the General on leaving him; it seemed as if she were glad to be rid of him.

"After all, she really was justified in doing that," thought Ivan Ilyitch; "they haven't learnt good manners. H'm! You, my friend, Porfiry, don't stand on ceremony," he said, addressing Pseldonymov. "You may have business to attend to . . . some arrangements . . . or something. . . . Please don't mind me . . ."

"Is he standing guard over me, or something?" he added to himself.

He found Pseldonymov unbearable, with his long neck and his stare fixed in his direction. In short, all this was not as it should be, not at all as it should be, but Ivan Ilyitch was still far from admitting this to himself.

*   *   *

The quadrille began.

"May I, Your Excellency . . . ?" asked Akim Petrovitch respectfully, holding the bottle in his hands, poised to fill His Excellency's glass.

"I . . . I really don't know whether . . ."

But Akim Petrovitch, his face beaming with reverence,

had already poured out the champagne. Filling one glass, he poured another for himself, furtively, stealthily, awkwardly grimacing, with one difference, that his own glass was about a finger's breadth less full, which seemed somehow more respectful. Seated beside his immediate superior, he felt like a woman in labour. What, in fact, was he to talk about? He felt in duty bound to entertain His Excellency, since he had the honour of his company. The champagne provided a way out of the situation, and besides, His Excellency welcomed the champagne—not for its own sake, for it was warm and quite horrible, but for the mere fact that it was being offered to him.

"The old fellow wants a drink himself," thought Ivan Ilyitch, "and doesn't dare to drink without me. I don't want to prevent him. And it would be odd for the bottle to stand neglected between us."

He took a gulp—at least it looked better than just sitting there like that.

"I am here, you see," he began, pausing and emphasizing each word, "you might say I just happen to be present, and, of course, some people might think it . . . so to speak . . . improper . . . for me to be present at such a gathering. . . ."

Akim Petrovitch remained silent and listened attentively with timid curiosity.

"But I hope you will understand why I am here. . . . After all, it's not just to drink wine that I've come, is it? . . . Ha! ha! ha!"

Akim Petrovitch wanted to laugh like His Excellency, but somehow broke off and once more failed to make a comforting response.

"I am here . . . as you might say, to sanction . . . to demonstrate, that is to say—the moral, that is to say, aim . . ." continued Ivan Ilyitch, getting annoyed with Akim Petrovitch for being so slow on the uptake; suddenly he fell silent too. He noticed that poor Akim Petrovitch was actually lowering his eyes in guilt. The General hastened, in some confusion, to take another gulp from his glass, while Akim Petrovitch, as if his whole salvation depended on it, seized the bottle and refilled the glass. "You certainly are dumb," thought Ivan Ilyitch, looking sternly at poor Akim Petrovitch. The latter, sensing the General's glance upon him, finally decided to remain silent and not to raise his eyes. Thus they remained seated opposite each other for about two minutes—two rather painful minutes for Akim Petrovitch.

Just one or two words about Akim Petrovitch. Timid as a rabbit, he was of the old school, brought up to accept subservience while at the same time being a kind and worthy man. He was a native of Petersburg, that is to say, his father and grandfather were born and bred in Petersburg and had worked there and never once been out of the town. Men like Akim Petrovitch belong to quite a peculiar class of Russian people. They know nothing about Russia, which really doesn't worry them. All their interests are centred in Petersburg, and particularly, in their place of employment. All their attention is directed to games of chance at kopeck points, to their place of work and their monthly salary. They do not know a single Russian custom nor a single Russian song except *Lutchinushka,* and this only thanks to the barrel organs. Incidentally, there exist two infallible signs by which one can immediately tell a true Russian from a Petersburg Russian: the first is that Petersburg Russians, without exception, never say *"The Petersburg Journal",* but always *"The Academic Journal".* The second and equally important sign is that they never say "breakfast", but always "Frühstück", with a special emphasis on the "Früh". By these well-established and distinctive signs one can recognize them anywhere. In brief, they represent a submissive type which has definitely emerged during the last thirty years. But Akim Petrovitch was no fool. Had the General asked him something within his sphere, he would have made an appropriate answer and kept up the conversation; but it would have been improper for a subordinate to reply to questions such as these, though Akim Petrovitch was dying to know something more definite about the immediate intentions of His Excellency. . . .

And meanwhile Ivan Ilyitch was sinking deeper and deeper into thought, into a state where his ideas revolved in a circle. Absent-mindedly, he took constant tiny sips at his glass. Eagerly Akim Petrovitch immediately replenished it. Both sat in silence. Ivan Ilyitch began to watch the dancing, and before long it held his attention. All at once, a certain occurrence rather surprised him.

The dances were indeed gay. Here they really danced out of the simplicity of their hearts, for the fun of it, letting themselves go. There were very few good dancers; but many awkward ones thumped so vigorously that one could have taken them for good dancers. The individual who distinguished himself above all was the officer; he particularly liked the part of the dance where he performed on his own, a kind of solo. He was amazingly supple; poised as straight as a ramrod, he would suddenly bend to one side, to such an extent that he seemed bound to topple over; but with the next step he suddenly bent to the opposite side, at the same acute angle to the floor. He maintained a solemn expression and danced in the conviction that everyone was admiring him. Another dancer fell asleep beside his partner during the second figure of the dance, having drunk too much beforehand, so that his partner had to dance alone. A young registrar, dancing energetically with the lady in the blue scarf, played the same trick in every figure, in fact, in all the five quadrilles danced that evening: that is, he fell a little behind his partner, seized the end of her scarf and, as he crossed over to his *vis-à-vis*, managed quickly to press a few dozen kisses to it. His lady floated before him, appearing quite oblivious to what was going on. The medical student actually did dance a solo on his head and provoked frenzied raptures, stamps of approval and screams of delight. In a word, the lack of inhibition was remarkable.

Ivan Ilyitch, who was also under the influence of the wine, at first began by smiling, but little by little a kind of bitter doubt began to seep into his soul: of course he very much approved of the easy manners and freedom; it is this that he has wanted, even in his heart willing this freedom when they had all hung back, but already it was getting out of control. For example, the lady in the well-worn blue velvet dress which looked as though it had been bought not second- but fourth-hand, had pinned it up so high during the sixth figure of the quadrille that it looked as if she wore trousers. This was that same Cleopatra Semyonovna, with whom one could risk anything, according to the expression used by her partner, the medical student. As for the medical student, no words could describe him: he was a wizard, a regular Fokine. How had it all happened? At one time they were diffident, and now they were rapidly becoming free and easy. Unimportant as this transition seemed, it was somehow strange and threatening; just as if they had completely forgotten

the existence of Ivan Ilyitch. Naturally, he was the first
to burst out laughing and even risked clapping. Akim
Petrovitch politely giggled in chorus with him, with obvious pleasure and no suspicion that His Excellency was
already beginning to nurture yet another viper in his
bosom.

"You dance famously, young man," Ivan Ilyitch felt
obliged to say to the student, who passed by at the end
of the quadrille.

The student turned sharply to him, made some sort of
grimace and rudely drawing up his face close to His Excellency's crowed like a cock at the top of his voice. This
was altogether too much. Ivan Ilyitch rose from the table. In spite of this, a volley of uncontrollable laughter
burst out, for the cock-crow sounded amazingly real, and
the grimace was quite unexpected. Ivan Ilyitch was still
standing perplexed, when suddenly Pseldonymov himself appeared and, bowing, invited him to supper. His
mother followed.

"Your Excellency, sir," she said, bowing, "do us the
honour—don't scorn our poverty . . ."

"I . . . I—really don't know . . ." began Ivan
Ilyitch. "I did not come for this. . . . I was just thinking
of going."

In fact, he was already holding his fur hat in his hands.
Moreover, at this very instant, he promised himself he
would go immediately, at all costs, and not stay for anything—but . . . he stayed.

A minute later he led the procession to the supper table. Pseldonymov and his mother walked before him,
clearing the way. They seated him in the place of honour
and again an unopened bottle of champagne appeared
before him. To begin with there was herring and vodka.
He stretched out his hand, filled himself a huge wineglass
of vodka and drained it. He never had before touched
vodka. He felt as if he were rolling downhill, flying, flying so that he must hold on, cling to something, but this
was no longer possible.

      •   •   •

Really, his position was becoming more and more of
an anomaly. Moreover, it seemed as though Fate was mocking at him. God knows what had happened to him in less

than an hour. On entering he had, so to speak, stretched
out his arms to embrace the whole of mankind and all
his subordinates; and here scarcely an hour had gone by
and he was painfully realizing only too clearly that he
hated Pseldonymov and cursed him, his wife and his wedding. As if that were not enough, he could see from Pseldonymov's face, by his eyes alone, that the latter hated
him too; he was staring at him almost saying: "Damn
you. What the hell have you tagged on to me for?" He
had long ago read all this in Pseldonymov's eyes.

Of course, even now, Ivan Ilyitch, as he sat down at
table, would sooner have had his hand cut off than
admit frankly, even to himself let alone out loud, that
all this was in fact so. That moment had not yet come; he
still retained some moral equilibrium, though something
was steadily gnawing at his heart. He felt his heart crying out for freedom, space to breathe and quietude. After
all, Ivan Ilyitch was too good a man, really!

Did he not know full well that he ought to have left
long ago; not merely left, but more, saved himself; that
all this had suddenly turned out very different from what
he had expected, from the way he had imagined things
when he was walking along the raised wooden pavement
earlier.

What did I come here for? Did I come here to eat and
drink? he asked himself as he helped himself to some herrings. He even felt certain misgivings. He felt a momentary sense of irony at his own actions; he began to ask
himself why he had entered. But how could he leave?
Simply to leave without seeing it through was impossible.
What will people say? They'll say I frequent the wrong
places. Indeed, that's what it'll look like if I don't see
things through to the end. What will they say tomorrow,
for instance (since the news is sure to spread)? What will
Stepan Nikiforovitch and Semyon Ivanovitch say, what
will they say at the office, at Shembel's, at Shubin's? No,
I must leave in such a way that they will all understand
why I came; I must reveal my moral aim. . . . Yet that
sublime moment declined to present itself. "They don't
even respect me," he continued. "What are they laughing about? They are so free and easy, as if they lack any
kind of feeling. . . . Yes, I have long suspected the
whole younger generation of lacking sensitivity. I must
stay, at all costs! . . . They have been dancing, but

now at table they will all be gathered together. . . . I shall talk about current affairs, reforms, the greatness of Russia . . . I may yet succeed in interesting them. Yes! Perhaps nothing is yet lost. . . . Perhaps this is how it always happens in real life. If only I knew how to set about winning them over. What sort of approach shall I make? I feel completely lost. . . . And what do they want, what are they asking for? I can see they are sniggering over there. Good Lord, surely not about me! But what is it I want? Why am I here, why don't I go away, what do I hope to accomplish? . . . He thought all this, and a kind of shame, a kind of deep, unbearable shame, rent his heart.

* * *

From then on, events took their own course.

Two minutes after he had sat down at table, he was struck by a terrible realization. He suddenly felt horribly drunk, not as he had been before, but totally, absolutely drunk. The cause of it was the glass of vodka which he had drained immediately after the champagne and which had taken effect at once. He felt, sensed with his whole being, that he was completely helpless. Of course, he appeared to be far more confident, but his consciousness did not forsake him and cried out: "It is wrong, very wrong, and also utterly revolting." Of course, the rambling, drunken thoughts could not concentrate on any one point; at once, almost tangibly, two opposing selves appeared within him. In the one self was confidence, the desire to gain a victory, surmount all obstacles, and the desperate conviction that he could reach his goal. The other made itself felt by anguish, by a kind of bleeding of the heart. "What will they say? How will all this end? What will happen tomorrow—Tomorrow . . . ?"

Earlier in the evening he had had a vague feeling that he had enemies among the guests. "That was because I was drunk when I came in," he thought, in agonizing doubt. To his increasing horror he now became convinced, through unmistakable signs, that some of those at table really were his enemies and that this could no longer be doubted.

"And why? What is it all for?" he mused.

At this table all the guests were seated, thirty of them;

among them some had finally passed out. The others conducted themselves with a somewhat negligent, flaunting independence, shouting at the tops of their voices, prematurely proposing toasts, shooting bread pellets at the ladies. One very ill-favoured individual in a dirty frock-coat fell off his chair as soon as he had seated himself at table and remained on the floor right to the end of the supper. Another was determined to climb on the table to propose a toast, and it was only the officer who restrained his ill-timed enthusiasm by seizing him by his coat-tails. The supper was quite commonplace, although a chef had been engaged, the serf of some general or other. There was brawn, tongue with potatoes, meat rissoles with green peas, and finally, blancmange for dessert. There was beer, vodka and sherry to drink. The bottle of champagne stood before the General alone, which obliged him to help himself and also Akim Petrovitch, who at supper did not dare to act on his own initiative. The other guests were meant to drink the toasts in bitters, or whatever they could get hold of. The table itself was made up of a number of smaller ones and included even a card table. They were covered with several tablecloths, among them a coloured Yaroslav one. Men and women were seated alternately at table. Pseldonymov's mother would not sit down; she bustled about and attended to the guests. And now a spiteful-looking female appeared who had not been there before; she wore a russet silk dress and the highest possible cap and had her face bandaged up as though she had toothache. This was the bride's mother, who had finally consented to come in to supper from the back room. Until then she had not left her room because of her irreconcilable hostility towards Pseldonymov's mother; but of this we shall speak later. The lady gave a malicious, almost scornful look at the General and evidently did not want to be introduced to him. Ivan Ilyitch was highly suspicious of her. But others were suspect besides, and instilled unwitting apprehension and uneasiness. It seemed almost as though they were involved in some conspiracy together directed against Ivan Ilyitch. At least, that is how it seemed to him, and as supper progressed he became more and more convinced of this. For example, there was an evil-looking gentleman with a small beard, some kind of self-styled artist; he actually looked several times at Ivan Ilyitch and then turned to whisper in the ear of his neighbour. Another, a student, admittedly completely drunk, judging by certain signs, was nevertheless suspect. There was little hope for the medical student either; even the officer was not entirely to be relied on. But it was the journalist from *The Firebrand* who was generating a peculiar and obvious hatred: he had a manner of lounging in his chair, with an extremely proud and arrogant air, sniffing with such self-assurance. And though the other guests paid no attention to the journalist (who had merely written four lines of verse for *The Firebrand*, which made him a liberal) and evidently positively disliked him, still when a small bread pellet suddenly fell beside Ivan Ilyitch, obviously intended for him, he was ready to swear that the culprit was none other than the contributor to *The Firebrand*.

Naturally, all this affected him for the worse.

He made yet another particularly unpleasant observation. Ivan Ilyitch was quite convinced that he was beginning to pronounce his words with difficulty and indistinctly; he wanted to say a great deal, but his tongue would not move; also his memory would suddenly have lapses and, worse still, he would suddenly burst out laughing for no reason at all. This condition soon passed after Ivan Ilyitch had helped himself to a glass of champagne without wanting it particularly, but suddenly gulping it down without further thought. As a result, he almost burst into tears. He felt he was succumbing to a most peculiar sentimentality. He began to love everyone again, even Pseldonymov, even the contributor to *The Firebrand*. He suddenly wanted to embrace them all, to forget everything and make peace with them. More, he wanted quite freely to tell them everything, everything, everything; that is, what a good and admirable fellow he was, what splendid abilities he possessed, what service he would be to his country, how well he could amuse the ladies, and, above all, how progressive he was, in what an idealistic manner he was prepared to condescend to all, even to the very lowest; and finally, to conclude, he would frankly describe all the motives that had induced him, an uninvited guest, to turn up at Pseldonymov's, drink two bottles of his champagne and give him the pleasure of his company.

"The truth above all, sacred truth and frankness; I'll

win them with frankness. They will believe me, I can see it so clearly; they look at me with positive hostility, but when I reveal everything I'll win them over, there's no doubt of it. They will fill up their glasses and drink my health. The officer, I am sure, will break his glass on his spur. They may even shout 'Hurrah!' Even if they should decide to toss me up in the Hussar manner, I would not resist that either; it might even be a good thing. I shall kiss the bride on the forehead; she is a sweet thing. Akim Petrovitch also is a very nice man. Pseldonymov, of course, will improve in time. He lacks the polish of the *beau monde.* . . . And though the whole of this new generation lacks that certain sensitivity, yet I shall tell them about Russia's standing among the Great Powers. I will also mention the peasant question, yes, and . . . they will all love me and I'll emerge crowned in glory. . . ."

These fantasies, naturally, were very pleasant; the only unpleasant thing amidst all these rosy hopes was that Ivan Ilyitch suddenly discovered in himself one more unexpected talent, that is, for spitting. At any rate, spittle began suddenly to spurt from his lips, quite involuntarily. He noticed it first of all on Akim Petrovitch, whose cheek he had bespattered and who, out of respect, sat there without daring to wipe it off. Ivan Ilyitch took a napkin and suddenly wiped it off himself. Yet at once this action seemed to him so absurd, so remote from all reason, that he fell silent and began to wonder. Akim Petrovitch, though he had had some drink, sat there just as if he had been scalded. Ivan Ilyitch now realized that he had been talking to him for almost a quarter of an hour on a most interesting subject, but Akim Petrovitch, as he listened to him, appeared not only embarrassed but even afraid of something. Also Pseldonymov, who was sitting one chair away from him, craned his long neck, and with his head on one side, seemed to be listening with a most unpleasant expression in his face. It was as if he was keeping an eye on him. . . . Glancing around at the guests he noticed that many were looking straight at him and roaring with laughter. But strangest of all, this did not embarrass him in the least; on the contrary, he sipped at his glass once more and began to talk so that everyone could hear.

"As I have just said to Akim Petrovitch," he began as loudly as possible, "ladies and gentlemen, Russia . . . particularly Russia . . . in one word, you understand what I want to s-say . . . Russia is experiencing, it is my deepest conviction, a mood of idealism . . ."

"Idealism!" echoed from the other end of the table.

"Hu-hu!"

"Tu-tu!"

Ivan Ilyitch was cut short. Pseldonymov rose from his chair and began to look round. Who was it who was shouting? Akim Petrovitch surreptitiously shook his head, as if reproving the guests. Ivan Ilyitch saw this clearly, but suffered in silence.

"Idealism," he continued stubbornly—"not long ago . . . just so . . . not long ago I said to Stepan Nikiforovitch . . . yes . . . that—that the rebirth, so to speak, of things . . ."

"Your Excellency!" somebody cried out from the other end of the table.

"Sir?" answered Ivan Ilyitch, interrupted, trying to make out who was addressing him.

"Nothing at all, Your Excellency, I got carried away. Continue! Co-on-tin-ue!" the same voice was heard again.

Ivan Ilyitch winced.

"The rebirth, so to speak, of these very things . . ."

"Your Excellency," shouted the same voice.

"What do you want?"

"How do you do!"

This time Ivan Ilyitch could stand it no longer. He broke off his speech and turned to the offender. He was still quite a young student, completely drunk, who looked exceedingly suspect. For a long time he had been shouting, and even broken a glass and two plates, asserting that this was the done thing at weddings. At the moment when Ivan Ilyitch turned to him, the officer had set about dealing severely with the rowdy.

"What's wrong; what are you yelling for? You should be sent out, that would be best."

"It's not about you, Your Excellency, not about you. Carry on!" cried the tipsy student, sprawling in his chair. "Carry on, I am listening and I am very pleased by you. It is praiseworthy, most praiseworthy."

"A drunken schoolboy!" Pseldonymov suggested in a whisper.

"I see he is drunk, but . . ."

"I have just told a funny story, Your Excellency," began the officer, "about a lieutenant of our regiment who talked to his superiors in just the same way; and the young man here is imitating him. He added to every word his superior said his own 'Praiseworthy' . . . For this he got discharged from the service ten years ago."

"What—what-t lieutenant was it?"

"One in our regiment, Your Excellency. He was mad about praising. At first he was cautioned, then later he was put under arrest. . . . His chief reproved him in a fatherly manner; but he only said 'praiseworthy'. It was strange, a fine sort of fellow he was—over six foot tall. They thought of having him tried, but then realized that he was insane."

"So he's a schoolboy. Well, one need not be too strict about schoolboy tricks. For my part, I am ready to forgive . . ."

"There was a medical examination, Your Excellency."

"How? Did they dissect him?"

"Good gracious, no; he was quite alive, sir."

A loud and almost universal burst of laughter came from the guests, who had at first tried to behave in a respectable manner. Ivan Ilyitch was embarrassed.

"Gentlemen, gentlemen," he cried, for the first time with hardly a stutter; "I am quite capable of grasping that one cannot dissect a living man. . . . I assumed that owing to his being insane he was no longer alive . . . that is to say, he was dead. . . . I mean to say . . . that you do not love me . . . whereas I love all of you; yes, I love Por . . . Porfiry. . . . I am lowering myself by speaking like this. . . ."

At that moment a huge gob of spittle flew out of Ivan Ilyitch's mouth and landed on the tablecloth with a splash, on a most conspicuous spot. Pseldonymov rushed to wipe it off with a napkin. This last misfortune finally crushed him.

"Gentlemen, this is just too much!" he cried out in despair.

"The man is tight, Your Excellency," Porfiry was on the point of putting in.

"Porfiry! I see that you . . . all . . . yes! I am saying that I hope . . . yes, I invite you all to say in what way I have lowered myself?" Ivan Ilyitch was on the verge of tears.

"Your Excellency, for goodness' sake, sir!"

"Porfiry, I appeal to you . . . Tell me, if I came . . . yes, yes, to the wedding, I had a purpose. I set out to raise your moral standards. . . . I wanted you to feel . . . I am appealing to you all: have I lowered myself very much in your eyes or have I not?"

Silence persisted. That was just it—dead silence, and after such a direct question, too! "Well, what would it cost them to say something at least?" flashed through His Excellency's mind. But the guests merely exchanged glances. Akim Petrovitch sat there more dead than alive, while Pseldonymov, struck dumb with fear, repeated the terrible question that had long before presented itself to him, under his breath: "And what will be the consequence of all this tomorrow?"

All of a sudden the contributor to *The Firebrand,* now completely drunk, who until then had been sitting in sullen silence, turned to Ivan Ilyitch and with flashing eyes began to answer on behalf of the whole company:

"Yes, sir!" he shouted in a thundering voice, "yes, sir, you have lowered yourself, yes, you are a reactionary . . . re-act-ionary!"

"Young man, come to your senses! Who d'you think you're talking to?" cried Ivan Ilyitch furiously, jumping up again from his chair.

"You; and furthermore, I am not 'young man' . . . you have come here to show off and to play for popularity."

"Pseldonymov, what is this?" cried out Ivan Ilyitch.

However, Pseldonymov had jumped up in such terror that he was rooted to the ground and was completely at a loss. The guests seated at the table had been struck dumb too. The artist and the student were applauding and shouting "Hear, hear!"

The journalist continued to shout with unrestrained fury:

"Yes, you came here to boast of your ideals. You have disrupted everyone's enjoyment. You have been drinking champagne and never considered that it was too expensive for a Government clerk on a salary of ten roubles a month. And I suspect that you are one of those chiefs who have a taste for the young wives of their employees. Not only that, but I am thoroughly convinced that you uphold the payment of compensation. . . . Yes, yes, yes!"

"Pseldonymov! Pseldonymov!" cried Ivan Ilyitch, stretching his arms towards him. He felt that each word of the journalist was a fresh dagger in his heart.

"At once, Your Excellency, please, don't worry," Pseldonymov cried hysterically, running up to the journalist, seizing him by the collar and dragging him away from the table. No one would have expected such a display of physical strength from the feeble Pseldonymov. But the journalist was very drunk, while Pseldonymov was completely sober. He punched him several times in the back and pushed him out of the door.

"You are all scoundrels," shouted the journalist. "I'll show you up in *The Firebrand* tomorrow. . . ."

Everyone rose.

"Your Excellency, Your Excellency," cried Pseldonymov, his mother and several of the guests, crowding round the General, "Your Excellency, calm yourself."

"No, no," cried the General, "I am destroyed. . . . I came . . . I wanted, so to speak, to give my blessing. . . . And this, for this . . ."

He sank on to a chair as if he were fainting, put both hands on the table and dropped his head on to them, straight into a plate of blancmange. No need to describe the general horror. After a minute he got up, evidently wanting to go away, staggered, tripped over the leg of a chair, fell on the floor with full force and began to snore. . . .

This kind of thing happens to people not accustomed to drink when by chance they do get drunk. Down to the last detail, up to the last moment they retain consciousness and then suddenly they black out completely. Ivan Ilyitch lay unconscious on the floor. Pseldonymov seized himself by the hair and stood rooted to the ground. The guests were breaking up hurriedly, each commenting on the occurrence in his own way. It was already nearly three o'clock in the morning.

· · ·

What complicated matters was that to Pseldonymov the affair was far worse than one could imagine, taking into account even the unpleasantness of the present situation. While Ivan Ilyitch is lying on the floor with Pseldonymov standing beside him tearing his hair in despair, let us digress to put in a few words of explanation about Porfiry Petrovitch Pseldonymov himself.

It was not more than a month before his wedding that he was on the verge of total and irrevocable disaster. He came from the provinces, where his father had held some post or other and had died while he was awaiting trial for some offence. When, five months before his wedding, Pseldonymov, who in Petersburg had been facing disaster for a whole year, obtained his appointment at ten roubles salary, he felt restored in body and soul, but he was soon humbled once again by circumstances. Of the Pseldonymov family there remained only two people in the whole world, himself and his mother, who had left her native place in the provinces after her husband's death. Mother and son lived in cold and hunger. There were days when Pseldonymov himself went with a mug to the Fontanka to get a drink of water. Having obtained a job, he and his mother managed to settle somewhere in a tenement. She set about washing linen for other people, while in four months he scraped together enough money to acquire a pair of boots and an old coat. And what misery he had to undergo in his office: his superiors would come up to him, asking when he had last had a bath. Rumour had it that whole nests of bugs had settled under the collar of his uniform. But Pseldonymov had a strong character. In appearance he was gentle and quiet; his education had been very sketchy, he was hardly ever heard to talk. I simply don't know whether he ever thought, ever made plans, evolved systems, ever indulged in day-dreaming at all. But instead of this he had developed an instinctive, determined unconscious resolve to work his way out of his unfortunate circumstances. He was as tenacious as an ant; if you destroy an ants' nest, they start building it again; destroy it a second time and they will start once more, and so on, without respite. He was an orderly and domesticated creature. It was written all over his face that he would make his way, build his nest and perhaps even put something by for a rainy day. His mother was the only person in the whole wide world who loved him, and she loved him passionately. She was strong, indefatigable, a hard-working woman, and at the same time, kind. They would have continued to live in their tenement for five or six years perhaps, until things had changed, had they not come across the retired Titular Councillor

Mlekopitayev. The latter was a former treasurer in a Government office of their native district, who had since established himself and settled with his family in Petersburg. He knew Pseldonymov, and had been in some way indebted to his father. He had not much money put by, of course, but he had some; how much, in fact, nobody knew, neither his wife, his eldest daughter, nor his relations. He had two daughters, and as he was pig-headed, a drunkard, a petty tyrant and, to crown it all, an invalid, he suddenly took it into his head to marry off one of his daughters to Pseldonymov: "I know him," he said, "his father was a good man, and the son will be a good man too." Whatever Mlekopitayev wanted to do, he did; and once he said a thing was to happen, it did happen. He was a singularly pig-headed man. He spent most of the time sitting in an arm-chair, as he had lost the use of his legs through some kind of illness, which, however, did not prevent him from drinking vodka. He spent whole days drinking and abusing people. He was a vicious man, and sure to be tormenting someone all the time. For this purpose he kept several distant relatives in the house; his sister, a sick and cantankerous woman, two of his wife's sisters, both bad-tempered and with long tongues; as well as his old aunt, who had managed to break a rib. Besides them, he kept another sponger, a Russified German woman, because of her talent for telling stories out of the *Arabian Nights*. His only pleasure was to nag these unfortunate hangers-on, to swear at them every minute, like a trooper, though none of them, not even his wife, who had been born with a chronic toothache, ever dared utter a word. He caused them to quarrel among themselves, invented and provoked gossip and dissensions, and then broke out into laughter, delighted to see them on the verge of coming to blows. He was very glad when his eldest daughter, who had lived in poverty for ten years with her officer husband, finally, when she was widowed, came to live in his house with her three small, sickly children. He could not bear her children, but because the number of victims on whom he could make his daily experiments increased with their arrival, the old man was very pleased. This whole crew of spiteful women and sick children were squeezed, together with their torturer, into a wooden house on the Petersburg Side. They never had enough food, because the old man was miserly and only gave money by kopecks, though he never grudged it for his vodka; they never had enough sleep because the old man suffered from insomnia and demanded to be amused. In short—all of them lived in misery and cursed their fate. It was at that time that Mlekopitayev noticed Pseldonymov. He was impressed by his long nose and his submissive manner. His sickly, plain youngest daughter was then just seventeen. Though she had been to a German school at one time, she had never learned much more than the alphabet. After that she continued to grow up, consumptive and anaemic, under the blows of her crippled and drunken father, in a turmoil of domestic gossip, spying and slander. She had no friends, and she was devoid of common sense. For a long time she had longed to get married. In the company of strangers she was silent but at home with her mother and the spongers she was spiteful, and sharp as a gimlet. She particularly liked to slap and pinch her sister's children, telling on them for taking sugar and bread, which caused eternal and ceaseless rows between her and her elder sister. The old man himself offered her hand to Pseldonymov. Poverty-stricken though the latter was, he still asked for a little time to reflect. He and his mother considered the proposal for quite a while. However, the house was to be transferred in the bride's name, and though it was wooden, one-storied and drab, all the same it was worth something. On top of that the old man was giving four hundred roubles—it was not so easy to save so much. "Do you know why I am taking a man into the house?" yelled the drunken tyrant. "First because all of you are women and I'm sick and tired of women. I want him to be under my thumb too, because I am his benefactor. Secondly, I'm taking him in because it's against your will and you are furious. I'll do it to spite you, see! What I say, I do. And you, Porfiry, thrash her when she's your wife; ever since she was born she has nurtured seven devils within her. Drive them all out. I'll have a stick ready."

Pseldonymov kept quiet, but he had already made up his mind. He and his mother were already taken into the house before the wedding; they were washed, clothed, shod and given money for the wedding. The old man was favouring them, perhaps simply because the whole family bore them malice. He even took a liking to Pseldonymov's mother, so that he controlled himself and did not nag her. Incidentally, while there was yet a week to go before the wedding, he made Pseldonymov himself dance the Kazatchek for him. "That will do, I wanted to see that you're not forgetting your place," he said at the end of the dance. As for wedding expenses, he gave the bare amount of money needed and then invited all his relatives and acquaintances. On Pseldonymov's side the only people asked were the contributor to *The Firebrand* and Akim Petrovitch, the guest of honour. Pseldonymov knew very well that his bride loathed him and would far rather have married an officer. But he bore it all, in accordance with the arrangements he and his mother had made. Throughout the day of the wedding, and the whole evening, the old man swore horribly as he sat drinking. Because of the wedding, the whole family had taken refuge in the back rooms and were so crowded together they were almost suffocating. The front rooms were intended for dancing and supper. At last, when, at eleven o'clock, the old man fell asleep, dead drunk, the bride's mother, who had been snarling at Pseldonymov's mother on that day more than ever, decided to change her tune and turn up at the party. The appearance of Ivan Ilyitch had upset everything. Mrs. Mlekopitayev was disconcerted; she was offended and began to scold them for not having warned her beforehand that the General himself was invited. She was assured that he had come of his own accord, uninvited, but she was so stupid that she would not believe this.

When champagne was required, all Pseldonymov's mother could find was just one rouble. Pseldonymov himself had not a kopeck. They were compelled to humble themselves before the angry Mrs. Mlekopitayev and beg money first for one bottle of champagne, then for another. They pointed out future business connections, the career to come, they did their utmost to persuade her. At last she consented to part with her money, but in return she nagged at Pseldonymov with such bitterness that he kept running into the chamber and throwing himself on the bridal couch, intended for heavenly delights, silently tearing his hair and trembling all over with impotent rage. Ivan Ilyitch had no idea of the price of the two bottles of champagne he had drunk that evening. How great was the terror of Pseldonymov, his anguish and even despair, when the business of Ivan Ilyitch took such an unexpected turn: he could anticipate the worries, the piercing shrieks and tears from the capricious bride, which would perhaps continue throughout the whole night, with reproaches from the bride's stupid relations. As it was, his head was already aching and he felt dazed. And here was Ivan Ilyitch requiring assistance; at three o'clock in the morning a doctor had to be found and a carriage to take him home; it had to be a carriage, since it would be impossible to dispatch such a personage, in such a state, to his home in a simple cab or sledge. But where was he to find the money even so much as for a carriage? Mrs. Mlekopitayev, enraged that the General had not spoken two words to her and had not even looked at her during the whole of supper, declared that she had not a kopeck. Perhaps she really had not got a kopeck to her name. But where was he to get the money? What was he to do? Yes, he had good reason to tear his hair.

Meanwhile, Ivan Ilyitch was carried to a little leather sofa that stood there ready in the dining-room. While the tables were cleared and sorted out, Pseldonymov rushed hither and thither to raise some money; he even tried to borrow from the servants, but he found that nobody had any. He dared to trouble Akim Petrovitch, who had stayed longer than the others. But kind as he was, at the sound of the word "money" he became so bewildered and indeed frightened that he talked a lot of surprising nonsense: "At any other time, I would with pleasure . . ." he mumbled, "but now . . . really you must excuse me . . ." And picking up his hat, he quickly fled from the house.

Only the kind-hearted young man who had told the story about the Book of Dreams gave some help, but even this was not of much avail. He also had stayed longer than the others, sympathetically participating in Pseldonymov's misfortune. At this Pseldonymov, his mother and the young man decided, after consultation, not to send for the doctor, but rather for a carriage to take the sick man home; and for the present, until the carriage arrived, to administer some home remedies to him, such as moistening the temples and applying ice-packs, and so on. All this was done by Pseldonymov's mother. The young man flew off to look for a carriage. As by that time of night there were no more cabs to be had on the Petersburg Side, he set off, quite a distance, for the coachmen's yard, and roused the coachmen. They began bargaining, declaring that at such an hour even five roubles would be too little for a carriage. They agreed, however, on three. But when the young man arrived in the carriage at Pseldonymov's at nearly four o'clock, there had already been a change of plan. It turned out that Ivan Ilyitch, who was still unconscious, had become so ill, had groaned and tosssed about so much, that it had become quite impossible to move him and take him home in such a state.

"What will come of all this?" said Pseldonymov, dejectedly. A new question rose; if the sick man were to be left in the house, then where was he to be carried and deposited? There were only two beds in the whole house; one, a huge double bed in which old Mlekopitayev and his wife slept, the other, also a double bed, of imitation walnut and newly acquired for the young couple. All the other inhabitants of the house slept on the floor, side by side, mostly on feather beds which were already partly worn and smelt—in brief, completely unsuitable, and there were in any case none to spare. Where was the sick man to be put? A feather bed might yet be found—in extreme need it could be pulled out from beneath someone —but where to put it? The upshot was that the bed must be made up in the drawing-room, the point farthest away from the bulk of the family and with its own exit. But what was the bed to be made up on? Simply on chairs? Everyone knows that only boys who are home from school for the weekend are made to sleep on chairs; for someone of Ivan Ilyitch's standing this would be most disrespectful. What would he say tomorrow at finding himself lying on a couple of chairs? Pseldonymov would not even hear of it. There was only one thing left to do: to carry him to the bridal couch. This bridal couch, as we have already said, had been set up in a little room leading from the dining-room. On the double bed was a newly bought, as yet unused mattress, clean bed linen, four pillows, in pink-coloured calico slips, under flounced muslin covers. The eiderdown was of pink satin, quilted in patterns. From a gilt ring above the bed fell muslin curtains. In a word, everything was as it should be, and the guests, who had nearly all visited the bedroom, had admired the fineries. The bride, though she could not bear Pseldonymov, had several times during the evening come into the room, quite secretly, to have a good look. Imagine her indignation, her fury, when she heard that they wanted to put the sick man, who was ill with cholera or something, on her bridal couch. The bride's mother began to take her part, cursed, and vowed she would complain the next day to her husband, but Pseldonymov held his own and insisted: Ivan Ilyitch was transferred to the double bed, and a bed was made up on chairs for the young couple in the drawing-room. The bride snivelled and wanted to pinch someone, but she dared not disobey; she knew well that Papa had a stick and that next day he would be sure to require a detailed report of what occurred.

To console her the pink quilt and the pillows in muslin covers were brought into the drawing-room. At that very moment the young man arrived with the carriage; when he heard that the carriage was no longer needed he had a terrible shock. He would have to pay for it himself, and he had never even possessed a twenty-kopeck piece. Pseldonymov announced that he was completely penniless. They tried to reason with the coachman, but he began to kick up a row to the extent of knocking at the shutters. How all this ended, I don't quite know. I believe the young man was driven in the carriage to Peski, on the fourth Rozhdestvenskaya Street, where he hoped to rouse a certain student who was passing the night with some acquaintances, to try to see whether he had any money. By the time the young couple were left to themselves and shut in the drawing-room it was five o'clock in the morning.

Pseldonymov's mother stayed all night by the bedside of the sufferer. She lay down on the floor on a small carpet and covered herself up with a shaggy fur coat, but she could not sleep as she constantly had to get up. Ivan Ilyitch had a terrible bout of sickness. Pseldonymov's mother, a brave and kind-hearted woman, herself undressed him, took off all his clothes, nursed him as if he were her own son, and throughout the night she fetched and carried between the bedroom and the corridor.

However, the misfortunes of that night were far from being at an end.

Ten minutes had hardly elapsed since the young couple had been shut away alone in the drawing-room, when a heart-rending cry rang out. There was nothing reassuring about that cry—it was a cry of the most sinister kind. Immediately following it a noise could be heard, a crash as if chairs were falling, and all at once a whole crowd of screaming and frightened women at every stage of undress rushed into the still, darkened room. These women were the bride's mother, her elder sister, who had abandoned her sick children for the time being, and three of her aunts—even the one with the broken rib had dragged herself along. The cook was there too; even the sponger, the German woman with the talent for telling stories, had come along. It was the latter's feather bed, the best in the house and her own and sole property, that had been forcibly removed from under her for the use of the young couple. All these shrewd respectable women had already, a quarter of an hour earlier, been stealing on tiptoe from the kitchen, through the corridor, and had been eavesdropping in the hall, consumed by the most inexplicable curiosity. Meanwhile, somebody hastily lit a candle and an unexpected sight was revealed. The chairs, unable to withstand the weight of two people and the broad feather bed which they supported on either side, had given way and the mattress had fallen between them to the floor. The bride was trembling with rage; this time she was wounded to her very heart. Pseldonymov, morally crushed, stood there like a criminal caught in the act. He did not even try to justify himself. Exclamations and shrieks were heard on all sides; hearing the noise, Pseldonymov's mother also came running up, but this time the bride's mother got the upper hand entirely. First she blamed Pseldonymov, for the most part unjustly saying: "What sort of a husband are you, my dear sir, in view of this? What use are you, my dear sir, after this disgrace?" and so on, and, finally, taking her daughter by the hand, led her away from her husband to her own room, taking it upon herself to account for this tomorrow when her fierce husband would demand an explanation. All the others departed with her, sighing and shaking their heads. His mother alone stayed with Pseldonymov and tried to comfort him. But he immediately drove her away.

He was in no condition to be comforted. He reached the sofa and sat down in a spirit of gloomy reflection; there he sat, barefooted, dressed only in his underwear. His mind was confused. Now and again he glanced in a mechanical fashion round the room where only recently there had been such wild dancing and where cigarette smoke still hung in the air. Cigarette-ends and sweet-papers were still scattered on the stained and dirty floor. The wreck of the bridal bed and the overturned chairs bore witness to the transitory nature of the best and truest earthly hopes and dreams. He remained like this for almost an hour. Depressing thoughts came into his head: what awaited him at the office? He realized that at all costs he would have to change his place of work; it would be impossible to stay on where he was after what had happened last night. Into his mind, too, came Mlekopitayev, who would probably on the morrow force him to dance the Kazatchek once more to test his docility. He realized that although Mlekopitayev had given fifty roubles towards the wedding expenses—which had all been spent to the last kopeck—he had not thought to let them have the four hundred roubles promised as dowry, nor even made further mention of them. Even the house had not been officially transferred to his name. His thoughts also turned to his wife, who had left him at the most critical moment of his life; he thought of the tall officer who had gone down on one knee before her. This he had already contrived to notice; he thought of the seven devils which possessed his wife, according to the personal testimony of her father, and of the stick ready to drive them out. . . . Of course, he felt he was capable of enduring much, but Fate had in the outcome allowed such surprises to assail him that it was finally understandable that he should doubt his own strength. Thus Pseldonymov grieved. Meanwhile the candle-end was burning low. Its flickering light, falling straight on to Pseldonymov's profile, reflected it on the wall in a huge image, with outstretched neck, a hooked nose and two tufts of hair sticking up over his forehead and at the back of his head. At last, when the first breath of morning freshness came, he got up, shivering and his feelings numbed, reached the feather bed which was lying between the chairs, and, without putting anything right, without blowing out the candle-end, without even slipping a pillow under his head, he crawled into the bed, overcome by that leaden, death-like sleep which is experienced perhaps by those who are condemned to public execution on the morrow.

. . .

On the other hand, what could compare with the agonizing night which Ivan Ilyitch Pralinski spent on the bridal couch of the unfortunate Pseldonymov? For a long time headache, vomiting and other most unpleasant attacks gave him not a moment's peace. This was infernal torment. His occasional flashes of awareness lit up such an abyss of terror, such grim and horrible images, that it would have been better for him to have remained unconscious. However, everything was still confused in his head. For instance, he recognized Pseldonymov's mother—he heard her gentle remonstrances: "Try to bear it, my pet, try to bear it, dearie, it'll be all right, you'll see." He recognized her but could not logically account for her presence. Horrible visions came to him: most often he saw Semyon Ivanovitch; but looking more closely he observed that it was not Semyon Ivanovitch at all, but Pseldonymov's nose. Before him flitted by the self-styled artist and the officer, the old woman with her face bound up. He was preoccupied most of all with the gilt ring hanging above his head, from which hung the muslin curtains. He made it out quite clearly in the dim light of the candle-end which illuminated the room, and all the time he was pondering; what was it made for? He asked the elderly woman about it several times, but evidently he said something other than what he intended, for she seemed not to understand him, however much he tried to explain. At last, as morning came near, the attacks ceased and he fell into a sound, dreamless sleep. He slept for the best part of an hour and when he awoke he was almost fully conscious; he felt he had an unbearable headache and the nastiest possible taste in his mouth and on his tongue which appeared to be made of woollen cloth. He raised himself on the bed, looked round, and reflected. The pale light of the breaking day penetrated through the chinks of the shutters in a narrow line, trembling on the wall. It was almost seven o'clock in the morning. But when Ivan Ilyitch suddenly realized and remembered all that had happened to him from the beginning of the previous evening; when he remembered all the mishaps at supper, his exploit that misfired, his speech at table; when suddenly, with terrifying vividness, the possible consequences of all this presented themselves to him, what people would now think and say about him; when he looked round and, finally, saw to what a sad and disordered state he had reduced the peaceful bridal couch of his subordinate—oh, then, such deadly shame, such torment filled his heart that he cried out, covered his face with his hands and, in despair, threw himself on to the pillow. A minute later he jumped out of bed and saw that his clothes were lying on the chair, neatly folded and already cleaned; he seized them and quickly began to struggle into them, looking around as if in dreadful fear of something. Here too, on the other chair, lay his fur coat, his fur hat with his yellow gloves. He was on the point of slipping quietly away. But suddenly the door opened and Pseldonymov's mother entered, carrying an earthenware basin and a jug. Over her shoulder hung a towel. She put the basin down and without further argument declared that he most certainly needed a wash.

"Come, come! My dear sir, you must wash, you can't go without washing. . . ."

In that instant Ivan Ilyitch realized that if there were a single person in the whole world before whom he need not be ashamed and whom he need not fear, it was this same elderly woman. He did wash. And long afterwards, in painful moments of his life, he remembered, along with other regrettable occasions, all the circumstances of this awakening: this earthenware basin and china jug filled with cold water in which bits of ice were still floating, the oval cake of soap with some kind of embossed lettering on it, wrapped in pink paper, which must have cost fifteen kopecks, bought evidently for the newlyweds and used by Ivan Ilyitch; and he remembered the elderly woman with the linen towel over her left shoulder. The cold water refreshed him; he rubbed himself dry and, without saying a word, without even thanking his nurse, he seized his fur hat, threw his fur coat, which Pseldonymov's mother handed to him, over his shoulder, and ran through the corridor, through the kitchen, where the cat was already mewing and the cook raising herself from her bed to look at him with avid curiosity, out into the street and flung himself into a passing cab. The morning was frosty, a chilly yellowish mist still blanketed the houses and everything else. Ivan Ilyitch turned up his collar. He felt that everybody was looking at him, that everybody knew him, that everybody would know . . .

.   .   .

For eight days he did not leave the house, nor did he appear at the office. He was ill, painfully ill, but more in his mind than his body. In those eight days he endured complete purgatory and, surely, they would be credited to him in the next world. There were moments when he thought of taking monastic vows. Truly, he had such moments; his imagination even began to play actively along those lines. He dreamed of quiet singing in cloisters, an open coffin, life in a solitary cell, woods and caves; but as soon as he came to himself he confessed that it was all terrible nonsense and exaggeration, and was ashamed of it. Then came pangs of mental anguish about his wasted life. Then shame once more filled his heart, overwhelmed it in an instant, and turned a knife in the wound. He shuddered as he recalled certain images. What would they say about him, what would they think about him when he entered the office, what whisperings would pursue him for a whole year, for ten years, for his whole life? The story of this disgraceful affair would be told to future generations. Sometimes he became so faint-hearted that he was ready to drive at once to Semyon Ivanovitch and ask him for forgiveness and for his friendship. He did not even try to justify himself, he blamed himself completely: he could find no excuse for himself and was ashamed of his inability to do so.

He also contemplated resigning his post immediately and dedicating himself, without fuss, in solitude, to the happiness of mankind. In any case, it was undoubtedly necessary to relinquish all his acquaintances and even to go so far as to eradicate all memory of himself. But then it occurred to him that this, too, was nonsense, and that with increased strictness towards his subordinates the whole thing could still be put right. This gave him hope and courage. Finally, after eight whole days of doubt and torment, he felt that he could no longer bear the uncertainty, and one fine morning he decided to set off for the office.

Previously, while he was still sitting at home in distress, he had pictured to himself a thousand times how he would enter his office. He was completely convinced that he was sure to hear ambiguous whisperings, that he would see suspicious faces, reap most malicious smiles. Imagine his surprise when, in fact, nothing of the kind happened. He was received respectfully; everyone bowed to him; all were serious; all were busy. When he reached his private room, joy filled his heart.

He at once and most conscientiously took up his work, listened to several reports and explanations, issued decisions. He felt that never till now had he reasoned and made decisions so well, with such judgment, so competently, as on that morning. He saw that they were pleased with him, respected him, esteemed him. The most sensitive susceptibility would have felt nothing. Everything went off splendidly.

At last Akim Petrovitch himself appeared with some papers. At sight of him Ivan Ilyitch felt as if something had struck him right to the heart, but only for a moment. He gave him his attention, talked in a measured manner, showed how things should be done and cleared up certain points. He noticed only that he avoided glancing for long at Akim Petrovitch, or, rather, that Akim Petrovitch was afraid to look at him. But then Akim Petrovitch had finished, and began to collect his papers.

"There is just one request," he began, as impassively as possible. "Official Pseldonymov asks to be transferred to the Department of ——. His Excellency Semyon Ivanovitch Shipulenko has promised him a position. Pseldonymov asks for your kind co-operation, Your Excellency."

"I see, he wishes to be transferred," said Ivan Ilyitch, feeling that a great weight had been taken off his mind. He glanced at Akim Petrovitch, and in that instant their eyes met.

"Well now, I, for my part . . . I will use . . ." replied Ivan Ilyitch, "I am prepared . . ."

It was plain to see that Akim Petrovitch wanted to slip away as quickly as possible. But suddenly Ivan Ilyitch, in a burst of magnanimity, decided to get the thing off his chest once and for all. He had evidently had another inspiration.

"Tell him," he began, directing a piercing and meaningful glance towards Akim Petrovitch. "Convey to Pseldonymov that I bear him no ill will. . . . Yes, I bear none. . . . That, on the contrary, I am quite prepared to forget the past, to forget everything, everything. . . ."

But suddenly, Ivan Ilyitch stopped short, amazed at the strange behaviour of Akim Petrovitch, when, for no reason whatever, he changed all of a sudden from a sensible person into a most awful fool. Instead of listening, and letting Ivan Ilyitch finish, he blushed very foolishly, bowing rather hurriedly and awkwardly, bobbing, at the same time receding towards the door. His whole appearance revealed the desire to sink through the floor, or, rather, to reach his desk as quickly as possible. Ivan Ilyitch, left alone, rose from his chair in confusion. He looked into the mirror and did not see his own face.

"No! discipline, discipline and again discipline," he whispered almost unconsciously, and suddenly his face burned. He felt more shame, more heaviness at heart, than he had experienced during even the most unbearable moments of his eight days of illness.

"I have failed to live up to my ideals!" he said to himself, and sank into his chair—helpless.

Notes from the Underground

TRANSLATED BY DAVID MAGARSHACK

Part I

Underground *

I

I AM A sick man. . . . I am a spiteful man. No, I am not
a pleasant man at all. I believe there is something wrong
with my liver. However, I don't know a damn thing
about my liver; neither do I know whether there is anything really wrong with me. I am not under medical treatment, and never have been, though I do respect medicine
and doctors. In addition, I am extremely superstitious, at
least sufficiently so to respect medicine. (I am well educated enough not to be superstitious, but I am superstitious for all that.) The truth is, I refuse medical treatment out of spite. I don't suppose you will understand
that. Well, I do. I don't expect I shall be able to explain to
you who it is I am actually trying to annoy in this case by
my spite; I realise full well that I can't "hurt" the doctors
by refusing to be treated by them; I realise better than
any one that by all this I am only hurting myself and no
one else. Still, the fact remains that if I refuse to be medi-
cally treated, it is only out of spite. My liver hurts me—
well, let it damn well hurt—the more it hurts the better.

* Both the author of the *Notes* and the *Notes* themselves are,
of course, fictitious. Nevertheless, such persons as the author
of such memoirs not only may, but must, exist in our society,
if we take into consideration the circumstances which led to
the formation of our society. It was my intention to bring before our reading public, more conspicuously than is usually
done, one of the characters of our recent past. He is one of the
representatives of a generation that is still with us. In this
extract, entitled *Underground*, this person introduces himself
and his views and, as it were, tries to explain those causes which
have not only led, but also were bound to lead, to his appearance
in our midst. In the subsequent extract (apropos of the Wet
Snow) we shall reproduce this person's *Notes* proper, dealing
with certain events of his life.

Fyodor Dostoevsky

I have been living like this a long time—about twenty years, I should think. I am forty now. I used to be in the Civil Service, but I am no longer there now. I was a spiteful civil servant. I was rude and took pleasure in being rude. Mind you, I never accepted any bribes, so that I had at least to find something to compensate myself for that. (A silly joke, but I shan't cross it out. I wrote it thinking it would sound very witty, but now that I have seen myself that I merely wanted to indulge in a bit of contemptible bragging, I shall let it stand on purpose!)

Whenever people used to come to my office on some business, I snarled at them and felt as pleased as Punch when I succeeded in making one of them really unhappy. I nearly always did succeed. They were mostly a timid lot: what else can you expect people who come to a government office to be? But among the fine gentlemen who used to come to me to make inquiries there was one officer in particular whom I could not bear. He would not submit with a good grace and he had a disgusting habit of rattling his sword. For sixteen months I waged a regular war with him over that sword. In the end, I got the better of him. He stopped rattling. However, all this happened a long time ago when I was still a young man. And do you know, gentlemen, what was the chief point about my spitefulness? Well, the whole point of it, I mean, the whole nasty, disgusting part of it was that all the time I was shamefully conscious—even at the moments of my greatest exasperation—that I was not at all a spiteful or even an exasperated man, but that I was merely frightening sparrows for no reason in the world, and being hugely amused by this pastime. I might foam at the mouth, but just present me with some litttle toy, give me a cup of tea with sugar in it, and I shouldn't be at all surprised if I calmed down completely, even be deeply touched, though afterwards I should most certainly snarl at myself and be overcome with shame and suffer from insomnia for months. That's the sort of man I am.

Incidentally, I was rather exaggerating just now when I said that I was a spiteful civil servant. All I did, as a matter of fact, was to indulge in a little innocent fun at the expense of the officer and the people who came to my office on business, for actually I never could become a spiteful man. I was always conscious of innumerable elements in me which were absolutely contrary to that. I felt them simply swarming in me all my life and asking to be allowed to come out, but I wouldn't let them. I would not let them! I would deliberately not let them. They tormented me to the point of making me ashamed of myself; they reduced me to a state of nervous exhaustion and, finally, I got fed up with them. Oh, how thoroughly I got fed up with them in the end! But doesn't it seem to you, gentlemen, that I might possibly be apologising to you for something? Asking you to forgive me for something? Yes, I'm sure it does. . . . Well, I assure you I don't care a damn whether it does seem so to you or not. . . .

Not only did I not become spiteful, I did not even know how to become anything, either spiteful or good, either a blackguard or an honest man, either a hero or an insect. And now I've been spending the last four years of my life in my funk-hole, consoling myself with the rather spiteful, though entirely useless, reflection that an intelligent man cannot possibly become anything in particular and that only a fool succeeds in becoming anything. Yes, a man of the nineteenth century must be, and is indeed morally bound to be, above all a characterless person; a man of character, on the other hand, a man of action, is mostly a fellow with a very circumscribed imagination. This is my conviction as a man of forty. I am forty now and, mind you, forty years is a whole lifetime. It is extreme old age. It is positively immoral, indecent, and vulgar to live more than forty years. Who lives longer than forty? Answer me that—sincerely and honestly. I'll tell you who—fools and blackguards—they do! I don't mind telling that to all old men to their face—all those worthy old men, all those silver-haired and ambrosial old men! I'll tell it to the whole world, damned if I won't. I have a right to say so, for I shall live to the age of sixty myself. I'll live to be seventy! I'll live to be eighty! Wait a minute, let me take your breath. . . .

I expect you must be thinking, gentlemen, that I want to amuse you. Well, you're mistaken there too. I'm not at all the jolly sort of person you think I am, or may think I am. However, if irritated with all this idle talk (and I feel that you are irritated), you were to ask me who I really am, then I should reply, I'm a retired civil servant of humble rank, a collegiate assessor. I got myself a job in the Civil Service because I had to eat (and only for that reason), and when a distant relative of mine left me six thousand roubles in his will last year, I immediately resigned from the Civil Service and settled in my little corner. I used to live in this corner before, but now I'm settled permanently here. My room is a dreadful, horrible hole, on the very outskirts of the town. My maidservant is an old country woman, bad-tempered from sheer stupidity, and there is, besides, always a bad smell about her. I'm told the Petersburg climate isn't good for me any more and that with my small means it is very expensive to live in Petersburg. I know that perfectly well, much better than all those experienced and wise mentors and counsellors. But I'm staying in Petersburg. I shall never leave Petersburg! I shan't leave it—oh, but it really makes no damned difference whether I leave it or not.

By the way, what does a decent chap talk about with the greatest possible pleasure?

Answer: about himself.

Very well, so I will talk about myself.

II

I should like to tell you now, gentlemen, whether you want to listen to me or not, why I've never been able to become even an insect. I declare to you solemnly that I've wished to become an insect many times. But even that has not been vouchsafed to me. I assure you, gentlemen, that to be too acutely conscious is a disease, a real, honest-to-goodness disease. It would have been quite sufficient for the business of everyday life to possess the ordinary human consciousness, that is to say, half or even a quarter of the share which falls to the lot of an intelligent man of our unhappy nineteenth century who, besides, has the double misfortune of living in Petersburg, the most abstract and premeditated city in the whole world. (There are premeditated and unpremeditated cities.) It would have been quite sufficient, for instance, to possess the sort of consciousness with which all the so-called plain men and men of action are endowed. I bet you think I'm writing all this just out of a desire to show off or to crack a joke at the expense of our men of action, and that if I'm rattling my sword like my army officer it is merely because I want to show off, and in rather bad taste, too. But, gentlemen, who wants to show off his own infirmities, let alone boast about them?

However, what am I talking about? Everyone does it; everyone does show off his infirmities, and I more than anyone else perhaps. But don't let us quibble about it; the point I raised was absurd. Still, I firmly believe that not only too much consciousness, but any sort of consciousness is a disease. I insist upon that. But let us leave that, too, for a moment. Tell me this: why did it invariably happen that just at those moments—yes, at those very moments—when I was acutely conscious of "the sublime and beautiful," as we used to call it in those days, I was not only conscious but also guilty of the most contemptible actions which—well, which, in fact, everybody is guilty of, but which, as though on purpose, I only happened to commit when I was most conscious that they ought not to be committed? The more conscious I became of goodness and all that was "sublime and beautiful," the more deeply did I sink into the mire and the more ready I was to sink into it altogether. And the trouble was that all this did not seem to happen to me by accident, but as though it couldn't possibly have happened otherwise. As though it were my normal condition, and not in the least a disease or a vice, so that at last I no longer even attempted to fight against this vice. It ended by my almost believing (and perhaps I did actually believe) that this was probably my normal condition. At first, at the very outset, I mean, what horrible agonies I used to suffer in that struggle! I did not think others had the same experience, and afterwards I kept it to myself as though it were a secret. I was ashamed (and quite possibly I still am ashamed); it got so far that I felt a sort of secret, abnormal, contemptible delight when, on coming home one one of the foulest nights in Petersburg, I used to realise intensely that again I had been guilty of some particularly dastardly action that day, and that once more it was no earthly use crying over spilt milk; and inwardly, secretly, I used to go on nagging myself, worrying myself, accusing myself, till at last the bitterness I felt turned into a sort of shameful, damnable sweetness, and finally, into real, positive delight! Yes, into delight. Into delight! I'm certain of it. As a matter of fact, I've mentioned this because I should like to know for certain whether other people feel the same sort of delight. Let me explain it to you. The feeling of delight was there just because I was so intensely aware of my own degradation; because I felt myself that I had come up against a blank wall; that no doubt, it was bad, but that it couldn't be helped; that there was no escape, and that I should never become a different man; that even if there still was any time or faith left to make myself into something different, I should most likely have refused to do so; and even if I wanted to I should still have done nothing, because as a matter of fact there was nothing I could change into. And above all—and this is the final point I want to make —whatever happened, happened in accordance with the normal and fundamental laws of intensified consciousness and by a sort of inertia which is a direct consequence of those laws, and that therefore you not only could not change yourself, but you simply couldn't make any attempt to. Hence it follows that as a result of that intensified consciousness you are quite right in being blackguard, as though it were any consolation to the blackguard that he actually is a blackguard. But enough. . . . Good Lord, I have talked a lot, haven't I? But have I explained anything? How is one to explain this feeling of delight? But I shall explain myself. I shall pursue the matter to the bitter end! That is why I've taken up my pen. . . .

Now, for instance, I'm very vain. I'm as suspicious and as quick to take offence as a hunchback or a dwarf, but as a matter of fact there were moments in my life when, if someone had slapped my face, I should perhaps have been glad even of that. I'm saying this seriously: I should quite certainly have found even there a sort of pleasure, the pleasure of despair, no doubt, but despair too has its moments of intense pleasure, intense delight, especially if you happen to be acutely conscious of the hopelessness of your position. And there, too, I mean, after you'd had your face slapped, you'd be overwhelmed by the consciousness of having been utterly humiliated and snubbed. The trouble is, of course, that however much I tried to find some excuse for what had happened, the conclusion I'd come to would always be that it was my own fault to begin with, and what hurt most of all was that though innocent I was guilty and, as it were, guilty according to the laws of nature. I was guilty, first of all, because I was cleverer than all the people round me. (I have always considered myself cleverer than any one else in the world, and sometimes, I assure you, I've been even ashamed of it. At least, all my life I looked away and I could never look people straight in the face.) I was, finally, guilty because even if I had had a grain of magnanimity in me, I should have suffered a thousand times more from the consciousness of its uselessness. For I should most certainly not have known what to do with my magnanimity —neither to forgive, since the man who would have slapped my face, would most probably have done it in obedience to the laws of nature; nor to forget, since though even if it is the law of nature, it hurts all the same. Finally, even if I had wanted to be utterly ungenerous and, on the contrary, had desired to avenge myself on the man who had offended me, I couldn't have avenged myself on anyone for anything because I should never have had the courage to do anything even if I could. Why shouldn't I have had the courage? Well, I'd like to say a few words about that by itself.

III

You see, people who know how to avenge themselves and, generally, how to stand up for themselves—how do they, do you think, do it? They are, let us assume, so seized by the feeling of revenge that while that feeling lasts there is nothing but that feeling left in them. Such a man goes straight to his goal, like a mad bull, with lowered horns, and only a stone wall perhaps will stop him. (Incidentally, before such a stone wall such people, that is to say, plain men and men of action, as a rule capitulate at once. To them a stone wall is not a challenge as it is, for instance, to us thinking men who, because we are thinking men, do nothing; it is not an excuse for turning aside, an excuse in which one of our sort does not believe himself, but of which he is always very glad. No, they capitulate in all sincerity. A stone wall exerts a sort of calming influence upon them, a sort of final and morally decisive influence, and perhaps even a mystic one. . . . But of the stone wall later.) Well, that sort of plain man I consider to be the real, normal man, such as his tender mother nature herself wanted to see him when she so lovingly brought him forth upon the earth. I envy such a man with all the forces of my embittered heart. He is stupid—I am not disputing that. But perhaps the normal man should be stupid. How are you to know? Why, perhaps this is even beautiful. And I'm all the more convinced of that—shall we say?—suspicion, since if we take, for instance, the antithesis of the normal man, that is to say, the man of great sensibility, who of course has sprung not out of the lap of nature, but out of a test tube (this is almost mysticism, gentlemen, but I, too, suspect it), then this test-tube-begotten man sometimes capitulates to his antithesis to such an extent that for all his intense sensibility he frankly considers himself a mouse and not a man. I grant you it is an intensely conscious mouse, but it's a mouse all the same, whereas the other is a man, and consequently . . . etc. And, above all, he himself—oh, yes, he in his own person—considers himself a mouse; no one asks him to do so; and this is an important point.

Well, let us now have a look at this mouse in action. Let us suppose, for instance, that its feelings are hurt (and its feelings are almost always hurt), and that it also wants to avenge itself. There will perhaps be a greater accumulation of spite in it than in *l'homme de la nature et de la vérité.* A nasty, mean little desire to repay whoever has offended it in his own coin stirs within it more nastily perhaps than in *l'homme de la nature et de la vérité;* for because of his inborn stupidity *l'homme de la nature et de la vérité* looks upon his revenge merely as a matter of justice whereas because of its intense sensibility the mouse denies that there is any question of justice here. At last we come to the business itself, to the act of revenge. The unhappy mouse has already succeeded in piling up—in the form of questions and doubts— a large number of dirty tricks in addition to its original dirty trick; it has accumulated such a large number of insoluble questions round every one question that it is drowned in a sort of deadly brew, a stinking puddle made up of its doubts, its flurries of emotion, and lastly, the contempt with which the plain men of action cover it from head to foot while they stand solemnly round as judges and dictators and split their sides with laughter at it. Well, of course, all that is left for it to do is to dismiss it with a disdainful wave of its little paw and with a smile of simulated contempt, in which it does not believe itself, and to scurry back ingloriously into its hole. There, in its stinking, disgusting, subterranean hole, our hurt, ridiculed, and beaten mouse plunges into cold, venomous, and, above all, unremitting spite. For forty years it will continuously remember its injury to the last and most shameful detail, and will, besides, add to it still more shameful details, worrying and exciting itself spitefully with the aid of its own imagination. It will be ashamed of its own fancies, but it will nevertheless remember everything, go over everything with the utmost care, think up all sorts of imaginary wrongs on the pretext that they, too, might have happened, and will forgive nothing. Quite likely it will start avenging itself, but, as it were, by fits and starts, in all sorts of trivial ways, from behind the stove, incognito, without believing in its right to avenge itself, nor in the success of its vengeance, and knowing beforehand that it will suffer a hundred times more itself from all its attempts at revenge than the person on whom it is revenging itself, who will most probably not care a hang about it. Even on its deathbed it will remember everything with the interest accumulated during all that time, and. . . . And it is just in that cold and loathsome half-despair and half-belief—in that conscious burying oneself alive for grief for forty years—in that intensely perceived, but to some extent uncertain, helplessness of one's position—in all that poison of unsatisfied desires that have turned inwards—in that fever of hesitations, firmly taken decisions, and regrets that follow almost instantaneously upon them—that the essence of that delight I have spoken of lies. It is so subtle and sometimes so difficult to grasp by one's conscious mind that people whose mental horizon is even a little bit circumscribed, or simply people with strong nerves will not understand anything of it. "Perhaps," you will add with a grin, "those who have never had their faces slapped will not understand it, either," and in that polite way give me a hint that I too have perhaps had my face slapped in my life and that for that reason I'm speaking about it with authority. I bet that's what you are thinking. But don't worry, gentlemen, I've never had my face slapped, and I don't care a damn what you may think about it. Very likely I am sorry not to have boxed the ears of a sufficient number of people in my lifetime. But enough! Not another word about this subject which seems to interest you so much.

Let me continue calmly about the people with strong nerves who do not understand the subtleties of the pleasure I have been speaking of. Though on some occasions these gentlemen may roar at the top of their voices like bulls, and though this, let us assume, does them the greatest credit, yet as I've already said, they at once capitulate in face of the impossible. The impossible is to them equivalent to a stone wall. What stone wall? Why, the laws of nature, of course, the conclusions of natural science, mathematics. When, for instance, it is proved to you that you are descended from a monkey, then it's no use pulling a long face about it: you just have to accept it. When they prove to you that one drop of your own fat must, as a matter of course, be dearer to you than a hundred thousand of your fellow-men and that all the so-called virtues and duties and other vain fancies and prejudices are, as a result of that consideration, of no importance whatever, then you have to accept it whether you like it or not, because twice-two—mathematics. Just try to refute that.

"Good Lord," they'll scream at you, "you can't possibly deny that: twice two *is* four! Never does nature ask you for your opinion; she does not care a damn for your wishes, or whether you like her laws or not. You are obliged to accept her as she is and, consequently, all her results. A stone wall, that is, is a stone wall . . . etc., etc." But, goodness gracious me, what do I care for the laws of nature and arithmetic if for some reason or other I don't like those laws of twice-two? No doubt I shall never be able to break through such a stone wall with my forehead, if I really do not possess the strength to do it, but I shall not reconcile myself to it just because I have to deal with a stone wall and haven't the strength to knock it down.

As though such a stone wall were really the same thing as peace of mind, and as though it really contained some word of comfort simply because a stone wall is merely the equivalent of twice-two-makes-four. Oh, what stuff and nonsense this is! Is it not much better to understand everything, to be aware of everything, to be conscious of all the impossibilities and stone walls? Not to be recon-

ciled to any of those impossibilities or stone walls if you
hate being reconciled to them? To reach by way of
the most irrefutable logical combinations the most hideous conclusions on the eternal theme that it is somehow
your own fault if there is a stone wall, though again it is
abundantly clear that it is not your fault at all, and therefore to abandon yourself sensuously to doing nothing,
silently and gnashing your teeth impotently, hugging the
illusion that there isn't really anyone you can be angry
with; that there is really no object for your anger and
that perhaps there never will be an object for it; that the
whole thing is nothing but some imposition, some hocus-
pocus, some card-sharping trick, or simply some frightful mess—no one knows what and no one knows who.
But in spite of these uncertainties and this hocus-pocus,
you have still got a headache, and the less you know
the more splitting the headache!

IV

"Ha-ha-ha! After this you'll no doubt be finding some
pleasure in toothache too!" you cry with a laugh.

"Well, why not? There's pleasure even in toothache,"
I reply.

I had toothache for a whole month, and I know there
is pleasure in it. For, you see, if you have toothache, you
don't lose your temper in silence. You groan. But these
groans of yours are not sincere groans. They are groans
mixed with malice. And it is the malice here that matters.
By these groans the sufferer expresses his pleasure. If he
did not feel any pleasure, he would not groan. That is an
excellent example, gentlemen, and I'm going to develop
it.

In these groans there is expressed, in the first place, the
whole purposelessness of your pain which is so humiliating to your consciousness; the crowning stroke of nature,
for which you, of course, don't care, but from which you
suffer all the same, while she goes scot free. They express
the consciousness of the fact that even though you had
no enemies, you do have pain; the consciousness that for
all the dentists in the world you are entirely at the
mercy of your teeth; that if someone should desire it,
your teeth would stop aching, and if he does not, they

will go on aching another three months; and that, finally, if you are still unconvinced and still keep on protesting, all that is left for your own gratification is to give yourself a thrashing or hit the wall with your fist as hard as you can, and absolutely nothing more.

Well, it is from these mortal injuries, from those gibes that come from goodness knows whom, that pleasure at last arises, pleasure that sometimes reaches the highest degree of voluptuousness. I beg of you, gentlemen, listen sometimes to the groans of an educated man of the nineteenth century who is suffering from toothache on—shall we say?—the second or third day of his indisposition, when he is beginning to groan in quite a different way from the way he groaned on the first day, that is, not simply because he has toothache, not like some coarse peasant, but like a man of culture and European civilisation, like a man "who has divorced himself from the soil and uprooted himself from his people," to use a phrase which is at present in vogue. His groans become nasty and offensively ill-tempered groans, and go on for days and nights. And yet he knows perfectly well that he is doing no good with his groaning; he knows better than anyone that he is merely irritating and worrying himself and others for nothing; he knows that the audience before whom he is performing with such zeal and all his family are listening to him with disgust, that they don't believe him in the least, and that in their hearts they know that, if he wished, he could have groaned differently and more naturally, without such trills and flourishes, and that he is only amusing himself out of spite and malice. Well, all those apprehensions and infamies are merely the expression of sensual pleasure. "I'm worrying you, am I?" he seems to say. "I'm breaking your hearts, I'm not letting anyone in the house sleep, am I? All right, don't sleep. I want you, too, to feel every minute that I have toothache. I'm no longer the same hero to you now as I tried to appear before, but just a loathsome little fellow, a nuisance? Very well then. So be it. I'm very glad you've found me out at last. You hate to listen to my mean little groans, do you? Well, all right. Hate it if you like. Just you listen to my next flourish. It'll be much worse than the one before, I promise you. . . ." You still don't understand, gentlemen? Well, it seems we have to develop still further and more thoroughly, we have to sharpen our consciousness still more, before we can fully appreciate all the twists and turns of this sort of voluptuous pleasure. You are laughing? I'm very glad, I'm sure. I'm afraid, gentlemen, my jokes are in very bad taste, they are lame and a bit confused, and show a lack of self-confidence, too. That is because I have no self-respect. But can a man of acute sensibility respect himself at all?

v

Well, can you expect a man who tries to find pleasure even in the feeling of his own humiliation to have an atom of respect for himself? I'm not saying this now from any hypersensitive feeling of remorse. And, anyway, I never could stand saying, "Sorry, father, I won't do it again,"—not because I'm not capable of saying it; on the contrary, because I'm too capable of saying it. Yes, indeed! I used to get into awful trouble on such occasions though I was not even remotely to be blamed for anything. That was the most horrible part of it. But every time that happened, I used to be touched to the very depth of my soul, I kept on repeating how sorry I was, shedding rivers of tears, and of course deceiving myself, though I was not pretending at all. It was my heart that somehow was responsible for all that nastiness. . . . Here one could not blame even the laws of nature, though the laws of nature have, in fact, always and more than anything else caused me infinite worry and trouble all through my life. It is disgusting to call to mind all this, and as a matter of fact it was a disgusting business even then. For after a minute or so I used to realise bitterly that it was all a lie, a horrible lie, a hypocritical lie, I mean, all those repentances, all those emotional outbursts, all those promises to turn over a new leaf. And if you ask why I tormented myself like that, the answer is because I was awfully bored sitting about and doing nothing, and that is why I started on that sort of song and dance. I assure you it is true. You'd better start watching yourselves more closely, gentlemen, and you will understand that it is so. I used to invent my own adventures, I used to devise my own life for myself, so as to be able to carry on somehow. How many times, for instance, used I to take offence without rhyme or reason, deliberately; and of course I realised very well that I had taken offence at nothing, that the whole thing was just a piece of play-acting, but in the end I would work myself up into such a state that I would be offended in good earnest. All my life I felt drawn to play such tricks, so that in the end I simply lost control of myself. Another time I tried hard to fall in love. This happened to me twice, as a matter of fact. And I can assure you, gentlemen, I suffered terribly. In my heart of hearts, of course, I did not believe that I was suffering, I'd even sneer at myself in a vague sort of way, but I suffered agonies none the less, suffered in the most genuine manner imaginable, as though I were really in love. I was jealous. I made scenes. And all because I was so confoundedly bored, gentlemen, all because I was so horribly bored. Crushed by doing nothing. For the direct, the inevitable, and the legitimate result of consciousness is to make all actions impossible, or—to put it differently—consciousness leads to thumb-twiddling. I've already said so before, but let me repeat, and repeat most earnestly: all plain men and men of action are active only because they are dull-witted and mentally undeveloped. How is that to be explained? Why, like this: owing to their arrested mental development they mistake the nearest and secondary causes for primary causes and in this way persuade themselves much more easily and quickly than other people that they have found a firm basis for whatever business they have in hand and, as a result, they are no longer worried, and that is really the main thing. For to start being active you must first of all be completely composed in mind and never be in doubt. But how can I, for instance, compose myself? Where am I to find the primary cause to lean against? Where am I to get the basis from? I am constantly exercising my powers of thought and, consequently, every primary cause with me at once draws another one after itself, one still more primary, and so *ad infinitum*. That, in fact, is the basis of every sort of consciousness and analysis. That, too, therefore is a law of nature. What is the result of it then? Why, the same. Remember I was speaking of revenge just now. (I don't suppose you grasped that.) I argued that a man revenges himself because he finds justice in it. This of course means that he has found a primary cause, a basis, namely justice. It follows therefore that now he is absolutely calm and, consequently, he revenges himself calmly and successfully, being convinced that what he does is both right and just. But I can't for the life of me see any justice here, and therefore if I should start revenging myself, it would be merely out of spite. Now spite, of course, could get the better of anything, of all my doubts, and so could very well take the place of any primary cause just because it is not a cause. But what can I do if I have not even spite (I began with that just now). Besides, my feeling of bitterness, too, is subject to the process of disintegration as a result of those damned laws of consciousness. One look and the object disappears into thin air, your reasons evaporate, there is no guilty man, the injury is no longer an injury but just fate, something in the nature of toothache for which no one can be blamed, and consequently there is only one solution left, namely, knocking your head against the wall as hard as you can. Well, so you just give it up because you've failed to find the primary cause. But try letting yourself be carried away by your emotions blindly, without reasoning, without any primary cause, letting your consciousness go hang at least for a time; hate or love just for the sake of not having to twiddle your thumbs. What will happen, of course, is that the day after tomorrow (and that at the latest) you will begin despising yourself for having knowingly duped yourself. As a result—a soap bubble and doing nothing again. As a matter of fact, gentlemen, the reason why I consider myself a clever man is simply because I could never in my life finish anything I'd started. All right, I am a talker, a harmless, boring talker as we all are. But what can I do if the direct and sole purpose of every intelligent man is to talk, that is to say, to waste his time deliberately?

VI

Oh, if only I had done nothing merely out of laziness! Lord, how I should have respected myself then. I should have respected myself just because I should at least have been able to be lazy; I should at least have possessed one quality which might be mistaken for a positive one and in which I could have believed myself. Question—who is he? Answer—a loafer. I must say it would have been a real pleasure to have heard that said about myself, for it would have meant that a positive definition had been found for me and that there was something one could say about me. "A loafer!"—why, it's a title, a purpose in life. It's a career, gentlemen, a career! Don't joke about it. It is so. I should then be a member of the most exclusive club by right and should have done nothing but gone on respecting myself continually. I knew a gentleman who all through his life was proud of the fact that he was a great connoisseur of Château Lafitte. He considered it a positive virtue and never had any misgivings. He died not only with a clear, but positively with a triumphant conscience, and he was absolutely right. So I, too, should have chosen a career for myself: I should have been a loafer and a glutton, but would, for instance, admire the sublime and beautiful in everything. How do you like that? I've been dreaming about it a long time. The "sublime and beautiful" has been a great worry to me during my forty years, but that was only *during* my forty years, at one time—oh, at one time it would have been different! I should at once have found an appropriate occupation for myself, namely, to drink to the health of the sublime and the beautiful. I should have made use of every opportunity to drop a tear into my glass and then drain it to all that was sublime and beautiful. I should then have turned everything in the world into something sublime and beautiful; I should have found the sublime and beautiful in the foullest and most unmistakable rubbish. I should have oozed tears like a sponge. The artist G., for instance, paints a picture. At once I drink to the health of the artist G. who has painted a picture because I love all that is sublime and beautiful. An author writes something to please "everybody"; at once I drink to the health of "everybody" because I love all that is sublime and beautiful.

I should demand respect for myself for acting like that, and I should persecute anyone who would not show me respect. I should be at peace with the world and die in the odour of sanctity—why, it's delightful, it's simply delightful! And I should have grown such a monumental belly, I should have propagated such a double chin, I should have acquired such a fiery nose that every man in the street would have said as he looked at me, "Now that's a fine chap! Here's something real, something positive!"

And say what you like, gentlemen, it is very pleasant to hear such tributes in this negative age.

VII

But these are just golden dreams. Oh, tell me who was it first said, who was it first proclaimed that the only reason man behaves dishonourably is because he does not know his own interests, and that if he were enlightened, if his eyes were opened to his real normal interests, he would at once cease behaving dishonourably and would at once become good and honourable because, being enlightened and knowing what is good for him, he would see that his advantage lay in doing good, and of course it is well known that no man ever knowingly acts against his own interests and therefore he would, as it were, willy-nilly start doing good. Oh, the babe! Oh, the pure innocent child! When, to begin with, in the course of all these thousands of years has man ever acted in accordance with his own interests? What is one to do with the millions of facts that bear witness that man *knowingly*, that is, fully understanding his own interests, has left them in the background and rushed along a different path to take a risk, to try his luck, without being in any way compelled to do it by anyone or anything, but just as though he deliberately refused to follow the appointed path, and obstinately, wilfully, opened up a new, a difficult, and an utterly preposterous path, groping for it almost in the dark. Well, what does it mean but that to man this obstinacy and wilfulness is pleasanter than any advantage. . . . Advantage! What is advantage? Can you possibly give an exact definition of the nature of human advantage? And what if *sometimes* a man's ultimate advantage not only may, but even must, in certain cases consist in his desiring something that is immediately harmful and not advantageous to himself? If that is so, if such a case can arise, then the whole rule becomes utterly worthless. What do you think? Are there cases where it is so? You are laughing? Well, laugh away, gentlemen, only tell me this: have men's advantages ever been calculated with absolute precision? Are there not some which have not only not fitted in, but cannot possibly be fitted in any classification? You, gentlemen, have, so far as I know, drawn up your entire list of positive human values by taking the averages of statistical figures and relying on scientific and economic formulae. What are your values? They are peace, freedom, prosperity, wealth and so on and so forth. So that any man who should, for instance, openly and knowingly act contrary to the whole of that list would, in your opinion, and in mine, too, for that matter, be an obscurantist or a plain madman, wouldn't he? But the remarkable thing surely is this: why does it always happen that when all these statisticians, sages, and lovers of the human race reckon up human values they always overlook one value? They don't even take it into account in the form in which it should be taken into account, and the whole calculation depends on that. What harm would there be if they did take it, that value, I mean, and add it to their list? But the trouble, you see, is that this peculiar good does not fall under any classification and cannot be included in any list. Now, I have a friend, for instance—why, good gracious, gentlemen, he is also a friend of yours, and indeed whose friend is he not? In undertaking any business, this gentleman at once explains to you in high-sounding and clear language how he intends to act in accordance with the laws of truth and reason. And not only that. He will talk to you, passionately and vehemently, all about real and normal human interests; he will scornfully reproach the shortsighted fools for not understanding their own advantages, nor the real meaning of virtue, and—exactly a quarter of an hour later, without any sudden or external cause but just because of some inner impulse which is stronger than any of his interests, he will do somthing quite different, that is to say, he will do something that is exactly contrary to what he has been saying himself: against the laws of reason and against his own interests, in short, against everything. . . . I'd better warn you, though, that my friend is a collective entity and that for that reason it is a little difficult to blame him alone. That's the trouble, gentlemen, that there exists something which is dearer to almost every man than his greatest good, or (not to upset the logic of my argument) that there exists one most valuable good (and one, too, that is being constantly overlooked, namely, the one we are talking about) which is greater and more desirable than all other goods, and for the sake of which a man, if need be, is ready to challenge all laws, that is to say, reason, honour, peace, prosperity —in short, all those excellent and useful things, provided he can obtain that primary and most desirable good which is dearer to him than anything in the world.

"Well," you say, "but they are values all the same, aren't they?"

Very well, I believe we shall soon understand each other, and, besides, this isn't a matter for quibbling. What is important is that this good is so remarkable just because it sets at naught all our classifications and shatters all the systems set up by the lovers of the human race for the happiness of the human race. In fact, it plays havoc with everything. But before I tell you what this good is, I should like to compromise myself personally and I therefore bluntly declare that all these fine systems, all these theories which try to explain to man all his normal interests so that, in attempting to obtain them by every possible means, he should at once become good and honourable, are in my opinion nothing but mere exercises in logic. Yes, exercises in logic. For to assert that you believed this theory of the regeneration of the whole human race by means of the system of its own advantages is, in my opinion, almost the same as—well, asserting, for instance, with Buckle, that civilisation softens man, who, consequently becomes less bloodthirsty and less liable to engage in wars. I believe he argues it very logically indeed. But man is so obsessed by systems and abstract deductions that he is ready to distort the truth deliberately, he is ready to deny the evidence of his senses, so long as he justifies his logic. That is why I take this example, for it is a most striking example. Well, just take a good look round you: rivers of blood are being spilt, and in the jolliest imaginable way, like champagne. Take all our nineteenth century in which Buckle lived. Look at Napoleon, the Great and the present one. Look at North America—the everlasting union. Look, finally, at Schleswig-Holstein. . . . And what, pray, does civilisation soften in us? All civilisation does is to develop in man the many-sidedness of his sensations, and nothing, absolutely nothing more. And through the development of his many-sidedness man, for all we know, may reach the stage when he will find pleasure in bloodshed. This has already happened to him. Have you noticed that the

most subtle shedders of blood have almost invariably been
most civilised men, compared with whom all the Attilas
and Stenka Razins were just innocent babes, and if they
are not so outstanding as Attila or Stenka Razin it is because we meet them so often, because they are *too* ordinary, and because we have got used to them. At any rate,
civilisation has made man, if not more bloodthirsty, then
certainly more hideously and more contemptibly bloodthirsty. In the past he looked on bloodshed as an act of
justice and exterminated those he thought necessary to
exterminate with a clear conscience; but now we consider bloodshed an abomination and we engage in this
abomination more than ever. Which is worse? You'd better decide for yourselves. They say that Cleopatra (if I
may take an instance from Roman history) loved to stick
golden pins into the breasts of her slave girls and enjoyed
their screams and contortions. You will say that this happened in relatively speaking barbarous times; but today,
too, we live in barbarous times because (again relatively
speaking) today, too, we stick pins into people; today, too,
though man has learnt to see things more clearly than in
barbarous times, he is still very far from having learnt to
act in accordance with the dictates of reason and science.
But I daresay you are firmly convinced that he will most
certainly learn to do so as soon as his so-called bad old
habits completely disappear and as soon as common sense
and science have completely re-educated human nature
and directed it along the road of normal behaviour. You
are convinced that, when this happens, man will stop making *deliberate* mistakes and perforce refuse to allow his
will to act contrary to his normal interests. And that is
not all. You say that science itself will then teach man
(though in my opinion it is an unnecessary luxury) that as
a matter of fact he possesses neither will nor uncontrollable desires, and never has done, and that he himself is
nothing more than a sort of piano-key or organ-stop, and
that, in addition, there are the laws of nature in the world;
so that whatever he does is not done of his own will at
all, but of itself, according to the laws of nature. Consequently, as soon as these laws of nature are discovered,
man will no longer have to answer for his actions and will
find life exceedingly easy. All human actions will then, no
doubt, be computed according to these laws, mathematically, something like the tables of logarithms, up to 108,-

000, and indexed accordingly. Or, better still, certain well-intentioned words will be published, something like our present encyclopaedic dictionaries, in which everything will be calculated and specified with such an exactness that there will be no more independent actions or adventures in the world.

Then—it is still you who are saying this—new economic relations will be established, relations all ready for use and calculated with mathematical exactitude, so that all sorts of problems will vanish in a twinkling simply because ready-made solutions will be provided for all of them. It is then that the Crystal Palace will be built. Then—why, in fact, the Golden Age will have dawned again. Of course, it is quite impossible to guarantee (it is I who am speaking now) that even then people will not be bored to tears (for what will they have to do when everything is calculated and tabulated), though, on the other hand, everything will be so splendidly rational. Of course, when you are bored, you are liable to get all sorts of ideas into your head. Golden pins, too, are after all stuck into people out of boredom. But all that would not matter. What is bad (and it is again I who am saying this) is that I'm afraid they will be glad even of golden pins then. For man is stupid, phenomenally stupid; I mean, he may not be really stupid, but on the other hand he is so ungrateful that you won't find anything like him in the whole wide world. I would not be at all surprised, for instance, if suddenly and without the slightest possible reason a gentleman of an ignoble or rather a reactionary and sardonic countenance were to arise amid all that future reign of universal common sense and, gripping his sides firmly with his hands, were to say to us all, "Well, gentlemen, what about giving all this common sense a mighty kick and letting it scatter in the dust before our feet simply to send all these logarithms to the devil so that we can again live according to our foolish will?" That wouldn't matter, either, but for the regrettable fact that he would certainly find followers: for man is made like that. And all, mind you, for the most stupid of reasons which seems hardly worth mentioning, namely, because man has always and everywhere—whoever he may be—preferred to do as he chose, and not in the least as his reason or advantage dictated; and one may choose to do something even if it is against one's own advantage, and sometimes one *positively should* (that is my idea). One's own free and unfettered choice, one's own whims, however wild, one's own fancy, overwrought though it sometimes may be to the point of madness—that is that same most desirable good which we overlooked and which does not fit into any classification, and against which all theories and systems are continually wrecked. And why on earth do all those sages assume that man must needs strive after some normal, after some rationally desirable good? All man wants is an absolutely *free* choice, however dear that freedom may cost him and wherever it may lead him to. Well, of course, if it is a matter of choice, then the devil only knows . . .

VIII

"Ha-ha-ha! But there's really no such thing as choice, as a matter of fact, whatever you may say," you interrupt me with a laugh. "Today science has succeeded in so far dissecting man that at least we now know that desire and the so-called free will are nothing but——"

One moment, gentlemen. I am coming to that myself, and I don't mind telling you that I was even feeling a little nervous. I was just about to say that choice depended on the devil only knows what and that that was all to the good, but I suddenly remembered science and—the words died on my lips. And you took advantage of it and began to speak. It is, of course, quite true that if one day they really discover some formula of all our desires and whims, that is to say, if they discover what they all depend on, by what laws they are governed, how they are disseminated, what they are aiming at in one case and another, and so on, that is, a real mathematical formula, man may perhaps at once stop feeling any desire and, I suppose, most certainly will. For who would want to desire according to a mathematical formula? And that is not all. He will at once be transformed from a man into an organ-stop, or something of the sort. For what is man without desires, without free will, and without the power of choice but a stop in an organ pipe? What do you think? Let us calculate the probabilities: is it or is it not likely to happen?

"Well," you decide, "in the majority of cases our desires are mistaken from a mistaken idea of what is to our advantage. Sometimes we desire absolute nonsense because in our stupidity we see in this nonsense the easiest way of attaining some conjectural good."

Very well, and when all that is explained and worked out on paper (which is quite possible, for it would be absurd and unreasonable to assume that man will never discover other laws of nature), the so-called desires will of course no longer exist. For when one day desire comes completely to terms with reason we shall of course reason and not desire, for it is obviously quite impossible to *desire* nonsense while retaining our reason and in that way knowingly go against our reason and wish to harm ourselves. And when all desires and reasons can be actually calculated (for one day the laws of our so-called free will are bound to be discovered) something in the nature of a mathematical table may in good earnest be compiled so that all our desires will in effect arise in accordance with this table. For if it is one day calculated and proved to me, for instance, that if I thumb my nose at a certain person it is because I cannot help thumbing my nose at him, and that I have to thumb my nose at him with that particular thumb, what *freedom* will there be left to me, especially if I happen to be a scholar and have taken my degree at a university? In that case, of course, I should be able to calculate my life for thirty years ahead. In short, if this were really to take place, there would be nothing left for us to do: we should have to understand everything whether we wanted to or not. And, generally speaking, we must go on repeating to ourselves incessantly that at a certain moment and in certain circumstances nature on no account asks us for our permission to do anything; that we have got to take her as she is, and not as we imagine her to be; and that if we are really tending towards mathematical tables and rules of thumb and—well—even towards test tubes, then what else is there left for us to do but to accept everything, test tube and all. Or else the test tube will come by itself and will be accepted whether you like it or not. . . .

Quite right, but there's the rub! I'm sorry, gentlemen, to have gone on philosophising like this: remember my forty years in the dark cellar! Do let me indulge my fancy for a moment. You see, gentlemen, reason is an excellent thing. There is no doubt about it. But reason is only reason, and it can only satisfy the reasoning ability of man, whereas volition is a manifestation of the whole of life, I mean, of the whole of human life, including reason with all its concomitant head-scratchings. And although our life, thus manifested, very often turns out to be a sorry business, it is life none the less and not merely extractions of square roots. For my part, I quite naturally want to live in order to satisfy all my faculties and not my reasoning faculty alone, that is to say, only some twentieth part of my capacity for living. What does reason know? Reason only knows what it has succeeded in getting to know (certain things, I suppose, it will never know; this may be poor comfort, but why not admit it frankly?), whereas human nature acts as a whole, with everything that is in it, consciously, and unconsciously, and though it may commit all sorts of absurdities, it persists. I cannot help thinking, gentlemen, that you look upon me with pity; you go on telling me over and over again that an enlightened and mentally developed man, such a man, in short, as the future man can be expected to be, cannot possibly desire deliberately something which is not a real "good," and that, you say, is mathematics. I quite agree. It is mathematics. But I repeat for the hundredth time that here is one case, one case only, when man can deliberately and consciously desire something that is injurious, stupid, even outrageously stupid, just because he wants *to have the right* to desire for himself even what is very stupid and not to be bound by an obligation to desire only what is sensible. For this outrageously stupid thing, gentlemen, this whim of ours, may really be more accounted by us than anything else on earth, especially in certain cases. And in particular it may be more valuable than any good even when it is quite obviously bad for us and contradicts the soundest conclusions of our reason about what is to our advantage, for at all events it preserves what is most precious and most important to us, namely, our personality and our individuality. Indeed some people maintain that this is more precious than anything else to man. Desire, of course, can, if it chooses, come to terms with reason, especially if people do not abuse it and make use of it in moderation; this is useful and sometimes even praiseworthy. But very often and indeed mostly desire is utterly and obstinately at loggerheads with reason and—and, do you know, that, too, is useful and occasionally even praiseworthy. Let us suppose, gentlemen, that man is not stupid. (As a matter of fact, it cannot possibly be said that man is stupid, if only from the one consideration that if he is, then who is wise?) But if he is not stupid, he is monstrously ungrateful. Phenomenally ungrateful. I'm even inclined to believe that the best definition of man is—a creature who walks on two legs and is ungrateful. But that is not all, that is not his principal failing; his greatest failing is his constant lack of moral sense, constant from the days of the Flood to the Schleswig-Holstein period of human history. Lack of moral sense and, consequently, lack of good sense; for it has long been known that lack of good sense is really the result of lack of moral sense. Well, try and cast your eye upon the history of mankind and what will you see? Grandeur? Yes, perhaps even grandeur. The Colossus of Rhodes, for instance, is worth something, isn't it? Well may Mr. Anayevsky bear witness to the fact that some people maintain that it is the work of human hands, while others assert that it was wrought by nature herself. Gaiety? Well, yes. Perhaps gaiety, too. One has only to think of the dress uniforms, military and civilian, of all peoples in all ages—that alone is worth something, and if we throw in the undress uniforms as well, we can only gasp in astonishment at the gaiety of it all; no historian, I am sure, will be able to resist it. Monotonous? Well, I suppose it is monotonous: they fight and fight, they are fighting now, they fought before, and they will fight again —you must admit this is rather monotonous. In short, you can say anything you like about world history, anything that might enter the head of a man with the most disordered imagination. One thing, though, you cannot possibly say about it: you cannot say that it is sensible. If you did, you would choke at the first word. And, moreover, this is the sort of curious thing you come across almost every minute: continually there crop up in life such sensible and moral people, such sages and lovers of humanity whose only object seems to be to live all their lives as sensibly and morally as possible, to be, as it were, a shining light to their neighbours for the sole purpose of proving to them that it is really possible to live morally and sensibly in the world. And what happens? We know that many of these altruists, sooner or later, towards the end of their lives, were untrue to themselves, committing some folly, sometimes indeed of a most indecent nature. Now let me ask you this question: what can you expect of man seeing that he is a being endowed with such strange qualities? Why, shower all the earthly blessings upon him, drown him in happiness, head over ears, so that only bubbles should be visible on its surface, as on the surface of water; bestow such economic prosperity upon him as would leave him with nothing else to do but sleep, eat cakes, and only worry about keeping world history going—and even then he will, man will, out of sheer ingratitude, out of sheer desire to injure you personally, play a dirty trick on you. He would even risk his cakes and ale and deliberately set his heart on the most deadly trash, the most uneconomic absurdity, and do it, if you please, for the sole purpose of infusing into this positive good sense his deadly fantastic element. It is just his fantastic dreams, his most patent absurdities, that he will desire above all else for the sole purpose of proving to himself (as though that were so necessary) that men are still men and not keys of a piano on which the laws of nature are indeed playing any tune they like, but are in danger of going on playing until no one is able to desire anything except a mathematical table. And that is not all: even if he really were nothing but a piano-key, even if this were proved to him by natural science and mathematically, even then he would refuse to come to his senses, but would on purpose, just in spite of everything, do something out of sheer ingratitude; actually, to carry his point. And if he has no other remedy, he will plan destruction and chaos, he will devise all sorts of sufferings, and in the end he will carry his point! He will send a curse over the world, and as only man can curse (this is his privilege which distinguishes him from other animals, he may by his curse alone attain his object, that is, really convince himself that he is a man and not a piano-key! If you say that this, too, can be calculated by the mathematical table—chaos, and darkness, and curses—so that the mere possibility of calculating it all beforehand would stop it all and reason would triumph in the end—well, if that were to happen man would go purposely mad in order to rid himself of reason and carry his point! I believe this is so, I give you my word for it; for it seems to me that the whole meaning of human life can be summed up in the one statement that man only exists for the purpose of proving to himself every minute that he is a man and not an organ-stop! Even if it means physical suffering, even if it means turning his back on civilisation, he will prove it. And how is one after that to resist the temptation to rejoice that all this has not happened yet and that so far desire depends on the devil alone knows what.

You shout at me (if, that is, you will deign to favour me with raising voices) that no one wants to deprive me of my free will, that all they are concerned with is to arrange things in such a way that my will should of itself, of its own will, coincide with my normal interests, with the laws of nature and arithmetic.

But, good Lord, gentlemen, what sort of a free will can it be once it is all a matter of mathematical tables and arithmetic, when the only thing to be taken into account will be that twice-two-makes-four? Twice-two will make four even without my will. Surely, free will does not mean that!

IX

Gentlemen, I am joking of course, and I'm afraid my jokes are rather poor, but you can't after all take everything as a joke. How do you know I'm not joking with a heavy heart? Gentlemen, I'm worried by all sorts of questions; please, answer them for me. For instance, you want to cure man of his old habits and reform his will in accordance with the demands of science and commonsense. But how do you know that man not only could but *should* be remade like that? And what leads you to conclude that human desires must *necessarily* be reformed? In short, how do you know that such a reformation will be a gain to man? And, if one is to put all one's cards on the table, why are you so *utterly* convinced that not to go counter to the real normal gains guaranteed by the conclusions of reason and arithmetic is always so certainly right for man and is a universal law so far as mankind is concerned? For at present it is only a supposition on your part. Let us assume it is a law of logic, but how do you know that it is also a human law? You don't by any chance think I'm mad, do you? Let me explain myself. I agree that man is above all a creative animal, condemned consciously to strive towards a goal and to occupy himself with the art of engineering, that is, always and incessantly clear with a path for himself *wherever it may lead*. And I should not be at all surprised if that were not the reason why he sometimes cannot help wishing to turn aside from the path just because he is condemned to clear it, and perhaps, too, because, however stupid the plain man of action may be as a rule, the thought will sometimes occur to him that the path almost always seems to lead *nowhere in particular*, and that the important point is not where it leads but that it should lead somewhere, and that a well-behaved child, disdaining the art of engineering, should not indulge in the fatal idleness which, as we all know, is the mother of all vices. Man likes to create and to clear paths—that is undeniable. But why is he also so passionately fond of destruction and chaos? Tell me that. But, if you don't mind, I'd like to say a few words about that myself. Is he not perhaps so fond of destruction and chaos (and it cannot be denied that he is sometimes very fond of it—that is a fact) because he is instinctively afraid of reaching the goal and completing the building he is erecting? How do you know, perhaps he only loves the building from a distance and not by any means at close quarters; perhaps he only loves building it and not living in it, preferring to leave it later *aux animaux domestiques*, such as ants, sheep, etc., etc. Now, ants are quite a different matter. They have one marvellous building of this kind, a building that is for ever indestructible—the ant-hill.

The excellent ants began with the ant-hill and with the ant-hill they will most certainly end, which does great credit to their steadfastness and perseverance. But man is a frivolous and unaccountable creature, and perhaps, like a chess-player, he is only fond of the process of achieving his aim, but not of the aim itself. And who knows (it is impossible to be absolutely sure about it), perhaps the whole aim mankind is striving to achieve on earth merely lies in this incessant process of achievement, or (to put it differently) in life itself, and not really in the attainment of any goal, which, needless to say, can be nothing else but twice-two-makes-four, that is to say, a formula; but twice-two-makes-four is not life, gentlemen. It is the beginning of death. At least, man seems always to have been afraid of this twice-two-makes-four, and I am afraid of it now. Let us assume that man does nothing but search for this twice-two-makes-four, sails across oceans and sacrifices his life in this search; but to succeed in his quest, really to find what he is looking for, he is afraid—yes, he really seems to be afraid of it. For he feels that when he has found it there will be nothing more for him to look for. When workmen have finished their work they at least receive their wages, and they go to a pub and later find themselves in a police cell—well, there's an occupation for a week. But where can man go? At all events, one observes a certain awkwardness about him every time he achieves one of these aims. He loves the process of achievement but not achievement itself, which, I'm sure you will agree, is very absurd. In a word, man is a comical creature; I expect there must be some sort of jest hidden in it all. But twice-two-makes-four is for all that a most insupportable thing. Twice-two-makes-four is, in my humble opinion, nothing but a piece of impudence. Twice-two-makes-four is a farcical, dressed-up fellow who stands across your path with arms akimbo and spits at you. Mind you, I quite agree that twice-two-makes-four is a most excellent thing; but if we are to give everything its due, then twice-two-makes-five is sometimes a most charming little thing, too.

And why are you so firmly, so solemnly, convinced that only the normal and positive, in short, only prosperity, is of benefit to man? Does not reason make mistakes about benefits? Is it not possible that man loves something besides prosperity? Perhaps he is just as fond of suffering? Perhaps suffering is just as good for him as prosperity? And man does love suffering very much sometimes. He loves it passionately. That is an undeniable fact. You need not even look up world history to prove that; ask yourself, if you are a man and have lived at all. As for my own personal opinion, I believe that to be fond of prosperity is, somehow, indecent even. Whether it is good or bad, it is sometimes very pleasant to smash things, too. Not that I'm particularly anxious to plead the cause of suffering, or of happiness, for that matter. All I plead for is that I should be allowed my whims, and that they should be guaranteed to me whenever I want them. In light comedies, for instance, suffering is not permitted, and I accept that. In the Crystal Palace it is unthinkable: suffering is doubt, it is negation, and what sort of Crystal Palace would it be if one were to have any doubts about it? And yet I am convinced that man will never renounce real suffering, that is to say, destruction and chaos. Suffering! Why, it's the sole cause of consciousness! And though at the beginning I did argue that consciousness was the greatest misfortune to man, yet I know that man loves it and will not exchange it for any satisfaction. Consciousness, for instance, is infinitely superior to twice-two. After twice-two there is nothing left for you to do, or even to learn. All you could do then would be to stop up your five senses and sink into contemplation. While if you hang on to your consciousness you may achieve the same result, that is to say, there will be nothing for you to do, either, you could at least administer a good thrashing to yourself from time to time, and that at any rate livens you up a bit. It may be a reactionary step, but it is better than nothing, isn't it?

X[1]

You believe in the Crystal Palace, forever indestructible, that is to say, in one at which you won't be able to stick out your tongue even by stealth or cock a snook even in your pocket. Well, perhaps I am afraid of this palace just because it is made of crystal and is forever indestructible, and just because I shan't be able to poke my tongue out at it even by stealth.

You see, if it were not a palace but a hencoop, and if it should rain, I might crawl into it to avoid getting wet, but I would never pretend that the hencoop was a palace out of gratitude to it for sheltering me from the rain. You laugh and you tell me that in such circumstances even a hencoop is as good as a palace. Yes, I reply, it certainly is if the only purpose in life is not to get wet.

But what is to be done if I've got it into my head that that is not the only purpose in life, and that if one has to live, one had better live in a palace? That is my choice; that is my desire. You can only force me to give it up when you change my desire. All right, do it. Show me something more attractive. Give me another ideal. For the time being, however, I refuse to accept a hencoop for a

---

[1] The censor so mangled this chapter that Dostoevsky later complained that he was made to contradict himself several times. *Translator.*

palace. The Crystal Palace may be just an idle dream, it may be against all laws of nature, I may have invented it because of my own stupidity, because of certain old and irrational habits of my generation. But what do I care whether it is against the laws of nature? What does it matter so long as it exists in my desires, or rather exists while my desires exist? You are not laughing again, are you? Laugh by all means; I am quite ready to put up with any jeers, but I will still refuse to say that I'm satisfied when I'm hungry. At all events I know that I shall never be content with a compromise, with an everlasting and recurring zero because it exists according to the laws of nature and *actually* exists. I will not accept as the crown of all my desires a big house with model flats for the poor on a lease of ninety-nine hundred and ninety-nine years, and, in case of emergency, with the dental surgeon Wagenheim on a signboard. Destroy my desires, eradicate my ideals, show me something better, and I will follow you. I daresay you will probably declare that it isn't worth your while having anything to do with me; but in that case I, too, can say the same to you. We are discussing this seriously; and if you are too proud to give me your attention, I shall have to do without it.

But while I'm still alive and have desires, I'd rather my right hand withered than let it bring even one small brick to such a house of model flats! I know that a short time ago I rejected the Crystal Palace myself for the sole reason that one would not be allowed to stick one's tongue out at it. But I did not say that because I am so fond of sticking out my tongue. Perhaps what I resented was that among all our buildings there has never been one at which one could not stick out one's tongue. On the contrary, I'd gladly have let my tongue be cut off out of gratitude if things could be so arranged that I should have no wish to stick it out at all. It is not my business if things cannot be arranged like that and if one has to be satisfied with model flats. Why then am I made with such desires? Surely, I have not been made for the sole purpose of drawing the conclusion that the way I am made is a piece of rank deceit? Can this be the sole purpose? I don't believe it.

However, do you know what? I am convinced that fellows like me who live in dark cellars must be kept under restraint. They may be able to live in their dark cellars for forty years and never open their mouths, but the moment they get into the light of day and break out they talk and talk and talk. . . .

XI

And, finally, gentlemen, it is much better to do nothing at all! Better passive awareness! And so three cheers for the dark cellar! Though I have said that I envy the normal man to the point of exasperation, I wouldn't care to be in his place in the circumstances in which I find him (though I shall never cease envying him. No, no, the dark cellar is, at any rate, of much greater advantage to me!). In the dark cellar one can at least. . . . Sorry, I'm afraid I am exaggerating. I am exaggerating because I know, as well as twice-two, that it is not the dark cellar that is better, but something else, something else altogether, something I long for but cannot find. To hell with the dark cellar!

Do you know what would be better? It would be better if I myself believed in anything I had just written. I assure you most solemnly, gentlemen, that there is not a word I've just written I believe in! What I mean is that perhaps I do believe, but at the same time I cannot help feeling and suspecting for some unknown reason that I'm lying like a cobbler.

"Then why have you written all this?" you ask me.

"Well, suppose I put you in a dark cellar for forty years without anything to do and then came to see you in your dark cellar after the forty years to find out what had become of you. Can a man be left for forty years with nothing to do?"

"But aren't you ashamed? Don't you feel humiliated?" you will perhaps say, shaking your head contemptuously. "You long for life, yet you try to solve the problems of life by a logical tangle! And how tiresome, how insolent your tricks are, and, at the same time, how awfully frightened you are! You talk a lot of nonsense and you seem to be very pleased with it; you say a lot of impudent things, and you are yourself always afraid and apologising for them. You assure us that you are afraid of nothing, and at the same time you try to earn our good opinion. You assure us that you are gnashing your teeth, but at the same time you crack jokes to make us laugh. You know your jokes are not amusing, but you seem to be highly pleased with their literary merit. You may perhaps have really suffered, but you don't seem to have the slightest respect for your suffering. There may be some truth in you, but there is no humility. You carry your truth to the market place out of the pettiest vanity to make a public show of it and to discredit it. No doubt you mean to say something, but you conceal your last word out of fear, because you haven't the courage to say it, but only craven insolence. You boast about your sensibility, but you merely don't know your own mind. For though your mind is active enough, your heart is darkened with corruption, and without a pure heart there can be no full or genuine sensibility. And how tiresome you are! How you impose yourself on people! The airs you give yourself! Lies, lies, lies!"

Now, of course, I've made up all this speech of yours myself. It, too, comes from the dark cellar. I've been listening to your words for forty years through a crack in the ceiling. I have invented them myself. It is the only thing I did invent. No wonder I got it pat and dressed it up in a literary form.

But are you really so credulous as to imagine that I would print all of this, and let you read it into the bargain? And there is another puzzle I'd like to solve: why on earth do I address you as "gentlemen," as though you really were my readers? Such confessions which I am now about to make are not printed, nor given to other people to read. At least I have not enough pluck for that, nor do I consider it necessary to have it. But, you see, a strange fancy has come into my head and I want to realise it, cost what may. It's like this:—

There are certain things in a man's past which he does not divulge to everybody but, perhaps, only to his friends. Again there are certain things he will not divulge even to his friends; he will divulge them perhaps only to himself, and that, too, as a secret. But, finally, there are things which he is afraid to divulge even to himself, and every decent man has quite an accumulation of such things in his mind. I can put it even this way: the more decent a man is, the larger will the number of such things be. At least I have allowed myself only recently to remember some of my early adventures, having till now avoided them rather uneasily. I'm afraid. Now, however, when I have not only remembered them, but have also made up my mind to write them down, I particularly want to put the whole thing to the test to see whether I can be absolutely frank with myself and not be afraid of the whole truth. Let me add, by the way: Heine says that true biographies are almost impossible, and that a man will most certainly tell a lot of lies about himself. In his view, Rousseau told a lot of lies about himself in his Confessions, and told them deliberately, out of vanity. I am sure Heine is right; I can understand perfectly how sometimes one tells all sorts of lies about oneself out of sheer vanity, even going so far as to confess to all sorts of crimes, and I can perfectly understand that sort of vanity. But Heine had in mind a man who made his confessions to the public. I, however, am writing for myself, and I should like to make it clear once and for all that if I address myself in my writings to a reader, I'm doing it simply as a matter of form, because I find it much easier to write like that. It is only a form, an empty show, for I know that I shall never have any readers. I have already intimated as much. . . .

I don't want to be hampered by any considerations in the editing of my Memoirs. I shan't bother about order or system. I shall put down whatever I remember.

Now, of course, I might, for instance, be taken at my word and asked if I really do not count on any readers, why do I now put down all sorts of conditions, and on paper, too, such as not to pay any attention to order or system, to write down what I remember, etc., etc. Why all these explanations? Why all these apologies?

"Ah," I reply, "now you're asking!"

There is, incidentally, a whole psychology in all this. Perhaps it's simply that I am a coward. Again, perhaps it is simply that I'm imagining an audience on purpose so as to observe the proprieties while I write. There are thousands of reasons, no doubt.

Then again there is this further puzzle: what do I want to write it down for? What is the object of it all? If I'm not writing for the reading public, why not simply recall these things in my mind without putting them down on paper?

Well, I suppose I could do that, but it will look more

dignified on paper. There is something imposing about that. There will be a greater sense of passing judgment on myself. The whole style, I'm sure, will be better. Moreover, I really may feel easier in my mind if I write it down. I have, for instance, been latterly greatly oppressed by the memory of some incident that happened to me a long time ago. I remembered it very vividly the other day, as a matter of fact, and it has since been haunting me like some annoying tune you can't get out of your head. And yet I simply must get rid of it. I have hundreds of such memories, but at times one of them stands out from the rest and oppresses me. So why shouldn't I try?

And, lastly, I'm awfully bored, and I have nothing to do. Writing down things is, in fact, a sort of work. People say work makes man better and more honest. Well, here's a chance for me at any rate.

Snow is falling today, almost wet snow, yellow, dirty. It was snowing yesterday, too, and the other day. I think it is because of the wet snow that I remembered the incident which gives me no rest now. So let it be a story apropos of the wet snow.

Part II

Apropos of the Wet Snow

When with a word of fervent conviction,
From the lowest dregs of dark affliction,
A soul from eternal doom I saved;
And in horror and in torments steeped,
Wringing your hands, you curses heaped
Upon the life that once you craved;
When your unheeding conscience at last
With your guilty memories flaying,
The dreadful story of your sin-stained past
To me you narrated, pardon praying;
And full of horror, full of shame,
Quickly in your hands you hid your face,
Unconscious of the flood of tears that came,
Shaken and indignant at your own disgrace. . . . etc., etc.

From the poetry of N. A. Nekrassov.

I

I was only twenty-four at the time. My life even then was gloomy, disorderly, and solitary to the point of savagery. I had no friends or acquaintances, avoided talking to people, and buried myself more and more in my hole. When at work in the office I tried not to look at anyone and I knew perfectly well that my colleagues not only regarded me as a queer fellow, but also—I couldn't help feeling that, too—looked upon me with a sort of loathing. I wondered why no one except me had ever had this feeling that people looked upon him with loathing. One of the clerks at the office had a repulsive, pock-marked face, the face, I should say, of a real villain. I should not have dared to look at anyone with such an indecent face. Another had such a filthy old uniform that one could not go near him without becoming aware of a bad smell. And yet these gentlemen did not seem to be in the least upset either about their clothes, or their faces, or the impression they created. Neither of them ever imagined that people looked at him with loathing; and I daresay it would not have made any difference to them if they had imagined it, so long as their superiors deigned to look at them. It is of course clear that, owing to my unbounded vanity and hence also to my over-sensitiveness where my own person was concerned, I often looked at myself with a sort of furious dissatisfaction which verged on loathing, and for that reason I could not help attributing my own views to other people. I hated my own face, for instance, finding it odious to a degree and even suspecting that it had rather a mean expression, and so every time I arrived at the office I went through agonies in my efforts to assume as independent an air as possible so as to make sure that my colleagues did not suspect me of meanness and so as to give my face as noble an expression as possible. "What do I care," I thought to myself, "whether my face is ugly or not, so long as it is also noble, expressive, and, above all, *extremely* intelligent." But I knew very well, I knew it agonisingly well, that it was quite impossible for my face to express such high qualities. But the really dreadful part of it was that I thought my face looked absolutely stupid. I would have been completely satisfied if it looked intelligent. Indeed, I'd have reconciled myself even to a mean expression so long as my face was at the same time generally admitted to be awfully intelligent.

I need hardly say that I hated all my colleagues at the office, one and all, and that I despised them all, and yet at the same time I was also in a way afraid of them. It sometimes happened that I thought of them more highly than of myself. It was a feeling that somehow came upon me suddenly: one moment I despised them and the next moment I thought of them as above me. A decent, educated man cannot afford the luxury of vanity without being exceedingly exacting with himself and without occasionally despising himself to the point of hatred. But whether I despised them or thought them superior to me, I used to drop my eyes almost every time I met any one of them. I even used to make experiments to see whether I would be able to meet without flinching the look of one or another of my colleagues, and it was always I who dropped my eyes first. That irritated me to the point of madness. I was also morbidly afraid of appearing ridiculous and for that reason I slavishly observed all the social conventions; I enthusiastically followed in the beaten track and was mortally afraid of any eccentricity. But how could I hope to keep it up? I was so highly developed mentally, as indeed a man of our age should be. They, on the other hand, were all so stupidly dull and as like one another as so many sheep. Perhaps I was the only one in our office who constantly thought that he was a coward and a slave, and I thought that just because I was so highly developed mentally. But the truth is that it was not only a matter of my imagining it, but that it actually was so: I was a coward and a slave. I say this without the slightest embarrassment. Every decent man of our age is, and indeed has to be, a coward and a slave. That is his normal condition. I am absolutely convinced of that. He is made like that, and he has been created for that very purpose. And not only at the present time or as a result of some fortuitous circumstances, but at all times and in general a decent man has to be a coward and a slave. This is the law of nature for all decent men on earth. If one of them does sometimes happen to pluck up courage about something or other, he need not derive any comfort from it or be pleased about it: he is quite sure to make a fool of himself over something else. Such is the inevitable and eternal result of his being what he is. Only donkeys and mules pretend not to be afraid, and even they do it only up to a point. It is hardly worth while taking any notice of them, however, since they do not amount to anything, anyway.

Another thing that used to worry me very much at that time was the quite incontestable fact that I was unlike anyone and that there was no one like me. "I am one, and they are *all*," I thought and—fell into a melancholy muse.

From all that it can be seen that I was still a very young man.

Sometimes, though, quite the reverse used to happen. I would loathe the thought of going to the office, and things went so far that many times I used to come home ill. But suddenly and for no reason at all a mood of scepticism would come upon me (everything was a matter of moods with me), and I would myself laugh at my intolerance and sensitiveness and reproach myself with being a *romantic*. Sometimes I'd hate to talk to anyone, and at other times I'd not only talk to people, but would even take it into my head to be friends with them. All my fastidiousness would suddenly and for no reason in the world disappear. Who knows, maybe I really had never been fastidious, but just acquired a taste for appearing fastidious out of books. I haven't thought of an answer to this question to this day. Once I got very friendly with them, began visiting their homes, playing preference, drinking vodka, talking of promotions. . . . But here you must let me make a digression.

We Russians, generally speaking, have never had those stupid starry-eyed German and, still more, French romantics on whom nothing produces any effect; though the very ground cracked beneath their feet, though the whole of France perished at the barricades, they would still be the same and would not change even for the sake of appearances, and they would go on singing their highly romantic songs to their last breath, as it were, because they were fools. In Russia, however, there are no fools; that is a well known fact and that is what makes us so different from other countries. Therefore no starry-eyed natures, pure and simple, can be found among us. All that has been invented by our "positive" publicists and critics who at the time were chasing after Gogol's and Goncharov's idealised landowners and, in their folly, mistook them for our ideal; they have traduced our romantics, thinking them the same starry-eyed sort as in Germany or France. On the contrary, the characteristics of our romantics are the exact and direct opposite of the starry-eyed European variety, and not a single European standard applies here. (I hope you don't mind my using the word "romantic"—it is an old, honourable, and highly estimable word and is familiar to all.) The characteristics of our romantic are to understand everything, *to see everything and to see it incomparably more clearly than the most positive of our thinkers;* to refuse to take anyone or anything for granted, but at the same time not to despise anything; to go round and round everything and to yield to everything out of policy; never to lose sight of the useful and the practical (rent-free quarters for civil servants, pensions of a sort, decorations)—and to discern this aim through all the enthusiasms and volumes of lyrical verses, and at the same time to preserve to his dying day a profound and indestructible respect for "the sublime and the beautiful," and, incidentally, also to preserve himself like some precious jewel wrapt in cotton-wool for the benefit, for instance, of the same "sublime and beautiful." Our romantic is a man of great breadth of vision and the most consummate rascal of all our rascals, I assure you—from experience. That, of course, is all true if our romantic is intelligent. Good Lord, what am I saying? The romantic is always intelligent. I only meant to observe that even if there were fools among our romantics, they need not be taken into account for the simple reason that they had transformed themselves into Germans when still in their prime and, to preserve that pristine jewel-like purity of theirs, gone and settled somewhere abroad, preferably in Weimar or the Black Forest.

Now, for instance, I had a sincere contempt for the Civil Service and if I did not show it, it was only out of sheer necessity, for I was myself sitting at a desk in a Government office and getting paid for it. As a result—note that, please!—I refrained from showing my contempt in any circumstances. Our romantic would sooner go off his head (which does not happen often, though) than show his contempt for his job if he has no other job in prospect, and he is never kicked out of a job, either, unless indeed he is carried off to a lunatic asylum as "the King of Spain," but even then only if he should go stark raving mad. However, only the very thin and fair people go off their heads in Russia. An innumerable host of romantics, on the other hand, usually end up by becoming civil servants of the highest grade. Quite a remarkable versatility! And what an ability they possess for the most contradictory sensations! Even in those days this thought used to console me mightily, and I am still of the same opinion. That is why we have such a great number of "expansive" natures who do not lose sight of their ideal even when faced with the most catastrophic disaster; and though they never lift a finger for their ideal, though they are the most thorough-paced villains and thieves, they respect their original ideal, are ready to shed bitter tears for it and are, besides, quite remarkably honest at heart. Yes, gentlemen, it is only among us that the most arrant knave can be perfectly and even sublimely honest at heart without at the same time ceasing to be a knave. I repeat, I have seen our romantics over and over again grown into the most businesslike rascals (I use the word "rascals" affectionately); they suddenly acquire such a wonderful grasp of reality and such a thorough knowledge of the practical world that their astonished superiors in the Civil Service and the public at large can only click their tongues in utter stupefaction.

Their many-sidedness is truly amazing, and goodness only knows into what it may be transformed and developed later on and what, as a result of it, the future may hold in store for us. And the material is far from unpromising! I do not say this out of some ridiculous or blustering patriotism. However, I'm sure you must be thinking again that I am pulling your legs. Well, I don't know. Perhaps I am wrong. I mean, perhaps you are convinced that this really is my opinion. In either case, gentlemen, I shall consider both these views as a singular honour and a matter of special gratification to me. And you will forgive me for my digression, won't you?

My friendship with my colleagues did not of course last. Within a very short time I was at loggerheads with them again and, owing to my youthful inexperience at the time, I even stopped exchanging greetings with them and, so to speak, cut them. That, however, only happened to me once. Generally speaking, I was always alone.

At home I mostly spent my time reading. I tried to stifle all that was seething within me by all sorts of outside distractions, and of all outside distractions reading was the most easily available to me. My reading of course helped a lot: it excited, delighted, and tormented me. But at times it also bored me terribly. I got heartily sick of sitting in my room; I wanted to go somewhere, to move about; and so I plunged into a sort of sombre, secret, disgusting—no, not dissipation, but vile, petty vice. My mean lusts were always acute and burning as a result of my continual morbid irritability. My outbursts of passion were hysterical, and always accompanied by tears and convulsions. Apart from my reading, I had nothing to occupy me. I mean, there was nothing in my surroundings which I could respect or to which I could feel attracted. In addition, I was terribly sick at heart; I felt a terrible craving for conflicts and contrasts, and so I plunged into a life of mean debauchery. Mind you, I have spoken at such great length now not at all because of any desire to justify myself. And yet—no! It's a lie! Of course I wanted to justify myself. I'm making this little note for my own use, gentlemen. I don't want to lie. I promised not to.

I pursued my vile amusements in solitude, at night, in secret, fearfully, filthily, with a feeling of shame that did no desert me in the mot sickening moments and that brought me in such moments to the point of calling down curses on my own head. Even in these days I carried the dark cellar about with me in my soul. I was terribly afraid of being seen, of meeting someone I knew, of being recognised. I frequented all sorts of rather obscure dens of vice.

One night as I was passing a small pub, I saw through a lighted window some men having a fight with billiard cues and one of them being thrown out of the window. At any other time I should have felt very much disgusted; but at the time I could not help feeling envious of the fellow who had been thrown out of the window. Indeed, so envious did I feel that I even went into the pub, walked straight into the billiard room, thinking that perhaps I too could pick a quarrel with the men there and be thrown out of the window.

I was not drunk, but what was I to do? To such a state of hysteria had my depression brought me! But nothing happened. It seemed that I was not even capable of jumping out of the window, and I went away without having a fight.

An army officer in the pub put me in my place from the very first.

I was standing beside the billiard table and, in my ignorance, was blocking the way. As he had to pass me, he took me by the shoulders and, without a word of warning or explanation, silently carried me bodily from where I was standing to another place and passed by as though he had not even noticed me. I could have forgiven him if he had given me a beating, but I could not forgive him for having moved me from one place to another as if I were a piece of furniture. I would have given anything at that moment for a real, a more regular, a more decent, and a more, so to speak, *literary* quarrel! But I had been treated like a fly. The army officer was over six foot, and I am a short, thin little fellow. The quarrel, however, was in my hands: if I had uttered one word of protest, I should most certainly have been thrown out of the window. But I changed my mind and preferred—to efface myself angrily.

I left the pub feeling wild and embarrassed and went straight home. On the following day I carried on with my mean dissipation even more timidly, more abjectly and miserably than before, as though with tears in my eyes, but I did carry on with it. Do not imagine, however, that I was afraid of the army officer because I am a coward; I never was a coward at heart, although I have invariably been a coward in action, but—don't be in such a hurry to laugh; I have an explanation for everything, don't you worry.

Oh, if that army officer had only been one of those who would accept a challenge to a duel! But no. He was most decidedly one of those gentlemen (alas, long extinct!) who preferred action with billiard cues or, like Gogol's lieutenant Pirogov, by lodging a complaint with the authorities. They never accepted a challenge, and in any case would have considered a duel with me, a low grade civil servant, as quite improper; as for duelling in general, they regarded it as something unthinkable, something that only a freethinker or a Frenchman would indulge in. But that did not prevent them from treading on any man's corns, and painfully, too, particularly as they were over six foot.

No, I was not afraid because I was a coward, but because of my unbounded vanity. I was not afraid of his six foot, nor of getting soundly thrashed and being thrown out of the window; I should have had sufficient physical courage for that, what I lacked was moral courage. What I was afraid of was that every one in the billiard room from the cheeky marker to the last rotten, pimply little government clerk in a greasy collar who was fawning upon everybody in the room, would misunderstand me and jeer at me when I protested and began addressing them in literary language. For even today we cannot speak of a point of honour—not of honour, mind you, but of a point of honour (*point d'honneur*) except in literary language. You cannot even mention a "point of honour" in ordinary language. I was absolutely convinced (the sense of reality in spite of all romanticism!) that they would all simply split their sides with laughter and that the officer would not just simply, that is to say, not inoffensively, thrash me, but would certainly push me round the billiard table with his knee and perhaps only then would he have taken pity on me and thrown me out of the window. With me a wretched incident like this would never, of course, end there. I often met that army officer in the street afterwards and made a careful note of him. What I am not quite sure about is whether he recognised me. I don't think he did, and I have come to this conclusion by certain signs. But I—I stared at him with hatred and malice, and that went on—oh, for several years. At first I began finding out quietly all I could about this officer. It was a difficult job, for I did not know anyone. But one day someone called him by his surname in the street just as I was trailing after him at a distance, as though I were tied to him by a string, and so I learnt his name. Another day I followed him to his home and for ten copecks I found out from the caretaker where he lived, on which floor, whether alone or with somebody, etc., in fact, everything one could learn from a caretaker. One morning, though I had never indulged in literary work, it suddenly occurred to me to write a story round this officer, a story in a satiric vein, in order to show him up for what he was. I wrote this story with real pleasure. I exposed, I did not hesitate even to libel him; at first I gave him a name which could be immediately recognised as his, but later, on second thoughts, I changed it, and sent the story to "Homeland Notes." But at that time exposures were not in fashion yet, and my story was not published. I felt very sore about it.

Sometimes my resentment became quite unbearable. At last I made up my mind to challenge my enemy to a duel. I wrote him a most beautiful, most charming letter, demanding an apology from him and, if he refused to apologise, hinting rather plainly at a duel. The letter was written in such a way that if the officer had had the least notion of "the sublime and the beautiful," he would certainly have come running to me, fallen on my neck, and offered me his friendship. And how wonderful that would have been! Oh, how wonderfully we should have got on together! He would have protected me by his rank of an army officer, and I would have enlarged his mind by my superior education and—well—by my ideas, and lots of things could have happened! Just consider, this was two years after he had insulted me, and my challenge was absurdly out of date, a pure anachronism, in fact, in spite of the cleverness of my letter explaining away and concealing the lapse of time. But, thank God (to this day I thank the Almighty with tears in my eyes!), I did not send my letter. A shiver runs down my spine when I think of what might have happened if I had sent it. And suddenly—suddenly I revenged myself in the simplest and most extraordinarily clever way! A most brilliant idea suddenly occurred to me.

Sometimes on a holiday I used to take a walk on Nevsky Avenue, on the sunny side of it, and about four o'clock in the afternoon. As a matter of fact, I did not really take a walk there, but went through a series of torments, humiliations, and bilious attacks; but I suppose that was really what I wanted. I darted along like a groundling in the most unbecoming manner imaginable among the people on the pavement, continuously making way for generals, officers of the guards and hussars, and ladies. At those moments I used to have sharp shooting pains in my heart and I used to feel all hot down the back at the mere thought of the miserable appearance of my clothes and the wretchedness of my darting little figure. It was a most dreadful torture, an incessant, unbearable humiliation at the thought, which grew into an uninterrupted and most palpable sensation, that in the eyes of all those high society people I was just a fly, an odious, obscene fly, more intelligent, more highly developed, more noble than anyone else (I had no doubts about that), but a fly that was always making way for everyone, a fly insulted and humiliated by every one. Why I suffered this torment, why I went for my walks on Nevsky Avenue, I do not know. But I was simply *drawn* there at every possible opportunity.

Already at that time I began experiencing the sudden onrush of those keen delights of which I spoke in the first part. But after the incident with the army officer, I felt drawn there more than ever: it was on Nevsky Avenue that I met him most frequently, and it was there that I took such delight in looking at him. He, too, used to take a walk there mostly on holidays. And though he, too, made way for generals and other persons of high rank, though he, too, darted like a groundling among them, he simply bore down on people like me, or even those who were a cut above me; he walked straight at them as though there were just an empty space in front of him, and never in any circumstances did he make way for them. I gloated spitefully as I looked at him and—made way for him resentfully every time he happened to bear down on me. I was tortured by the thought that even in the street I could not be on the same footing as he. "Why do you always have to step aside first?" I asked myself over and over again in a sort of hysterical rage, sometimes waking up at three o'clock in the morning. "Why always you and not he? There is no law about it, is there? There's nothing written down about it, is there? Why can't you arrange it so that each of you should make way for the other, as usually happens when two well-bred men meet in the street? He yields you half of his pavement and you half of yours, and you pass one another with mutual respect." But it never happened like that. It was always I who stepped aside, while he did not even notice that I made way for him.

And it was then the brilliant idea occurred to me. "And what," thought I, "what if I should meet him and—and not move aside? Just not do it on purpose, even if I have to give him a push. Well, what would happen then?" This brazen thought took such a hold of me that it gave me no rest. I thought of it continually and went for a walk on Nevsky Avenue more frequently so as to make quite sure of the way in which I was going to do it when I did do it.

I felt transported. This plan seemed to me more and more feasible and promising. "Of course I'm not going to give him a real push," I thought, feeling much kindlier disposed towards him in my joy. "I'll simply not make way for him. Knock against him, taking good care not to hurt him very much, just shoulder against shoulder, just as much as the laws of propriety allow. I shall only knock against him as much as he knocks against me."

At last my mind was firmly made up. But my preparations took a long time. The first thing I had to take into account was that when I carried out my plan I had to take good care to be as well dressed as possible. I had therefore to see about my clothes. "Just in case, for instance, there should be a public scandal (and there was sure to be quite an audience there: a countess taking a walk, Prince D. taking a walk, the whole literary world taking a walk), one had to be decently dressed. Good clothes impress people and will immediately put us on an equal footing in the eyes of society." Accordingly, I obtained an advance of salary and bought myself a pair of black gloves and a smart hat at Churkin's. Black gloves seemed to me more impressive and more elegant than canary-coloured ones which I had thought of buying first. "Too bright a colour. Looks as though a man wants to show off too much!" So I did not take the canary-coloured ones. I had long ago got ready an excellent shirt with white bone studs; but my overcoat delayed the carrying out of my plan for a long time. My overcoat was not at all bad. It kept me warm. But it was wadded and had a raccoon collar, which made one look altogether too much a flunkey. The collar had to be changed at all costs for a beaver one, like one of those army officers wore. To acquire such a collar, I began visiting the Arcade, and after a few attempts decided to buy a cheap German beaver. These German beavers may soon look shabby and worn, but at first, when new, they look very decent indeed. And I wanted it for one occasion only. I asked the price: it was much too expensive. On thinking it over, I decided to sell my raccoon collar and to borrow the rest of the money (and a considerable sum it was, too) from the head of my department, Anton Antonovich Setochkin, a quiet man, but serious and dependable, who never lent any money to any one, but to whom I had been particularly recommended years ago on entering the service by an important personage who got me the job. I went through hell before taking this step. To ask Anton Antonovich for a loan seemed to me a monstrous and shameful thing. I did not sleep for two or three nights and, as a matter of fact, I did not sleep well at the time generally, feeling very feverish. My heart seemed to be either beating very faintly or suddenly began thumping, thumping, thumping! . . . Anton Antonovich looked rather surprised at first, then he frowned, then he pondered, and in the end he did lend me the money, having made me sign a promissory note authorising him to deduct the money from my salary in a fortnight. In this way everything was settled at last; the beautiful beaver reigned in the place of the odious raccoon, and gradually I set about making the final arrangements. This sort of thing could not be done without careful preparation, without thought. It had to be done skilfully and without hurry. But I must admit that after many attempts to carry my plan into execution, I began to give way to despair: however much I tried, we just did not knock against each other, and there seemed to be nothing I could do about it! Hadn't I got everything ready? Hadn't I made up my mind to go through with it? And did it not now seem that we ought to knock against each other any minute? And yet, when the moment came I made way for him again and he passed without taking any notice of me. I even offered up a prayer when I approached him, beseeching God to fill me with the necessary determination to see the business through. Once I had quite made up my mind, but it all ended by my tripping up and falling down in front of him, for at the last moment, at a distance of only a few feet, my courage failed me. He calmly strode over me, and I was hurled to one side like a ball. That night I was again in a fever and delirious. And suddenly everything came to a most satisfactory conclusion. The night before I had made up my mind most definitely not to go through with my luckless enterprise and to forget all about it, and with that intention I went for a walk on Nevsky Avenue for the last time, just to see how I would forget all about it. Suddenly, only three paces from my enemy, I quite unexpectedly made up my mind, shut my eyes, and —we knocked violently against each other, shoulder to shoulder. I did not budge an inch and passed him absolutely on an equal footing! He did not even look round and pretended not to have noticed anything. But he was only pretending: I am quite sure of that. Yes, to this day I am quite sure of that! Of course I got the worst of it, for he was stronger. But that was not the point. The point was that I had done what I had set out to do, that I had kept up my dignity, that I had not yielded an inch, and that I had put myself publicly on the same social footing as he. I came back home feeling that I had completely revenged myself for everything. I was beside myself with delight. I was in the seventh heaven and sang Italian arias. I shall not, of course, describe to you what happened to me three days later. If you have read my first chapter, you will be able to guess for yourselves. The officer was afterwards transferred somewhere. I have not seen him for fourteen years now. I wonder how the dear fellow is getting on now. Who is he bullying now?

II

But when my mood for odious little dissipations came to an end I used to feel dreadfully flat and miserable. I had an awful conscience about it, but I did my best not to think of it: I felt too miserable for that. Little by little, however, I got used to that, too. I got used to everything, or rather I did not really get used to it, but just made up my mind to grin and bear it. But I had a solution which made up for everything, and that was to seek salvation in all that was "sublime and beautiful," in my dreams, of course. I would give myself up entirely to dreaming. I would dream for three months on end, skulking in my corner. And, believe me, at those moments I bore no resemblance to the gentleman who in his pigeon-livered confusion had sewed a piece of German beaver to the collar of his overcoat. I suddenly became a hero. I shouldn't have admitted my six-foot lieutenant to my rooms even if he had come to pay a call on me. I could not even picture him before me at the time. What exactly my dreams were about, or how I could be content with them, it is difficult to say now, but I was content with them at the time. As a matter of fact, I feel even now a certain glow of satisfaction at the memory of it. It was after my phase of dissipation had passed that I took special pleasure in my dreams which seemed sweeter and more vivid then. They came to me with repentance and tears, with curses and transports of delight. I had moments of such positive intoxication, of such intense happiness, that, I assure you, I did not feel even the faintest stir of derision within me. What I had was faith, hope, and love. The trouble was that in those days I believed blindly that by some miracle, by some outside event, all this would suddenly draw apart and expand, that I would suddenly catch a glimpse of a vista of some suitable activity, beneficent and beautiful, and, above all, an activity that was absolutely ready-made (what sort of activity I never knew, but the great thing was that it was to be all ready-made), and then I would suddenly emerge into the light of day, almost mounted on a white horse and with a laurel wreath on my head. I could not even imagine any place of secondary importance for myself, and for that very reason I quite contentedly occupied the most insignificant one in real life. Either a hero or dirt—there was no middle way. That turned out to be my undoing, for while wallowing in dirt I consoled myself with the thought that at other times I was a hero, and the hero overlaid the dirt: an ordinary mortal, as it were, was ashamed to wallow in dirt, but a hero was too exalted a person to be entirely covered in dirt, and hence I could wallow in dirt with an easy conscience. It is a remarkable fact that these attacks of the "sublime and beautiful" came to me even during my spells of odious dissipation, and more particularly at the time when I was touching bottom. They came quite unexpectedly, in separate outbursts, as though reminding me of themselves, but their appearance never brought my debauch to an end; on the contrary, they seemed to stimulate it by contrast, and they only lasted for as long as it was necessary for them to carry out the function of a good sauce. In this case the sauce consisted of contradictions and suffering, of torturing inner analysis, and all these pangs and torments added piquancy and even meaning to my odious little dissipation—in short, fully carried out the function of a good sauce. All this had a certain profundity, too. For I could never have been content to indulge in the simple, vulgar, direct, sordid debauchery of some office clerk and reconcile myself to all that filth! What else could I have found so attractive in it to draw me into the street at night? No, gentlemen, I had a noble loophole for every thing. . . .

But how much love, good Lord, how much love I used

to experience in those dreams of mine, during those hours of "salvation through the sublime and the beautiful"; fantastic though that sort of love was and though in reality it had no relation whatever to anything human, there was so much of it, so much of this love, that one did not feel the need of applying it in practice afterwards; that would indeed have been a superfluous luxury. Everything, however, always ended most satisfactorily in an indolent and rapturous transition to art, that is, to the beautiful forms of existence, all ready-made, snatched forcibly from the poets and novelists and adapted to every possible need and requirement. For instance, I triumphed over everything; all of course lay in the dust at my feet, compelled of their own free will to acknowledge all my perfections, and I forgave them all. I was a famous poet and court chamberlain, and I fell in love; I became a multi-millionaire and at once devoted all my wealth to the improvement of the human race, and there and then confessed all my hideous and shameful crimes before all the people; needless to say, my crimes were, of course, not really hideous or shameful, but had much in them that was "sublime and beautiful," something in the style of Manfred. All would weep and kiss me (what damned fools they'd have been otherwise!), and I'd go off, barefoot and hungry, to preach new ideas and inflict another Waterloo on the reactionaries. Then the band would be brought out and strike up a march, a general amnesty would be granted, and the Pope would agree to leave Rome for Brazil; then there would be a ball for the whole of Italy at the Villa Borghese on the banks of Lake Como, Lake Como being specially transferred for that occasion to the neighbourhood of Rome; this would be followed by the scene in the bushes, and so on and so forth—don't tell me you don't know it! You will say it is mean and contemptible now to shout it all from the housetops after all the raptures and tears which I have myself confessed to. But why, pray, is it mean? Surely, you don't think I'm ashamed of it, do you? You don't imagine by any chance that all this was much sillier than what ever happened in your life, gentlemen? And let me assure you that certain things were not so badly worked out by me, either. . . . It did not all take place on the banks of Lake Como. Of course, on the other hand, you are quite right. As a matter of fact, it is mean and contemptible. And what is even meaner is that now I should be trying to justify myself to you. Enough of this, though, or I should never finish: things are quite sure to get meaner and meaner anyway.

I was never able to spend more than three months of dreaming at a time without feeling an irresistible urge to plunge into social life. To me plunging into social life meant paying a call on the head of my department, Anton Antonovich Setochkin. He was the only permanent acquaintance I have had in my life, and I can't help being surprised at it myself now. But I used to call on him only when I was in the right mood for such a visit, when, that is, my dreams had reached such a pinnacle of bliss that I felt an instant and irresistible urge to embrace all my fellow-men and all humanity. But to do that one had at least to have one man who actually existed. However, it was only on Tuesdays that one could call on Anton Antonovich (Tuesday was his at home day), and therefore it was necessary to work myself up into the right mood for embracing all mankind on that day. This Anton Antonovich Setochkin lived at Five Corners, on the fourth floor, in four little rooms with low ceilings, one smaller than the other, and all of a most frugal and jaundiced appearance. He had two daughters and their aunt who used to pour out the tea. One of the daughters was thirteen and the other fourteen; both had snub noses and both used to embarrass me terribly because they kept whispering to each other and giggling. The master of the house was usually in his study. He sat on a leather sofa in front of his desk, with some grey-haired visitor, a civil servant from our department or, occasionally, from some other department. I never saw more than two or three visitors there, and always the same. The usual topic of conversation was excise duties, the hard bargaining in the Senate, salaries, promotions, His Excellency, the best way to please him, etc., etc. I had the patience to sit like a damn fool beside these people for hours, listening to them, neither daring to speak to them, nor knowing what to say. I got more and more bored, broke out into a sweat, and was in danger of getting an apoplectic stroke. But all this was good and useful to me. When I came home, I would put off for a time my desire to embrace all mankind.

I had, by the way, another acquaintance of a sort, a

fellow by the name of Simonov, an old schoolfellow of mine. I suppose I must have had quite a lot of schoolfellows in Petersburg, but I had nothing to do with them and even stopped exchanging greetings with them in the street. I expect the real reason why I had got myself transferred to another department in the Civil Service was that I did not want to have anything to do with them any more. I wanted to cut myself off completely from the hateful years of my childhood. To hell with that school and those terrible years of slavery! In short, I broke with my schoolfellows as soon as I began to shift for myself. There were only two or three of them left with whom I still exchanged greetings in the street. One of them was Simonov, who was a very quiet boy at school, of an equable nature and not particularly brilliant, but I discerned in him a certain independence of character and even honesty. I don't think he was a dull fellow at all. Not very dull, anyway. We had had some bright times together, but I'm afraid they did not last long and somehow or other got lost in a mist rather suddenly. I had a feeling that he did not exactly relish being reminded of those times and that he seemed to be always afraid that I might adopt the same tone with him again. I suspected that he really loathed the sight of me, but as I was never quite sure about it, I went on visiting him.

So that one Thursday afternoon, unable to bear my solitude any longer and knowing that on Thursdays Anton Antonovich's door would be closed, I thought of Simonov. As I was climbing up to his rooms on the fourth floor, I could not help thinking that this particular gentleman must be sick and tired of me and that I was wasting my time going to see him. But as it invariably happened that such reflections merely spurred me on to put myself into an equivocal position, I went in. It was almost a year since I had last seen Simonov.

III

I found two more of my former schoolfellows with him. They seemed to be discussing some highly important matter. None of them took any particular notice of my arrival, which struck me as rather odd considering that I had not seen them for years. No doubt they regarded me as some sort of common fly. I had never been treated like that even at school, though they all hated me there. I realised, of course, that they could not help despising me now for my failure to get on in the Civil Service, for my having sunk so low, going about shabbily dressed, etc., which in their eyes was, as it were, an advertisement of my own incompetence and insignificance. But all the same I had never expected so great a contempt for me. Simonov could not even disguise his surprise at my visit. He always used to be surprised at my visits, at least that was the impression I got. All this rather upset me. I sat down, feeling somewhat put out, and began listening to their conversation.

They were discussing very earnestly, and even with some warmth, the question of a farewell dinner which they wanted to give next day to a friend of theirs, an army officer by the name of Zverkov, who was due to leave for some remote place in the provinces. Zverkov too had been at school with me all the time, but I grew to hate him particularly in the upper forms. In the lower forms he had been just a good-looking, high-spirited boy, who was a favourite with everybody. I had dated him, however, even in the lower forms just because he was so good-looking and high-spirited a boy. He was never good at lessons, and as time went on he got worse and worse. But he got his school certificate all right because he had powerful connections. During his last year at school he came into an inheritance, an estate with two hundred peasants, and as almost all of us were poor, he even began showing off to us. He was superlatively vulgar, but a good fellow in spite of it, even when he gave himself airs. And in spite of the superficial, fantastic, and rather silly ideas of honour and fair play we had at school, all but a few of us grovelled before Zverkov, and the more he showed off, the more anxious were they to get into his good books. And they did it not because of any selfish motives, but simply because he had been favoured with certain gifts by nature. Besides, Zverkov was for some reason looked upon by us as an authority on smartness and good manners. The last point in particular used to infuriate me. I hated the brusque, self-assured tone of his voice, the way he enjoyed his own jokes, which, as a matter of fact, were awfully silly, though he always was rather daring in his expressions; I hated his handsome but rather vapid face (for which, by the way, I would

have gladly exchanged my *clever* one) and his free and
easy military manners which were in vogue in the forties. I hated the way in which he used to talk of his future conquests (he did not have the courage to start an
affair with a woman before getting his officer's epaulettes,
and was looking forward to them with impatience), and
of the duels he would be fighting almost every minute.
I remember how I, who had always been so reserved and
taciturn, had a furious argument with Zverkov when he
was discussing his future love affairs with his cronies during playtime and, becoming as playful as a puppy in the
sun, suddenly declared that on his estate he would not
leave a single peasant girl who was a virgin without his at-
tentions, that that was his *droit de seigneur,* and that if
any of his peasants dared to protest he would have them
flogged and double the tax on them, too, the bearded rascals. Our oafs applauded him, but I got my teeth into him
not because I was sorry for the virgins or their fathers,
but just because they were applauding such an insect. I
got the better of him then, but though a great fool, Zverkov was an impudent and jolly fellow, so he laughed the
whole affair off, and did it so well that I didn't really get
the better of him in the end: the laugh was against me.
He got the better of me several times afterwards, but
without malice and as though it were all a great lark,
with a casual sort of laugh. I would not reply to him,
keeping resentfully and contemptuously silent. When we
left school, Zverkov seemed anxious to be friends with
me, and feeling flattered, I did not object; but we soon,
and quite naturally, drifted apart. Afterward I heard of
his barrackroom successes as a lieutenant and of the *gay*
life he was leading. Then other rumours reached me of
his *progress* in the army. Already he began cutting me
dead in the street, and I suspected he was afraid of compromising himself by greeting so insignificant a person as
me. I also saw him at the theatre once, in the circle, already wearing shoulder-straps. He was bowing and scraping to the daughters of some ancient general. In three
years he had lost his youthful looks, though he still was
quite handsome and smart. He was beginning to put on
weight and looked somewhat bloated. It was pretty clear
that by the time he was thirty he would go completely fat
and flabby. It was to this Zverkov, who was now leaving
the capital, that our friends were going to give a din-

ner. They had been his boon companions, though I felt sure that in their hearts they never thought themselves his equal.

Of Simonov's two friends one was Ferfichkin, a Russian of German origin, a little fellow with the face of a monkey and one of my worst enemies from our earliest days at school. He was an utterly contemptible, impudent, conceited fellow who liked to parade his claims to a most meticulous sense of honour, but who really was a rotten little coward at heart. He belonged to those of Zverkov's admirers who fawned on him for selfish reasons and who, in fact, often borrowed money from him. Simonov's other visitor, Trudolyubov, was not in any way remarkable. He was an army officer, tall, with rather a cold countenance, fairly honest, but a great admirer of every kind of success and only capable of discussing promotions. He seemed to be a distant relative of Zverkov's, and that, foolish as it may sound, invested him with a certain prestige among us. He always regarded me as a man of no importance, but if not polite, his treatment of me was tolerant.

"Well," said Trudolyubov, "I suppose if we contribute seven roubles each we'll have twenty-one roubles, and for that we ought to be able to get a damn good dinner. Zverkov, of course, won't pay."

"Naturally," Simonov agreed, "if we're inviting him."

"Surely you don't suppose," Ferfichkin interjected superciliously and with some warmth, like an impudent footman who was boasting about the decorations of his master the general, "surely you don't suppose Zverkov will let us pay for him, do you? He might let us pay for the dinner out of a feeling of delicacy, but I bet you anything he'll contribute half a dozen bottles of champagne."

"Half a dozen for the four of us is a bit too much, isn't it?" remarked Trudolyubov, paying attention only to the half-dozen.

"So the three of us then, with Zverkov making four, twenty-one roubles, at the Hôtel de Paris at five o'clock tomorrow," Simonov, who had been chosen as the organiser of the dinner, concluded finally.

"How do you mean twenty-one?" I said in some agitation, pretending to be rather offended. "If you count me, you'll have twenty-eight roubles, and not twenty-one."

I felt that to offer myself suddenly and so unexpectedly

as one of the contributors to the dinner was rather a handsome gesture on my part and that they would immediately accept my offer with enthusiasm and look at me with respect.

"You don't want to contribute, too, do you?" Simonov observed without concealing his displeasure and trying not to look at me.

He could read me like a book.

I felt furious that he should be able to read me like a book.

"But why shouldn't I? I'm an old school friend of his, am I not? I must say I can't help resenting being passed over like that!" I spluttered again.

"And where do you suppose were we to find you?" Ferfichkin broke in, rudely.

"You were never on good terms with Zverkov, you know," Trudolyubov added, frowning.

But I had got hold of the idea and I was not to give it up so easily.

"I don't think anyone has a right to express an opinion about that," I replied with a tremor in my voice, as though goodness knows what had happened. "It is just because I was not on very good terms with him before that I might like to meet him now."

"Well," Trudolyubov grinned, "who can make you out —all those fine ideals——"

"Very well," Simonov made up his mind, "we'll put your name down. Tomorrow at five o'clock at the Hôtel de Paris. Don't forget."

"But the money!" Ferfichkin began in an undertone, addressing Simonov and nodding in my direction, but he stopped short, for even Simonov felt embarrassed.

"All right," Trudolyubov said, getting up, "let him come, if he really wants to so much."

"But, damn it all, it's only a dinner for a few intimate friends," Ferfichkin remarked crossly as he, too, picked up his hat. "It's not an official gathering. How do you know we want you at all?"

They went away. As he went out, Ferfichkin did not even think it necessary to say goodbye to me. Trudolyubov just nodded, without looking at me. Simonov, with whom I now remained alone, seemed perplexed and puzzled, and he gave me a strange look. He did not sit down, nor did he ask me to take a seat.

"Mmmm—yes—tomorrow then. Will you let me have the money now? I mean, I'd like to know—" he murmured, looking embarrassed.

I flushed and, as I did so, I remembered that I had owed Simonov fifteen roubles for years, which, incidentally I never forgot, though I never returned the money.

"But look here, Simonov, you must admit that I couldn't possibly have known when I came here that—I mean, I am of course very sorry I forgot——"

"All right, all right! It makes no difference. You can pay me tomorrow at the dinner. I just want to know, that's all. Please, don't——"

He stopped short and began pacing the room noisily, looking more vexed than ever. As he paced the room, he raised himself on his heels and stamped even more noisily.

"I'm not keeping you, am I?" I asked after a silence of two minutes.

"Oh, no, not at all!" He gave a sudden start. "I mean, as a matter of fact, you are. You see I have an appointment with someone,—er—not far from here," he added in an apologetic sort of voice, a little ashamed.

"Good Lord, why didn't you tell me?" I cried, seizing my cap with rather a nonchalant air, though goodness only knows where I got it from.

"Oh, it's not far really—only a few steps from here," Simonov repeated, seeing me off to the front door with a bustling air, which did not become him at all. "So tomorrow at five o'clock sharp!" he shouted after me as I was going down the stairs.

He seemed very glad indeed to see me go, but I was mad with rage.

"What possessed me to do it?" I muttered, grinding my teeth, as I walked along the street. "And for such a rotter, such a swine as Zverkov. Of course I mustn't go. Of course to hell with the lot of them. Why should I? I'm not obliged to, am I? I'll let Simonov know tomorrow. Drop him a line by post."

But the reason why I was so furious was because I knew perfectly well that I should go, that I should go deliberately; and that the more tactless, the more indecent my going was, the more certainly would I go.

And there was a good reason why I should not go: I had not got the money. All in all, I had nine roubles, but of that I had to give seven to my servant Apollon tomorrow for his monthly wages, out of which he paid for his board. Not to pay him was quite out of the question, knowing as I did the sort of man Apollon was. But of that fiend, of that scourge of mine, I shall speak another time.

Anyway, I knew very well that I wouldn't pay him, but would quite certainly go to the dinner.

That night I had the most hideous dreams. And no wonder. The whole evening I was haunted by memories of my hateful days at school, and I could not get rid of them. I was sent to the school by some distant relations of mine, on whom I was dependent and of whom I have not heard anything since. They dumped me there, an orphan already crushed by their reproaches, already accustomed to brood for hours on end, always silent, one who looked sullenly on everything around him. My schoolmates overwhelmed me with spiteful and pitiless derision because I was not like any of them. And derision was the only thing I could not stand. I did not find it at all as easy to make friends with people as they did to make friends among themselves. I at once conceived a bitter hatred for them and withdrew from them all into my own shell of wounded, timid, and excessive pride. Their coarseness appalled me. They laughed cynically at my face, at my ungainly figure. And yet how stupid their own faces were! At our school the faces of the boys seemed to undergo an extraordinary change and grow particularly stupid. Lots of nice looking children entered our school, but after a few years one could not look at them without a feeling of revulsion. Even at the age of sixteen I wondered morosely at them. Even at that time I was amazed at the pettiness of their thoughts, the silliness of their occupations, their games, their conversations. They did not understand even the most necessary things; they were not interested in anything that was out of the ordinary, in anything that was conducive to thought, so that I could not help looking on them as my inferiors. It was not injured vanity that drove me to it, and don't for goodness' sake come to me with your hackneyed and nauseating objections, such as, for instance, that I was only dreaming, while they understood the real meaning of life even then. They understood nothing. They had not the faintest idea of real life. Indeed, it was just that I could not stand most of all about them. On the contrary, they had a most fantastic and absurd notion of the most simple, most ordinary facts, and already at that early age they got into the habit of admiring success alone. Everything that was just but looked down upon and oppressed, they laughed at shamelessly and heartlessly. Rank they mistook for brains. Even at sixteen all they were discussing was cushy jobs. A great deal of it, no doubt, was due to their stupidity, to the bad examples with which they had been surrounded in their childhood and adolescence. And they were abominably vicious. I suppose much of that, too, was only on the surface, much of their depravity was just affected cynicism, and even in their vices one could catch a glimpse of youth and of a certain freshness. But that freshness had nothing attractive about it, and it took the form of a kind of rakishness. I hated them terribly, though I suppose I was really much worse than they. They repaid me in the same coin and did not conceal their loathing of me. But I was no longer anxious for them to like me; on the contrary, I longed continually to humiliate them. To escape their ridicule, I purposely began to apply myself more diligently to my studies and was soon among the top boys in my form. This did make an impression on them. Moreover, they all began gradually to realise that I was already reading books they could not read, and that I understood things (not included in our school curriculum) of which they had not even heard. They looked sullenly and sardonically on all this, but they had to acknowledge my moral superiority, particularly as even the teachers took notice of me on account of it. Their jeering stopped, but their hostility remained, and henceforth our relations became strained and frigid. In the end I could no longer stand it myself: the older I became, the more I longed for the society of men and the more I was in need of friends. I tried to become friends with some of them, but my friendship with them always somehow appeared unnatural and came to an end of itself. I did have a sort of a friend once, but by that time I was already a tyrant at heart: I wanted to exercise complete authority over him, I wanted to implant a contempt for his surroundings in his heart, I demanded that he should break away from these surroundings, scornfully and finally. I frightened him with my passionate friendship. I reduced him to tears, to hysterics.

He was a simple and devoted soul, but the moment I felt that he was completely in my power I grew to hate him and drove him from me, as though I only wanted him for the sake of gaining a victory over him, for the sake of exacting his complete submission to me. But I could not get the better of them all. My friend, too, was unlike any of the others; he was, in fact, a rare exception. The first thing I did on leaving school was to give up the career for which I had been trained so as to break all the ties that bound me to my past, which I loathed and abominated. . . . And I'm damned if I know why after all that I should go trotting off to see that Simonov! . . .

Early next morning I jumped out of bed in a state of tremendous excitement, as though everything were about to happen there and then. But I really did believe that there was going to be some radical break in my life and that it would most certainly come that day. Whether it was because I was not used to change or for some other reason, but all through my life I could not help feeling that any extraneous event, however trivial, would immediately bring about some radical alteration in my life. However, I went to the office as usual, but slipped away home two hours early to get ready. The important thing, I thought, was not to arrive there first, or they might think that I was really glad to be in their company. But there were thousands of such important things to think of, and they excited me so much that in the end I felt a physical wreck. I gave my boots another polish with my own hands; Apollon would not have cleaned them twice a day for anything in the world, for he considered that a most irregular procedure. I polished them with the brushes I had sneaked from the passage to make sure he did not know anything about it, for I did not want him to despise me for it afterwards. Then I submitted my clothes to a most meticulous inspection and found that everything was old, worn, and covered with stains. I had certainly grown much too careless of my appearance. My Civil Service uniform was not so bad, but I could not go out to dinner in my uniform, could I? The worst of it was that there was a huge yellow stain on the knee of my trousers. I had a presentiment that that stain alone would rob me of nine-tenths of my self-respect. I knew, too, that it was a thought unworthy of me. "But this is no time for thinking: now I have to face reality," I thought with a sinking heart. I knew, of course, perfectly well at the time that I was monstrously exaggerating all these facts. But what could I do? It was too late for me to control my feelings, and I was shaking with fever. I imagined with despair how patronisingly and how frigidly that "rotter" Zverkov would meet me; with what dull and irresistible contempt that blockhead Trudolyubov would look at me; with what unbearable insolence that insect Ferfichkin would titter at me in order to curry favour with Zverkov; how perfectly Simonov would understand it all and how he would despise me for the baseness of my vanity and want of spirit, and, above all, how paltry, *unliterary*, and commonplace the whole affair would be. Of course, the best thing would be not to go at all. But that was most of all out of the question: once I felt drawn into something, I was drawn into it head foremost. All my life I should have jeered at myself afterwards: "So you were afraid, were you? Afraid of *life!* Afraid!" On the contrary, I longed passionately to show all that "rabble" that I was not such a coward as even I imagined myself to be. And that was not all by any means: in the most powerful paroxysms of my cowardly fever I dreamed of getting the upper hand, of sweeping the floor with them, of forcing them to admire and like me—if only for my "lofty thoughts and indisputable wit." They would turn their backs on Zverkov, he would be left sitting by himself in some corner, silent and ashamed, utterly crushed by me. Afterwards, no doubt, I would make it up with him and we would drink to our everlasting friendship. But what was most galling and infuriating to me was that even then I knew without a shadow of doubt that, as a matter of fact, I did not want any of this at all, that, as a matter of fact, I had not the least desire to get the better of them, to crush them, to make them like me, and that if I ever were to do so, I should not give a rap for it. Oh, how I prayed for the day to pass quickly! Feeling utterly miserable I walked up again and again to the window, opened the small ventilating pane, and peered out into the murky haze of the thickly falling wet snow. . . .

At last my cheap clock wheezed out five. I seized my hat and, trying not to look at Apollon, who had been waiting for his wages ever since the morning but was too big a fool to speak to me about it first, slipped past him through the door, and in a smart sledge, which cost me my last fifty copecks, drove up in great style to the Hôtel de Paris.

IV

I had had a feeling the day before that I'd be the first to arrive. But it was no longer a question of arriving first. For not only were they not there, but I could hardly find the room. Nor was the table laid. What did it mean? After many inquiries I found out at last from the waiters that the dinner had been ordered for six and not for five o'clock. I had that confirmed at the bar, too. I even began feeling ashamed to go on making those inquiries. It was only twenty-five minutes past five. If they had changed the dinner hour, they should at least have let me know—what was the post for?—and not have exposed me to such "humiliation" in my own eyes and—and certainly not in the eyes of the waiters. I sat down. A waiter began laying the table. I felt even more humiliated in his presence. Towards six o'clock they brought in candles in addition to the burning lamps. The waiter, however, had never thought of bringing them in as soon as I arrived. In the next room two gloomy gentlemen were having dinner at separate tables; they looked angry and were silent. People in one of the other rooms were kicking up a terrible shindy, shouting at the top of their voices; I could hear the loud laughter of a whole crowd of people, interspersed with some disgustingly shrill shrieks in French: there were ladies at the dinner. The whole thing, in short, could not have been more nauseating. I don't remember ever having had such a bad time, so that when, punctually at six, they arrived all together, I was at first very glad to see them, as though they were my deliverers, and I almost forgot that I ought to be looking offended.

Zverkov entered the room ahead of everybody, quite obviously the leading spirit of the whole company. He and his companions were laughing. But as soon as he caught sight of me, he pulled himself up and, walking up to me unhurriedly, bent his body slightly from the waist, as though showing off what a fine gentleman he was. He shook hands with me affably, though not too affably, with a sort of watchful politeness, almost as though he were already a general, and as though in giving me his hand he was protecting himself against something. I had imagined that as soon as he came in he would, on the contrary, break into his customary high-pitched laugh, intermingled with shrill shrieks, and at once start making his insipid jokes and witticisms. It was to deal with this that I had been preparing myself since last evening, but I had never expected such condescending affability, such grand manners of a person of the highest rank. So he already considered himself infinitely superior to me in every respect, did he? If he only meant to insult me with the superior airs of a general, it would not matter, I thought to myself; but what if, without the least desire to offend me, the fool had really got the preposterous idea into his head that he was immeasurably superior to me and could not look at me but with a patronising air? The very thought of it made me choke with resentment.

"I was surprised to hear of your desire to join us," he began, mouthing and lisping, which he never used to do before. "I'm afraid we haven't seen much of each other recently. You seem to avoid us. A pity. We're not so terrible as you think. Anyway, I'm glad to—er—re-e-sume —er——" and he turned away casually to put down his hat on the windowsill.

"Been waiting long?" asked Trudolyubov.

"I arrived at precisely five o'clock as I was told to yesterday," I replied in a loud voice and with an irritation that threatened an early explosion.

"Didn't you let him know that we had changed the hour?" Trudolyubov asked, turning to Simonov.

"I'm afraid I didn't—forgot all about it," Simonov replied unrepentantly and, without a word of apology to me, went off to order the *hors d'œuvres*.

"You poor fellow, so you've been waiting here for a whole hour, have you?" Zverkov exclaimed sarcastically, for, according to his notions, this was really very funny.

That awful cad Ferfichkin broke into a nasty, shrill chuckle, like the yapping of a little dog. My position seemed to him too ludicrous and too embarrassing for words.

"It isn't funny at all!" I cried to Ferfichkin, getting more and more irritated. "It was somebody's else's fault, not mine. I expect I wasn't considered important enough to be told. This—this—this is simply idiotic!"

"No only idiotic, but something else as well," Trudolyubov muttered, naïvely taking my part. "You're much too nice about it. It's simply insulting. Unintentional, no doubt. And how could Simonov—well!"

"If anyone had played that kind of joke on me," observed Ferfichkin, "I'd——"

"You'd have ordered something for yourself," Zverkov interrupted him, "or simply asked for dinner without waiting for us."

"But you must admit I could have done as much without your permission," I rapped out. "If I waited, I——"

"Let's take our seats, gentlemen," Simonov cried, coming in. "Everything's ready. I can answer for the champagne—it's been excellently iced. . . . I'm sorry," he suddenly turned to me, but again somehow avoiding looking at me, "but I didn't know your address, and so I couldn't possibly have got hold of you, could I?"

He must have had something against me. Must have changed his mind after my visit last night.

All sat down; so did I. The table was a round one. Trudolyubov was on my left and Simonov on my right. Zverkov was sitting opposite with Ferfichkin next to him, between him and Trudolyubov.

"Tell me plea-ea-se are you—er—in a Government department?" Zverkov continued to be very attentive to me.

He saw how embarrassed I was and he seriously imagined that it was his duty to be nice to me and, as it were, cheer me up.

"Does he want me to throw a bottle at his head?" I thought furiously. As I was unaccustomed to these surroundings, I was getting irritated somehow unnaturally quickly.

"In the . . . office," I replied abruptly, my eyes fixed on my plate.

"Good Lord, and do-o-o you find it re-mu-nerative? Tell me, plea-ea-se, what indu-u-uced you to give up your old job?"

"What indu-u-uced me was simply that I got fed up with my old job," I answered, drawing out the words three times as much as he and scarcely able to control myself.

Ferfichkin snorted. Simonov glanced ironically at me. Trudolyubov stopped eating and began observing me curiously.

Zverkov winced, but pretended not to have noticed anything.

"We-e-e-ell, and what's your screw?"

"Which screw?"

"I mean, what's your sa-a-alary?"

"You're not by any chance cross-examining me, are you?"

However, I told him at once what my salary was. I was blushing terribly.

"Not much," Zverkov observed importantly.

"No," Ferfichkin added insolently, "hardly enough to pay for your dinners at a restaurant."

"I think it's simply beggarly," Trudolyubov said, seriously.

"And how thin you've grown, how you've changed since—er—those days," added Zverkov, no longer without venom, examining my clothes with a sort of impudent compassion.

"Stop embarrassing the poor fellow," Ferfichkin exclaimed, giggling.

"You're quite mistaken, sir," I burst out at last, "I'm not at all embarrassed. Do you hear? I'm dining here at this restaurant, sir, at my own expense, and not at other people's. Make a note of that, Mr. Ferfichkin."

"What do you mean?" Ferfichkin flew at me, turning red as a lobster and glaring furiously at me. "And who, sir, isn't dining at his own expense here? You seem to——"

"I mean what I said," I replied, feeling that I had gone too far, "and I think we'd better talk of something more intelligent."

"You're not by any chance anxious to show off your intelligence, are you?"

"I shouldn't worry about that, if I were you. It would be entirely out of place here."

"What are you talking about, my dear sir? You haven't gone out of your mind at that _le_partment of yours, have you?"

"Enough, enough, gentlemen!" Zverkov cried in a commanding voice.

"How damn silly!" Simonov muttered.

"It is damn silly," Trudolyubov said, addressing himself rudely to me alone. "Here we are, a few good friends, met to wish godspeed to a comrade, and you're trying to settle old scores! It was you who invited yourself to join us yesterday, so why are you now upsetting the friendly atmosphere of this dinner?"

"Enough, enough, gentlemen!" Zverkov cried again. "Drop it,

gentlemen. This is hardly the time or place for a brawl. Let me rather tell you how I nearly got married the other day!"

And off he went to tell some scandalous story of how he had nearly got married a few days before. There was, by the way, not a word about the marriage. The story was all about generals, colonels, and even court chamberlains, and Zverkov, of course, played the most important part among them. It was followed by a burst of appreciative laughter, Ferfichkin's high-pitched laugh breaking into loud shrieks.

None of them paid any attention to me, and I sat there feeling crushed and humiliated.

"Good heavens, is this the sort of company for me?" I thought. "And what an ass I've made of myself in front of them! I let Ferfichkin go too far, though. The idiots think they do me an honour by letting me sit down at the same table with them. They don't seem to realise that it is I who am doing them an honour, and not they me. 'You look so thin! Your clothes!' Damn my trousers! I'm sure Zverkov noticed the stain on the knee the moment he came in. . . . But what the hell am I doing here? I'd better get up at once, this minute, take my hat, and simply go without a word. . . . Show them how much I despise them! Don't care a damn if I have to fight a duel tomorrow. The dirty rotters! Do they really think I care about the seven roubles? They might, though. . . . To hell with it! I don't care a damn about the seven roubles! I'll go this minute!"

But, of course, I stayed.

In my despair I drank glass after glass of sherry and Château Lafitte. As I was unused to drink, I got drunk very quickly, and the more drunk I got the hotter did my resentment grow. I suddenly felt like insulting them in the most insolent way and then going. Waiting for the right moment, then showing them the kind of man I was, and in that way forcing them to admit that, though I might be absurd, I was clever and—and—oh, to hell with them!

I looked impudently at them with leaden eyes. But they seemed to have entirely forgotten me. *They* were noisy, clamorous, happy. Zverkov was talking all the time. I started listening. He was talking about some ravishingly beautiful woman whom he had brought to the point of declaring her love to him at last (he was of course lying like a trooper), and how an intimate friend of his, a prince of sorts, a hussar by the name of Kolya, who owned three thousand peasants, was particularly helpful to him in this affair.

"And yet this friend of yours, the chap with the three thousand peasants, isn't here, is he? To see you off, I mean," I broke into the conversation.

For a minute there was dead silence.

"I believe you're quite tight now." Trudolyubov at last condescended to notice me, throwing a disdainful glance in my direction.

Zverkov stared at me in silence, examining me as though I were an insect. Simonov quickly began pouring out the champagne.

Trudolyubov raised his glass, all the others except myself following his example.

"To your health and a pleasant journey!" he cried to Zverkov. "To our past, gentlemen, and to our future! Hurrah!"

They drained their glasses and rushed to embrace Zverkov. I did not stir; my full glass stood untouched before me.

"Aren't you going to drink?" roared Trudolyubov, losing patience and addressing me menacingly.

"I want to make a speech too—er—a special speech and—and then I'll drink, Mr. Trudolyubov."

"Unmannerly brute!" muttered Simonov.

I drew myself up in my chair and took up my glass feverishly, preparing myself for something extraordinary, though I hardly knew myself what I was going to say.

"Silence!" cried Ferfichkin. "Now we're going to hear something really clever!"

Zverkov waited gravely, realising what was in the wind.

"Lieutenant Zverkov," I began, "I'd like you to know that I hate empty phrases, phrasemongers, and tight waists. . . . That is the first point I should like to make. The second will follow presently."

They all stirred uneasily.

"My second point: I hate smutty stories and the fellows who tell them. Especially the fellows who tell them. My third point: I love truth, frankness, and honesty," I went on almost mechanically, for I was beginning to freeze with terror myself, quite at a loss how I came to talk like this. "I love thought, Mr. Zverkov. I love true comradeship where all are equal, and not—er—yes. I love—but what the hell! Why not? I'll drink to your health too, Mr. Zverkov. Seduce the Caucasian maidens, shoot the enemies of our country and—and—to your health, Mr. Zverkov!"

Zverkov got up from his seat, bowed, and said, "Very much obliged to you, I'm sure."

He was terribly offended and even turned pale.

"Damn it all!" Trudolyubov roared, striking the table with his fist.

"Why, sir," Ferfichkin squealed, "people get a punch on the nose for that!"

"Let's kick him out!" muttered Simonov.

"Not another word, gentlemen, please!" Zverkov cried solemnly, putting a stop to the general indignation. "I thank you all, but leave it to me to show him how much value I attach to his words."

"Mr. Ferfichkin," I said in a loud voice, addressing myself importantly to Ferfichkin, "I expect you to give me full satisfaction tomorrow for your words just now!"

"You mean a duel, do you? With pleasure, sir!" Ferfichkin replied, but I must have looked so ridiculous as I challenged him, and the whole thing, in fact, must have looked so incongruous in view of my small stature, that everyone, including Ferfichkin, roared with laughter.

"Oh, leave him alone for goodness' sake," Trudolyubov said with disgust. "The fellow's tight!"

"I shall never forgive myself for having put his name down," Simonov muttered again.

"Now is the time to throw a bottle at them," I thought, picked up the bottle and—poured myself out another glass.

". . . No, I'd better see it through to the end!" I went on thinking to myself. "You'd be pleased if I went away, gentlemen, wouldn't you? But I shan't go. Oh, no. Not for anything in the world. I'll go on sitting here on purpose—and drinking—to the end just to show you that I don't care a damn for you. I'll go on sitting and drinking because this is nothing but a low-class pub and, besides, I paid for everything. I'll sit and drink because I think you're a lot of nobodies, a lot of miserable, paltry nobodies. I'll sit and drink and—and sing, if I like. Yes, sing! For, damn it, I've a right to sing—er—yes."

But I did not sing. I just did my best not to look at them,

assumed most independent attitudes, and waited patiently for them to speak to me *first*. But, alas, they did not speak to me. And how I longed—oh, how I longed at that moment to be reconciled to them! It struck eight, then at last nine. They moved from the table to the sofa. Zverkov made himself comfortable on the sofa, placing one foot on a little round table. They took the wine with them. Zverkov did actually stand them three bottles of champagne. He did not of course invite me to join them. They all sat round him on the sofa, listening to him almost with reverence. It was clear that they were fond of him. "But why? Why?" I asked myself. From time to time they were overcome with drunken enthusiasm and kissed each other. They talked about the Caucasus, about the nature of real passion, about cards, about cushy jobs in the service; about the income of the hussar Podkharzhevsky, whom none of them knew personally, and they were glad he had such a large income; about the marvellous grace and beauty of princess D., whom none of them had ever seen, either; and at last they finished up with the statement that Shakespeare was immortal.

I was smiling contemptuously, walking up and down at the other end of the room, directly opposite the sofa, along the wall, from the table to the stove, and back again. I did my best to show them that I could do without them, at the same time deliberately stamping on the floor, raising myself up and down on my heels. But it was all in vain. *They* paid no attention to me. I had the patience to pace the room like that right in front of them from eight till eleven o'clock, always in the same place, from the table to the stove, and back again. "Here I am, walking up and down, just as I please, and no one can stop me!" The waiter, who kept coming into the room, stopped and looked at me a few times. I was beginning to feel giddy from turning round so frequently, and there were moments when I thought I was delirious. Three times during those three hours I got wet through with perspiration and three times I got dry again. At times the thought would flash through my mind and stab my heart with fierce, intense pain that ten, twenty, forty years would pass and I would still remember after forty years with humiliation and disgust those beastly, ridiculous and horrible moments of my life. It was quite impossible for anyone to abase himself more disgracefully and do it

more willingly, and I realised it fully—fully—and yet I
went on pacing the room from the table to the stove, and
from the stove to the table. "Oh, if only you knew the
thoughts and feelings I'm capable of and how intelligent
I am!" I thought again and again, addressing myself mentally to the sofa on which my enemies were sitting. But
my enemies behaved as though I were not in the room at
all. Once, only once, they turned to me, just when Zverkov
began talking about Shakespeare and I burst out laughing
contemptuously. I guffawed in so affected and disgusting
a manner that they at once interrupted their conversation
and watched me silently for a couple of minutes, with a
grave air and without laughing, walking up and down
along the wall from the table to the stove, *taking no notice
of them*. But nothing came of it: they said nothing to me,
and two minutes later stopped taking any notice of me
again. It struck eleven.

"Gentlemen," Zverkov cried, getting up from the sofa,
"now let's all go *there!*"

"Of course, of course," the others said.

I turned abruptly to Zverkov. I was so exhausted, so
dead beat, that I would have gladly cut my own throat to
put an end to my misery. I was feverish. My hair, wet
with perspiration, stuck to my forehead and temples.

"Zverkov," I said sharply and determinedly, "I'm sorry.
Ferfichkin and all of you, all of you, I hope you'll forgive
me—I've offended you all!"

"Aha! Got frightened of the duel, have you?" Ferfichkin hissed venomously.

I felt as though he had stabbed me to the heart.

"No, Ferfichkin, I'm not afraid of the duel. I'm ready
to fight you tomorrow, if you like, but only after we've
made it up. Yes, I even insist on it, and you can't possibly
refuse me. I want to show you that I'm not afraid of a
duel. You can fire first, and I'll fire in the air!"

"Pleased with himself, isn't he?" Simonov remarked.

"Talking through his hat, if you ask me," Trudolyubov
declared.

"Get out of my way, will you?" Zverkov said contemptuously. "What are you standing in my way for? What do
you want?"

They were all red in the face; their eyes were shining;
they had been drinking heavily.

"I ask you for your friendship, Zverkov. I offended you, but——"

"Offended me? *You* offended *me*? Don't you realise, sir, that you couldn't possibly offend me under any circumstances?"

"We've had enough of you," Trudolyubov summed up the position. "Get out! Come on, let's go!"

"Olympia's mine, gentlemen! Agreed?" Zverkov exclaimed.

"Agreed! Agreed!" they answered him, laughing.

I stood there utterly humiliated. The whole party left the room noisily. Trudolyubov began singing some stupid song. Simonov stayed behind for a second to tip the waiters. I suddenly went up to him.

"Simonov," I said firmly and desperately, "let me have six roubles!"

He gazed at me in utter amazement, with a sort of stupefied look in his eyes. He, too, was drunk.

"But you're not coming *there* with us, are you?"

"Yes, I am!"

"I haven't any money!" he snapped out with a contemptuous grin, and left the room.

I caught him by the overcoat. It was a nightmare.

"Simonov, I saw you had money. Why do you refuse me? Am I a scoundrel? Be careful how you refuse me: if you knew, if you knew why I'm asking! Everything depends on it, my whole future, all my plans! . . ."

Simonov took out the money and almost flung it at me.

"Take it if you're so utterly without shame!" he said, pitilessly, and rushed away to overtake them.

For a moment I remained alone. The general disorder in the room, the remains of the dinner, the broken wine-glass on the floor, the cigarette-stubs, the fumes of wine and the delirium in my head, the piercing anguish in my heart, and, finally, the waiter who had seen and heard everything and was now peering curiously into my eyes.

"*There!*" I cried. "Either they'll implore me for my friendship on their knees or—or I'll slap Zverkov's face!"

v

"So this is it—this is it at last—a head-on clash with real life!" I murmured, racing down the stairs. "This is quite a different proposition from your Pope leaving Rome for Brazil! This isn't your ball on Lake Como!"

"You're a swine," the thought flashed through my mind, "if you laugh at this now!"

"I don't care," I cried in answer to myself. "Now everything is lost anyway!"

There was not a trace of them to be seen in the street, but that did not worry me: I knew where they had gone.

At the front steps of the hotel stood a solitary night-sledge with its driver in a rough, peasant coat, thickly covered with wet and, as it were, warm snow which was still falling. It was steamy and close. His little shaggy, pie-bald horse was also covered thickly with snow and was coughing—I remember it all very well. I rushed to the wooden sledge, raised a leg to get into it, and was suddenly so stunned by the memory of how Simonov had just given me the six roubles that I fell into the sledge like a sack.

"Oh, I shall have to do a lot to get my own back," I cried. "But I shall do it or perish on the spot tonight. Come on, driver, start!"

We started. My thoughts were in a whirl.

"They won't go down on their knees to ask me to be their friend. That's an illusion, a cheap, romantic, fantastic, horrible illusion—just another ball on Lake Como. And that's why I *must* slap Zverkov's face! I simply must do it. Well, that's settled then. I'm flying now to slap his face! Hurry up, driver!"

The driver tugged at the reins.

"As soon as I go in I'll slap his face. Ought I perhaps to say a few words before slapping his face by way of introduction? No. I'll just go in and slap his face. They'll be all sitting in the large room, and he'll be on the sofa with Olympia. That blasted Olympia! She made fun of my face once and refused me. I shall drag Olympia by the hair and then drag Zverkov by the ears. No. Better by one ear. I shall take him all round the room by the ear. Quite likely they'll all start beating me and will kick me out. That's almost certain. But never mind. I'd have slapped his face first all the same. My initiative. And by the rules of hon-our that's everything. He would be branded for life and he couldn't wipe off the slap by any blows—no, by noth-ing but a duel. We will have to fight. Yes, let them beat me now. Let them, the ungrateful swine! I expect

Trudolyubov will do most of the beating: he's so strong. Ferfichkin will hang on to me from the side and quite certainly by the hair—yes, quite certainly by the hair. Well, let him. Let him. That's the whole idea of my going there. The silly fools will be forced to realise at last that there's something tragic here! When they're dragging me to the door, I'll shout to them that as a matter of fact they're not worth my little finger. Come on, driver, hurry up!" I cried to the sledge-driver.

He gave a start and whipped up his horse—I shouted so fiercely.

"We shall fight at dawn, that's settled. It's all over with the department. Ferfichkin had said *le*partment instead of *de*partment at dinner. But where am I to get the pistols? Nonsense! I'll ask for an advance of salary and buy them. But the powder, the bullets? That's not my business. Let the second worry about that. But how can I get it all done by daybreak? And where am I to get a second? I have no friends. . . . Nonsense!" I cried, getting more and more carried away. "Nonsense! The first man I meet in the street is bound to be my second, as he would be bound to drag a drowning man out of the water. I must make allowances for the most improbable incidents. Why, even if I were to ask the head of my department himself tomorrow morning to be my second, he too would have to agree, if only from a feeling of chivalry, and keep the secret into the bargain! Anton Antonovich——"

The truth is that at that very moment the whole hideous absurdity of my plans became clearer and more obvious to me than to anyone else in the world. I saw clearly the other side of the medal, and yet——

"Faster, driver! Faster, you rascal! Faster!"

"Lord, sir," said the son of the soil.

A cold shiver ran suddenly down my spine.

"But wouldn't it be better—wouldn't it be a hundred times better to—to go straight home? Oh, dear God, why did I have to invite myself to this dinner yesterday? But no—that's impossible! And what about my walking up and down the room from the table to the stove for three hours? No, they—they alone will have to make amends to me for that walk! They must wipe out that dishonour! Drive on!

". . . And what if they should hand me over to the police? They won't dare! They'll be afraid of a scandal!

And what if Zverkov contemptuously refused to fight a duel? That's most likely, but if that happens I'll show them —I'll go to the posting station when he is leaving tomorrow, seize him by the leg, drag his overcoat off him when he gets into the carriage. I'll hang on to his arm with my teeth. I'll bite him. 'See to what lengths a desperate man can be driven?' Let him punch me on the head and the others on the back. I'll shout to all the people around, 'Look, here's a young puppy who's going off to the Caucasus to captivate the girls there with my spit on his face!'

"Of course, after that everything will be over. The department will have vanished off the face of the earth. I shall be arrested. I shall be tried. I shall be dismissed from the Civil Service, thrown into prison, sent to Siberia, to one of the convict settlements there. Never mind. Fifteen years later, after they let me out of jail, I shall set out in search of him, in rags, a beggar, and at last I shall find him in some provincial city. He will be married and happy. He will have a grown-up daughter. I shall say, 'Look, monster, look at my hollow cheeks and my rags! I've lost everything—my career, my happiness, art, science, *the woman I loved*, and all through you. Here are the pistols. I've come to discharge my pistol and—and I forgive you!' And then I shall fire into the air, and he won't hear of me again. . . ."

I almost broke into tears, though I knew very well at that moment that the whole thing was from *Silvio* and from Lermontov's *Masquerade*. And all of a sudden I felt terribly ashamed, so ashamed that I stopped the sledge, got out of it, and stood in the snow in the middle of the road. The driver sighed and looked at me in astonishment.

"What am I to do? I can't go there, for the whole thing is absurd. But I couldn't leave things like that, either, because if I did, it would——Good Lord, how could I possibly leave it like that? And after such insults, too! No!" I cried, rushing back to the sledge. "It's ordained! It's fate! Drive on! Drive on, there!"

And in my impatience I hit the driver in the back with my fist.

"What's the matter with you? What are you hitting me for?" the poor man shouted, but he whipped up the horse so that it began kicking.

The wet snow was falling in large flakes. I unbuttoned my overcoat—I didn't mind the snow. I forgot everything, for I had finally made up my mind to slap Zverkov in the face, and I couldn't help feeling with horror that now it was going to happen *for certain* and that *nothing in the world could stop it.* Solitary street-lamps flickered gloomily in the snowy haze like torches at a funeral. The snow was drifting under my overcoat, under my coat, and under my collar where it melted. I did not button myself up: all was lost, anyway!

At last we arrived. I jumped out and, hardly knowing what I was doing, rushed up the steps and began banging at the door with my fists and feet. My legs, especially at the knees, felt terribly weak. The door was opened more quickly than I expected, as though they knew about my arrival. (Simonov, as a matter of fact, had warned them that someone else might arrive, and in this place it was necessary to give notice beforehand and, generally, to take precautions. It was one of those "fashion shops" which were long ago closed by the police. In the daytime it really was a shop, but at night those who had an introduction could go there to be entertained.) I walked rapidly through the dark shop into the familiar large room where there was only one candle burning and stopped dead, looking utterly bewildered: there was no one there.

"But where are they?" I asked someone.

But, of course, they had already gone their separate ways.

Before me was standing a person who looked at me with a stupid smirk on her face. It was the proprietress herself who knew me slightly. A moment later a door opened and another person came in.

I walked up and down the room without paying any attention to them and, I believe, I was talking to myself. It was as though I had been saved from death, and I felt it joyfully with every fibre of my being. For I should most certainly have slapped his face—oh, most certainly! But they were not there and everything—everything had vanished, everything had changed! I looked round. I was still unable to think clearly. I looked up mechanically at the girl who had just entered: I caught sight of a fresh, young, somewhat pale face, with straight dark eyebrows, and with a serious, as it were, surprised look in her eyes. I liked that at once. I should have hated her if she had been smiling. I began looking at her more intently and with a certain effort: I could not collect my thoughts even yet.

There was something kind and good-humoured about her face, but also something strangely serious. I was sure that was to her disadvantage here, and that not one of those fools had noticed her. However, you could hardly have called her a beauty, although she was tall, strong, and well-built. She was dressed very simply. Something vile came over me: I went straight up to her.

I caught sight of myself accidentally in a mirror. My flustered face looked utterly revolting to me: pale, evil, mean, with dishevelled hair. "It's all right, I'm glad of it," I thought. "I'm glad that I'll seem repulsive to her. I like that. . . ."

VI

Somewhere behind the partition, as though under some great pressure, as though someone were strangling it, the clock began wheezing. After the unnaturally protracted wheezing there came a thinnish, disagreeable, and, somehow, unexpectedly rapid chime, as though it had suddenly taken a leap forward. It struck two. I woke up, though I hadn't been really asleep and had only lain in a state of semi-consciousness.

The small, narrow, low-ceilinged room, filled with a huge wardrobe and cluttered up with cardboard boxes, clothes, and all sorts of rags, was almost completely dark. The guttered end of a candle which was burning on the table at the other end of the room was on the point of going out, and only from time to time did it flicker faintly. In a few moments the room would be plunged in darkness.

It did not take me long to recover: everything came back to me in a flash, without the slightest effort, as though it had only been waiting for an opportunity to pounce upon me again. And even while I was fast asleep there always remained some sort of a point in my memory which I never forgot and round which my drowsy dreams revolved wearily. But the strange thing was that everything that had happened to me during the previous day seemed to me now, on awakening, to have occurred a long, long time ago, as though I had long ago shaken it all off.

My head was heavy. Something seemed to be hovering over me, provoking me, exciting and worrying me. Resentiment and black despair were again surging up in me and seeking an outlet. Suddenly, close beside me, I saw two wide-open eyes observing me intently and curiously. The look in those eyes was coldly indifferent and sullen, as though it were utterly detached, and it made me feel terribly depressed.

A peevish thought stirred in my mind and seemed to pass all over my body like some vile sensation, resembling the sensation you experience when you enter a damp and stale cellar. It seemed somehow unnatural that those two eyes should have been scrutinising me only now. I remembered, too, that for two whole hours I had never said a word to this creature, and had not even thought it necessary to do so; that, too, for some reason appealed to me. Now, however, I suddenly saw clearly how absurd and hideous like a spider was the idea of vice which, without love, grossly and shamelessly begins where true love finds its consummation. We went on looking at each other like that for a long time, but she did not drop her eyes before mine, nor did she change her expression, so that in the end it made me for some reason feel creepy.

"What's your name?" I asked abruptly, to put an end to this unbearable situation.

"Lisa," she replied, almost in a whisper, but somehow without attempting to be agreeable, and turned her eyes away.

I said nothing for the next few moments.

"The weather was beastly yesterday—snow—horrible!" I said, almost as though I were speaking to myself, putting my arm disconsolately under my head and staring at the ceiling.

She made no answer. The whole thing was hideous.

"Were you born here?" I asked after a minute's silence, almost angry with her, and turning my head slightly towards her.

"No."

"Where do you come from?"

"Riga," she replied reluctantly.

"German?"

"No, I'm a Russian."

"Have you been here long?"

"Where?"

"In this house."

"A fortnight."

She spoke more and more abruptly. The candle went out. I could no longer make out her face.

"Have you any parents?"

"No—yes—I have."

"Where are they?"

"They are there—in Riga."

"Who are they?"

"Oh——"

"Oh? How do you mean? Who are they? What are they?"

"Tradespeople."

"Did you live with them all the time?"

"Yes."

"How old are you?"

"Twenty."

"Why did you leave them?"

"Oh——"

This "oh" meant leave me alone, I'm fed up. We were silent.

Goodness only knows why I did not go away. I felt more and more cheerless and disconsolate myself. The events of the previous day passed disjointedly through my mind, as though of themselves and without any effort on my part. I suddenly remembered something I had seen in the street that morning when, worried and apprehensive, I was hurrying to the office.

"I saw them carrying out a coffin yesterday and they nearly dropped it," I suddenly said aloud, without wishing to start a conversation and almost, as it were, by accident.

"A coffin?"

"Yes, in the Hay Market. They were carrying it out of a cellar."

"A cellar?"

"Well, not exactly a cellar. A basement—you know— down there, below—from a disorderly house. There was such filth everywhere—litter, bits of shell—an evil smell —oh, it was horrible."

Silence.

"It was a rotten day for a funeral," I began again, simply because I did not want to be silent.

"Why rotten?"

"Snow—slush——" I yawned.

"What difference does it make?" she said suddenly after a moment's silence.

"No, it was horrible—(I yawned again)—I expect the

grave-diggers must have been swearing at getting wet by the snow. And there must have been water in the grave."

"Why should there be water in the grave?" she asked with a strange sort of curiosity, but speaking even more abruptly and harshly than before.

Something inside me suddenly began egging me on to carry on with the conversation.

"Of course there's water there. About a foot of water at the bottom. You can't dig a dry grave in Volkovo cemetery."

"Oh? Why not?"

"How do you mean? The whole place is a swamp. Marshy ground everywhere. Saw it for myself—many a time."

(I had never seen it, nor have I ever been in Volkovo cemetery. All I knew about it was from what I had heard people say.)

"Don't you mind it at all—dying, I mean?"

"But why should I die?" she replied, as though defending herself.

"You will die one day, you know, and I expect you'll die the same way as that girl whose coffin I saw yesterday morning. She too was a—a girl like you. Died of consumption."

"The slut would have died in the hospital too," she said.

("She knows all about it," I thought to myself, "and she said 'slut' and not girl.")

"She owed money to the woman who employed her," I replied, feeling more and more excited by the discussion. "She worked for her to the very end, though she was in a consumption. The cabmen were talking about it with some soldiers in the street, and they told them that. They were laughing. Promised to have a few drinks to her memory at the pub."

(Much of that was pure invention on my part.)

Silence. Profound silence. She did not even stir.

"You don't suppose it's better to die in a hospital, do you?" she asked, adding a little later, irritably, "What difference does it make? And why on earth should I die?"

"If not now, then later——"

"Later? Oh, well——"

"Don't be so sure of yourself! Now you're young, good-looking, fresh, and that's why they put such a high value on you. But after a year of this sort of life you'll be different. You'll lose your looks."

"After one year?"

"Well, after one year your price will have dropped, anyway," I went on maliciously. "You'll find yourself in some lower establishment then. In another house. In another year—in a third house, lower and lower. And in about seven years you'll get to the cellar in the Hay Market. That wouldn't be so terrible, but, you see, the trouble is that you may fall ill—a weakness in the chest —or catch a cold, or something. In this sort of life it's not so easy to shake off an illness. Once you fall ill you'll find it jolly difficult to get well again. And so you will die."

"All right, so I'll die," she replied, very spitefully, and made a quick movement.

"But aren't you sorry?"

"Sorry? For what?"

"For your life."

Silence.

"You've been engaged to be married, haven't you?"

"Why don't you mind your own business?"

"I'm sorry. I'm not trying to cross-examine you. What the hell do I care? Why are you so angry? I expect you must have all sorts of trouble. It's not my business, of course. But I can't help feeling sorry. That's all."

"Sorry for whom?"

"Sorry for you."

"Not worth it," she whispered in a hardly audible voice and stirred again.

That incensed me. Good Lord, I had been so gentle with her, and she. . . .

"Well, what do you think about it? You think you're on the right path, do you?"

"I don't think anything."

"That's what's wrong with you—you don't think. Come, get back your senses while there's still time. You're still young, you're good-looking, you might fall in love, be married, be happy——"

"Not all married women are happy, are they?" she snapped out, in her former harsh, quick, and abrupt manner.

"Why, no. Not all, of course. But it's much better than here, anyway. A hundred times better. For if you love, you can live even without happiness. Life is sweet even in sorrow. It's good to be alive, however hard life is. But what have you got here? Nothing but foulness. Phew!"

I turned away in disgust. I was no longer reasoning coldly. I was myself beginning to react emotionally to my words and getting worked up. I was already longing to expound my own favourite *little* notions which I had nursed so lovingly in my funk-hole. Suddenly something flared up in me, a sort of aim had *appeared*.

"Don't pay any attention to me," I said. "I mean, that I am here. I'm not an example for you. I'm probably much worse than you. Anyway, I was drunk when I came here," I hastened, however, to justify myself. "Besides, a man is no example for a woman. It's different. Though I may be defiling and degrading myself, I'm not anyone's slave: now I'm here, but I shall be gone soon and you won't see me again. I can shake it all off and be a different man. But you—why, you're a slave from the very start. Yes, a slave! You give away everything. All your freedom. And even if one day you should want to break your chains, you won't be able to: you'll only get yourself more and more entangled in them. That's the kind of damnable chain it is! I know it. And I'm not mentioning anything else, for I don't suppose you'll understand it. Tell me one thing, though. Do you owe money to the woman who employs you? You do, don't you? Ah, there you are!" I added, though she did not reply, but merely listened in silence, with all her being. "So that's your chain. You'll never be able to pay off your debt. They'll see to that. Why, it's the same as selling your soul to the devil! And, besides, perhaps for all you know I'm every bit as wretched as you are and wallow in filth on purpose—because I, too, am sick at heart. People take to drink because they are unhappy, don't they? Well, I, too, am here because I am unhappy. Now, tell me what is there so good about all this? Here you and I were making love to one another—a few hours ago—and we never said a word to each other all the time, and it was only afterwards that you began staring at me like a wild thing. And I at you. Is that how people love one another? Is that how one human being should make love to another? It's disgusting that's what it is!"

"Yes!" she agreed with me, sharply and promptly.

The promptness with which she had uttered that "yes"

even surprised me. So the same thought must have occurred to her too when she was looking so intently at me. So she, too, was capable of the same thoughts. "Damn it, this is interesting—this means that we are *akin* to one another," I thought, almost rubbing my hands with glee. And how indeed should I not be able to cope with a young creature like that?

What appealed to me most was the sporting side of it.

She turned her head closer to me—so it seemed to me in the dark—propping herself up on her arm. Perhaps she was examining me. I was so sorry I could not see her eyes. I heard her deep breathing.

"Why did you come here?" I began, already with a certain note of authority in my voice.

"Oh——"

"But it's nice to be living in your father's house, isn't it? Warm, free—your own home."

"But what if it's much worse than it is here?"

"I must find the right tone," the thought flashed through my mind. "I shan't get far by being sentimental with her, I'm afraid."

However, it was only a momentary thought. She most certainly did interest me. Besides, I was feeling rather exhausted and irritable, and guile accommodates itself so easily to true feeling.

"I don't doubt it for a moment," I hastened to reply. "Everything's possible. You see, I'm sure someone must have wronged you and it's *their* fault rather than yours. Mind, I don't know anything of your story, but it's quite clear to me that a girl like you wouldn't have come here of her own inclination, would she?"

"What kind of girl am I?" she murmured in a hardly audible whisper, but I heard it.

Damn it all, I was flattering her! That was horrible. But perhaps it was not. Perhaps it was all right. . . . She was silent.

"Look here, Lisa, I'll tell you about myself. If I had had a home when I was a child, I should not be what I am now. I often think of it. For however bad life in a family can be your father and your mother are not your enemies, are they? They are not strangers, are they? Though perhaps only once a year, they will still show their love for you. And however bad it may be, you know you are at home. But I grew up without a home. That's why I suppose I am what I am—a man without feeling. . . ."

Again I waited for some response.

"I don't suppose she understands what I am talking about, after all," I thought. "Besides, it's ridiculous—all this moralising!"

"If I were a father and had a daughter of my own, I think I'd love my daughter more than my sons—I would indeed!" I began indirectly as though I never intended to draw her out at all. I must confess, I blushed.

"But why's that?" she asked.

Oh, so she was listening!

"Just—well, I don't really know, Lisa. You see, I once knew a father who was very strict, a very stern man he was, but he used to go down on his knees to his daughter, kiss her hands and feet, never grew tired of looking at her. Yes, indeed. She would spend the evening dancing at some party, and he'd stand for five hours in the same place without taking his eyes off her. He was quite mad about her. I can understand that. At night she'd get tired and fall asleep, and he'd go and kiss her in her sleep and make the sign of the cross over her. He would go about in a dirty old coat, he was a miser to everyone else, but on her he'd lavish everything he had. He'd buy her expensive presents and be overjoyed if she were pleased with them. Fathers always love their daughters more than mothers do. Many a girl finds life at home very pleasant indeed. I don't think I'd ever let my daughter marry!"

"But why ever not?" she asked with a faint smile.

"I'd be jealous. Indeed I would. I mean I'd hate the thought of her kissing someone else. Loving a stranger more than her father. Even the thought of it is painful to me. Of course, it's all nonsense. Of course, every father would come to his senses in the end. But I'm afraid I'd worry myself to death before I'd let her marry. I'd certainly find fault with all the men who proposed to her. But in the end I daresay I should let her marry the man she herself loved. For the man whom his daughter loves always seems to be the worst to the father. That's how it is. There's a lot of trouble in families because of that."

"Some parents are glad to sell their daughters, let alone marry them honourably," she said suddenly.

Oh, so that's what it was!

"That, Lisa, only happens in those infamous families where there is neither God nor love," I interjected warmly. "For where there's no love, there's no decency, either. It's true there are such families, but I'm not speaking of them. You can't have known any kindness in your family, if you talk like that. Indeed, you must be very unlucky. Yes, I expect this sort of thing mostly happens because of poverty."

"But is it any better in rich families? Honest people live happily even if they are poor."

"Well, yes, I suppose so. And come to think of it, Lisa, a man only remembers his misfortunes. He never remembers his good fortune. If he took account of his good fortune as well, he'd have realised that there's a lot of that too for his share. But what if all goes well with the family? If with the blessing of God your husband is a good man, loves you, cherishes you, never leaves you for a moment? Oh, such a family is happy, indeed! Even if things don't turn out so well sometimes, it is still all right. For where is there no sorrow? If you ever get married, *you'll find it out for yourself*. Then again if you take the first years of your marriage to a man you love—oh, what happiness, what happiness there is in it sometimes! Why, it's a common enough experience. At first even your quarrels with your husband end happily. There are many women who the more they love their husbands, the more ready they are to quarrel with them. I tell you I knew such a woman myself. 'You see,' she used to say, 'I love you very much, and it's just because I love you so much that I'm tormenting you, and you ought to realise that!' Do you know that one can torment a person just because one loves him? Women do it mostly. They say to themselves, 'But I shall love him so dearly, I shall cherish him so much afterwards that it doesn't matter if I torment him a little now.' And everyone in the house is happy looking at you, everything's so nice, so jolly, so peaceful, and so honest. . . . Other women, of course, are jealous. If her husband happens to go off somewhere (I knew a woman who was like that), she won't be happy till she runs out of the house at night and finds out on the quiet where he is, whether he is in that house or with that woman. That's bad. That's very bad. And she knows herself it is wrong. Her heart fails her and she suffers agonies, but, you see, she loves him: it's all through love. And how nice it is to make it up after a quarrel, to admit that she was wrong, or to forgive him! And how happy they are suddenly. So happy that it seems as though they had met for the first time, as though they had only just got married, as though they had fallen in love for the first time. And no one, no one ought to know what passes between man and wife, if they love one another. And however much they quarrel, they ought not to call in their own mother to adjudicate between them, and to tell tales of one another. They are their own judges. Love is a mystery that God alone only comprehends and should be hidden from all eyes whatever happens. If that is done, it is more holy, and better. They are more likely to respect one another, and a lot depends on their respect for one another. And if once there has been love, if at first they married for love, there is no reason why their love should pass away. Surely, they can keep it! It hardly ever happens that it cannot be kept. Well, and if the husband is a good and honest man, why should love pass away? It is true they will not love one another as they did when they were married, but afterwards their love will be better still, for then they will be united in soul as well as in body, they will manage their affairs in common, there will be no secrets between them—the important thing is to love and have courage. In such circumstances even hard work is a joy; even if you have to go hungry sometimes for the sake of your children, it is a joy. For they will love you for it afterwards; for you are merely laying up treasures for yourself: as the children grow up, you feel that you are an example for them, that you are their support, that even when you die your thoughts and feelings will live with them, for they have received them from you, for they are like you in everything. It is therefore a duty, a great duty. Indeed, the father and the mother cannot help drawing closer together. People say children are a great trouble. But who says it? It is the greatest happiness people can have on earth! Are you fond of little children, Lisa? I am very fond of them. Just imagine a rosy little baby boy sucking at your breast—what husband's heart is not touched at the sight of his wife nursing his child? Oh, such a plump and rosy baby! He sprawls, he snuggles up to you, his little hands are so pink and chubby, his nails are so clean and tiny—so tiny that it makes you laugh to look at them, and his eyes gaze at you as if he understands everything. And while he sucks he pulls at your breast with his sweet little hand—plays. If his father comes near, he tears himself away from the breast, flings himself back, looks at his father and laughs as if goodness only knows how funny it is—and then he begins sucking greedily again. Or again, when his teeth are beginning to come through he will just bite his mother's breast, looking slyly at her with his eyes—'See? I'm biting you!' Isn't everything here happiness when the three of them—husband, wife, and child—are together? One can forgive a great deal for the sake of these moments. Yes, Lisa, one has to learn to live first before blaming others."

"It is with pictures, with pictures like these, that you will beguile her," I thought to myself, though, goodness knows, I spoke with real feeling, and suddenly blushed. "And what if she should suddenly burst out laughing? What a priceless ass I'd look then!" This thought made me furious. Towards the end of my speech I really grew excited, and now my vanity was somewhat hurt. I almost felt like nudging her.

"What are you——" she began suddenly and stopped.

But I understood everything: there was quite a different note in her trembling voice, something that was no longer harsh and crude and unyielding as a short while ago, but something soft and shy, so that I suddenly felt somehow ashamed of her myself. I felt guilty.

"What?" I asked with curiosity.

"Why, you——"

"What?"

"Why, you—you're speaking as though you were reading from a book," she said, and something that sounded like irony could suddenly be heard in her voice.

I resented that remark very deeply. It was not what I was expecting.

I did not realise that by her irony she was deliberately concealing her own feelings, that this was the usual last stratagem of people with pure and chaste hearts against those who impudently and unceremoniously attempt to pry into the inmost recesses of their minds, and that, out of pride, such people do not give in till the very last moment, that they are afraid to show their feelings before you. I should have guessed that from the timidity with which after several tries she approached her ironic remark, and from the shy way in which she made it at last.

But I did not guess, and a feeling of vicious spite took possession of me.

"You wait!" I thought.

VII

"Good Lord, Lisa, what sort of a book am I supposed to be reading from when I, who cannot possibly have any interest in what happens to you, feel so sick myself. But as a matter of fact I'm not indifferent, either. All that has now awakened in my heart——Surely, surely, you yourself must be sick to death of being here. Or does habit really mean so much? Hang it all, habit can apparently make anything of a man! Do you really seriously believe that you will never grow old, that you will always be good-looking, and that they will keep you here for ever and ever? To say nothing of the vileness of your present way of life. However, let me tell you this about this business here, about your present way of life. Though you are now young, attractive, pretty, sensitive, warm-hearted, I—well, you know, the moment I woke up a few minutes ago, I couldn't help feeling disgusted at being with you here! It is only when you're drunk that you come to a place like this. But if you were anywhere else, if you lived as all good, decent people live, I should not only have taken a fancy to you, but fallen head over ears in love with you. I'd have been glad if you'd only looked at me, let alone spoken to me. I'd have hung round your door. I'd have gone down on my knees before you. I'd have been happy if you'd have consented to marry me, and deemed it an honour, too. I shouldn't have dared to harbour a single indecent thought about you. But here I know that I have only to whistle and, whether you like it or not, you'll have to come with me, and that it is not I who have to consult your wishes, but you mine. Even if the meanest peasant hires himself out as a labourer, he does not make a slave of himself entirely, and, besides, he knows that after a certain time he will be his own master again. But when can you say as much for yourself? Just think what you are giving up here. What is it you're enslaving? Why, it is your soul, your soul over which you have no power, together with your body! You're giving your love to every drunkard to mock at! Love? Why, that's everything, that's a precious jewel, a girl's dearest treasure—that's what love is! To win this love, a man would be ready to give his soul, to face death itself! And how much is your love worth now? You can be all bought, all of you! And why should anyone try to win your love when he can get everything without love? Why, there is no greater insult for a girl than that. Don't you see it? I am told that to please you, poor fools, they let you have lovers here. But good Lord, what is it but just insulting you? What is it but sheer deceit? Why, they are just laughing at you, and you believe them! Or do you really believe that lover of yours loves you? I don't believe it. How can he love you when he knows that you can be called away from him any moment? He'd be nothing but a pimp after that! And could such a man have an atom of respect for you? What have you in common with him? He's just laughing at you, and robbing you into the bargain—that's what his love amounts to. You're lucky if he doesn't beat you. Perhaps he does, too. Ask him, if you have such a lover, whether he will marry you. Why, he'll laugh in your face, if, that is, he doesn't spit in it or give you a beating, and he himself is probably not worth twopence. And why have you ruined your life here? For what? For the coffee they give you to drink? For the good meals? Have you ever thought why they feed you so well here? Another woman, an honest woman, could not swallow such food, for she would know why she was being fed so well. You are in debt here—well, take my word for it, you'll never be able to repay your debt, you'll remain in debt to the very end, till the visitors here begin to scorn you. And all that will be much sooner than you think. You need not count on your good looks. They don't last very long here, you know. And then you'll be kicked out. And that's not all by any means: long before you're kicked out they'll start finding fault with you, reproaching you, reviling you, as though you had not sacrificed your health for them, ruined your youth and your soul for them, without getting anything in return, but as though you had ruined them, robbed them, beggared them. And don't expect any of the other girls to take your part: they, those friends of yours, will turn against you, too, for the sake of currying favour with your employer, for you are all slaves here, you've all lost all conscience and pity long ago. They have sunk too low, and there's nothing in the world filthier, more odious, and more insulting than their abuse. And you'll leave everything here, everything you possess, without any hope of ever getting it back—your health, your beauty, and your hopes, and at twenty-two you'll look like a woman of thirty-five, and you'll be lucky if you're not ill —pray God for that. I shouldn't be at all surprised if you were not thinking now that you're having a lovely time— no work, just a life of pleasure! But let me tell you that there is no work in the world harder or more oppressive —and there never has been. It is a wonder you haven't long ago cried your heart out. And when they turn you out you won't dare to say a word, not even as much as a syllable, and you'll go away as though it is you who were to blame. You'll pass on to another place, then to a third, then again to some other place, till at last you'll find yourself in the Hay Market. And there they'll start beating you as a matter of course. It's a lovely custom they have there. A visitor there does not know how to be kind without first giving you a good thrashing. You don't believe it's so horrible there? Well, go and have a look for yourself some time and you'll perhaps see with your own eyes. Once, on New Year's Eve, I saw a girl there. She had been turned out by her friends as a joke, to cool off a little in the frost, because she had been howling too much, and they locked the door behind her. At nine o'clock in the morning she was already dead drunk, dishevelled, half naked, beaten black and blue. Her face was made up, but she had two black eyes; she was bleeding from the nose and mouth; she sat down on the stone steps, holding some salt fish in her hands; she was shrieking at the top of her voice bewailing her 'bad luck,' and striking the salt fish against the steps, while a crowd of cabmen and drunken soldiers were standing round and making fun of her. You don't believe that you, too, will be like her one day? Well, I shouldn't like to believe it, either, but how do you know? Perhaps ten or eight years ago the same girl, the girl with the salt fish, arrived here as fresh as a child, innocent and pure, knowing no evil and blushing at every word. Perhaps she was like you, proud, quick to take offence, quite unlike the others, looking like a queen, and quite certain that she would make the man who fell in love with her and whom she loved the happiest man in the world. But you see how it all ended, don't you? And what if at the very moment when she was striking the grimy

steps with that fish, dirty and dishevelled, what if at that
moment she recalled all the innocent years she had once
spent at her father's house, when she used to go to school
and the son of their neighbours waited for her on the way
and assured her that he would love her as long as he
lived, that he would devote his whole future to her, and
when they vowed to love one another for ever and be
married as soon as they grew up? No, Lisa, you'd be
lucky, you'd be very lucky, if you were to die soon, very
soon, of consumption, in some corner, in some cellar like
that woman I told you of. In a hospital, you say? You'll
be fortunate if they take you to a hospital, for, you see,
you may still be wanted by your employer. Consumption
is a queer sort of illness. It is not like a fever. A consumptive goes on hoping to the last minute. To the very last
he goes on saying that there is nothing the matter with
him, that he is not ill—deceiving himself. And your em-
ployers are only too pleased. Don't worry, it is so. I assure
you. You've sold your soul and you owe money into the
bargain, so you daren't say a word. But when you are dying, all will abandon you, all will turn away from you, for
what more can they get out of you? If anything, they'll
reproach you for taking up room without paying for it,
for not dying quickly enough. You beg and beg for a
drink of water, and when at last they bring it to you
they'll abuse you at the same time. 'When are you going
to die, you dirty baggage, you? You don't let us sleep,
moaning all the time, and the visitors don't like it.' That's
true. I've heard such things said myself. And when you are
really dying, they'll drag you to the most foul-smelling
corner of the cellar, in the damp and the darkness, and
what will your thoughts be as you are lying by yourself?
When you die, strangers will lay you out, hurriedly,
impatiently, grumbling. No one will bless you. No one
will sigh for you. Get you quickly out of the way—that's
all they'll be concerned about. They'll buy a cheap coffin,
take you to the cemetery as they took that poor girl yesterday, and then go to a pub to talk about you. Your grave
will be full of slush and dirt and wet snow—they won't
put themselves out for you—not they! 'Let her down,
boy! Lord, just her "bad luck," I suppose. Gone with her
legs up here too, the slut! Shorten the ropes, you young
rascal!' 'It's all right!' 'All right, is it? Can't you see she's
lying on her side? She's been a human being herself once,

ain't she? Oh, all right, fill it up!' And they won't be wasting much time in abusing each other over you, either. They will fill in your grave with wet blue clay and go off to a pub. . . . That will be the end of your memory on earth. Other women have children to visit their graves, fathers, husbands, but there will be neither tears, nor sighs, nor any remembrance for you. No one, no one in the world will ever come to you. Your name will vanish from the face of the earth as though you had never been born! Dirt and mud, dirt and mud, though you knock at your coffin lid at night when the dead arise as hard as you please, crying, 'Let me live in the world, good people! I lived, but I knew no real life. I spent my life as a doormat for people to wipe their dirty boots on. My life has been drunk away at a pub in the Hay Market. Let me live in the world again, good people!' "

I worked myself up into so pathetic a state that I felt a lump rising to my throat and—all of a sudden I stopped, raised myself in dismay, and, bending over apprehensively, began to listen with a violently beating heart. I had good reason to feel embarrassed.

I had felt for a long while that I had cut her to the quick and wrung her heart, and the more I became convinced of it, the more eager I was to finish what I had set out to do as expeditiously and as thoroughly as possible. It was the sport of it, the sport of it, that carried me away. However, it was not only the sport of it.

I knew I was speaking in a stiff, affected, even bookish manner, but as a matter of fact I could not speak except "as though I was reading from a book." But that did not worry me, for I knew, I had a feeling that I would be understood, that this very bookishness would assist rather than hinder matters. But now that I had succeeded in making an impression, I got frightened. No, never, never had I witnessed such despair! She lay prone on the bed, with her face buried in the pillow, which she clasped tightly with both her hands. Her bosom was heaving spasmodically. Her young body was writhing as though in convulsions. The sobs which she tried to suppress seemed to deprive her of breath and rend her bosom, and suddenly they broke out into loud moans and cries. It was then that she clung more tightly to the pillow. She did not want anyone here, not a soul, to know of her agonies and tears. She bit the pillow, she bit her arm till it bled (I saw it afterwards), or clutching at her dishevelled hair with her fingers, went rigid with that superhuman effort, holding her breath and clenching her teeth. I began saying something to her, asking her to calm herself, but I felt that I dared not go on, and all at once, shivering as though in a fever and almost in terror, I began groping for my clothes, intending to dress myself quickly and go. It was dark. However much I tried, I could not finish dressing quickly. Suddenly my hand touched a box of matches and a candle-stick with a new unused candle. The moment the candle lit up the room, Lisa jumped up, sat up on the bed, and with a strangely contorted face and a half-crazy smile looked at me with an almost vacant expression. I sat down beside her and took her hands. She recollected herself, flung herself at me as though wishing to embrace me, but did not dare and slowly bowed her head before me.

"Lisa, my dear, I'm sorry, I—I shouldn't have——" I began, but she squeezed my hands in her fingers with such force that I realised that I was saying the wrong thing and stopped.

"Here's my address, Lisa. Come and see me."

"I will," she whispered firmly, but still not daring to raise her head.

"I'm going now. Goodbye. You will come, won't you?"

I got up. She too got up, and suddenly blushed crimson, gave a shudder, seized a shawl from a chair, threw it over her shoulders and muffled herself up to the chin. Having done that, she again smiled a rather sickly smile, blushed and looked at me strangely. I was deeply sorry for her. I was longing to go, to sink through the floor.

"Wait a minute," she said suddenly in the entrance hall, at the very door, and stopped me by catching hold of my overcoat.

She quickly put down the candle and ran off. She must have remembered something or wanted to show me something. As she was running away, she again blushed all over, her eyes were shining, a smile flitted over her lips— what could it mean? I waited against my will. She came back in a minute and looked at me as though asking forgiveness for something. It was altogether a different face, altogether a different look from a few hours ago—sullen, mistrustful, and obstinate. Now her eyes were soft and beseeching, and at the same time trustful, tender, and shy. So do children look at people they are very fond of and from whom they expect some favour. She had light-brown eyes, beautiful and full of life, eyes which could express love as well as sullen hatred.

Without a word of explanation, as though I, like a sort of higher being, ought to know everything without explanations, she held out a piece of paper to me. At that moment her whole face was radiant with the most naïve, most childlike, triumph. I unfolded it. It was a letter to her from some medical student or someone of the sort—a highly flamboyant and flowery, but also extremely respectful declaration of love. I cannot recall its exact words now, but I remember very well that through that grandiloquent style there peered a genuine feeling which cannot be faked. When I had finished reading the letter, I met her fervent, curious, and childishly impatient gaze fixed on me. Her eyes were glued to my face, and she was waiting with impatience to hear what I had to say. In a few words, hurriedly, but, somehow, joyfully and as though proudly, she explained to me that she had been to a dance in a private house, a family of "very, very nice people, who *knew nothing*, nothing at all," for she had only been here a short time and she did not really intend to stay—no, she had made up her mind not to stay, and she was indeed quite certainly going to leave as soon as she paid her debt. . . . Well, anyway, at that party she had met a student who had danced the whole evening with her. He had talked to her, and it appeared that he had known her as a child in Riga when they used to play together, but that was a long time ago. And he knew her parents too, but he knew nothing, nothing whatever about *this*, and he had not the slightest suspicion even! And the day after the dance (three days ago) he had sent her that letter through a girl friend of hers with whom she had gone to the dance and—and—"well, that is all."

She lowered her shining eyes somewhat shyly as she finished telling me her story.

Poor child, she was keeping the letter of that student as a treasure and ran to fetch that one treasure of hers not wishing that I should go away without knowing that she, too, was loved sincerely and honestly, that people addressed her, too, with respect. That letter, I knew, would most certainly remain in her box without leading to anything. But that did not matter. I was sure she would keep it all her life, guarding it as a priceless treasure, as her pride and justification, and now at such a moment she had remembered it and brought it to boast about naïvely to me, to vindicate herself in my eyes, so that I should see it and commend her for it. I said nothing, pressed her hand, and went out. I longed to get away. . . .

I walked home all the way, though the wet snow kept falling all the time in large flakes. I felt dead tired, depressed, bewildered. But the truth was already blazing through my bewilderment. The disgusting truth!

VIII

However, it took me some time before I acknowledged that truth to myself. Waking up next morning after a few hours of heavy, leaden sleep and immediately remembering all that had occurred the previous day, I was utterly amazed at my *sentimentality* with Lisa the night before, and all "those horrors and commiserations of last night."

"I must have been suffering from an attack of nerves just like a silly old woman," I decided. "Lord, what a fool I was! And why did I give her my address? What if she should come? However, what does it matter if she does come? Let her come, I don't mind. . . ."

But *obviously* that was not the chief and most important thing. What I had to do now, and that quickly too, was to save my reputation in the eyes of Zverkov and Simonov. That was the chief thing. And so preoccupied was I with the other affair that I forgot all about Lisa that morning.

First of all I had immediately to return the money I had borrowed from Simonov the day before. I decided on a desperate step: to borrow fifteen roubles from Anton Antonovich. As it happened, he was in an excellent mood that morning and lent me the money as soon as I asked him for it. That made me feel so happy that, as I signed the promissory note, I told him *casually* with a sort of devil-may-care air that "we had a very gay party last night at the Hôtel de Paris; seeing off a friend, I suppose I might almost say a friend of my childhood. An awful rake, you know, terribly spoilt and, well, of course, of a good family, a man of considerable means, a brilliant career, witty, charming, has affairs with society women,

you understand. Drank an additional 'half-dozen' and——
And it went off all right," I said it all very glibly, confidently, and complacently.

As soon as I got home I wrote to Simonov.

To this day, as I recall that letter of mine to Simonov,
I am lost in admiration at the gentlemanly, good-humoured, frank tone of it. Very dexterously, with perfect
grace, and, above all, without any superfluous words, I
candidly acknowledged myself to have been completely
in the wrong. My only excuse, "if there can possibly be
an excuse for the way I behaved," was that, being utterly
unaccustomed to drink, I got drunk after the first glass
which (I lied) I had drunk before they arrived, while I
was waiting for them at the Hôtel de Paris between five
and six o'clock. I apologised principally to Simonov, and
I asked him to convey my explanations to all the others,
especially to Zverkov, whom "I remember as though in a
dream" I seem to have insulted. I added that I would
have apologised personally to every one of them myself,
but I had a terrible headache and—to be quite frank—
was too ashamed to face them. I was particularly pleased
with the "certain lightness," almost off-handedness (by no
means discourteous, by the way) which was so unexpectedly reflected in my style and gave them to understand at
once better than any arguments that I took a very detached view of "all that ghastly business of last night";
that I was not at all so crushed as you, gentlemen, probably imagine, but on the contrary look upon it just as any
self-respecting gentleman ought to look on it. "A young
man," as it were, "can hardly be blamed for every indiscretion he commits."

"Damned if there isn't a certain marquis-like playfulness about it!" I thought admiringly as I read over my
letter. "And it's all because I'm such a well-educated person! Others in my place wouldn't have known how to
extricate themselves, but I've wriggled out of it and I'm as
bright and merry as ever, and all because I am 'an educated man, a modern intellectual.'"

And really the whole ghastly business had most probably been due to the wine. Well, perhaps not to the wine.
As a matter of fact, I didn't have any drinks between five
and six when I was waiting for them. I had lied to
Simonov. I had told him the most shameless lie, but I'm
not in the least sorry for it even now. . . .

Anyway, to hell with it! The main thing is that I've got out of it.

I put six roubles in the letter, sealed it, and asked Apollon to take it to Simonov. When he learnt that there was money in the letter, Apollon became more respectful and agreed to take it to Simonov. Towards evening I went out for a walk. My head was still aching from the night before and I was feeling sick. But the further the evening wore on and the darker it grew, the more my impressions and—after them—my thoughts changed and grew confused. Inside me, deep down in my heart and conscience, something kept stirring, would not die, and manifested itself in a feeling of poignant anguish. Mostly I walked aimlessly along the most crowded business streets, along Meshchanskaya, Sadovaya, and Yussupov Park. I always particularly liked taking a stroll along these streets at dusk just when crowds of workers and tradespeople with cross and worried faces were going home from their daily work. What I liked about it was just that common bustle, the every-day, prosaic nature of it all. That evening all that rush and bustle in the streets irritated me more than ever. I could not cope with my own feelings. I could not find an explanation for them. Something was rising up, rising up incessantly in my soul, painfully, something that wouldn't quieten down. I returned home feeling greatly upset. It was as though I had a crime on my conscience.

The thought that Lisa might come worried me constantly. I found it very strange that of all the memories of the day before, the memory of her seemed to torment me in particular, and, as it were, apart from the rest. Everything else I had been successful in dismissing from my mind completely by the evening; I just dismissed it all and was still perfectly satisfied with my letter to Simonov. But so far as Lisa was concerned, I somehow did not feel satisfied. As if it were the thought of Lisa alone that made me so unhappy. "What if she comes?" I kept thinking all the time. "Well, what if she does? Let her. H'm . . . For one thing, I don't want her to see how I live. Last night I seemed—er—a hero to her and—er —now—h'm! It is certainly a nuisance that I let myself go to pieces like that. Everything in my room is so poor and shabby. And how could I have gone out to dinner in such clothes last night! And that American cloth sofa of mine with the stuffing sticking out of it! And my dressing gown in which I can't even wrap myself decently! Rags and tatters. . . . And she will see it all, and she will see Apollon, too. The swine will probably insult her. He'll be rude to her just to be rude to me. And I, of course, will get into a funk as usual, start striking attitudes before her, drape myself in the skirts of my dressing gown, start smiling, start telling lies. Ugh! Sickening! And it isn't this that's really so sickening. There's something more important, more horrible, more contemptible! Yes, more contemptible! And again to assume that dishonest, lying mask —again, again!"

Having come thus far in my thoughts, I couldn't help flaring up.

"Why dishonest? In what way is it dishonest? I was speaking sincerely last night. I remember there was some genuine feeling in me, too. I wanted to awaken honourable feelings in her. . . . If she cried a little, it was all to the good. It's sure to have a highly beneficent effect on her. . . ."

All that evening, even when I had returned home, even after nine o'clock when I knew that Lisa could not possibly come, I still could not get her out of my mind, and, above all, I remembered her in one and the same position. Yes, one moment of that night's incident seemed to stand out in my memory with particular clarity, namely, when I struck a match and saw her pale, contorted face and that tortured look in her eyes. What a pitiful, what an unnatural, what a twisted smile she had at that moment! But I did not know then that fifteen years later I should still see Lisa in my mind's eye with the same pitiful, inappropriate smile which was on her face at that moment.

Next day I was once more quite ready to dismiss it all as nonsense, as a result of overstrained nerves, and, above all, as—an *exaggeration*. I was always aware of that weakness of mine, and sometimes I was very much afraid of it. "I always exaggerate—that's my trouble," I used to remind myself almost every hour. But still—"still, Lisa will probably show up all the same," that was the constant refrain of my thoughts at the time. I was so worried about it that I sometimes flew into a blind rage: "She'll come! She's quite certain to come!" I stormed, pacing my room. "If not today, then tomorrow, but come she will! She'll seek me out! For such is the damned romanticism of all those *pure hearts!* Oh, the loathsomeness, oh, the stupidity, oh, the insensibility of these blasted 'sentimental souls!' How could she fail to understand? Why, anyone would have seen through it!"

But here I would stop, overcome with embarrassment.

And how few, how few words were necessary, I thought in passing, how few idyllic descriptions were necessary (and those, too, affected, bookish, insincere) to shape a whole human life at once according to my will! There's innocence for you! Virgin soil!

Sometimes I wondered whether I ought not to go and see her, "tell her everything," and ask her not to come to me. But there, at that thought, I'd fly into such a rage that it seemed to me that I should have crushed that "damned" Lisa if she had happened to be near me at the time. I should have humiliated her. I should have heaped mortal insults upon her, driven her out, beaten her!

However, one day passed, and another, and a third, and she did not come, and I was beginning to feel easier in my mind. I felt particularly cheerful and let my fancy run riot after nine o'clock, and at times I even began indulging in rather sweet daydreams. For instance, "I'm saving Lisa just because she's coming regularly to see me and I'm talking to her. . . . I'm educating her, enlarging her mind. At last I notice that she is in love with me. I pretend not to understand (I don't know why I am pretending, though, just for the sheer beauty of it, I suppose). In the end, all embarrassed, beautiful, trembling and sobbing, she flings herself at my feet and says that I have saved her and that she loves me more than anything in the world. I look surprised, but—'Lisa,' I say, 'surely you don't imagine I haven't noticed that you love me, do you? I saw everything, I guessed everything, but I did not dare lay claim to your heart first because I knew you were under my influence and was afraid that, out of gratitude, you would deliberately force yourself to respond to my love, that you would rouse a feeling in your heart which perhaps did not really exist, and I did not want this because it—it would be sheer despotism on my part—it would have been indelicate. . . . (Well, in short, here I got myself entangled in a sort of European, Geroge-Sandian, inexpressibly noble subtleties.) But now, now you're mine, you are my creation, you are pure and beautiful, you are—my beautiful wife!"

> And my house, fearlessly and freely,
> As mistress you can enter now!

And then we live happily ever after, go abroad, etc., etc. In short, I got so thoroughly fed up with myself in the end that I finished up by sticking out my tongue at myself.

"Besides, they won't let her go, the 'tart!'" I thought to myself. "I don't think they are allowed to go out very much and certainly not in the evening (for some reason I took it into my head that she would come in the evening and exactly at seven o'clock). However, she told me herself that she was not entirely at their beck and call and that she was given special privileges, and that means— h'm! Damn it, she will come! She will most certainly turn up!"

Fortunately, Apollon took my mind off Lisa by his churlish behaviour. I lost my patience with him completely! He was the bane of my life, the punishment Providence had imposed upon me. For years on end we had been continually squabbling, and I hated him. Lord, how I hated him! I don't think I ever hated anyone as much as him, particularly at certain times. He was an elderly, pompous man, who did some tailoring in his spare time. For some unknown reason he despised me beyond measure, and looked down upon me in a way that was simply maddening. He looked down upon everyone, as a matter of fact. Take one look at that fair, smoothly brushed head, at the tuft of hair which he fluffed out over his forehead and smeared with lenten oil, at that gravely pursed mouth, always compressed into the shape of the letter V—and you felt that you were in the presence of a creature who was never in doubt. He was pedantic to a degree, the greatest pedant, in fact, I ever met in my life, and, in addition, possessed of a vanity that was worthy only of Alexander the Great. He was in love with every button on his coat, with every hair on his head. Yes, in love, most decidedly in love with them! And he looked it. His attitude towards me was utterly despotic. He hardly ever spoke to me, and if occasionally he did deign to look at me, his look was so hard, so majestically self-confident, and invariably so contemptuous, that it alone was sometimes sufficient to drive me into a fury. He carried out his duties with an air of conferring the greatest favour upon me. As a matter of fact, he hardly ever did anything for me, and he did not even consider himself bound to do anything for me. There could be no doubt whatever that he looked upon me as the greatest fool on earth, and if he graciously permitted me "to live with him," it was only because he could get his wages from me every month. He did not mind "doing nothing" for me for seven roubles a month. I'm certain many of my sins will be forgiven me for what I suffered from him. At times I hated him so bitterly that I was almost thrown into a fit when I heard him walking about. But what I loathed most of all was his lisp. His tongue must have been a little too long, or something of the sort, and because of that he always lisped and minced his words, and, I believe, he was terribly proud of it, imagining that it added to his dignity. He spoke in a slow, measured voice, with his hands behind his back and his eyes fixed on the ground. He infuriated me particularly when he began reading the psalter in his room behind the partition. I have fought many battles over that reading. But he was terribly fond of reading aloud of an evening, in a slow, even, sing-song voice, as though he were chanting psalms for the dead. It is interesting that he is doing just that at present: he hires himself out to read psalms over the dead and exterminates rats and manufactures a boot polish as well. But at that time I could not get rid of him, as though he formed one chemical substance with me. Besides, he would never have consented to leave me for anything in the world. I could not afford to live in furnished rooms. I lived in an unfurnished self-contained flat —it was my shell, the case into which I hid from humanity, and for some confounded reason Apollon seemed to be an integral part of my flat, and for seven years I could not get rid of him.

To be behind with his wages even for two or three days, for instance, was quite out of the question. He'd have made such a fuss that I shouldn't have known how to keep out of his way. But at that time I was feeling so exasperated with everyone that for a reason I did not myself clearly understand I made up my mind to *punish* Apollon by withholding his wages for a whole fortnight. I had been intending to do it for a long time, for the last two years, just to show him that he had no business to treat me with such insolence and that if I liked I could always refuse to pay him his wages. I decided to say nothing to him about it and to ignore the whole thing deliberately so as to crush his pride and force him to speak about his wages first. Then I would take the seven roubles out of the drawer, show him that I had the money, that I had purposely put it aside, and say that "I won't, I won't, I simply won't give you your wages! I won't just because *I don't want to*," because I was the master in this house, because he had been disrespectful, because he had been rude; but if he were to ask me nicely, I might relent and give it to him; otherwise he would have to wait a fortnight, or three weeks, or maybe a month even. . . .

But furious though I was with him, he got the better of me in the end. I could not hold out for four days even. He started, as he always did start in such circumstances, for they had already happened before, I had already tried it on before (and, let me add, I knew all this beforehand, I knew all his contemptible tactics by heart)—he started by fixing me with a stern glare which he kept up for several minutes at a time, particularly when he used to meet me or when I went out of the house. If I did not shrink back and pretended not to notice his glances, he would set about—still in silence—to inflict more tortures upon me. He would suddenly and without any excuse whatever enter my room quietly and smoothly when I was either reading or pacing my room, and remain standing at the door, with one hand behind his back and one foot thrust forward, and stare fixedly at me. This time his stare was not only stern, but witheringly contemptuous. If I suddenly asked him what he wanted, he would not reply, but continue to stare straight at me for a few more seconds, then he would purse his lips with a specially significant expression, turn round slowly, and slowly go back to his room. About two hours later he would leave his room again, and again appear before me in the same manner. Sometimes, beside myself with rage, I did not even ask him what he wanted, but just raised my head sharply and imperiously and began staring back at him. We would thus stare at each other for about two minutes till at last he would turn round, slowly and pompously, and again go back for two hours.

If that did not make me come to my senses and I continued to be rebellious, he would suddenly break into sighs as he stared at me, as though measuring with each sigh the whole depth of my moral turpitude and, of course, it all ended in his complete victory over me: I raved, I shouted, but I still had to do what was expected of me.

No sooner did this manœuvre of stern looks begin this time than I lost my temper at once and flew at him in a blind rage.

"Stop!" I shouted, beside myself, as he was turning round slowly and silently, with one hand behind his back, to go back to his room. "Stop! Come back, I tell you! Come back!"

I must have roared at him in so unnatural a voice that he turned round again and began looking at me with surprise. He still said nothing, and that maddened me.

"How dare you come into my room without knocking and stare at me like that? Come on, answer me!"

But after looking calmly at me for half a minute, he started turning round again.

"Stop!" I roared, rushing up to him. "Don't you dare to move! Ah, that's better! Now answer me: what did you come in to look at me for?"

"If there is anything, sir, you want me to do for you now, it is my duty to carry it out," he replied, once more pausing a little before speaking, with his slow and measured lisp, raising his eyebrows and calmly inclining his head first to one side and then to another, and all this with the most exasperating self-composure.

"That's not what I asked you about, you tormentor!" I screamed, trembling with rage. "I'll tell you myself, you tormentor, why you come here. You see I'm not giving you your wages, and being too proud to come and ask for them yourself, you come here to stare at me stupidly in order to punish me, in order to torment me, without suspect-ing, tormentor that you are, how damned silly, silly, silly, silly it all is!"

He was about to turn round again silently, but I caught hold of him.

"Look," I shouted to him, "here's the money! Do you see? Here it is! (I took it out of the table drawer.) All the seven roubles. But you won't get them, you—will—not—get—them, until you come to me respectfully, acknowledge your fault, and say you are sorry! Do you hear?"

"That will never be!" he answered with a sort of unnatural self-confidence.

"It shall be!" I screamed. "I give you my word of honour—it shall be!"

"There's nothing I have to apologise for," he went on, as though not noticing my screams, "because you, sir, called me 'tormentor,' for which I can lodge a complaint against you at the police station."

"Go and lodge your complaint!" I roared. "Go at once, this very minute, this very second! You are a tormentor! A tormentor! A tormentor!"

But he only gave me a look, then turned round and, without paying any attention to my screams to stop, went out to his room with a measured step and without turning round.

"But for Lisa this would never have happened!" I said to myself. Then, after standing still for a minute, I went myself to his room behind the partition, gravely and solemnly, and without hurrying, though my heart was thumping slowly and violently. "Apollon," I said quietly and with great emphasis, though rather breathlessly, "go at once and fetch the police inspector. At once!"

He had in the meantime seated himself at his table, put on his spectacles, and settled down to his sewing. But, hearing my order, he burst into a loud guffaw.

"Go at once! This minute! Go, I say, or I shan't be responsible for what happens!"

"You must be off your head, sir," he remarked, without even raising his head, with his usual, slow lisp, calmly threading the needle. "Whoever heard of a man going to report to the police against himself! But, of course, sir, if you want to frighten me, then you might as well save yourself the trouble, for nothing will come of it."

"Go!" I screamed, grasping him by the shoulder. I felt that I was going to strike him any minute.

But I did not hear the door from the passage open quietly and slowly at that instant and someone come in, stand still, and start gazing at us in bewilderment. I looked up, nearly fainted with shame, and rushed back to my room. There, clutching at my hair with both hands and leaning my head against the wall, I remained motionless in that position.

About two minutes later I heard Apollon's slow footsteps.

"There's a certain young lady to see you, sir," he said, looking rather severely at me.

He then stood aside to let Lisa in. He did not seem to want to go, and stood staring at us sarcastically.

"Go! Go!" I ordered him, completely thrown off my balance.

At that moment my clock made a tremendous effort, and, wheezing, struck seven.

IX

And my house, fearlessly and freely,
As mistress you can enter now!

By the same poet.

I stood before her, feeling utterly crushed, disgraced, and shockingly embarrassed, and, I think, I smiled, trying desperately to wrap myself in the skirts of my tattered, wadded old dressing gown, exactly as a short while ago in one of the moments of complete depression I had imagined I would do. After watching us for a few minutes, Apollon went away, but that did not make me feel any better. Worst of all, she too was suddenly overcome with confusion, which I had hardly expected.

"Sit down," I said mechanically, placing a chair for her near the table.

I myself sat down on the sofa. She sat down at once, obediently, looking at me with wide-open eyes and evidently expecting something from me at any moment. It was this naïve expectancy of hers that incensed me, but I controlled myself.

If she had had any sense, she would have pretended not to have noticed anything, as though everything had been as usual, but instead she . . .

And I felt vaguely that I would make her pay dearly for *all this*.

"I'm afraid you've found me in a rather strange situation, Lisa," I began, stammering, and realising perfectly well that I shouldn't have opened the conversation like that. "No, no, don't think there's anything wrong," I exclaimed, seeing that she had suddenly blushed. "I'm not ashamed of my poverty. On the contrary, I look on it with pride. I'm a poor but honourable man. One can be poor and honourable, you know," I stammered. "However, will you have some tea?"

"No, thank you," she began.

"Wait a minute!"

I jumped up and ran out to Apollon. I had to get out of her sight somehow.

"Apollon," I whispered feverishly, talking very fast and flinging down on the table before him the seven roubles I had been keeping in my clenched hand all the time, "here are your wages. You see, I give them to you. But for that you must save me: go at once and fetch a pot of tea and a dozen rusks from the tea-shop. If you won't go, you'll make me the unhappiest man in the world! You don't know what a fine woman she is! She's wonderful! You may be thinking there's something—er—but you don't know what a fine woman she is!"

Apollon, who had sat down to his work and put on his spectacles again, at first looked silently at the money without putting down the needle; then, without paying any attention to me or replying to me, he went on busying himself with the needle, which he was still threading. I waited for three minutes, standing in front of him with my hands crossed *a la Napoléon*. My temples were wet with perspiration; I was very pale—I could feel it. But, thank God, he must have felt sorry as he looked at me, for having finished threading his needle, he slowly rose from his place, slowly pushed back his chair, slowly took off his glasses, slowly counted the money, and at last, asking me over his shoulder whether he should get a pot of tea for two, slowly left the room. As I was going back to Lisa, the thought occurred to me whether it would not be a good idea to run away just as I was in my dressing gown, run away no matter where, and let things take their course.

I sat down again. She regarded me uneasily. For a few minutes neither of us spoke.

"I'll murder him!" I suddenly screamed, banging my fist on the table with such violence that the ink spurted out of the ink-well.

"Good heavens, what are you saying?" she cried, startled.

"I'll murder him! I'll murder him!" I screamed, banging the table, beside myself with rage, but realising very well at the same time how stupid it was to be in such a rage.

"You can't imagine, Lisa, what a tormentor he is to me. He's my tormentor. He's gone out for some rusks now—he——"

And suddenly I burst into tears. It was a nervous attack. In between my sobs I felt awfully ashamed, but I could do nothing to stop them.

She was frightened. "What's the matter? What's the matter?" she kept asking, standing helplessly over me.

"Water . . . Give me some water, please. It's over there!" I murmured in a weak voice, realising very well at the same time that I could have managed without a drink of water and without murmuring in a weak voice. But I was, what is called, *play-acting* to save appearances, though my fit was real enough.

She gave me water, looking at me in utter confusion. At that moment Apollon brought in the tea. I felt that this ordinary, prosaic tea was very inappropriate and paltry after all that had happened, and I blushed. Lisa looked at Apollon almost in terror. He went out without a glance at us.

"Do you despise me, Lisa?" I said, looking straight at her and trembling with impatience to know what she was thinking of.

She was overcome with confusion and did not know what to say.

"Drink your tea," I said, angrily.

I was angry with myself, but of course it was she who would suffer for it. A terrible resentment against her suddenly blazed up in my heart. I believe I could have killed her. To revenge myself on her, I took a silent vow not to say a single word to her while she was in my room. "She's to blame for everything," I thought.

Our silence went on for almost five minutes. The tea stood on the table, but she did not touch it. I had got so far that I deliberately did not want to start drinking it in order to make her feel even more embarrassed. And she could not very well start drinking it alone. She glanced at me a few times in mournful perplexity. I kept obstinately silent. I was, of course, the chief sufferer, for I fully realised the whole despicable meanness of my spiteful stupidity, and yet I could do nothing to restrain myself.

"I—I want to get away from that—place for good," she began in an effort to do something to break the silence, but, poor thing, that was just what she should not have spoken about at the moment, for it was a stupid thing to say and especially to a man who was as stupid as I. Even I felt a pang of pity in my heart for her clumsiness and unnecessary frankness. But something hideous inside me at once stifled my feeling of pity. It provoked me even more—to hell with it all! Another five minutes passed.

"I haven't come at the wrong time, have I?" she began shyly in a hardly audible whisper, and made to get up.

But the moment I saw the first signs of injured dignity, I shook with spite and burst out at once.

"What have you come here for? Answer me! Answer!" I began, gasping for breath and paying no attention to the logical order of my words. I wanted to blurt it all out at once, and I didn't care a damn what I started with, "I'll tell you, my dear girl, what you have come for. You've come because I made *pathetic speeches* to you the other night. So you were softened and now you want more of these pathetic speeches. Well, I may as well tell you at once that I was laughing at you then. And I'm laughing at you now. What are you shuddering for? Yes, I was laughing at you! I had been insulted before, at dinner, by the fellows who came before me that night. I came to your place intending to thrash one of them, an army officer, but I was too late. He had already gone. So to avenge my wounded pride on someone, to get my own back, I vented my spite on you and I laughed at you. I had been humiliated, so I too wanted to humiliate someone; they wiped the floor with me, so I too wanted to show my power. That's what happened, and you thought I'd come there specially to save you, did you? You thought so, didn't you? You did, didn't you?"

I knew that she would probably be confused and unable to make head or tail of it, but I knew, too, that she would grasp the gist of it perfectly. And so it was. She turned white as a sheet, tried to say something, her lips painfully twisted. But before she could say anything, she collapsed in a chair as though she had been felled by an axe. And afterwards she listened to me all the time with parted lips and wide-open eyes, trembling with terror. The cynicism, the cynicism of my words crushed her. . . .

"To save you!" I went on, jumping up from my chair and running up and down the room in front of her. "Save you from what? Why, I'm probably much worse than you. Why didn't you throw it in my teeth when I was reading that lecture to you? 'But why did you come to us yourself? To read me a lecture on morality?' I wanted power. Power was what I wanted then. I wanted sport. I wanted to see you cry. I wanted to humiliate you. To make you hysterical. That's what I wanted. I couldn't keep it up because I'm nothing but a rag myself. I got frightened, and I'm damned if I know why I told you where I lived. I was a bloody fool. That's why, I suppose. So even before I got home that night I was cursing and swearing at you for having given you my address. I hated you already because of the lies I had been telling you. For all I wanted was to make a few fine speeches, to have something to dream about. And do you know what I really wanted? What I wanted was that you should all go to hell! That's what I wanted. The thing I must have at any cost is peace of mind. To get that peace of mind, to make sure that no one worried me, I'd sell the whole world for a farthing. Is the world to go to rack and ruin or am I to have my cup of tea? Well, so far as I'm concerned, blow the world so long as I can have my cup of tea. Did you know that, or didn't you? Well, anyway, I know I'm a blackguard, a cad, an egoist, a loafer. Here I've been shivering in a fever for the last three days for fear that you might come. And do you know what I was so worried about in particular during those three days? I'll tell you. What I was so worried about was that I was making myself out to be such a hero before you and that you'd find me here in this torn old dressing gown of mine, poor and loathsome. Only a few minutes ago I told you that I was not ashamed of my poverty. Well, it's not true. I am ashamed of my poverty. I'm ashamed of it more than of anything. I'm afraid of it more than of anything, more than of being a thief, because I'm so confoundedly vain that at times I feel as though I had been skinned and every puff of air hurt me. Don't you realise now that I shall never forgive you for having found me in this tattered old dressing gown and just when, like a spiteful cur, I flew at Apollon's throat? Your saviour, your former hero, flings himself like some mangy, shaggy mongrel on his valet, and his valet is laughing at him! And I shall never forgive you for the tears which I was shedding before you a minute ago, like some silly old woman who had been put to shame. Nor shall I ever forgive *you* for what I'm now confessing to you! Yes, you alone must answer for it all because you just happened to come at that moment, because I'm a rotter, because I'm the most horrible, the most ridiculous, the most petty, the most stupid, the most envious of all the worms on earth who are not a bit better than me, but who—I'm damned if I know why —are never ashamed or embarrassed, while I shall be insulted all my life by every louse because that's the sort of fellow I am! And what the hell do I care if you don't understand what I'm talking about? And what the hell do I care what happens to you? Whether you're going to rack and ruin there or not? And do you realise that now that I've told you all this I shall hate you for having been here and listened to me? Why, it's only once in a lifetime that a man speaks his mind like this, and that, too, when he is in hysterics. What more do you want? Why after all this do you still stand here before me torturing me? Why don't you get out of here?"

But here a very odd thing happened.

I was so used to imagining everything and to thinking of everything as it happened in books, and to picturing to myself everything in the world as I had previously made it up in my dreams, that at first I could not all at once grasp the meaning of this occurrence. What occurred was this: Lisa, humiliated and crushed by me, understood much more than I imagined. She understood from all this what a woman who loves sincerely always understands first of all, namely, that I was unhappy.

The frightened and resentful look on her face first gave place to one of sorrowful astonishment. But when I began to call myself a cad and a blackguard and my tears began to flow (I had spoken the whole of that tirade with tears), her whole face began to work convulsively. She was about to get up and stop me, and when I finished, it was not my cries of why she was here and why she did not go away to which she paid attention; what she felt was that I must have found it very hard indeed to say all this. And besides, she was so crushed, poor girl. She considered herself so inferior to me. Why should she feel angry or offended? She suddenly jumped up from her chair with a kind of irresistible impulse and, all drawn towards me but still feeling very shy and not daring to move from her place, held out her hands to me. . . . It was here that my heart failed me. Then she rushed to me, flung her arms round my neck, and burst into tears. I could not restrain myself, either, and burst out sobbing as I had never in my life sobbed before. . . .

"They—they won't let me—I—I can't be good!" I could hardly bring myself to say, then I stumbled to the sofa, fell on it face downwards, and for a quarter of an hour sobbed hysterically. She clung to me, put her arms round me, and seemed to remain frozen in that embrace.

But the trouble was that my hysterical fit could not go on for ever. And so (it is the loathsome truth I am writing), lying prone on the sofa, clinging tightly to it, and my face buried in my cheap leather cushion, I began gradually, remotely, involuntarily but irresistibly to feel that I should look an awful ass if I raised my head now and looked Lisa straight in the face. What was I ashamed of? I don't know. All I know is that I was ashamed. It also occurred to me just then, overwrought as I was, that our parts were now completely changed, that she was the heroine now, while I was exactly the same crushed and humiliated creature as she had appeared to me that night —four days before. . . . And all this flashed through my mind while I was still lying prone on the sofa!

Good God, was I really envious of her then?

I don't know. To this day I cannot possibly say whether I was envious of her or not, and at the time of course I was less able to understand it than now. I cannot live without feeling that I have someone completely in my power, that I am free to tyrannise over some human being. But—you can't explain anything by reasoning and consequently it is useless to reason.

I soon pulled myself together, however, and raised my head; I had to do it sooner or later. . . . And, well, to this day I can't help thinking that it was because I was ashamed to look at her that another feeling was suddenly kindled and blazed up in my heart—a feeling of domination and possession! My eyes flashed with passion and I clasped her hands violently. How I hated her and how I was drawn to her at that moment! One feeling intensified the other. This was almost like vengeance! . . . At first she looked bewildered and even frightened, but only for one moment. She embraced me warmly and rapturously.

X

A quarter of an hour later I was rushing up and down the room in furious impatience. Every minute I walked up to the screen and looked through the narrow slit at Lisa. She was sitting on the floor, her head leaning against the edge of the bed, and, I suppose, was crying.

But she did not go away, and that irritated me. This time she knew everything. I had insulted her finally, but—there is no need to speak about it. She guessed that my outburst of passion was nothing but revenge, a fresh insult for her, and that to my earlier, almost aimless, hatred, there was now added a *personal, jealous* hatred of her. . . . However, I can't be certain that she did understand it all so clearly; what she certainly did understand was that I was a loathsome man and that, above all, I was incapable of loving her.

I know I shall be told that it is incredible—that it is incredible that anyone could be as spiteful and as stupid as I was; and I daresay it will be added that it was improbable that I should not love her or, at any rate, appreciate her love. But why is it improbable? First of all, I could not possibly have loved anyone because, I repeat, to me love meant to tyrannise and to be morally superior. I have never in my life been able to imagine any other sort of love, and I have reached the point that sometimes I cannot help thinking even now that love only consists in the right to tyrannise over the woman you love, who grants you this right of her own free will. Even in my most secret dreams I could not imagine love except as a struggle, and always embarked on it with hatred and ended it with moral subjugation, and afterwards I did not have the faintest idea what to do with the woman I had subjugated. And indeed what is there improbable about it when I had at last reached such a state of moral depravity, when I had lost touch so much with "real life," that only a few hours before I had thought of reproaching her for having come to me to listen to "pathetic speeches," and did not even guess that she had not come to listen to my pathetic speeches at all, but to love me, for it is only in love that a woman can find her true resurrection, her true salvation from any sort of calamity, and her moral regeneration, and she cannot possibly find it in anything else. Still, I did not hate her so much after all when I was pacing the room and looked at her through the chink in the screen. I merely felt unbearably distressed at her being there. I wanted her to disappear. I longed for "peace." I wanted to be left alone in my funk-hole. "Real life"—so unaccustomed was I to it—had crushed me so much that I found it difficult to breathe.

But a few minutes passed and still she did not get up,

as though she were unconscious. I had the meanness to knock quietly at the screen to remind her. . . . She gave a start, got up quickly, and began looking for her kerchief, her hat, her fur coat, as though her only thought were how to run away from me as quickly as possible. . . .

Two minutes later she came out slowly from behind the screen and looked hard at me. I grinned maliciously, though I must confess I had to force myself to do it, *for the sake of appearances*, and turned away from her gaze.

"Goodbye," she said, going to the door.

I ran up to her suddenly, seized her hand, opened it, put something in it and—closed it again. Then I turned at once and rushed away quickly to the other corner of the room so as not to see her at least.

I almost told a lie this very minute. I was about to write that I did not do it deliberately, that I did it because I did not realise what I was doing, having in my folly completely lost my head. But I don't want to lie, and therefore I say frankly that I opened her hand and put something in it—out of spite. The thought came into my head when I was running up and down the room and she was sitting behind the screen. But this I can say in all truth: I did that cruel thing deliberately, I did it not because my heart, but because my wicked brain prompted me to do it. This cruelty was so insincere, so much thought out, so deliberately invented, so *bookish*, that I couldn't stand it myself even for a minute, but first rushed away to a corner so as not to see anything, and then, overwhelmed with shame and despair, rushed after Lisa. I opened the front door and began listening.

"Lisa! Lisa!" I cried down the stairs, but in a halting voice, in an undertone.

There was no answer, but I thought I heard her footsteps, lower down on the stairs.

"Lisa!" I called in a louder voice.

No answer. But at that moment I heard the heavy glass street-door open with a creak and with difficulty and slam heavily. The noise reverberated on the stairs.

She was gone. I returned musing to my room, feeling terribly ill at ease.

I stopped at the table beside the chair on which she had sat and looked disconsolately before me. A minute passed. Suddenly I gave a start: straight before me on the table I saw a crumpled blue five-rouble note, the same which a minute before I had pressed into her hand. It *was* the same note. It could be no other, for there was no other in the house. She therefore had just enough time to fling it on the table at the moment when I rushed to the other end of the room.

Well, of course, I might have expected it of her. Might have expected it? No, I was too great an egoist, I had too little respect for people to have been able even to imagine that she would do it. That was too much. That I could not bear. A moment later I began to dress madly, putting on hurriedly whatever clothes I could lay my hands on, and rushed headlong after her. She had hardly had time to walk more than a hundred yards when I ran out into the street.

The street was quiet and deserted. It was snowing heavily, the snowflakes falling almost perpendicularly and piling up in deep drifts on the pavement and on the empty road. There was not a soul to be seen, not a sound to be heard. The street-lamps twinkled desolately and uselessly. I ran about a hundred yards to the cross-roads and stopped.

Where had she gone? And why was I running after her? Why? To fall on my knees before her, to sob with remorse, to kiss her feet, to beseech her to forgive me! I wanted to do so, my breast was being torn to pieces, and never, never shall I be able to recall that moment with indifference. But—why? I could not help thinking. Would I not hate her fiercely tomorrow perhaps just because I had been kissing her feet today? Could I make her happy? Had I not learnt today for the hundredth time what I was really worth? Should I not torture her to death?

I stood in the snow, peering into the dim haze, and thought of that.

"And will it not be better, will it not be much better," I thought afterwards at home, giving full rein to my imagination and suppressing the living pain in my heart, "will it not be much better that she should now carry that insult away with her for ever? What is an insult but a sort of purification? It is the most corrosive and painful form of consciousness! Tomorrow I should have bespattered her soul with mud, I should have wearied her heart by thrusting myself upon her, while now the memory of the insult will never die in her, and however horrible the filth that lies in store for her, the memory of that humiliation will raise her and purify her—by hatred, and, well, perhaps also by forgiveness. Still, will that make things easier for her?"

And, really, here am I already putting the idle question to myself—which is better: cheap happiness or exalted suffering? Well, which is better?

So I went on dreaming as I sat at home that evening, almost dead with the pain in my heart. Never before had I endured such suffering and remorse. But didn't I know perfectly well when I ran out of my flat that I should turn back half-way? I never met Lisa again, and have heard nothing of her. I may as well add that I remained for a long time pleased with the *phrase* about the usefulness of insults and hatred in spite of the fact that I almost fell ill at the time from blank despair.

Even now, after all these years, I somehow feel *unhappy* to recall all this. Lots of things make me unhappy now when I recall them, but—why not finish my "memoirs" at this point? I can't help thinking that I made a mistake in starting to write them. At any rate, I have felt ashamed all the time I have been writing this *story:* so it seems this is no longer literature, but a corrective punishment. For to tell long stories and how I have, for instance, spoilt my life by a moral disintegration in my funk-hole, by my unsociable habits, by losing touch with life, and by nursing my spite in my dark cellar—all this, I'm afraid, is not interesting. A novel must have a hero, and here I seemed to have *deliberately* gathered together all the characteristics of an anti-hero, and, above all, all this is certain to produce a most unpleasant impression because we have all lost touch with life, we are all cripples, every one of us—more or less. We have lost touch so much that occasionally we cannot help feeling a sort of disgust with "real life," and that is why we are so angry when people remind us of it. Why, we have gone so far that we look upon "real life" almost as a sort of burden, and we are all agreed that "life" as we find it in books is much better. And why do we make such a fuss sometimes? Why do we make fools of ourselves? What do we want? We don't know ourselves. For as a matter of fact we should fare much worse if our nonsensical prayers were granted. Why, just try, just give us, for instance, more independence, untie the hands of any one of us, widen the sphere of our activities, relax discipline, and we—yes, I assure you—we should immediately be begging for the discipline to be reimposed upon us. I know that very likely you will be angry with me for saying this, that you will start shouting and stamping, "Speak for yourself and for your miserable life in that dark cellar of yours and don't you dare to say 'all of us.'" But, good Lord, gentlemen, I'm not trying to justify myself by this *all-of-usness*. For my part, I have merely carried to extremes in my life what you have not dared to carry even half-way, and, in addition, you have mistaken your cowardice for common sense and have found comfort in that, deceiving yourselves. So that, as a matter of fact, I seem to be much more alive than you. Come, look into it more closely! Why, we do not even know where we are to find real life, or what it is, or what it is called. Leave us alone without any books, and we shall at once get confused, lose ourselves in a maze, we shall not know what to cling to, what to hold on to, what to love and what to hate, what to respect and what to despise. We even find it hard to be men, men of *real* flesh and blood, *our own* flesh and blood. We are ashamed of it. We think it a disgrace. And we do our best to be some theoretical "average" men. We are stillborn, and for a long time we have been begotten not by living fathers, and that's just what we seem to like more and more. We are getting a taste for it. Soon we shall invent some way of being somehow or other begotten by an idea. But enough—I don't want to write any more "from a Dark Cellar. . . ."

(This is not, by the way, the end of the "Memoirs" of this paradoxical fellow. He could not resist and went on and on. But it seems to us, too, that we may stop here.)

The Gambler

(From the Diary of a Young Man)

TRANSLATED BY CONSTANCE GARNETT

Chapter 1

AT LAST I have come back from my fortnight's absence. Our friends have already been two days in Roulettenburg. I imagined that they were expecting me with the greatest eagerness; I was mistaken, however. The General had an extremely independent air, he talked to me condescendingly and sent me away to his sister. I even fancied that the General was a little ashamed to look at me. Marya Filippovna was tremendously busy and scarcely spoke to me; she took the money, however, counted it, and listened to my whole report. They were expecting Mezentsov, the little Frenchman, and some Englishman; as usual, as soon as there was money there was a dinner-party; in the Moscow style. Polina Alexandrovna, seeing me, asked why I had been away so long, and without waiting for an answer went off somewhere. Of course, she did that on purpose. We must have an explanation, though. Things have accumulated.

They had assigned me a little room on the fourth storey of the hotel. They know here that I belong to the *General's suite*. It all looks as though they had managed to impress the people. The General is looked upon by everyone here as a very rich Russian grandee. Even before dinner he commissioned me, among other things, to change two notes for a thousand francs each. I changed them at the office of the hotel. Now we shall be looked upon as millionaires for a whole week, at least. I wanted to take Misha and Nadya out for a walk, but on the stairs I was summoned back to the General; he had graciously bethought him to inquire where I was taking them. The man is absolutely unable to look me straight in the face; he would like to very much, but every time I meet his eyes with an intent, that is, disrespectful air, he seems overcome with embarrassment. In very bombastic language, piling one sentence on another, and at last losing his thread altogether, he gave me to understand that I was to take the children for a walk in the park, as far as possible from the Casino. At last he lost his temper completely, and added sharply: "Or else maybe you'll be taking them into the gambling saloon. You must excuse me," he added, "but I know you are still rather thoughtless and capable, perhaps, of gambling. In any case, though, I am not your mentor and have no desire to be, yet I have the right, at any rate, to desire that you will not compromise me, so to speak. . . ."

"But I have no money," I said calmly; "one must have it before one can lose it."

"You shall have it at once," answered the General, flushing a little; he rummaged in his bureau, looked up in an account book, and it turned out that he had a hundred and twenty roubles owing me.

"How are we to settle up?" he said. "We must change it into thalers. Come, take a hundred thalers—the rest, of course, won't be lost."

I took the money without a word.

"Please don't be offended by my words, you are so ready to take offence. . . . If I did make an observation, it was only, so to speak, by way of warning, and, of course, I have some right to do so. . . ."

On my way home before dinner, with the children, I met a perfect cavalcade. Our party had driven out to look at some ruin. Two magnificent carriages, superb horses! In one carriage was Mlle. Blanche with Marya Filippovna and Polina; the Frenchman, the Englishman and our General were on horseback. The passers-by stopped and stared; a sensation was created; but the General will have a bad time, all the same. I calculated that with the four thousand francs I had brought, added to what they had evidently managed to get hold of, they had now seven or eight thousand francs; but that is not enough for Mlle. Blanche.

Mlle. Blanche, too, is staying at the hotel with her mother; our Frenchman is somewhere in the house, too. The footman calls him "Monsieur le Comte." Mlle. Blanche's mother is called "Madame la Comtesse"; well, who knows, they may be Comte and Comtesse.

I felt sure that M. le Comte would not recognize me when we assembled at dinner. The General, of course, would not have thought of introducing us or even saying a word to him on my behalf; and M. le Comte has been in Russia himself, and knows what is called an *outchitel* is very small fry. He knows me very well, however. But I must confess I made my appearance at dinner unbidden; I fancy the General forgot to give orders, or else he would certainly have sent me to dine at the *table d'hôte*. I came of my own accord, so that the General looked at me with astonishment. Kind-hearted Marya Filippovna immediately made a place for me; but my meeting with Mr. Astley saved the situation, and I could not help seeming to belong to the party.

I met this strange Englishman for the first time in the train in Prussia, where we sat opposite to one another, when I was travelling to join the family; then I came across him as I was going into France, and then again in Switzerland: in the course of that fortnight twice—and now I suddenly met him in Roulettenburg. I never met a man so shy in my life. He is stupidly shy and, of course, is aware of it himself, for he is by no means stupid. He is very sweet and gentle, however. I drew him into talk at our first meeting in Prussia. He told me that he had been that summer at North Cape, and that he was very anxious to visit the fair at Nizhni Novgorod. I don't know how he made acquaintance with the General; I believe that he is hopelessly in love with Polina. When she came in he glowed like a sunset. He was very glad that I was sitting beside him at the table and seemed already to look upon me as his bosom friend.

At dinner the Frenchman gave himself airs in an extraordinary way; he was nonchalant and majestic with every one. In Moscow, I remember, he used to blow soap bubbles. He talked a great deal about finance and Russian politics. The General sometimes ventured to contradict, but discreetly, and only so far as he could without too great loss of dignity.

I was in a strange mood; of course, before we were half through dinner I had asked myself my usual invariable question: "Why I went on dancing attendance on this General, and had not left them long ago?" From time to time I glanced at Polina Alexandrovna. She took no notice of me whatever. It ended by my flying into a rage and making up my mind to be rude.

I began by suddenly, apropos of nothing, breaking in on the conversation in a loud voice. What I longed to do above all things was to be abusive to the Frenchman. I turned round to the General and very loudly and distinctly, I believe, interrupted him. I observed that this summer it was utterly impossible for a Russian to dine at *table d'hôte*. The General turned upon me an astonished stare.

"If you are a self-respecting man," I went on, "you will certainly be inviting abuse and must put up with affronts to your dignity. In Paris, on the Rhine, even in Switzerland, there are so many little Poles, and French people who sympathize with them, that there's no chance for a Russian to utter a word."

I spoke in French. The General looked at me in amazement. I don't know whether he was angry or simply astonished at my so forgetting myself.

"It seems some one gave you a lesson," said the Frenchman, carelessly and contemptuously.

"I had a row for the first time with a Pole in Paris," I answered; "then with a French officer who took the Pole's part. And then some of the French came over to my side, when I told them how I tried to spit in Monseigneur's coffee."

"Spit?" asked the General, with dignified perplexity, and he even looked about him aghast.

The Frenchman scanned me mistrustfully.

"Just so," I answered. "After feeling convinced for two whole days that I might have to pay a brief visit to Rome about our business, I went to the office of the Papal Embassy to get my passport *viséed*. There I was met by a little abbé, a dried-up little man of about fifty, with a frost-bitten expression. After listening to me politely, but extremely drily, he asked me to wait a little. Though I was in a hurry, of course I sat down to wait, and took up *L'Opinion Nationale* and began reading a horribly abusive attack on Russia. Meanwhile, I heard some one in the next room ask to see Monseigneur; I saw my abbé bow to him. I addressed the same request to him again; he asked me to wait—more drily than ever. A little later some one else entered, a stranger, but on business, some Austrian; he was listened to and at once conducted upstairs. Then I felt very much vexed; I got up, went to the abbé and said resolutely, that as Monseigneur was receiving, he might settle my business, too. At once the abbé drew back in great surprise. It was beyond his comprehension that an insignificant Russian should dare to put himself on a level with Monseigneur's guests. As though delighted to have an opportunity of insulting me, he looked me up and down, and shouted in the most insolent tone: 'Can you really suppose that Monseigneur is going to leave his coffee on your account?' Then I shouted, too, but more loudly than he: 'Let me tell you I'm ready to spit in your Monseigneur's coffee! If you don't finish with my passport this minute, I'll go to him in person.'

" 'What! When the Cardinal is sitting with him!' cried the abbé, recoiling from me with horror, and, flinging wide his arms, he stood like a cross, with an air of being ready to die rather than let me pass.

"Then I answered him that 'I was a heretic and a barbarian, *que je suis hérétique et barbare,*' and that I cared nothing for all these Archbishops, Cardinals, Monseigneurs and all of them. In short, I showed I was not going to give way. The abbé looked at me with uneasy ill-humour, then snatched my passport and carried it upstairs. A minute later it had been *viséed.* Here, wouldn't you like to see it?" I took out the passport and showed the Roman *visé.*

"Well, I must say . . ." the General began.

"What saved you was saying that you were a heretic and barbarian," the Frenchman observed, with a smile. "*Cela n'était pas si bête.*"

"Why, am I to model myself upon our Russians here? They sit, not daring to open their lips, and almost ready to deny they are Russians. In Paris, anyway in my hotel, they began to treat me much more attentively when I told every one about my passage-at-arms with the abbé. The fat Polish *pan,* the person most antagonistic to me at *table d'hôte,* sank into the background. The Frenchmen did not even resent it when I told them that I had, two years previously, seen a man at whom, in 1812, a French *chasseur* had shot simply in order to discharge his gun. The man was at that time a child of ten, and his family had not succeeded in leaving Moscow."

"That's impossible," the Frenchman boiled up; "a French soldier would not fire at a child!"

"Yet it happened," I answered. "I was told it by a most respectable captain on the retired list, and I saw the scar on his cheek from the bullet myself."

The Frenchman began talking rapidly and at great length. The General began to support him, but I recommended him to read, for instance, passages in the "Notes" of General Perovsky, who was a prisoner in the hands of the French in 1812. At last Marya Filippovna began talking of something else to change the conversation. The General was very much displeased with me, for the Frenchman and I had almost begun shouting at one another. But I fancy my dispute with the Frenchman pleased Mr. Astley very much. Getting up from the table, he asked me to have a glass of wine with him.

In the evening I duly succeeded in getting a quarter of an hour's talk with Polina Alexandrovna. Our conversation took place when we were all out for a walk. We all went into the park by the Casino. Polina sat down on a seat facing the fountain, and let Nadenka play with some children not far from her. I, too, let Misha run off to the fountain, and we were at last left alone.

We began, of course, at first with business. Polina simply flew into a rage when I gave her only seven hundred guldens. She had reckoned positively on my pawning her diamonds in Paris for two thousand guldens, if not more.

"I must have money, come what may," she said. "I must get it or I am lost."

I began asking her what had happened during my absence.

"Nothing, but the arrival of two pieces of news from Petersburg: first that Granny was very ill, and then, two days later, that she seemed to be dying. The news came from Timofey Petrovitch," added Polina, "and he's a trustworthy man. We are expecting every day to hear news of the end."

"So you are all in suspense here?" I asked.

"Of course, all of us, and all the time; we've been hoping for nothing else for the last six months."

"And are *you* hoping for it?" I asked.

"Why, I'm no relation. I am only the General's stepdaughter. But I am sure she will remember me in her will."

"I fancy you'll get a great deal," I said emphatically.

"Yes, she was fond of me; but what makes *you* think so?"

"Tell me," I answered with a question, "our *marquis* is initiated into all our secrets, it seems?"

"But why are you interested in that?" asked Polina, looking at me drily and austerely.

"I should think so; if I'm not mistaken, the General has already succeeded in borrowing from him."

"You guess very correctly."

"Well, would he have lent the money if he had not known about your 'granny'? Did you notice at dinner, three times speaking of her, he called her 'granny.' What intimate and friendly relations!"

"Yes, you are right. As soon as he knows that I have come into something by the will, he will pay his addresses to me at once. That is what you wanted to know, was it?"

"He will only begin to pay you his addresses? I thought he had been doing that a long time."

"You know perfectly well that he hasn't!" Polina said, with anger. "Where did you meet that Englishman?" she added, after a minute's silence.

"I knew you would ask about him directly."

I told her of my previous meetings with Mr. Astley on my journey.

"He is shy and given to falling in love, and, of course, he's fallen in love with you already."

"Yes, he's in love with me," answered Polina.

"And, of course, he's ten times as rich as the Frenchman. Why, is it certain that the Frenchman has anything? Isn't that open to doubt?"

"No, it is not. He has a château of some sort. The General has spoken of that positively. Well, are you satisfied?"

"If I were in your place I should certainly marry the Englishman."

"Why?" asked Polina.

"The Frenchman is better-looking, but he is nastier; and the Englishman, besides being honest, is ten times as rich," I snapped out.

"Yes, but on the other hand, the Frenchman is a *marquis* and clever," she answered, in the most composed manner.

"But it is true?" I went on, in the same way.

"It certainly is."

Polina greatly disliked my questions, and I saw that she was trying to make me angry by her tone and the strangeness of her answers. I said as much to her at once.

"Well, it really amuses me to see you in such a rage. You must pay for the very fact of my allowing you to ask such questions and make such suppositions."

"I certainly consider myself entitled to ask you any sort of question," I answered calmly, "just because I am prepared to pay any price you like for it, and I set no value at all on my life now."

Polina laughed.

"You told me last time at the Schlangenberg, that you were prepared, at a word from me, to throw yourself head foremost from the rock, and it is a thousand feet high, I believe. Some day I shall utter that word, solely in order to see how you will pay the price, and trust me, I won't give way. You are hateful to me, just because I've allowed you to take such liberties, and even more hateful because you are so necessary to me. But so long as you are necessary to me, I must take care of you."

She began getting up. She spoke with irritation. Of late she had always ended every conversation with me in anger and irritation, real anger.

"Allow me to ask you, what about Mlle. Blanche?" I asked, not liking to let her go without explanation.

"You know all about Mlle. Blanche. Nothing more has happened since. Mlle. Blanche will, no doubt, be Madame la Générale, that is, if the rumour of Granny's death is confirmed, of course, for Mlle. Blanche and her mother and her cousin twice removed, the *marquis*—all know very well that we are ruined."

"And is the General hopelessly in love?"

"That's not the point now. Listen and remember: take these seven hundred florins and go and play. Win me as much as you can at roulette; I must have money now, come what may."

Saying this, she called Nadenka and went into the Casino, where she joined the rest of the party. I turned into the first path to the left, wondering and reflecting. I felt as though I had had a blow on the head after the command to go and play roulette. Strange to say, I had plenty to think about, but I was completely absorbed in analyzing the essential nature of my feeling towards Polina. It was true I had been more at ease during that fortnight's absence than I was now on the day of my return, though on the journey I had been as melancholy and restless as a madman, and at moments had even seen her in my dreams. Once, waking up in the train (in Switzerland), I began talking aloud, I believe, with Polina, which amused all the passengers in the carriage with me. And once more now I asked myself the question: "Do I love her?" And again I could not answer it, or, rather, I answered for the hundredth time that I hated her. Yes, she was hateful to me. There were moments (on every occasion at the end of our talks) when I would have given

my life to strangle her! I swear if it had been possible on
the spot to plunge a sharp knife in her bosom, I believe
I should have snatched it up with relish. And yet I swear
by all that's sacred that if at the Schlangenberg, at the
fashionable peak, she really had said to me, "Throw
yourself down," I should have thrown myself down at
once, also with positive relish. I knew that. In one way
or another it must be settled. All this she understood wonderfully well, and the idea that I knew, positively and
distinctly, how utterly beyond my reach she was, how
utterly impossible my mad dreams were of fulfilment, that
thought, I am convinced, afforded her extraordinary satisfaction; if not, how could she, cautious and intelligent
as she was, have been on such intimate and open terms
with me? I believe she had hitherto looked on me as that
empress of ancient times looked on the slave before whom
she did not mind undressing because she did not regard
him as a human being. Yes, often she did not regard me
as a human being!

I had her commission, however, to win at roulette, at
all costs. I had no time to consider why must I play, and
why such haste, and what new scheme was hatching in
that ever-calculating brain. Moreover, it was evident
that during that fortnight new facts had arisen of which
I had no idea yet. I must discover all that and get to the
bottom of it and as quickly as possible. But there was no
time now; I must go to roulette.

Chapter 2

I confess it was disagreeable to me. Though I had
made up my mind that I would play, I had not proposed
to play for other people. It rather threw me out of my
reckoning, and I went into the gambling saloon with
very disagreeable feelings. From the first glance I disliked everything in it. I cannot endure the flunkeyishness
of the newspapers of the whole world, and especially our
Russian papers, in which, almost every spring, the jour-
nalists write articles upon two things: first, on the extraordinary magnificence and luxury of the gambling saloons
on the Rhine, and secondly, on the heaps of gold which
are said to lie on the tables. They are not paid for it; it is
simply done from disinterested obsequiousness. There

was no sort of magnificence in these trashy rooms, and not only were there no piles of gold lying on the table, but there was hardly any gold at all. No doubt some time, in the course of the season, some eccentric person, either an Englishman or an Asiatic of some sort, a Turk, perhaps (as it was that summer), would suddenly turn up and lose or win immense sums; all the others play for paltry guldens, and on an average there is very little money lying on the tables.

As soon as I went into the gambling saloon (for the first time in my life), I could not for some time make up my mind to play. There was a crush besides. If I had been alone, even then, I believe I should soon have gone away and not have begun playing. I confess my heart was beating and I was not cool. I knew for certain, and had made up my mind long before, that I should not leave Roulettenburg unchanged, that some radical and fundamental change would take place in my destiny; so it must be and so it would be. Ridiculous as it may be that I should expect so much for myself from roulette, yet I consider even more ridiculous the conventional opinion accepted by all that it is stupid and absurd to expect anything from gambling. And why should gambling be worse than any other means of making money —for instance, commerce? It is true that only one out of a hundred wins, but what is that to me?

In any case I determined to look about me first and not to begin anything in earnest that evening. If anything did happen that evening it would happen by chance and be something slight, and I staked my money accordingly. Besides, I had to study the game; for, in spite of the thousand descriptions of roulette which I had read so eagerly, I understood absolutely nothing of its working until I saw it myself.

In the first place it all struck me as so dirty, somehow, morally horrid and dirty. I am not speaking at all of the greedy, uneasy faces which by dozens, even by hundreds, crowd round the gambling tables. I see absolutely nothing dirty in the wish to win as quickly and as much as possible. I always thought very stupid the answer of that fat and prosperous moralist, who replied to some one's excuse "that he played for a very small stake," "So much the worse, it is such petty covetousness." As though covetousness were not exactly the same, whether on a big scale or a petty one. It is a matter of proportion. What is paltry to Rothschild is wealth to me, and as for profits and winnings, people, not only at roulette, but everywhere, do nothing but try to gain or squeeze something out of one another. Whether profits or gains are nasty is a different question. But I am not solving that question here. Since I was myself possessed by an intense desire of winning, I felt as I went into the hall all this covetousness, and all this covetous filth if you like, in a sense congenial and convenient. It is most charming when people do not stand on ceremony with one another, but act openly and aboveboard. And, indeed, why deceive oneself? Gambling is a most foolish and imprudent pursuit! What was particularly ugly at first sight, in all the rabble round the roulette table, was the respect they paid to that pursuit, the solemnity and even reverence with which they all crowded round the tables. That is why a sharp distinction is drawn here between the kind of game that is *mauvais genre* and the kind that is permissible to well-bred people. There are two sorts of gambling: one the gentlemanly sort: the other the plebeian, mercenary sort, the game played by all sorts of riff-raff. The distinction is sternly observed here, and how contemptible this distinction really is! A gentleman may stake, for instance, five or ten louis d'or, rarely more; he may, however, stake as much as a thousand francs if he is very rich; but only for the sake of the play, simply for amusement, that is, simply to look on at the process of winning or of losing, but must on no account display an interest in winning. If he wins, he may laugh aloud, for instance; may make a remark to one of the bystanders; he may even put down another stake, and may even double it, but solely from curiosity, for the sake of watching and calculating the chances, and not from the plebeian desire to win. In fact, he must look on all gambling, roulette, *trente et quarante*, as nothing else than a pastime got up entirely for his amusement. He must not even suspect the greed for gain and the shifty dodges on which the bank depends.

It would be extremely good form, too, if he should imagine that all the other gamblers, all the rabble, trembling over a gulden, were rich men and gentlemen like himself and were playing simply for their diversion and amusement. This complete ignorance of reality and innocent view of people would be, of course, extremely aristocratic. I have seen many mammas push forward their daughters, innocent and elegant misses of fifteen and sixteen, and, giving them some gold coins, teach them how to play. The young lady wins or loses, invariably smiles and walks away, very well satisfied. Our General went up to the table with solid dignity; a flunkey rushed to hand him a chair, but he ignored the flunkey; he, very slowly and deliberately, took out his purse, very slowly and deliberately took three hundred francs in gold from his purse, staked them on the black, and won. He did not pick up his winnings, but left them on the table. Black turned up again; he didn't pick up his winnings that time either; and when, the third time, red turned up, he lost at once twelve hundred francs. He walked away with a smile and kept up his dignity. I am positive he was raging inwardly, and if the stake had been two or three times as much he would not have kept up his dignity but would have betrayed his feelings. A Frenchman did, however, before my eyes, win and lose as much as thirty thousand francs with perfect gaiety and no sign of emotion. A real gentleman should not show excitement even if he loses his whole fortune. Money ought to be so much below his gentlemanly dignity as to be scarcely worth noticing. Of course, it would have been extremely aristocratic not to notice the sordidness of all the rabble and all the surroundings. Sometimes, however, the opposite pose is no less aristocratic—to notice —that is, to look about one, even, perhaps, to stare through a lorgnette at the rabble; though always taking the rabble and the sordidness as nothing else but a diversion of a sort, as though it were a performance got up for the amusement of gentlemen. One may be jostled in that crowd, but one must look about one with complete conviction that one is oneself a spectator and that one is in no sense part of it. Though, again, to look very attentively is not quite the thing; that, again, would not be gentlemanly because, in any case, the spectacle does not deserve much, or close, attention. And, in fact, few spectacles do deserve a gentleman's close attention. And yet it seemed to me that all this was deserving of very close attention, especially for one who had come not only to observe it, but sincerely and genuinely reckoned himself as one of the rabble. As for my hidden moral convictions, there is no place for them, of course, in my present reasonings. Let that be enough for the present. I speak to relieve my conscience. But I notice one thing: that of late it has become horribly repugnant to me to test my thoughts and actions by any moral standard whatever. I was guided by something different. . . .

The rabble certainly did play very sordidly. I am ready to believe, indeed, that a great deal of the most ordinary thieving goes on at the gambling table. The croupiers who sit at each end of the table look at the stakes and reckon the winnings; they have a great deal to do. They are rabble, too! For the most part they are French. However, I was watching and observing, not with the object of describing roulette. I kept a sharp look-out for my own sake, so that I might know how to behave in the future. I noticed, for instance, that nothing was more common than for some one to stretch out his hand and snatch what one had won. A dispute would begin, often an uproar, and a nice job one would have to find witnesses and to prove that it was one's stake!

At first it was all an inexplicable puzzle to me. All I could guess and distinguish was that the stakes were on the numbers, on odd and even, and on the colours. I made up my mind to risk a hundred guldens of Polina Alexandrovna's money. The thought that I was not playing for myself seemed to throw me out of my reckoning. It was an extremely unpleasant feeling, and I wanted to be rid of it as soon as possible. I kept feeling that by beginning for Polina I should break my own luck. Is it impossible to approach the gambling table without becoming infected with superstition? I began by taking out five friedrichs d'or (fifty gulden) and putting them on the even. The wheel went round and thirteen turned up—I had lost. With a sickly feeling I staked another five friedrichs d'or on red, simply in order to settle the matter and go away. Red turned up. I staked all the ten friedrichs d'or—red turned up again. I staked all the money again on the same, and again red turned up. On receiving forty friedrichs d'or I staked twenty upon the twelve middle figures, not knowing what would come of it. I was paid three times my stake. In this way from ten friedrichs d'or I had all at once eighty. I was overcome by a strange, unusual feeling which was so unbearable that I made up my mind to go away. It seemed to me that I should not have been playing at all like that if I had been playing for myself. I staked the whole eighty friedrichs d'or, however, on even. This time four turned up; another eighty friedrichs d'or was poured out to me, and, gathering up the whole heap of a hundred and sixty friedrichs d'or, I set off to find Polina Alexandrovna.

They were all walking somewhere in the park and I only succeeded in seeing her after supper. This time the Frenchman was not of the party, and the General unbosomed himself. Among other things he thought fit to observe to me that he would not wish to see me at the gambling tables. It seemed to him that it would compromise him if I were to lose too much: "But even if you were to win a very large sum I should be compromised, too," he added significantly. "Of course, I have no right to dictate your actions, but you must admit yourself . . ." At this point he broke off, as his habit was. I answered, drily, that I had very little money, and so I could not lose very conspicuously, even if I did play. Going upstairs to my room I succeeded in handing Polina her winnings, and told her that I would not play for her another time.

"Why not?" she asked, in a tremor.

"Because I want to play on my own account," I answered, looking at her with surprise; "and it hinders me."

"Then you still continue in your conviction that roulette is your only escape and salvation?" she asked ironically.

I answered very earnestly, that I did; that as for my confidence that I should win, it might be absurd; I was ready to admit it, but that I wanted to be let alone.

Polina Alexandrovna began insisting I should go halves with her in to-day's winnings, and was giving me eighty friedrichs d'or, suggesting that I should go on playing on those terms. I refused the half, positively and finally, and told her that I could not play for other people, not because I didn't want to, but because I should certainly lose.

"Yet I, too," she said, pondering, "stupid as it seems, am building all my hopes on roulette. And so you must go on playing, sharing with me, and—of course—you will."

At this point she walked away, without listening to further objections.

Chapter 3

Yet all yesterday she did not say a single word to me about playing, and avoided speaking to me altogether. Her manner to me remained unchanged: the same absolute carelessness on meeting me; there was even a shade of contempt and dislike. Altogether she did not care to conceal her aversion; I noticed that. In spite of that she did not conceal from me, either, that I was in some way necessary to her and that she was keeping me for some purpose. A strange relation had grown up between us, incomprehensible to me in many ways when I considered her pride and haughtiness with every one. She knew, for instance, that I loved her madly, even allowed me to speak of my passion; and, of course, she could not have shown greater contempt for me than by allowing me to speak of my passion without hindrance or restriction. It was as much as to say that she thought so little of my feelings that she did not care in the least what I talked about to her and what I felt for her. She had talked a great deal about her own affairs before, but had never been completely open. What is more, there was this peculiar refinement in her contempt for me: she would know, for instance, that I was aware of some circumstance in her life, or knew of some matter that greatly concerned her, or she would tell me herself something of her circumstances, if to forward her objects she had to make use of me in some way, as a slave or an errand-boy; but she would always tell me only so much as a man employed on her errands need know, and if I did not know the whole chain of events, if she saw herself how worried and anxious I was over her worries and anxieties, she never deigned to comfort me by giving me her full confidence as a friend; though she often made use of me for commissions that were not only troublesome, but dangerous, so that to my thinking she was bound to be open with me. Was it worth her while, indeed, to trouble herself about my feelings, about my being worried, and perhaps three times as much worried and tormented by her anxieties and failures as she was herself?

I knew of her intention to play roulette three weeks before. She had even warned me that I should have to play for her, and it would be improper for her to play herself. From the tone of her words, I noticed even then that she had serious anxieties, and was not actuated simply by a desire for money. What is money to her for its own sake? She must have some object, there must be some circumstance at which I can only guess, but of which so far I have no knowledge. Of course, the humiliation and the slavery in which she held me might have made it possible for me (it often does) to question her coarsely and bluntly. Seeing that in her eyes I was a slave and utterly insignificant, there was nothing for her to be offended at in my coarse curiosity. But the fact is, that though she allowed me to ask questions, she did not answer them, and sometimes did not notice them at all. That was the position between us.

A great deal was said yesterday about a telegram which had been sent off four days before, and to which no answer had been received. The General was evidently upset and preoccupied. It had, of course, something to do with Granny. The Frenchman was troubled, too. Yesterday, for instance, after dinner, they had a long, serious talk. The Frenchman's tone to all of us was unusually high and mighty, quite in the spirit of the saying: "Seat a pig at table and it will put its feet on it." Even with Polina he was casual to the point of rudeness; at the same time he gladly took part in the walks in the public gardens and in the rides and drives into the country. I had long known some of the circumstances that bound the Frenchman to the General: they had made plans for establishing a factory together in Russia; I don't know whether their project had fallen through, or whether it was being discussed. Moreover, I had by chance come to know part of a family secret. The Frenchman had actually, in the previous year, come to the General's rescue, and had given him thirty thousand roubles to make up a deficit of Government monies missing when he resigned his duties. And, of course, the General is in his grip; but now the principal person in the whole business is Mlle. Blanche; about that I am sure I'm not mistaken.

What is Mlle. Blanche? Here among us it is said that she is a distinguished Frenchwoman, with a colossal fortune and a mother accompanying her. It is known, too, that she is some sort of relation of our *marquis,* but a very distant one: a cousin, or something of the sort. I am told that before I went to Paris, the Frenchman and Mlle. Blanche were on much more ceremonious, were, so to speak, on a more delicate and refined footing; now their acquaintance, their friendship and relationship, was of a rather coarse and more intimate character. Perhaps our prospects seemed to them so poor that they did not think it very necessary to stand on ceremony and keep up appearances with us. I noticed even the day before yesterday how Mr. Astley looked at Mlle. Blanche and her mother. It seemed to me that he knew them. It even seemed to me that our Frenchman had met Mr. Astley before. Mr. Astley, however, is so shy, so reserved and silent, that one can be almost certain of him—he won't wash dirty linen in public. Anyway, the Frenchman barely bows to him and scarcely looks at him, so he is not afraid of him. One can understand that, perhaps, but why does Mlle. Blanche not look at him either? Especially when the *marquis* let slip yesterday in the course of conversation—I don't remember in what connection—that Mr. Astley had a colossal fortune and that he—the *marquis*—knew this for a fact; at that point Mlle. Blanche might well have looked at Mr. Astley. Altogether the General was uneasy. One can understand what a telegram announcing his aunt's death would mean!

Though I felt sure Polina was, apparently for some object, avoiding a conversation with me, I assumed a cold and indifferent air: I kept thinking that before long she would come to me of herself. But both to-day and yesterday I concentrated my attention principally on Mlle. Blanche. Poor General! He is completely done for! To fall in love at fifty-five with such a violent passion is a calamity, of course! When one takes into consideration the fact that he is a widower, his children, the ruin of his estate, his debts, and, finally, the woman it is his lot to fall in love with. Mlle. Blanche is handsome. But I don't know if I shall be understood if I say that she has a face of the type of which one might feel frightened. I, anyway, have always been afraid of women of that sort. She is probably five-and-twenty. She is well grown and broad, with sloping shoulders; she has a magnificent throat and bosom; her complexion is swarthy yellow. Her hair is as black as Indian ink, and she has a tremendous lot of it, enough to make two ordinary coiffures. Her eyes are black with yellowish whites; she has an insolent look in her eyes;

her teeth are very white; her lips are always painted; she smells of musk. She dresses effectively, richly and with *chic*, but with much taste. Her hands and feet are exquisite. Her voice is a husky contralto. Sometimes she laughs, showing all her teeth, but her usual expression is a silent and impudent stare—before Polina and Marya Filippovna, anyway (there is a strange rumour that Marya Filippovna is going back to Russia). I fancy that Mlle. Blanche has had no sort of education. Possibly she is not even intelligent; but, on the other hand, she is striking and she is artful. I fancy her life has not passed without adventures. If one is to tell the whole truth, it is quite possible that the *marquis* is no relation of hers at all, and that her mother is not her mother. But there is evidence that in Berlin, where we went with them, her mother and she had some decent acquaintances. As for the *marquis* himself, though I still doubt his being a *marquis*, yet the fact that he is received in decent society—among Russians, for instance, in Moscow, and in some places in Germany—is not open to doubt. I don't know what he is in France. They say he has a château.

I thought that a great deal would have happened during this fortnight, and yet I don't know if anything decisive has been said between Mlle. Blanche and the General. Everything depends on our fortune, however; that is, whether the General can show them plenty of money. If, for instance, news were to come that Granny were not dead, I am convinced that Mlle. Blanche would vanish at once. It surprises and amuses me to see what a gossip I've become. Oh! how I loathe it all! How delighted I should be to drop it all, and them all! But can I leave Polina, can I give up spying round her? Spying, of course, is low, but what do I care about that?

I was interested in Mr. Astley, too, to-day and yesterday. Yes, I am convinced he's in love with Polina. It is curious and absurd how much may be expressed by the eyes of a modest and painfully chaste man, moved by love, at the very time when the man would gladly sink into the earth rather than express or betray anything by word or glance. Mr. Astley very often meets us on our walks. He takes off his hat and passes by, though, of course, he is dying to join us. If he is invited to do so, he immediately refuses. At places where we rest—at the Casino, by the bandstand, or before the fountain—he always stands somewhere not far from our seat; and wherever we may be—in the park, in the wood, or on the Schlangenberg—one has only to glance round, to look about one, and somewhere, either in the nearest path or behind the bushes, Mr. Astley's head appears. I fancy he is looking for an opportunity to have a conversation with me apart. This morning we met and exchanged a couple of words. He sometimes speaks very abruptly. Without saying "good-morning," he began by blurting out—

"Oh, Mlle. Blanche! . . . I have seen a great many women like Mlle. Blanche!"

He paused, looking at me significantly. What he meant to say by that I don't know. For on my asking what he meant, he shook his head with a sly smile, and added, "*Oh*, well, that's how it is. Is Mlle. Pauline very fond of flowers?"

"I don't know; I don't know at all," I answered.

"What? You don't even know that!" he cried, with the utmost amazement.

"I don't know; I haven't noticed at all," I repeated, laughing.

"H'm! That gives me a queer idea."

Then he shook his head and walked away. He looked pleased, though. We talked the most awful French together.

Chapter 4

To-day has been an absurd, grotesque, ridiculous day. Now it is eleven o'clock at night. I am sitting in my little cupboard of a room, recalling it. It began with my having to go to roulette to play for Polina Alexandrovna. I took the hundred and sixty friedrichs d'or, but on two conditions: first, that I would not go halves—that is, if I won I would take nothing for myself; and secondly, that in the evening Polina should explain to me why she needed to win, and how much money. I can't, in any case, suppose that it is simply for the sake of money. Evidently the money is needed, and as quickly as possible, for some particular object. She promised to explain, and I set off. In the gambling hall the crowd was awful. How insolent and how greedy they all were! I forced my way into the middle and

stood near the croupier; then I began timidly experiment-
ing, staking two or three coins at a time. Meanwhile, I
kept quiet and looked on; it seemed to me that calculation
meant very little, and had by no means the importance
attributed to it by some players. They sit with papers before them scrawled over in pencil, note the strokes,
reckon, deduce the chances, calculate, finally stake and—
lose exactly as we simple mortals who play without calculations. On the other hand, I drew one conclusion which
I believe to be correct: that is, though there is no system,
there really is a sort of order in the sequence of casual
chances—and that, of course, is very strange. For instance, it happens that after the twelve middle numbers
come the twelve later numbers; twice, for instance, it
turns up on the twelve last numbers and passes to the
twelve first numbers. After falling on the twelve first numbers, it passes again to numbers in the middle third, turns
up three or four times in succession on numbers between
thirteen and twenty-four, and again passes to numbers in
the last third; then, after turning up two numbers between
twenty-five and thirty-six, it passes to a number among
the first twelve, turns up once again on a number among
the first third, and again passes for three strokes in succession to the middle numbers; and in that way goes on
for an hour and a half or two hours. One, three and two—
one, three and two. It's very amusing. One day or one
morning, for instance, red will be followed by black and
back again almost without any order, shifting every minute, so that it never turns up red or black for more than
two or three strokes in succession. Another day, or another evening, there will be nothing but red over and over
again, turning up, for instance, more than twenty-two
times in succession, and so for a whole day. A great deal
of this was explained to me by Mr. Astley, who spent the
whole morning at the tables, but did not once put down a
stake.

As for me, I lost every farthing very quickly. I staked
straight off twenty friedrichs d'or on even and won, staked
again and again won, and went on like that two or three
times. I imagine I must have had about four hundred
friedrichs d'or in my hands in about five minutes. At that
point I ought to have gone away, but a strange sensation
rose up in me, a sort of defiance of fate, a desire to challenge it, to put out my tongue at it. I laid down the largest

stake allowed—four thousand gulden—and lost it. Then, getting hot, I pulled out all I had left, staked it on the same number, and lost again, after which I walked away from the table as though I were stunned. I could not even grasp what had happened to me, and did not tell Polina Alexandrovna of my losing till just before dinner. I spent the rest of the day sauntering in the park.

At dinner I was again in an excited state, just as I had been three days before. The Frenchman and Mlle. Blanche were dining with us again. It appeared that Mlle. Blanche had been in the gambling hall that morning and had witnessed my exploits. This time she addressed me, it seemed, somewhat attentively. The Frenchman set to work more directly, and asked me: Was it my own money I had lost? I fancy he suspects Polina. In fact, there is something behind it. I lied at once and said it was.

The General was extremely surprised. Where had I got such a sum? I explained that I had begun with ten frie-drichs d'or, that after six or seven times staking success-fully on equal chances I had five or six hundred gulden, and that afterwards I had lost it all in two turns.

All that, of course, sounded probable. As I explained this I looked at Polina, but I could distinguish nothing from her face. She let me lie, however, and did not set it right; from this I concluded that I had to lie and conceal that I was in collaboration with her. In any case, I thought to myself, she is bound to give me an explanation, and promised me this morning to reveal something.

I expected the General would have made some remark to me, but he remained mute; I noticed, however, signs of disturbance and uneasiness in his face. Possibly in his straitened circumstances it was simply painful to him to hear that such a pile of gold had come into, and within a quarter of an hour had passed out of, the hands of such a reckless fool as me.

I suspect that he had a rather hot encounter with the Frenchman yesterday. They were shut up together talking for a long time. The Frenchman went away seeming irri-tated, and came to see the General again early this morn-ing—probably to continue the conversation of the previ-ous day.

Hearing what I had lost, the Frenchman observed bit-ingly, even spitefully, that one ought to have more sense. He added—I don't know why—that though a great many

Russians gamble, Russians were not, in his opinion, well qualified even for gambling.

"In my mind," said I, "roulette is simply made for Russians."

And when at my challenge the Frenchman laughed contemptuously, I observed that I was, of course, right, for to speak of the Russians as gamblers was abusing them far more than praising them, and so I might be believed.

"On what do you base your opinion?" asked the Frenchman.

"On the fact that the faculty of amassing capital has, with the progress of history, taken a place—and almost the foremost place—among the virtues and merits of the civilized man of the West. The Russian is not only incapable of amassing capital, but dissipates it in a reckless and unseemly way. Nevertheless we Russians need money, too," I added, "and consequently we are very glad and very eager to make use of such means as roulette, for instance, in which one can grow rich all at once, in two hours, without work. That's very fascinating to us; and since we play badly, recklessly, without taking trouble, we usually lose!"

"That's partly true," observed the Frenchman complacently.

"No, it is not true, and you ought to be ashamed to speak like that of your country," observed the General, sternly and impressively.

"Allow me," I answered. "I really don't know which is more disgusting: Russian unseemliness or the German faculty of accumulation by honest toil."

"What an unseemly idea!" exclaimed the General.

"What a Russian idea!" exclaimed the Frenchman.

I laughed; I had an intense desire to provoke them.

"Well, I should prefer to dwell all my life in a Kirgiz tent," I cried, "than bow down to the German idol."

"What idol?" cried the General, beginning to be angry in earnest.

"The German faculty for accumulating wealth. I've not been here long, but yet all I have been able to observe and verify revolts my Tatar blood. My God! I don't want any such virtue! I succeeded yesterday in making a round of eight miles, and it's all exactly as in the edifying German picture-books: there is here in every house a *vater* horribly virtuous and extraordinarily honest—so honest that you are afraid to go near him. I can't endure honest people whom one is afraid to go near. Every such German *vater* has a family, and in the evening they read improving books aloud. Elms and chestnut trees rustle over the house. The sun is setting; there is a stork on the roof, and everything is extraordinarily practical and touching. . . . Don't be angry, General; let me tell it in a touching style. I remember how my father used to read similar books to my mother and me under the lime-trees in the garden. . . . So I am in a position to judge. And in what complete bondage and submission every such family is here. They all work like oxen and all save money like Jews. Suppose the *vater* has saved up so many gulden and is reckoning on giving his son a trade or a bit of land; to do so, he gives his daughter no dowry, and she becomes an old maid. To do so, the youngest son is sold into bondage or into the army, and the money is added to the family capital. This is actually done here; I've been making inquiries. All this is done from nothing but honesty, from such intense honesty that the younger son who is sold believes that he is sold from nothing but honesty: and that is the ideal when the victim himself rejoices at being led to the sacrifice. What more? Why, the elder son is no better off: he has an Amalia and their hearts are united, but they can't be married because the pile of gulden is not large enough. They, too, wait with perfect morality and good faith, and go to the sacrifice with a smile. Amalia's cheeks grow thin and hollow. At last, in twenty years, their prosperity is increased; the gulden have been honestly and virtuously accumulating. The *vater* gives his blessing to the forty-year-old son and his Amalia of thirty-five, whose chest has grown hollow and whose nose has turned red. . . . With that he weeps, reads them a moral sermon, and dies. The eldest son becomes himself a virtuous *vater* and begins the same story over again. In that way, in fifty or seventy years, the grandson of the first *vater* really has a considerable capital, and he leaves it to his son, and he to his, and he to his, till in five or six generations one of them is a Baron Rothschild or goodness knows who. Come, isn't that a majestic spectacle? A hundred or two hundred years of continuous toil, patience, intelligence, honesty, character, determination, prudence, the stork on the roof! What more do you want? Why, there's nothing loftier than that; and from that standpoint

they are beginning to judge the whole world and to punish the guilty; that is, any who are ever so little unlike
them. Well, so that's the point: I would rather waste my
substance in the Russian style or grow rich at roulette. I
don't care to be Goppe and Co. in five generations. I want
money for myself, and I don't look upon myself as something subordinate to capital and necessary to it. I know
that I have been talking awful nonsense, but, never mind,
such are my convictions."

"I don't know whether there is much truth in what you
have been saying," said the General thoughtfully, "but I
do know you begin to give yourself insufferable airs as
soon as you are permitted to forget yourself in the
least . . ."

As his habit was, he broke off without finishing. If our
General began to speak of anything in the slightest degree
more important than his ordinary everyday conversation,
he never finished his sentences. The Frenchman listened
carelessly with rather wide-open eyes; he had scarcely
understood anything of what I had said. Polina gazed
with haughty indifference. She seemed not to hear my
words, or anything else that was said that day at table.

Chapter 5

She was unusually thoughtful, but directly we got up
from table she bade me escort her for a walk. We took
the children and went into the park towards the fountain.

As I felt particularly excited, I blurted out the crude
and stupid question: why the Marquis de Grieux, our
Frenchman, no longer escorted her when she went out
anywhere, and did not even speak to her for days together.

"Because he is a rascal," she answered me strangely.

I had never heard her speak like that of De Grieux, and
I received it in silence, afraid to interpret her irritability.

"Have you noticed that he is not on good terms with
the General to-day?"

"You want to know what is the matter?" she answered
drily and irritably. "You know that the General is completely mortgaged to him; all his property is his, and if
Granny doesn't die, the Frenchman will come into possession of everything that is mortgaged to him."

"And is it true that everything is mortgaged? I had heard it, but I did not know that everything was."

"To be sure it is."

"Then farewell to Mlle. Blanche," said I. "She won't be the General's wife, then! Do you know, it strikes me the General is so much in love that he may shoot himself if Mlle. Blanche throws him over. It is dangerous to be so much in love at his age."

"I fancy that something will happen to him, too," Polina Alexandrovna observed musingly.

"And how splendid that would be!" I cried. "They couldn't have shown more coarsely that she was only marrying him for his money! There's no regard for decency, even; there's no ceremony about it whatever. That's wonderful! And about Granny—could there be anything more comic and sordid than to be continually sending telegram after telegram: 'Is she dead, is she dead'? How do you like it, Polina Alexandrovna?"

"That's all nonsense," she said, interrupting me with an air of disgust. "I wonder at your being in such good spirits. What are you so pleased about? Surely not at having lost my money?"

"Why did you give it to me to lose? I told you I could not play for other people—especially for you! I obey you, whatever you order me to do, but I can't answer for the result. I warned you that nothing would come of it. Are you very much upset at losing so much money? What do you want so much for?"

"Why these questions?"

"Why, you promised to explain to me . . . Listen: I am absolutely convinced that when I begin playing for myself (and I've got twelve friedrichs d'or) I shall win. Then you can borrow as much from me as you like."

She made a contemptuous grimace.

"Don't be angry with me for such a suggestion," I went on. "I am so deeply conscious that I am nothing beside you—that is, in your eyes—that you may even borrow money from me. Presents from me cannot insult you. Besides, I lost yours."

She looked at me quickly, and seeing that I was speaking irritably and sarcastically, interrupted the conversation again.

"There's nothing of interest to you in my circumstances. If you want to know, I'm simply in debt. I've borrowed money and I wanted to repay it. I had the strange and mad idea that I should be sure to win here at the gambling table. Why I had the idea I can't understand, but I believed in it. Who knows, perhaps I believed it because no other alternative was left me."

"Or because it was quite *necessary* you should win. It's exactly like a drowning man clutching at a straw. You will admit that if he were not drowning he would not look at a straw as a branch of a tree."

Polina was surprised.

"Why," she said, "you were reckoning on the same thing yourself! A fortnight ago you said a great deal to me about your being absolutely convinced that you would win here at roulette, and tried to persuade me not to look upon you as mad; or were you joking then? But I remember you spoke so seriously that it was impossible to take it as a joke."

"That's true," I answered thoughtfully. "I am convinced to this moment that I shall win. I confess you have led me now to wonder why my senseless and unseemly failure to-day has not left the slightest doubt in me. I am still fully convinced that as soon as I begin playing for myself I shall be certain to win."

"Why are you so positive?"

"If you will have it—I don't know. I only know that I *must* win, that it is the only resource left me. Well, that's why, perhaps, I fancy I am bound to win."

"Then you, too, absolutely *must* have it, since you are so fanatically certain?"

"I wager you think I'm not capable of feeling that I *must* have anything?"

"That's nothing to me," Polina answered quietly and indifferently. "Yes, if you like. I doubt whether anything troubles you in earnest. You may be troubled, but not in earnest. You are an unstable person, not to be relied on. What do you want money for? I could see nothing serious in the reasons you brought forward the other day."

"By the way," I interrupted, "you said that you had to repay a debt. A fine debt it must be! To the Frenchman, I suppose?"

"What questions! You're particularly impertinent to-day. Are you drunk, perhaps?"

"You know that I consider myself at liberty to say any-

thing to you, and sometimes ask you very candid questions. I repeat, I'm your slave, and one does not mind
what one says to a slave, and cannot take offence at anything he says."

"And I can't endure that 'slave' theory of yours."

"Observe that I don't speak of my slavery because I
want to be your slave. I simply speak of it as a fact which
doesn't depend on me in the least."

"Tell me plainly, what do you want money for?"

"What do you want to know that for?"

"As you please," she replied, with a proud movement
of her head.

"You can't endure the 'slave' theory, but insist on slav-
ishness: 'Answer and don't argue.' So be it. Why do I want
money? you ask. How can you ask? Money is everything!"

"I understand that, but not falling into such madness
from wanting it! You, too, are growing frenzied, fatalistic.
There must be something behind it, some special object.
Speak without beating about the bush; I wish it."

She seemed beginning to get angry, and I was awfully
pleased at her questioning me with such heat.

"Of course there is an object," I answered, "but I don't
know how to explain what it is. Nothing else but that
with money I should become to you a different man, not
a slave."

"What? How will you manage that?"

"How shall I manage it? What, you don't even understand how I could manage to make you look at me as anything but a slave? Well, that's just what I don't care for,
such surprise and incredulity!"

"You said this slavery was a pleasure to you. I thought
it was myself."

"You thought so!" I cried, with a strange enjoyment.
"Oh, how delightful such naïveté is from you! Oh, yes,
yes, slavery to you is a pleasure. There is—there is a pleasure in the utmost limit of humiliation and insignificance!"
I went on maundering. "Goodness knows, perhaps there
is in the knout when the knout lies in the back and tears
the flesh. . . . But I should perhaps like to enjoy another
kind of enjoyment. Yesterday, in your presence, the General thought fit to read me a lecture for the seven hundred
roubles a year which perhaps I may not receive from him
after all. The Marquis de Grieux raises his eyebrows and

stares at me without noticing me. And I, perhaps, have a passionate desire to pull the Marquis de Grieux by the nose in your presence!"

"That's the speech of a milksop. One can behave with dignity in any position. If there is a struggle, it is elevating, not humiliating."

"That's straight out of a copybook. You simply take for granted that I don't know how to behave with dignity; that is, that perhaps I am a man of moral dignity, but that I don't know how to behave with dignity. You understand that that perhaps may be so. Yes, all Russians are like that; and do you know why? Because Russians are too richly endowed and many-sided to be able readily to evolve a code of manners. It is a question of good form. For the most part we Russians are so richly endowed that we need genius to evolve our code of manners. And genius is most often absent, for, indeed, it is a rarity at all times. It's only among the French, and perhaps some other Europeans, that the code of manners is so well defined that one may have an air of the utmost dignity and yet be a man of no moral dignity whatever. That's why good form means so much with them. A Frenchman will put up with an insult, a real, moral insult, without blinking, but he wouldn't endure a flip on the nose for anything, because that is a breach of the received code, sanctified for ages. That's why our Russian young ladies have such a weakness for Frenchmen, that their manners are so good. Though, to my thinking, they have no manners at all; it's simply the cock in them, le coq gaulois. I can't understand it, though; I'm not a woman. Perhaps cocks are nice. And, in fact, I've been talking nonsense, and you don't stop me. You must stop me more often. When I talk to you I long to tell you everything, everything, everything. I am oblivious of all good manners. I'll even admit that I have no manners, no moral qualities either. I tell you that. I don't even worry my head about moral qualities of any sort; everything has come to a standstill in me now; you know why. I have not one human idea in my head. For a long time past I've known nothing that has gone on in the world, either in Russia or here. Here I've been through Dresden, and I don't remember what Dresden was like. You know what has swallowed me up. As I have no hope whatever and am nothing in your eyes, I speak openly: I see nothing but you everywhere, and all the rest is naught to me. Why and how I love you I don't know. Perhaps you are not at all nice really, you know. Fancy! I don't know whether you are good or not, even to look at. You certainly have not a good heart; your mind may very well be ignoble."

"Perhaps that's how it is you reckon on buying me with money," she said, "because you don't believe in my sense of honour."

"When did I reckon on buying you with money?" I cried.

"You have been talking till you don't know what you are saying. If you don't think of buying me, you think of buying my respect with your money."

"Oh no, that's not it at all. I told you it was difficult for me to explain. You are overwhelming me. Don't be angry with my chatter. You know why you can't be angry with me: I'm simply mad. Though I really don't care, even if you are angry. When I am upstairs in my little garret I have only to remember and imagine the rustle of your dress, and I am ready to bite off my hands. And what are you angry with me for? For calling myself your slave? Make use of my being your slave, make use of it, make use of it! Do you know that I shall kill you one day? I shall kill you not because I shall cease to love you or be jealous, I shall simply kill you because I have an impulse to devour you. You laugh. . . ."

"I'm not laughing," she answered wrathfully. "I order you to be silent."

She stood still, almost breathless with anger. Upon my word, I don't know whether she was handsome, but I always liked to look at her when she stood facing me like that, and so I often liked to provoke her anger. Perhaps she had noticed this and was angry on purpose. I said as much to her.

"How disgusting!" she said, with an air of repulsion.

"I don't care," I went on. "Do you know, too, that it is dangerous for us to walk together? I often have an irresistible longing to beat you, to disfigure you, to strangle you. And what do you think—won't it come to that? You are driving me into brain fever. Do you suppose I am afraid of a scandal? Your anger—why, what is your anger to me? I love you without hope, and I know that after this I shall love you a thousand times more than ever. If ever I do kill you I shall have to kill myself, too. Oh, well,

I shall put off killing myself as long as possible, so as to go on feeling this insufferable pain of being without you. Do you know something incredible? I love you *more* every day, and yet that is almost impossible. And how can I help being a fatalist? Do you remember the day before yesterday, on the Schlangenberg, I whispered at your provocation, 'Say the word, and I will leap into that abyss?' If you had said that word I should have jumped in then. Don't you believe that I would have leapt down?"

"What stupid talk!" she cried.

"I don't care whether it is stupid or clever!" I cried. "I know that in your presence I must talk, and talk, and talk —and I do talk. I lose all self-respect in your presence, and I don't care."

"What use would it be for me to order you to jump off the Schlangenberg?" she said in a dry and peculiarly insulting manner. "It would be absolutely useless to me."

"Splendid," I cried; "you said that splendid 'useless' on purpose to overwhelm me. I see through you. Useless, you say? But pleasure is always of use, and savage, unbounded power—if only over a fly—is a pleasure in its way, too. Man is a despot by nature, and loves to be a torturer. You like it awfully."

I remember she looked at me with peculiar fixed attention. My face must have expressed my incoherent and absurd sensations. I remember to this moment that our conversation actually was almost word for word exactly as I have described it here. My eyes were bloodshot. There were flecks of foam on my lips. And as for the Schlangenberg, I swear on my word of honour even now, if she had told me to fling myself down I should have flung myself down! If only for a joke she had said it, with contempt, if with a jeer at me she had said it, I should even then have leapt down!

"No, why? I believe you," she pronounced, as only she knows how to speak, with such contempt and venom, with such scorn that, by God, I could have killed her at the moment.

She risked it. I was not lying about that, too, in what I said to her.

"You are not a coward?" she asked me suddenly.

"Perhaps I am a coward. I don't know. . . . I have not thought about it for a long time."

"If I were to say to you, 'Kill this man,' would you kill him?"

"Whom?"

"Whom I choose."

"The Frenchman?"

"Don't ask questions, but answer. Whom I tell you. I want to know whether you spoke seriously just now?"

She waited for my answer so gravely and impatiently that it struck me as strange.

"Come, do tell me, what has been happening here?" I cried. "What are you afraid of—me, or what? I see all the muddle here for myself. You are the stepdaughter of a mad and ruined man possessed by a passion for that devil —Blanche. Then there is this Frenchman, with his mysterious influence over you, and—here you ask me now so gravely . . . such a question. At any rate let me know, or I shall go mad on the spot and do something. Are you ashamed to deign to be open with me? Surely you can't care what I think of you?"

"I am not speaking to you of that at all. I asked you a question and I'm waiting for the answer."

"Of course I will kill any one you tell me to," I cried. "But can you possibly . . . could you tell me to do it?"

"Do you suppose I should spare you? I shall tell you to, and stand aside and look on. Can you endure that? Why, no, as though you could! You would kill him, perhaps, if you were told, and then you would come and kill me for having dared to send you."

I felt as though I were stunned at these words. Of course, even then I looked upon her question as half a joke, a challenge; yet she had spoken very earnestly. I was struck, nevertheless, at her speaking out so frankly, at her maintaining such rights over me, at her accepting such power over me and saying so bluntly: "Go to ruin, and I'll stand aside and look on." In those words there was something so open and cynical that to my mind it was going too far. That, then, was how she looked at me. This was something more than slavery or insignificance. If one looks at a man like that, one exalts him to one's own level, and absurd and incredible as all our conversation was, yet there was a throb at my heart.

Suddenly she laughed. We were sitting on a bench, be-fore the playing children, facing the place where the carriages used to stop and people used to get out in the avenue before the Casino.

"Do you see that stout baroness?" she cried. "That is Baroness Burmerhelm. She has only been here three days. Do you see her husband—a tall, lean Prussian with a stick? Do you remember how he looked at us the day before yesterday? Go up to the Baroness at once, take off your hat, and say something to her in French."

"Why?"

"You swore that you would jump down the Schlangenberg; you swear you are ready to kill any one if I tell you. Instead of these murders and tragedies I only want to laugh. Go without discussing it. I want to see the Baron thrash you with his stick."

"You challenge me; you think I won't do it?"

"Yes, I do challenge you. Go; I want you to!"

"By all means, I am going, though it's a wild freak. Only, I say, I hope it won't be unpleasant for the General, and through him for you. Upon my honour, I am not thinking of myself, but of you and the General. And what a mad idea to insult a woman!"

"Yes, you are only a chatterer, as I see," she said contemptuously. "Your eyes were fierce and bloodshot, but perhaps that was only because you had too much wine at dinner. Do you suppose that I don't understand that it is stupid and vulgar, and that the General would be angry? I simply want to laugh; I want to, and that's all about it! And what should you insult a woman for? Why, just to be thrashed."

I turned and went in silence to carry out her commission. Of course it was stupid, and of course I did not know how to get out of it, but as I began to get closer to the Baroness I remember, as it were, something within myself urging me on; it was an impulse of schoolboyish mischief. Besides, I was horribly overwrought, and felt just as though I were drunk.

Chapter 6

Now two days have passed since that stupid day. And what a noise and fuss and talk and uproar there was! And how unseemly and disgraceful, how stupid and vulgar, it was! And I was the cause of it all. Yet at times it's laughable—to me, at any rate. I can't make up my mind what happened to me, whether I really was in a state of frenzy, or whether it was a momentary aberration and I behaved disgracefully till I was pulled up. At times it seemed to me that my mind was giving way. And at times it seems to me that I have not outgrown childhood and schoolboyishness, and that it was simply a crude school-boy's prank.

It was Polina, it was all Polina! Perhaps I shouldn't have behaved like a schoolboy if it hadn't been for her. Who knows? perhaps I did it out of despair (stupid as it seems, though, to reason like that). And I don't under-stand, I don't understand what there is fine in her! She is fine, though; she is; I believe she's fine. She drives other men off their heads, too. She's tall and graceful, only very slender. It seems to me you could tie her in a knot or bend her double. Her foot is long and narrow—torment-ing. Tormenting is just what it is. Her hair has a reddish tint. Her eyes are regular cat's eyes, but how proudly and disdainfully she can look with them. Four months ago, when I had only just come, she was talking hotly for a long while one evening with De Grieux in the drawing-room, and looked at him in such a way . . . that after-wards, when I went up to my room to go to bed, I imag-ined that she must have just given him a slap in the face. She stood facing him and looked at him. It was from that evening that I loved her.

To come to the point, however.

I stepped off the path into the avenue, and stood wait-ing for the Baron and the Baroness. When they were five paces from me I took off my hat and bowed.

I remember the Baroness was wearing a light grey dress of immense circumference, with flounces, a crinoline, and a train. She was short and exceptionally stout, with such a fearful double chin that she seemed to have no neck. Her face was crimson. Her eyes were small, spiteful and insolent. She walked as though she were doing an honour to all beholders. The Baron was lean and tall. Like most Germans, he had a wry face covered with thousands of fine wrinkles, and wore spectacles; he was about forty-five. His legs seemed to start from his chest: that's a sign of race. He was as proud as a peacock. He was rather clumsy. There was something like a sheep in the expression of his face that would pass with them for profundity.

All this flashed upon my sight in three seconds.

My bow and the hat in my hand gradually arrested their attention. The Baron slightly knitted his brows. The Baroness simply sailed straight at me.

"*Madame la baronne,*" I articulated distinctly, emphasizing each word, "*j'ai l'honneur d'être votre esclave.*"

Then I bowed, replaced my hat, and walked past the Baron, turning my face towards him with a polite smile.

She had told me to take off my hat, but I had bowed and behaved like an impudent schoolboy on my own account. Goodness knows what impelled me to! I felt as though I were plunging into space.

"*Hein!*" cried, or rather croaked, the Baron, turning towards me with angry surprise.

I turned and remained in respectful expectation, still gazing at him with a smile. He was evidently perplexed, and raised his eyebrows as high as they would go. His face grew darker and darker. The Baroness, too, turned towards me, and she, too, stared in wrathful surprise. The passers-by began to look on. Some even stopped.

"*Hein!*" the Baron croaked again, with redoubled gutturalness and redoubled anger.

"*Ja wohl!*" I drawled, still looking him straight in the face.

"*Sind Sie rasend?*" he cried, waving his stick and beginning, I think, to be a little nervous. He was perhaps perplexed by my appearance. I was very well, even foppishly, dressed, like a man belonging to the best society.

"*Ja wo-o-ohl!*" I shouted suddenly at the top of my voice, drawling the *o* like the Berliners, who use the expression *Ja wohl* in every sentence, and drawl the letter *o* more or less according to the shade of their thought or feeling.

The Baron and Baroness turned away quickly and almost ran away from me in terror. Of the spectators, some were talking, others were gazing at me in amazement. I don't remember very clearly, though.

I turned and walked at my ordinary pace to Polina Alexandrovna.

But when I was within a hundred paces of her seat, I saw her get up and walk with the children towards the hotel.

I overtook her at the door.

"I have performed . . . the foolery," I said, when I reached her.

"Well, what of it? Now you can get out of the scrape," she answered. She walked upstairs without even glancing at me.

I spent the whole evening walking about the park. I crossed the park and then the wood beyond and walked into another state. In a cottage I had an omelette and some wine; for that idyllic repast they extorted a whole thaler and a half.

It was eleven o'clock before I returned home. I was at once summoned before the General.

Our party occupied two suites in the hotel; they have four rooms. The first is a big room—a drawing-room with a piano in it. The next, also a large room, is the General's study. Here he was awaiting me, standing in the middle of the room in a majestic pose. De Grieux sat lolling on the sofa.

"Allow me to ask you, sir, what have you been about?" began the General, addressing me.

"I should be glad if you would go straight to the point, General," said I. "You probably mean to refer to my encounter with a German this morning?"

"A German? That German was Baron Burmerhelm, a very important personage! You insulted him and the Baroness."

"Not in the least."

"You alarmed them, sir!" cried the General.

"Not a bit of it. When I was in Berlin the sound was for ever in my ears of that *ja wohl*, continually repeated at every word and disgustingly drawled out by them. When I met them in the avenue that *Ja wohl* suddenly came into my mind, I don't know why, and—well, it had an irritating effect on me. . . . Besides, the Baroness, who has met me three times, has the habit of walking straight at me as though I were a worm who might be trampled underfoot. You must admit that I, too, may have my proper pride. I took off my hat and said politely (I assure you I said it politely): '*Madame, j'ai l'honneur d'être votre esclave.*' When the Baron turned round and said, '*Hein!*' I felt an impulse to shout, '*Ja wohl!*' I shouted it twice: the first time in an ordinary tone, and the second—I drawled it as much as I could. That was all."

I must own I was intensely delighted at this extremely

schoolboyish explanation. I had a strange desire to make the story as absurd as possible in the telling.

And as I went on, I got more and more to relish it.

"Are you laughing at me?" cried the General. He turned to the Frenchman and explained to him in French that I was positively going out of my way to provoke a scandal! De Grieux laughed contemptuously and shrugged his shoulders.

"Oh, don't imagine that; it was not so at all!" I cried. "My conduct was wrong, of course; I confess that with the utmost candour. My behaviour may even be called a stupid and improper schoolboy prank, but—nothing more. And do you know, General, I heartily regret it. But there is one circumstance which, to my mind at least, almost saves me from repentance. Lately, for the last fortnight, indeed, I've not been feeling well: I have felt ill, nervous, irritable, moody, and on some occasions I lose all control of myself. Really, I've sometimes had an intense impulse to attack the Marquis de Grieux and . . . However, there's no need to say, he might be offended. In short, it's the sign of illness. I don't know whether the Baroness Burmerhelm will take this fact into consideration when I beg her pardon (for I intend to apologize). I imagine she will not consider it, especially as that line of excuse has been somewhat abused in legal circles of late. Lawyers have taken to arguing in criminal cases that their clients were not responsible at the moment of their crime, and that it was a form of disease. 'He killed him,' they say, 'and has no memory of it.' And only imagine, General, the medical authorities support them— and actually maintain that there are illnesses, temporary aberrations, in which a man scarcely remembers anything, or has only a half or a quarter of his memory. But the Baron and Baroness are people of the older generation; besides, they are Prussian *junkers* and landowners, and so are probably unaware of this advance in the world of medical jurisprudence, and will not accept my explanation. What do you think, General?"

"Enough, sir," the General pronounced sharply, with surprised indignation; "enough! I will try once for all to rid myself of your mischievous pranks. You are not going to apologize to the Baron and Baroness. Any communication with you, even though it were to consist solely of your request for forgiveness, would be beneath their dignity. The Baron has learnt that you are a member of my household; he has already had an explanation with me at the Casino, and I assure you that he was within an ace of asking me to give him satisfaction. Do you understand what you have exposed me to—me, sir? I—I was forced to ask the Baron's pardon, and gave him my word that immediately, this very day, you would cease to be a member of my household."

"Allow me, allow me, General; then did he insist on that himself, that I should cease to belong to your household, as you were pleased to express it?"

"No, but I considered myself bound to give him that satisfaction, and, of course, the Baron was satisfied. We must part, sir. There is what is owing to you, four friedrichs d'or and three florins, according to the reckoning here. Here is the money, and here is the note of the account; you can verify it. Good-bye. From this time forth we are strangers. I've had nothing but trouble and unpleasantness from you. I will call the *kellner* and inform him from this day forth that I am not responsible for your hotel expenses. I have the honour to remain your obedient servant."

I took the money and the paper upon which the account was written in pencil, bowed to the General, and said to him very seriously—

"General, the matter cannot end like this. I am very sorry that you were put into an unpleasant position with the Baron, but, excuse me, you were to blame for it yourself. Why did you take it upon yourself to be responsible for me to the Baron? What is the meaning of the expression that I am a member of your household? I am simply a teacher in your house, that is all. I am neither your son nor your ward, and you cannot be responsible for my actions. I am a legally responsible person, I am twenty-five, I am a graduate of the university, I am a nobleman, I am not connected with you in any way. Nothing but my unbounded respect for your dignity prevents me now from demanding from you the fullest explanation and satisfaction for taking upon yourself the right to answer for me."

The General was so much amazed that he flung up his hands, then turned suddenly to the Frenchman and hurriedly informed him that I had just all but challenged him to a duel.

The Frenchman laughed aloud.

"But I am not going to let the Baron off," I said, with complete composure, not in the least embarrassed by M. de Grieux's laughter; "and as, General, you consented to listen to the Baron's complaint to-day and have taken up his cause, and have made yourself, as it were, a party in the whole affair, I have the honour to inform you that no later than to-morrow morning I shall ask the Baron on my own account for a formal explanation of the reasons which led him to apply to other persons—as though I were unable or unfit to answer for myself."

What I foresaw happened. The General, hearing of this new absurdity, became horribly nervous.

"What, do you mean to keep up this damnable business?" he shouted. "What a position you are putting me in —good heavens! Don't dare, don't dare, sir, or, I swear! . . . There are police here, too, and I . . . I . . . in fact, by my rank . . . and the Baron's, too . . . in fact, you shall be arrested and turned out of the state by the police, to teach you not to make a disturbance. Do you understand that, sir?" And although he was breathless with anger, he was also horribly frightened.

"General," I answered, with a composure that was insufferable to him, "you can't arrest any one for making a disturbance before they have made a disturbance. I have not yet begun to make my explanations to the Baron, and you don't know in the least in what form or on what grounds I intend to proceed. I only wish to have an explanation of a position insulting to me, *i.e.* that I am under the control of a person who has authority over my freedom of action. There is no need for you to be so anxious and uneasy."

"For goodness' sake, for goodness' sake, Alexey Ivanovitch, drop this insane intention!" muttered the General, suddenly changing his wrathful tone for one of entreaty, and even clutching me by the hand. "Fancy what it will lead to! Fresh unpleasantness! You must see for yourself that I must be particular here . . . particularly now! particularly now! . . . Oh, you don't know, you don't know all my circumstances! . . . When we leave this place I shall be willing to take you back again; I was only speaking of now, in fact—of course, you understand there are reasons!" he cried in despair. "Alexey Ivanovitch, Alexey Ivanovitch . . ."

Retreating to the door, I begged him more earnestly not to worry himself, promised him that everything should go off well and with propriety, and hastily withdrew.

The Russian abroad is sometimes too easily cowed, and is horribly afraid of what people will say, how they will look at him, and whether this or that will be the proper thing. In short, they behave as though they were in corsets, especially those who have pretensions to consequence. The thing that pleases them most is a certain established traditional etiquette, which they follow slavishly in hotels, on their walks, in assemblies, on a journey. . . . But the General had let slip that, apart from this, there was a particular circumstance, that he must be "particular." That was why he so weakly showed the white feather and changed his tone with me. I took this as evidence and made a note of it; and, of course, he might have brought my folly to the notice of the authorities, so that I really had to be careful.

I did not particularly want to anger the General, however; but I did want to anger Polina. Polina had treated me so badly, and had thrust me into such a stupid position, that I could not help wanting to force her to beg me to stop. My schoolboyish prank might compromise her, too. Moreover, another feeling and desire was taking shape in me: though I might be reduced to a nonentity in her presence, that did not prove that I could not hold my own before other people, or that the Baron could thrash me. I longed to have the laugh against them all, and to come off with flying colours. Let them see! She would be frightened by the scandal and call me back again, or, even if she didn't, at least she would see that I could hold my own.

(A wonderful piece of news! I have just heard from the nurse, whom I met on the stairs, that Marya Filippovna set off to-day, entirely alone, by the evening train to Karlsbad to see her cousin. What's the meaning of that? Nurse says that she has long been meaning to go; but how was it no one knew of it? Though perhaps I was the only one who did not know it. The nurse let slip that Marya Filippovna had words with the General the day before yesterday. I understand. No doubt that is Mlle. Blanche. Yes, something decisive is coming.)

Chapter 7

In the morning I called for the *kellner* and told him to make out a separate bill for me. My room was not such an expensive one as to make me feel alarmed and anxious to leave the hotel. I had sixteen friedrichs d'or, and there . . . there perhaps was wealth! Strange to say, I have not won yet, but I behave, I feel and think, like a rich man, and cannot imagine anything else.

In spite of the early hour I intended to go at once to see Mr. Astley at the Hotel d'Angleterre, which was quite close by, when suddenly De Grieux came in to me. That had never happened before, and, what is more, that gentleman and I had for some time past been on very queer and strained terms. He openly displayed his contempt for me, even tried not to conceal it; and I—I had my own reasons for disliking him. In short, I hated him. His visit greatly surprised me. I at once detected that something special was brewing.

He came in very politely and complimented me on my room. Seeing that I had my hat in my hand, he inquired whether I could be going out for a walk so early. When he heard that I was going to see Mr. Astley on business, he pondered, he reflected, and his face assumed an exceedingly careworn expression.

De Grieux was like all Frenchmen; that is, gay and polite when necessary and profitable to be so, and insufferably tedious when the necessity to be gay and polite was over. A Frenchman is not often naturally polite. He is always polite, as it were, to order, with a motive. If he sees the necessity for being fantastic, original, a little out of the ordinary, then his freakishness is most stupid and unnatural, and is made up of accepted and long-vulgarized traditions. The natural Frenchman is composed of the most plebeian, petty, ordinary practical sense —in fact, he is one of the most wearisome creatures in the world. In my opinion, only the innocent and inexperienced—especially Russian young ladies—are fascinated by Frenchmen. To every decent person the conventionalism of the established traditions of drawing-room politeness, ease and gaiety are at once evident and intolerable.

"I have come to see you on business," he began, with marked directness, though with courtesy, "and I will not disguise that I have come as an ambassador, or rather as a mediator, from the General. As I know Russian very imperfectly I understood very little of what passed yesterday, but the General explained it to me in detail, and I confess . . ."

"But, listen, M. de Grieux," I interrupted; "here you have undertaken to be a mediator in this affair. I am, of course, an *outchitel*, and have never laid claim to the honour of being a great friend of this family, nor of being on particularly intimate terms with it, and so I don't know all the circumstances; but explain: are you now entirely a member of the family? You take such an interest in everything and are certain at once to be a mediator . . ."

This question did not please him. It was too transparent for him, and he did not want to speak out.

"I am connected with the General partly by business, partly by *certain special* circumstances," he said drily. "The General has sent me to ask you to abandon the intentions you expressed yesterday. All you thought of doing was no doubt very clever; but he begged me to represent to you that you would be utterly unsuccessful; what's more, the Baron will not receive you, and in any case is in a position to rid himself of any further unpleasantness on your part. You must see that yourself. Tell me, what is the object of going on with it? The General promises to take you back into his home at the first convenient opportunity, and until that time will continue your salary, *vos appointements*. That will be fairly profitable, won't it?"

I retorted very calmly that he was rather mistaken; that perhaps I shouldn't be kicked out at the Baron's, but, on the contrary, should be listened to; and I asked him to admit that he had probably come to find out what steps I was going to take in the matter.

"Oh, heavens! Since the General is so interested, he will, of course, be glad to know how you are going to behave, and what you are going to do."

I proceeded to explain, and he began listening, stretching himself at his ease and inclining his head on one side towards me, with an obvious, undisguised expression of irony on his face. Altogether he behaved very loftily. I tried with all my might to pretend that I took a very serious view of the matter. I explained that since the Baron had addressed a complaint of me to the General as though I were the latter's servant, he had, in the first place, deprived me thereby of my position; and secondly, had treated me as a person who was incapable of answering for himself and who was not worth speaking to. Of course, I said, I felt with justice that I had been insulted; however, considering the difference of age, position in society, and so on, and so on (I could scarcely restrain my laughter at this point), I did not want to rush into fresh indiscretion by directly insisting on satisfaction from the Baron, or even proposing a duel to him; nevertheless, I considered myself fully entitled to offer the Baron, and still more the Baroness, my apologies, especially since of late I had really felt ill, overwrought, and, to say, fanciful, and so on, and so on. However, the Baron had, by his applying to the General, which was a slight to me, and by his insisting that the General should deprive me of my post, put me in such a position that now I could not offer him and the Baroness my apologies, because he and the Baroness and all the world would certainly suppose that I came to apologize because I was frightened and in order to be reinstated in my post. From all this it followed that I found myself now compelled to beg the Baron first of all to apologize to me in the most formal terms; for instance, to say that he had no desire to insult me. And when the Baron said this I should feel that my hands were set free, and with perfect candour and sincerity I should offer him my apologies. In brief, I concluded, I could only beg the Baron to untie my hands.

"Fie! how petty and how far-fetched! And why do you want to apologize? Come, admit, *monsieur . . . monsieur . . .* that you are doing all this on purpose to vex the General . . . and perhaps you have some special object . . . *mon cher monsieur . . . pardon, j'ai oublié votre nom, M. Alexis? . . . N'est-ce pas?*"

"But, excuse me, *mon cher marquis*, what has it to do with you?"

"*Mais le général . . .*"

"But what about the General? He said something last night, that he had to be particularly careful . . . and was so upset . . . but I did not understand it."

"There is, there certainly is a particular circumstance," De Grieux caught me up in an insistent voice, in which a note of vexation was more and more marked, "You know Mlle. de Cominges . . . ?"

"That is, Mlle. Blanche?"

"Why, yes, Mlle. Blanche de Cominges . . . *et madame sa mère.* You see for yourself, the General . . . in short, the General is in love; in fact . . . in fact, the marriage may be celebrated here. And fancy, scandal, gossip . . ."

"I see no scandal or gossip connected with the marriage in this."

"But *le baron est si irascible, un caractère Prussien, vous savez, enfin il fera une querelle d'Allemand.*"

"With me, then, and not with you, for I no longer belong to the household. . . ." (I tried to be as irrational as possible on purpose.) "But, excuse me, is it settled, then, that Mlle. Blanche is to marry the General? What are they waiting for? I mean, why conceal this from us, at any rate from the members of the household?"

"I cannot . . . however, it is not quite . . . besides . . . you know, they are expecting news from Russia; the General has to make arrangements . . ."

"*Ah! ah! La baboulinka!*"

De Grieux looked at me with hatred.

"In short," he interrupted, "I fully rely on your innate courtesy, on your intelligence, on your tact. . . . You will certainly do this for the family in which you have been received like one of themselves, in which you have been liked and respected . . ."

"Excuse me, I've been dismissed! You maintain now that that is only in appearance; but you must admit, if you were told: 'I won't send you packing, but, for the look of the thing, kindly take yourself off' . . . You see, it comes almost to the same thing."

"Well, if that's how it is, if no request will have any influence on you," he began sternly and haughtily, "allow me to assure you that steps will be taken. There are authorities here; you'll be turned out to-day—*que diable! Un blanc-bec comme vous* wants to challenge a personage like the Baron! And do you think that you will not be interfered with? And, let me assure you, nobody is afraid of you here! I have approached you on my own account, because you have been worrying the General. And do you imagine that the Baron will not order his flunkeys to turn you out of the house?"

"But, you see, I'm not going myself," I answered, with the utmost composure. "You are mistaken, M. de Grieux; all this will be done much more decorously than you imagine. I am just setting off to Mr. Astley, and I am going to ask him to be my intermediary; in fact, to be my second. The man likes me, and certainly will not refuse. He will go to the Baron, and the Baron will receive him. Even if I am an *outchitel* and seem to be something subordinate and, well, defenceless, Mr. Astley is a nephew of a lord, of a real lord; every one knows that— Lord Pibroch—and that lord is here. Believe me, the Baron will be courteous to Mr. Astley and will listen to him. And if he won't listen, Mr. Astley will look upon it as a personal affront (you know how persistent Englishmen are), and will send a friend to call on the Baron; he has powerful friends. You may reckon, now, upon things not turning out quite as you expect."

The Frenchman was certainly scared; all this was really very much like the truth, and so it seemed that I really might be able to get up a scandal.

"Come, I beg you," he said in a voice of actual entreaty, "do drop the whole business! It seems to please you that it will cause a scandal! It is not satisfaction you want, but a scandal! As I have told you, it is very amusing and even witty—which is perhaps what you are aiming at. But, in short," he concluded, seeing that I had got up and was taking my hat, "I've come to give you these few lines from a certain person; read them; I was charged to wait for an answer."

Saying this, he took out of his pocket a little note, folded and sealed with a wafer, and handed it to me.

It was in Polina's handwriting.

"I fancy that you intend to go on with this affair, but there are special circumstances which I will explain to you perhaps later; please leave off and give way. It is all such silliness! I need you, and you promised yourself to obey me. Remember the Schlangenberg; I beg you to be obedient, and, if necessary, I command you.—Your P.

"P.S.—If you are angry with me for what happened yesterday, forgive me."

Everything seemed to be heaving before my eyes when I read these lines. My lips turned white and I began to tremble. The accursed Frenchman watched me with an exaggerated air of discretion, with his eyes turned away as though to avoid noticing my confusion. He had better have laughed at me outright.

"Very good," I answered; "tell Mademoiselle that she may set her mind at rest. Allow me to ask you," I added sharply, "why you have been so long giving me this letter. Instead of chattering about all sorts of nonsense, I think you ought to have begun with that . . . if you came expressly with that object."

"Oh, I wanted . . . all this is so strange that you must excuse my natural impatience. I was in haste to learn from you in person what you intended to do. Besides, I don't know what is in that note, and I thought there was no hurry for me to give it you."

"I understand: the long and the short of it is you were told only to give me the letter in case of the utmost necessity, and if you could settle it by word of mouth you were not to give it to me. Is that right? Tell me plainly, M. de Grieux."

"*Peut-être*," he said, assuming an air of peculiar reserve, and looking at me with a peculiar glance.

I took off my hat; he took off his hat and went out. It seemed to me that there was an ironical smile on his lips. And, indeed, what else could one expect?

"We'll be quits yet, Frenchy; we'll settle our accounts," I muttered as I went down the stairs. I could not think clearly; I felt as though I had had a blow on my head. The air revived me a little.

Two minutes later, as soon as ever I was able to reflect clearly, two thoughts stood out vividly before me: the *first* was that such trivial incidents, that a few mischievous and far-fetched threats from a mere boy, had caused such *universal* consternation! The *second* thought was: what sort of influence had this Frenchman over Polina? A mere word from him and she does anything he wants—writes a note and even *begs* me. Of course, their relations have always been a mystery to me from the very beginning, ever since I began to know them; but of late I have noticed in her a positive aversion and even contempt for him, while he did not even look at her, was absolutely rude to her. I had noticed it. Polina herself had spoken of him to me with aversion; she had dropped some extremely significant admissions . . . so he simply had her in his power. She was in some sort of bondage to him.

Chapter 8

On the promenade, as it is called here, that is, in the chestnut avenue, I met my Englishman.

"Oh, oh!" he began, as soon as he saw me. "I was coming to see you, and you are on your way to me. So you have parted from your people?"

"Tell me, first, how it is that you know all this?" I asked in amazement. "Is it possible that everybody knows of it?"

"Oh, no, every one doesn't; and, indeed, it's not worth their knowing. No one is talking about it."

"Then how do you know it?"

"I know, that is, I chanced to learn it. Now, where are you going when you leave here? I like you and that is why I was coming to see you."

"You are a splendid man, Mr. Astley," said I (I was very much interested, however, to know where he could have learnt it), "and since I have not yet had my coffee, and most likely you have not had a good cup, come to the café in the Casino. Let us sit down and have a smoke there, and I will tell you all about it, and . . . you tell me, too. . . ."

The café was a hundred steps away. They brought us some coffee. We sat down and I lighted a cigarette. Mr. Astley did not light one and, gazing at me, prepared to listen.

"I am not going anywhere. I am staying here," I began.

"And I was sure you would," observed Mr. Astley approvingly.

On my way to Mr. Astley I had not meant to tell him anything of my love for Polina, and, in fact, I expressly intended to say nothing to him about it. All that time I had hardly said one word to him about it. He was, besides, very reserved. From the first I noticed that Polina had made a great impression upon him, but he never uttered her name. But, strange to say, now no sooner had he sat down and turned upon me his fixed, pewtery eyes, I felt, I don't know why, a desire to tell him everything, that is, all about my love in all its aspects. I was talking to him for half an hour and it was very pleasant to me; it was the first time I had talked of it! Noticing that at certain ardent sentences he was embarrassed, I purposely exaggerated my ardour. Only one thing I regret: I said, perhaps, more than I should about the Frenchman. . . .

Mr. Astley listened, sitting facing me without moving, looking straight into my eyes, not uttering a word, a sound; but when I spoke of the Frenchman, he suddenly pulled me up and asked me, severely, whether I had the right to refer to this circumstance which did not concern me? Mr. Astley always asked questions very strangely.

"You are right. I am afraid not," I answered.

"You can say nothing definite, nothing that is not supposition about that *marquis* and Miss Polina?"

I was surprised again at such a point-blank question from a man so reserved as Mr. Astley.

"No, nothing definite," I answered; "of course not."

"If so, you have done wrong, not only in speaking of it to me, but even in thinking of it yourself."

"Very good, very good; I admit it, but that is not the point now," I interrupted, wondering at myself. At this point I told him the whole of yesterday's story in full detail: Polina's prank, my adventure with the Baron, my dismissal, the General's extraordinary dismay, and, finally, I described in detail De Grieux's visit that morning. Lastly I showed him the note.

"What do you deduce from all this?" I asked. "I came on purpose to find out what you think. For my part, I could kill that Frenchman, and perhaps I shall."

"So could I," said Mr. Astley. "As regards Miss Polina, you know . . . we may enter into relations even with people who are detestable to us if we are compelled by necessity. There may be relations of which you know nothing, dependent upon outside circumstances. I think you may set your mind at rest—to some extent, of course. As for her action yesterday, it was strange, of course; not that she wanted to get rid of you and expose you to the Baron's walking-stick (I don't understand why he did not use it, since he had it in his hand), but because such a prank is improper . . . for such an . . . exquisite young lady. Of course, she couldn't have expected that you would carry out her jesting wish so literally . . ."

"Do you know what?" I cried suddenly, looking intently at Mr. Astley. "It strikes me that you have heard about this already—do you know from whom? From Miss Polina herself!"

Mr. Astley looked at me with surprise.

"Your eyes are sparkling and I can read your suspicion in them," he said, regaining his former composure; "but you have no right whatever to express your suspicions. I cannot recognize the right, and I absolutely refuse to answer your question."

"Enough! There's no need," I cried, strangely perturbed, and not knowing why it had come into my head. And when, where and how could Mr. Astley have been chosen by Polina to confide in? Though, of late, indeed, I had, to some extent, lost sight of Mr. Astley, and Polina was always an enigma to me, such an enigma that now, for instance, after launching into an account of my passion to Mr. Astley, I was suddenly struck while I was speaking by the fact that there was scarcely anything positive and definite I could say about our relations. Everything was, on the contrary, strange, unstable, and, in fact, quite unique.

"Oh, very well, very well. I am utterly perplexed and there is a great deal I can't understand at present," I answered, gasping as though I were breathless. "You are a good man, though. And now, another matter, and I ask not your advice, but your opinion."

After a brief pause I began.

"What do you think? Why was the General so scared? Why did he make such a to-do over my stupid practical joke? Such a fuss that even De Grieux thought it necessary to interfere (and he interferes only in the most important matters); visited me (think of that!), begged and besought me—he, De Grieux—begged and besought me! Note, finally, he came at nine o'clock, and by that time Miss Polina's letter was in his hands. One wonders when it was written. Perhaps they waked Miss Polina up on purpose! Apart from what I see clearly from this, that Miss Polina is his slave (for she even begs my forgiveness!)—apart from that, how is she concerned in all this, she personally; why is she so much interested? Why are they frightened of some Baron? And what if the Gen-

eral is marrying Mlle. Blanche de Cominges? They say
that, owing to that circumstance, they must *be particular*
but you must admit that this is somewhat too particular!
What do you think? I am sure from your eyes you know
more about it than I do!"

Mr. Astley laughed and nodded.

"Certainly. I believe I know much more about it than
you," he said. "Mlle. Blanche is the only person concerned, and I am sure that is the absolute truth."

"Well, what about Mlle. Blanche?" I cried impatiently.
(I suddenly had a hope that something would be disclosed
about Mlle. Polina.)

"I fancy that Mlle. Blanche has at the moment special
reasons for avoiding a meeting with the Baron and Baroness, even more an unpleasant meeting, worse still, a
scandalous one."

"Well, well . . ."

"Two years ago Mlle. Blanche was here at Roulettenburg in the season. I was here, too. Mlle. Blanche was not
called Mlle. de Cominges then, and her mother, Madame
la maman Cominges, was non-existent then. Anyway,
she was never mentioned. De Grieux—De Grieux was
not here either. I cherish the conviction that, far from
being relations, they have only very recently become acquainted. He—De Grieux—has only become a marquis
very recently, too—I am sure of that from one circumstance. One may assume, in fact, that his name has not
been De Grieux very long either. I know a man here who
has met him passing under another name."

"But he really has a very respectable circle of acquaintances."

"That may be. Even Mlle. Blanche may have. But two
years ago, at the request of that very Baroness, Mlle.
Blanche was invited by the police to leave the town, and
she did leave it."

"How was that?"

"She made her appearance here first with an Italian, a
prince of some sort, with an historical name—Barberini,
or something like it—a man covered with rings and diamonds, not false ones either. They used to drive about in
a magnificent carriage. Mlle. Blanche used to play *trente
et quarante*, at first winning, though her luck changed
later on, as far as I remember. I remember one evening she
lost a considerable sum. But, worse still, *un beau matin*

her prince vanished; the horses and the carriage vanished too, everything vanished. The bills owing at the hotels were immense. Mlle. Selma (she suddenly ceased to be Barberini, and became Mlle. Selma) was in the utmost despair. She was shrieking and wailing all over the hotel, and rent her clothes in her fury. There was a Polish count staying here at the hotel (all Polish travellers are counts), and Mlle. Selma, rending her garments and scratching her face like a cat with her beautiful perfumed fingers, made some impression on him. They talked things over, and by dinner-time she was consoled. In the evening he made his appearance at the Casino with the lady on his arm. As usual, Mlle. Selma laughed very loudly, and her manner was somewhat more free and easy than before. She definitely showed that she belonged to the class of ladies who, when they go up to the roulette table, shoulder the other players aside to clear a space for themselves. That's particularly *chic* among such ladies. You must have noticed it?"

"Oh, yes."

"It's not worth noticing. To the annoyance of the decent public they are not moved on here—at least, not those of them who can change a thousand-rouble note every day, at the roulette table. As soon as they cease to produce a note to change they are asked to withdraw, however. Mlle. Selma still went on changing notes, but her play became more unlucky than ever. Note that such ladies are very often lucky in their play; they have a wonderful self-control. However, my story is finished. One day the count vanishes just as the prince had done. However, Mlle. Selma made her appearance at the roulette table alone; this time no one came forward to offer her his arm. In two days she had lost everything. After laying down her last louis d'or and losing it, she looked around, and saw, close by her, Baron Burmerhelm, who was scrutinizing her intently and with profound indignation. But Mlle. Selma, not noticing his indignation, accosted the Baron with that smile we all know so well, and asked him to put down ten louis d'or on the red for her. In consequence of a complaint from the Baroness she received that evening an invitation not to show herself at the Casino again. If you are surprised at my knowing all these petty and extremely improper details, it is because I have heard them from Mr. Fider, one of my relations, who carried off Mlle.

Selma in his carriage from Roulettenburg to Spa that very evening. Now, remember, Mlle. Blanche wishes to become the General's wife; probably in order in future not to receive such invitations as that one from the police at the Casino, the year before last. Now she does not play; but that is because, as it seems, she has capital of her own which she lends out at a percentage to gamblers here. That's a much safer speculation. I even suspect that the luckless General is in debt to her. Perhaps De Grieux is, too. Perhaps De Grieux is associated with her. You will admit that, till the wedding, at any rate, she can hardly be anxious to attract the attention of the Baron and Baroness in any way. In short, in her position, nothing could be more disadvantageous than a scandal. You are connected with their party and your conduct might cause a scandal, especially as she appears in public every day either arm-in-arm with the General or in company with Miss Polina. Now do you understand?"

"No, I don't!" I cried, thumping the table so violently that the garçon ran up in alarm.

"Tell me, Mr. Astley," I said furiously. "If you knew all this story and, therefore, know positively what Mlle. Blanche de Cominges is, why didn't you warn me at least, the General, or, most of all, most of all, Miss Polina, who has shown herself here at the Casino in public, arm-in-arm with Mlle. Blanche? Can such a thing be allowed?"

"I had no reason to warn you, for you could have done nothing," Mr. Astley answered calmly. "Besides, warn them of what? The General knows about Mlle. Blanche perhaps more than I do, yet he still goes about with her and Miss Polina. The General is an unlucky man. I saw Mlle. Blanche yesterday, galloping on a splendid horse with M. de Grieux and that little Russian Prince, and the General was galloping after them on a chestnut. He told me in the morning that his legs ached, but he sat his horse well. And it struck me at that moment that he was an utterly ruined man. Besides, all this is no business of mine, and I have only lately had the honour of making Miss Polina's acquaintance. However" (Mr. Astley caught himself up), "I've told you already that I do not recognize your right to ask certain questions, though I have a genuine liking for you . . ."

"Enough," I said, getting up. "It is clear as daylight to

me now, that Miss Polina knows all about Mlle. Blanche, but that she cannot part from her Frenchman, and so she brings herself to going about with Mlle. Blanche. Believe me, no other influence would compel her to go about with Mlle. Blanche and to beg me in her letter not to interfere with the Baron! Damn it all, there's no understanding it!"

"You forget, in the first place, that Mlle. de Cominges is the General's *fiancée*, and in the second place that Miss Polina is the General's stepdaughter, that she has a little brother and sister, the General's own children, who are utterly neglected by that insane man and have, I believe, been robbed by him."

"Yes, yes, that is so! To leave the children would mean abandoning them altogether; to remain means protecting their interests and, perhaps, saving some fragments of their property. Yes, yes, all that is true. But still, still! . . . Ah, now I understand why they are all so concerned about Granny!"

"About whom?" asked Mr. Astley.

"That old witch in Moscow who won't die, and about whom they are expecting a telegram that she is dying."

"Yes, of course, all interest is concentrated on her. Everything depends on what she leaves them! If he comes in for a fortune the General will marry, Miss Polina will be set free, and De Grieux . . ."

"Well, and De Grieux?"

"And De Grieux will be paid; that is all he is waiting for here."

"Is that all, do you think that is all he's waiting for?"

"I know nothing more." Mr. Astley was obstinately silent.

"But I do, I do!" I repeated fiercely. "He's waiting for the inheritance too, because Polina will get a dowry, and as soon as she gets the money will throw herself on his neck. All women are like that! Even the proudest of them turn into the meanest slaves! Polina is only capable of loving passionately: nothing else. That's my opinion of her! Look at her, particularly when she is sitting alone, thinking; it's something predestined, doomed, fated! She is capable of all the horrors of life, and passion . . . she . . . she . . . but who is that calling me?" I exclaimed suddenly. "Who is shouting? I heard some one shout in

Russian: Alexey Ivanovitch! A woman's voice. Listen, listen!"

At this moment we were approaching the hotel. We had left the café long ago, almost without noticing it.

"I did hear a woman calling, but I don't know who was being called; it is Russian. Now I see where the shouts come from," said Mr. Astley. "It is that woman sitting in a big armchair who has just been carried up the steps by so many flunkeys. They are carrying trunks after her, so the train must have just come in."

"But why is she calling me? She is shouting again; look, she is waving to us."

"I see she is waving," said Mr. Astley.

"Alexey Ivanovitch! Alexey Ivanovitch! Mercy on us, what a dolt he is!" came desperate shouts from the hotel steps.

We almost ran to the entrance. I ran up the steps and . . . my hands dropped at my sides with amazement and my feet seemed rooted to the ground.

Chapter 9

At the top of the broad steps at the hotel entrance, surrounded by footmen and maids and the many obsequious servants of the hotel, in the presence of the *ober-kellner* himself, eager to receive the exalted visitor, who had arrived with her own servants and with so many trunks and boxes, and had been carried up the steps in an invalid-chair, was seated—*Granny!* Yes, it was she herself, the terrible old Moscow lady and wealthy landowner, Antonida Vassilyevna Tarasyevitchev, the *Granny* about whom telegrams had been sent and received, who had been dying and was not dead, and who had suddenly dropped upon us in person, like snow on our heads. Though she was seventy-five and had for the last five years lost the use of her legs and had to be carried about everywhere in a chair, yet she had arrived and was, as always, alert, captious, self-satisfied, sitting upright in her chair, shouting in a loud, peremptory voice and scolding every one. In fact, she was exactly the same as she had been on the only two occasions that I had the honour of seeing her during the time I had been tutor in the

General's family. Naturally I stood rooted to the spot with amazement. As she was being carried up the steps, she had detected me a hundred paces away, with her lynx-like eyes, had recognized me and called me by my name, which she had made a note of, once for all, as she always did. And this was the woman they had expected to be in her coffin, buried, and leaving them her property. That was the thought that flashed into my mind. "Why, she will outlive all of us and every one in the hotel! But, my goodness! what will our friends do now, what will the General do? She will turn the whole hotel upside down!"

"Well, my good man, why are you standing with your eyes starting out of your head?" Granny went on shouting to me. "Can't you welcome me? Can't you say 'How do you do'? Or have you grown proud and won't? Or, perhaps, you don't recognize me? Potapitch, do you hear?" She turned to her butler, an old man with grey hair and a pink bald patch on his head, wearing a dress-coat and white tie. "Do you hear? he doesn't recognize me. They had buried me! They sent telegram upon telegram to ask whether I was dead or not! You see, I know all about it! Here, you see, I am quite alive."

"Upon my word, Antonida Vassilyevna, why should I wish you harm?" I answered gaily, recovering myself. "I was only surprised. . . . And how could I help being surprised at such an unexpected . . ."

"What is there to surprise you? I just got into the train and came. The train was comfortable and not jolting. Have you been for a walk?"

"Yes, I've been a walk to the Casino."

"It's pleasant here," said Granny, looking about her. "It's warm and the trees are magnificent. I like that! Are the family at home? The General?"

"Oh, yes, at this time they are sure to be all at home."

"So they have fixed hours here, and everything in style? They set the tone. I am told they keep their carriage, *les seigneurs russes!* They spend all their money and then they go abroad. And is Praskovya with them?"

"Yes, Polina Alexandrovna, too."

"And the Frenchy? Oh, well, I shall see them all for myself. Alexey Ivanovitch, show me the way straight to him. Are you comfortable here?"

"Fairly so, Antonida Vassilyevna."

"Potapitch, tell that dolt, the *kellner,* to give me a nice convenient set of rooms, not too high up, and take my things there at once. Why are they all so eager to carry me? Why do they put themselves forward? Ech, the slavish creatures! Who is this with you?" she asked, addressing me again.

"This is Mr. Astley," I answered.

"What Mr. Astley?"

"A traveller, a good friend of mine; an acquaintance of the General's, too."

"An Englishman. To be sure he stares at me and keeps his mouth shut. I like Englishmen, though. Well, carry me upstairs, straight to their rooms. Where are they?"

They carried Granny up; I walked up the broad staircase in front. Our procession was very striking. Every one we met stopped and stared. Our hotel is considered the best, the most expensive, and the most aristocratic in the place. Magnificent ladies and dignified Englishmen were always to be met on the staircase and in the corridors. Many people were making inquiries below of the *ober-kellner,* who was greatly impressed. He answered, of course, that this was a distinguished foreign lady, *une russe, une comtesse, grande dame,* and that she was taking the very apartments that had been occupied the week before by *la grande duchesse de N.* Granny's commanding and authoritative appearance as she was carried up in the chair was chiefly responsible for the sensation she caused. Whenever she met any one fresh she scrutinized him inquisitively and questioned me about him in a loud voice. Granny was powerfully built, and though she did not get up from her chair, it could be seen that she was very tall. Her back was as straight as a board and she did not lean back in her chair. Her big grey head with its large, bold features was held erect; she had a positively haughty and defiant expression; and it was evident that her air and gestures were perfectly natural. In spite of her seventy-five years there was still a certain vigour in her face: and even her teeth were almost perfect. She was wearing a black silk dress and a white cap.

"She interests me very much," Mr. Astley, who was going up beside me, whispered to me.

"She knows about the telegrams," I thought. "She knows about De Grieux, too, but I fancy she does not know much about Mlle. Blanche as yet." I communicated this thought to Mr. Astley.

Sinful man that I was, after the first surprise was over, I was immensely delighted at the thunderbolt that we were launching at the General. I was elated; and I walked in front feeling very gay.

Our apartments were on the third floor. Without announcing her arrival or even knocking at the door, I simply flung it wide-open and Granny was carried in, in triumph. All of them were, as by design, assembled in the General's study. It was twelve o'clock and, I believe, some excursion was being planned for the whole party. Some were to drive, others were to ride on horseback, some acquaintances had been asked to join the party. Besides the General and Polina, with the children and their nurse, there were sitting in the study De Grieux, Mlle. Blanche, again wearing her riding-habit, her mother, the little Prince, and a learned German traveller whom I had not seen before.

Granny's chair was set down in the middle of the room, three paces from the General. My goodness! I shall never forget the sensation! As we went in the General was describing something, while De Grieux was correcting him. I must observe that Mlle. Blanche and De Grieux had for the last few days been particularly attentive to the little Prince, *à la barbe du pauvre général,* and the tone of the party was extremely gay and genially intimate, though, perhaps, it was artificial. Seeing Granny, the General was struck dumb. His mouth dropped open and he broke off in the middle of a word. He gazed at her open-eyed, as though spellbound by the eye of a basilisk. Granny looked at him in silence, too, immovably, but what a triumphant, challenging and ironical look it was! They gazed at each other for ten full seconds in the midst of profound silence on the part of all around them. For the first moment De Grieux was petrified, but immediately afterwards a look of extreme uneasiness flitted over his face. Mlle. Blanche raised her eyebrows, opened her mouth and gazed wildly at Granny. The Prince and the learned German stared at the whole scene in great astonishment. Polina's eyes expressed the utmost wonder and perplexity, and she suddenly turned white as a handkerchief; a minute later the blood rushed rapidly into her face, flushing her cheeks. Yes, this was a catastrophe for all of them! I kept turning my eyes from Granny to all surrounding her and back again. Mr. Astley stood on one side, calm and polite as usual.

"Well, here I am! Instead of a telegram!" Granny broke the silence by going off into a peal of laughter. "Well, you didn't expect me?"

"Antonida Vassilyevna . . . Auntie . . . But how on earth . . ." muttered the unhappy General.

If Granny had remained silent for a few seconds longer, he would, perhaps, have had a stroke.

"How on earth what? I got into the train and came. What's the railway for? You all thought that I had been laid out, and had left you a fortune? You see, I know how you sent telegrams from here. What a lot of money you must have wasted on them! They cost a good bit from here. I simply threw my legs over my shoulders and came off here. Is this the Frenchman? M. de Grieux, I fancy?"

"*Oui, madame,*" De Grieux responded; "*et croyez, je suis si enchanté . . . votre santé . . . c'est un miracle . . . vous voir ici . . . une surprise charmante. . . .*"

"*Charmante,* I daresay; I know you, you mummer. I haven't this much faith in you," and she pointed her little finger at him. "Who is this?" she asked, indicating Mlle. Blanche. The striking-looking Frenchwoman, in a riding-habit with a whip in her hand, evidently impressed her. "Some one living here?"

"This is Mlle. Blanche de Cominges, and this is her mamma, Madame de Cominges; they are staying in this hotel," I explained.

"Is the daughter married?" Granny questioned me without ceremony.

"Mlle. de Cominges is an unmarried lady," I answered, purposely speaking in a low voice and as respectfully as possible.

"Lively?"

"I do not understand the question."

"You are not dull with her? Does she understand Russian? De Grieux picked it up in Moscow. He had a smattering of it."

I explained that Mlle. de Cominges had never been in Russia.

"*Bonjour,*" said Granny, turning abruptly to Mlle. Blanche.

"*Bonjour, madame.*" Mlle. Blanche made an elegant and ceremonious curtsey, hastening, under the cover of modesty and politeness, to express by her whole face and figure her extreme astonishment at such a strange question and manner of address.

"Oh, she casts down her eyes, she is giving herself airs and graces; you can see the sort she is at once; an actress of some kind. I'm stopping here below in the hotel," she said, turning suddenly to the General. "I shall be your neighbour. Are you glad or sorry?"

"Oh, Auntie! do believe in my sincere feelings . . . of pleasure," the General responded. He had by now recovered himself to some extent, and as, upon occasion, he could speak appropriately and with dignity, and even with some pretension of effectiveness, he began displaying his gifts now. "We have been so alarmed and upset by the news of your illness. . . . We received such despairing telegrams, and all at once . . ."

"Come, you are lying, you are lying," Granny interrupted at once.

"But how could you"—the General, too, made haste to interrupt, raising his voice and trying not to notice the word "lying"—"how could you bring yourself to undertake such a journey? You must admit that at your age and in your state of health . . . at any rate it is all so unexpected that our surprise is very natural. But I am so pleased . . . and we all" (he began smiling with an ingratiating and delighted air) "will try our utmost that you shall spend your season here as agreeably as possible. . . ."

"Come, that's enough; that's idle chatter; you are talking nonsense, as usual. I can dispose of my time for myself. Though I've nothing against you, I don't bear a grudge. You ask how I could come? What is there surprising about it? It was the simplest thing. And why are you so surprised? How are you, Praskovya? What do you do here?"

"How do you do, Granny?" said Polina, going up to her. "Have you been long on the journey?"

"Well, she's asked a sensible question—the others could say nothing but oh and ah! Why, you see, I lay in bed and lay in bed and was doctored and doctored, so I sent the doctors away and called in the sexton from St. Nicolas. He had cured a peasant woman of the same disease by means of hayseed. And he did me good, too. On the third day I was in a perspiration all day and I got up. Then my Germans gathered round again, put on their spectacles and began to argue. 'If you were to go abroad now,' said they, 'and take a course of the waters, all your symptoms would disappear.' And why shouldn't I? I thought. The fools of Zazhigins began sighing and moaning: 'Where are you off to?' they said. Well, so here I am! It took me a day to get ready, and the following week, on a Friday, I took a maid, and Potapitch, and the footman, Fyodor, but I sent Fyodor back from Berlin, because I saw he was not wanted, and I could have come quite alone. I took a special compartment and there are porters at all the stations, and for twenty kopecks they will carry you wherever you like. I say, what rooms he has taken!" she said in conclusion, looking about her. "How do you get the money, my good man? Why, everything you've got is mortgaged. What a lot of money you must owe to this Frenchman alone! I know all about it; you see, I know all about it!"

"Oh, Auntie . . ." said the General, all confusion. "I am surprised, Auntie . . . I imagine that I am free to act . . . Besides, my expenses are not beyond my means, and we are here . . ."

"They are not? You say so! Then you must have robbed your children of their last farthing—you, their trustee!"

"After that, after such words," began the General, indignant, "I really don't know . . ."

"To be sure you don't! I'll be bound you are always at roulette here? Have you whistled it all away?"

The General was so overwhelmed that he almost spluttered in the rush of his feelings.

"Roulette! I? In my position . . . I? Think what you are saying, Auntie; you must still be unwell . . ."

"Come, you are lying, you are lying. I'll be bound they can't tear you away; it's all lies! I'll have a look to-day what this roulette is like. You, Praskovya, tell me where to go and what to see, and Alexey Ivanovitch here will show me, and you, Potapitch, make a note of all the places to go to. What is there to see here?" she said, addressing Polina again.

"Close by are the ruins of the castle; then there is the Schlangenberg."

"What is it, the Schlangenberg? A wood or what?"

"No, not a wood, it's a mountain; there is a peak there . . ."

"What do you mean by a peak?"

"The very highest point on the mountain. It is an enclosed place—the view from it is unique."

"What about carrying my chair up the mountain? They wouldn't be able to drag it up, would they?"

"Oh, we can find porters," I answered.

At this moment, Fedosya, the nurse, came up to greet Granny and brought the General's children to her.

"Come, there's no need for kissing! I cannot bear kissing children, they always have dirty noses. Well, how do you get on here, Fedosya?"

"It's very, very nice here, Antonida Vassilyevna," answered Fedosya. "How have you been, ma'am? We've been so worried about you."

"I know, you are a good soul. Do you always have visitors?"—she turned to Polina again. "Who is that wretched little rascal in spectacles?"

"Prince Nilsky," Polina whispered.

"Ah, a Russian. And I thought he wouldn't understand! Perhaps he didn't hear. I have seen Mr. Astley already. Here he is again," said Granny, catching sight of him. "How do you do?"—she turned to him suddenly.

Mr. Astley bowed to her in silence.

"Have you no good news to tell me? Say something! Translate that to him, Polina."

Polina translated it.

"Yes. That with great pleasure and delight I am looking at you, and very glad that you are in good health," Mr. Astley answered seriously, but with perfect readiness. It was translated to Granny and it was evident she was pleased.

"How well Englishmen always answer," she observed. "That's why I always like Englishmen. There's no comparison between them and Frenchmen! Come and see me," she said, addressing Mr. Astley again. "I'll try not to worry you too much. Translate that to him, and tell him that I am here below—here below—do you hear? Below, below," she repeated to Mr. Astley, pointing downwards.

Mr. Astley was extremely pleased at the invitation.

Granny looked Polina up and down attentively and with a satisfied air.

"I was fond of you, Praskovya," she said suddenly. "You're a fine wench, the best of the lot, and as for will

—my goodness! Well, I have will too; turn round. That's not a false chignon, is it?"

"No, Granny, it's my own."

"To be sure. I don't care for the silly fashion of the day. You look very nice. I should fall in love with you if I were a young gentleman. Why don't you get married? But it is time for me to go. And I want to go out, for I've had nothing but the train and the train . . . Well, are you still cross?" she added, turning to the General.

"Upon my word, Auntie, what nonsense!" cried the General, delighted. "I understand at your age . . ."

"Cette vieille est tombée en enfance," De Grieux whispered to me.

"I want to see everything here. Will you let me have Alexey Ivanovitch?" Granny went on to the General.

"Oh, as much as you like, but I will myself . . . and Polina, M. de Grieux . . . we shall all think it a pleasure to accompany you."

"Mais, madame, cela sera un plaisir" . . . De Grieux addressed her with a bewitching smile.

"A *plaisir*, to be sure; you are absurd, my good sir. I am not going to give you any money, though," she added suddenly. "But now to my rooms; I must have a look at them, and then we'll go the round of everything. Come, lift me up." Granny was lifted up again and we all flocked downstairs behind her chair. The General walked as though stunned by a blow on the head. De Grieux was considering something. Mlle. Blanche seemed about to remain, but for some reason she made up her mind to come with the rest. The Prince followed her at once, and no one was left in the General's study but Madame de Cominges and the German.

Chapter 10

At watering-places and, I believe, in Europe generally, hotelkeepers and *ober-kellners*, in assigning rooms to their visitors, are guided not so much by the demands and desires of the latter as by their own personal opinion of them, and, one must add, they are rarely mistaken. But for some reason I cannot explain, they had assigned Granny such a splendid suite that they had quite overshot the mark. It consisted of four splendidly furnished rooms with a bathroom, quarters for the servants and a special room for the maid, and so on. Some *grande duchesse* really had been staying in those rooms the week before, a fact of which the new occupant was informed at once, in order to enhance the value of the apartments. Granny was carried, or rather wheeled, through all the rooms, and she looked at them attentively and severely. The *ober-kellner*, an elderly man with a bald head, followed her respectfully at this first survey.

I don't know what they all took Granny to be, but apparently for a very important and, above all, wealthy lady. They put down in the book at once: *"Madame la générale princesse de Tarasyevitchev,"* though Granny had never been a princess. Her servants, her special compartment in the train, the mass of useless bags, portmanteaus, and even chests that had come with Granny, probably laid the foundation of her prestige; while her invalid-chair, her abrupt tone and voice, her eccentric questions, which were made with the most unconstrained air that would tolerate no contradiction—in short, Granny's whole figure, erect, brisk, imperious—increased the awe in which she was held by all. As she looked at the rooms, Granny sometimes told them to stop her chair, pointed to some object in the furniture and addressed unexpected questions to the *ober-kellner,* who still smiled respectfully, though he was beginning to feel nervous. Granny put her questions in French, which she spoke, however, rather badly, so that I usually translated. The *ober-kellner's* answers for the most part did not please her and seemed unsatisfactory. And, indeed, she kept asking about all sorts of things quite irrelevant. Suddenly, for instance, stopping before a picture, a rather feeble copy of some well-known picture of a mythological subject, she would ask—

"Whose portrait is that?"

The *ober-kellner* replied that no doubt it was some countess.

"How is it you don't know? You live here and don't know. Why is it here? Why is she squinting?"

The *ober-kellner* could not answer these questions satisfactorily, and positively lost his head.

"Oh, what a blockhead!" commented Granny, in Russian.

She was wheeled on. The same performance was repeated with a Dresden statuette, which Granny looked at for a long time, and then ordered them to remove, no one knew why. Finally, she worried the *ober-kellner* about what the carpets in the bedroom cost, and where they had been woven! The *ober-kellner* promised to make inquiries.

"What asses," Granny grumbled, and concentrated her whole attention on the bed. "What a gorgeous canopy! Open the bed."

They opened the bed.

"More, more, turn it all over. Take off the pillows, the pillows, lift up the feather-bed."

Everything was turned over. Granny examined it attentively.

"It's a good thing there are no bugs. Take away all the linen! Make it up with my linen and my pillows. But all this is too gorgeous. Such rooms are not for an old woman like me. I shall be dreary all alone. Alexey Ivanovitch, you must come and see me very often when your lessons with the children are over."

"I left the General's service yesterday," I answered, "and am living in the hotel quite independently."

"How is that?"

"A German of high rank, a Baron, with his Baroness, came here from Berlin the other day. I addressed him yesterday in German without keeping to the Berlin accent."

"Well, what then?"

"He thought it an impertinence and complained to the General, and yesterday the General discharged me."

"Why, did you swear at the Baron, or what? (though if you had it wouldn't have mattered!)"

"Oh, no. On the contrary, the Baron raised his stick to thrash me."

"And did you, sniveller, allow your tutor to be treated like that?" she said suddenly, addressing the General; "and turned him out of his place too! Noodles! you're all a set of noodles, as I see."

"Don't disturb yourself, Auntie," said the General, with a shade of condescending familiarity; "I can manage my own business. Besides, Alexey Ivanovitch has not given you quite a correct account of it."

"And you just put up with it?"—she turned to me.

"I meant to challenge the Baron to a duel," I answered, as calmly and as modestly as I could, "but the General opposed it."

"Why did you oppose it?"—Granny turned to the General again. ("And you can go, my good man; you can come when you are called," she said, addressing the *oberkellner;* "no need to stand about gaping. I can't endure this Nürnberg rabble!")

The man bowed and went out, not, of course, understanding Granny's compliments.

"Upon my word, Auntie, surely a duel was out of the question."

"Why out of the question? Men are all cocks; so they should fight. You are all noodles, I see, you don't know how to stand up for your country. Come, take me up, Potapitch; see that there are always two porters: engage them. I don't want more than two. I shall only want them to carry me up and down stairs, and to wheel me on the levels in the street. Explain that to them; and pay them beforehand—they will be more respectful. You will always be with me yourself, and you, Alexey Ivanovitch, point out that Baron to me when we are out: that I may have a look at the von Baron. Well, where is the roulette?"

I explained that the roulette tables were in rooms in the Casino. Then followed questions: Were there many of them? Did many people play? Did they play all day long? How was it arranged? I answered at last, that she had much better see all this with her own eyes, and that it was rather difficult to describe it.

"Well, then, take me straight there! You go first, Alexey Ivanovitch!"

"Why, Auntie, don't you really mean to rest after your journey?" the General asked anxiously. He seemed rather flurried and, indeed, they all seemed embarrassed and were exchanging glances. Probably they all felt it rather risky and, indeed, humiliating to accompany Granny to the Casino, where, of course, she might do something eccentric, and in public; at the same time they all proposed to accompany her.

"Why should I rest? I m not tired and, besides, I've been sitting still for three days. And then we will go and see the springs and medicinal waters; where are they? And then . . . we'll go and see, what was it you said, Praskovya?—peak, wasn't it?"

"Yes, Granny."

"Well, peak, then, if it is a peak. And what else is there here?"

"There are a great many objects of interests, Granny," Polina exerted herself to say.

"Why don't you know them! Marfa, you shall come with me, too," she said, addressing her maid.

"But why should she come?" the General said fussily; "and in fact it's out of the question, and I doubt whether Potapitch will be admitted into the Casino."

"What nonsense! Am I to abandon her because she is a servant? She's a human being, too; here we have been on our travels for a week; she wants to have a look at things, too. With whom could she go except me? She wouldn't dare show her nose in the street by herself."

"But, Granny . . ."

"Why, are you ashamed to be with me? Then stay at home; you are not asked. Why, what a General! I am a General's widow myself. And why should you all come trailing after me? I can look at it all with Alexey Ivanovitch."

But De Grieux insisted that we should all accompany her, and launched out into the most polite phrases about the pleasure of accompanying her, and so on. We all started.

Elle est tombée en enfance," De Grieux repeated to the General; "*seule, elle fera des bêtises . . .*" I heard nothing more, but he evidently had some design, and, possibly, his hopes had revived.

It was half a mile to the Casino. The way was through an avenue of chestnuts to a square, going round which, they came out straight on the Casino. The General was to some extent reassured, for our procession, though somewhat eccentric, was, nevertheless, decorous and presentable. And there was nothing surprising in the fact of an invalid who could not walk putting in an appearance at the Casino; but, anyway, the General was afraid of the Casino; why should an invalid unable to walk, and an old lady, too, go into the gambling saloon? Polina and Mlle. Blanche walked on each side of the bath-chair. Mlle. Blanche laughed, was modestly animated and even sometimes jested very politely with Granny, so much so that the latter spoke of her approvingly at last. Polina, on the other side, was obliged to be continually answering Granny's innumerable questions, such as: "Who was that passed? Who was that woman driving past? Is it a big town? Is it a big garden? What are those trees? What's that hill? Do eagles fly here? What is that absurd-looking roof?" Mr. Astley walked beside me and whispered that he expected a great deal from that morning. Potapitch and Marfa walked in the background close behind the bath-chair, Potapitch in his swallow-tailed coat and white tie, but with a cap on his head, and Marfa (a red-faced maid-servant, forty years old and beginning to turn grey) in a cap, cotton gown, and creaking goatskin slippers. Granny turned to them very often and addressed remarks to them. De Grieux was talking with an air of determination. Probably he was reassuring the General, evidently he was giving him some advice. But Granny had already pronounced the fatal phrase: "I am not going to give you money." Perhaps to De Grieux this announcement sounded incredible, but the General knew his aunt. I noticed that De Grieux and Mlle. Blanche were continually exchanging glances. I could distinguish the Prince and the German traveller at the further end of the avenue; they had stopped, and were walking away from us.

Our visit to the Casino was a triumph. The porters and attendants displayed the same deference as in the hotel. They looked at us, however, with curiosity. Granny began by giving orders that she should be wheeled through all the rooms. Some she admired, others made no impression on her; she asked questions about them all. At last we came to the roulette room. The lackeys, who stood like sentinels at closed doors, flung the doors wide open as though they were impressed.

Granny's appearance at the roulette table made a profound impression on the public. At the roulette tables and at the other end of the room, where there was a table with *trente et quarante*, there was a crowd of a hundred and fifty or two hundred players, several rows deep. Those who had succeeded in squeezing their way right up to the table, held fast, as they always do, and would not give up their places to any one until they had lost; for simple spectators were not allowed to stand at the tables and occupy the space. Though there were chairs set round the table, few of the players sat down, especially when there was a great crowd, because standing one could get closer and consequently pick out one's place and put down one's stake more conveniently. The second and the third rows pressed up upon the first, waiting and watching for their turn; but sometimes a hand would be impatiently thrust forward through the first row to put down a stake. Even from the third row people managed to seize chances of poking forward their stakes; consequently every ten or even five minutes there was some "scene" over disputed stakes at one end of the hall or another. The police of the Casino were, however, fairly good. It was, of course, impossible to prevent crowding; on the contrary, the owners were glad of the rush of people because it was profitable, but eight croupiers sitting round the table kept a vigilant watch on the stakes: they even kept count of them, and when disputes arose they could settle them. In extreme cases they called in the police, and the trouble was over in an instant. There were police officers in plain clothes stationed here and there among the players, so that they could not be recognized. They were especially on the look-out for thieves and professional pickpockets, who are very numerous at the roulette tables, as it affords them excellent opportunity for exercising their skill. The fact is, elsewhere thieves must pick pockets or break locks, and such enterprises, when unsuccessful, have a very troublesome ending. But in this case the thief has only to go up to the roulette table, begin playing, and all at once, openly and publicly, take another person's winnings and put them in his pocket. If a dispute arises, the cheat insists loudly that the stake was his. If the trick is played cleverly and the witnesses hesitate, the thief may often succeed in carrying off the money, if the sum is not a very large one, of course. In that case the croupiers or some one of the other players are almost certain to have been keeping an eye on it. But if the sum is not a large one, the real owner sometimes actually declines to keep up the dispute, and goes away shrinking from the scandal. But if they succeed in detecting a thief, they turn him out at once with contumely.

All this Granny watched from a distance with wild curiosity. She was much delighted at a thief's being turned out. *Trente et quarante* did not interest her very much; she was more pleased at roulette and the rolling of the little ball. She evinced a desire at last to get a closer view of the game. I don't know how it happened, but the attendants and other officious persons (principally Poles who had lost, and who pressed their services on lucky players and foreigners of all sorts) at once, and in spite of the crowd, cleared a place for Granny in the very middle of the table beside the chief croupier, and wheeled her chair to it. A number of visitors who were not playing, but watching the play (chiefly Englishmen with their families), at once crowded round the table to watch Granny from behind the players. Numbers of lorgnettes were turned in her direction. The croupiers' expectations rose. Such an eccentric person certainly seemed to promise something out of the ordinary. An old woman of over seventy, who could not walk, yet wished to play, was, of course, not a sight to be seen every day. I squeezed my way up to the table too, and took my stand beside Granny. Potapitch and Marfa were left somewhere in the distance among the crowd. The General, Polina, De Grieux, and Mlle. Blanche stood aside, too, among the spectators.

At first Granny began looking about at the players. She began in a half whisper asking me abrupt, jerky questions. Who was that man and who was this woman? She was particularly delighted by a young man at the end of the table, who was playing for very high stakes, putting down thousands and had, as people whispered around, already won as much as forty thousand francs, which lay before him in heaps of gold and banknotes. He was pale; his eyes glittered and his hands were shaking; he was staking now without counting, by handfuls, and yet he kept on winning and winning, kept raking in and raking in the money. The attendants hung about him solicitously, set a chair for him, cleared a place round him that he might have more room, that he might not be crowded— all this in expectation of a liberal tip. Some players, after they have won, tip the attendants without counting a handful of coins in their joy. A Pole had already established himself at his side, and was deferentially but continually whispering to him, probably telling him what to stake on, advising and directing his play—of course, he, too, expecting a tip later on! But the player scarcely looked at him. He staked at random and kept winning. He evidently did not know what he was doing.

Granny watched him for some minutes.

"Tell him," Granny said suddenly, growing excited

and giving me a poke, "tell him to give it up, to take his money quickly and go away. He'll lose it all directly, he'll lose it all!" she urged, almost breathless with agitation. "Where's Potapitch? Send Potapitch to him. Come, tell him, tell him," she went on, poking me. "Where is Potapitch? *Sortez! Sortez!*"—she began herself shouting to the young man.

I bent down to her and whispered resolutely that she must not shout like this here, that even talking aloud was forbidden, because it hindered counting and that we should be turned out directly.

"How vexatious! The man's lost! I suppose it's his own doing. . . . I can't look at him, it quite upsets me. What a dolt!" and Granny made haste to turn in another direction.

On the left, on the other side of the table, there was conspicuous among the players a young lady, and beside her a sort of dwarf. Who this dwarf was, and whether he was a relation or brought by her for the sake of effect, I don't know. I had noticed the lady before; she made her appearance at the gambling table every day, at one o'clock in the afternoon, and went away exactly at two; she always played for an hour. She was already known, and a chair was set for her at once. She took out of her pocket some gold, some thousand-franc notes, and began staking quietly, coolly, prudently, making pencil notes on a bit of paper of the numbers about which the chances grouped themselves, and trying to work out a system. She staked considerable sums. She used to win every day —one, two, or at the most three thousand francs—not more, and instantly went away. Granny scrutinized her for a long time.

"Well, that one won't lose! That one there won't lose! Of what class is she! Do you know? Who is she?"

"She must be a Frenchwoman, of a certain class, you know," I whispered.

"Ah, one can tell the bird by its flight. One can see she has a sharp claw. Explain to me now what every turn means and how one has to bet!"

I explained as far as I could to Granny all the various points on which one could stake: *rouge et noir, pair et impair, manque et passe,* and finally the various subtleties in the system of the numbers. Granny listened attentively, remembered, asked questions, and began to master it. One could point to examples of every kind, so that she very quickly and readily picked up a great deal.

"But what is *zéro*? You see that croupier, the curly-headed one, the chief one, showed *zéro* just now? And why did he scoop up everything that was on the table? Such a heap, he took it all for himself. What is the meaning of it?"

"*Zéro*, Granny, means that the bank wins all. If the little ball falls on *zéro*, everything on the table goes to the bank. It is true you can stake your money so as to keep it, but the bank pays nothing."

"You don't say so! And shall I get nothing?"

"No, Granny, if before this you had staked on *zéro* you would have got thirty-five times what you staked."

"What! thirty-five times, and does it often turn up? Why don't they stake on it, the fools."

"There are thirty-six chances against it, Granny."

"What nonsense. Potapitch! Potapitch! Stay, I've money with me—here." She took out of her pocket a tightly packed purse, and picked out of it a friedrich d'or. "Stake it on the *zéro* at once."

"Granny, *zéro* has only just turned up," I said; "so now it won't turn up for a long time. You will lose a great deal; wait a little, anyway."

"Oh, nonsense; put it down!"

"As you please, but it may not turn up again till the evening. You may go on staking thousands; it has happened."

"Oh, nonsense, nonsense. If you are afraid of the wolf you shouldn't go into the forest. What? Have I lost? Stake again!"

A second friedrich d'or was lost: she staked a third. Granny could scarcely sit still in her seat. She stared with feverish eyes at the little ball dancing on the spokes of the turning wheel. She lost a third, too. Granny was beside herself, she could not sit still, she even thumped on the table with her fist when the croupier announced, "*trente-six*" instead of the *zéro* she was expecting.

"There, look at it," said Granny angrily; "isn't that cursed little *zéro* coming soon? As sure as I'm alive, I'll sit here till *zéro* does come! It's that cursed curly-headed croupier's doing; he'll never let it come! Alexey Ivanovitch, stake two gold pieces at once! Staking as much as you do, even if *zéro* does come you'll get nothing by it."

"Granny!"

"Stake, stake! it is not your money."

I staked two friedrichs d'or. The ball flew about the wheel for a long time, at last it began dancing about the spokes. Granny was numb with excitement, and squeezed my fingers, and all at once—

"*Zéro!*" boomed the croupier.

"You see, you see!"—Granny turned to me quickly, beaming and delighted. "I told you so. The Lord Himself put it into my head to stake those two gold pieces! Well, how much do I get now? Why don't they give it me? Potapitch, Marfa, where are they? Where have all our people got to? Potapitch, Potapitch!"

"Granny, afterwards," I whispered; "Potapitch is at the door, they won't let him in. Look, Granny, they are giving you the money, take it!" A heavy roll of printed blue notes, worth fifty friedrichs d'or, was thrust towards Granny and twenty friedrichs d'or were counted out to her. I scooped it all up in a shovel and handed it to Granny.

"*Faites le jeu, messieurs! Faites le jeu, messieurs! Rien ne va plus?*" called the croupier, inviting the public to stake, and preparing to turn the wheel.

"Heavens! we are too late. They're just going to turn it. Put it down, put it down!" Granny urged me in a flurry. "Don't dawdle, make haste!" She was beside herself and poked me with all her might.

"What am I to stake it on, Granny?"

"On *zéro*, on *zéro*! On *zéro* again! Stake as much as possible! How much have we got altogether? Seventy friedrichs d'or. There's no need to spare it. Stake twenty friedrichs d'or at once."

"Think what you are doing, Granny! Sometimes it does not turn up for two hundred times running! I assure you, you may go on staking your whole fortune."

"Oh, nonsense, nonsense! Put it down! How your tongue does wag! I know what I'm about." Granny was positively quivering with excitement.

"By the regulations it's not allowed to stake more than twelve roubles on *zéro* at once, Granny; here I have staked that."

"Why is it not allowed? Aren't you lying? Monsieur! Monsieur!"—she nudged the croupier, who was sitting near her on the left, and was about to set the wheel turning. *"Combien zéro? Douze? Douze?"*

I immediately interpreted the question in French.

"Oui, madame," the croupier confirmed politely; "as the winnings from no single stake must exceed four thousand florins by the regulations," he added in explanation.

"Well, there's no help for it, stake twelve."

"Le jeu est fait," cried the croupier. The wheel rotated, and thirty turned up. She had lost.

"Again, again, again! Stake again!" cried Granny. I no longer resisted, and, shrugging my shoulders, staked another twelve friedrichs d'or. The wheel turned a long time. Granny was simply quivering as she watched the wheel. "Can she really imagine that *zéro* will win again?" I thought, looking at her with wonder. Her face was beaming with a firm conviction of winning, an unhesitating expectation that in another minute they would shout *"Zéro!"* The ball jumped into the cage.

"Zéro!" cried the croupier.

"What!!!" Granny turned to me with intense triumph.

I was a gambler myself, I felt that at the moment my arms and legs were trembling, there was a throbbing in my head. Of course, this was a rare chance that *zéro* should have come up three times in some dozen turns; but there was nothing particularly wonderful about it. I had myself seen *zéro* turn up three times *running* two days before, and a gambler who had been zealously noting down the lucky numbers, observed aloud that, only the day before, *zéro* had turned up only once in twenty-four hours.

Granny's winnings were counted out to her with particular attention and deference as she had won such a large sum. She received four hundred and twenty friedrichs d'or, that is, four thousand florins and seventy friedrichs d'or. She was given twenty friedrichs d'or in gold, and four thousand florins in banknotes.

This time Granny did not call Potapitch; she had other preoccupations. She did not even babble or quiver outwardly! She was, if one may so express it, quivering inwardly. She was entirely concentrated on something, absorbed in one aim.

"Alexey Ivanovitch, he said that one could only stake

four thousand florins at once, didn't he? Come, take it, stake the whole four thousand on the red," Granny commanded.

It was useless to protest, the wheel began rotating.

"*Rouge*," the croupier proclaimed.

Again she had won four thousand florins, making eight in all.

"Give me four, and stake four again on red," Granny commanded.

Again I staked four thousand.

"*Rouge*," the croupier pronounced again.

"Twelve thousand altogether! Give it me all here. Pour the gold here into the purse and put away the notes. That's enough! Home! Wheel my chair out."

Chapter 11

The chair was wheeled to the door at the other end of the room. Granny was radiant. All our party immediately thronged round her with congratulations. However eccentric Granny's behaviour might be, her triumph covered a multitude of sins, and the General was no longer afraid of compromising himself in public by his relationship with such a strange woman. With a condescending and familiarly good-humoured smile, as though humouring a child, he congratulated Granny. He was, however, evidently impressed, like all the other spectators. People talked all round and pointed at Granny. Many passed by to get a closer view of her! Mr. Astley was talking of her aside, with two English acquaintances. Some majestic ladies gazed at her with majestic amazement, as though at a marvel. . . . De Grieux positively showered congratulations and smiles upon her.

"*Quelle victoire!*" he said.

"*Mais, madame, c'était du feu,*" Mlle. Blanche commented, with an ingratiating smile.

"Yes, I just went and won twelve thousand florins! Twelve indeed; what about the gold? With the gold it makes almost thirteen. What is that in our money? Will it be six thousand?"

I explained that it made more than seven, and in the present state of exchange might even amount to eight.

"Well, that's something worth having, eight thousand!

And you stay here, you noodles, and do nothing! Pota-pitch, Marfa, did you see?"

"My goodness! how did you do it, ma'am? Eight thousand!" exclaimed Marfa, wriggling.

"There! there's five gold pieces for you, here!"

Potapitch and Marfa flew to kiss her hand.

"And give the porters, too, a friedrich d'or each. Give it them in gold, Alexey Ivanovitch. Why is that flunkey bowing and the other one too? Are they congratulating me? Give them a friedrich d'or too."

"*Madame la princesse . . . un pauvre expatrié . . . malheur continuel . . . les princes russes sont si généreux . . .*" A person with moustaches and an obsequious smile, in a threadbare coat and gay-coloured waistcoat, came cringing about Granny's chair, waving his hat in his hand.

"Give him a friedrich d'or too. . . . No, give him two; that's enough, or there will be no end to them. Lift me up and carry me out, Praskovya"—she turned to Polina Alex-androvna—"I'll buy you a dress tomorrow, and I'll buy Mlle. . . . what's her name, Mlle. Blanche, isn't it? I'll buy her a dress too. Translate that to her, Praskovya!"

"*Merci, madame.*" Mlle. Blanche made a grateful curtsey while she exchanged an ironical smile with De Grieux and the General. The General was rather embarrassed and was greatly relieved when we reached the avenue.

"Fedosya—won't Fedosya be surprised," said Granny, thinking of the General's nurse. "I must make her a present of a dress. Hey, Alexey Ivanovitch, Alexey Ivanovitch, give this to the poor man."

A man in rags, with bent back, passed us on the road, and looked at us.

"And perhaps he is not a poor man, but a rogue, Granny."

"Give him a gulden, give it him!"

I went up to the man and gave it him. He looked at me in wild amazement, but took the gulden, however. He smelt of spirits.

"And you, Alexey Ivanovitch. Have you not tried your luck yet?"

"No, Granny."

"But your eyes were burning, I saw them."

"I shall try, Granny, I certainly shall later."

"And stake on *zéro* straight away. You will see! How much have you in hand?"

"Only twenty friedrichs d'or, Granny."

"That's not much. I will give you fifty friedrichs d'or. I will lend it if you like. Here, take this roll—but don't you expect anything, all the same, my good man, I am not going to give you anything," she said, suddenly addressing the General.

The latter winced, but he said nothing. De Grieux frowned.

"Que diable, c'est une terrible vieille!" he muttered to the General through his teeth.

"A beggar, a beggar, another beggar!" cried Granny. "Give him a gulden, too, Alexey Ivanovitch."

This time it was a grey-headed old man with a wooden leg, in a long-skirted blue coat and with a long stick in his hand. He looked like an old soldier. But when I held out a gulden to him he stepped back and looked at me angrily.

"Was ist's der Teufel," he shouted, following up with a dozen oaths.

"Oh, he's a fool," cried Granny, dismissing him with a wave of her hand. "Go on! I'm hungry! Now we'll have dinner directly; then I'll rest a little, and back here again."

"You want to play again, Granny!" I cried.

"What do you expect? That you should all sit here and sulk while I watch you?"

"Mais, madame—" De Grieux drew near—*"les chances peuvent turner, une seule mauvaise chance et vous perdrez tout . . . surtout avec votre jeu . . . C'est terrible!"*

"Vous perdrez absolument," chirped Mlle. Blanche.

"But what is it to do with all of you? I shouldn't lose your money, but my own! And where is that Mr. Astley?" she asked me.

"He stayed in the Casino, Granny."

"I'm sorry, he's such a nice man."

On reaching home Granny met the *ober-kellner* on the stairs, called him and began bragging of her winnings; then she sent for Fedosya, made her a present of three friedrichs d'or and ordered dinner to be served. Fedosya and Marfa hovered over her at dinner.

"I watched you, ma'am," Marfa cackled, "and said to Potapitch, 'What does our lady want to do?' And the money on the table—saints alive! the money! I haven't seen so much money in the whole of my life, and all round were gentlefolk—nothing but gentlefolk sitting. 'And wherever do all these gentlefolk come from, Potapitch?'

said I. May our Lady Herself help her, I thought. I was praying for you, ma'am, and my heart was simply sinking, simply sinking; I was all of a tremble. Lord help her, I thought, and here the Lord has sent you luck. I've been trembling ever since, ma'am. I'm all of a tremble now."

"Alexey Ivanovitch, after dinner, at four o'clock, get ready and we'll go. Now good-bye for a time; don't forget to send for a doctor for me. I must drink the waters, too. Go, or maybe you'll forget."

As I left Granny I was in a sort of stupor. I tried to imagine what would happen now to all our people and what turn things would take. I saw clearly that they (especially the General) had not yet succeeded in recovering from the first shock. The fact of Granny's arrival instead of the telegram which they were expecting from hour to hour to announce her death (and consequently the inheritance of her fortune) had so completely shattered the whole fabric of their plans and intentions that Granny's further exploits at roulette threw them into positive bewilderment and a sort of stupefaction seemed to have come over all of them.

Meanwhile this second fact was almost more important than the first; for though Granny had repeated twice that she would not give the General any money, yet, who knows?—there was no need to give up all hope yet. De Grieux, who was involved in all the General's affairs, had not lost hope. I am convinced that Mlle. Blanche, also much involved in the General's affairs (I should think so: to marry a General and with a considerable fortune!), would not have given up hope, and would have tried all her fascinating arts upon Granny—in contrast with the proud and incomprehensible Polina, who did not know how to curry favour with any one. But now, now that Granny had had such success at roulette, now that Granny's personality had shown itself so clearly and so typically (a refractory and imperious old lady, *et tombée en enfance*), now, perhaps, all was lost. Why, she was as pleased as a child, so pleased that she would go on till she was ruined and had lost everything. Heavens! I thought (and, God forgive me, with a malignant laugh), why, every friedrich d'or Granny staked just now must have been a fresh sore in the General's heart, must have maddened De Grieux and infuriated Mlle. de Cominges, who saw the cup slipping from her lips. Another fact: even in

her triumph and joy of winning, when Granny was giving
money away to every one, and taking every passer-by for
a beggar, even then she had let fall to the General, "I'm
not going to give you anything, though!" That meant that
she had fastened upon that idea, was sticking to it, had
made up her mind about it. There was danger! danger!

All these reflections were revolving in my mind as I
mounted the front stairs from Granny's apartments to
my garret in the very top storey. All this interested me
strongly. Though, of course, I could before have divined
the strongest leading motives prompting the actors before
me, yet I did not know for certain all the mysteries and
intrigues of the drama. Polina had never been fully open
with me. Though it did happen at times that she revealed
her feelings to me, yet I noticed that almost always after
such confidences she would make fun of all she had said,
or would try to obscure the matter and put it in a different
light. Oh, she had hidden a great deal! In any case, I foresaw that the *dénouement* of this mysterious and constrained position was at hand. One more shock—and
everything would be ended and revealed. About my fortunes, which were also involved in all this, I scarcely
troubled. I was in a strange mood: I had only twenty
friedrichs d'or in my pocket; I was in a foreign land without a job or means of livelihood, without hope, without
prospects, and—I did not trouble my head about it! If it
had not been for the thought of Polina, I should have
abandoned myself to the comic interest of the approaching catastrophe, and should have been shouting with
laughter. But I was troubled about Polina; her fate was
being decided, I divined that; but I regret to say that it
was not altogether her fate that troubled me. I wanted to
fathom her secrets; I wanted her to come to me and say:
"I love you," and if not that, if that was senseless insanity,
then . . . well, what was there to care about? Did I know
what I wanted? I was like one demented: all I wanted was
to be near her, in the halo of her glory, in her radiance,
always, for ever, all my life. I knew nothing more! And
could I leave her?

In their passage on the third storey I felt as though
something nudged me. I turned round and, twenty paces
or more from me, I saw coming out of a door Polina. She
seemed waiting: and as soon as she saw me beckoned to
me.

"Polina Alexandrovna . . ."

"Hush!" she said.

"Imagine," I whispered to her, "I felt as though some one had nudged me just now; I looked round—you! It seems as though there were a sort of electricity from you!"

"Take this letter," Polina articulated anxiously with a frown, probably not hearing what I had said, "and give it into Mr. Astley's own hands at once. Make haste, I beg you. There is no need of an answer. He will . . ."

She did not finish.

"Mr. Astley?" I repeated in surprise.

But Polina had already disappeared behind the door.

"Aha, so they are in correspondence!" I ran at once, of course, to Mr. Astley; first to his hotel, where I did not find him, then to the Casino, where I hurried through all the rooms: and at last, as I was returning home in vexation, almost in despair, I met him by chance, with a party of Englishmen and Englishwomen on horseback. I beckoned to him, stopped him and gave him the letter: we had not time even to exchange a glance. But I suspect that Mr. Astley purposely gave rein to his horse.

Was I tortured by jealousy? Anyway, I was in an utterly shattered condition. I did not even want to find out what they were writing to one another about. And so he was trusted by her! "Her friend, her friend," I thought, "and that is clear (and when has he had time to become her friend), but is there love in the case? Of course not," common-sense whispered to me. But common-sense alone counts for little in such cases; anyway, this, too, had to be cleared up. Things were growing unpleasantly complicated.

Before I had time to go into the hotel, first the porter and then the *ober-kellner*, coming out of his room, informed me that I was wanted, that I had been asked for, three times they had sent to ask: where was I?—that I was asked to go as quickly as possible to the General's rooms. I was in the most disagreeable frame of mind. In the General's room I found, besides the General himself, De Grieux and Mlle. Blanche—alone, without her mother. The mother was evidently an official one, only used for show. But when it came to real *business* she acted for herself. And probably the woman knew little of her so-called daughter's affairs.

They were, however, consulting warmly about some-

thing, and the doors of the study were actually locked—
which had never happened before. Coming to the door, I
heard loud voices—De Grieux's insolent and malignant
voice, Blanche's shrill fury, and the General's pitiful tones,
evidently defending himself about something. Upon my
entrance they all, as it were, pulled themselves up and restrained themselves. De Grieux smoothed his hair and
forced a smile into his angry face—that horrid official
French smile which I so detest. The crushed and desperate General tried to assume an air of dignity, but it was
a mechanical effort. Only Mlle. Blanche's countenance,
blazing with anger, scarcely changed. She only ceased
speaking while she fixed her eyes upon me in impatient
expectation. I may mention that hitherto she had treated
me with extraordinary casualness, had even refused to
respond to my bows, and had simply declined to see me.

"Alexey Ivanovitch," the General began in a soft mol-
lifying tone, "allow me to tell you that it is strange, exceedingly strange . . . in fact, your conduct in regard
to me and my family . . . in fact, it is exceedingly
strange . . ."

"*Eh! ce n'est pas ça*," De Grieux interposed, with vexation and contempt. (There's no doubt he was the leading
spirit.) "*Mon cher monsieur, notre cher général se
trompe*, in taking up this tone" (I translate the rest of his
speech in Russian), "but he meant to say . . . that is to
warn you, or rather to beg you most earnestly not to ruin
him—yes, indeed, not to ruin him! I make use of that expression."

"But how, how?" I interrupted.

"Why, you are undertaking to be the guide (or how
shall I express it?) of this old woman, *cette pauvre terrible
vieille*"—De Grieux himself hesitated—"but you know
she'll lose everything; she will gamble away her whole fortune! You know yourself, you have seen yourself, how she
plays! If she begins to lose, she will never leave off from
obstinacy, from anger, and will lose everything, she will
gamble away everything, and in such cases one can never
regain one's losses and then . . . then . . ."

"And then," the General put in, "then you will ruin the
whole family! I and my family are her heirs, she has no
nearer relations. I tell you openly: my affairs are in a bad
way, a very bad way. You know my position to some extent. . . . If she loses a considerable sum or even (Lord

help us!) her whole fortune, what will become of me, of my children!" (The General looked round at De Grieux.) "Of me." (He looked round at Mlle. Blanche, who turned away from him with contempt.) "Alexey Ivanovitch, save us, save us! . . ."

"But how, General, how, how can I? . . . What influence have I in the matter?"

"Refuse, refuse, give her up! . . ."

"Then some one else will turn up," I said.

"*Ce n'est pas ça, ce n'est pas ça,*" De Grieux interrupted again, "*que diable!* No, don't desert her, but at least advise her, dissuade her, draw her away . . . don't let her play too much, distract her in some way."

"But how can I do that? If you would undertake the task yourself, M. de Grieux," I added, as naïvely as I could.

Here I caught a rapid, fiery, questioning glance from Mlle. Blanche at M. de Grieux. And in De Grieux's own face there was something peculiar, something he could not himself disguise.

"The point is, she won't accept me now!" De Grieux cried, with a wave of his hand. "If only . . . later on . . ."

De Grieux looked rapidly and meaningly at Mlle. Blanche.

"*O, mon cher M. Alexis, soyez si bon.*" Mlle. Blanche herself took a step towards me with a most fascinating smile, she seized me by both hands and pressed them warmly. Damn it all! That diabolical face knew how to change completely in one moment. At that instant her face was so imploring, so sweet, it was such a child-like and even mischievous smile; at the end of the phrase she gave me such a sly wink, unseen by all the rest, she meant to do for me completely, and it was successfully done; only it was horribly coarse.

Then the General leapt up, positively leapt up. "Alexey Ivanovitch, forgive me for beginning as I did just now. I did not mean that at all. . . . I beg you, I beseech you, I bow down before you in Russian style—you alone, you alone can save us. Mlle. de Cominges and I implore you—you understand, you understand, of course." He besought me, indicating Mlle. Blanche with his eyes. He was a very pitiful figure.

At that instant there came three subdued and respectful knocks at the door; it was opened—the corridor attendant was knocking and a few steps behind him stood Potapitch. They came with messages from Granny; they were charged to find and bring me at once. "She is angry," Potapitch informed me.

"But it is only half-past three."

"She could not get to sleep; she kept tossing about, and then at last she got up, sent for her chair and for you. She's at the front door now."

"Quelle mégère," cried De Grieux.

I did, in fact, find Granny on the steps, out of all patience at my not being there. She could not wait till four o'clock.

"Come," she cried, and we set off again to roulette.

Chapter 12

Granny was in an impatient and irritable mood; it was evident that roulette had made a deep impression on her mind. She took no notice of anything else and was altogether absent-minded. For instance, she asked me no questions on the road as she had done before. Seeing a luxurious carriage whirling by, she was on the point of raising her hand and asking: What is it? Whose is it?—but I believe she did not hear what I answered: her absorption was continually interrupted by abrupt and impatient gesticulations. When I pointed out to her Baron and Baroness Burmerhelm, who were approaching the Casino, she looked absent-mindedly at them and said, quite indifferently, "Ah!" and, turning round quickly to Potapitch and Marfa, who were walking behind her, snapped out to them—

"Why are you hanging upon us? We can't take you every time! Go home! You and I are enough," she added, when they had hurriedly turned and gone home.

They were already expecting Granny at the Casino. They immediately made room for her in the same place, next to the croupier. I fancy that these croupiers, who are always so strictly decorous and appear to be ordinary officials who are absolutely indifferent as to whether the bank wins or loses, are by no means so unconcerned at the bank's losses and, of course, receive instructions for attracting players and for augmenting the profits—for which they doubtless receive prizes and bonuses. They looked upon Granny, anyway, as their prey.

Then just what we had expected happened.

This was how it was.

Granny pounced at once on *zéro* and immediately ordered me to stake twelve friedrichs d'or. She staked once, twice, three times—*zéro* never turned up.

"Put it down! Put it down!" Granny nudged me, impatiently. I obeyed.

"How many times have we staked?" she asked at last, grinding her teeth with impatience.

"I have staked twelve times, Granny. I have put down a hundred and forty-four friedrichs d'or. I tell you, Granny, very likely till evening . . ."

"Hold your tongue!" Granny interrupted. "Stake on *zéro*, and stake at once a thousand gulden on red. Here, take the note."

Red won, and *zéro* failed once more; a thousand gulden was gained.

"You see, you see!" whispered Granny, "we have gained almost all that we have lost. Stake again on *zéro*; we'll stake ten times more and then give it up."

But the fifth time Granny was thoroughly sick of it.

"The devil take that filthy *zéro*. Come, stake the whole four thousand gulden on the red," she commanded me.

"Granny! it will be so much; why, what if red does not turn up?" I besought her; but Granny almost beat me. (Indeed, she nudged me so violently that she might almost be said to have attacked me.) There was no help for it, I staked on red the whole four thousand won that morning. The wheel turned. Granny sat calmly and proudly erect, never doubting that she would certainly win.

"*Zéro!*" boomed the croupier.

At first Granny did not understand, but when she saw the croupier scoop up her four thousand gulden together with everything on the table, and learned that *zéro*, which had not turned up for so long and on which we had staked in vain almost two hundred friedrichs d'or, had, as though to spite her, turned up just as Granny was abusing it, she groaned and flung up her hands in view of the whole hall. People around actually laughed.

"Holy saints! The cursed thing has turned up!" Granny wailed, "the hateful, hateful thing! That's your doing! It's all your doing"—she pounced upon me furiously, pushing me. "It was you persuaded me."

"Granny, I talked sense to you; how can I answer for chance?"

"I'll chance you," she whispered angrily. "Go away."

"Good-bye, Granny." I turned to go away.

"Alexey Ivanovitch, Alexey Ivanovitch! stop. Where are you off to? Come, what's the matter, what's the matter? Ach, he's in a rage! Stupid, come, stay, stay; come, don't be angry; I am a fool myself! Come, tell me what are we to do now!"

"I won't undertake to tell you, Granny, because you will blame me. Play for yourself, tell me and I'll put down the stakes."

"Well, well! Come, stake another four thousand gulden on red! Here, take my pocket-book." She took it out of her pocket and gave it me. "Come, make haste and take it, there's twenty thousand roubles sterling in it."

"Granny," I murmured, "such stakes . . ."

"As sure as I am alive, I'll win it back. . . . Stake." We staked and lost.

"Stake, stake the whole eight!"

"You can't, Granny, four is the highest stake! . . ."

"Well, stake four!"

This time we won. Granny cheered up.

"You see, you see," she nudged me; "stake four again!" She staked—she lost; then we lost again and again.

"Granny, the whole twelve thousand is gone," I told her.

"I see it's all gone," she answered with the calm of fury, if I may so express it. "I see, my good friend, I see," she muttered, with a fixed, as it were, absent-minded stare. "Ech, as sure I am alive, stake another four thousand gulden!"

"But there's no money, Granny; there are some of our Russian five per cents. and some bills of exchange of some sort, but no money."

"And in the purse?"

"There's some small change, Granny."

"Are there any money-changers here? I was told one could change any of our notes," Granny inquired resolutely.

"Oh, as much as you like, but what you'll lose on the exchange . . . would horrify a Jew!"

"Nonsense! I'll win it all back. Take me! Call those blockheads!"

I wheeled away the chair; the porters appeared and we went out of the Casino.

"Make haste, make haste, make haste," Granny commanded. "Show us the way, Alexey Ivanovitch, and take us the nearest . . . Is it far?"

"Two steps, Granny."

But at the turning from the square into the avenue we were met by our whole party: the General, De Grieux, Mlle. Blanche and her mamma. Polina Alexandrovna was not with them, nor Mr. Astley either.

"Well! Don't stop us!" cried Granny. "Well, what do you want? I have no time to spare for you now!"

I walked behind; De Grieux ran up to me.

"She's lost all she gained this morning and twelve thousand gulden as well. We are going to change some five per cents.," I whispered to him quickly.

De Grieux stamped and ran to tell the General. We went on wheeling Granny.

"Stop, stop!" the General whispered to me frantically.

"You try stopping her," I whispered.

"Auntie!" said the General, approaching, "Auntie . . . we are just . . . we are just . . ." his voice quivered and failed him, "hiring a horse and driving into the country . . . a most exquisite view . . . the peak . . . We were coming to invite you."

"Oh, bother you and your peak." Granny waved him off irritably.

"There are trees there . . . we will have tea . . ." the General went on, utterly desperate.

"*Nous boirons du lait, sur l'herbe fraîche*," added De Grieux, with ferocious fury.

Du lait, de l'herbe fraîche, that is the Paris bourgeois notion of the ideally idyllic; that is, as we all know, his conception of *nature et la vérité!*

"Oh, go on with you and your milk! Lap it up yourself; it gives me the bellyache. And why do you pester me?" cried Granny. "I tell you I've no time to waste."

"It's here, Granny," I said; "it's here!"

We had reached the house where the bank was. I went in to change the notes; Granny was left waiting at the entrance; De Grieux, the General and Blanche stood apart waiting, not knowing what to do. Granny looked wrathfully at them, and they walked away in the direction of the Casino.

They offered me such ruinous terms that I did not accept them, and went back to Granny for instructions.

"Ah, the brigands!" she cried, flinging up her hands. "Well, never mind! Change it," she cried resolutely; "stay, call the banker out to me!"

"One of the clerks, Granny, do you mean?"

"Yes, a clerk, it's all the same. Ach, the brigands!"

The clerk consented to come when he learned that it was an invalid and aged countess, unable to come in, who was asking for him. Granny spent a long time loudly and angrily reproaching him for swindling her, and haggled with him in a mixture of Russian, French and German, while I came to the rescue in translating. The grave clerk listened to us in silence and shook his head. He looked at Granny with an intent stare that was hardly respectful; at last he began smiling.

"Well, get along with you," cried Granny. "Choke yourself with the money! Change it with him, Alexey Ivanovitch; there's no time to waste, or we would go elsewhere. . . ."

"The clerk says that other banks give even less."

I don't remember the sums exactly, but the banker's charges were terrible. I received close upon twelve thousand florins in gold and notes, took the account and carried it to Granny.

"Well, well, well, it's no use counting it," she said, with a wave of her hand. "Make haste, make haste, make haste!

"I'll never stake again on that damned *zéro* nor on the red either," she pronounced, as she was wheeled up to the Casino.

This time I did my very utmost to impress upon her the necessity of staking smaller sums, trying to persuade her that with the change of luck she would always be able to increase her stake. But she was so impatient that, though she agreed at first, it was impossible to restrain her when the play had begun; as soon as she had won a stake of ten, of twenty friedrichs d'or——

"There, you see, there, you see," she would begin nudging me; "there, you see, we've won; if only we had staked four thousand instead of ten, we should have won four thousand, but as it is what's the good? It's all your doing, all your doing!"

And, vexed as I felt, watching her play, I made up my mind at last to keep quiet and to give no more advice.

Suddenly De Grieux skipped up.

The other two were close by; I noticed Mlle. Blanche standing on one side with her mother, exchanging amenities with the Prince. The General was obviously out of favour, almost banished. Blanche would not even look at him, though he was doing his utmost to cajole her! The poor General! He flushed and grew pale by turns, trembled and could not even follow Granny's play. Blanche and the Prince finally went away; the General ran after them.

"Madame, madame," De Grieux whispered in a honeyed voice to Granny, squeezing his way close up to her ear. "Madame, such stakes do not answer. . . . No, no, it's impossible . . ." he said, in broken Russian. "No!"

"How, then? Come, show me!" said Granny, turning to him.

De Grieux babbled something rapidly in French, began excitedly advising, said she must wait for a chance, began reckoning some numbers. . . . Granny did not understand a word. He kept turning to me, for me to translate; tapped the table with his fingers, pointed; finally took a pencil and was about to reckon something on paper. At last Granny lost patience.

"Come, get away, get away! You keep talking nonsense! 'Madame, madame,' he doesn't understand it himself; go away."

"*Mais, madame,*" De Grieux murmured, and he began once more showing and explaining.

"Well, stake once as he says," Granny said to me; "let us see: perhaps it really will answer."

All De Grieux wanted was to dissuade her from staking large sums; he suggested that she should stake on numbers, either individually or collectively. I staked as he directed, a friedrich d'or on each of the odd numbers in the first twelve and five friedrichs d'or respectively on the groups of numbers from twelve to eighteen and from eighteen to twenty-four, staking in all sixteen friedrichs d'or.

The wheel turned.

"*Zéro!*" cried the croupier.

We had lost everything.

"You blockhead!" cried Granny, addressing De Grieux. "You scoundrelly Frenchman! So this is how he advises, the monster. Go away, go away! He knows nothing about it and comes fussing round!"

Fearfully offended, De Grieux shrugged his shoulders, looked contemptuously at Granny, and walked away. He felt ashamed of having interfered; he had been in too great a hurry.

An hour later, in spite of all our efforts, we had lost everything.

"Home," cried Granny.

She did not utter a single word till we got into the avenue. In the avenue and approaching the hotel she began to break into exclamations—

"What a fool! What a silly fool! You're an old fool, you are!"

As soon as we got to her apartments—

"Tea!" cried Granny. "And pack up at once! We are going!"

"Where does your honour mean to go?" Marfa was beginning.

"What has it to do with you? Mind your own business! Potapitch, pack up everything: all the luggage. We are going back to Moscow. I have thrown away fifteen thousand roubles!"

"Fifteen thousand, madame! My God!" Potapitch cried, flinging up his hands with deep feeling, probably meaning to humour her.

"Come, come, you fool! He is beginning to whimper! Hold your tongue! Pack up! The bill, make haste, make haste!"

"The next train goes at half-past nine, Granny," I said, to check her furore.

"And what is it now?"

"Half-past seven."

"How annoying! Well, it doesn't matter! Alexey Ivanovitch, I haven't a farthing. Here are two more notes. Run there and change these for me too. Or I have nothing for the journey."

I set off. Returning to the hotel half an hour later, I found our whole party at Granny's. Learning that Granny was going off to Moscow, they seemed to be even more upset than by her losses. Even though her going might save her property, what was to become of the General? Who would pay De Grieux? Mlle. Blanche would, of course, decline to wait for Granny to die and would certainly now make up to the Prince or to somebody else. They were all standing before Granny, trying to console her and persuade her. Again Polina was not there. Granny was shouting at them furiously.

"Let me alone, you devils! What business is it of yours? Why does that goat's beard come forcing himself upon me?" she cried at De Grieux; "and you, my fine bird?" she cried, addressing Mlle. Blanche, "what are you after?"

"Diantre!" whispered Mlle. Blanche, with an angry flash of her eyes, but suddenly she burst out laughing and went out of the room.

"Elle vivra cent ans!" she called to the General, as she went out of the door.

"Ah, so you are reckoning on my death?" Granny yelled to the General. "Get away! Turn them all out, Alexey Ivanovitch! What business is it of yours? I've fooled away my own money, not yours!"

The General shrugged his shoulders, bowed and went out. De Grieux followed him.

"Call Praskovya," Granny told Marfa.

Five minutes later Marfa returned with Polina. All this time Polina had been sitting in her own room with the children, and I fancy had purposely made up her mind not to go out all day. Her face was serious, sad and anxious.

"Praskovya," began Granny, "is it true, as I learned by accident just now, that that fool, your stepfather, means to marry that silly featherhead of a Frenchwoman—an actress is she, or, something worse? Tell me, is it true?"

"I don't know anything about it for certain, Granny," answered Polina, "but from the words of Mlle. Blanche herself, who does not feel it necessary to conceal anything, I conclude . . ."

"Enough," Granny broke in vigorously, "I understand! I always reckoned that he was capable of it and I have always thought him a most foolish and feather-headed man. He thinks no end of himself, because he is a General (he was promoted from a Colonel on retiring), and he gives himself airs. I know, my good girl, how you kept sending telegram after telegram to Moscow, to ask if your old Granny would soon be laid out. They were on the look-out for my money; without money that nasty hussy, what's her name—De Cominges—wouldn't take him for her footman, especially with his false teeth. She has a lot of money herself, they say, lends at interest, has made a lot. I am not blaming you, Praskovya, it wasn't you who sent the telegrams; and I don't want to remember the past, either. I know you've got a bad temper—a wasp! You can sting to hurt; but I'm sorry for you because I was fond of your mother, Katerina. Well, you throw up everything here and come with me. You've nowhere to go, you know; and it's not fitting for you to be with them now. Stop!" cried Granny, as Polina was about to speak; "I've finished. I ask nothing of you. As you know, I have in Moscow a palace; you can have a whole storey to yourself and not come and see me for weeks at a time if my temper does not suit you! Well, will you or not?"

"Let me ask you first: do you really mean to set off at once?"

"Do you suppose I'm joking, my good girl! I've said I'm going and I'm going. I've wasted fifteen thousand roubles to-day over your damned roulette. Five years ago I promised to rebuild a wooden church with stone on my estate near Moscow, and instead of that I've thrown away my money here. Now, my girl, I'm going home to build the church."

"And the waters, Granny? You came to drink the waters?"

"Bother you and the waters, too. Don't irritate me, Praskovya; are you doing it on purpose? Tell me, will you come or not?"

"I thank you very, very much," Polina began, with feeling, "for the home you offer me. You have guessed my position to some extent. I am so grateful to you that I shall perhaps come to you soon; but now there are reasons . . . important reasons . . . and I can't decide at once, on the spur of the moment. If you were staying only a fortnight . . ."

"You mean you won't?"

"I mean I can't. Besides, in any case I can't leave my brother and sister, as . . . as . . . as it may actually happen that they may be left abandoned, so . . . if you would take me with the children, Granny, I certainly would come, and, believe me, I would repay you for it!"

she added warmly; "but without the children I can't come, Granny."

"Well, don't whimper." (Polina had no intention of whimpering—indeed, I had never seen her cry.) "Some place will be found for the chickens, my henhouse is big enough. Besides, it is time they were at school. Well, so you are not coming now! Well, Praskovya, mind! I wished for your good, but I know why you won't come! I know all about it, Praskovya. That Frenchman will bring you no good."

Polina flushed crimson. I positively shuddered. (Every one knows all about it. I am the only one to know nothing!)

"Come, come, don't frown. I am not going to say anything more. Only take care no harm comes of it, understand. You are a clever wench; I shall be sorry for you. Well, that's enough. I should not like to look on you as on the others! Go along, good-bye!"

"I'll come to see you off," said Polina.

"There's no need, don't you interfere; I am sick of you all."

Polina was kissing Granny's hand, but the latter pulled it away and kissed her on the cheek.

As she passed me, Polina looked at me quickly and immediately turned away her eyes.

"Well, good-bye to you, too. Alexey Ivanovitch, there's only an hour before the train starts, and I think you must be tired out with me. Here, take these fifty pieces of gold."

"I thank you very much, Granny; I'm ashamed . . ."

"Come, come!" cried Granny, but so vigorously and angrily that I dared say no more and took it.

"When you are running about Moscow without a job come to me: I will give you some introductions. Now, get along with you!"

I went to my room and lay down on my bed. I lay there for half an hour on my back, with my hands clasped behind my head. The catastrophe had come at last, I had something to think about. I made up my mind to talk earnestly to Polina. The nasty Frenchman! So it was true then! But what could there be at the bottom of it? Polina and De Grieux! Heavens! what a pair!

It was all simply incredible. I suddenly jumped up, beside myself, to look for Mr. Astley, and at all costs to make him speak out. No doubt in this matter, too, he knew more than I did. Mr. Astley? He was another riddle to me!

But suddenly there was a tap at my door. I looked up. It was Potapitch.

"Alexey Ivanovitch, you are wanted to come to my lady!"

"What's the matter? Is she setting off? The train does not start for twenty minutes."

"She's uneasy, she can't sit still. 'Make haste, make haste!' she says, meaning to fetch you, sir. For Christ's sake, don't delay."

I ran downstairs at once. Granny was being wheeled out into the passage, her pocket-book was in her hand.

"Alexey Ivanovitch, go on ahead; we're coming."

"Where, Granny?"

"As sure as I'm alive, I'll win it back. Come, march, don't ask questions! Does the play go on there till midnight?"

I was thunderstruck. I thought a moment, but at once made up my mind.

"Do as you please, Antonida Vassilyevna, I'm not coming."

"What's that for? What now? Have you all eaten too many pancakes, or what?"

"Do as you please, I should blame myself for it afterwards; I won't. I won't take part in it or look on at it; spare me, Antonida Vassilyevna. Here are your fifty friedrichs d'or back; good-bye!" And, laying the fifty friedrichs d'or on the little table near which Granny's chair was standing, I bowed and went out.

"What nonsense!" Granny shouted after me. "Don't come if you don't want to, I can find the way by myself! Potapitch, come with me! Come, lift me up, carry me!"

I did not find Mr. Astley and returned home. It was late, after midnight, when I learned from Potapitch how Granny's day ended. She lost all that I had changed for her that evening—that is, in Russian money, another ten thousand roubles. The little Pole, to whom she had given two friedrichs d'or the day before, had attached himself to her and had directed her play the whole time. At first, before the Pole came, she had made Potapitch put down the stakes, but soon she dismissed him; it was at that moment the Pole turned up. As ill-luck would have it, he understood Russian and babbled away in a mixture of three languages, so that they understood each other after a fashion. Granny abused him mercilessly the whole time; and though he incessantly "laid himself at his lady's feet," "yet he couldn't be compared with you, Alexey Ivanovitch," said Potapitch. "She treated you *like a gentleman,* while the other—I saw it with my own eyes, God strike me dead—stole her money off the table. She caught him at it herself twice. She did give it to him with all sorts of names, sir, even pulled his hair once, upon my word she did, so that folks were laughing round about. She's lost everything, sir, everything, all you changed for her; we brought her back here—she only asked for a drink of water, crossed herself and went to bed. She's worn out, to be sure; she fell asleep at once. God send her heavenly dreams. Och! these foreign parts!" Potapitch wound up. "I said it would lead to no good. If only we could soon be back in Moscow! We'd everything we wanted at home in Moscow: a garden, flowers such as you don't have here, fragrance, the apples are swelling, plenty of room everywhere. No, we had to come abroad. Oh, oh, oh . . ."

Chapter 13

Now almost a whole month has passed since I touched these notes of mine, which were begun under the influence of confused but intense impressions. The catastrophe which I felt to be approaching has actually come, but in a form a hundred times more violent and startling than I had expected. It has all been something strange, grotesque and even tragic—at least for me. Several things have happened to me that were almost miraculous; that is, at least, how I look upon them to this day—though from another point of view, particularly in the whirl of events in which I was involved at that time, they were only somewhat out of the common. But what is most marvellous to me is my own attitude to all these events. To this day I cannot understand myself, and it has all floated by like a dream—even my passion—it was violent and sincere, but . . . what has become of it now? It is true that sometimes the thought flashes through my brain: "Wasn't I out of my mind then, and wasn't I all that time somewhere in a madhouse and perhaps I'm there now, so that was all my fancy and still is my fancy . . ." I put my notes together and read them over. (Who knows—perhaps to convince myself that I did not write them in a madhouse.) Now I am entirely alone. Autumn is coming on and the leaves are turning yellow. I'm still in this dismal little town (oh! how dismal the little German towns are!), and instead of considering what to do next, I go on living under the influence of the sensations I have just passed through, under the influence of memories still fresh, under the influence of the whirl of events which caught me up and flung me aside again. At times I fancy that I am still caught up in that whirlwind, that that storm is still raging, carrying me along with it, and again I lose sight of all order and measure and I whirl round and round again. . . .

However, I may, perhaps, leave off whirling and settle down in a way if, so far as I can, I put clearly before my mind all the incidents of the past month. I feel drawn to my pen again. Besides, I have sometimes nothing at all to do in the evenings. I am so hard up for something to do that, odd as it seems, I even take from the scurvy lending library here the novels of Paul de Kock (in a German translation), though I can't endure them; yet I read them and wonder at myself. It is as though I were afraid of breaking the spell of the recent past by a serious book or any serious occupation. It is as though that grotesque dream, with all the impressions left by it, was so precious to me that I am afraid to let anything new touch upon it for fear it should all vanish in smoke. Is it all so precious to me? Yes, of course it is precious. Perhaps I shall remember it for forty years. . . .

And so I take up my writing again. I can give a brief account of it to some extent now: the impressions are not at all the same.

In the first place, to finish with Granny. The following day she lost everything. It was what was bound to happen. When once any one is started upon the road, it is like a man in a sledge flying down a snow mountain more and more swiftly. She played all day till eight o'clock in the evening; I was not present and only know what happened from what I was told.

Potapitch was in attendance on her at the Casino all day. Several Poles in succession guided Granny's operations in the course of the day. She began by dismissing the Pole whose hair she had pulled the day before and taking on another, but he turned out almost worse. After dismissing the second, and accepting again the first, who had never left her side, but had been squeezing himself in behind her chair and continually poking his head in during the whole period of his disgrace, she sank at last into complete despair. The second Pole also refused to move away; one stationed himself on her right and the other on her left. They were abusing one another the whole time and quarrelling over the stakes and the game, calling each other *"laidak"* and other Polish civilities, making it up again, putting down money recklessly and playing at random. When they quarrelled they put the money down regardless of each other—one, for instance, on the red and the other on the black. It ended in their completely bewildering and overwhelming Granny, so that at last, almost in tears, she appealed to the old croupier, begging him to protect her and to send them away. They were, in fact, immediately turned out in spite of their outcries and protests; they both shouted out at once and tried to prove that Granny owed them something, that she had deceived them about something and had treated them basely and dishonourably. The luckless Potapitch told me all this the same evening almost with tears, and complained that they stuffed their pockets with money, that he himself had seen them shamelessly steal and continually thrust the money in their pockets. One, for instance, would beg five friedrichs d'or for his trouble and begin putting them down on the spot side by side with Granny's stakes. Granny won, but the man shouted that his stake was the winning one and that Granny's had lost. When they were dismissed Potapitch came forward and said that their pockets were full of gold. Granny at once bade the croupier to look into it and, in spite of the outcries of the Poles (they cackled like two cocks caught in the hand), the police came forward and their pockets were immediately emptied for Granny's benefit. Granny enjoyed unmistakable prestige among the croupiers and the whole staff of the Casino all that day, until she had lost everything. By degrees her fame spread all over the town. All the visitors at the watering-place, of all nations, small and great, streamed to look on at *"une vieille comtesse russe tombée en enfance,"* who had already lost "some millions."

But Granny gained very, very little by being rescued

from the two Poles. They were at once replaced by a third, who spoke perfectly pure Russian and was dressed like a gentleman, though he did look like a flunkey with a huge moustache and a sense of his own importance. He, too "laid himself at his lady's feet and kissed them," but behaved haughtily to those about him, was despotic over the play; in fact, immediately behaved like Granny's master rather than her servant. Every minute, at every turn in the game, he turned to her and swore with awful oaths that he was himself a "*pan* of good position," and that he wouldn't take a kopeck of Granny's money. He repeated this oath so many times that Granny was completely intimidated. But as this *pan* certainly seemed at first to improve her luck, Granny was not willing to abandon him on her own account. An hour later the two Poles who had been turned out of the Casino turned up behind Granny's chair again, and again proffered their services if only to run errands for her. Potapitch swore that the "*pan* of good position" winked at them and even put something in their hands. As Granny had no dinner and could not leave her chair, one of the Poles certainly was of use: he ran off once to the dining-room of the Casino and brought her a cup of broth and afterwards some tea. They both ran about, however. But towards the end of the day, when it became evident to everyone that she would stake her last banknote, there were behind her chair as many as six Poles who had never been seen or heard of before. When Granny was playing her last coin, they not only ceased to obey her, but took no notice of her whatever, squeezed their way up to the table in front of her, snatched the money themselves, put down the stakes and made their own play, shouted and quarrelled, talked to the "*pan* of good position" as to one of themselves, while the "*pan* of good position" himself seemed almost oblivious of Granny's existence. Even when Granny, after losing everything, was returning after eight o'clock to the hotel, three or four Poles ran at the side of her bath-chair, still unable to bring themselves to leave her; they kept shouting at the top of their voices, declaring in a hurried gabble that Granny had cheated them in some way and must give them something. They followed her in this way right up to the hotel, from which they were at last driven away with blows.

By Potapitch's reckoning Granny had lost in all ninety

thousand roubles that day, apart from what she had lost the day before. All her notes, her exchequer bonds, all the shares she had with her, she had changed, one after another. I marvelled how she could have stood those seven or eight hours sitting there in her chair and scarcely leaving the table, but Potapitch told me that three or four times she had begun winning considerably; and, carried on by fresh hope, she could not tear herself away. But gamblers know how a man can sit for almost twenty-four hours at cards, without looking to right or to left.

Meanwhile, very critical events were taking place all that day at the hotel. In the morning, before eleven o'clock, when Granny was still at home, our people— that is, the General and De Grieux—made up their minds to take the final step. Learning that Granny had given up all idea of setting off, but was going back to the Casino, they went in full conclave (all but Polina) to talk things over with her finally and even *openly*. The General, trembling and with a sinking heart in view of the awful possibilities for himself, overdid it. After spending half an hour in prayers and entreaties and making a clean breast of everything—that is, of all his debts and even his passion for Mlle. Blanche (he quite lost his head), the General suddenly adopted a menacing tone and even began shouting and stamping at Granny; cried that she was disgracing their name, had become a scandal to the whole town, and finally . . . finally: "You are shaming the Russian name," cried the General, and he told her that the police would be called in! Granny finally drove him from her with a stick (an actual stick). The General and De Grieux consulted once or twice that morning, and the question that agitated them was whether it were not possible in some way to bring in the police, on the plea that an unfortunate but venerable old lady, sinking into her dotage, was gambling away her whole fortune, and so on; whether, in fact, it would be possible to put her under any sort of supervision or restraint. . . . But De Grieux only shrugged his shoulders and laughed in the General's face, as the latter pranced up and down his study talking excitedly. Finally, De Grieux went off with a wave of his hand. In the evening we learned that he had left the hotel altogether, after having been in very earnest and mysterious confabulation with Mlle. Blanche. As for Mlle. Blanche, she had taken her measures early in the morning: she threw the General over completely and would not even admit him to her presence. When the General ran to the Casino in search of her and met her arm-in-arm with the Prince, neither she nor Madame de Cominges deigned to notice him. The Prince did not bow to him either. Mlle. Blanche spent that whole day hard at work upon the Prince, trying to force from him a definite declaration. But alas! she was cruelly deceived in her reckoning! This little catastrophe took place in the evening. It suddenly came out that he was as poor as a church mouse, and, what is more, was himself reckoning on borrowing from her on an I O U to try his luck at roulette. Blanche turned him out indignantly and locked herself up in her room.

On the morning of that day I went to Mr. Astley—or, to be more exact, I went in search of Mr. Astley, but could find him nowhere. He was not at home, or in the park, or in the Casino. He was not dining at his hotel that day. It was past four o'clock when I suddenly saw him walking from the railway station towards the Hotel d'Angleterre. He was in a hurry and was very much preoccupied, though it was hard to trace any anxiety or any perturbation whatever in his face. He held out his hand to me cordially, with his habitual exclamation "Ah!" but without stopping walked on with rather a rapid step. I attached myself to him, but he managed to answer me in such a way that I did not succeed in even asking him about anything. Moreover, I felt, for some reason, ashamed to begin speaking of Polina; he did not ask a word about her. I told him about Granny. He listened attentively and seriously and shrugged his shoulders.

"She will gamble away everything," I observed.

"Oh, yes," he answered; "she went in to play just as I was going away, and afterwards I learnt for a fact that she had lost everything. If there were time I would look in at the Casino, for it is curious."

"Where have you been?" I cried, wondering that I had not asked before.

"I've been in Frankfurt."

"On business?"

"Yes, on business."

Well, what more was there for me to ask? I did, however, continue walking beside him, but he suddenly turned into the Hôtel des Quatre Saisons, nodded to me and van-

ished. As I walked home I gradually realized that if I had
talked to him for a couple of hours I should have learnt
absolutely nothing, because . . . I had nothing to ask
him! Yes, that was so, of course! I could not possibly
formulate my question.

All that day Polina spent walking with the children
and their nurse in the park, or sitting at home. She had
for a long time past avoided the General, and scarcely
spoke to him about anything—about anything serious, at
any rate. I had noticed that for a long time past. But
knowing what a position the General was in to-day, I
imagined that he could hardly pass her over—that is,
there could not but be an important conversation about
family affairs between them. When, however, I returned
to the hotel, after my conversation with Mr. Astley, I
met Polina with the children. There was an expression of
the most unruffled calm on her face, as though she alone
had remained untouched by the family tempest. She nodded in response to my bow. I returned home feeling quite
malignant.

I had, of course, avoided seeing her and had seen nothing of her since the incident with the Burmerhelms. There
was some affectation and pose in this; but as time went
on, I felt more and more genuinely indignant. Even if she
did not care for me in the least, she should not, I
thought, have trampled on my feelings like that and have
received my declarations so contemptuously. She knew
that I really loved her; she admitted me, she allowed me
to speak like that! It is true that it had begun rather
strangely. Some time before, long ago, in fact, two months
before, I began to notice that she wanted to make me her
friend, her *confidant*, and indeed was in a way testing me.
But somehow this did not come off then; instead of that
there remained the strange relations that existed between
us; that is how it was I began to speak to her like that.
But if my love repelled her, why did she not directly forbid me to speak of it?

She did not forbid me; indeed she sometimes provoked
me to talk of it and . . . and, of course, she did this for
fun. I know for certain. I noticed it unmistakably—it was
agreeable to her to listen and to work me up to a state
of misery, to wound me by some display of the utmost
contempt and disregard. And, of course, she knew that
I could not exist without her. It was three days since the

affair with the Baron and I could not endure our separation any longer. When I met her just now near the Casino, my heart throbbed so that I turned pale. But she could not get on without me, either! She needed me and—surely, surely not as a buffoon, a clown?

She had a secret—that was clear! Her conversation with Granny had stabbed my heart. Why, I had urged her a thousand times to be open with me, and she knew that I was ready to give my life for her. But she always put me off, almost with contempt, or had asked of me, instead of the sacrifice of my life, such pranks as the one with the Baron!

Was not that enough to make one indignant? Could that Frenchman be all the world to her? And Mr. Astley? But at that point the position became utterly incomprehensible—and meanwhile, my God! what agonies I went through!

On getting home, in an access of fury I snatched up my pen and scribbled the following letter to her—

"Polina Alexandrovna, I see clearly that the *dénouement* is at hand which will affect you also. I repeat for the last time: do you need my life or not? If I can be of use in *any way whatever*, dispose of me as you think fit, and I will meanwhile remain in my room and not go out at all. If you need me, write to me or send for me."

I sealed up this note and sent it off by the corridor attendant, instructing him to give it into her hands. I expected no answer, but three minutes later the attendant returned with the message that "she sent her greetings."

It was past six when I was summoned to the General. He was in his study, dressed as though he were on the point of going out. His hat and coat were lying on the sofa. It seemed to me as I went in that he was standing in the middle of the room with his legs wide apart and his head hanging, talking aloud to himself. But as soon as he saw me, he rushed at me almost crying out, so that I involuntarily stepped back and was almost running away, but he seized me by both hands and drew me to the sofa; sat down on the sofa himself, made me sit down in an armchair just opposite himself, and, keeping tight hold of my hand, with trembling lips and with tears suddenly glistening on his eyelashes, began speaking in an imploring voice.

"Alexey Ivanovitch, save, save me, spare me."

It was a long while before I could understand. He kept talking and talking and talking, continually repeating, "Spare me, spare me!" At last I guessed that he expected something in the way of advice from me; or, rather, abandoned by all in his misery and anxiety, he had thought of me and had sent for me, simply to talk and talk and talk to me.

He was mad, or at any rate utterly distraught. He clasped his hands and was on the point of dropping on his knees before me to implore me (What do you suppose?) to go at once to Mlle. Blanche and to beseech, to urge her to return to him and marry him.

"Upon my word, General," I cried; "why, Mlle. Blanche is perhaps scarcely aware of my existence. What can I do?"

But it was vain to protest; he didn't understand what was said to him. He fell to talking about Granny, too, but with terrible incoherence; he was still harping on the idea of sending for the police.

"Among us, among us," he began, suddenly boiling over with indignation; "among us, in a well-ordered state, in fact, where there is a Government in control of things, such old women would have been put under guardianship at once! Yes, my dear sir, yes," he went on, suddenly dropping into a scolding tone, jumping up from his chair and pacing about the room; "you may not be aware of the fact, honoured sir," he said, addressing some imaginary "honoured sir" in the corner, "so let me tell you . . . yes . . . among us such old women are kept in order, kept in order; yes, indeed. . . . Oh, damn it all!"

And he flung himself on the sofa again, and a minute later, almost sobbing, gasping for breath, hastened to tell me that Mlle. Blanche would not marry him because Granny had come instead of the telegram, and that now it was clear he would not come into the inheritance. He imagined that I knew nothing of this till then. I began to speak of De Grieux; he waved his hand: "He has gone away! Everything of mine he has in pawn; I'm stripped of everything! That money you brought . . . that money —I don't know how much there is, I think seven hundred francs are left and that's enough, that's all and what's to come—I don't know, I don't know! . . ."

"How will you pay your hotel bill?" I cried in alarm; "and . . . afterwards what will you do?"

He looked at me pensively, but I fancy he did not understand and perhaps did not hear what I said. I tried to speak of Polina Alexandrovna, of the children; he hurriedly answered: "Yes! yes!" but at once fell to talking of the Prince again, saying that Blanche would go away with him now and "then . . . then, what am I to do. Alexey Ivanovitch?" he asked, addressing me suddenly. "I vow, by God! I don't know what to do; tell me, isn't this ingratitude? Isn't this ingratitude?"

Finally he dissolved into floods of tears.

There was no doing anything with such a man; it would be dangerous to leave him alone, too—something might happen to him. I got rid of him somehow, but let nurse know she must look in upon him pretty frequently, and also spoke to the corridor attendant, a very sensible fellow; he, too, promised me to keep an eye on the General.

I had hardly left the General when Potapitch came to summon me to Granny. It was eight o'clock and she had only just come back from the Casino after losing everything. I went to her; the old lady was sitting in an armchair, utterly worn out and evidently ill. Marfa was giving her a cup of tea and almost forcing her to drink it. And Granny's tone and voice were utterly changed.

"Good-day, Alexey Ivanovitch, my good sir," she said, bending her head slowly, and with dignity; "excuse me for troubling you once more, you must excuse an old woman. I have left everything behind there, my friend, nearly a hundred thousand roubles. You did well not to come with me yesterday. Now I have no money, not a farthing. I don't want to delay a moment, at half-past nine I'm setting off. I have sent to that Englishman of yours—what's his name, Astley—I want to ask him to lend me three thousand francs for a week. So you must persuade him not to take it amiss and refuse. I am still fairly well off, my friend. I have still three villages and two houses. And there is still some money. I didn't bring it all with me. I tell you this that he may not feel any doubts . . . Ah, here he is! One can see he is a nice man."

Mr. Astley had hastened to come at Granny's first summons. With no hesitation and without wasting words he promptly counted out three thousand francs for an I O U which Granny signed. When this business was settled he made haste to take his leave and go away.

"And now you can go, too, Alexey Ivanovitch. I have only a little over an hour left. I want to lie down: my bones ache. Don't be hard on an old fool like me. Henceforward I won't blame young people for being flighty, and it would be a sin for me now to blame that luckless fellow, your General, either. I won't give him any money, though, as he wants me to, because—to my thinking he is utterly silly; only, old fool as I am, I've no more sense than he. Verily God seeks out and punishes pride, even in old age. Well, good-bye. Marfa, lift me up!"

I wanted to see Granny off, however. What's more, I was in a state of suspense; I kept expecting that in another minute something would happen. I could not sit quietly in my room. I went out into the corridor, even for a moment went for a saunter along the avenue. My letter to her had been clear and decisive and the present catastrophe was, of course, a final one. I heard in the hotel that De Grieux had left. If she rejected me as a friend, perhaps she would not reject me as a servant. I was necessary to her, I was of use to her, if only to run her errands, it was bound to be so!

When the train was due to start I ran to the station and saw Granny into the train. Her whole party were together, in a special reserved compartment. "Thank you, my good friend, for your disinterested sympathy," she said, at parting from me; "and tell Praskovya, in reference to what we were discussing yesterday, I shall expect her."

I went home. Passing the General's rooms I met the old nurse and inquired after the General. "Oh, he's all right, sir," she answered me dolefully. I went in, however, but stood still in positive amazement. Mlle. Blanche and the General were both laughing heartily. Madame de Cominges was sitting on the sofa close by. The General was evidently beside himself with delight. He was murmuring incoherently and going off into prolonged fits of nervous laughter, during which his face was puckered with innumerable wrinkles and his eyes disappeared from sight. Afterwards I learnt from Blanche herself that, having dismissed the Prince and having heard how the General was weeping, she had taken it into her head to comfort him by going to see him for a minute. But the poor General did not know that at that time his fate was decided, and that Mlle. Blanche had already packed to set off for Paris by the first train next morning.

Stopping in the doorway of the General's study, I changed my mind and went away unnoticed. Going up to my own room and opening the door, I suddenly noticed a figure in the half-darkness sitting on a chair in the corner by the window. She did not get up when I went in. I went up quickly, looked, and—my heart stood still: it was Polina.

Chapter 14

I positively cried out aloud.

"What is it? What is it?" she asked me strangely. She was pale and looked gloomy.

"You ask what is it? You? Here in my room!"

"If I come, then I come *altogether*. That's my way. You'll see that directly; light the candle."

I lighted a candle. She got up, went up to the table, and put before me an open letter.

"Read it," she ordered me.

"It's—it's De Grieux's handwriting," I cried, taking the letter. My hands trembled and the lines danced before my eyes. I have forgotten the exact wording of the letter, but here is the main drift of it, if not the actual words:

"Mademoiselle," wrote De Grieux, "an unfortunate circumstance compels me to go away at once. You have, no doubt, observed that I have purposely avoided a final explanation with you until such time as the whole position might be cleared up. The arrival of your old relation (*de la vieille dame*) and her absurd behaviour have put an end to my doubts. The unsettled state of my own affairs forbids me to cherish further the sweet hopes which I permitted myself to indulge for some time. I regret the past, but I trust that you will not detect in my behaviour anything unworthy of a gentleman and an honest man (*gentilhomme et honnête homme*). Having lost almost all my money in loans to your stepfather, I find myself compelled to make the utmost use of what is left to me; I have already sent word to my friend in Petersburg to arrange at once for the sale of the estates he has mortgaged to me; knowing, however, that your frivolous stepfather has squandered your private fortune I have determined to forgive him fifty thousand francs, and I am returning him part of my claims on his property equivalent to that sum, so that you are now put in a position to regain all that you have lost by demanding the property from him by legal process. I hope, Mademoiselle, that in the present position of affairs my action will be very advantageous to you. I hope, too, that by this action I am fully performing the duty of a man and a gentleman. Rest assured that your memory is imprinted upon my heart for ever."

"Well, that's all clear," I said, turning to Polina; "surely you could have expected nothing else," I added, with indignation.

"I expected nothing," she answered, with apparent composure, though there was a tremor in her voice. "I had made up my mind long ago; I read his mind and knew what he was thinking. He thought that I was trying—that I should insist . . ." (She broke off without finishing her sentence, bit her lips and was silent.) "I purposely doubled my scorn towards him," she began again. "I waited to see what was coming from him. If a telegram had come telling of the inheritance I'd have flung him the money borrowed from that idiot, my stepfather, and would have sent him about his business. He has been hateful to me for ages and ages. Oh! he was not the same man! A thousand times over, I tell you, he was different! but now, now . . . Oh, with what happiness I could fling that fifty thousand in his nasty face and spit and stamp . . ."

"But the security, the I O U for that fifty thousand, is in the General's hands. Take it and return it to De Grieux."

"Oh, that's not the same thing, that's not the same thing . . ."

"Yes, that's true, it's not the same thing. Besides, what is the General capable of now? And Granny!" I cried suddenly.

Polina looked at me, as it were absent-mindedly and impatiently.

"Why Granny?" asked Polina, with vexation. "I can't go to her . . . And I don't want to ask any one's pardon," she added irritably.

"What's to be done!" I cried, "and how, oh, how could you love De Grieux! Oh, the scoundrel, the scoundrel! If you like I will kill him in a duel! Where is he now?"

"He's at Frankfurt, and will be there three days."

"One word from you and I'll set off to-morrow by the first train," I said, with stupid enthusiasm.

She laughed.

"Why, he'll say, maybe: 'Give me back the fifty thousand francs first.' Besides, what should you fight him for? . . . What nonsense it is!"

"But where, where is one to get that fifty thousand francs?" I repeated, grinding my teeth as though it had been possible to pick them up from the floor. "I say—Mr. Astley," I suggested, turning to her with a strange idea dawning upon me.

Her eyes flashed.

"What, do you mean to say *you yourself* want me to turn from you to that Englishman!" she said, looking in my face with a searching glance and smiling bitterly. For the first time in her life she addressed me in the second person singular.

I believe she was giddy with emotion at the moment, and all at once she sat down on the sofa as though she were exhausted.

It was as though I had been struck by a flash of lightning. I stood up and could not believe my eyes, could not believe my ears! Why, then she loved me! She had come to me and not to Mr. Astley!

She, she, a young girl, had come to my room in a hotel, so she had utterly compromised herself by her own act, and I, I was standing before her and still did not understand.

One wild idea flashed through my mind.

"Polina, give me only one hour. Stay here only one hour and . . . I'll come back. That's . . . that's essential! You shall see! Be here, be here!"

And I ran out of the room, not responding to her amazed questioning look; she called something after me but I did not turn back.

Sometimes the wildest idea, the most apparently impossible thought, takes possession of one's mind so strongly that one accepts it at last as something substantial . . . more than that, if the idea is associated with a strong passionate desire, then sometimes one will accept it at last as something fated, inevitable, predestined—as something bound to be, and bound to happen. Perhaps there is something else in it, some combination of presentiments, some extraordinary effort of will, self-poisoning by one's own fancy—or something else—I don't know what, but on that evening (which I shall never in my life forget) something marvellous happened to me. Though it is quite justified by the laws of arithmetic, nevertheless it is a marvel to me to this day. And why, why had that conviction so long before taken such firm and deep root in my mind? I had certainly thought about it—I repeat—not as a chance among others which might or might not come to pass, but as something which was absolutely bound to happen!

It was a quarter past ten. I went into the Casino with a confident expectation and at the same time with an excitement I had never experienced before. There were still a good many people in the gambling hall, though not half as many as in the morning.

Between ten and eleven there are still to be found in the gambling halls the genuine desperate gamblers for whom nothing exists at a spa but roulette, who have come for that alone, who scarcely notice what is going on around them and take no interest in anything during the whole season, but play from morning till night and would be ready perhaps to play all night till dawn, too, if it were possible. And they always disperse with annoyance when at twelve o'clock the roulette hall is closed. And when the senior croupier announces, just before midnight. *"Les trois derniers coups, messieurs,"* they are ready to stake on those last three strokes all they have in their pockets—and do, in fact, lose most at that time. I went up to the very table where Granny had sat that day. It was not crowded, and so I soon took my place at the table standing. Exactly before me was the word *Passe* scrawled on the green cloth.

Passe is the series of numbers from nineteen inclusive to thirty-six.

The first series of numbers from one to eighteen inclusive is called *manque;* but what was that to me? I was not calculating, I had not even heard what had been the winning number last, and I did not ask about it when I began to play—as every player of any prudence would do.

I pulled out all my twenty friedrichs d'or and staked them on *passe,* the word which lay before me.

"*Vingt-deux,*" cried the croupier.

I had won and again staked all: including my winnings.

"*Trente-et-un,*" cried the croupier.

I had won again. I had in all eighty friedrichs d'or. I staked the whole of that sum on the twelve middle numbers (my winnings would be three to one, but the chances were two to one against me). The wheel rotated and stopped at twenty-four. I was passed three rolls each of fifty friedrichs d'or in paper and ten gold coins; I had now two hundred friedrichs d'or.

I was as though in delirium and I moved the whole heap of gold to red—and suddenly thought better of it. And for the only time that whole evening, all the time I was playing, I felt chilled with terror and a shudder made my arms and legs tremble, I felt with horror and instantly realized what losing would mean for me now! My whole life was at stake.

"*Rouge,*" cried the croupier, and I drew a breath; fiery pins and needles were tingling all over my body. I was paid in banknotes. It came to four thousand florins and eighty friedrichs d'or (I could still keep count at that stage).

Then, I remember, I staked two thousand florins on the twelve middle numbers, and lost: I staked my gold, the eighty friedrichs d'or, and lost. I was seized with fury: I snatched up the two hundred florins I had left and staked them on the first twelve numbers—haphazard, at random, without thinking! There was, however, an instant of suspense, like, perhaps, the feeling experienced by Madame Blanchard when she flew from a balloon in Paris to the earth.

"*Quatre!*" cried the croupier.

Now with my stake I had six thousand florins. I looked triumphant already. I was afraid of nothing—nothing, and staked four thousand florins on black. Nine people followed my example and staked on black. The croupiers exchanged glances and said something to one another. People were talking all round in suspense.

Black won. I don't remember my winnings after, nor what I staked on. I only remember as though in a dream that I won, I believe, sixteen thousand florins; suddenly three unlucky turns took twelve thousand from it; then I staked the last four thousand on *passe* (but I scarcely felt anything as I did so; I simply waited in a mechanical, senseless way)—and again I won; then I won four times running. I only remember that I gathered up money in thousands; I remember, too, that the middle twelve won most often and I kept to it. It turned up with a sort of regularity, certainly three or four times in succession, then it did not turn up twice running and then it followed three or four times in succession. Such astonishing regularity is sometimes met with in streaks, and that is what throws inveterate gamblers who calculate with a pencil in their hands out of their reckoning. And what horrible ironies of fate happen sometimes in such cases!

I believe not more than half an hour had passed since I came into the room, when suddenly the croupier informed me that I had won thirty thousand florins, and as the bank did not meet claims for a larger sum at one time the roulette would be closed till next morning. I snatched up all my gold, dropped it into my pockets, snatched up all my notes, and at once went into the other room where there was another roulette table; the whole crowd streamed after me; there at once a place was cleared for me and I fell to staking again haphazard without reckoning. I don't understand what saved me!

At times, however, a glimmer of prudence began to dawn upon my mind. I clung to certain numbers and combinations, but soon abandoned them and staked almost unconsciously. I must have been very absent-minded; I remember the croupiers several times corrected me. I made several gross mistakes. My temples were soaked with sweat and my hands were shaking. The Poles ran up, too, with offers of their services, but I listened to no one. My luck was unbroken! Suddenly there were sounds of loud talk and laughter, and every one cried "Bravo, bravo!" some even clapped their hands. Here, too, I collected three hundred thousand florins, and the bank closed till next day.

"Go away, go away," a voice whispered on my right.

It was a Frankfurt Jew; he was standing beside me all the time, and I believe sometimes helped me in my play.

"For goodness' sake go," another voice whispered in my left ear.

I took a hurried glance. It was a lady about thirty, very

soberly and quietly dressed, with a tired, pale, sickly face which yet bore traces of having once been beautiful. At that moment I was stuffing my pockets with the notes, which I crumpled up anyhow, and gathering up the gold that lay on the table. Snatching up the last roll of notes, I succeeded in putting it into the pale lady's hands quite without attracting notice; I had an intense desire to do so at the time, and I remember her pale slim fingers pressed my hand warmly in token of gratitude. All that took place in one instant.

Having collected quickly all my winnings I went quickly to the *trente et quarante*.

Trente et quarante is frequented by the aristocratic public. Unlike roulette, it is a game of cards. Here the bank will pay up to a hundred thousand thalers at once. The largest stake is here also four thousand florins. I knew nothing of the game, and scarcely knew how to bet on it, except the red and the black upon which one can bet in this game too. And I stuck to red and black. The whole Casino crowded round. I don't remember whether I once thought of Polina all this time. I was experiencing an overwhelming enjoyment in scooping up and taking away the notes which grew up in a heap before me.

It seemed as though fate were urging me on. This time, as luck would have it, a circumstance occurred which, however, is fairly frequent in the game. Chance favours red, for instance, ten or even fifteen times in succession. I had heard two days before that in the previous week red had turned up twenty-two times in succession; it was something which had never been remembered in roulette, and it was talked of with amazement. Every one, of course, abandoned red at once, and after the tenth time, for instance, scarcely any one dared to stake on it. But none of the experienced players staked on black either. The experienced gambler knows what is meant by this "freak of chance." It would mean that after red had won sixteen times, at the seventeenth time the luck would infallibly fall on black. Novices at play rush to this conclusion in crowds, double and treble their stakes, and lose terribly.

But, noticing that red had turned up seven times running, by strange perversity I staked on it. I am convinced that vanity was half responsible for it; I wanted to impress the spectators by taking a mad risk, and—oh, the strange sensation—I remember distinctly that, quite apart from the promptings of vanity, I was possessed by an intense craving for risk. Perhaps passing through so many sensations my soul was not satisfied but only irritated by them and craved still more sensation—and stronger and stronger ones—till utterly exhausted. And, truly I am not lying, if the regulations had allowed me to stake fifty thousand florins at once, I should certainly have staked them. People around shouted that it was madness—that red had won fourteen times already!

"Monsieur a gagné déjà cent mille florins," I heard a voice say near me.

I suddenly came to myself. What? I had won during that evening a hundred thousand florins! And what more did I want? I fell on my banknotes, crumpled them up in my pockets without counting them, scooped up all my gold, all my rolls of notes, and ran out of the Casino. Every one was laughing as I went through the room, looking at my bulging pockets and at the way I staggered under the weight of gold. I think it weighed over twenty pounds. Several hands were held out to me; I gave it away in handfuls as I snatched it up. Two Jews stopped me at the outer door.

"You are bold—you are very bold," they said to me, "but be sure to go away to-morrow as soon as possible, or else you will lose it all—you will lose it all. . . ."

I didn't listen to them. The avenue was so dark that I could not see my hand before my face. It was half a mile to the hotel. I had never been afraid of thieves or robbers even as a small boy; I did not think of them now either. I don't remember what I thought of on the road; I had no thoughts. I was only aware of an immense enjoyment —success, victory, power—I don't know how to express it. Polina's image hovered before my mind too; I remembered her and was conscious I was going to her; I should be with her in a moment, should be telling her and showing her . . . But I hardly remembered what she had said to me earlier, and why I had gone, and all the sensations I had felt, not more than an hour and a half before, seemed to me something long past, transformed, grown old—something of which we should say no more because everything now would begin anew. Almost at the end of the avenue a sudden panic came upon me. What if I were robbed and murdered at this instant? At every step my panic grew greater. I almost ran. Suddenly, at the end of the avenue there was the glare of our hotel with its many windows lighted up—thank God, home!

I ran up to my storey and rapidly opened the door. Polina was there, sitting on the sofa with her arms crossed, with a lighted candle before her. She looked at me with amazement, and no doubt at that moment I must have looked rather strange. I stood before her and began flinging down all my piles of money on the table.

Chapter 15

I remember she fixed a very intent look on my face, but without even moving from her seat or changing her position.

"I've won two hundred thousand francs!" I cried, as I flung down the last roll of notes.

The huge bundles of notes and piles of gold filled up the whole table; I could not take my eyes off it. At moments I completely forgot Polina. At one moment I began arranging the heap of banknotes, folding them up together, at the next I began undoing the rolls of gold and heaping them up in one pile; then I abandoned it all and strode rapidly up and down the room, lost in thought, then went up to the table, counting the money again. Suddenly, as though coming to myself, I ran to the door and locked it with two turns of the key. Then I stood pondering before my little portmanteau.

"Shall I put it in the portmanteau till to-morrow?" I said, suddenly remembering Polina and turning towards her.

She was still sitting in the same place without stirring, but watching me attentively. Her expression was somehow strange; I did not like that expression. I am not mistaken if I say that there was hatred in it.

I went up to her quickly.

"Polina, here are twenty-five thousand florins—that's fifty thousand francs—more, in fact. Take it, throw it in his face to-morrow."

She did not answer me.

"If you like I will take you away early in the morning. Shall I?"

She suddenly burst out laughing. She laughed for a long time.

I looked at her with wonder and a mortified feeling. That laugh was very much like sarcastic laughter at my expense, which had always been so frequent at the times of my most passionate declarations.

At last she ceased laughing and frowned; she looked at me sternly from under her brows.

"I won't take your money," she declared contemptuously.

"How? What's this?" I cried. "Polina, why?"

"I won't take money for nothing."

"I offer it you as a friend; I offer you my life."

She looked at me with a long, penetrating look, as though she would pierce me through with it.

"You give too much," she said, with a laugh; "De Grieux's mistress is not worth fifty thousand francs."

"Polina, how can you talk to me like that!" I cried, reproachfully. "Am I a De Grieux?"

"I hate you! Yes . . . yes! . . . I love you no more than De Grieux," she cried, her eyes suddenly flashing.

Then she suddenly covered her face with her hands and went into hysterics. I rushed to her.

I realized that something had happened to her while I was away. She seemed quite out of her mind.

"Buy me! Do you want to? Do you want to? For fifty thousand francs, like De Grieux?" broke from her with convulsive sobs.

I held her in my arms, kissed her hands, her feet, fell on my knees before her.

Her hysterics passed off. She put both hands on my shoulders, and looked at me intently; she seemed trying to read something in my face. She listened to me, but evidently did not hear what I was saying to her. Some doubt and anxiety betrayed itself in her face. I was anxious about her; it seemed to me that her brain was giving way. Then she began softly drawing me to her; a trustful smile began straying over her face; but she suddenly pushed me away, and again fell to scanning me with a darkened look.

Suddenly she fell to embracing me.

"You love me, you love me, don't you?" she said. "Why, you . . . why, you . . . wanted to fight the Baron for my sake!"

And suddenly she burst out laughing—as though she had recalled something sweet and funny. She cried and laughed all at once. Well, what was I to do? I was in a fever myself. I remember she began saying something to me—but I could scarcely understand anything. It was a sort of delirium—a sort of babble—as though she wanted to tell me something as rapidly as possible—a delirium which was interrupted from time to time with the merriest laughter, which at last frightened me. "No, no; you are sweet, sweet," she repeated. "You are my faithful one!" And again she put her hand on my shoulders, again she looked at me and repeated, "You love me . . . love me . . . will love me?" I could not take my eyes off her; I had never seen her before in such a mood of love and tenderness; it is true this, of course, was delirium, but . . . noticing my passionate expression, she suddenly began smiling slyly; apropos of nothing she began suddenly talking of Mr. Astley.

She talked incessantly of Mr. Astley, however (she talked of him particularly when she had been trying to tell me of something that evening), but what she meant exactly I could not quite grasp; she seemed to be actually laughing at him. She repeated continually that he was waiting and that, did I know, he was certainly standing under the window?

"Yes, yes, under the window; come open it: look out: look out: he certainly is here! She pushed me to the window, but as soon as I made a movement to go she went off into peals of laughter and I remained with her, and she fell to embracing me.

"Shall we go away? shall we go away to-morrow?" The question suddenly came into her mind uneasily. "Well . . ." (and she sank into thought) "Well, shall we overtake Granny; what do you think? I think we might overtake her at Berlin. What do you think she will say when she sees us? And Mr. Astley? . . . Well, he won't leap off the Schlangenberg—what do you think?" (she burst out laughing) "Come, listen, do you know where he is going next summer? He wants to go to the North Pole for scientific investigations, and he has asked me to go with him, ha-ha-ha! He says that we Russians can do nothing without Europeans and are incapable of anything. . . . But he is good-natured, too! Do you know he makes excuses for the General? He says that Blanche . . . that passion

—oh, I don't know, I don't know," she repeated, as though she didn't know what she was talking about. "They are poor—how sorry I am for them, and Granny . . . Come, listen, listen, how could you kill De Grieux? And did you really imagine you could kill him? Oh, silly fellow! Can you really think I would let you fight with De Grieux? Why, you did not even kill the Baron," she added, suddenly laughing. "Oh, how funny you were then with the Baron. I looked at you both from the seat; and how unwilling you were to go then, when I sent you. How I laughed then, how I laughed," she added, laughing.

And suddenly she kissed and embraced me again. Again she pressed her face to mine passionately and tenderly. I heard nothing and thought of nothing more. My head was in a whirl. . . .

I think it was about seven o'clock in the morning when I woke up. The sun was shining into the room. Polina was sitting beside me and looking about her strangely, as though she were waking from some darkness and trying to collect her thoughts. She, too, had only just woken up and was gazing at the table and the money. My head ached and was heavy. I tried to take Polina by the hand: she pushed me away and jumped up from the sofa. The dawning day was overcast. Rain had fallen before sunrise. She went to the window, she opened it, put out her head and shoulders and with her face in her hands and her elbows on the window-sill, stayed for three minutes looking out without turning to me or hearing what I said to her. I wondered with dread what would happen now and how it would end. All at once she got up from the window, went up to the table and, looking at me with infinite hatred, with lips trembling with anger, she said to me—

"Well, give me my fifty thousand francs now?"

"Polina, again, again?" I was beginning.

"Or have you changed your mind? Ha-ha-ha! Perhaps you regret it now."

Twenty-five thousand florins, counted out the evening before, were lying on the table; I took the money and gave it to her.

"It's mine now, isn't it? That's so, isn't it? Isn't it?" she asked me, spitefully holding the money in her hand.

"Yes, it was always yours," I answered.

"Well, there are your fifty thousand francs for you!"

With a swing of her arm she flung the money at me. It hit me a stinging blow in the face and the coins flew all over the table. After doing this Polina ran out of the room.

I know that at that moment she was certainly not in her right mind, though I don't understand such temporary insanity. It is true that she is still ill, even now, a month later. What was the cause of her condition, and, above all, of this whim? Was it wounded pride? Despair at having brought herself to come to me? Had I shown any sign of priding myself on my happiness, and did I, like De Grieux, want to get rid of her by giving her fifty thousand francs? But that was not so; I know that, on my conscience. I believe that her vanity was partly responsible; her vanity prompted her to distrust and insult me, although all that perhaps was not clear, even to herself. In that case, of course, I was punished for De Grieux and was made responsible, though I was not much to blame. It is true that all this was almost only delirium; it is true, too, that I knew she was in delirium and . . . did not take that fact into consideration; perhaps she cannot forgive me for that now. Yes, but that is now; but then, then? Why, she was not in such a delirium and so ill then as to be utterly oblivious of what she was doing; when she came to me with De Grieux's letter she knew what she was doing.

I made haste to thrust all my notes and my heap of gold into the bed, covered it over and went out ten minutes after Polina. I made sure she would run home, and I thought I would slip in to them on the sly, and in the hall ask the nurse how the young lady was. What was my astonishment when I learnt from Nurse, whom I met on the stairs, that Polina had not yet returned home and that Nurse was coming to me for her.

"She only just left my room about ten minutes ago; where can she have gone?"

Nurse looked at me reproachfully.

And meanwhile it had caused a regular scandal, which by now was all over the hotel. In the porter's room and at the *ober-kellner's* it was whispered that Fräulein had run out of the hotel in the rain at six o'clock in the morning in the direction of the Hôtel d'Angleterre. From what they said and hinted, I noticed that they all knew already that she had spent the night in my room. However, stories were being told of the whole family: it had become known all through the hotel that the General had gone out of his mind and was crying. The story was that Granny was his mother, who had come expressly from Russia to prevent her son's marriage with Mlle. de Cominges, and was going to cut him out of her will if he disobeyed her; and, as he certainly would disobey her, the Countess had purposely thrown away all her money at roulette before his eyes, so that he should got nothing. *"Diese Russen!"* repeated the *ober-kellner,* shaking his head indignantly. The others laughed. The *ober-kellner* was making out his bill. My winning was known about already. Karl, my corridor attendant, was the first to congratulate me. But I had no thought for any of them. I rushed to the Hôtel d'Angleterre.

It was early; Mr. Astley was seeing no one; learning that it was I, he came out into the corridor to me and stopped before me, turning his pewtery eyes upon me in silence, waiting to hear what I should say. I inquired about Polina.

"She is ill," answered Mr. Astley, looking at me as fixedly as before.

"Then she really is with you?"

"Yes, she is."

"Then, what do you . . . do you mean to keep her?"

"Yes."

"Mr. Astley, it will make a scandal; it's impossible. Besides, she is quite ill; perhaps you don't see it?"

"Oh, yes, I notice it, and I've just told you she is ill. If she had not been ill she would not have spent the night with you."

"Then you know that?"

"Yes, I know it. She came here yesterday and I would have taken her to a relation of mine, but as she was ill, she made a mistake and went to you."

"Fancy that! Well, I congratulate you, Mr. Astley. By the way, you've given me an idea: weren't you standing all night under our window? Miss Polina was making me open the window and look out all night to see whether you were standing under the window; she kept laughing about it."

"Really? No, I didn't stand under the window; but I was waiting in the corridor and walking round."

"But she must be looked after, Mr. Astley."

"Oh, yes, I've sent for the doctor, and, if she dies, you will answer to me for her death."

I was amazed.

"Upon my word, Mr. Astley, what do you want?"

"And is it true that you won two hundred thousand thalers yesterday?"

"Only a hundred thousand florins."

"Well, do you see, you had better go off to Paris this morning!"

"What for?"

"All Russians who have money go to Paris," Mr. Astley explained, in a tone of voice as though he had read this in a book.

"What could I do now in Paris, in the summer? I love her, Mr. Astley, you know it yourself."

"Really? I am convinced you don't. If you remain here you will certainly lose all you have won and you will have nothing left to go to Paris with. But, good-bye, I am perfectly certain you will go to Paris to-day."

"Very well, good-bye, only I shan't go to Paris. Think, Mr. Astley, what will be happening here? The General . . . and now this adventure with Miss Polina—why, that will be all over the town."

"Yes, all over the town; I believe the General is not thinking about that: he has no thoughts to spare for that. Besides, Miss Polina has a perfect right to live where she likes. In regard to that family, one may say quite correctly that the family no longer exists."

I walked away laughing at this Englishman's strange conviction that I was going to Paris. "He wants to shoot me in a duel, though," I thought, "if Mlle. Polina dies—what a complication!" I swear I was sorry for Polina, but, strange to say, from the very moment when I reached the gambling tables the previous evening and began winning a pile of money, my love had retreated, so to speak, into the background. I say this now; but at the time I did not realize all this clearly. Can I really be a gambler? Can I really . . . have loved Polina so strangely? No, I love her to this day. God is my witness! And then, when I left Mr. Astley and went home, I was genuinely miserable and blaming myself. But . . . at this point a very strange and silly thing happened to me.

I was hurrying to see the General, when suddenly not

far from his rooms, a door was opened and some one called me. It was Madame *la veuve* Cominges, and she called me at the bidding of Mlle. Blanche. I went in to see Mlle. Blanche.

They had a small suite of apartments, consisting of two rooms. I could hear Mlle. Blanche laugh and call out from the bedroom.

She was getting up.

"Ah, c'est lui! Viens donc, bête! It is true, *que tu as gagné une montagne d'or et d'argent? J'aimerais mieux l'or."*

"Yes, I did win," I answered, laughing.

"How much?"

"A hundred thousand florins."

"Bibi, comme tu es bête. Why, come in here. I can't hear anything. *Nous ferons bombance, n'est-ce pas?"*

I went in to her. She was lying under a pink satin quilt, above which her robust, swarthy, wonderfully swarthy, shoulders were visible, shoulders such as one only sees in one's dreams, covered to some extent by a batiste nightgown bordered with white lace which was wonderfully becoming to her dark skin.

"Mon fils, as-tu du cœur?" she cried, seeing me, and burst out laughing. She laughed very good-humouredly, and sometimes quite genuinely.

"Tout autre," I began, paraphrasing Corneille.

"Here you see, *vois-tu,"* she began babbling; "to begin with, find my stockings, help me to put them on; and then, *si tu n'es pas trop bête, je te prends à Paris.* You know I am just going."

"Just going?"

"In half an hour."

All her things were indeed packed. All her portmanteaus and things were ready. Coffee had been served some time before.

"Eh bien, if you like, *tu verras Paris. Dis donc qu'est-ce que c'est qu'un outchitel? Tu étais bien bête, quand tu étais outchitel.* Where are my stockings? Put them on for me?"

She thrust out some positively fascinating feet, little dark-skinned feet, not in the least misshapen, as feet that look so small in shoes always are. I laughed and began drawing her silk stockings on for her. Meanwhile Mlle. Blanche sat up in bed, prattling away.

"*Eh bien, que feras-tu, si je te prends avec?* To begin with, I want fifty thousand francs. You'll give them to me at Frankfurt. *Nous allons à Paris;* there we'll play together: *et je te ferai voir des étoiles en plein jour.* You will see women such as you have never seen before. Listen . . ."

"Wait a minute, so if I give you fifty thousand francs, what will be left for me?"

"*Et cent cinquante mille francs,* you have forgotten: and what's more, I consent to live with you a month, two months: *que sais-je!* In those two months we shall certainly get through that hundred and fifty thousand francs, you see, *je suis bonne enfant,* and I tell you beforehand, *mais tu verras des étoiles.*"

"What! all in two months!"

"Why! does that horrify you? *Ah, vil esclave!* But, do you know? one month of such a life is worth your whole existence. One month—*et après, le déluge! Mais tu ne peux comprendre; va!* Go along, go along, you are not worth it! *Aie, que fais-tu?*"

At that moment I was putting a stocking on the other leg, but could not resist kissing it. She pulled it away and began hitting me on the head with the tip of her foot. At last, she turned me out altogether.

"*Eh bien! mon outchitel, je t'attends, si tu veux;* I am starting in a quarter of an hour!" she called after me.

On returning home I felt as though my head were going round. Well, it was not my fault that Mlle. Polina had thrown the whole pile of money in my face, and had even yesterday preferred Mr. Astley to me. Some of the banknotes that had been scattered about were still lying on the floor; I picked them up. At that moment the door opened and the *ober-kellner* himself made his appearance (he had never deigned to look into my room before) with a suggestion that I might like to move downstairs to a magnificent suite of apartments which had just been vacated by Count V.

I stood still and thought a little.

"My bill—I am just leaving, in ten minutes," I cried. "If it's to be Paris, let it be Paris," I thought to myself; "it seems it was fated at my birth!"

A quarter of an hour later we were actually sitting in a reserved compartment, Mlle. Blanche, Madame *la veuve* Cominges and I. Mlle. Blanche, looking at me, laughed till she was almost hysterical. Madame de Cominges followed suit; I cannot say that I felt cheerful. My life had broken in two, but since the previous day I had grown used to staking everything on a card. Perhaps it is really the truth that my sudden wealth was too much for me and had turned my head. *Pent-être, je ne demandais pas mieux*. It seemed to me for a time—but only for a time, the scenes were shifted. "But in a month I shall be here, and then ... and then we will try our strength, Mr. Astley!" No, as I recall it now, I was awfully sad then, though I did laugh as loudly as that idiot, Blanche.

"But what is the matter with you? How silly you are! Oh! how silly you are!" Blanche kept exclaiming, interrupting her laughter to scold me in earnest. "Oh well, oh well, we'll spend your two hundred thousand francs: but in exchange *mais tu seras heureux comme un petit roi;* I will tie your cravat myself and introduce you to Hortense. And when we have spent all our money, you will come back here and break the bank again. What did the Jews tell you? The great thing is—boldness, and you have it, and you will bring me money to Paris more than once again. *Quant à moi je veux cinquante mille francs de rentes et alors . . .*"

"And the General?" I asked her.

"Why, the General, as you know, comes to see me every day with a bouquet. This time I purposely asked him to get me some very rare flowers. The poor fellow will come back and will find the bird has flown. He'll fly after us, you will see. Ha-ha-ha! I shall be awfully pleased to see him. He'll be of use to me in Paris; Mr Astley will pay his bill here. . . ."

And so that was the way in which I went to Paris.

Chapter 16

What shall I say about Paris? It was madness, of course, and foolery. I only spent a little over three weeks in Paris, and by the end of that time my hundred thousand francs was finished. I speak only of a hundred thousand. The other hundred thousand I gave to Mlle. Blanche in hard cash—fifty thousand at Frankfurt and three days later in Paris I gave her an I O U for another fifty thousand francs, though a week later she exchanged this for cash from me. *"Et les cent mille francs, qui nous restent, tu les mangeras avec moi, mon outchitel."* She always called me an *outchitel*, *i.e.*, a tutor. It is difficult to imagine anything in the world meaner, stingier and more niggardly than the class of creatures to which Mlle. Blanche belonged. But that was in the spending of her own money. As regards my hundred thousand francs, she openly informed me, later on, that she needed them to establish herself in Paris, "as now I am going to settle in decent style once for all, and now no one shall turn me aside for a long time; at least, that is my plan," she added. I hardly saw that hundred thousand, however; she kept the money the whole time, and in my purse, into which she looked every day, there was never more than a hundred francs, and always less and less.

"What do you want money for?" she would say, sometimes, in the simplest way, and I did not dispute with her. But she furnished and decorated her flat very nicely with that money, and afterwards, when she took me to her new abode, as she showed me the rooms, she said: "You see what care and taste can do even with the scantiest means." These "scanty means" amounted to fifty thousand francs, however. With the second fifty thousand she provided herself with a carriage and horses. Moreover, we gave two balls, that is, two evening parties at which were present Hortense, Lizette and Cléopatra, women remarkable in very many respects and even quite good-looking. At those two evenings I had to play the very foolish part of host, to receive and entertain the stupidest rich tradesmen, incredibly ignorant and shameless, various army lieutenants and miserable little authors and journalistic insects, who appeared in the most fashionable swallow-tails and straw-coloured gloves, and displayed a vanity and affectation whose proportions were beyond anything conceivable in Petersburg—and that is saying a great deal. Many of them thought fit to jeer at me; but I got drunk with champagne and lolled at full length in a back room. To me it was all loathsome to the last degree. *"C'est un outchitel,"* Blanche kept saying about me, *"il a gagné deux cent mille francs.* Without me he wouldn't have known how to spend it. And afterwards he will be an *outchitel* again; don't you know of a place for one? we ought to do something for him."

I had recourse to champagne very often, because I was often sad and dreadfully bored. I lived in the most bourgeois, in the most mercenary surroundings in which every *sou* was reckoned and accounted for. Blanche disliked me for the first fortnight: I noticed that; it is true, she dressed me like a dandy, and tied my cravat for me every day, but in her soul she genuinely despised me. I did not pay the slightest attention to that. Bored and dispirited, I used to go usually to the Château de Fleurs, where regularly every evening I got drunk and practised the *cancan* (which they dance so disgustingly there), and acquired in the end a kind of celebrity.

At last Blanche gauged my true character. She had for some reason conceived the idea that I should spend all the time we were together walking after her with a pencil and paper in my hand, and should always be reckoning how much she had spent, how much she had stolen, how much she would spend and how much more she would steal. And she was, of course, convinced that we should have a regular battle over every ten-franc piece. She had an answer in readiness for every attack that she anticipated from me; but when she found I did not attack her, she could not at first refrain from defending herself, unprovoked. Sometimes she would begin with great heat, but seeing that I remained silent as a rule, lying on a sofa gazing at the ceiling—at last, she was surprised. At first she thought I was simply stupid, *"un outchitel,* and merely cut short her explanations, probably thinking to herself: "Why, he's a fool. There's no need to lay it on for him, since he doesn't understand." She would go away but come back again ten minutes later (this happened at a time when she was spending most ferociously, spending on a scale quite out of proportion to our means: she had, for instance, got rid of the horses first bought and bought another pair for sixteen thousand francs).

"Well, so you are not cross, *bibi?*" she said, coming up to me.

"N—n—n—no! You weary me!" I said, removing her hands from me, but this seemed to her so curious, that she immediately sat down beside me.

"You see, I only decided to pay so much because they could be sold later on if need be. They can be sold again for twenty thousand francs."

"No doubt, no doubt; they are splendid horses, and you have a fine turnout now; it suits you; well, that's enough."

"Then you are not cross?"

"Why should I be? You are sensible to provide yourself with things that are necessary to you. All that will be of use to you afterwards. I see that it is quite necessary for you to establish yourself in such a style; otherwise you will never save up your million. Our hundred thousand francs is only a beginning; a drop in the ocean."

Blanche had expected from me anything but such reflections (instead of outcries and reproaches). She seemed to drop from the clouds.

"So that's what you are like! *Mais tu as l'esprit pour comprendre. Sais-tu, mon garçon,* though you are an *outchitel* you ought to have been born a prince. So you don't grudge the money's going so quickly?"

"Bother the money! The quicker the better!"

"*Mais sais-tu . . . mais dis donc,* are you rich? *Mais sais-tu,* you really despise money too much. *Qu'est-ce que tu feras après, dis donc?*"

"*Après,* I shall go to Homburg and win another hundred thousand francs."

"*Oui, oui, c'est ça, c'est magnifique!* And I know you will certainly win it and bring it here. *Dis donc,* why you will make me really love you. *Eh bien,* I will love you all the time for being like that, and won't once be unfaithful to you. You see, I have not loved you all this time, *parceque je croyais que tu n'étais qu'un outchitel (quelque chose comme un laquais, n'est-ce pas?),* but I have been faithful to you all the same, *parceque je suis bonne fille.*"

"Come, you are lying! How about Albert, that swarthy-faced little officer; do you suppose I didn't see last time?"

"*Oh, oh, mais tu es . . .*"

"Come, you are lying, you are lying; why, do you suppose I should be angry? Why, it's no matter; *il faut que la jeunesse se passe.* And there's no need for you to send him away if you had him before me and are fond of him. Only don't give him money, do you hear?"

"So you are not angry about it? *Mais tu es un vrai philosophe, sais-tu? Un vrai philosophe!*" she cried enthusiastically.

"*Eh bien! je t'aimerai, je t'aimerai—tu verras, tu seras content!*"

And from that time she really did seem to be attached

to me, to be really affectionate; and so our last ten days passed. The "stars" promised me I did not see. But in some respects she really did keep her word. What is more, she introduced me to Hortense, who really was a remarkable woman in her own way, and in our circle was called *Thérèse philosophe.* . . .

. However, there is no need to enlarge upon that; all that might make a separate story, in a different tone, which I do not want to introduce into this story. The fact is, I longed above everything for all this episode to be over. But our hundred thousand francs lasted, as I have mentioned already, almost a month—at which I was genuinely surprised; eighty thousand of that, at least, Blanche spent on things for herself, and we lived on no more than twenty thousand francs, and—yet it was enough. Blanche, who was in the end almost open with me (or, at any rate, did not lie to me about some things), declared that, anyway, the debts she had been obliged to make would not fall upon me: "I have never given you bills or I O U's to sign," she said, "because I was sorry for you; but any other girl would have certainly done it and got you into prison. You see, you see how I loved you and how good I am! Think of what that devil of a wedding alone is going to cost me!"

We really were going to have a wedding. It took place at the very end of my month, and it may be assumed that the last remains of my hundred thousand francs went upon it; that was how the thing ended; that is, my month ended with that, and after it I received my formal dismissal.

This was how it happened: a week after our arrival in Paris the General suddenly turned up. He came straight to Blanche, and from his first call almost lived with us. He had a lodging of his own, it is true. Blanche received him joyfully, with shrieks of laughter, and even flew to embrace him; as things had turned out, she was unwilling to let him go: and he had to follow her about everywhere, on the boulevards, and to the theatres, and to call on her acquaintances, and to take her for drives. The General was still of use for such purposes; he was of rather imposing and decorous appearance—he was above the average in height, with dyed whiskers and moustaches (he had once served in the Cuirassiers); he was still presentable-looking, though his face was puffy. His manners were superb; he looked well in evening dress. In Paris he began wearing his decorations. The promenade on the boulevard with a man like this was not only possible, but *advantageous*. The good-natured and senseless General was immensely delighted with all this; he had not reckoned upon it at all when he came to see us on arriving in Paris. He had come, then, almost trembling with terror; he was afraid that Blanche would make an uproar and order him to be turned out; and so he was highly delighted at the changed aspect of the position, and spent the whole month in a sort of senseless rapture: and he was in the same state when I left him. I learnt that on the morning of our sudden departure from Roulettenburg he had had some sort of a fit. He had fallen insensible, and had been all that week almost like a madman, talking incessantly. He was being nursed and doctored, but he suddenly threw up everything, got into the train and flew off to Paris. Of course, Blanche's reception was the best cure for him; but the traces of his illness remained long after, in spite of his joy and his enthusiastic condition. He was utterly incapable of reflection or even of carrying on a conversation on any serious subject; when any such topic was brought forward, he confined himself to nodding his head and ejaculating, "H'm!" at every word. He often laughed, but it was a nervous, sickly laugh, as though he were giggling; another time he would sit for hours looking as black as night, knitting his bushy brows. Of many things he had no recollection whatever; he had become absent-minded to an unseemly degree, and had acquired the habit of talking to himself. Blanche was the only person who could rouse him; and, indeed, his attacks of gloom and depression, when he hid himself in a corner, meant nothing but that he hadn't seen Blanche for a long time, or that Blanche had gone off somewhere without taking him, or had not been nice to him before going. At the same time he could not say what he wanted, and did not know why he was depressed and miserable. After sitting for two or three hours (I noticed this on two or three occasions when Blanche had gone out for the whole day, probably to see Albert), he would suddenly begin to look about him in a nervous fluster, to stare round, to recollect himself, and seem to be looking for something; but seeing no one and not remembering the question he meant to ask, he sank into forgetfulness again till Blanche reappeared, gay, frisky, gorgeously dressed, with her ringing laugh; she would run up to him, begin teasing him, and even kissing him—a favour which she did not often, however, bestow upon him. Once the General was so delighted to see her that he even burst into tears—I really marvelled at him.

From the very first, Blanche began to plead his cause before me. Indeed, she waxed eloquent in his behalf; reminded me that she had betrayed the General for my sake, that she was almost engaged to him, had given him her word; that he had abandoned his family on her account, and, lastly, that I had been in his service and ought to remember that, and that I ought to be ashamed. . . . I said nothing while she rattled away at a terrific pace. At last I laughed: and with that the matter ended, that is, at first, she thought I was a fool: and at last came to the conclusion that I was a very nice and accommodating man. In fact, I had the good fortune to win in the end the complete approval of that excellent young woman. (Blanche really was, though, a very good-natured girl— in her own way, of course; I had not such a high opinion of her at first.) "You're a kind and clever man," she used to say to me towards the end, "and . . . and . . . it's only a pity you are such a fool! You never, never, save anything!"

"Un vrai russe, un calmouk!" Several times she sent me to take the General for a walk about the streets, exactly as she might send her lapdog out with her footman. I took him, however, to the theatre, and to the Bal-Mabille, and to the restaurants. Blanche gave me the money for this, though the General had some of his own, and he was very fond of taking out his pocket-book before people. But I had almost to use force to prevent him from buying a brooch for seven hundred francs, by which he was fascinated in the Palais Royal and of which he wanted, at all costs, to make Blanche a present. But what was a brooch of seven hundred francs to her? The General hadn't more than a thousand francs altogether. I could never find out where he had got that money from. I imagine it was from Mr. Astley, especially as the latter had paid their bill at the hotel. As for the General's attitude to me all this time, I believe that he did not even guess at my relations with Blanche. Though he had heard vaguely that I had won a fortune, yet he probably supposed that I was with Blanche

in the capacity of a private secretary or even a servant. Anyway, he always, as before, spoke to me condescendingly, authoritatively, and even sometimes fell to scolding me. One morning he amused Blanche and me immensely at breakfast. He was not at all ready to take offence, but suddenly he was huffy with me—why?—I don't know to this day. No doubt he did not know himself. In fact, he made a speech without a beginning or an end, *à bâtons rompus*, shouted that I was an impudent boy, that he would give me a lesson . . . that he would let me know it . . . and so on. But no one could make out anything from it. Blanche went off into peals of laughter. At last he was somehow appeased and taken out for a walk. I noticed sometimes, however, that he grew sad, that he was regretting some one and something, he was missing something, in spite of Blanche's presence. On two such occasions he began talking to me of himself, but could not express himself clearly, alluded to his times in the army, to his deceased wife, to his family affairs, to his property. He would stumble upon some phrase—and was delighted with it and would repeat it a hundred times a day, though perhaps it expressed neither his feelings nor his thoughts. I tried to talk to him about his children: but he turned off the subject with incoherent babble, and passed hurriedly to another topic: "Yes, yes, my children, you are right, my children!" Only once he grew sentimental—we were with him at the theatre: "Those unhappy children!" he began suddenly. "Yes, sir, those un—happy children!" And several times afterwards that evening he repeated the same words: "unhappy children!" Once, when I began to speak of Polina, he flew into a frenzy. "She's an ungrateful girl," he cried. "She's wicked and ungrateful! She has disgraced her family. If there were laws here I would make her mind her p's and q's. Yes, indeed, yes, indeed!" As for De Grieux, he could not bear even to hear his name: "He has been the ruin of me," he would say, "he has robbed me, he has destroyed me! He has been my nightmare for the last two years! He has haunted my dreams for whole months! It's, it's, it's . . . Oh, never speak to me of him!"

I saw there was an understanding between them, but, as usual, I said nothing. Blanche announced the news to me, first—it was just a week before we parted: *"Il a du chance,"* she babbled. "Granny really is ill this time, and certainly will die. Mr. Astley has sent a telegram. You must admit that the General is her heir, anyway, and even if he were not, he would not interfere with me in anything. In the first place, he has his pension, and in the second place, he will live in a back room and will be perfectly happy. I shall be 'Madame la Générale.' I shall get into a good set" (Blanche was continually dreaming of this), "in the end I shall be a Russian landowner, *j'aurai un château, des moujiks, et puis j'aurai toujours mon million.*"

"Well, what if he begins to be jealous, begins to insist . . . on goodness knows what—do you understand?"

"Oh, no, *non, non, non!* How dare he! I have taken precautions, you needn't be afraid. I have even made him sign some I O U's for Albert. The least thing—and he will be arrested; and he won't dare!"

"Well, marry him. . . ."

The marriage was celebrated without any great pomp; it was a quiet family affair. Albert was invited and a few other intimate friends. Hortense, Cléopatra and company were studiously excluded. The bridegroom was extremely interested in his position. Blanche herself tied his cravat with her own hands, and pomaded his head: and in his swallow-tailed coat with his white tie he looked *très comme il faut.*

"*Il est pourtant très comme il faut,*" Blanche herself observed to me, coming out of the General's room, as though the idea that the General was *très comme il faut* was a surprise even to her. Though I assisted at the whole affair as an idle spectator, yet I·took so little interest in the details that I have to a great extent forgotten the course of events. I only remember that Blanche turned out not to be called "De Cominges," and her mamma not to be *la veuve* "Cominges," but "Du Placet." Why they had been both "De Cominges" till then, I don't know. But the General remained very much pleased with that, and "Du Placet" pleased him, in fact, better than "De Cominges." On the morning of the wedding, fully dressed for the part, he kept walking to and fro in the drawing-room, repeating to himself with a grave and important air, "Mlle. Blanche du Placet! Blanche du Placet, du Placet!" . . . and his countenance beamed with a certain complacency. At church, before the *maire*, and at the wedding breakfast at home, he was not only joyful but proud. There was a change in both of them. Blanche, too, had an air of peculiar dignity.

"I shall have to behave myself quite differently now," she said to me, perfectly seriously: "*mais vois-tu,* I never thought of one very horrid thing: I even fancy, to this day, I can't learn my surname. Zagoryansky, Zagozyansky, Madame la Générale de Sago—Sago, *ces diables de noms russes, enfin madame la générale a quatorze consonnes! Comme c'est agréable, n'est-ce pas?*"

At last we parted, and Blanche, that silly Blanche, positively shed tears when she said good-bye to me. "*Tu étais bon enfant,*" she said, whimpering. "*Je te croyais bête et tu en avais l'air,* but it suits you." And, pressing my hand at parting, she suddenly cried, "*Attends!*" rushed to her boudoir and, two minutes later, brought me a banknote for two thousand francs. That I should never have believed possible! "It may be of use to you. You may be a very learned *outchitel,* but you are an awfully stupid man. I am not going to give you more than two thousand, for you'll lose it gambling, anyway. Well, good-bye! *Nous serons toujours bon amis,* and if you win, be sure to come to me again, *et tu seras heureux!*"

I had five hundred francs left of my own. I had besides a splendid watch that cost a thousand francs, some diamond studs, and so on, so that I could go on a good time longer without anxiety. I am staying in this little town on purpose to collect myself, and, above all, I am waiting for Mr. Astley. I have learnt for a fact that he will pass through the town and stay here for twenty-four hours on business. I shall find out about everything; and then— then I shall go straight to Homburg. I am not going to Roulettenburg; not till next year anyway. They say it is a bad omen to try your luck twice running at the same tables; and Homburg is the real place for play.

Chapter 17

It is a year and eight months since I looked at these notes, and only now in sadness and dejection it has occurred to me to read them through. So I stopped then at my going to Homburg. My God! With what a light heart, comparatively speaking, I wrote those last lines! Though not with a light heart exactly, but with a sort of self-confidence, with undaunted hopes! Had I any doubt of myself? And now more than a year and a half has passed, and I am, to my own mind, far worse than a beggar! Yes, what is being a beggar? A beggar is nothing! I have simply ruined myself! However, there is nothing I can compare myself with, and there is no need to give myself a moral lecture! Nothing could be stupider than moral reflections at this date! Oh, self-satisfied people, with what proud satisfaction these prattlers prepare to deliver their lectures! If only they knew how thoroughly I understand the loathsomeness of my present position, they would not be able to bring their tongues to reprimand me. Why, what, what can they tell me that I do not know? And is that the point? The point is that—one turn of the wheel, and all will be changed, and those very moralists will be the first (I am convinced of that) to come up to congratulate me with friendly jests. And they will not all turn away from me as they do now. But, hang them all! What am I now? Zero. What may I be to-morrow? To-morrow I may rise from the dead and begin to live again! There are still the makings of a man in me.

I did, in fact, go to Homburg then, but . . . afterwards I went to Roulettenburg again, and to Spa. I have even been in Baden, where I went as valet to the councillor Gintse, a scoundrel, who was my master here. Yes, I was a lackey for five whole months! I got a place immediately after coming out of prison. (I was sent to prison in Roulettenburg for a debt I made here.) Some one, I don't know who, paid my debt—who was it? Was it Mr. Astley? Polina? I don't know, but the debt was paid; two hundred thalers in all, and I was set free. What could I do? I entered the service of this Gintse. He is a young man and frivolous, he liked to be idle, and I could read and write in three languages. At first I went into his service as a sort of secretary at thirty guldens a month; but I ended by becoming a regular valet: he had not the means to keep a secretary; and he lowered my wages; I had nowhere to go, I remained—and in that way became a lackey by my own doing. I had not enough to eat or to drink in his service, but on the other hand, in five months I saved up seventy gulden. One evening in Baden, however, I announced to him that I intended parting from him; the same evening I went to roulette. Oh, how my heart beat! No, it was not money that I wanted. All that I wanted then was that next day all these Gintses, all these *ober-kellners*, all these magnificent Baden ladies—that they might be all talking about me, repeating my story, wondering at me, admiring me, praising me, and doing homage to my new success. All these are childish dreams and desires, but . . . who knows, perhaps I should meet Polina again, too, I should tell her, and she would see that I was above all these stupid ups and downs of fate. . . . Oh, it was not money that was dear to me! I knew I should fling it away to some Blanche again and should drive in Paris again for three weeks with a pair of my own horses, costing sixteen thousand francs. I know for certain that I am not mean; I believe that I am not even a spendthrift—and yet with what a tremor, with what a thrill at my heart, I hear the croupier's cry: *trente-et-un, rouge, impair et passe,* or: *quatre, noir, pair et manque!* With what avidity I look at the gambling table on which louis d'or, friedrichs d'or and thalers lie scattered: on the piles of gold when they are scattered from the croupier's shovel like glowing embers, or at the piles of silver a yard high that lie round the wheel. Even on my way to the gambling hall, as soon as I hear, two rooms away, the clink of the scattered money I almost go into convulsions.

Oh! that evening, when I took my seventy gulden to the gambling table, was remarkable too. I began with ten gulden, staking them again on *passe.* I have a prejudice in favour of *passe.* I lost. I had sixty gulden left in silver money; I thought a little and chose *zéro.* I began staking five gulden at a time on *zéro;* at the third turn the wheel stopped at *zéro;* I almost died of joy when I received one hundred and seventy-five gulden; I had not been so delighted when I won a hundred thousand gulden. I immediately staked a hundred gulden on *rouge*—it won; the two hundred on *rouge*—it won; the whole of the four hundred on *noir*—it won; the whole eight hundred on *manque*—it won; altogether with what I had before it made one thousand seven hundred gulden and that—in less than five minutes! Yes, at moments like that one forgets all one's former failures! Why, I had gained this by risking more than life itself, I dared to risk it, and—there I was again, a man among men.

I took a room at the hotel, locked myself in and sat till three o'clock counting over my money. In the morning I woke up, no longer a lackey. I determined the same day to go to Homburg: I had not been a lackey or been in prison there. Half an hour before my train left, I set off to stake on two hazards, no more, and lost fifteen hundred florins. Yet I went to Homburg all the same, and I have been here for a month. . . .

I am living, of course, in continual anxiety. I play for the tiniest stakes, and I keep waiting for something, calculating, standing for whole days at the gambling table and watching the play; I even dream of playing—but feel that in all this, I have, as it were, grown stiff and wooden, as though I had sunk into a muddy swamp. I gather this from my feeling when I met Mr. Astley. We had not seen each other since that time, and we met by accident. This was how it happened: I was walking in the gardens and reckoning that now I was almost without money, but that I had fifty gulden—and that I had, moreover, three days before paid all I owed at the hotel. And so it was possible for me to go once more to roulette—if I were to win anything, I might be able to go on playing; if I lost I should have to get a lackey's place again, if I did not come across Russians in want of a tutor. Absorbed in these thoughts, I went my daily walk, across the park and the forest in the adjoining principality.

Sometimes I used to walk like this for four hours at a time, and go back to Homburg hungry and tired. I had scarcely gone out of the gardens into the park, when suddenly I saw on one of the seats Mr. Astley. He saw me before I saw him, and called to me. I sat down beside him. Detecting in him a certain dignity of manner, I instantly moderated my delight; though I was awfully delighted to see him.

"And so you are here! I thought I should meet you," he said to me. "Don't trouble yourself to tell me your story; I know, I know all about it; I know every detail of your life during this last year and eight months."

"Bah! What a watch you keep on your old friends!" I answered. "It is very creditable in you not to forget. . . . Stay, though, you have given me an idea. Wasn't it you bought me out of prison at Roulettenburg where I was imprisoned for debt for two hundred gulden? Some unknown person paid it for me."

"No, oh, no; it was not I who bought you out when you were in prison at Roulettenburg for a debt of two hundred gulden. But I knew that you were imprisoned for a debt of two hundred gulden."

"Then you know who did pay my debt?"

"Oh, no, I can't say that I know who bought you out."

"Strange; I don't know any of our Russians; besides, the Russians here, I imagine, would not do it; at home in Russia the Orthodox may buy out other Orthodox Christians. I thought it might have been some eccentric Englishman who did it as a freak."

Mr. Astley listened to me with some surprise. I believe he had expected to find me dejected and crushed.

"I am very glad, however, to find that you have quite maintained your independence of spirit and even your cheerfulness," he pronounced, with a rather disagreeable air.

"That is, you are chafing inwardly with vexation at my not being crushed and humiliated," I said, laughing.

He did not at once understand, but when he understood, he smiled.

"I like your observations: I recognize in those words my clever, enthusiastic and, at the same time, cynical old friend; only Russians can combine in themselves so many opposites at the same time. It is true, a man likes to see even his best friend humiliated; a great part of friendship rests on humiliation. But in the present case I assure you that I am genuinely glad that you are not dejected. Tell me, do you intend to give up gambling?"

"Oh, damn! I shall give it up at once as soon as I . . ."

"As soon as you have won back what you have lost! Just what I thought; you needn't say any more—I know —you have spoken unawares, and so you have spoken the truth. Tell me, have you any occupation except gambling?"

"No, none. . . ."

He began cross-examining me. I knew nothing. I scarcely looked into the newspapers, and had literally not opened a single book all that time.

"You've grown rusty," he observed. "You have not only given up life, all your interests, private and public, the duties of a man and a citizen, your friends (and you really had friends)—you have not only given up your objects, such as they were, all but gambling—you have even given up your memories. I remember you at an intense and ardent moment of your life; but I am sure you have forgotten all the best feelings you had then; your dreams, your most genuine desires now do not rise above *pair, impair, rouge, noir*, the twelve middle numbers, and so on, I am sure!"

"Enough, Mr. Astley, please, please don't remind me," I cried with vexation, almost with anger, "let me tell you, I've forgotten absolutely nothing; but I've only for a time put everything out of my mind, even my memories, until I can make a radical improvement in my circumstances; then . . . then you will see, I shall rise again from the dead!"

"You will be here still in ten years' time," he said. "I bet you I shall remind you of this on this very seat, if I'm alive."

"Well, that's enough," I interrupted impatiently; "and to prove to you that I am not so forgetful of the past, let me ask: where is Miss Polina now? If it was not you who got me out of prison, it must have been her doing. I have had no news of her of any sort since that time."

"No, oh no, I don't believe she did buy you out. She's in Switzerland now, and you'll do me a great favour if you leave off asking about Miss Polina," he said resolutely, and even with some anger.

"That means that she has wounded you very much!" I laughed with displeasure.

"Miss Polina is of all people deserving of respect the very best, but I repeat—you will do me a great favour if you cease questioning me concerning Miss Polina. You never knew her: and her name on your lips I regard as an insult to my moral feelings."

"You don't say so! you are wrong, however; besides, what have I to talk to you about except that, tell me that? Why, all our memories really amount to that! Don't be uneasy, though; I don't want to know your private secret affairs. . . . I am only interested, so to say, in Miss Polina's external affairs. That you could tell me in a couple of words."

"Certainly, on condition that with those two words all is over. Miss Polina was ill for a long time; she's ill even now. For some time she stayed with my mother and sister in the north of England. Six months ago, her grandmother—you remember that madwoman?—died and left her, personally, a fortune of seven thousand pounds. At the present time Miss Polina is travelling with the family of my married sister. Her little brother and sister, too, were provided for by their grandmother's will, and are at school in London. The General, her stepfather, died a month ago in Paris of a stroke. Mlle. Blanche treated him well, but succeeded in getting possession of all he received from the grandmother. . . . I believe that's all."

"And De Grieux? Is not he travelling in Switzerland, too?"

"No, De Grieux is not travelling in Switzerland: and I don't know where De Grieux is; besides, once for all, I warn you to avoid such insinuations and ungentlemanly coupling of names, or you will certainly have to answer for it to me."

"What! in spite of our friendly relations in the past?"

"Yes, in spite of our friendly relations in the past."

"I beg a thousand pardons, Mr. Astley. But allow me, though: there is nothing insulting or ungentlemanly about it; I am not blaming Miss Polina for anything. Besides— a Frenchman and a Russian young lady, speaking generally—it's a combination, Mr. Astley, which is beyond your or my explaining or fully comprehending."

"If you will not mention the name of De Grieux in company with another name, I should like you to explain what you mean by the expression of 'the Frenchman and the Russian young lady.' What do you mean by that 'combination'? Why the Frenchman exactly and why the Russian young lady?"

"You see you are interested. But that's a long story, Mr. Astley. You need to understand many things first. But it is an important question, however absurd it may seem at first sight. The Frenchman, Mr. Astley, is the product of a finished beautiful tradition. You, as a Briton, may not agree with this; I, as a Russian, do not either, from envy maybe; but our young ladies may be of a different opinion. You may think Racine artificial, affected and perfumed; probably you won't even read him. I, too, think him artificial, affected and perfumed—from one point of view even absurd; but he is charming. Mr. Astley, and, what is more, he is a great poet, whether we like it or not. The national type of Frenchman, or, rather, of Parisian, had been moulded into elegant forms while we were still bears. The revolution inherited the traditions of the aristocracy. Now even the vulgarest Frenchman

has manners, modes of address, expressions and even
thoughts, of perfectly elegant form, though his own initiative, his own soul and heart, have had no part in the
creation of that form; it has all come to him through inheritance. Well, Mr. Astley, I must inform you now that
there is not a creature on the earth more confiding, and
more candid, than a good, clean and not too sophisticated
Russian girl. De Grieux, appearing in a peculiar role, mas-
querading, can conquer her heart with extraordinary
ease; he has elegance of form, Mr. Astley, and the young
lady takes this form for his individual soul, as the natural
form of his soul and his heart, and not as an external
garment, which has come to him by inheritance. Though
it will greatly displease you, I must tell you that Englishmen are for the most part awkward and inelegant, and
Russians are rather quick to detect beauty, and are eager
for it. But to detect beauty of soul and originality of character needs incomparably more independence and freedom than is to be found in our women, above all in our
young ladies—and of course ever so much more experience. Miss Polina—forgive me, the word is spoken
and one can't take it back—needs a long, long time to
bring herself to prefer you to the scoundrel De Grieux.
She thinks highly of you, becomes your friend, opens all
her heart to you; but yet the hateful scoundrel, the base
and petty money-grubber, De Grieux, will still dominate
her heart. Mere obstinacy and vanity, so to say, will
maintain his supremacy, because at one time this De
Grieux appeared to her with the halo of an elegant marquis, a disillusioned liberal, who is supposed to have
ruined himself to help her family and her frivolous stepfather. All these shams have been discovered later on.
But the fact that they have been discovered makes no
difference: anyway, what she wants is the original De
Grieux—that's what she wants! And the more she hates
the present De Grieux the more she pines for the original
one, though he existed only in her imagination. You are a
sugar-boiler, Mr. Astley."

"Yes, I am a partner in the well-known firm, Lovel &
Co."

"Well, you see, Mr. Astley, on one side—a sugar-boiler,
and on the other—Apollo Belvedere; it is somewhat incongruous. And I am not even a sugar-boiler; I am simply
a paltry gambler at roulette, and have even been a lackey,

which I think Miss Polina knows very well, as I fancy she has good detectives."

"You are exasperated, and that is why you talk all this nonsense," Mr. Astley said coolly, after a moment's thoughts. "Besides, there is nothing original in what you say."

"I admit that! But the awful thing is, my noble friend, that however stale, however hackneyed, however farcical my statements may be—they are nevertheless true! Anyway, you and I have made no way at all!"

"That's disgusting nonsense . . . because, because . . . let me tell you!" Mr. Astley, with flashing eyes, pronounced in a quivering voice, "let me tell you, you ungrateful, unworthy, shallow and unhappy man, that I am come to Homburg expressly at her wish, to see you, to have a long and open conversation with you and to tell her everything—what you are feeling, thinking, hoping, and . . . what you remember!"

"Is it possible? Is it possible?" I cried, and tears rushed in streams from my eyes.

I could not restrain them. I believe it was the first time it happened in my life.

"Yes, unhappy man, she loved you, and I can tell you that, because you are—a lost man! What is more, if I were to tell you that she loves you to this day—you would stay here just the same! Yes, you have destroyed yourself. You had some abilities, a lively disposition, and were not a bad fellow; you might have even been of service to your country, which is in such need of men, but—you will remain here, and your life is over. I don't blame you. To my mind all Russians are like that, or disposed to be like that. If it is not roulette it is something similar. The exceptions are very rare. You are not the first who does not understand the meaning of work (I am not talking of your peasantry). Roulette is a game pre-eminently for the Russians. So far you've been honest and preferred serving as a lackey to stealing. . . . But I dread to think what may come in the future. Enough, good-bye! No doubt you are in want of money? Here are ten louis d'or from me. I won't give you more, for you'll gamble it away in any case. Take it and good-bye! Take it!"

"No, Mr. Astley, after all you have said."

"Ta—ake it!" he cried. "I believe that you are still an honourable man, and I give it as a true friend gives to another friend. If I were sure that you would throw up gambling, leave Homburg and would return to your own country, I would be ready to give you at once a thousand pounds to begin a new career. But I don't give you a thousand pounds: I give you only ten louis d'or just because a thousand pounds and ten louis d'or are just the same to you now; it's all the same—you'll gamble it away. Take it and good-bye."

"I will take it if you will let me embrace you at parting."

"Oh, with pleasure!"

We embraced with sincere feeling, and Mr. Astley went away.

No, he is wrong! If I was crude and silly about Polina and De Grieux, he was crude and hasty about Russians. I say nothing of myself. However . . . however, all that is not the point for the time: that is all words, words, and words, deeds are what are wanted! Switzerland is the great thing now! To-morrow . . . Oh, if only it were possible to set off to-morrow! To begin anew, to rise again. I must show them. . . . Let Polina know that I still can be a man. I have only to . . . But now it's too late—but to-morrow . . . oh, I have a presentiment and it cannot fail to be! I have now fifteen louis d'or, and I have begun with fifteen gulden! If one begins carefully . . . and can I, can I be such a baby! Can I fail to understand that I am a lost man, but—can I not rise again! Yes! I have only for once in my life to be prudent and patient and—that is all! I have only for once to show will power and in one hour I can transform my destiny! The great thing is will power. Only remember what happened to me seven months ago at Roulettenburg just before my final failure. Oh! it was a remarkable instance of determination: I had lost everything then, everything. . . . I was going out of the Casino, I looked, there was still one gulden in my waistcoat pocket: "Then I shall have something for dinner," I thought. But after I had gone a hundred paces I changed my mind and went back. I staked that gulden on *manque* (that time it was on *manque*), and there really is something peculiar in the feeling when, alone in a strange land, far from home and from friends, not knowing whether you will have anything to eat that day—you stake your last gulden, your very last! I won, and twenty minutes later I went out of the Casino, having a hundred and seventy gulden in my pocket. That's a fact! That's what the last gulden can sometimes do! And what if I had lost heart then? What if I had not dared to risk it? . . .

To-morrow, to-morrow it will all be over!

The Eternal Husband

TRANSLATED BY CONSTANCE GARNETT

Chapter 1

Velchaninov

THE SUMMER had come and, contrary to expectations, Velchaninov remained in Petersburg. The trip he had planned to the south of Russia had fallen through, and the end of his case was not in sight. This case—a lawsuit concerning an estate—had taken a very unfortunate turn. Three months earlier it had appeared to be quite straightforward, almost impossible to contest; but suddenly everything was changed. "And, in fact, everything has changed for the worse!" Velchaninov began frequently and resentfully repeating that phrase to himself. He was employing an adroit, expensive, and distinguished lawyer, and was not sparing money; but through impatience and lack of confidence he had been tempted to meddle in the case himself too. He read documents and wrote statements which the lawyer rejected point-blank, ran from one court to another, collected evidence, and probably hindered everything; the lawyer complained, at any rate, and tried to pack him off to a summer villa. But Velchaninov could not even make up his mind to go away. The dust, the stifling heat, the white nights of Petersburg, that always fret the nerves were what he was enjoying in town. His flat was near the Grand Theatre; he had only recently taken it, and it, too, was a failure. "Everything is a failure!" he thought. His nervousness increased every day; but he had for a long time past been subject to nervousness and hypochondria.

He was a man whose life had been full and varied, he was by no means young, thirty-eight or even thirty-nine, and his "old age," as he expressed it himself, had come upon him "quite unexpectedly"; but he realized himself that he had grown older less by the number than by the quality, so to say, of his years, and that if he had begun to be aware of waning powers, the change was rather from within than from without. In appearance he was still strong and hearty. He was a tall, sturdily-built fellow, with thick flaxen hair without a sign of greyness and a long fair beard almost half-way down his chest; at first sight he seemed somewhat slack and clumsy, but if you looked more attentively, you would detect at once that he was a man of excellent breeding, who had at some time received the education of an aristocrat. Velchaninov's manners were still free, assured and even gracious, in spite of his acquired grumpiness and slackness. And he was still, even now, full of the most unhesitating, the most snobbishly insolent self-confidence, the depth of which he did not himself suspect, although he was a man not merely intelligent, but even sometimes sensible, almost cultured and unmistakably gifted. His open and ruddy face had been in old days marked by a feminine softness of complexion which attracted the notice of women; and even now some people, looking at him, would say: "What a picture of health! What a complexion!" And yet this picture of health was cruelly subject to nervous depression. His eyes were large and blue, ten years earlier they had possessed great fascination; they were so bright, so gay, so careless that they could not but attract every one who came in contact with him. Now that he was verging on the forties, the brightness and good-humour were almost extinguished. Those eyes, which were already surrounded by tiny wrinkles, had begun to betray the cynicism of a worn-out man of doubtful morals, a duplicity, an ever-increasing irony and another shade of feeling, which was new: a shade of sadness and of pain—a sort of absent-minded sadness as though about nothing in particular and yet acute. This sadness was especially marked when he was alone. And, strange to say, this man who had been only a couple of years before fond of noisy gaiety, careless and good-humoured, who had been so capital a teller of funny stories, liked nothing now so well as being absolutely alone. He purposely gave up a great number of acquaintances whom he need not have given up even now, in spite of his financial difficulties. It is true that his vanity counted for something in this. With his vanity and mistrustfulness he could not have endured the society of his old acquaintances. But, by degrees, in solitude even his vanity began to change its character. It grew no less, quite the contrary, indeed; but it began to develop into a special sort of vanity which was new in him; it began at times to suffer from different causes— from unexpected causes which would have formerly been quite inconceivable, from causes of a "higher order" than ever before—"if one may use such an expression, if there really are higher or lower causes. . . ." This he added on his own account.

Yes, he had even come to that; he was worrying about some sort of *higher* ideas of which he would never have thought twice in earlier days. In his own mind and in his conscience he called "higher" all "ideas" at which (he found to his surprise) he could not laugh in his heart—there had never been such hitherto—in his secret heart only, of course; oh, in company it was a different matter! He knew very well, indeed, that—if only the occasion were to arise—he would the very next day, in spite of all the mysterious and reverent resolutions of his conscience, with perfect composure disavow all these "higher ideas" and be the first to turn them into ridicule, without, of course, admitting anything. And this was really the case, in spite of a certain and, indeed, considerable independence of thought, which he had of late gained at the expense of the "lower ideas" that had mastered him till then. And how often, when he got up in the morning, he began to be ashamed of the thoughts and feelings he had passed through during a sleepless night! And he had suffered continually of late from sleeplessness. He had noticed for some time past that he had become excessively sensitive about everything, trifles as well as matters of importance, and so he made up his mind to trust his feelings as little as possible. But he could not overlook some facts, the reality of which he was forced to admit. Of late his thoughts and sensations were sometimes at night completely transformed, and for the most part utterly unlike those which came to him in the early part of the day. This struck him—and he even consulted a distinguished doctor who was, however, an acquaintance; he spoke to him about it jocosely, of course. The answer he received was that the transformation of ideas and sensations, and even the possession of two distinct sets of thoughts and sensations, was a universal fact among persons "who think and feel," that the convictions of a whole lifetime were sometimes transformed under the melancholy influences of night and sleeplessness; without rhyme or reason most momentous decisions were taken; but all this, of course, was only true up to a certain point —and, in fact, if the subject were too conscious of the double nature of his feelings, so that it began to be a source of suffering to him, it was certainly a symptom of approaching illness; and then steps must be taken at once. The best thing of all was to make a radical change in the mode of life, to alter one's diet, or even to travel. Relaxing medicine was beneficial, of course.

Velchaninov did not care to hear more; but to his mind it was conclusively shown to be illness.

"And so all this is only illness, all these 'higher ideas' are mere illness and nothing more!" he sometimes exclaimed to himself resentfully. He was very loth to admit this.

Soon, however, what had happened exclusively in the hours of the night began to be repeated in the morning, only with more bitterness than at night, with anger instead of remorse, with irony instead of emotion. What really happened was that certain incidents in his past, even in his distant past, began suddenly, and God knows why, to come more and more frequently back to his mind, but they came back in quite a peculiar way. Velchaninov had, for instance, complained for a long time past of loss of memory: he would forget the faces of acquaintances, who were offended by his cutting them when they met; he sometimes completely forgot a book he had read months before; and yet in spite of this loss of memory, evident every day (and a source of great uneasiness to him), everything concerning the remote past, things that had been quite forgotten for ten or fifteen years, would sometimes come suddenly into his mind now with such amazing exactitude of details and impressions that he felt as though he were living through them again. Some of the facts he remembered had been so completely forgotten that it seemed to him a miracle that they could be recalled. But this was not all, and, indeed, what man of wide experience has not some memory of a peculiar sort? But the point was that all that was recalled came back now with a quite fresh, surprising and, till then, inconceivable point of view, and seemed as though some one were leading up to it on purpose. Why did some things he remembered strike him now as positive crimes? And it was not a question of the judgments of his mind only: he would have put little faith in his gloomy, solitary and sick mind; but it reached the point of curses and almost of tears, of inward tears. Why, two years before, he would not have believed it if he had been told that he would ever shed tears! At first, however, what he remembered was rather of a mortifying than of a sentimental character: he recalled certain failures and humiliations in society; he remembered, for instance, how he had been slandered by an intriguing fellow, and in consequence refused admittance to a certain house; how, for instance, and not so long ago, he had been publicly and unmistakably insulted, and had not challenged the offender to a duel; how in a circle of very pretty women he had been made the subject of an extremely witty epigram and had found no suitable answer. He even recollected one or two unpaid debts—trifling ones, it is true, but debts of honour —owing to people whom he had given up visiting and even spoke ill of. He was also worried (but only in his worst moments) by the thought of the two fortunes, both considerable ones, which he had squandered in the stupidest way possible. But soon he began to remember things of a "higher order."

Suddenly, for instance, apropos of nothing, he remembered the forgotten, utterly forgotten, figure of a harmless, grey-headed and absurd old clerk, whom he had once, long, long ago, and with absolute impunity, insulted in public simply to gratify his own conceit, simply for the sake of an amusing and successful jest, which was repeated and increased his prestige. The incident had been so completely forgotten that he could not even recall the old man's surname, though all the surroundings of the incident rose before his mind with incredible clearness. He distinctly remembered that the old man was defending his daughter, who was unmarried, though no longer quite young, and had become the subject of gossip in the town. The old man had begun to answer angrily, but he suddenly burst out crying before the whole company, which made some sensation. They had ended by making him drunk with champagne as a joke and getting a hearty laugh out of it. And now when, apropos of nothing, Velchaninov remembered how the poor old man had sobbed and hidden his face in his hands like a child, it suddenly seemed to him as though he had never forgotten it. And, strange to say, it had all seemed to him very amusing at the time, especially some of the details, such as the way he had covered his face with his hands; but now it was quite the contrary.

Later, he recalled how, simply as a joke, he had slandered the very pretty wife of a schoolmaster, and how the slander had reached the husband's ears. Velchaninov had left the town soon after and never knew what the final consequences of his slander had been, but now he began to imagine how all might have ended—and there is no knowing to what lengths his imagination might not have gone if this memory had not suddenly been succeeded by a much more recent reminiscence of a young girl of the working-class, to whom he had not even felt attracted, and of whom, it must be admitted, he was actually ashamed. Yet, though he could not have said what had induced him, he had got her into trouble and had simply abandoned her and his child without even saying good-bye (it was true, he had no time to spare), when he left Petersburg. He had tried to find that girl for a whole year afterwards, but he had not succeeded in tracing her. He had, it seemed, hundreds of such reminiscences—and each one of them seemed to bring dozens of others in its train. By degrees his vanity, too, began to suffer.

We have said already that his vanity had degenerated into something peculiar. That was true. At moments (rare moments, however), he even forgot himself to such a degree that he ceased to be ashamed of not keeping his own carriage, that he trudged on foot from one court to another, that he began to be somewhat negligent in his dress. And if some one of his own acquaintance had scanned him with a sarcastic stare in the street or had simply refused to recognize him, he might really have had pride enough to pass him by without a frown. His indifference would have been genuine, not assumed for effect. Of course, this was only at times: these were only the moments of forgetfulness and nervous irritation, yet his vanity had by degrees grown less concerned with the subjects that had once affected it, and was becoming concentrated on one question, which haunted him continually.

"Why, one would think," he began reflecting satirically sometimes (and he almost always began by being satirical when he thought about himself), "why, one would think some one up aloft were anxious for the reformation of my morals, and were sending me these cursed reminiscences and 'tears of repentance'! So be it, but it's all useless! It is all shooting with blank cartridges! As though I did not know for certain, more certainly than certainty, that in spite of these fits of tearful remorse and self-reproach, I haven't a grain of independence for all my foolish middle age! Why, if the same temptation were to turn up to-morrow, if circumstances, for instance, were to make it to my interest to spread a rumour that the schoolmaster's wife had taken presents from me, I should certainly spread it, I shouldn't hesitate—and it would be even worse, more loathsome than the first time, just because it would be the second time and not the first time. Yes, if I were insulted again this minute by that little prince whose leg I shot off eleven years ago, though he was the only son of his mother, I should challenge him at once and condemn him to crutches again. So they are no better than blank cartridges, and there's no sense in them! And what's the good of remembering the past when I've not the slightest power of escaping from myself?"

And though the adventure with the schoolmaster's wife was not repeated, though he did not condemn any one else to crutches, the very idea that it inevitably would be the same, if the same circumstances arose, almost killed him . . . at times. One cannot, in reality, suffer from memories all the time; one can rest and enjoy oneself in the intervals.

So, indeed, Velchaninov did: he was ready to enjoy himself in the intervals; yet his sojourn in Petersburg grew more and more unpleasant as time went on. July was approaching. Intermittently he had flashes of determination to give up everything, the lawsuit and all, and to go away somewhere without looking back, to go suddenly, on the spur of the moment, to the Crimea, for instance. But, as a rule, an hour later he had scorned the idea and had laughed at it: "These hateful thoughts won't stop short at sending me to the south, if once they've begun and if I've any sense of decency, and so it's useless to run away from them, and, indeed, there's no reason to.

"And what's the object of running away?" he went on brooding in his despondency; "it's so dusty here, so stifling, everything in the house is so messy. In those lawcourts where I hang about among those busy people, there is such a scurrying to and fro like mice, such a mass of sordid cares! All the people left in town, all the faces that flit by from morning till night so naïvely and openly betray their self-love, their guileless insolence, the cowardice of their little souls, the chicken-heartedness of their little natures—why, it's a paradise for a melancholy man, seriously speaking! Everything is open, everything is clear, no one thinks it necessary to hide anything as they do among our gentry in our summer villas or at watering-places abroad—and so it's more deserving of respect, if only for its openness and simplicity! . . . I won't go away! I'll stay here if I burst!"

Chapter 2

The Gentleman with Crape on His Hat

It was the third of July. The heat and stuffiness were insufferable. The day had been a very busy one for Velchaninov; he had had to spend the whole morning in walking and driving from place to place, and he had before him the prospect of an unavoidable visit that evening to a gentleman—a lawyer and a civil councillor—whom he hoped to catch unawares at his villa out of town. At six o'clock Velchaninov went at last into a restaurant (the fare was not beyond criticism, though the cooking was French) on the Nevsky Prospect, near the Police Bridge. He sat down at the little table in his usual corner and asked for the dinner of the day.

He used to eat the dinner that was provided for a rouble and paid extra for the wine, and he regarded this as a sacrifice to the unsettled state of his finances and an act of prudence on his part. Though he wondered how he could possibly eat such stuff, he nevertheless used to devour it to the last crumb—and every time with as much appetite as though he had not eaten for three days before. "There's something morbid about it," he would mutter to himself sometimes, noticing his appetite. But on this occasion he took his seat at his little table in a very bad humour, tossed his hat down angrily, put his elbows on the table, and sank into thought.

Though he could be so polite and, on occasion, so loftily imperturbable, he would probably now, if some one dining near him had been noisy, or the boy waiting on him had failed to understand at the first word, have been as blustering as a *junker* and would perhaps have made a scene.

The soup was put before him. He took up the ladle, but before he had time to help himself, he dropped it, and almost jumped up from the table. A surprising idea suddenly dawned upon him: at that instant—and God knows by what process—he suddenly realized the cause of his depression, of the special extra depression which had tormented him of late for several days together, had for some unknown reason fastened upon him and for some unknown cause refused to be shaken off; now he suddenly saw it all and it was as plain as a pikestaff.

"It's all that hat," he muttered as though inspired. "It's nothing but that cursed bowler hat with that beastly mourning crape that is the cause of it all!"

He began pondering—and the more he pondered the more morose he grew, and the more extraordinary "the whole adventure" seemed to him.

"But . . . it is not an adventure, though," he protested, distrustful of himself. "As though there were anything in the least like an adventure about it!"

All that had happened was this. Nearly a fortnight before (he did not really remember, but he fancied it was about a fortnight), he had first met somewhere in the street, near the corner of Podyatchesky Street and Myestchansky Street, a gentleman with crape on his hat. The gentleman was like any one else, there was nothing peculiar about him, he passed quickly, but he stared somewhat too fixedly at Velchaninov, and for some reason at once attracted his attention in a marked degree. His countenance struck Velchaninov as familiar. He had certainly at some time met it somewhere. "But I must have seen thousands of faces in my life, I can't remember them all!"

Before he had gone twenty paces further he seemed to have forgotten the encounter, in spite of the impression made at first. But the impression persisted the whole day —and it was somewhat singular, it took the form of a peculiar undefined annoyance. Now, a fortnight later, he remembered all that distinctly; he remembered, too, what he had failed to grasp at the time—that is, what his annoyance was due to; and he had so utterly failed to grasp it that he had not even connected his ill-humour all that evening with the meeting that morning.

But the gentleman had lost no time in recalling himself to Velchaninov's mind, and next day had come across the latter in the Nevsky Prospect again, and again stared at him rather strangely. Velchaninov dismissed him with a curse and immediately afterwards wondered why he cursed. It is true that there are faces that at once arouse an undefined and aimless aversion.

"Yes, I certainly have met him somewhere," he muttered thoughtfully, an hour after the meeting. And he remained in a very bad humour the whole evening afterwards; he even had a bad dream at night, and yet it never entered his head that the whole cause of this new fit of despondency was nothing but that gentleman in mourning, although he did not once think of him that evening! He had even been wrathful at the moment that such a "wretched object" could occupy his attention as long as it did and would certainly have thought it degrading to ascribe his agitation to him, if it had ever occurred to his mind to do so. Two days later they met again in a crowd coming off one of the Nevsky steamers. On this third occasion Velchaninov was ready to swear that the gentleman with the crape on his hat recognized him and made a dash for him, but was borne away in the crush; he fancied he had even had the "effrontery" to hold out his hand to him; perhaps he had even cried out and shouted his name. That, however, Velchaninov had not heard distinctly, but . . . "Who is the low fellow, though, and why does he not come up to me, if he really does know me, and if he is so anxious to?" he thought angrily, as he got into a cab and drove towards Smolny monastery. Half-an-hour later he was noisily arguing with his lawyer, but in the evening and the night he was suffering again from the most abominable and most fantastic attack of acute depression. "Am I in for a bilious attack?" he wondered uneasily, looking at himself in the looking-glass.

This was the third meeting. Afterwards, for five days in succession, he met "no one," and not a sign was seen of the low fellow. And yet the gentleman with the crape on his hat was continually in his mind. With some surprise Velchaninov caught himself wondering: "What's the matter with me—am I sick on his account, or what? H'm! . . . and he must have a lot to do in Petersburg, too—and for whom is he wearing crape? He evidently recognized me, but I don't recognize him. And why do these people put on crape? It's out of keeping with him somehow. . . . I fancy if I look at him closer, I shall recognize him. . . ."

And something seemed faintly stirring in his memory, like some familiar but momentarily forgotten word, which one tries with all one's might to recall; one knows it very well and knows that one knows it; one knows exactly what it means, one is close upon it and yet it refuses to be remembered, in spite of one's efforts.

"It was . . . It was long ago . . . and it was somewhere . . . There was . . . there was . . . but, damn the fellow, whatever there was or wasn't. . . ." he cried angrily all at once; "it is not worth while to demean and degrade myself over that wretched fellow. . . ."

He grew horribly angry, but in the evening, when he suddenly remembered that he had been angry that morning, and "horribly" angry, it was extremely disagreeable to him; he felt as though some one had caught him in something shameful. He was bewildered and surprised.

"Then there must be reasons for my being so angry . . . apropos of nothing . . . at a mere reminiscence . . ." He left the thought unfinished.

And next day he felt angrier than ever, but this time he fancied he had grounds for it, and that he was quite right in feeling so; "It was unheard-of insolence," he thought. What had happened was the fourth meeting. The gentleman with crape on his hat had suddenly made his appearance again, as though he had sprung out of the earth. Velchaninov had just caught in the street the indispensable civil councillor before mentioned, of whom he was still in pursuit, meaning to pounce on him unawares at his summer villa, for the gentleman, whom Velchaninov scarcely knew, though it was so necessary to see him about his business, on that occasion as on this eluded him, and was evidently keeping out of sight and extremely reluctant to meet him. Delighted at coming across him at last, Velchaninov walked hurriedly beside him, glancing into his face and straining every effort to bring the wily old fellow to the discussion of a certain subject, in which the latter might be indiscreet enough to let slip the facts of which he had so long been on the track; but the crafty old man had his own views, and kept putting him off with laughter or silence—and it was just at this extremely absorbing moment that Velchaninov descried on the opposite pavement the gentleman with crape on his hat. He was standing staring at them both—he was watching them, that was evident, and seemed to be jeering at them.

"Damnation!" cried Velchaninov in a fury, as he left the civil councillor at his destination and ascribed his failure with him to the sudden appearance of that "impudent fellow." "Damnation! is he spying on me? He's evidently following me. Hired by some one, perhaps, and . . . and . . . and, by Jove! he was jeering at me! By Jove! I'll thrash him. . . . I'm sorry I've no stick with me! I'll buy a stick! I won't let it pass. Who is he? I insist on knowing who he is."

It was three days after this fourth meeting that Velchaninov was at his restaurant, as we have described him, agitated in earnest and even somewhat overwhelmed. He could not help being conscious of it himself, in spite of his pride. He was forced at last, putting all the circumstances together, to suspect that all his depression—all this *peculiar* despondency and the agitation that had persisted for the last fortnight—was caused by no other than this gentleman in mourning, "nonentity as he was."

"I may be a hypochondriac," thought Velchaninov, "and so I am ready to make a mountain out of a molehill, but does it make it any better for me that all this is *perhaps* only fancy! Why, if every rogue like that is going to be able to upset one in this way, why . . . it's . . . why? . . ."

Certainly in the meeting of that day (the fifth), which had so agitated Velchaninov, the mountain had proved to be little more than a mole-hill: the gentleman had as before darted by him, but this time without scrutinizing Velchaninov, and without, as before, betraying that he recognized him; on the contrary, he dropped his eyes and seemed to be very anxious to escape being noticed. Velchaninov turned round and shouted at the top of his voice—

"Hi! you with the crape on your hat! Hiding now! Stop! Who are you?"

The question (and his shouting altogether) was very irrational, but Velchaninov only realized that after he had uttered it. The gentleman turned round at the shout, stood still for a minute disconcerted, smiled, seemed on the point of doing or saying something, was obviously for a minute in a state of the utmost indecision, then he suddenly turned and rushed away without looking back. Velchaninov looked after him with astonishment.

"And what if it's a case of my forcing myself on him, not his forcing himself on me?" he thought. "And that's all it amounts to?"

When he had finished dinner he made haste to set off to the summer villa to see the civil councillor. He did not find him; he was informed that "his honour had not returned that day, and probably would not come back till three or four o'clock in the morning, as he was staying in town to a birthday party." This was so mortifying that, in his first fury, Velchaninov decided himself to go to the birthday party, and even set off to do so; but reflecting on the road that it was a long way to go, he dismissed the cab and trudged home on foot to his flat near the Grand Theatre. He felt that he wanted exercise. He must, at all costs, overcome his usual sleeplessness, and sleep sound that night, to soothe his excited nerves; and in order to sleep he must anyway be tired. And, as it was a long walk, it was half-past ten before he reached home, and he certainly was very tired.

Though he so criticized the flat that he had taken the previous March, and abused it so malignantly—excusing himself to himself on the plea that he was only "camping there temporarily," and stranded in Petersburg through that "damned lawsuit"—the flat was by no means so bad and so unsuitable as he made out. The approach was certainly rather dark and "grubby" under the gateway, but the flat itself, on the second storey, consisted of two big, lofty and bright rooms, separated from one another by a dark entry, and looking one into the street, the other into the courtyard. Adjoining the room the windows of which looked into the courtyard was a small study, which had been designed for a bedroom; but Velchaninov kept it littered with books and papers; he slept in one of the larger rooms, the one that looked into the street. He had a bed made up on the sofa. The furniture was quite decent, though second-hand, and he had besides a few articles of value—the relics of his former prosperity: bronze and china, and big, genuine Bokhara rugs; even two good pictures had been preserved; but everything had been unmistakably untidy and even dusty and nothing had been put in its place ever since his servant, Pelagea, had gone home to Novgorod for a holiday and left him alone.

The oddity of having a solitary female servant for a bachelor and man of the world who was still anxious to keep up the style of a gentleman almost made Velchaninov blush, though he was very well satisfied with his Pelagea. The girl had come to him when he was taking the flat in the spring, from a family of his acquaintance who were going abroad, and she had put the flat to rights. But when she went away he could not bring himself to engage another woman; to engage a manservant was not worth while for a short time; besides, he did not like menservants. And so it was arranged that the sister of the porter's wife should come in every morning to clear up and that Velchaninov should leave the key at the porter's lodge when he went out. She did absolutely nothing, merely pocketed her wages; and he suspected her of pilfering. Yet he dismissed everything with a shrug and was positively glad that he was left quite alone in the flat. But there are limits to everything; and at some jaundiced moments the "filth" was absolutely insufferable to his nerves, and he almost always went into his rooms with a feeling of repugnance on returning home.

But this time he barely gave himself time to undress; flinging himself on the bed, he irritably resolved to think of nothing, but to go to sleep "this minute," whatever might happen; and, strange to say, he did fall asleep as soon as his head touched the pillow; such a thing had not happened to him for almost a month.

He slept for nearly three hours, but his sleep was uneasy, and he had strange dreams such as one has in fever. He dreamed of some crime which he had committed and concealed and of which he was accused by people who kept coming up to him. An immense crowd collected, but more people still came, so that the door was not shut but remained open. But his whole interest was centered on a strange person, once an intimate friend of his, who was dead, but now somehow suddenly came to see him. What made it most worrying was that Velchaninov did not know the man, had forgotten his name and could not recall it. All he knew was that he had once liked him very much. All the other people who had come up seemed expecting from this man a final word that would decide Velchaninov's guilt or innocence, and all were waiting impatiently. But he sat at the table without moving, was mute and would not speak. The noise did not cease for a moment, the general irritation grew more intense, and suddenly in a fury Velchaninov struck the man for refusing to speak, and felt a strange enjoyment in doing it. His heart thrilled with horror and misery at what he had done, but there was enjoyment in that thrill. Utterly exasperated, he struck him a second time and a third, and, drunk with rage and terror, which reached the pitch of madness, but in which there was an intense enjoyment, he lost count of his blows, and went on beating him without stopping. He wanted to demolish *it* all, all. Suddenly something happened: they all shrieked horribly and turned round to the door, as though expecting something, and at that instant there came the sound of a ring at the bell, repeated three times, with violence enough to pull the bell off. Velchaninov woke up and was wideawake in an instant. He leapt headlong out of bed and rushed to the door; he was absolutely convinced that the ring at the bell was not a dream and that some one really had rung at his bell that moment. "It would be too unnatural for such a distinct, such a real, palpable ring to be only a dream!"

But to his surprise the ring at the bell turned out to be a dream, too. He opened the door, went out on the landing, even peeped down the stairs—there was absolutely no one there. The bell hung motionless. Surprised, but relieved, he went back into his room. When he had lighted a candle he remembered that he had left the door closed but not locked or bolted. He had sometimes in the past forgotten when he came home to lock the door for the night, not thinking it of much importance.

Pelagea had often given him a talking-to about it. He went back into the passage, shut the door, opened it once more and looked out on the landing, but only fastened the door on the inside with the hook, without taking the trouble to turn the key. The clock struck half-past two; so he must have slept three hours.

His dream had so disturbed him that he did not want to go to bed again at once, and made up his mind to walk up and down his room for half an hour or—"Time enough to smoke a cigar"—he thought. Hastily dressing, he went to the window and lifted the thick stuff curtain and the white blind behind it. It was already daylight in the street. The light summer nights of Petersburg always worked on his nerves and of late had intensified his insomnia, so that it was expressly on this account that he had, a fortnight previously, put up thick stuff curtains which completely excluded the light when they were fully drawn. Letting in the daylight and forgetting the lighted candle on the table, he fell to pacing up and down the room, still oppressed by a sort of sick and heavy feeling. The impression of the dream was still upon him. A real feeling of distress that he should have been capable of raising his hand against that man and beating him still persisted.

"That man doesn't exist, and never has existed; it's all a dream. Why am I worrying about it?"

He began thinking with exasperation, as though all his troubles were concentrated on this, that he was certainly beginning to be ill—"A sick man."

It was always painful to him to think that he was getting old and growing feebler, and in his bad moments he exaggerated his age and failing powers on purpose to irritate himself.

"Old age," he muttered; "I'm getting quite old, I'm losing my memory, I see apparitions, I dream dreams, bells ring. . . . Damn it all, I know from experience that such dreams are always a sign of fever with me. . . . I am convinced that all this business with the crape gentleman is a dream too. I was certainly right yesterday: it's I, I, who am pestering him, not he me. I've woven a romance about him, and I am hiding under the table in my fright at it. And why do I call him a low fellow? He may be a very decent person. His face is not attractive, certainly, though there is nothing particularly ugly about it; he's dressed like any one else. Only in his eyes there's something. . . . Here I'm at it again! I'm thinking about him again!! What the devil does the look in his eyes matter to me? Can't I get on without that? . . ."

Among the thoughts that kept starting up in his mind, one rankled painfully: he felt suddenly convinced that this gentleman with the crape on his hat had once been an acquaintance on friendly terms with him, and now sneered at him when he met him because he knew some great secret about him in the past and saw him now in such a humiliating position. He went mechanically to the window, meaning to open it and get a breath of the night air, and—and he suddenly shuddered all over: it seemed to him that something incredible and unheard-of was suddenly happening before his eyes.

He had not yet opened the window but he made haste to slip behind the corner of the window and hide himself: on the deserted pavement opposite he had suddenly seen directly facing the house the man with the crape on his hat. The gentleman was standing on the pavement looking towards his windows, but evidently not noticing him, stared inquisitively at the house as though considering something. He seemed to be deliberating and unable to decide: he lifted his hand and seemed to put his finger to his forehead. At last he made up his mind: he took a cursory glance round, and began stealthily on tiptoe crossing the street. Yes: he had gone in at the gateway by the little gate (which sometimes in summer was left unbolted till three o'clock).

"He's coming to me," flashed on Velchaninov's mind, and, also on tiptoe, he ran headlong to the door and stood before it silent and numb with suspense, softly laying his trembling right hand on the hook of the door he had just fastened, listening intently for the sound of footsteps on the stairs.

His heart beat so violently that he was afraid he might not hear the stranger come up on tiptoe. He did not understand what it meant, but he felt it all with tenfold intensity. His dream seemed to have melted into reality. Velchaninov was by temperament bold. He sometimes liked to display fearlessness in the face of danger even if he were only admiring himself with no one else to look at him. But now there was something else as well. The man who had so lately been given up to hypochondria and nervous depression was completely transformed; he was not the same man. A nervous, noiseless laugh broke from him. From behind the closed door he divined every movement of the stranger.

"Ah! now he's coming in, he has come in, he's looking about him; he's listening downstairs; he's holding his breath, stealing up . . . ah! He has taken hold of the handle, he's pulling it, trying it! He reckoned on its not being locked! So he knows I sometimes forget to lock it! He's pulling at the handle again; why, does he imagine that the hook will come out? It's a pity to part! Isn't it a pity to let him go like this?"

And indeed everything must have happened just as he pictured it; someone really was standing on the other side of the door, and was softly and noiselessly trying the lock, and was pulling at the handle and—"Of course, he had his object in doing so." But by now Velchaninov had resolved to settle the question, and with a sort of glee got ready for the moment. He had an irresistible longing to unfasten the hook, suddenly to fling open the door, and to confront the "bugbear" face to face. "What may you be doing here, pray, honoured sir?"

And so he did: seizing the moment, he suddenly lifted the hook, pushed the door and—almost fell over the gentleman with crape on his hat.

Chapter 3

Pavel Pavlovitch Trusotsky

The latter stood speechless, rooted to the spot. They stood facing one another in the doorway, and stared fixedly into each other's faces. Some moments passed and suddenly—Velchaninov recognized his visitor!

At the same time the visitor evidently realized that Velchaninov recognized him fully. There was a gleam in his eye that betrayed it. In one instant his whole face melted into a sugary smile.

"I have the pleasure, I believe, of addressing Alexey Ivanovitch?" he almost chanted in a voice of deep feeling, ludicrously incongruous with the circumstances.

"Surely you are not Pavel Pavlovitch Trusotsky?" Velchaninov brought out with an air of perplexity.

"We were acquainted nine years ago at T——, and if you will allow me to remind you—we were intimately acquainted."

"Yes . . . to be sure, but now it's three o'clock, and for the last ten minutes you've been trying whether my door was locked or not."

"Three o'clock!" cried the visitor, taking out his watch and seeming positively grieved and surprised; "why, so it is. Three! I beg your pardon, Alexey Ivanovitch, I ought to have considered before coming up: I'm quite ashamed. I'll come again and explain, in a day or two, but now . . ."

"No! If there's to be an explanation will you kindly give it me this minute!" Velchaninov caught him up. "Please walk inside, into this room—no doubt you intended to come into the room yourself, and have not turned up in the middle of the night simply to try the lock."

He was excited and at the same time disconcerted, and felt that he could not grasp the position. He was even somewhat ashamed—there proved to be neither mystery nor danger. The whole phantasmagoria had proved to be nothing; all that had turned up was the foolish figure of some Pavel Pavlovitch. And yet he did not believe that it was all so simple; he had a vague presentiment and dread of something. Making his visitor sit down in an arm-chair, he seated himself impatiently on his bed, not a yard away, bent forward with his hands on his knees and waited irritably for him to speak. He scanned him greedily and remembered him. But, strange to say, the man was silent, quite silent, and seemed not to realize that he was "in duty bound" to speak at once; on the contrary, he, too, gazed at Velchaninov with a look of expectation. It was possible that he was simply timid, feeling at first a certain awkwardness like a mouse in a trap; but Velchaninov flew into a rage.

"What do you mean by it!" he cried; "you are not a phantom or a dream, I suppose! You've not come to play at being dead, surely? Explain yourself, my good man!"

The visitor fidgeted, smiled, and began warily—

"So far as I see, what strikes you most of all is my coming at such an hour and under such peculiar circumstances. . . . So that, remembering all the past, and how we parted—it's really strange to me now. . . . Though, indeed, I had no intention of calling, and it has only happened by accident. . . ."

"How by accident? Why, I saw you through the window run across the street on tiptoe!"

"Ah, you saw me! So perhaps you know more about it all than I do! But I'm only irritating you. . . . You see, I arrived here three weeks ago on business of my own. . . . I am Pavel Pavlovitch Trusotsky, you know; you recognized me yourself. I am here to try to get transferred to another province, and to a post in another department considerably superior. . . . But all that's neither here nor there, though . . . The point is, if you must know, that I have been hanging about here for the last three weeks, and I seem to be spinning out my business on purpose—that is, the business of my transfer—and really, if it comes off I do believe I shan't notice that it has come off and shall stay on in your Petersburg, feeling as I do now. I hang about as though I had lost sight of my object and, as it were, pleased to have lost sight of it—feeling as I do! . . ."

"Feeling how?" Velchaninov asked, frowning.

The visitor raised his eyes to him, lifted his hat and pointed to the crape on it.

"Why, look; that's how I'm feeling."

Velchaninov gazed blankly first at the crape and then at the countenance of his visitor. Suddenly the colour rushed into his cheeks and he grew terribly agitated.

"Surely not Natalya Vassilyevna?"

"Yes! Natalya Vassilyevna! Last March . . . consumption, and almost suddenly, after two or three months' illness! And I am left—as you see!"

As he said this the visitor, in deep emotion, put out his hands on each side, the hat with the crape on it flapping in his left one, while he made a low bow that displayed his bald head for ten seconds at least.

His air and his gesture seemed to revive Velchaninov; an ironical and even provocative smile hovered on his lips—but only for a moment: the news of the death of this lady (whom he had known so long ago and had long ago succeeded in forgetting) gave him a shock which was a complete surprise to him.

"Is it possible?"—he muttered the first words that came to his tongue—"and why didn't you come straight and tell me?"

"I thank you for you sympathy. I see it and appreciate it, in spite of . . ."

"In spite of?"

"In spite of so many years of separation, you have just shown such sympathy for my sorrow and even for me that I am, of course, sensible of gratitude. That was all I wanted to express. It's not that I had doubts of my friends: I can find here the truest friends at once— Stepan Mihalovitch Bagautov, for instance. But you know, Alexey Ivanovitch, our acquaintance with you— friendship rather, as I gratefully recall it—was over nine years ago, you never came back to us; there was no interchange of letters. . . ."

The visitor chanted his phrases as though to music, but all the while that he was holding forth he looked at the floor, though, no doubt, all the time he saw everything. But Velchaninov had by now regained his composure.

With a very strange impression, which grew stronger and stronger, he listened to Pavel Pavlovitch and watched him, and when the latter suddenly paused, the most incongruous and surprising ideas rushed in a sudden flash into his mind.

"But how was it I didn't recognize you till now?" he cried, growing more animated. "Why, we've stumbled across each other five times in the street!"

"Yes; I remember that, too; you were constantly crossing my path—twice, or perhaps three times. . . ."

"That is, *you* were constantly coming upon me, not I upon you."

Velchaninov stood up and suddenly, quite unexpectedly, he began laughing. Pavel Pavlovitch paused, looked at him attentively, but at once continued—

"And as for your not recognizing me, you might well have forgotten me, and, besides, I've had smallpox and it has left some traces on my face."

"Smallpox? To be sure, he has had smallpox! However did you——"

"Manage that? Anything may happen. One never can tell, Alexey Ivanovitch; one does have such misfortunes."

"Only it's awfully funny all the same. But continue, continue, my dear friend!"

"Though I met you, too . . ."

"Stay! Why did you say 'manage that' just now? I meant to use a much more polite expression. But go on, go on!"

For some reason he felt more and more good-humoured. The feeling of shock was completely effaced by other emotions. He walked up and down the room with rapid steps.

"Even though I met you, and though when I set out for Petersburg I intended to seek you out, yet now, I repeat, I have been feeling so broken in spirit . . . and mentally shattered ever since March . . ."

"Oh, yes! shattered since March. . . . Stop a minute. Don't you smoke?"

"As you know, in old days when Natalya Vassilyevna was living I . . ."

"To be sure, to be sure; and since March?"

"Just a cigarette, perhaps."

"Here is a cigarette. Light it—and go on! Go on, it's awfully——"

And, lighting a cigar, Velchaninov quickly settled himself on the bed again.

Pavel Pavlovitch paused.

"But how excited you are yourself. Are you quite in good health?"

"Oh, damn my health!" Velchaninov was suddenly exasperated. "Continue!"

The visitor, for his part, looking at his companion's agitation, seemed better pleased and grew more self-confident.

"But what is there to continue?" he began again. "Imagine, Alexey Ivanovitch, in the first place, a man destroyed—that is, not simply destroyed, but fundamentally, so to say; a man whose existence is transformed after twenty years of married life, wandering about the streets with no consistent object, as though in a wilderness, almost in a state of oblivion, and finding a certain fascination in that oblivion. It is natural that sometimes when I meet an acquaintance, even a real friend, I purposely go out of my way to avoid approaching him, at such a moment of oblivion, I mean. And at another moment one remembers everything so, and so longs to see any one who has witnessed that recent past, gone now never to return, and has taken part in it, and one's heart beats so violently that one is ready to risk throwing oneself upon a friend by night as well as by day, even though one might have to wake him up at four o'clock in the morning on purpose. . . . I have made a mistake about the time only, not about our friendship; for this moment more than makes up for it. And as for the time, I really thought it was only twelve, feeling as I do. One drinks the cup of one's sorrow till one is drunk with it. And it's not sorrow, indeed, but the novelty of my state that crushes me. . . ."

"How strangely you express yourself!" Velchaninov observed gloomily, becoming extremely grave again.

"Yes, I do express myself strangely. . . ."

"And you're . . . not joking?"

"Joking!" exclaimed Pavel Pavlovitch in pained surprise, "and at the moment when I am announcing the sad . . ."

"Ach, don't speak of that, I entreat you!"

Velchaninov got up and began pacing the room again.

So passed five minutes. The visitor seemed about to get up too, but Velchaninov shouted: "Sit still, sit still!" and Pavel Pavlovitch obediently sank back into his arm-chair at once.

"But, how you have changed though," Velchaninov began again, suddenly stopping before him as though all at once struck by the thought. "You're dreadfully changed! Extraordinarily! Quite a different person."

"That's not strange: nine years."

"No, no, no, it's not a question of years! It's incredible how you've changed in appearance; you've become a different man!"

"That, too, may well be, in nine years."

"Or is it since March!"

"He—he!" Pavel Pavlovitch sniggered slyly. "That's a funny idea of yours. . . . But if I may venture—what is the change exactly?"

"You ask what! The Pavel Pavlovitch I used to know was such a solid, decorous person, that Pavel Pavlovitch was such a clever chap, and now—this Pavel Pavlovitch is a regular *vaurien!*"

He was at that stage of irritability in which even reserved people say more than they ought.

"*Vaurien!* You think so? And not a clever chap now—not clever?" Pavel Pavlovitch chuckled with relish.

"Clever chap be damned! Now I daresay you really are too clever."

"I'm insolent, but this low fellow's more so and . . . and what is his object?" Velchaninov was thinking all the while.

"Ach, dearest, most precious friend!" cried the visitor suddenly, growing extremely agitated and turning round in his chair. "What are we saying? We are not in the world now, we're not in the society of the great and the worldly! We're two old friends, very old friends! And we've come together in the fullest sincerity to recall to one another the priceless bond of friendship of which the dear departed was the precious link!"

And he was so carried away by the ecstasy of his feeling that he bowed his head as before, hiding his face in his hat. Velchaninov watched him with aversion and uneasiness.

"What if he's simply a buffoon," flashed through his mind; "but n-no, n-no! I don't think he's drunk—he may be drunk, though: his face is red. Even if he were drunk —it comes to the same thing. What's he driving at? What does the low fellow want?"

"Do you remember, do you remember," cried Pavel Pavlovitch, removing the hat a little and seeming more and more carried away by his reminiscences, "do you remember our expeditions into the country, our evenings and little parties with dancing and innocent games at the house of His Excellency, our most hospitable Semyon Semyonovitch? And how we used to read together, the three of us, in the evening! And our first acquaintance with you, when you called on me that morning to make inquiries about your business, and even began to speak rather warmly, and suddenly Natalya Vassilyevna came in, and within ten minutes you had become a real friend of the family and so you were for a whole year, exactly as in Turgenev's play *A Provincial Lady*."

Velchaninov paced slowly up and down, looked at the floor, listened with impatience and repulsion, but—listened intently.

"The thought of *A Provincial Lady* never entered my head," he interrupted, somewhat confused, "and you never used to talk in such a shrill voice and such . . . unnatural language. What is that for?"

"I certainly used to be more silent—that is, I was more reserved," Pavel Pavlovitch interposed hurriedly. "You know I used to prefer listening while the dear departed talked. You remember how she used to talk, how wittily. . . . And in regard to *A Provincial Lady* and Stupendyev particularly, you are quite right, for I remember it was we ourselves, the precious departed and I, used to speak of that at quiet moments after you'd gone away—comparing our first meeting with that drama, for there really was a resemblance. About Stupendyev especially."

"What Stupendyev? Damn him!" cried Velchaninov, and he actually stamped, utterly disconcerted at the mention of "Stupendyev," owing to a disturbing recollection that was evoked by the name.

"Stupendyev is a character, a character in a play, the husband in *A Provincial Lady*," Pavel Pavlovitch piped in a voice of honeyed sweetness; "but it belonged to a different series of our precious and happy memories, when after your departure Stepan Mihalovitch Bagautov bestowed his friendship on us, exactly as you did, for five whole years."

"Bagautov? What do you mean? What Bagautov?" Velchaninov stood still as though petrified.

"Bagautov, Stepan Mihalovitch, who bestowed his friendship on us, a year after you and . . . and exactly as you did."

"Good heavens, yes! I know that!" cried Velchaninov, recovering himself at last. "Bagautov! Why, of course, he had a berth in your town. . . ."

"He had, he had! At the Governor's! From Petersburg. A very elegant young man, belonging to the best society!" Pavel Pavlovitch exclaimed in a positive ecstasy.

"Yes, yes, yes! What was I thinking of? Why, he, too . . ."

"He too, he too," Pavel Pavlovitch repeated in the same ecstasy, catching up the word his companion had incautiously dropped. "He too! Well, we acted *A Provincial Lady* at His Excellency's, our most hospitable Semyon Semyonovitch's private theatre—Stepan Mihalovitch was the 'count,' I was the 'husband,' and the dear departed was 'The Provincial Lady'—only they took away the 'husband's' part from me, Natalya Vassilyevna insisted on it, so that I did not act the 'husband' because I was not fitted for the part. . . ."

"How the devil could you be Stupendyev? You're preeminently Pavel Pavlovitch Trusotsky and not Stupendyev," said Velchaninov, speaking with coarse rudeness and almost trembling with irritation. "Only, excuse me; Bagautov's in Petersburg, I saw him myself in the spring! Why don't you go and see him too?"

"I have been every blessed day, for the last fortnight. I'm not admitted! He's ill, he can't see me! And, only fancy, I've found out from first-hand sources that he really is very dangerously ill! The friend of six years. Ach, Alexey Ivanovitch, I tell you and I repeat it, that sometimes one's feelings are such that one longs to sink into the earth; yes, really; at another moment one feels as though one could embrace any one of those who have been, so to say, witnesses and participators of the past and simply that one may weep, absolutely for nothing else but that one may weep. . . ."

"Well, anyway, I've had enough of you for to-day,

haven't I?" Velchaninov brought out abruptly.
"More than enough, more!" Pavel Pavlovitch got up
from his seat at once. "It's four o'clock, and, what's
worse, I have so selfishly upset you. . . ."

"Listen, I will be sure to come and see you myself, and
then, I hope . . . Tell me straight out, tell me frankly,
you are not drunk to-day?"

"Drunk! Not a bit of it. . . ."

"Hadn't you been drinking just before you came, or
earlier?"

"Do you know, Alexey Ivanovitch, you're in a regular
fever."

"I'll come and see you to-morrow morning before one
o'clock."

"And I've been noticing for a long time that you seem,
as it were, delirious," Pavel Pavlovitch interrupted with
zest, still harping on the same subject. "I feel conscience-
stricken, really, that by my awkwardness . . . but I'm
going, I'm going! And you lie down and get some sleep!"

"Why, you haven't told me where you're living," Velchaninov called hastily after him.

"Didn't I tell you? At the Pokrovsky Hotel."

"What Pokrovsky Hotel?"

"Why, close to the Pokrovsky Church, close by, in the
side street. I've forgotten the name of the street and I've
forgotten the number, only it's close by the Pokrovsky
Church."

"I shall find it!"

"You'll be very welcome."

He was by now on his way downstairs.

"Stay," Velchaninov shouted after him again; "you
are not going to give me the slip?"

"How do you mean, give you the slip?" cried Pavel
Pavlovitch, staring at him open-eyed and turning round
to smile on the third step.

Instead of answering, Velchaninov shut the door with
a loud slam, carefully locked it and fastened the hook.
Returning to the room, he spat as though he had been in
contact with something unclean.

After standing for some five minutes in the middle of
the room, he flung himself on the bed without undressing
and in one minute fell asleep. The forgotten candle burnt
itself out on the table.

Chapter 4

The Wife, the Husband and the Lover

He slept very soundly and woke up at half-past nine; he remembered everything instantly, sat down on his bed and began at once thinking of "that woman's death." The shock of the sudden news of that death the night before had left a certain agitation and even pain. That pain and agitation had only for a time been smothered by a strange idea while Pavel Pavlovitch was with him.

But now, on waking up, all that had happened nine years before rose before his mind with extraordinary vividness.

This woman, this Natalya Vassilyevna, the wife of "that Trusotsky," he had once loved, and he had been her lover for the whole year that he had spent at T——, ostensibly on business of his own (that, too, was a lawsuit over a disputed inheritance), although his presence had not really been necessary for so long. The real cause of his remaining was this intrigue. The *liaison* and his love had such complete possession of him that it was as though he were in bondage to Natalya Vassilyevna, and he would probably have been ready on the spot to do anything, however monstrous and senseless, to satisfy that woman's slightest caprice.

He had never felt anything of the sort before. At the end of the year, when separation was inevitable, although it was expected to be only a brief one, Velchaninov was in such despair, as the fatal time drew near, that he proposed to Natalya Vassilyevna that she should elope with him, that he should carry her off from her husband, that they should throw up everything and that she should come abroad with him for ever. Nothing but the jibes and firm determination of the lady (who had, probably from boredom, or to amuse herself, quite approved of the project at first) could have dissuaded him and forced him to go alone. And actually, before two months had passed, he was asking himself in Petersburg the question which had always remained unanswered. Had he really loved that woman or had it been nothing but an "infatuation"? And it was not levity or the influence of some new passion that had given rise to this question: for those first two months in Petersburg he had been plunged in a sort of stupefaction and had scarcely noticed any woman, although he had at once mixed with his former acquaintances again and had seen a hundred women. At the same time he knew that if he were transported that moment to T—— he would promptly fall under the yoke of that woman's fascination again, in spite of any questions. Even five years later his conviction was unchanged. But five years later he used to admit this to himself with indignation and he even thought of "that woman" herself with hatred. He was ashamed of that year at T——; he could not even understand how such a "stupid" passion could have been possible for him, Velchaninov. All his memories of that passion had become absurd to him; and he blushed to the point of tears and was tormented by conscience-pricks at the thought of it. It is true that a few years later he had become somewhat calmer; he tried to forget it all—and almost succeeded. And now, all at once, nine years afterwards, all this had so suddenly and strangely risen up before him again, after hearing that night of the death of Natalya Vassilyevna.

Now, sitting on his bed, with confused thoughts crowding in disorder on his mind, he felt and realized clearly one thing only—that in spite of the "shock" he had felt at the news, he was nevertheless quite undisturbed by the fact of her death. "Can it be that I have no feeling for her?" he asked himself. It is true that he had now no feeling of hatred for her, and that he could criticize her more impartially, more fairly. In the course of those nine years of separation he had long since formulated the view that Natalya Vassilyevna belonged to the class of absolutely ordinary provincial ladies moving in good provincial society "and, who knows? perhaps she really was such, perhaps it was only I who idealized her so fantastically." He had always suspected, however, that there might be an error in that view; and he felt it even now. And, indeed, the facts were opposed to it; this Bagautov, too, had for several years been connected with her and apparently he, too, had been "under the yoke of her fascination." Bagautov certainly was a young man belonging to the best Petersburg society and, as he was a most "empty-headed fellow," he could only have had a successful career in Petersburg (Velchaninov used to say of him). Yet he had neglected Petersburg—that is, sacrificed his most important interests—and remained for five years in T—— solely on account of that woman! Yes, and he had finally returned to Petersburg, perhaps only because he, too, had been cast off like "an old, worn-out shoe." So there must have been in that woman something exceptional—a power of attracting, of enslaving, of dominating.

And yet one would have thought that she had not the gifts with which to attract and to enslave. She was not exactly pretty; perhaps she was actually plain. She was twenty-eight when Velchaninov first knew her. Though not altogether beautiful, her face was sometimes charmingly animated, but her eyes were not pretty: there was something like an excess of determination in them. She was very thin. On the intellectual side she had not been well educated; her keen intelligence was unmistakable, though she was one-sided in her ideas. Her manners were those of a provincial lady and at the same time, it is true, she had a great deal of tact; she had artistic taste, but showed it principally in knowing how to dress. In character she was resolute and domineering; she could never make up her mind to compromise in anything: it was all or nothing. In difficult positions her firmness and stoicism were amazing. She was capable of generosity and at the same time would be utterly unjust. To argue with that lady was impossible: "twice two makes four" meant nothing to her. She never thought herself wrong or to blame in anything. Her continual deception of her husband and the perfidies beyond number which she practised upon him did not weigh on her in the least. But, to quote Velchaninov's own comparison, she was like the "Madonna of the Flagellants," who believes implicitly herself that she is the mother of God—so Natalya Vassilyevna believed implicitly in everything she did.

She was faithful to her lover, but only as long as he did not bore her. She was fond of tormenting her lover, but she liked making up for it too. She was of a passionate, cruel and sensual type. She hated depravity and condemned it with exaggerated severity and—was herself depraved. No sort of fact could have made her recognize her own depravity. "Most likely she *genuinely* does not know it," Velchaninov thought about her even before he left T——. (We may remark, by the way, that he was the accomplice of her depravity.) "She is one of those women who are born to be unfaithful wives. Such women never become old maids; it's a law of their nature to be married to that end. The husband is the first lover, but never till after the wedding. No one gets married more adroitly and easily than this type of woman. For her first infidelity the husband is always to blame. And it is all accompanied by the most perfect sincerity: to the end they feel themselves absolutely right and, of course, entirely innocent."

Velchaninov was convinced that there really was such a type of woman; but, on the other hand, he was also convinced that there was a type of husband corresponding to that woman, whose sole vocation was to correspond with that feminine type. To his mind, the essence of such a husband lay in his being, so to say, "the eternal husband," or rather in being, all his life, a husband and nothing more. "Such a man is born and grows up only to be a husband, and, having married, is promptly transformed into a supplement of his wife, even when he happens to have unmistakable character of his own. The chief sign of such a husband is a certain decoration. He can no more escape wearing horns than the sun can help shining; he is not only unaware of the fact, but is bound by the very laws of his nature to be unaware of it." Velchaninov firmly believed in the existence of these two types and in Pavel Pavlovitch Trusotsky's being a perfect representative of one of them. The Pavel Pavlovitch of the previous night was, of course, very different from the Pavel Pavlovitch he had known at T——. He found him incredibly changed, but Velchaninov knew that he was bound to have changed and that all that was perfectly natural; Trusotsky could only as long as his wife was alive have remained all that he used to be, but, as it was, he was only a fraction of a whole, suddenly cut off and set free; that is, something wonderful and unique.

As for the Pavel Pavlovitch of the past at T——, this is how Velchaninov remembered him and recalled him now.

"Of course, at T——, Pavel Pavlovitch had been simply a husband," and nothing more. If he were, for instance, an official in the service as well, it was solely because such a position was one of the obligations of his married life; he was in the service for the sake of his wife and her social position in T——, though he was in himself zealous in his duties. He was thirty-five then and was possessed of some little fortune. He showed no special ability in his department and showed no special lack of it either. He used to mix with all the best people in the province and was said to be on an excellent footing with them. Natalya Vassilyevna was deeply respected in T——; she did not, however, greatly appreciate that, accepting it as simply her due, but in her own house she was superb at entertaining guests, and Pavel Pavlovitch had been so well trained by her that he was able to behave with dignity even when entertaining the highest magnates of the province. Perhaps (it seemed to Velchaninov) he had intelligence too, but as Natalya Vassilyevna did not like her spouse to talk too much, his intelligence was not very noticeable. Perhaps he had many natural good qualities, as well as bad ones. But his good qualities were kept under a shade, as it were, and his evil propensities were almost completely stifled.

Velchaninov remembered, for instance, that Pavel Pavlovitch sometimes betrayed a disposition to laugh at his neighbours, but this was sternly forbidden him. He was fond, too, at times of telling anecdotes; but a watch was kept on that weakness too, and he was only allowed to tell such as were brief and of little importance. He had a weakness for a festive glass outside the house and was even capable of drinking too much with a friend; but this failing had been severely nipped in the bud. And it is noteworthy that no outside observer would have said that Pavel Pavlovitch was a hen-pecked husband; Natalya Vassilyevna seemed an absolutely obedient wife, and most likely believed herself to be one. It was possible that Pavel Pavlovitch loved Natalya Vassilyevna passionately; but no one noticed it, and, indeed, it was impossible to notice it, and this reserve was probably due to her domestic discipline. Several times during his life at T—— Velchaninov had asked himself whether the husband had any suspicion at all of his wife's intrigue. Several times he questioned Natalya Vassilyevna seriously about it, and always received the answer, uttered with a certain annoyance, that her husband knew nothing and never could know anything about it and that "it was no concern of his." Another characteristic of hers was that she never laughed at Pavel Pavlovitch and did not consider him absurd or very plain and would, indeed, have taken his part very warmly if any one had dared to show him incivility. Having no children, she was naturally bound to become a society woman, but her home life, too, was essential to her. Social pleasures never had complete sway of her, and at home she was very fond of needlework and looking after the house. Pavel Pavlovitch had recalled, that night, the evenings they had spent in reading; it happened that sometimes Velchaninov read aloud and sometimes Pavel Pavlovitch: to Velchaninov's surprise he read aloud excellently. Meanwhile, Natalya Vassilyevna did sewing as she listened, always calmly and serenely. They read a novel of Dickens, something from a Russian magazine, sometimes even something "serious." Natalya Vassilyevna highly appreciated Velchaninov's culture, but appreciated it in silence, as something final and established, of which there was no need to talk. Altogether, her attitude to everything intellectual and literary was rather one of indifference, as to something irrelevant though perhaps useful. Pavel Pavlovitch sometimes showed considerable warmth on the subject.

The *liaison* at T—— was broken suddenly when on Velchaninov's side it had reached its zenith—that is, almost the point of madness. In reality he was abruptly dismissed, though it was all so arranged that he went away without grasping that he had been cast off "like a worthless old shoe."

Six weeks before his departure, a young artillery officer who had just finished at the training college arrived in T—— and took to visiting the Trusotskys. Instead of three, they were now a party of four. Natalya Vassilyevna welcomed the boy graciously but treated him as a boy. No suspicion crossed Velchaninov's mind and indeed he had no thought to spare for it, for he had just been told that separation was inevitable. One of the hundreds of reasons urged by Natalya Vassilyevna for his leaving her as soon as possible was that she believed herself to be with child: and therefore, naturally, he must disappear at once for three or four months at least, so that it would not be so easy for her husband to feel any doubt if there were any kind of gossip afterwards. It was rather a far-fetched argument. After a stormy proposition on the part of Velchaninov that she should fly with him to Paris or America, he departed alone to Petersburg, "only for a brief moment, of course," that is, for no more than three months, or nothing would have induced him to go, in spite of any reason or argument. Exactly two months later he received in Petersburg a letter from Natalya Vassilyevna asking him never to return, as she already loved another; she informed him that she had been mistaken about her condition. This information was superfluous. It was all clear to him now: he remembered the young officer. With that it was all over for good. He chanced to hear afterwards, some years later, that Bagautov had appeared on the scene and spent five whole years there. He explained the disproportionate duration of that affair partly by the fact that Natalya Vassilyevna, by now, was a good deal older, and so more constant in her attachments.

He remained sitting on his bed for nearly an hour: at last he roused himself, rang for Mavra to bring his coffee, drank it hastily, and at eleven o'clock set out to look for the Pokrovsky Hotel. In going there he had a special idea which had only come to him in the morning. He felt somewhat ashamed of his behaviour to Pavel Pavlovitch the night before and now he wanted to efface the impression.

The whole fantastic business with the door handle, the night before, he now put down to chance, to the tipsy condition of Pavel Pavlovitch and perhaps to something else, but he did not really know, exactly, why he was going now to form new relations with the former husband, when everything had so naturally and of its own accord ended between them. Something attracted him. He had received a peculiar impression and he was attracted in consequence of it.

Chapter 5

Liza

Pavel Pavlovitch had no idea of "giving him the slip," and goodness knows why Velchaninov had asked him the question the night before; he was, indeed, at a loss to explain it himself. At his first inquiry at a little shop near the Pokrovsky Church, he was directed to the hotel in the side street a couple of paces away. At the hotel, it was explained that M. Trusotsky was staying in the lodge close by in the courtyard, in furnished rooms at Marya Sysoevna's. Going up the narrow, wet and very dirty stone stairs to the second storey, where these rooms were, he suddenly heard the sound of crying. It seemed like the crying of a child of seven or eight; the sound was distressing; he heard smothered sobs which would break out and with them the stamping of feet and shouts of fury, which were smothered, too, in a hoarse falsetto voice, evidently that of a grown-up man. This man seemed to be trying to suppress the child and to be very anxious that her crying should not be heard, but was making more noise than she was. The shouts sounded pitiless, and the child seemed to be begging forgiveness. In a small passage at the top, with doors on both sides of it, Velchaninov met a tall, stout, slovenly-looking peasant woman of forty and asked for Pavel Pavlovitch. She pointed towards the door from which the sounds were coming. There was a look of some indignation on the fat, purple face of this woman.

"You see how he amuses himself!" she said gruffly and went downstairs.

Velchaninov was just about to knock at the door, but on second thoughts he walked straight in. In a small room, roughly though amply furnished with common painted furniture, stood Pavel Pavlovitch without his coat and waistcoat. With a flushed and exasperated face he was trying, by means of shouts, gesticulations and even (Velchaninov fancied) kicks, to silence a little girl of eight, shabbily dressed in a short, black, woollen frock. She seemed to be actually in hysterics, she gasped hysterically and held out her hands to Pavel Pavlovitch as though she wanted to clutch at him, to hug him, to beseech and implore him about something. In one instant the whole scene was transformed: seeing the visitor, the child cried out and dashed away into a tiny room adjoining, and Pavel Pavlovitch, for a moment disconcerted, instantly melted into smiles, exactly as he had done the night before when Velchaninov flung open the door upon him on the stairs.

"Alexey Ivanovitch!" he cried, in genuine surprise. "I could never have expected . . . but come in, come in! Here, on the sofa, or here in the arm-chair, while I . . ."

And he rushed to put on his coat, forgetting to put on his waistcoat.

"Stay as you are, don't stand on ceremony."

Velchaninov sat down in the chair.

"No, allow me to stand on ceremony; here, now I am more respectable. But why are you sitting in the corner? Sit here in the arm-chair, by the table. . . . Well, I didn't expect you, I didn't expect you!"

He, too, sat down on the edge of a rush-bottomed chair, not beside his "unexpected" visitor, but setting his chair at an angle so as to sit more nearly facing him. "Why didn't you expect me? Why, I told you last night that I would come at this time."

"I thought you wouldn't come; and when I reflected on all that happened yesterday, on waking this morning, I despaired of ever seeing you again."

Meanwhile Velchaninov was looking about him. The room was in disorder, the bed was not made, clothes were lying about, on the table were glasses with dregs of coffee in them, crumbs and a bottle of champagne, half full, with the cork out and a glass beside it. He stole a glance towards the next room, but there all was quiet; the child was in hiding and perfectly still.

"Surely you are not drinking that now?" said Velchaninov, indicating the champagne.

"The remains . . ." said Pavel Pavlovitch in confusion.

"Well, you have changed!"

"It's a bad habit, come upon me all at once; yes, really, since that date. I'm not lying! I can't restrain myself. Don't be uneasy, Alexey Ivanovitch. I'm not drunk now, and I'm not going to play the fool now as I did at your flat yesterday; but I'm telling the truth, it's all since then. And if any one had told me six months ago that I should break down like this, if I'd been shown myself in the looking-glass—I shouldn't have believed it."

"You were drunk last night, then?"

"I was," Pavel Pavlovitch admitted in a low voice, looking down in embarrassment. "And you see I wasn't exactly drunk then, but I had been a little before. I want to explain, because I'm always worse a little while after. If I get ever so little tipsy, it is followed by a sort of violence and foolishness, and I feel my grief more intensely too. It's because of my grief, perhaps, I drink. Then I'm capable of playing all sorts of pranks and I push myself forward quite stupidly and insult people for nothing. I must have presented myself very strangely to you yesterday?"

"Do you mean to say you don't remember?"

"Not remember! I remember it all. . . ."

"You see, Pavel Pavlovitch, that's just what I thought," Velchaninov said in a conciliatory voice. "What's more, I was myself rather irritable with you last night and . . . too impatient, I readily admit it. I don't feel quite well at times, and then your unexpected arrival last night . . ."

"Yes, at night, at night!" Pavel Pavlovitch shook his head, as though surprised and disapproving. "And what possessed me! Nothing would have induced me to come in to you if you had not opened the door yourself; I should have gone away from the door. I came to you a week ago, Alexey Ivanovitch, and you were not at home, but perhaps I should never have come again. I have some pride, too, Alexey Ivanovitch, although I do recognize the position I am in. We met in the street, too, and I kept thinking: 'Why, he must recognize me and yet he turns away; nine years are no joke,' and I couldn't make up my mind to come. And last night I had wandered from the Petersburg Side and I forgot the time. It all came from that" (he pointed to the bottle), "and from my feelings. It was stupid! Very! And if it had been any one but you —for you've come to see me even after what happened yesterday, for the sake of old times—I should have given up all hope of renewing our acquaintance!"

Velchaninov listened attentively. The man seemed to him to be speaking sincerely and even with a certain dignity; and yet he did not believe one word he had heard since he came into the room.

"Tell me, Pavel Pavlovitch, you are not alone here, then? Whose little girl is that I found with you just now?"

Pavel Pavlovitch was positively amazed and raised his eyebrows, but he looked frankly and pleasantly at Velchaninov.

"Whose little girl? Why, it's Liza!" he said, with an affable smile.

"What Liza?" muttered Velchaninov, with a sort of inward tremor. The shock was too sudden. When he came in and saw Liza, just before, he was surprised, but had absolutely no presentiment of the truth, and thought nothing particular about her.

"Yes, our Liza, our daughter Liza!" Pavel Pavlovitch smiled.

"Your daughter? Do you mean that you and Natalya . . . Natalya Vassilyevna had children?" Velchaninov asked timidly and mistrustfully, in a very low voice.

"Why, of course! But there, upon my word, how should you have heard of it? What am I thinking about! It was after you went away, God blessed us with her!"

Pavel Pavlovitch positively jumped up from his chair in some agitation, though it seemed agreeable too.

"I heard nothing about it," said Velchaninov, and he turned pale.

"To be sure, to be sure; from whom could you have heard it?" said Pavel Pavlovitch, in a voice weak with emotion. "My poor wife and I had lost all hope, as no doubt you remember, and suddenly God sent us this blessing, and what it meant to me—He only knows! Just a year after you went away, I believe. No, not a year, not nearly a year. Wait a bit; why, you left us, if my memory does not deceive me, in October or November, I believe."

"I left T—— at the beginning of September, the twelfth of September; I remember it very well."

"In September, was it? H'm! . . . what was I thinking about?" cried Pavel Pavlovitch, much surprised. "Well, if that's so, let me see: you went away on the twelfth of September, and Liza was born on the eighth of May, so —September—October—November—December—January—February—March—April—a little over eight months! And if you only knew how my poor wife . . ."

"Show me . . . call her . . ." Velchaninov faltered in a breaking voice.

"Certainly!" said Pavel Pavlovitch fussily, at once breaking off what he was saying, as though it were of no consequence. "Directly, directly, I'll introduce her!"

And he went hurriedly into the other room to Liza.

Fully three or perhaps four minutes passed; there was a hurried, rapid whispering in the room, and he just caught the sound of Liza's voice. "She's begging not to be brought in," thought Velchaninov. At last they came out.

"You see, she's all confusion," said Pavel Pavlovitch; "she's so shy, and so proud . . . the image of my poor wife!"

Liza came in, looking down and no longer tearful; her father was holding her hand. She was a tall, slim, very pretty little girl. She raised her big blue eyes to glance with curiosity at the visitor, looked at him sullenly, and dropped them again at once. Her eyes were full of that gravity one sees in children when they are left alone with a stranger and, retreating into a corner, look out solemnly and mistrustfully at the unfamiliar visitor; but she had, perhaps, some other thought, by no means childish, in her mind—so Velchaninov fancied.

Her father led her straight up to him.

"This is an uncle Mother used to know long ago; he was our friend. Don't be shy, hold out your hand."

The child bent forward a little, and timidly held out her hand.

"Natalya Vassilyevna would not have her trained to curtsey, but taught her to make a little bow, and hold out her hand in the English fashion," he added by way of explanation to Velchaninov, watching him intently.

Velchaninov knew that he was being watched, but had quite ceased to trouble himself to conceal his emotion; he sat perfectly still in his chair, held Liza's hand in his and gazed at the child. But Liza was in great anxiety about something, and, forgetting her hand in the visitor's hand, she kept her eyes fixed on her father. She listened apprehensively to all that he said. Velchaninov recognized those big blue eyes at once, but what struck him most of all was the wonderful soft whiteness of her face and the colour of her hair; these characteristics were so marked and so significant. Her features and the lines of the lips reminded him vividly of Natalya Vassilyevna. Meanwhile, Pavel Pavlovitch had for some time been telling him something, speaking, it seemed, with very great warmth and feeling, but Velchaninov did not hear him. He only caught the last sentence—

". . . so that you can't imagine our joy at this gift from the Lord, Alexey Ivanovitch! She became everything to me as soon as she came to us, so that I used to think that even if my tranquil happiness should, by God's will, be at an end, Liza would always be left me; that I reckoned upon for certain!"

"And Natalya Vassilyevna?" Velchaninov queried.

"Natalya Vassilyevna?" said Pavel Pavlovitch affectedly. "You know her way, you remember that she never cared to say a great deal, but the way she said good-bye to her on her death-bed . . . everything came out then! I said just now 'on her death-bed,' but yet only a day before her death she was upset and angry, said that they were trying to cure her with drugs, that there was nothing wrong with her but an ordinary fever, and that neither of our doctors understood it, and that as soon as Koch came back (do you remember our old friend the army doctor?)

she would be up again in a fortnight! But there! five hours before her decease she remembered that in three weeks' time we must visit her aunt, Liza's godmother, on her name day . . ."

Velchaninov suddenly got up from his chair, still holding the child's hand. Among other things it struck him that there was something reproachful in the intense look the child kept fixed upon her father.

"She's not ill?" he asked hurriedly and somewhat strangely.

"I don't think so, but . . . our circumstances are here so . . ." said Pavel Pavlovitch, with mournful solicitude. "She's a strange child and nervous at all times; after her mother's death she was ill for a fortnight, hysterical. Why, what a weeping and wailing we had just before you came in . . . do you hear, Liza, do you hear? And what was it all about? All because I go out and leave her; she says it shows I don't love her any more as I used to when mother was alive—that's her complaint against me. And a child like that who ought to be playing with her toys, instead of fretting over a fantastic notion like that. Though here she has no one to play with."

"Why, how . . . you're surely not alone here?"

"Quite alone; the servant only comes in once a day."

"And you go out and leave her like this alone?"

"What else could I do? And when I went out yesterday I locked her in, into that little room there, that's what the tears have been about to-day. But what else could I do? Judge for yourself: the day before yesterday she went down when I was out, and a boy threw a stone at her in the yard and hit her on the head. Or else she begins crying and runs round to all the lodgers in the yard, asking where I've gone. And that's not nice, you know. And I'm a nice one, too; I go out for an hour and come back next morning; that's what happened yesterday. It was a nice thing, too, that while I was away the landlady let her out, sent for a locksmith to break the lock—such a disgrace— I literally feel myself a monster. All mental aberration, all mental aberration. . . ."

"Father!" the child said timidly and uneasily.

"There you are, at it again! You're at the same thing again. What did I tell you just now?"

"I won't, I won't!" Liza repeated in terror, hurriedly clasping her hands before him.

"You can't go on like this in these surroundings," Velchaninov said impatiently, in a voice of authority. "Why, you . . . why, you're a man of property; how is it you're living like this—in this lodge and in such surroundings?"

"In the lodge? But, you see, we may be going away in a week's time, and we've wasted a great deal of money already, even though I have property. . . ."

"Come, that's enough, that's enough," Velchaninov cut him short with increasing impatience, as it were expressing plainly "There's no need to talk. I know all that you have to say, and I know with what feelings you are speaking."

"Listen, I'll make a suggestion. You said just now that you'll be staying a week, maybe possibly even a fortnight. I know a household here, that is, a family where I'm quite at home—have known them twenty years. The father, Alexandr Pavlovitch Pogoryeltsev, is a Privy Councillor; he might be of use to you in your business. They are at their summer villa now. They've got a splendid villa. Klavdia Petrovna is like a sister to me or a mother. They have eight children. Let me take Liza to them at once . . . that we may lose no time. They will be delighted to take her in for the whole time you are here, and will treat her like their own child, their own child!"

He was terribly impatient and did not disguise it.

"That's scarcely possible," said Pavel Pavlovitch, with a grimace, looking, so Velchaninov fancied, slily in his face.

"Why, why impossible?"

"Why, how can I let the child go so suddenly—with such a real friend as you, of course—I don't mean, but into a house of strangers, and of such high rank, where I don't know how she'd be received either?"

"But I've told you that I'm like one of the family!" cried Velchaninov, almost wrathfully. "Klavdia Petrovna will be delighted to take her at a word from me— as though it were my child. Damn it all! Why, you know yourself that you only say all this for the sake of saying something . . . there's nothing to discuss!"

He positively stamped his foot.

"I only mean, won't it seem strange? I should have to go and see her once or twice anyway, or she would be left without a father! He—he! . . . and in such a grand household."

"But it's the simplest household, not 'grand' at all!"

shouted Velchaninov. "I tell you there are a lot of children. She'll revive there, that's the whole object. . . . And I'll introduce you myself to-morrow, if you like. And of course you would have to go to thank them; we'll drive over every day, if you like."

"It's all so . . ."

"Nonsense! And, what's more, you know that yourself! Listen. Come to me this evening, and stay the night, perhaps, and we'll set off early in the morning so as to get there at twelve."

"My benefactor! And even to stay the night with you . . ." Pavel Pavlovitch agreed suddenly in a tone of fervent feeling. "You are doing me a charity literally. . . . Where is their villa?"

"Their villa is in Lyesnoe."

"Only, I say, what about her dress? For, you know, in such a distinguished household and in their summer villa, too, you know yourself . . . a father's heart . . ."

"What about her dress? She's in mourning. She couldn't be dressed differently, could she? It's the most suitable one could possibly imagine! The only thing is she ought to have clean linen . . . a clean tucker . . ."

Her tucker and what showed of her underlinen were, in fact, very dirty.

"She must change her things at once," said Pavel Pavlovitch fussily, "and we'll get together the rest of what she needs in the way of underclothes; Marya Sysoevna has got them in the wash."

"Then you should tell them to fetch a carriage," Velchaninov interposed; "and make haste if you can."

But a difficulty presented itself: Liza resolutely opposed it; she had been listening all the time in terror, and, if Velchaninov had had time to look at her attentively while he was persuading Pavel Pavlovitch, he would have seen a look of utter despair upon her little face.

"I am not going," she said firmly, in a low voice.

"There, there! You see, she's her mother over again."

"I'm not my mother over again, I'm not my mother over again!" cried Liza in despair, wringing her little hands, and as it were trying to defend herself before her father from the awful reproach of being like her mother. "Father, Father, if you leave me . . ."

She suddenly turned on Velchaninov, who was in dismay.

"If you take me I'll . . ."

But before she had time to say more, Pavel Pavlovitch clutched her by the arm and with undisguised exasperation dragged her almost by the collar into the little room. Whispering followed for some minutes; there was the sound of suppressed crying. Velchaninov was on the point of going in himself, but Pavel Pavlovitch came out and with a wry smile announced that she was coming directly. Velchaninov tried not to look at him and kept his eyes turned away.

Marya Sysoevna appeared. She was the same peasant woman that he had met just before in the passage; she began packing the linen she had brought with her in a pretty little bag belonging to Liza.

"Are you taking the little girl away then, sir?" she asked, addressing Velchaninov. "Have you a family, then? It's a good deed, sir: she's a quiet child; you are taking her from a perfect Bedlam."

"Come, come, Marya Sysoevna!" muttered Pavel Pavlovitch.

"Marya Sysoevna, indeed! That's my name, right enough. It is a Bedlam here, isn't it? Is it the proper thing for a child that can understand to see such disgraceful goings-on? They've fetched you a carriage, sir—to Lyesnoe, is it?"

"Yes, yes."

"Well, it's a blessing you came!"

Liza came out pale and, looking down, took her bag. Not one glance in Velchaninov's direction; she restrained herself and did not, as before, rush to embrace her father, even at parting; evidently she was unwilling to look at him either. Her father kissed her decorously on the head and patted it; her lips twitched as he did so and her little chin quivered, but still she did not raise her eyes to her father. Pavel Pavlovitch looked pale, and his hands were trembling—Velchaninov noticed that distinctly, though he was doing his utmost not to look at him. The one thing he longed for was to get away as quickly as possible.

"After all, it's not my fault," he thought. "It was bound to be so."

They went downstairs; there Marya Sysoevna kissed Liza good-bye, and only when she was sitting in the carriage Liza lifted her eyes to her father, flung up her hands and screamed; another minute and she would have flung herself out of the carriage to him, but the horses had started.

Chapter 6

A New Fancy of an Idle Man

"Are you feeling ill?" asked Velchaninov in alarm. "I will tell them to stop, I'll tell them to bring water. . . ."

She turned her eyes upon him and looked at him passionately, reproachfully.

"Where are you taking me?" she asked sharply and abruptly.

"It's a very nice family, Liza. They're in a delightful summer villa now; there are a lot of children; they'll love you; they are kind. Don't be angry with me, Liza; I only wish for your good."

How strange it would have seemed to all who knew him if any one could have seen him at that moment.

"How . . . how . . . how . . . how horrid you are!" said Liza, choking with stifled tears, glaring at him with her beautiful eyes full of anger.

"Liza, I . . ."

"You are wicked, wicked, wicked, wicked!"

She wrung her hands. Velchaninov was completely at a loss.

"Liza, darling, if you knew how despairing you make me!"

"Is it true that he will come to-morrow? Is it true?" she asked peremptorily.

"Yes, yes, I'll bring him myself; I'll take him with me and bring him."

"He'll deceive me," she whispered, looking down.

"Doesn't he love you, Liza?"

"He doesn't love me."

"Does he ill-treat you? Does he?"

Liza looked at him gloomily and was mute. She turned away from him again and sat with her eyes obstinately cast down. He began trying to coax her; he talked to her warmly, he was in a perfect fever. Liza listened with mistrust and hostility, but she did listen. Her attention delighted him extremely; he even began explaining to her what was meant by a man's drinking. He told her that he

loved her himself and would look after her father. Liza
lifted her eyes at last and looked at him intently. He began telling her how he used to know her mother and he
saw that what he told her interested her. Little by little
she began answering his questions, though cautiously and
in monosyllables. She still stubbornly refused to answer
his leading questions; she remained obstinately silent
about everything to do with her relations with her father
in the past. As he talked to her, Velchaninov took her
hand in his as before and held it; she did not pull it away.
The child was not silent all the time, however; she let out
in her confused answers that she loved her father more
than her mother, because he had always been fonder of
her, and her mother had not cared so much for her, but
that when her mother was dying she had kissed her and
cried a great deal when every one had gone out of the
room and they were left alone . . . and that now she
loved her more than any one, more than any one, more
than any one in the world, and every night she loved her
more than any one. But the child was certainly proud.
Realizing that she had spoken too freely, she suddenly
shrank into herself again and glanced with positive hatred
at Velchaninov, who had led her into saying so much.
Towards the end of the journey her hysterical agitation
almost passed off, but she sank into brooding and had the
look of a wild creature, sullen and gloomily, resolutely
stubborn. The fact that she was being taken to a strange
family, in which she had never been before, seemed for
the time being not to trouble her much. What tormented
her was something else.

Velchaninov saw that; he guessed that she was
ashamed before *him*, that she was ashamed of her father's
having so easily let her go with him, of his having, as it
were, flung her into his keeping.

"She is ill," he thought, "perhaps very ill; she's been
worried to death. . . . Oh, the drunken, abject beast! I
understand him now!"

He urged on the driver; he rested his hopes on the
country, the fresh air, the garden, the children, and the
new, unfamiliar life, and then, later on . . . But of what
would come afterwards he had no doubts at all; of the
future he had the fullest, brightest hopes. One thing only
he knew for certain: that he had never before felt what

he was experiencing now and that it would never leave him all his life.

"Here was an object, here was life!" he thought triumphantly.

A great many thoughts flashed upon his mind, but he did not dwell upon them and obstinately put away details; so long as he avoided details it all seemed clear and unassailable. His plan of action was self-evident.

"It will be possible to work upon that wretch," he mused, "by our united forces, and he will leave Liza in Petersburg at the Pogoryeltsevs', though at first only temporarily, for a certain time, and will go away alone, and Liza will be left to me; that's the whole thing. What more do I want? And . . . of course, he wants that himself; or else why does he torment her?"

At last they arrived. The Pogoryeltsevs' country home really was a charming place; they were met first of all by a noisy crowd of children, flocking out into the porch. Velchaninov had not been there for a long time, and the children were in a frenzy of delight; they were fond of him. The elder ones shouted to him at once, before he got out of the carriage—

"And how about the case, how is your case getting on?"

The cry was caught up even by the smallest, and they shrieked it mirthfully in imitation of their elders. They used to tease him about the lawsuit. But, seeing Liza, they surrounded her at once and began scrutinizing her with intent, dumb, childish curiosity. Klavdia Petrovna came out, followed by her husband. She and her husband, too, began with a laughing question about the lawsuit.

Klavdia Petrovna was a lady about thirty-seven, a plump and still good-looking brunette, with a fresh, rosy face. Her husband was fifty-five, a shrewd and clever man, but above everything good-natured. Their house was in the fullest sense of the word "a home" to Velchaninov, as he had said himself. But underlying this was the special circumstance that, twenty years before, Klavdia Petrovna had been on the point of marrying Velchaninov, then a student, hardly more than a boy. It was a case of first love, ardent, ridiculous and splendid. It had ended, however, in her marrying Pogoryeltsev. Five years later they had met again, and it had all ended in a quiet, serene friendship. A certain warmth, a peculiar glow suffusing their relations, had remained for ever. All was pure and irreproachable in Velchaninov's memories of this friendship, and it was the dearer to him for being perhaps the solitary case in which this was so. Here in this family he was simple, unaffected and kind; he used to fondle the children, he admitted all his failings, confessed his short-comings, and never gave himself airs. He swore more than once to the Pogoryeltsevs that he should before long give up the world, come and live with them and never leave them again. In his heart he thought of this project seriously.

He told them all that was necessary about Liza in some detail; but a mere request from him was enough, without any special explanations. Klavdia Petrovna kissed the "orphan" and promised for her part to do everything. The children took possession of Liza and carried her off to play in the garden.

After half an hour of lively conversation Velchaninov got up and began saying good-bye. He was so impatient that every one noticed it. They were all astonished; he had not been to see them for three weeks and now he was going in half an hour. He laughed and pledged him-self to come next day. They remarked that he seemed to be in a state of great excitement; he suddenly took Klavdia Petrovna's hand and, on the pretext of having forgotten to tell her something important, drew her aside into another room.

"Do you remember what I told you—you alone—what even your husband does not know—of my year at T——?"

"I remember perfectly; you often talked of it."

"It was not talking, it was a confession, to you alone, to you alone! I never told you the surname of that woman; she was the wife of this man Trusotsky. She is dead, and Liza is her daughter—my daughter!"

"Is it certain? You are not mistaken?" Klavdia Pe-trovna asked with some excitement.

"It's perfectly certain, perfectly certain; I am not mis-taken!" Velchaninov pronounced ecstatically.

And as briefly as he could, in haste and great excite-ment, he told her everything. Klavdia Petrovna already knew the whole story, but not the lady's name.

Velchaninov had always been so alarmed at the very idea that any one who knew him might ever meet Madame Trusotsky and think that *he* could *so* have loved that woman, that he had not till that day dared to reveal "that woman's" name even to Klavdia Petrovna, his one friend.

"And the father knows nothing?" asked Klavdia Petrovna, when she had heard his story.

"Y-yes, he does know. . . . It worries me that I've not got to the bottom of it yet!" Velchaninov went on eagerly. "He knows, he knows; I noticed it to-day and yesterday. But I must know how much he knows. That's why I'm in a hurry now. He is coming to me this evening. I can't imagine, though, how he can have found out—found out *everything*, I mean. He knows about Bagautov, there's no doubt of that. But about me? You know how clever women are in reassuring their husbands in such cases! If an angel came down from heaven—the husband would not believe him, but he would believe his wife! Don't shake your head and don't blame me; I blame myself and have blamed myself, for the whole affair, long ago, long ago! . . . You see, I was so certain he knew when I was there this morning that I compromised myself before him. Would you believe it, I felt so wretched and ashamed at having met him so rudely yesterday (I will tell you all about it fully afterwards). He came to me yesterday from an irresistible, malicious desire to let me know that he knew of the wrong done him, and knew who had done it; that was the whole reason of his stupid visit when he was drunk. But that was so natural on his part! He simply came to work off his resentment! I was altogether too hasty with him this morning and yesterday! Careless—stupid! I betrayed myself to him. Why did he turn up at a moment when I was upset? I tell you he's even been tormenting Liza, tormenting the child, and probably that, too, was to work off his resentment—to vent his malice if only on the child! Yes, he is spiteful—insignificant as he is, yet he is spiteful; very much so, indeed. In himself he is no more than a buffoon, though, God knows, in old days he seemed to be a very decent fellow within his limits—it's so natural that he should be going to the dogs! One must look at it from a Christian point of view! And you know, my dear, my best of friends, I want to be utterly different to him; I want to be kind to him. That would be really a 'good deed' on my part. For, you know, after all, I have wronged him! Listen, you know there's something else I must tell you. On one occasion in T—— I was in want of four thousand roubles, and he lent me the money on the spot, with no security, and showed genuine pleasure at being of use to me; and, do you know, I took it then, I took it from his hands. I borrowed money from him, do you understand, as a friend!"

"Only be more careful," Klavdia Petrovna anxiously observed, in response to all this. "And what a state of ecstasy you're in; I feel uneasy about you! Of course, Liza will be like a child of my own now. But there's so much, so much still to be settled! The great thing is that you must be more circumspect; you absolutely must be more circumspect when you are happy or so ecstatic; you're too generous when you are happy," she added, with a smile.

They all came out to see Velchaninov off. The children, who had been playing with Liza in the garden, brought her with them. They seemed to look at her with more amazement now than at first. Liza was overcome with shyness when, at parting, Velchaninov kissed her before them all, and warmly repeated his promise to come next day with her father. To the last minute she was silent and did not look at him, but then suddenly she clutched at his arm and drew him aside, fixing an imploring look on him; she wanted to tell him something. He promptly took her away into another room.

"What is it, Liza?" he asked her tenderly and reassuringly; but she, still looking about her apprehensively, drew him into the furthest corner; she wanted to be hidden from them all.

"What is it, Liza? What's the matter?"

She was dumb, she could not bring herself to speak; she gazed fixedly with her blue eyes into his face, and every feature of her little face expressed nothing but frantic terror.

"He'll . . . hang himself!" she whispered, as though in delirium.

"Who will hang himself?" asked Velchaninov in dismay.

"He, he! He tried to hang himself with a cord in the night!" the child said breathlessly. "I saw him! He tried to hang himself with a cord, he told me so, he told me so! He meant to before, he always meant to . . . I saw him in the night. . . ."

"Impossible," whispered Velchaninov in amazement. She suddenly fell to kissing his hands; she cried, almost choking with sobs, begged and besought him, but he could make nothing of her hysterical whisperings. And the tortured face of that terror-stricken child who looked to him as her last hope remained printed on his memory for ever, haunting him awake and visiting his dreams.

"And can she, can she really love him so much?" he thought, jealously and enviously, as with feverish impatience he returned to town. "She had told me herself that morning that she loved her mother more . . . perhaps she hated him and did not love him at all! . . . And what did that mean: he will hang himself? What did she mean by that? Would the fool hang himself?" . . . He must find out, he must certainly find out! He must get to the bottom of it as soon as possible—once and for all.

Chapter 7

The Husband and the Lover Kiss Each Other

He was in terrible haste "to find out."

"This morning I was so overwhelmed. This morning I hadn't the time to realize the position," he thought, recalling his first sight of Liza, "but now I must find out." To find out more quickly he was on the point of telling the driver to take him to Trusotsky's lodging, but on second thoughts decided: "No, better let him come to me, and meanwhile I'll make haste and get this accursed legal business off my hands."

He set to work feverishly; but this time he was conscious himself that he was very absent-minded and that he was hardly capable that day of attending to business. At five o'clock, when he went out to dinner, he was struck for the first time by an absurd idea: that perhaps he really was only hindering the progress of his case, by meddling in the lawsuit himself, fussing about in the law-courts and hunting up his lawyer, who was already beginning to hide from him. He laughed gaily at his supposition. "If this idea had occurred to me yesterday, I should have been dreadfully distressed," he added, even more gaily. In spite of his gaiety, he grew more and more preoccupied and more and more impatient. He fell to musing at last; and though his restless thought clutched at one thing after another, he could arrive at nothing that would satisfy him.

"I must have that man!" he decided finally. "I must solve the riddle of that man, and then make up my mind. It's—a duel!"

Returning home at seven o'clock, he did not find Pavel Pavlovitch and was extremely surprised, then extremely wrathful, and later still extremely depressed; finally he began to be actually frightened.

"God knows, God knows how it will end!" he repeated, as he walked about the room or stretched himself on the sofa, continually looking at his watch. At last, about nine o'clock, Pavel Pavlovitch appeared. "If the fellow were trying to dupe me, he couldn't have caught me at a more favourable time—I feel so unhinged at this moment," he thought, his confidence completely restored and his spirits rising again.

To his brisk and cheerful inquiry why he was so late coming, Pavel Pavlovitch gave a wry smile, seated himself with a free and easy air, very different from his manner the night before, and carelessly threw his hat with the crape on it on another chair close by. Velchaninov at once noticed this free and easy manner and made a note of it.

Calmly, without wasting words, with none of the excitement he had shown in the morning, he told him, as though giving a report, how he had taken Liza, how kindly she had been received, how good it would be for her, and little by little, as though forgetting Liza, he imperceptibly turned the conversation entirely on the Pogoryeltsevs—what charming people they were, how long he had known them, what a splendid and influential man Pogoryeltsev was, and so on. Pavel Pavlovitch listened inattentively and from time to time glanced up from under his brows at the speaker with an ill-humoured and crafty sneer.

"You're an impulsive person," he muttered, with a particularly disagreeable smile.

"You're rather ill-humoured to-day, though," Velchaninov observed with vexation.

"And why shouldn't I be ill-humoured, like every one else!" Pavel Pavlovitch cried out suddenly, just as though he had only been waiting for that to bounce out.

"You're at liberty to please yourself," laughed Velchaninov. "I wondered if anything had happened to you."

"So it has!" the other exclaimed, as though boasting that something had happened.

"What is it?"

Pavel Pavlovitch delayed answering for a little.

"Why, our Stepan Mihalovitch has played me a trick . . . Bagautov, that elegant young Petersburg gentleman of the best society."

"Was he not at home again?"

"No, this time he was at home. For the first time I was admitted, and I gazed upon his face . . . only he was dead!"

"Wha-at! Bagautov is dead?" Velchaninov was awfully surprised, though there was no apparent reason for his being so surprised.

"Yes. For six years our true and constant friend! Only yesterday, almost at midday, he died, and I knew nothing of it! I was going maybe that very minute to inquire after his health. To-morrow there will be the service and the funeral, he's already in his coffin. The coffin is lined with crimson-coloured velvet trimmed with gold . . . he died of brain fever. I was admitted—I was admitted to gaze upon his face! I told them at the door that I was an intimate friend, that was why I was admitted. What's one to think of the way he's treated me now, my true and constant friend for six long years—I ask you that? Perhaps it was only on his account I came to Petersburg!"

"But what are you angry with him for?" laughed Velchaninov. "Why, he did not die on purpose!"

"But I speak with my heart full of regret; he was a precious friend; this was what he meant to me."

And all at once, quite unexpectedly, Pavel Pavlovitch put up his two fingers like two horns on his bald forehead and went off into a low, prolonged chuckle. He sat like that, chuckling, for a full half-minute, staring into Velchaninov's face in a frenzy of malignant insolence. The latter was petrified as though at the sight of some ghost. But his stupefaction lasted but one brief instant; a sarcastic and insolently composed smile came slowly upon his lips.

"What's the meaning of that?" he asked, carelessly drawling the words.

"The meaning of it is—horns!" Pavel Pavlovitch rapped out, taking away his fingers from his forehead at last.

"That is . . . your horns?"

"My own, generously bestowed!" Pavel Pavlovitch said with a very nasty grimace. Both were silent.

"You're a plucky fellow, I must say!" Velchaninov pronounced.

"Because I showed you my decorations? Do you know, Alexey Ivanovitch, you'd better offer me something! You know I entertained you every blessed day for a whole year at T——. Send for just one bottle, my throat is dry."

"With pleasure; you should have said so before. What will you have?"

"Why you? Say we; we'll drink together, won't we?" said Pavel Pavlovitch, gazing into his face with a challenging but at the same time strangely uneasy look.

"Champagne?"

"What else? It's not the time for vodka yet. . . ."

Velchaninov got up deliberately, rang for Mavra and gave instructions.

"To the joy of our delightful meeting after nine years' absence," said Pavel Pavlovitch, with a quite superfluous and inappropriate snigger. "Now you, and you only, are the one friend left me! Stepan Mihalovitch Bagautov is no more! As the poet says—

" 'Great Patrocus is no more,
    Vile Thersites still lives on!' "

And at the word "Thersites" he poked himself in the chest.

"You'd better hurry up and speak out, you swine; I don't like hints," Velchaninov thought to himself. His anger was rising and for a long time he had hardly been able to restrain himself.

"Tell me," he said in a tone of vexation, "since you accuse Stepan Mihalovitch" (he could not call him simply Bagautov now), "I should have thought you would have been glad that the man who has wronged you is dead; why are you angry about it?"

"Glad? Why glad?"

"I imagine those must be your feelings."

"He—he! You are quite mistaken about my feelings on that subject; as some wise man has said, 'A dead enemy is good, but a living one is better,' he—he!"

"But you saw him living every day for five years, I believe; you had time to get tired of the sight of him," Velchaninov observed, with spiteful impertinence.

"But you don't suppose I knew then . . . you don't suppose I knew?" Pavel Pavlovitch blurted out suddenly, just as though he had bounced out from behind a corner again, and as though he were delighted to be asked a question he had long been waiting for.

"What do you take me for, then, Alexey Ivanovitch?" And there was a gleam in his face of something quite new and unexpected, which seemed to transform his countenance, till then full of spite and abjectly grimacing.

"Is it possible you didn't know, then?" said Velchaninov, disconcerted and completely taken by surprise.

"Is it possible I knew? Is it possible I knew? Oh, you race of Jupiters! For you a man's no more than a dog, and you judge all according to your own petty nature. I tell you that! You can swallow that!" And he banged frantically on the table with his fist, but was at once dismayed at the bang and began to look apprehensive.

Velchaninov assumed an air of dignity.

"Listen, Pavel Pavlovitch. It's absolutely nothing to me, as you can see for yourself, whether you knew, or whether you didn't. If you didn't know, it's to your credit in any case, though . . . I can't understand, however, why you've chosen to make this confidence to me" . . . ?

"I didn't mean you . . . don't be angry. I didn't mean you . . ." muttered Pavel Pavlovitch, looking down.

Mavra came in with the champagne.

"Here it is!" cried Pavel Pavlovitch, evidently relieved at her entrance. "Glasses, my good girl, glasses; splendid! We ask for nothing more, my dear. And uncorked already! Honour and glory to you, charming creature! Come, you can go!"

And with renewed courage he looked impudently at Velchaninov again.

"Confess," he chuckled suddenly, "that all this is very interesting and by no means 'absolutely nothing to you,' as you were pleased to declare; so much so that you would be disappointed if I were to get up this minute and go away without explaining myself."

"I really shouldn't be disappointed."

"Oh, that's a lie!" was what Pavel Pavlovitch's smile expressed.

"Well, let's come to business!" And he filled his glass.

"Let's drink," he pronounced, taking up the glass, "to the health of our friend departed in God, Stepan Mihalovitch."

He raised his glass, and drank it.

"I'm not going to drink such a health," said Velchaninov, putting down his glass.

"Why not? It's a pleasant toast."

"I say, weren't you drunk when you came in just now?"

"I had had a little. But why?"

"Nothing particular, but I thought last night, and this morning still more, that you were genuinely grieved at the loss of Natalya Vassilyevna."

"And who told you that I'm not genuinely grieved at the loss of her now?" Pavel Pavlovitch bounced out again, exactly as though he were worked by springs.

"And I didn't mean that; but you must admit that you may be mistaken about Stepan Mihalovitch, and it is— a grave matter."

Pavel Pavlovitch smiled craftily and winked.

"And wouldn't you like to know how I found out about Stepan Mihalovitch?"

Velchaninov flushed.

"I tell you again that it's nothing to me." . . . "Hadn't I better chuck him out this minute, bottle and all?" he thought furiously, and he flushed a deeper crimson.

"That's all right!" said Pavel Pavlovitch, as though trying to encourage him, and he poured himself out another glass.

"I will explain at once how I found out all about it, and so gratify your ardent desire . . . for you are an ardent man, Alexey Ivanovitch, a terribly ardent man! He—he! Only give me a cigarette, for ever since March . . . !"

"Here's a cigarette for you."

"I have gone to the dogs since March, Alexey Ivanovitch, and I'll tell you how it's all happened—listen. Consumption, as you know yourself, my best of friends," he grew more and more familiar, "is a curious disease. Consumptives have scarcely a suspicion they may be dying to-morrow and then all in a minute they're dead. I tell you that only five hours before, Natalya Vassilyevna was planning a visit a fortnight later to her aunt, thirty miles away. You are aware, too, probably, of the practice, or rather bad habit—common in many ladies and very likely in their admirers as well—of preserving all sorts of rubbish in the way of love-letters. . . . It would be much safer to put them in the stove, wouldn't it? No, every scrap of paper is carefully stored away in a box or a *nécessaire;* even docketed in years, and in months, and in series. Whether it's a comfort to them—I don't know; but, no doubt, it's for the sake of agreeable memories. Since only five hours before her end she was arranging to go to visit her aunt, Natalya Vassilyevna naturally had no thought of death to the very last hour. She was still expecting Koch. So it happened that Natalya Vassilyevna died, and an ebony box inlaid with mother-of-pearl and silver was left standing on her bureau. And it was a charming box, with a lock and key, an heirloom that had come to her from her grandmother. In that box everything lay revealed, absolutely everything; all, without exception, with the year and the day, everything for the last twenty years. And as Stepan Mihalovitch had a distinct literary bent (he actually sent a passionate love story to a journal), his contributions ran into the hundreds—to be sure they were spread out over five years. Some specimens had been annotated in Natalya Vassilyevna's own handwriting. A pleasant surprise for a husband. What do you think of it?"

Velchaninov reflected hurriedly and felt sure that he had never sent Natalya Vassilyevna a single letter, not a note of any kind. Though he had written twice from Petersburg, his letters, in accordance with a compact between them, had been addressed to the husband as well as the wife. To Natalya Vassilyevna's last letter, in which she had decreed his banishment, he had never answered.

When he had ended his story, Pavel Pavlovitch paused for a full minute with an importunate and expectant smile.

"Why do you give me no answer to my little question?" he brought out at last, with evident anxiety.

"What little question?"

"Why, the pleasant surprise for a husband on opening that box."

"Oh! what is it to do with me!" exclaimed Velchaninov, with a gesture of disgust, and he got up and walked about the room.

"And I bet you're thinking now, you're a swine to have shown me your shame. He—he! You're a very fastidious man . . . you are."

"I think nothing about it. On the contrary, you are so much exasperated by the death of the man who wronged you and you've drunk so much wine, too. I see nothing extraordinary in all this; I quite understand why you wanted Bagautov alive, and I am ready to respect your annoyance: but . . ."

"And what did I want Bagautov for, do you suppose?"

"That's your affair."

"I bet that you were thinking of a duel!"

"Damn it all!" cried Velchaninov, growing more and more unable to control himself. "I imagine that a decent man . . . in such cases does not stoop to ridiculous babble, to stupid antics, to ludicrous complaints and disgusting insinuations, by which he only degrades himself more, but acts openly, directly, straightforwardly—like a decent man!"

"He—he! but perhaps I'm not a decent man!"

"That's your affair again . . . but in that case, what the devil did you want Bagautov alive for?"

"Why, if only to see a friend. We'd have had a bottle and drunk together."

"He wouldn't have drunk with you."

"Why not? *Noblesse oblige!* Here, you're drinking with me; in what way is he better than you?"

"I haven't drunk with you."

"Why such pride all of a sudden?"

Velchaninov suddenly broke into a nervous and irritable laugh.

"Damnation! Why, you are really a 'predatory type'! I thought you were only 'the eternal husband,' and nothing more!"

"What do you mean by 'the eternal husband,' what's that?" Pavel Pavlovitch suddenly pricked up his ears.

"Oh, it's one type of husband . . . it would be a long story. You'd better clear out, it's time you were gone; I'm sick of you."

"And predatory? You said 'predatory'!"

"I said you were a 'predatory type'; I said it ironically."

"What do you mean by a 'predatory type'? Tell me, please, Alexey Ivanovitch, for God's sake, or for Christ's sake!"

"Come, that's enough, that's enough!" cried Velchaninov, suddenly growing horribly angry. "It's time you were off. Get along."

"No, it's not enough!" Pavel Pavlovitch flared up; "even though you are sick of me it's not enough, for we must drink together and clink glasses! Let us drink together, and then I'll go, but as it is it's not enough!"

"Pavel Pavlovitch! Will you go to the devil to-day or will you not?"

"I can go to the devil, but first we'll drink! You said that you would not drink *with me*; but I *want* you to drink with me!"

There was no grimacing, no sniggering about him now. He seemed all at once entirely transformed, and to have become in his whole tone and appearance so completely the opposite of the Pavel Pavlovitch of the moment before that Velchaninov was quite taken aback.

"Do let us drink, Alexey Ivanovitch! Don't refuse me," Pavel Pavlovitch persisted, gripping his hand tightly and looking strangely into his eyes.

Clearly there was more at stake than merely drinking.

"Yes, if you like," muttered Velchaninov; "but how can we? . . . There's nothing left but the dregs. . . ."

"There are just two glasses left, it's thick, but we'll drink it and clink glasses! Here, take your glass."

They clinked their glasses and emptied them.

"Since that's so—since that's so . . . Ach!"

Pavel Pavlovitch clutched his forehead in his hand and remained for some moments in that position. Velchaninov had a feeling every moment that he would speak out and utter the very *final* word. But Pavel Pavlovitch uttered nothing; he simply gazed at him and smiled again the same sly, knowing smile.

"What do you want of me, you drunken fellow! You're playing the fool with me!" Velchaninov shouted furiously, stamping.

"Don't shout, don't shout; what is there to shout for?" cried Pavel Pavlovitch, gesticulating hurriedly. "I'm not playing the fool, I'm not playing the fool! Do you know what you are to me now?"

And he suddenly seized his hand and kissed it. Velchaninov was utterly taken aback.

"That's what you mean to me now! And now—and now I'll go to the devil as soon as you please!"

"Wait a minute, stay!" cried Velchaninov, recovering himself. "I forgot to tell you. . . ."

Pavel Pavlovitch turned back from the door.

"You see," muttered Velchaninov, very quickly, flushing crimson and looking away, "you must be at the Pogoryeltsevs' to-morrow . . . to make their acquaintance and thank them; you must . . ."

"Certainly, I must. I understand that, of course!" Pavel Pavlovitch acquiesced with the utmost readiness, waving his hand quickly as though to protest that there was no need to remind him.

"And besides, Liza is very anxious to see you. I promised her . . ."

"Liza!" Pavel Pavlovitch turned back. "Liza? Do you know what Liza has meant to me and means? Has meant and still means!" he cried all at once, almost frantically. "But . . . But of that later, all that can be later. . . . But now it's not enough that we've drunk together, Alexey Ivanovitch, I must have something else to be satisfied. . . ."

He laid his hat on a chair and gazed at him, gasping for breath a little as he had done just before.

"Kiss me, Alexey Ivanovitch!" he suggested suddenly.

"You're drunk!" Velchaninov declared, stepping back.

"Yes, but kiss me all the same, Alexey Ivanovitch. Oh, kiss me! Why, I kissed your hand just now."

For some minutes Velchaninov was silent, as though stunned by a blow on the head. But suddenly he bent down to Pavel Pavlovitch, whose face was on a level with his shoulder, and kissed him on the lips, which smelt very strongly of spirits. He was not, however, perfectly certain that he had kissed him.

"Well, now, now. . . ." Pavel Pavlovitch cried again in a drunken frenzy, his drunken eyes flashing; "now I'll tell you; I thought then, What if he too? What if that one, I thought, what if he too . . . whom can I trust after that!"

Pavel Pavlovitch suddenly burst into tears.

"So you understand, you're the one friend left me now!"

And he ran with his hat out of the room. Velchaninov again stood still for some minutes in the same place, just as he had done after Pavel Pavlovitch's first visit.

"Ah! a drunken fool and nothing more!" He waved his hand, dismissing the subject.

"Absolutely nothing more," he repeated energetically as he undressed and got into bed.

Chapter 8

Liza Ill

Next morning Velchaninov walked about his room expecting Pavel Pavlovitch, who had promised to arrive in good time to go to the Pogoryeltsevs. As he smoked and sipped his coffee he was conscious at every moment that he was like a man who on waking up in the morning cannot forget for one instant that he has received a slap in the face overnight. "H'm! . . . he quite understands the position and will take his revenge on me through Liza!" he thought with horror.

The charming figure of the poor child rose mournfully before him for a moment. His heart beat faster at the thought that he would soon, within two hours, see *his* Liza again. "Ah! it's no use talking about it!" he decided hotly—"It's my whole life and my whole object now! what do slaps in the face or memories of the past matter? What has my life been till now? Muddle and sadness . . . but now . . . it's all different, everything's changed!"

But in spite of his enthusiasm, he grew more and more doubtful.

"He is tormenting me by means of Liza—that's clear! And he is tormenting Liza too. It's in that way he will devour me utterly in revenge for everything. H'm! . . . Of course, I can't allow him to go on as he did yesterday" —he flushed crimson all at once—"and . . . here it's twelve o'clock, though, he doesn't come"

He waited a long time, till half-past twelve, and his depression grew more and more acute. Pavel Pavlovitch did not appear. At last the thought that had long been stirring in his mind, that Pavel Pavlovitch had not come on purpose, simply in order to get up another scene like that of the night before, put the finishing touch to his irritation. "He knows that I depend on him, and what a state Liza will be in now. And how can I appear before her without him?"

At last he could stand it no longer, and at one o'clock he rushed off to the Pokrovsky Hotel alone. At the lodging he was told that Pavel Pavlovitch had not slept at home, but had only turned up at nine o'clock in the morning, had stayed no more than a quarter of an hour, and then gone out again. Velchaninov stood at the door of Pavel Pavlovitch's room, listening to what the servant said, and mechanically turned the handle of the locked door and pulled it backwards and forwards. Realizing what he was doing, he uttered a curse and asked the servant to take him to Marya Sysoevna. But the landlady, hearing he was there, came out readily.

She was a good-natured woman. "A woman with generous feelings," as Velchaninov said of her when he was reporting his conversation afterwards to Klavdia Petrovna. Inquiring briefly about his journey with the child the day before, Marya Sysoevna launched out into accounts of Pavel Pavlovitch's doings. In her words: "If it had not been for the child, she would have sent him about his business long ago. He was turned out of the hotel because of his disorderly behaviour. Wasn't it wicked to bring home a wench with him when there was a child here old enough to understand? He was shouting: 'She will be your mother, if I choose!' And, would you believe it? what that street wench did, she even spat in his face. 'You're not my daughter, but he's a ——!' she cried."

"Really!" Velchaninov was horrified.

"I heard it myself. Though the man was drunk till he was almost senseless, yet it was very wrong before the child; though she is but young, she broods over everything in her mind! The child cries. I can see she is worried to death. And the other day there was a terrible thing done in our building: a clerk, so folks say, took a room in the hotel overnight, and in the morning hanged himself. They say he had squandered all his money. People flocked to see. Pavel Pavlovitch was not at home, and the child was running about with no one to look after her; I looked, and there she was in the passage among the people, and peeping in behind the others: she was looking so strangely at the body. I brought her away as quickly as I could. And what do you think—she was all of a tremble, she looked quite black in the face, and as soon as I brought her in she flopped on the floor in a faint. She struggled and writhed, and it was all I could do to bring her round. It was a fit, and she's been poorly ever since that hour. He heard of it, came home, and pinched her all over—for he's not one for beating, he's more given to pinching her, and afterwards, when he came home after having a drop, he'd frighten her: 'I'll hang myself too,' he'd say; 'you'll make me hang myself; on this blind-cord here,' he'd say; and he'd make a noose before her eyes. And she'd be beside herself—she'd scream and throw her little arms round him: 'I won't!' she'd cry, 'I never will again.' It was pitiful."

Though Velchaninov had expected something strange, this story amazed him so much that he could not believe it.

Marya Sysoevna told him a great deal more; on one occasion, for instance, had it not been for Marya Sysoevna Liza might have thrown herself out of the window.

Velchaninov went out of the house reeling as though he were drunk.

"I'll knock him on the head like a dog!" was the thought that floated before his mind. And for a long time he kept repeating it to himself.

He took a cab and drove to the Pogoryeltsevs. On the way the carriage was obliged to stop at the cross-roads, near the bridge on the canal, over which a long funeral procession was passing. And on both sides of the bridge there were several carriages waiting in a block; people on foot were stopped too. It was a grand funeral and there was a very long string of carriages following it, and lo and behold! in the windows of one of these carriages Velchaninov caught a passing glimpse of the face of Pavel Pavlovitch. He would not have believed his eyes if Pavel Pavlovitch had not thrust his head out and nodded to him with a smile. Evidently he was delighted at recognizing Velchaninov; he even began beckoning to him from the carriage. Velchaninov jumped out of his cab and, in spite of the crush, in spite of the police, and in spite of the fact that Pavel Pavlovitch's carriage was driving on to the bridge, he ran right up to the window. Pavel Pavlovitch was alone.

"What's the matter with you?" cried Velchaninov; "why didn't you come? How is it you are here?"

"I'm repaying a debt. Don't shout, don't shout, I am

repaying a debt," sniggered Pavel Pavlovitch, screwing up his eyes, jocosely. "I'm following the mortal remains of my faithful friend, Stepan Mihalovitch."

"That's all nonsense, you drunken, senseless man," Velchaninov shouted louder than ever, though he was taken aback for an instant. "Get out this minute and come into the cab with me."

"I can't, it's a duty. . . ."

"I'll drag you out!" Velchaninov yelled.

"And I'll scream! I'll scream!" said Pavel Pavlovitch, sniggering as jocosely as before, as though it were a game, though he did huddle into the furthest corner of the carriage. . . .

"Look out, look out! you'll be run over!" shouted a policeman.

At the further end of the bridge a carriage cutting across the procession did, in fact, cause a commotion. Velchaninov was forced to skip back; the stream of carriages and the crowd of people immediately carried him further away. With a curse he made his way back to the cab.

"No matter, I couldn't have taken a fellow like that with me, at any rate!" he thought, with a feeling of bewildered anxiety that persisted.

When he told Klavdia Petrovna Marya Sysoevna's story and described the strange meeting in the funeral procession, she grew very thoughtful.

"I feel afraid for you," she said. "You ought to break off all relations with him, and the sooner the better."

"He's a drunken fool and nothing more!" Velchaninov cried passionately; "as though I could be afraid of him! And how can I break off relations with him when there's Liza to be considered. Think of Liza!"

Liza meanwhile was lying ill; she had begun to be feverish the evening before and they were expecting a celebrated doctor, for whom they had sent an express messenger to the town in the morning. This completed Velchaninov's distress.

Klavdia Petrovna took him to the invalid.

"I watched her very carefully yesterday," she observed, stopping outside Liza's room. "She's a proud and reserved child; she is ashamed that she is here, and that her father has cast her off; that's the whole cause of her illness, to my thinking."

"How cast her off? Why do you say he's cast her off?"

"The very fact that he let her come here, among complete strangers and with a man . . . who's almost a stranger, too, or on such terms . . ."

"But it was I took her, I took her by force; I don't perceive . . ."

"Oh, my God, and even Liza, a child, perceives it! It's my belief that he simply won't come at all."

Liza was not astonished when she saw Velchaninov alone; she only smiled mournfully and turned her feverishly hot little head to the wall. She made no response to Velchaninov's timid efforts to comfort her and his fervent promises to bring her father next day without fail. On coming away from her, he suddenly burst into tears.

It was evening before the doctor came. After examining the patient, he alarmed them all from the first word, by observing that they had done wrong not to have sent for him before. When it was explained to him that the child had been taken ill only the evening before, he was at first incredulous.

"It all depends how things go on to-night," he said in conclusion. After giving various instructions, he went away, promising to come again next day as early as possible. Velchaninov would have insisted on staying the night, but Klavdia Petrovna begged him once more "to try and bring that monster."

"Try once more," Velchaninov retorted in a frenzy. "Why, this time I'll tie him hand and foot and carry him here in my arms!" The idea of tying Pavel Pavlovitch hand and foot and carrying him there took possession of him and made him violently impatient to carry it out. "I don't feel in the least guilty towards him now, not in the least!" he said to Klavdia Petrovna, as he said good-bye. "I take back all the abject, snivelling things I said here yesterday," he added indignantly.

Liza was lying with her eyes shut, apparently asleep; she seemed to be better. When Velchaninov cautiously bent over her head, to say good-bye and to kiss, if only the edge of her garment, she suddenly opened her eyes, as though she had been expecting him, and whispered to him—

"Take me away!"

It was a gentle, pitiful prayer, without a shade in it of the irritability of the previous day, but at the same time he could hear in it the conviction that he would not do what she asked. Velchaninov, in complete despair, began trying to persuade her that this was impossible.

In silence she closed her eyes and did not utter another word, as though she did not see or hear him.

On getting into Petersburg he told the driver to take him straight to Pokrovsky Hotel. It was ten o'clock; Pavel Pavlovitch was not in his lodging. Velchaninov spent a full half-hour in waiting for him and walking up and down the passage in sickening suspense. Marya Sysoevna assured him at last that Pavel Pavlovitch would not be back till early next morning. "Then I will come early in the morning," Velchaninov decided, and, beside himself, he set off for home.

But what was his astonishment when, at the door of his flat, he learned from Mavra that his yesterday's visitor had been waiting for him since ten o'clock.

"And has been pleased to drink tea here, and has sent out for wine again, and has given me a blue note to get it."

Chapter 9

An Apparition

Pavel Pavlovitch had made himself exceedingly comfortable. He was sitting in the same chair as the day before, smoking a cigarette, and had just poured himself out the fourth and last glass from a bottle of wine. The teapot and an unfinished glass of tea were standing on a table close by. His flushed face was beaming with bliss. He had even taken off his coat, as it was warm, and was sitting in his waistcoat.

"Excuse me, most faithful of friends!" he cried, seeing Velchaninov and jumping up to put on his coat. "I took it off for the greater enjoyment of the moment. . . ."

Velchaninov went up to him menacingly.

"Are you not quite drunk yet? Is it still possible to talk to you?"

Pavel Pavlovitch was a little flustered.

"No, not quite. . . . I've been commemorating the deceased, but . . . not quite. . . ."

"Will you understand me too?"

"That's what I've come for, to understand you."

"Well, then; I begin by telling you straight out that you are a worthless scoundrel!" cried Velchaninov.

"If you begin like that, how will you end?" Pavel Pavlovitch protested, evidently cowed, but Velchaninov went on shouting without heeding him.

"Your daughter is dying, she is ill; have you abandoned her or not?"

"Can she really be dying?"

"She is ill, ill, exceedingly, dangerously ill!"

"Possibly some little fit . . ."

"Don't talk nonsense! She is ex—ceed—ing—ly, dangerously ill! You ought to have gone if only to . . ."

"To express my gratitude, my gratitude for their hospitality! I quite understand that! Alexey Ivanovitch, my precious, perfect friend"—he suddenly clutched Velchaninov's hand in both of his, and with drunken sentimentality, almost with tears, as though imploring forgiveness, he kept crying out: "Alexey Ivanovitch, don't shout, don't shout! Whether I die or fall drunk into the Neva—what does it matter in the real significance of things? We have plenty of time to go to Mr. Pogoryeltsev. . . ."

Velchaninov pulled himself together and restrained himself a little.

"You're drunk, and so I don't understand the sense of what you are saying," he observed sternly. "I am always ready to have things out with you, shall be glad to, in fact, as soon as possible. . . . I've come indeed. . . . But first of all I warn you that I shall take steps: you must stay the night here! To-morrow morning I'll take you and we'll go together. I won't let you go," he yelled again. "I'll tie you up and carry you there in my arms! . . . Would you like this sofa?" he said breathlessly, pointing to a wide, soft sofa, which stood opposite the one against the other wall, where he used to sleep himself.

"By all means, I can sleep anywhere. . . ."

"Not anywhere, but on that sofa! Here, take your sheets, your quilt, your pillow." All these Velchaninov took out of the cupboard and hurriedly flung them to Pavel Pavlovitch, who held out his arms submissively. "Make the bed at once, make it at once!"

Pavel Pavlovitch, loaded with his burden, stood in the middle of the room as though hesitating, with a broad drunken grin on his drunken face. But at a second menacing shout from Velchaninov he suddenly began bustling about at full speed; he pushed back the table and began, sighing and groaning, to unfold the sheets and make the bed. Velchaninov went to assist him; he was, to some extent, appeased by the alarm and submissiveness of his visitor.

"Finish your glass and go to bed," he ordered him again; he felt as though he could not help giving orders. "You sent for that wine yourself, didn't you?"

"Yes. . . . I knew you wouldn't send for any more, Alexey Ivanovitch."

"It was well you knew it, and there is something more you must know too. I tell you once more I've taken measures, I won't put up with any more of your antics, I won't put up with your drunken kisses as I did yesterday."

"I understand myself, Alexey Ivanovitch, that that was only possible once," sniggered Pavel Pavlovitch.

Hearing his answer, Velchaninov, who had been striding up and down the room, stopped almost solemnly before Pavel Pavlovitch.

"Pavel Pavlovitch, tell me frankly! You're a sensible man, I've recognized that again, but I assure you, you are on the wrong tack! Speak straightforwardly, act straightforwardly and I give you my word of honour I will answer any question you like."

Pavel Pavlovitch grinned his broad grin again, which was enough in itself to drive Velchaninov to fury.

"Stop!" Velchaninov shouted again. "Don't sham, I see through you! I repeat: I give you my word of honour, that I am ready to answer *anything* and you shall receive every satisfaction possible, that is every sort, even the impossible! Oh, how I wish you could understand me! . . ."

"Since you are so good"—Pavel Pavlovitch moved cautiously towards him—"I was much interested in what you said last night about a 'predatory type'! . . ."

Velchaninov, with a curse, fell to pacing about the room more rapidly than ever.

"No, Alexey Ivanovitch, don't curse, because I'm so much interested, and have come on purpose to make sure. . . . I'm not very ready with my tongue, but you must forgive me. You know of that 'predatory type,' and of that 'peaceable type' I read in a magazine, in the literary criticism. I remembered it this morning . . . only I had forgotten it, and to tell the truth I did not understand it at the time. This is what I wanted you to explain: the deceased, Stepan Mihalovitch Bagautov—was he 'predatory' or 'peaceable'? How do you classify him?"

Velchaninov still remained silent, and did not cease his pacing up and down.

"The predatory type," he began, stopping suddenly in exasperation, "is the man who would sooner have put poison in Bagautov's glass when drinking champagne with him in honour of their delightful meeting, as you drank with me yesterday, than have followed his coffin to the cemetery as you have to-day, the devil only knows from what secret, underground, loathsome impulse and distorted feeling that only degrades you! Yes, degrades you!"

"It's true that I shouldn't have gone," Pavel Pavlovitch assented; "but you do pitch into me. . . ."

"It's not the man," Velchaninov, getting hotter, went on shouting, without heeding him; "it's not the man who poses to himself as goodness knows what, who reckons up his score of right and wrong, goes over and over his grievance as though it were a lesson, frets, goes in for all sorts of antics and apishness, hangs on people's necks—and most likely he has been spending all his time at it too! Is it true that you tried to hang yourself—is it?"

"When I was drunk, I did talk wildly—I don't remember. It isn't quite seemly, Alexey Ivanovitch, to put poison in wine. Apart from the fact that I am a civil servant of good repute, you know I have money of my own, and, what's more, I may want to get married again."

"Besides, you'll be sent to the gallows."

"To be sure, that unpleasantness also, though nowadays they admit many extenuating circumstances in the law-courts. I'll tell you a killing little anecdote, Alexey Ivanovitch. I thought of it this morning in the carriage. I wanted to tell you of it then. You said just now 'hangs on people's necks.' You remember, perhaps, Semyon Petrovitch Livtsov, he used to come and see us when you were in T——; well, his younger brother, who was also a young Petersburg swell, was in attendance on the governor at V——, and he, too, was distinguished for various qualities. He had a quarrel with Golubenko, a colonel, in the presence of ladies and the lady of his heart, and considered himself insulted, but he swallowed the affront and concealed it; and, meanwhile, Golubenko cut him out with the lady of his heart and made her an offer. And what do you think? This Livtsov formed a genuine friendship with Golubenko, he quite made it up with him, and, what's more, insisted on being his best man, he held the wedding crown, and when they came from under the wedding crown, he went up to kiss and congratulate Golubenko; and in the presence of the governor and all the honourable company, with his swallow-tail coat, and his hair in curl, he sticks the bridegroom in the stomach with a knife—so that he rolled over! His own best man! What a disgrace! And, what's more, when he'd stabbed him like that, he rushed about crying: 'Ach! what have I done! Oh, what is it I've done!' with floods of tears, trembling all over, flinging himself on people's necks, even ladies. 'Ach, what have I done!' he kept saying. 'What have I done now!' He—he—he! he was killing. Though one feels sorry for Golubenko, perhaps, but after all he recovered."

"I don't see why you told me the story," observed Velchaninov, frowning sternly.

"Why, all because he stuck the knife in him, you know," Pavel Pavlovitch tittered; "you can see he was not the type, but a snivelling fellow, since he forgot all good manners in his horror and flung himself on the ladies' necks in the presence of the governor—but you see he stabbed him, he got his own back! That was all I meant."

"Go to hell!" Velchaninov yelled suddenly, in a voice not his own, as though something had exploded in him. "Go to hell with your underground vileness; you are nothing but underground vileness. You thought you'd scare me—you base man, torturing a child; you scoundrel, you scoundrel, you scoundrel!" he shouted, beside himself, gasping for breath at every word.

A complete revulsion came over Pavel Pavlovitch which actually seemed to sober him; his lips quivered.

"It is you, Alexey Ivanovitch, call me a scoundrel, *you* call *me?*"

But Velchaninov had already realized what he had done.

"I am ready to apologize," he answered, after a pause

of gloomy hesitation; "but only if you will act straight-forwardly at once yourself."

"In your place I would apologize without any ifs, Alexey Ivanovitch."

"Very good, so be it," said Velchaninov, after another slight pause. "I apologize to you; but you'll admit your-self, Pavel Pavlovitch, that, after all this, I need not consider that I owe you anything. I'm speaking with reference to the *whole* matter and not only to the present incident."

"That's all right, why consider?" Pavel Pavlovitch snig-gered, though he kept his eyes on the ground.

"So much the better, then, so much the better! Finish your wine and go to bed, for I won't let you go, anyway. . . ."

"Oh, the wine. . . ." Pavel Pavlovitch seemed, as it were, a little disconcerted. He went to the table, how-ever, and finished the last glass of wine he had poured out so long before.

Perhaps he had drunk a great deal before, for his hand trembled and he spilt part of the wine on the floor, and on his shirt and waistcoat. He finished it all, however, as though he could not bear to leave a drop, and respect-fully replacing the empty glass on the table, he went sub-missively to his bed to undress.

"But wouldn't it be better for me not to stay the night?" he brought out for some reason, though he had taken off one boot and was holding it in his hand.

"No, it wouldn't," Velchaninov answered wrathfully, still pacing up and down the room without looking at him.

Pavel Pavlovitch undressed and got into bed. A quarter of an hour later Velchaninov went to bed too, and put out the candle.

He fell asleep uneasily. The new element that had turned up unexpectedly and complicated the whole busi-ness more than ever worried him now, and at the same time he felt that he was for some reason ashamed of his uneasiness. He was just dozing off, but he was waked up all at once by a rustling sound. He looked round at once towards Pavel Pavlovitch's bed. The room was dark (the curtains were drawn), but Velchaninov fancied that Pavel Pavlovitch was not lying down, but was sitting on the bed.

"What's the matter?" Velchaninov called to him.

"A ghost," Pavel Pavlovitch said, scarcely audibly, after a brief pause.

"What do you mean, what sort of ghost?"

"There in that room, I seem to see a ghost in the doorway."

"Whose ghost?" Velchaninov asked again, after a pause.

"Natalya Vassilyevna's."

Velchaninov stood up on the rug, and looked across the passage, into the other room, the door of which always stood open. There were only blinds instead of curtains on the window, and so it was much lighter there.

"There's nothing in that room and you are drunk. Go to bed!" said Velchaninov. He got into bed and wrapped himself in the quilt.

Pavel Pavlovitch got into bed, too, without uttering a word.

"And have you ever seen ghosts before?" Velchaninov asked suddenly, ten minutes afterwards.

Pavel Pavlovitch, too, was silent for a while.

"I thought I saw one once," he responded faintly.

Silence followed again.

Velchaninov could not have said for certain whether he had been asleep or not, but about an hour had passed when he suddenly turned round again: whether he was roused again by a rustle, he was not sure, but felt as though in the pitch-dark something white was standing over him, not quite close, but in the middle of the room. He sat up in bed and for a full minute gazed into the darkness.

"Is that you, Pavel Pavlovitch?" he said, in a failing voice.

His own voice ringing out suddenly in the stillness and the dark seemed to him somehow strange.

No answer followed, but there could be no doubt that some one was standing there.

"Is that you . . . . Pavel Pavlovitch?" he repeated, more loudly—so loudly, in fact, that if Pavel Pavlovitch had been quietly asleep in his bed he would certainly have waked up and answered.

But again no answer came, yet he fancied that the white, hardly distinguishable figure moved nearer to him. Then something strange followed: something seemed to explode within him, exactly as it had that evening, and he shouted at the top of his voice, in a most hideous, frantic voice, gasping for breath at each word:

"If you . . . drunken fool . . . dare to imagine . . . that you can . . . frighten me, I'll turn over to the wall, I'll put the bedclothes over my head, and won't turn round again all night . . . to show you how much I care . . . if you were to stand there till morning . . . like a fool . . . and I spit upon you . . ."

And he spat furiously in the direction, as he supposed, of Pavel Pavlovitch, turned over to the wall, drew the bedclothes over his head as he had said and grew numb in that position, not stirring a muscle. A deathlike silence followed. Whether the phantom was moving nearer or standing still he could not tell, but his heart was beating, beating, beating violently. Fully five minutes passed, and suddenly, two steps from him, he heard the meek and plaintive voice of Pavel Pavlovitch.

"I got up, Alexey Ivanovitch, to look for the . . ." (and he mentioned a quite indispensable domestic article). "I didn't find one there. . . . I meant to look quietly under your bed."

"Why didn't you speak when I shouted?" Velchaninov asked in a breaking voice, after an interval of half a minute.

"I was frightened, you shouted so. . . . I was frightened."

"There in the corner on the left, in the little cupboard. Light the candle. . . ."

"I can do without the candle," Pavel Pavlovitch brought out meekly, making for the corner. "Forgive me, Alexey Ivanovitch, for disturbing you so. . . . I was so bewildered . . ."

But Velchaninov made no reply. He still lay with his face to the wall, and lay so all night, without once turning over. Whether it was that he wanted to do as he had said and so show his contempt—he did not know himself what he was feeling; his nervous irritability passed at last almost into delirium, and it was a long time before he went to sleep. Waking next morning between nine and ten, he jumped up and sat up in bed, as though some one had given him a shove—but Pavel Pavlovitch was not in the room—the unmade bed stood there empty; he had crept away at dawn.

"I knew it would be so," cried Velchaninov, slapping himself on the forehead.

Chapter 10

In the Cemetery

The doctor's fears turned out to be justified; Liza was suddenly worse—worse than Velchaninov and Klavdia Petrovna had imagined possible the evening before. Velchaninov found the invalid conscious in the morning, though she was in a high fever; afterwards he declared that she had smiled and even held out her feverish little hand to him. Whether this was really so, or whether he had imagined it, in an unconscious effort to comfort himself, he had no time to make sure; by nightfall the sick child was unconscious, and she remained so till the end. Ten days after her coming to the Pogoryeltsevs she died.

It was a sorrowful time for Velchaninov; the Pogoryeltsevs were very anxious about him. He spent those bitter days for the most part with them. During the last days of Liza's illness he would sit for whole hours together in a corner apparently thinking of nothing; Klavdia Petrovna attempted to distract his mind, but he made little response, and seemed to find it a burden even to talk to her. Klavdia Petrovna had not expected that "all this would have such an effect upon him." The children succeeded best in rousing him; in their company he sometimes even laughed, but almost every hour he would get up from his chair and go on tiptoe to look at the invalid. He sometimes fancied that she recognized him. He had no hope of her recovery, nor had any one, but he could not tear himself away from the room in which she lay dying, and usually sat in the next room.

On two occasions in the course of those days, however, he showed great activity: he roused himself and rushed off to Petersburg to the doctors, called on all the most distinguished of them, and arranged for a consultation. The second and last consultation took place the evening before Liza's death. Three days before that Klavdia Petrovna urged upon Velchaninov the necessity of seeking out M. Trusotsky: pointing out that "if the worst happened, the funeral would be impossible without him."

Velchaninov mumbled in reply that he would write to him. Pogoryeltsev thereupon declared that he would undertake to find him through the police. Velchaninov did finally write a note of two lines and took it to the Pokrovsky Hotel. Pavel Pavlovitch, as usual, was not at home, and he left the letter for him with Marya Sysoevna.

At last Liza died, on a beautiful summer evening at sunset, and only then Velchaninov seemed to wake up. When they dressed the dead child in a white frock that belonged to one of Klavdia Petrovna's daughters and was kept for festivals, and laid her on the table in the drawing-room with flowers in her folded hands, he went up to Klavdia Petrovna with glittering eyes, and told her that he would bring the "murderer" at once. Refusing to listen to their advice to put off going till next day, he set off for Petersburg at once.

He knew where to find Pavel Pavlovitch; he had not only been to fetch the doctors when he went to Petersburg before. He had sometimes fancied during those days that if he brought her father to Liza, and she heard his voice, she might come to herself; so he had fallen to hunting for him like one possessed. Pavel Pavlovitch was in the same lodging as before, but it was useless for him to inquire there: "He hasn't slept here for the last three nights or been near the place," Marya Sysoevna reported; "and if he does come he's bound to be drunk, and before he's been here an hour he's off again: he's going to rack and ruin." The waiter at the Pokrovsky Hotel told Velchaninov, among other things, that Pavel Pavlovitch used to visit some young women in Voznesensky Prospect. Velchaninov promptly looked up these young women. When he had treated them and made them presents these persons readily remembered their visitor, chiefly from the crape on his hat, after which, of course, they abused him roundly for not having been to see them again. One of them, Katya, undertook "to find Pavel Pavlovitch any time, because nowadays he was always with Mashka Prostakov, and he had no end of money, and she ought to have been Mashka Prohvostov (*i. e.* scoundrelly) instead of Prostakov (*i. e.* simple), and she'd been in the hospital, and if she (the speaker) liked she could pack the wench off to Siberia—she had only to say the word." Katya did not, however, look up Pavel Pavlovitch on that occasion, but she promised faithfully to do so another time. It was on her help that Velchaninov was reckoning now.

On reaching Petersburg at ten o'clock, he went at once to ask for her, paid the keeper to let her go, and set off to search with her. He did not know himself what he was going to do with Pavel Pavlovitch: whether he would kill him, or whether he was looking for him simply to tell him of his daughter's death and the necessity of his presence at the funeral. At first they were unsuccessful. It turned out that this Mashka had had a fight with Pavel Pavlovitch two days before, and that a cashier "had broken his head with a stool." In fact, for a long time the search was in vain, and it was only at two o'clock in the afternoon that Velchaninov, coming out of an "establishment," to which he had been sent as a likely place, unexpectedly hit up against him.

Pavel Pavlovitch, hopelessly drunk, was being conducted to this "establishment" by two ladies, one of whom was holding his arm and supporting him. They were followed by a tall, sturdy fellow, who was shouting at the top of his voice and threatening Pavel Pavlovitch with all sorts of horrors. He bawled among other things that "Pavel Pavlovitch was exploiting him and poisoning his existence." There seemed to have been some dispute about money; the women were much frightened and flustered. Seeing Velchaninov, Pavel Pavlovitch rushed to him with outstretched hands and screamed as though he were being murdered:

"Brother, defend me!"

At the sight of Velchaninov's athletic figure the bully promptly disappeared; Pavel Pavlovitch in triumph shook his fist after him with a yell of victory; at that point Velchaninov seized him by the shoulder in a fury, and, without knowing why he did it, shook him until his teeth chattered. Pavel Pavlovitch instantly ceased yelling and stared at his tormentor in stupid, drunken terror. Probably not knowing what to do with him next, Velchaninov folded him up and sat him on the curbstone.

"Liza is dead!" he said to him.

Pavel Pavlovitch, still staring at Velchaninov, sat on the curbstone supported by one of the ladies. He understood at last, and his face suddenly looked pinched.

"Dead . . . ." he whispered strangely. Whether his face wore his loathsome, drunken grin, or whether it was contorted by some feeling, Velchaninov could not distinguish, but a moment later Pavel Pavlovitch, with an effort, lifted his trembling hand to make the sign of the cross; his trembling hand dropped again without completing it. A little while after he slowly got up from the curbstone, clutched at his lady and, leaning upon her, went on his way, as though oblivious—as though Velchaninov had not been present. But the latter seized him by the shoulder again.

"Do you understand, you drunken monster, that without you she can't be buried?" he shouted breathlessly.

Pavel Pavlovitch turned his head towards him.

"The artillery . . . the lieutenant . . . do you remember him?" he stammered.

"Wha—at!" yelled Velchaninov, with a sickening pang.

"There's her father for you! Find him—for the burial."

"You're lying," Velchaninov yelled like one distraught. "You say that from spite. . . . I knew you were preparing that for me."

Beside himself, he raised his terrible fist to strike Pavel Pavlovitch. In another minute he might have killed him at one blow; the ladies squealed and were beating a retreat, but Pavel Pavlovitch did not turn a hair. His face was contorted by a frenzy of ferocious hatred.

"Do you know," he said, much more steadily, almost as though he were sober, "our Russian . . . ?" (and he uttered an absolutely unprintable term of abuse). "Well, you go to it, then!"

Then with a violent effort he tore himself out of Velchaninov's hands, stumbled and almost fell down. The ladies caught him and this time ran away, squealing and almost dragging Pavel Pavlovitch after them. Velchaninov did not follow them.

On the afternoon of the next day a very presentable-looking, middle-aged government clerk in uniform arrived at the Pogoryeltsevs' villa and politely handed Klavdia Petrovna an envelope addressed to her by Pavel Pavlovitch Trusotsky. In it was a letter enclosing three hundred roubles and the legal papers necessary for the burial. Pavel Pavlovitch wrote briefly, respectfully, and most properly. He warmly thanked Her Excellency for the kind sympathy she had shown for the little motherless girl, for which God alone could repay her. He wrote vaguely that extreme ill-health would prevent him from coming to arrange the funeral of his beloved and unhappy daughter, and he could only appeal to the angelic kindness of Her Excellency's heart. The three hundred roubles were, as he explained later in the letter, to pay for the funeral, and the expenses caused by the child's illness. If any of this money were left over he must humbly and respectfully beg that it might be spent on "a perpetual mass for the rest of the soul of the departed." The clerk who brought the letter could add nothing in explanation; it appeared, indeed, from what he said that it was only at Pavel Pavlovitch's earnest entreaty that he had undertaken to deliver the letter to Her Excellency. Pogoryeltsev was almost offended at the expression "the expenses caused by the child's illness," and after setting aside fifty roubles for the funeral—since it was impossible to prevent the father from paying for his child's burial—he proposed to send the remaining two hundred and fifty roubles back to M. Trusotsky at once. Klavdia Petrovna finally decided not to send back the two hundred and fifty roubles, but only a receipt from the cemetery church for that sum in payment for a perpetual mass for the repose of the soul of the deceased maiden Elizaveta. This receipt was afterwards given to Velchaninov to be despatched to Pavel Pavlovitch. Velchaninov posted it to his lodging.

After the funeral he left the villa. For a whole fortnight he wandered about the town aimless and alone, so lost in thought that he stumbled against people in the street. Sometimes he would lie stretched out on his sofa for days together, forgetting the commonest things of everyday life. Several times the Pogoryeltsevs went to ask him to go to them; he promised to go, but immediately forgot. Klavdia Petrovna even went herself to see him, but did not find him at home. The same thing happened to his lawyer; the lawyer had, indeed, something to tell him: his lawsuit had been very adroitly settled and his opponents had come to an amicable arrangement, agreeing to accept an insignificant fraction of the disputed inheritance. All that remained was to obtain Velchaninov's own consent. When at last he did find him at home, the lawyer was surprised at the apathy and indifference with which Velchaninov, once such a troublesome client, listened to his explanation.

The very hottest days of July had come, but Velchaninov was oblivious of time. His grief ached in his heart like a growing abscess, and he was distinctly conscious of it and every moment with agonizing acuteness. His chief suffering was the thought that, before Liza had had time to know him, she had died, not understanding with what anguish he loved her! The object in life of which he had had such a joyful glimpse had suddenly vanished into everlasting darkness. That object—he thought of it every moment now—was that Liza should be conscious of his love every day, every hour, all her life. "No one has a higher object and no one could have," he thought sometimes, with gloomy fervour. "If there are other objects none can be holier than that!" "By my love for Liza," he mused, "all my old putrid and useless life would be purified and expiated; to make up for my own idle, vicious and wasted life I would cherish and bring up that pure and exquisite creature, and for her sake everything would be forgiven me and I could forgive myself everything."

All these *conscious* thoughts always rose before his mind, together with the vivid, ever-present and ever-poignant memory of the dead child. He re-created for himself her little pale face, remembered every expression on it: he thought of her in the coffin decked with flowers, and as she had lain unconscious in fever, with fixed and open eyes. He suddenly remembered that when she was lying on the table he had noticed one of her fingers, which had somehow turned black during her illness; this had struck him so much at the time, and he had felt so sorry for that poor little finger, that for the first time he thought of seeking out Pavel Pavlovitch and killing him; until that time he had been "as though insensible." Was it wounded pride that had tortured her wounded heart, or was it those three months of suffering at the hands of her father, whose love had suddenly changed to hatred, who had insulted her with shameful words, laughing at her terror, and had abandoned her at last to strangers? All this he dwelt upon incessantly in a thousand variations. "Do you know what Liza has been to me?"—he suddenly recalled the drunkard's exclamation and felt that that exclamation was sincere, not a pose, and that there was love in it. "How could that monster be so cruel to a child whom he had loved so much, and is it credible?" But every time he made haste to dismiss that question and, as it were, brush it aside; there was something awful in that question, something he could not bear and could not solve.

One day, scarcely conscious where he was going, he

wandered into the cemetery where Liza was buried and found her little grave. He had not been to the cemetery since the funeral; he had always fancied it would be too great an agony, and had been afraid to go. But, strange to say, when he had found her little grave and kissed it, his heart felt easier. It was a fine evening, the sun was setting; all round the graves the lush green grass was growing; the bees were humming in a wild rose close by; the flowers and wreaths left by the children and Klavdia Petrovna on Liza's grave were lying there with the petals half dropping. There was a gleam of something like hope in his heart after many days.

"How serene!" he thought, feeling the stillness of the cemetery, and looking at the clear, peaceful sky.

A rush of pure, calm faith flooded his soul.

"Liza has sent me this, it's Liza speaking to me," he thought.

It was quite dark when he left the cemetery and went home. Not far from the cemetery gates, in a low-pitched wooden house on the road, there was some sort of eating-house or tavern; through the windows he could see people sitting at the tables. It suddenly seemed to him that one of them close to the window was Pavel Pavlovitch, and that he saw him, too, and was staring at him inquisitively. He walked on, and soon heard some one pursuing him; Pavel Pavlovitch was, in fact, running after him; probably he had been attracted and encouraged by Velchaninov's conciliatory expression as he watched him from the window. On overtaking him he smiled timidly, but it was not his old drunken smile; he was actually not drunk.

"Good-evening," he said.

"Good-evening," answered Velchaninov.

Chapter 11

Pavel Pavlovitch Means to Marry

As he responded with this "Good-evening," he was surprised at himself. It struck him as extremely strange that he met this man now without a trace of anger, and that in his feeling for him at that moment there was something quite different, and actually, indeed, a sort of impulse towards something new.

"What an agreeable evening," observed Pavel Pavlovitch, looking into his face.

"You've not gone away yet," Velchaninov observed, not by way of a question, but simply making that reflection aloud as he walked on.

"Things have dragged on, but—I've obtained a post with an increase of salary. I shall be going away the day after to-morrow for certain."

"You've got a post?" he said this time, asking a question.

"Why shouldn't I?" Pavel Pavlovitch screwed up his face.

"Oh, I only asked . . ." Velchaninov said, disclaiming the insinuation, and, with a frown, he looked askance at Pavel Pavlovitch.

To his surprise, the attire, the hat with the crape band and the whole appearance of M. Trusotsky were incomparably more presentable than they had been a fortnight before.

"What was he sitting in that tavern for?" he kept wondering.

"I was intending, Alexey Ivanovitch, to communicate with you on a subject for rejoicing," Pavel Pavlovitch began again.

"Rejoicing?"

"I'm going to get married."

"What?"

"After sorrow comes rejoicing, so it is always in life; I should be so gratified, Alexey Ivanovitch, if . . . but—I don't know, perhaps you're in a hurry now, for you appear to be . . ."

"Yes, I am in a hurry . . . and I'm unwell too."

He felt a sudden and intense desire to get rid of him; his readiness for some new feeling had vanished in a flash.

"I should have liked . . ."

Pavel Pavlovitch did not say what he would have liked; Velchaninov was silent.

"In that case it must be later on, if only we meet again . . ."

"Yes, yes, later on," Velchaninov muttered rapidly, without stopping or looking at him.

They were both silent again for a minute; Pavel Pavlovitch went on walking beside him.

"In that case, good-bye till we meet again," Pavel Pavlovitch brought out at last.

"Good-bye; I hope . . ."

Velchaninov returned home thoroughly upset again. Contact with "that man" was too much for him. As he got into bed he asked himself again: "Why was he at the cemetery?"

Next morning he made up his mind to go to the Pogoryeltsevs. He made up his mind to go reluctantly; sympathy from any one, even from the Pogoryeltsevs, was too irksome for him now. But they were so anxious about him that he felt absolutely obliged to go. He suddenly had a foreboding that he would feel horribly ashamed at their first meeting again.

Should he go or not, he thought, as he made haste to finish his breakfast; when, to his intense amazement, Pavel Pavlovitch walked in.

In spite of their meeting the day before Velchaninov could never have conceived that the man would come to see him again, and was so taken aback that he stared at him and did not know what to say. But Pavel Pavlovitch was equal to the occasion. He greeted him, and sat down on the very same chair on which he had sat on his last visit. Velchaninov had a sudden and peculiarly vivid memory of that visit, and gazed uneasily and with repulsion at his visitor.

"You're surprised?" began Pavel Pavlovitch, interpreting Velchaninov's expression.

He seemed altogether much more free and easy than on the previous day, and at the same time it could be detected that he was more nervous than he had been then. His appearance was particularly curious. M. Trusotsky was not only presentably but quite foppishly dressed— in a light summer jacket, light-coloured trousers of a smart, close-fitting cut, a light waistcoat; gloves, a gold lorgnette, which he had suddenly adopted for some reason. His linen was irreproachable; he even smelt of scent. About his whole get-up there was something ridiculous, and at the same time strangely and unpleasantly suggestive.

"Of course, Alexey Ivanovitch," he went on, wriggling, "I'm surprising you by coming, and I'm sensible of it. But there is always, so I imagine, preserved between people, and to my mind there should be preserved, something higher, shouldn't there? Higher, I mean, than all the conditions and even unpleasantnesses that may come to pass. . . . Shouldn't there?"

"Pavel Pavlovitch, say what you have to say quickly, and without ceremony," said Velchaninov, frowning.

"In a couple of words," Pavel Pavlovitch began hastily, "I'm going to get married and I am just setting off to see my future bride. They are in a summer villa too. I should like to have the great honour to make bold to introduce you to the family, and have come to ask an unusual favour," (Pavel Pavlovitch bent his head humbly) "to beg you to accompany me. . . ."

"Accompany you, where?" Velchaninov stared with open eyes.

"To them, that is, to their villa. Forgive me, I am talking as though in a fever, and perhaps I've not been clear; but I'm so afraid of your declining."

And he looked plaintively at Velchaninov.

"Do you want me to go with you now to see your future bride?" Velchaninov repeated, scrutinizing him rapidly, unable to believe his eyes or ears.

"Yes," said Pavel Pavlovitch, extremely abashed. "Don't be angry, Alexey Ivanovitch. It's not impudence; I only beg you most humbly as a great favour. I had dreamed that you might not like, that being so, to refuse. . . ."

"To begin with, it's utterly out of the question." Velchaninov turned round uneasily.

"It is merely an intense desire on my part and nothing more," Pavel Pavlovitch went on, imploring him. "I will not conceal, either, that there are reasons for it, but I should have preferred not to have revealed them till later, and for the present to confine myself to the very earnest request. . . ."

And he positively got up from his seat to show his deference.

"But in any case it is quite impossible, you must admit that yourself. . . ."

Velchaninov, too, stood up.

"It is quite possible, Alexey Ivanovitch. I was proposing to present you as a friend; and besides, you are an acquaintance of theirs already; you see, it's to Zahlebinin's, to his villa. The civil councillor, Zahlebinin."

"What?" cried Velchaninov.

It was the civil councillor for whom he had been constantly looking for a month before, and had never found at home. He had, as it turned out, been acting in the interests of the other side.

"Yes, yes; yes, yes," said Pavel Pavlovitch, smiling and seeming to be greatly encouraged by Velchaninov's great astonishment; "the very man, you remember, whom you were walking beside, and talking to, while I stood opposite watching you; I was waiting to go up to him when you had finished. Twenty years ago we were in the same office, and that day, when I meant to go up to him after you had finished, I had no idea of the sort. It occurred to me suddenly, only a week ago."

"But, upon my word, they are quite a decent family," said Velchaninov, in naïve surprise.

"Well, what then, if they are?" Pavel Pavlovitch grimaced.

"No, of course, I didn't mean . . . only as far as I've observed when I was there . . ."

"They remember, they remember your being there," Pavel Pavlovitch put in joyfully; "only you couldn't have seen the family then; but he remembers you and has a great esteem for you. We talked of you with great respect."

"But when you've only been a widower three months?"

"But you see the wedding will not be at once; the wedding will be in nine or ten months, so that the year of mourning will be over. I assure you that everything is all right. To begin with, Fedosey Petrovitch has known me from a boy; he knew my late wife; he knows my style of living, and what people think of me, and what's more, I have property, and I'm receiving a post with increase of salary—so all that has weight."

"Why, is it his daughter?"

"I will tell you all about it." Pavel Pavlovitch wriggled ingratiatingly. "Allow me to light a cigarette. And you'll see her yourself to-day too. To begin with, such capable men as Fedosey Petrovitch are sometimes very highly thought of here in Petersburg, if they succeed in attracting notice. But you know, apart from his salary and the additional and supplementary fees, bonuses, hotel expenses, and moneys given in relief, he has nothing—that is, nothing substantial that could be called a capital. They are comfortably off, but there is no possibility of saving where there's a family. Only imagine: Fedosey Petrovitch has eight girls, and only one son, still a child. If he were to die to-morrow there would be nothing left but a niggardly pension. And eight girls! just imagine—only imagine—what it must run into simply for their shoes! Of these eight girls five are grown up, the eldest is four-and-twenty (a most charming young lady, as you will see) and the sixth, a girl of fifteen, is still at the high school. Of course, husbands must be found for the five elder ones, and that ought to be done in good time, as far as possible, so their father ought to bring them out, and what do you suppose that will cost? And then I turn up, the first suitor they have had in the house, and one they know all about, that I really have property, I mean. Well, that's all."

Pavel Pavlovitch explained with fervour.

"You're engaged to the eldest?"

"N-no, I . . . no, not to the eldest; you see, I'm proposing for the sixth, the one who is still at the high school."

"What?" said Velchaninov, with an involuntary smile. "Why, you say she's only fifteen!"

"Fifteen now; but in nine months she'll be sixteen, she'll be sixteen and three months, so what of it? But as it would be improper at present, there will be no open engagement but only an understanding with the parents. . . . I assure you that everything is all right!"

"Then it's not settled yet?"

"Yes, it is settled, it's all settled. I assure you, all is as it should be."

"And does she know?"

"Well, it's only in appearance, for the sake of propriety, that they are not telling her; of course she knows." Pavel Pavlovitch screwed up his eyes insinuatingly. "Well, do you congratulate me, Alexey Ivanovitch?" Pavel Pavlovitch concluded very timidly.

"But what should I go there for? However," he added hurriedly, "since I'm not going in any case, don't trouble to find a reason."

"Alexey Ivanovitch . . . ."

"But do you expect me to get in beside you and drive off there with you? Think of it!"

The feeling of disgust and aversion came back after the momentary distraction of Pavel Pavlovitch's chatter about his future bride. In another minute he would have turned him out. He even felt angry with himself for some reason.

"Do, Alexey Ivanovitch, do, and you won't regret it!" Pavel Pavlovitch implored him in a voice fraught with feeling. "No, no, no!"—he waved his hands, catching an impatient and determined gesture from Velchaninov. "Alexey Ivanovitch, Alexey Ivanovitch, wait a bit before you decide! I see that you have perhaps misunderstood me. Of course, I know only too well that you cannot be to me, nor I to you . . . that we're not comrades; I am not so absurd as not to understand that. And that the favour I'm asking of you will not pledge you to anything in the future. And, indeed, I'm going away after to-morrow altogether, absolutely; just as though nothing had happened. Let this day be a solitary exception. I have come to you resting my hopes on the generosity of the special feelings of your heart, Alexey Ivanovitch—those feelings which might of late have been awakened . . . I think I'm speaking clearly, am I not?"

Pavel Pavlovitch's agitation reached an extreme point. Velchaninov looked at him strangely.

"You ask for some service from me?" he questioned, hesitatingly, "and are very insistent about it. That strikes me as suspicious; I should like to know more about it."

"The only service is that you should come with me. And afterwards, on our way back, I will unfold all to you as though at confession. Alexey Ivanovitch, believe me!"

But Velchaninov still refused, and the more stubbornly because he was conscious of an oppressive and malignant impulse. This evil impulse had been faintly stirring within him from the very beginning, ever since Pavel Pavlovitch had talked of his future bride: whether it was simply curiosity, or some other quite obscure prompting, he felt tempted to consent. And the more he felt tempted, the more he resisted. He sat with his elbow on one hand, and hesitated.

Pavel Pavlovitch beside him kept coaxing and persuading.

"Very good, I'll come," he consented all at once, uneasily and almost apprehensively, getting up from his seat.

Pavel Pavlovitch was extremely delighted.

"But, Alexey Ivanovitch, you must change your clothes

now," Pavel Pavlovitch cajoled him, hanging gleefully about him; "put on your best suit."

"And why must he meddle in this, too, strange fellow?" Velchaninov thought to himself.

"This is not the only service I'm expecting of you, Alexey Ivanovitch. Since you have given your consent, please be my adviser."

"In what, for example?"

"The great question, for instance, of crape. Which would be more proper, to remove the crape, or keep it on?"

"As you prefer."

"No, I want you to decide; what would you do yourself in my place, that is, if you had crape on your hat? My own idea is that, if I retain it, it points to the constancy of my feelings, and so is a flattering recommendation."

"Take it off, of course."

"Do you really think it's a matter of course?" Pavel Pavlovitch hesitated. "No, I think I had better keep it. . . ."

"As you like."

"He doesn't trust me, that's a good thing," thought Velchaninov.

They went out; Pavel Pavlovitch gazed with satisfaction at Velchaninov's smartened appearance; his countenance seemed to betray an even greater degree of deference and of dignity! Velchaninov wondered at him and even more at himself. A very good carriage stood waiting for them at the gate.

"So you had a carriage all ready too? So you felt sure I should come?"

"I engaged the carriage for myself, but I did feel confident that you would consent to accompany me," Pavel Pavlovitch replied, with the air of a perfectly happy man.

"Ah, Pavel Pavlovitch," Velchaninov said, laughing as it were irritably when they were in the carriage and had set off, "weren't you too sure of me?"

"But it's not for you, Alexey Ivanovitch, it's not for you to tell me that I'm a fool for it," Pavel Pavlovitch responded, in a voice full of feeling.

"And Liza," thought Velchaninov, and at once hastened to dismiss the thought of her as though afraid of sacrilege. And it suddenly seemed to him that he was so petty, so insignificant at that moment; it struck him that the thought that had tempted him was a thought so small and nasty . . . and he longed again, at all costs, to fling it all up, and to get out of the carriage at once, even if he had to thrash Pavel Pavlovitch. But the latter began talking and the temptation mastered his heart again,

"Alexey Ivanovitch, do you know anything about jewels?"

"What sort of jewels?"

"Diamonds."

"Yes."

"I should like to take a little present. Advise me, should I or not?"

"I think you shouldn't."

"But I feel I should so like to," returned Pavel Pavlovitch, "only, what am I to buy? A whole set, that is, a brooch, earrings, bracelets, or simply one article?"

"How much do you want to spend?"

"About four hundred or five hundred roubles?"

"Ough!"

"Is it too much, or what?" asked Pavel Pavlovitch in a flutter.

"Buy a single bracelet for a hundred roubles."

Pavel Pavlovitch was positively mortified; he was so eager to spend more and buy a "whole set" of jewels. He persisted. They drove to a shop. It ended, however, in his only buying a bracelet, and not the one that he wanted to, but the one that Velchaninov fixed upon. Pavel Pavlovitch wanted to take both. When the jeweller, who had asked a hundred and seventy-five roubles for the bracelet, consented to take a hundred and fifty for it, Pavel Pavlovitch was positively vexed; he would have paid two hundred if that sum had been asked, he was so eager to spend more.

"It doesn't matter, does it, my being in a hurry with presents?" he gushed blissfully, when they had set off again. "They're not grand people, they are very simple. The innocent creatures are fond of little presents," he said, with a sly and good-humoured grin. "You smiled just now, Alexey Ivanovitch, when you heard she was fifteen; but that's just what bowled me over; that she was still going to school with the satchel on her arm full of copy books and pens, he—he! That satchel fascinated me! It's innocence that charms me, Alexey Ivanovitch;

it's not so much beauty of face, it's that. She giggles in the corner with her school friend, and how she laughs, my goodness! And what at? It's all because the kitten jumped off the chest of drawers on to the bed and was curled up like a little ball. . . . And then there's that scent of fresh apples! Shall I take off the crape?"

"As you please."

"I will take it off."

He took off his hat, tore off the crape and flung it in the road. Velchaninov saw that his face was beaming with the brightest hopes, as he replaced his hat upon his bald head.

"Can it be that he is really like this?" he thought, feeling genuinely angry; "can it be there isn't some trick in his inviting me? Can he be really reckoning on my generosity?" he went on, almost offended at the last supposition. "What is he—a buffoon, a fool, or the 'eternal husband'—but it's impossible!"

Chapter 12

At the Zahlebinins'

The Zahlebinins were really a "very decent family," as Velchaninov had expressed it, and Zahlebinin himself had an assured position in a government office and was well thought of by his superiors. All that Pavel Pavlovitch had said about their income was true too: "They live very comfortably, but if he dies there'll be nothing left."

Old Zahlebinin gave Velchaninov a warm and affable welcome, and his former "foe" seemed quite like a friend.

"I congratulate you, it was better so," he began at the first word, with a pleasant and dignified air. "I was in favour of settling it out of court myself and Pyotr Karlovitch (Velchaninov's lawyer) is priceless in such cases. Well, you get sixty thousand without any bother, without delay and dispute! And the case might have dragged on for three years!"

Velchaninov was at once presented to Madame Zahlebinin, an elderly lady of redundant figure, with a very simple and tired-looking face. The young ladies, too, began to sail in one after the other or in couples. But a very great many young ladies made their appearance; by degrees they gathered to the number of ten or twelve—Velchaninov lost count of them; some came in, others went out. But among them several were girl friends from the neighbouring villas. The Zahlebinins' villa, a large wooden house, built in quaint and whimsical style, with parts added at different periods, had the advantage of a big garden; but three or four other villas looked into the garden on different sides, and it was common property, an arrangement which naturally led to friendly relations among the girls of the different households. From the first words of conversation Velchaninov observed that he was expected, and that his arrival in the character of a friend of Pavel Pavlovitch, anxious to make their acquaintance, was hailed almost triumphantly.

His keen and experienced eye quickly detected something special; from the over-cordial welcome of the parents, from a certain peculiar look about the girls and their get-up (though, indeed, it was a holiday), from all that, the suspicion dawned upon him that Pavel Pavlovitch had been scheming and, very possibly, without, of course, saying it in so many words, had been suggesting a conception of him as a bachelor of property and of the "best society," who was suffering from ennui and very, very likely to make up his mind to "change his state and settle down," especially as he had just come into a fortune. The manner and the appearance of the eldest Mademoiselle Zahlebinin, Katerina Fedosyevna, the one who was twenty-four and who had been described by Pavel Pavlovitch as a charming person, struck him as being in keeping with that idea. She was distinguished from her sisters by her dress and the original way in which her luxuriant hair was done. Her sisters and the other girls all looked as though they were firmly convinced that Velchaninov was making their acquaintance "on Katya's account" and had come "to have a look at her." Their glances and even some words, dropped in the course of the day, confirmed him in this surmise. Katerina Fedosyevna was a tall blonde of generous proportions, with an exceedingly sweet face, of a gentle, unenterprising, even torpid character. "Strange that a girl like that should still be on hand," Velchaninov could not help thinking, watching her with pleasure. "Of course, she has no dowry and she'll soon grow too fat, but meantime lots of men would admire her. . . ." All the other sisters, too, were nice-looking, and among their friends there were several amusing and even pretty faces. It began to divert him; he had come, moreover, with special ideas.

Nadyezhda Fedosyevna, the sixth, the schoolgirl and Pavel Pavlovitch's bride-elect, did not appear till later. Velchaninov awaited her coming with an impatience which surprised him and made him laugh at himself. At last she made her entrance, and not without effect, accompanied by a lively, keen-witted girl friend, a brunette with a comical face whose name was Marie Nikititchna, and of whom, as was at once apparent, Pavel Pavlovitch stood in great dread. This Marie Nikititchna, a girl of twenty-three, with a mocking tongue and really clever, was a nursery governess in a friend's family. She had long been accepted by the Zahlebinins as one of themselves and was thought a great deal of by the girls. It was evident that Nadya found her indispensable now. Velchaninov discerned at once that all the girls were antagonistic to Pavel Pavlovitch, even the friends, and two minutes after Nadya's arrival he had made up his mind that she *detested* him. He observed, too, that Pavel Pavlovitch either failed to notice this or refused to.

Nadya was unquestionably the handsomest of the lot —a little brunette with a wild, untamed look and the boldness of a nihilist; a roguish imp with blazing eyes, with a charming but often malicious smile, with wonderful lips and teeth, slender and graceful, her face still childlike but glowing with the dawn of thought. Her age was evident in every step she took, in every word she uttered. It appeared afterwards that Pavel Pavlovitch did see her for the first time with an American leather satchel on her arm, but this time she had not got it.

The presentation of the bracelet was a complete failure, and, indeed, made an unpleasant impression. As soon as Pavel Pavlovitch saw his "future bride" come into the room he went up to her with a smirk. He presented it as a testimony "of the agreeable gratification he had experienced on his previous visit on the occasion of the charming song sung by Nadyezhda Fedosyevna at the piano. . . ." He stammered, could not finish, and stood helpless, holding out the case with the bracelet and thrusting it into the hand of Nadyezhda Fedosyevna, who did not

want to take it, and, crimson with shame and anger, drew
back her hands. She turned rudely to her mother, whose
face betrayed embarrassment, and said aloud:

"I don't want to take it, *maman!*"

"Take it and say thank you," said her father, with calm
severity: but he, too, was displeased. "Unnecessary, quite
unnecessary!" he muttered reprovingly to Pavel Pavlovitch.

Nadya, seeing there was no help for it, took the case
and, dropping her eyes, curtsied, as tiny children curtsey
—that is, suddenly bobbed down, and popped up again
as though on springs. One of her sisters went up to look
at it and Nadya handed her the case unopened, showing,
for her part, that she did not care to look at it. The bracelet was taken out and passed from one to the other; but
they all looked at it in silence, and some even sarcastically. Only the mother murmured that the bracelet was
very charming. Pavel Pavlovitch was ready to sink into
the earth.

Velchaninov came to the rescue.

He began talking, loudly and eagerly, about the first
thing that occurred to him, and before five minutes were
over he had gained the attention of every one in the
drawing-room. He was a brilliant master of the art of
small talk—that is, the art of seeming perfectly frank and
at the same time appearing to consider his listeners as
frank as himself. He could, with perfect naturalness, appear when necessary to be the most light-hearted and
happy of men. He was very clever, too, in slipping in a
witty remark, a jibe, a gay insinuation or an amusing pun,
always as it were accidentally and as though unconscious
of doing it—though the epigram or pun and the whole
conversation, perhaps, had been prepared and rehearsed
long, long before and even used on more than one previous occasion. But at the present moment nature and
art were at one, he felt that he was in the mood and that
something was drawing him on; he felt the most absolute
confidence in himself and knew that in a few minutes all
these eyes would be turned upon him, all these people
would be listening only to him, talking to no one but him,
and laughing only at what he said. And, in fact, the laughter soon came, by degrees the others joined in the conversation—and he was exceedingly clever in making
other people talk—three or four voices could be heard at

once. The bored and weary face of Madame Zahlebinin was lighted up almost with joy; it was the same with Katerina Fedosyevna, who gazed and listened as though enchanted. Nadya watched him keenly from under her brows; it was evident that she was prejudiced against him. This spurred him on the more. The "mischievous" Marie Nikititchna succeeded in getting in rather a good thrust at him; she asserted quite fictitiously that Pavel Pavlovitch had introduced him as the friend of his boyhood, so putting with obvious intent at least seven years on to his age. But even the malicious Marie Nikititchna liked him. Pavel Pavlovitch was completely nonplussed. He had, of course, some idea of his friend's abilities and at first was delighted at his success; he tittered himself and joined in the conversation; but by degrees he seemed to sink into thoughtfulness, and finally into positive dejection, which was clearly apparent in his troubled countenance.

"Well, you're a visitor who doesn't need entertaining," old Zahlebinin commented gaily, as he got up to go upstairs to his own room, where, in spite of the holiday, he had some business papers awaiting his revision; "and, only fancy, I thought of you as the most gloomy, hypochondriacal of young men. What mistakes one makes!"

They had a piano; Velchaninov asked who played, and suddenly turned to Nadya:

"I believe you sing?"

"Who told you?" Nadya snapped out.

"Pavel Pavlovitch told me just now."

"It's not true. I only sing for fun. I've no voice."

"And I've no voice either, but I sing."

"Then you'll sing to us? Well, then, I'll sing to you," said Nadya, her eyes gleaming; "only not now, but after dinner. I can't endure music," she added. "I'm sick of the piano: they're all singing and playing from morning to night here—Katya's the only one worth hearing."

Velchaninov at once took this up, and it appeared that Katerina Fedosyevna was the only one who played the piano seriously. He at once begged her to play. Every one was evidently pleased at his addressing Katya, and the mamma positively flushed crimson with gratification, Katerina Fedosyevna got up, smiling, and went to the piano, and suddenly, to her own surprise, she flushed crimson and was horribly abashed that she, such a big girl, four-and-twenty and so stout, should be blushing like a child—and all this was written clearly on her face as she sat down to play. She played something from Haydn and played it carefully though without expression, but she was shy. When she had finished Velchaninov began warmly praising to her, not her playing but Haydn, and especially the little thing which she had played, and she was evidently so pleased and listened so gratefully and happily to his praises, not of herself but of Haydn, that he could not help looking at her with more friendliness and attention: "Ah, but you are a dear!" was reflected in the gleam of his eye—and every one seemed instantly to understand that look, especially Katerina Fedosyevna herself.

"You have a delightful garden," he said, suddenly addressing the company and looking towards the glass door that led on to the balcony. "What do you say to our all going into the garden?"

"Let us, let us!" they shrieked joyfully, as though he had guessed the general wish.

They walked in the garden till dinner-time. Madame Zahlebinin, though she had been longing to have a nap, could not resist going out with them, but wisely sat down to rest on the verandah, where she at once began to doze. In the garden Velchaninov and the girls got on to still more friendly terms. He noticed that several very young men from the villas joined them; one was a student and another simply a high school boy. They promptly made a dash each for *his* girl, and it was evident that they had come on their account; the third, a very morose and dishevelled-looking youth of twenty, in huge blue spectacles, began, with a frown, whispering hurriedly with Marie Nikititchna and Nadya. He scanned Velchaninov sternly, and seemed to consider it incumbent upon himself to treat him with extraordinary contempt. Some of the girls suggested that they should play games. To Velchaninov's question, what games they played, they said all sorts of games, and catch-catch, but in the evening they would play proverbs—that is, all would sit down and one would go out, the others choose a proverb—for instance: "More haste, less speed," and when the one outside is called in, each in turn has to say one sentence to him. One, for instance, must say a sentence in which there is the word "more," the second, one in which there is the word "haste," and so on. And from their sentences he must guess the proverb.

"That must be very amusing," said Velchaninov.

"Oh, no, it's awfully boring," cried two or three voices at once.

"Or else we play at acting," Nadya observed, suddenly addressing him. "Do you see that thick tree, round which there's a seat: behind that tree is behind the scenes, and there the actors sit, say a king, a queen, a princess, a young man—just as any one likes; each one enters when he chooses and says anything that comes into his head, and that's the game."

"But that's delightful!" Velchaninov repeated again.

"Oh, no, it's awfully dull! At first it did turn out amusing, but lately it's always been senseless, for no one knows how to end it; perhaps with you, though, it will be more interesting. We did think you were a friend of Pavel Pavlovitch's, though, but it seems he was only bragging. I'm very glad you have come . . . for one thing. . . ."

She looked very earnestly and impressively at Velchaninov and at once walked away to Marie Nikititchna.

"We're going to play proverbs this evening," one of the girl friends whom Velchaninov had scarcely noticed before, and with whom he had not exchanged a word, whispered to him confidentially. "They're all going to make fun of Pavel Pavlovitch, and you will too, of course."

"Ah, how nice it is that you've come, we were all so dull," observed another girl in a friendly way. She was a red-haired girl with freckles, and a face absurdly flushed from walking and the heat. Goodness knows where she had sprung from; Velchaninov had not noticed her till then.

Pavel Pavlovitch's uneasiness grew more and more marked. In the garden Velchaninov made great friends with Nadya. She no longer looked at him from under her brows as she had at first; she seemed to have laid aside her critical attitude towards him, and laughed, skipped about, shrieked, and twice even seized him by the hand; she was extremely happy, she continued to take not the slightest notice of Pavel Pavlovitch, and behaved as though she were not aware of his existence. Velchaninov felt certain that there was an actual plot against Pavel Pavlovitch; Nadya and the crowd of girls drew Velchaninov aside, while some of the other girl friends lured Pavel Pavlovitch on various pretexts in another direction; but the latter broke away from them, and ran full speed straight to them—that is, to Velchaninov and Nadya, and suddenly thrust his bald head in between them with uneasy curiosity. He hardly attempted to restrain himself; the naïveté of his gestures and actions were sometimes amazing. He could not resist trying once more to turn Velchaninov's attention to Katerina Fedosyevna; it was clear to her now that he had not come on her account, but was much more interested in Nadya; but her expression was just as sweet and good-humoured as ever. She seemed to be happy simply at being beside them and listening to what their new visitor was saying; she, poor thing, could never keep up her share in a conversation cleverly.

"What a darling your sister Katerina Fedosyevna is!" Velchaninov said aside to Nadya.

"Katya! No one could have a kinder heart than she has. She's an angel to all of us. I adore her," the girl responded enthusiastically.

At last dinner came at five o'clock; and it was evident that the dinner, too, was not an ordinary meal, but had been prepared expressly for visitors. There were two or three very elaborate dishes, which evidently were not part of their ordinary fare, one of them so strange that no one could find a name for it. In addition to the everyday wine there was a bottle of Tokay, obviously for the benefit of the visitors; at the end of dinner champagne was brought in for some reason. Old Zahlebinin took an extra glass, became extraordinarily good-humoured and ready to laugh at anything Velchaninov said.

In the end Pavel Pavlovitch could not restrain himself. Carried away by the spirit of rivalry he suddenly attempted to make a pun too; at the end of the table, where he was sitting by Madame Zahlebinin, there was a sudden roar of loud laughter from the delighted girls.

"Papa, Papa! Pavel Pavlovitch has made a pun too," the fourth and fifth Zahlebinin girls shouted in unison. "He says we're 'damsels who dazzle all. . . .' "

"Ah, so he's punning too! Well, what was his pun?" the old man responded sedately, turning patronizingly to Pavel Pavlovitch and smiling in readiness for the expected pun.

"Why, he says we're 'damsels who dazzle all.'"

"Y-yes, well, and what then?" The old man did not understand and smiled more good-humouredly in expectation.

"Oh, Papa, how tiresome you are; you don't understand. Why, 'damsels' and then 'dazzle'; 'damsel' is like 'dazzle,' 'damsels who dazzle all. . . .'"

"A-a-ah," the old man drawled in a puzzled voice. "H'm, well, he'll make a better one next time!"

And the old man laughed good-humouredly.

"Pavel Pavlovitch, you can't have all the perfections at once," Marie Nikititchna jerked aloud. "Oh, my goodness! he's got a bone in his throat," she exclaimed, jumping up from her chair.

There was a positive hubbub, but that was just what Marie Nikititchna wanted. Pavel Pavlovitch had simply choked over the wine which he was sipping to cover his confusion, but Marie Nikititchna vowed and declared that it was a "fish bone," that she had seen it herself and that people sometimes died of it.

"Slap him on the nape of the neck," some one shouted.

"Yes, really that's the best thing to do!" the old man approved aloud.

Eager volunteers were already at him; Marie Nikititchna and the red-haired girl (who had also been invited to dinner), and, finally, the mamma herself, greatly alarmed; every one wanted to slap Pavel Pavlovitch on the back. Jumping up from the table, Pavel Pavlovitch wriggled away and was for a full minute asseverating that he had swallowed his wine too quickly and that the cough would soon be over, while the others realized that it was all a trick of Marie Nikititchna's.

"But, really, you tease . . . !" Madame Zahlebinin tried to say sternly to Marie Nikititchna: but she broke down and laughed as she very rarely did, and that made quite a sensation of a sort.

After dinner they all went out on the verandah to drink coffee.

"And what lovely days we're having!" said the old man, looking with pleasure into the garden, and serenely admiring the beauties of nature. "If only we could have some rain. Enjoy yourselves and God bless you! And you enjoy yourself too," he added, patting Pavel Pavlovitch on the shoulder as he went out.

When they had all gone out into the garden again, Pavel Pavlovitch suddenly ran up to Velchaninov and pulled him by the sleeve.

"Just one minute," he whispered impatiently.

They turned into a lonely side path.

"No, in this case, excuse me, no, I won't give up . . ." he stuttered in a furious whisper, clutching Velchaninov's arm.

"What? what?" Velchaninov asked, opening his eyes in amazement.

Pavel Pavlovitch stared at him mutely, his lips moved, and he smiled furiously.

"Where are you going? Where are you? Everything's ready," they heard the ringing, impatient voices of the girls.

Velchaninov shrugged his shoulders and returned to the rest of the party.

Pavel Pavlovitch, too, ran after him.

"I'll bet he asked you for a handkerchief," said Marie Nikititchna; "he forgot one last time too."

"He'll always forget it!" the fifth Zahlebinin girl put in.

"He's forgotten his handkerchief, Pavel Pavlovitch has forgotten his handkerchief, Mamma, Pavel Pavlovitch has forgotten his pocket-handkerchief, Mamma, Pavel Pavlovitch has a cold in his head again!" cried voices.

"Then why doesn't he say so! You do stand on ceremony, Pavel Pavlovitch!" Madame Zahlebinin drawled in a sing-song voice. "It's dangerous to trifle with a cold; I'll send you a handkerchief directly. And why has he always got a cold in his head?" she added, as she moved away, glad of an excuse for returning home.

"I have two pocket-handkerchiefs and I haven't a cold in my head!" Pavel Pavlovitch called after her, but the lady apparently did not grasp what he said, and a minute later, when Pavel Pavlovitch was ambling after the others, keeping near Velchaninov and Nadya, a breathless maid-servant overtook him and brought him a handkerchief.

"Proverbs, a game of proverbs," the girls shouted on all sides, as though they expected something wonderful from "a game of proverbs."

They fixed on a place and sat down on a seat; it fell to Marie Nikititchna's lot to guess; they insisted that she should go as far away as possible and not listen; in her absence they chose a proverb and distributed the words.

Marie Nikititchna returned and guessed the proverb at once. The proverb was: "It's no use meeting troubles half-way."

Marie Nikititchna was followed by the young man with dishevelled hair and blue spectacles. They insisted on even greater precautions with him—he had to stand in the arbour and keep his face to the fence. The gloomy young man did what was required of him contemptuously, and seemed to feel morally degraded by it. When he was called he could guess nothing, he went the round of all of them and listened to what they said twice over, spent a long time in gloomy meditation, but nothing came of it. They put him to shame. The proverb was: "To pray to God and serve the Czar ne'er fail of their reward."

"And the proverb's disgusting!" the exasperated young man exclaimed indignantly, as he retreated to his place.

"Oh, how dull it is!" cried voices.

Velchaninov went out; he was hidden even further off; he, too, failed to guess.

"Oh, how dull it is!" more voices cried.

"Well, now, I'll go out," said Nadya.

"No, no, let Pavel Pavlovitch go out now, it's Pavel Pavlovitch's turn," they all shouted, growing more animated.

Pavel Pavlovitch was led away, right up to the fence in the very corner, and made to stand facing it, and that he might not look round, the red-haired girl was sent to keep watch on him. Pavel Pavlovitch, who had regained his confidence and almost his cheerfulness, was determined to do his duty properly and stood stock-still, gazing at the fence and not daring to turn round. The red-haired girl stood on guard twenty paces behind him nearer to the party in the arbour, and she exchanged signals with the girls in some excitement; it was evident that all were expecting something with trepidation; something was on foot. Suddenly the red-haired girl waved her arms as a signal to the arbour. Instantly they all jumped up and ran off at breakneck speed.

"Run, you run, too," a dozen voices whispered to Velchaninov, almost with horror at his not running.

"What's the matter? What has happened?" he asked, hurrying after them.

"Hush, don't shout! Let him stand there staring at the fence while we all run away. See, Nastya is running."

The red-haired girl (Nastya) was running at breakneck speed, waving her hands as though something extraordinary had happened. They all ran at last to the other side of the pond, the very opposite corner of the garden. When Velchaninov had got there he saw that Katerina Fedosyevna was hotly disputing with the others, especially with Nadya and Marie Nikititchna.

"Katya, darling, don't be angry!" said Nadya, kissing her.

"Very well, I won't tell Mamma, but I shall go away myself, for it's very horrid. What must he be feeling at the fence there, poor man!"

She went away—from pity—but all the others were merciless and as ruthless as before. They all insisted sternly that when Pavel Pavlovitch came back, Velchaninov should take no notice of him, as though nothing had happened.

"And let us all play catch-catch!" cried the red-haired girl ecstatically.

It was at least a quarter of an hour before Pavel Pavlovitch rejoined the party. For two-thirds of that time he had certainly been standing at the fence. The game was in full swing, and was a great success—everybody was shouting and merry. Frantic with rage, Pavel Pavlovitch went straight up to Velchaninov and pulled at his sleeve again.

"Just half a minute!"

"Good gracious, what does he want with his half-minutes!"

"He's borrowing a handkerchief again," was shouted after him once more.

"Well, this time it was you; now it's all your doing. . . ."

Pavel Pavlovitch's teeth chattered as he said this.

Velchaninov interrupted him, and mildly advised him to be livelier, or they would go on teasing him. "They tease you because you are cross when all the rest are enjoying themselves." To his surprise, these words of advice made a great impression on Pavel Pavlovitch; he subsided at once—so much so, in fact, that he went back to the party with a penitent air and submissively took his place in the game; after which they left him alone and treated him like the rest—and before half an hour had passed he had almost regained his spirits. In all the games when he had to choose a partner he picked out by preference the red-haired traitress, or one of the Zahlebinin sisters. But to his still greater surprise Velchaninov noticed that Pavel Pavlovitch did not dare try to speak to Nadya, although he continually hovered about her. At any rate he accepted his position, as an object of scorn and neglect to her, as though it were a fitting and natural thing. But towards the end they played a prank upon him again.

The game was "hide-and-seek." The one who hid, however, was allowed to run anywhere in the part of the garden allotted him. Pavel Pavlovitch, who had succeeded in concealing himself completely in some thick bushes, conceived the idea of running out and making a bolt for the house. He was seen and shouts were raised; he crept hurriedly upstairs to the first floor, knowing of a place behind a chest of drawers where he could hide. But the red-haired girl flew up after him, crept on tiptoe to the door and turned the key on him. All left off playing and ran just as they had done before to the other side of the pond, at the further end of the garden. Ten minutes later, Pavel Pavlovitch, becoming aware that no one was looking for him, peeped out of the window. There was no one to be seen. He did not dare to call out for fear of waking the parents; the maids had been sternly forbidden to answer Pavel Pavlovitch's call or go to him. Katerina Fedosyevna might have unlocked him, but, returning to her room and sitting down to dream a little, she had unexpectedly fallen asleep too. And so he stayed there about an hour. At last the girls came, as it were by chance, in twos and threes.

"Pavel Pavlovitch, why don't you come out to us? Oh, it has been fun! We've been playing at acting. Alexey Ivanovitch has been acting 'a young man.' "

"Pavel Pavlovitch, why don't you come, we want to admire you!" others observed as they passed.

"Admire what now?" they suddenly heard the voice of Madame Zahlebinin, who had only just woken up and made up her mind to come out into the garden and watch the "children's" games while waiting for tea.

"But here's Pavel Pavlovitch," they told her, pointing to the window where Pavel Pavlovitch's face, pale with anger, looked out with a wry smile.

"It's an odd fancy for a man to sit alone, when you're all enjoying yourselves!" said the mamma, shaking her head.

Meanwhile, Nadya had deigned to give Velchaninov an explanation of her words that she "was glad he had come for one reason."

The explanation took place in a secluded avenue. Marie Nikititchna purposely summoned Velchaninov, who was taking part in some game and was horribly bored, and left him alone in the avenue with Nadya.

"I am absolutely convinced," she said boldly, in a rapid patter, "that you are not such a great friend of Pavel Pavlovitch's as he boasted you were. I am reckoning on you as the one person who can do me a very great service." She took the case out of her pocket. "I humbly beg you to give this back to him at once, as I shall never speak to him again in my life. You can say so from me, and tell him not to dare to force his company and his presents on me. I'll let him know the rest through other people. Will you be so kind as to do what I want?"

"Oh, for mercy's sake, spare me!" Velchaninov almost cried out, waving his hand.

"What? Spare you?" Nadya was extraordinarily surprised at his refusal, and she gazed at him round-eyed.

The tone she had assumed for the occasion broke down immediately, and she was almost in tears.

Velchaninov laughed.

"I don't mean that. . . . I should be very glad . . . but I have my own account to settle with him. . . ."

"I knew that you were not his friend and that he was telling lies!" Nadya interrupted quickly and passionately. "I'll never marry him, I tell you! Never! I can't understand how he could presume . . . Only you must give him back his disgusting present or else what shall I do? I particularly, particularly want him to have it back today, the same day, so that his hopes may be crushed, and if he sneaks about it to Papa he shall see what he gets by it."

And from behind the bushes there suddenly emerged the young man in the blue spectacles.

"It's your duty to return the bracelet," he blurted out furiously, pouncing on Velchaninov. "If only from respect for the rights of women, that is—if you are capable of rising to the full significance of the question."

But before he had time to finish Nadya tugged at his sleeve with all her might, and drew him away from Velchaninov.

"My goodness, how silly you are, Predposylov!" she cried. "Go away, go away, go away, and don't dare to lisen; I told you to stand a long way off!" . . . She stamped her little foot at him, and when he had crept back into the bushes she still walked up and down across the path, with her eyes flashing and her arms folded before her, as though she were beside herself with anger.

"You wouldn't believe how silly they are!" She stopped suddenly before Velchaninov. "It amuses you, but think what it means to me."

"That's not *he*, it's not *he*, is it?" laughed Velchaninov.

"Of course it isn't, and how could you imagine it!" cried Nadya, smiling and blushing. "That's only his friend. But I can't understand the friends he chooses; they all say that he's a 'future leader,' but I don't understand it. . . . Alexey Ivanovitch, I've no one I can appeal to; I ask you for the last time, will you give it back?"

"Oh, very well, I will; give it me."

"Ah, you are kind, you are good!" she cried, delighted, handing him the case. "I'll sing to you the whole evening for that, for I sing beautifully, do you know. I told you a fib when I said I didn't like music. Oh, you must come again—once at any rate; how glad I should be. I would tell you everything, everything, everything, and a great deal more besides, because you're so kind—as kind, as kind, as—as Katya!"

And when they went in to tea she did sing him two songs, in an utterly untrained and hardly mature, but pleasant and powerful voice. When they came in from the garden Pavel Pavlovitch was stolidly sitting with the parents at the tea-table, on which the big family samovar was already boiling, surrounded by cups of Sèvres china. He was probably discussing very grave matters with the old people, as two days later he was going away for nine whole months. He did not glance at the party as they came in from the garden, and particularly avoided looking at Velchaninov. It was evident, too, that he had not been sneaking and that all was serene so far.

But when Nadya began singing he put himself forward at once. Nadya purposely ignored one direct question he addressed her, but this did not disconcert Pavel

Pavlovitch, or make him hesitate. He stood behind her chair and his whole manner showed that this was his place and he was not going to give it up to any one.

"Alexey Ivanovitch sings, Mamma; Alexey Ivanovitch wants to sing, Mamma!" almost all the girls shouted at once, crowding round the piano at which Velchaninov confidently installed himself, intending to play his own accompaniment. The old people came in, and with them Katerina Fedosyevna, who had been sitting with them, pouring out the tea.

Velchaninov chose a song of Glinka's, now familiar to almost every one—

"In the glad hour when from thy lips
Come murmurs tender as a dove's."

He sang it, addressing himself entirely to Nadya, who was standing at his elbow nearer to him than any one. His voice had passed its prime, but what was left of it showed that it had once been a fine one. Velchaninov had, twenty years before, when he was a student, the luck to hear that song for the first time sung by Glinka himself, at the house of a friend of the composer's. It was at a literary and artistic bachelor gathering, and Glinka, growing expansive, played and sang his own favourite compositions, among them this song. He, too, had little voice left then, but Velchaninov remembered the great impression made by that song. A drawing-room singer, however skilful, would never have produced such an effect. In that song the intensity of passion rises, mounting higher and higher at every line, at every word; and, from this very intensity, the least trace of falsity, of exaggeration or unreality, such as passes muster so easily at an opera, would distort and destroy the whole value of it. To sing that slight but exceptional song it was essential to have truth, essential to have real inspiration, real passion, or a complete poetical comprehension of it. Otherwise the song would not only be a failure but might even appear unseemly and almost shameless: without them it would be impossible to express such intensity of passion without arousing repulsion, but truth and simplicity saved it. Velchaninov remembered that he had made a success with this song on some occasion. He had almost reproduced Glinka's manner of singing, but now, from the first note, from the first line, there was a gleam of inspiration in his singing which quivered in his voice.

At every word the torrent of feeling was more fervent and more boldly displayed; in the last lines the cry of passion is heard, and when, with blazing eyes, Velchaninov addressed the last words of the song to Nadya—

> "Grown bolder, in thine eyes I gaze;
> Draw close my lips, can hear no more,
> I long to kiss thee, kiss thee, kiss thee!
> I long to kiss thee, kiss thee, kiss thee!"—

she trembled almost with alarm, and even stepped back; the colour rushed into her cheeks, and at the same time Velchaninov seemed to catch a glimpse of something responsive in her abashed and almost dismayed little face. The faces of all the audience betrayed their enchantment and also their amazement: all seemed to feel that it was disgraceful and impossible to sing like that, and yet at the same time all their faces were flushed and all their eyes glowed and seemed to be expecting something more. Among those faces Velchaninov had a vision especially of the face of Katerina Fedosyevna, which looked almost beautiful.

"What a song," old Zahlebinin muttered, a little flabbergasted; "but . . . isn't it too strong? charming, but strong. . . ."

"Yes . . ." Madame Zahlebinin chimed in, but Pavel Pavlovitch would not let her go on; he dashed forward suddenly like one possessed, so far forgetting himself as to seize Nadya by the arm and pull her away from Velchaninov; he skipped up to him, gazed at him with a desperate face and quivering lips that moved without uttering a sound.

"Half a minute," he uttered faintly at last.

Velchaninov saw that in another minute the man might be guilty of something ten times as absurd; he made haste to take his arm and, regardless of the general amazement, drew him out into the verandah, and even took some steps into the garden with him, where it was now almost dark.

"Do you understand that you must go away with me this minute?" said Pavel Pavlovitch.

"No, I don't understand. . . ."

"Do you remember," Pavel Pavlovitch went on, in his

frenzied whisper, "do you remember that you insisted that I should tell you everything, *everything* openly, 'the very last word . . .' do you remember? Well, the time has come to say that word . . . let us go!"

Velchaninov thought a minute, looked at Pavel Pavlovitch and agreed to go.

The sudden announcement of their departure upset the parents, and made all the girls horribly indignant.

"At least have another cup of tea," said Madame Zahlebinin plaintively.

"Come, what's upset you?" old Zahlebinin said in a tone of severity and displeasure, addressing Pavel Pavlovitch, who stood simpering and silent.

"Pavel Pavlovitch, why are you taking Alexey Ivanovitch away?" the girls began plaintively, looking at him with exasperation.

Nadya gazed at him so wrathfully that he positively squirmed, but he did not give way.

"You see, Pavel Pavlovitch has reminded me—many thanks to him for it—of a very important engagement which I might have missed," Velchaninov said, smiling, as he shook hands with Zahlebinin, and bowed to the mamma and the girls, especially distinguishing Katerina Fedosyevna in a manner apparent to all.

"We are very grateful for your visit and shall always be glad to see you," Zahlebinin said ponderously, in conclusion.

"Ah, we shall be so delighted . . ." the mamma chimed in with feeling.

"Come again, Alexey Ivanovitch, come again!" numerous voices were heard calling from the verandah, when he had already got into the carriage with Pavel Pavlovitch; there was perhaps one voice that called more softly than the others, "Come again, dear, dear Alexey Ivanovitch."

"That's the red-haired girl," thought Velchaninov.

Chapter 13

On Whose Side Most?

He might think about the red-haired girl, and yet his soul was in agonies of vexation and remorse. And, indeed, during the whole of that day, which seemed on the surface so amusingly spent, a feeling of acute depression had scarcely left him. Before singing the song he did not know how to get away from it; perhaps that was why he had sung it with such fervour.

"And I could demean myself like that . . . tear myself away from everything," he began reproaching himself, but he hurriedly cut short his thoughts. Indeed, it seemed to him humiliating to lament; it was a great deal more pleasant to be angry with some one.

"Fool!" he whispered wrathfully, with a side glance at the silent figure of Pavel Pavlovitch sitting beside him in the carriage.

Pavel Pavlovitch remained obstinately silent, perhaps concentrated on preparing what he had got to say. With an impatient gesture he sometimes took off his hat and wiped his brow with his handkerchief.

"Perspiring!" Velchaninov thought spitefully.

On one occasion only Pavel Pavlovitch addressed a question to the coachman. "Is there going to be a storm?" he asked.

"Storm, indeed! Not a doubt of it; it's been brewing up all day."

The sky was indeed growing dark and there were flashes of lightning in the distance.

They reached the town about half-past ten.

"I am coming in with you, of course," Pavel Pavlovitch warned him, not far from the house.

"I understand, but I must tell you that I feel seriously unwell."

"I won't stay, I won't stay long."

When they went in at the gate, Pavel Pavlovitch ran in at the porter's lodge to find Mavra.

"What were you running off there for?" Velchaninov said sternly, as the latter overtook him and they went into the room.

"Oh . . . nothing . . . the driver . . ."

"I won't have you drink!"

No answer followed. Velchaninov lighted the candle, and Pavel Pavlovitch at once sat down on the chair. Velchaninov remained standing before him, with a frown on his face.

"I, too, promised to say my 'last' word," he began, with an inward, still suppressed irritation. "Here it is—that word: I consider on my conscience that everything between us is over, so that, in fact, there is nothing for us to talk about—do you hear?—nothing; and so wouldn't it be better for you to go away at once, and I'll close the door after you?"

"Let us settle our account, Alexey Ivanovitch," said Pavel Pavlovitch, looking in his face, however, with peculiar mildness.

"Set-tle our ac-count!" repeated Velchaninov, greatly surprised. "That's a strange thing to say! Settle what account? Bah! Isn't that perhaps that 'last word' you promised . . . to reveal to me?"

"It is."

"We've no account to settle; we settled our account long ago!" Velchaninov pronounced proudly.

"Can you really think so?" Pavel Pavlovitch brought out in a voice full of feeling, clasping his hands strangely and holding them before his breast.

Velchaninov made him no answer, but continued pacing up and down the room. "Liza! Liza!" he was moaning in his heart.

"What did you want to settle, though?" he asked him, frowning, after a rather prolonged silence.

Pavel Pavlovitch had been following him about the room with his eyes all this time, still holding his hands clasped before him.

"Don't go there again," he almost whispered in a voice of entreaty, and he suddenly got up from his chair.

"What! So that's all you are thinking about?" Velchaninov laughed spitefully. "You've surprised me all day, though!" he was beginning malignantly, but suddenly his whole face changed. "Listen," he said mournfully, with deep and sincere feeling; "I consider that I have never lowered myself as I have to-day—to begin with, by consenting to go with you, and then—by what happened there. . . . It was so paltry, so pitiful. . . . I've defiled and debased myself by mixing myself up in it . . . and forgetting . . . But there!" he cried hastily. "Listen, you attacked me to-day in an unguarded moment when I was nervous and ill . . . but there's no need to justify myself! I'm not going there again, and I assure you I take no interest in them whatever," he concluded resolutely.

"Really, really?" cried Pavel Pavlovitch, not disguising his relief and excitement.

Velchaninov looked at him contemptuously, and began pacing up and down the room again.

"You seem to have made up your mind to be happy?" he could not refrain from observing.

"Yes," Pavel Pavlovitch repeated naïvely, in a low voice.

"What is it to me," Velchaninov reflected, "that he's a buffoon and only spiteful through stupidity? I can't help hating him, though he isn't worth it!"

"I am 'the eternal husband'!" said Pavel Pavlovitch, with an abjectly submissive smile at his own expense. "I heard that expression from you, Alexey Ivanovitch, long ago, when you were staying with us in those days. I remember a great many of your sayings in that year. Last time, when you said here, 'the eternal husband,' I reflected."

Mavra came in with a bottle of champagne and two glasses.

"Forgive me, Alexey Ivanovitch; you know that I can't get on without it! Don't think it's impudence; look upon me as an outsider not on your level."

"Yes . . ." Velchaninov muttered with repugnance, "but I assure you I feel unwell. . . ."

"Directly . . . directly . . . in one minute," said Pavel Pavlovitch fussily; "just one little glass because my throat . . ."

He greedily tossed off a glassful at a gulp and sat down, looking almost tenderly at Velchaninov.

Mavra went out.

"How beastly!" Velchaninov murmured.

"It's only those girl friends," Pavel Pavlovitch said confidently, all of a sudden completely revived.

"What? Ah, yes, you are still at that. . . ."

"It's only those girl friends! And then she's so young; we have our little airs and graces! They're charming, in fact. But then—then, you know, I shall be her slave; when she's treated with deference, when she sees something of society . . . she'll be transformed."

"I shall have to give him back that bracelet, though," thought Velchaninov, scowling, as he felt the case in his pocket.

"You say that I'm resolved to be happy? I must get married, Alexey Ivanovitch," Pavel Pavlovitch went on confidentially and almost touchingly, "or what will become of me? You see for yourself!" He pointed to the bottle. "And that's only one-hundredth of my vices. I can't get on at all without marriage and—without new faith; I shall have faith and shall rise up again."

"But why on earth do you tell me this?" Velchaninov asked, almost bursting with laughter. It all struck him as wild. "But tell me," he cried, "what was your object in dragging me out there? What did you want me there for?"

"As a test . . ." Pavel Pavlovitch seemed suddenly embarrassed.

"A test of what?"

"The effect. . . . You see, Alexey Ivanovitch, it's only a week altogether . . . I've been looking round there." (Pavel Pavlovitch grew more and more confused.) "Yesterday I met you and thought: 'I've never yet seen her in outside, so to say, society, that is, in men's, except my own. . . .' A stupid idea; I feel that myself now; unnecessary. I expected too much . . . it's my horrible character. . . ."

He suddenly raised his head and flushed crimson.

"Can he be telling the whole truth?" Velchaninov was petrified with surprise.

"Well, and what then?" he asked.

Pavel Pavlovitch gave a sugary and, as it were, crafty smile.

"It's only charming childishness! It's all those girl friends! Only forgive me for my stupid behaviour before you to-day, Alexey Ivanovitch; I never will again; and indeed it will never happen again."

"And I shan't be there again," said Velchaninov, with a smile.

"That's partly what I mean."

Velchaninov felt a little piqued.

"But I'm not the only man in the world, you know," he observed irritably.

Pavel Pavlovitch flushed again.

"It's sad for me to hear that, Alexey Ivanovitch, and, believe me, I've such a respect for Nadyezhda Fedosyevna . . ."

"Excuse me, excuse me, I didn't mean anything; it only seems a little strange to me that you have such an exaggerated idea of my attractions . . . and . . . such genuine confidence in me."

"I had such confidence just because it was after all . . . that happened in the past."

"Then if so, you look upon me even now as a most honourable man?" said Velchaninov, suddenly halting.

At another time he would have been horrified at the naïveté of his own question.

"I always thought you so," said Pavel Pavlovitch, dropping his eyes.

"Why, of course. . . . I didn't mean that; that is, not in that sense. I only meant to say that, in spite of any . . . preconceptions . . ."

"Yes, in spite of preconceptions."

"When you came to Petersburg?" Velchaninov could not resist asking, though he felt how utterly monstrous was his curiosity.

"When I came to Petersburg, too, I looked upon you as the most honourable of men. I always respected you, Alexey Ivanovitch."

Pavel Pavlovitch raised his eyes and looked candidly, without a trace of embarrassment, at his opponent. Velchaninov was suddenly panic-stricken; he was not at all anxious that anything should happen, or that anything should overstep a certain line, especially as he had provoked it.

"I loved you, Alexey Ivanovitch," Pavel Pavlovitch articulated, as though he had suddenly made up his mind to speak, "and all that year at T—— I loved you. You did not notice it," he went on, in a voice that quivered, to Velchaninov's positive horror; "I was too insignificant, compared with you, to let you see it. And there was no need, indeed, perhaps. And I've thought of you all these nine years, because there has never been another year in my life like that one." (Pavel Pavlovitch's eyes began to glisten.) "I remembered many of your phrases and sayings, your thoughts. I always thought of you as a man with a passion for every noble feeling, a man of education, of the highest education and of ideas: 'Great ideas spring not so much from noble intelligence as from noble feeling.' You said that yourself; perhaps you've forgotten it, but I remembered it. I always looked on you, therefore, as a man of noble feeling . . . and therefore believed in you—in spite of anything . . ."

His chin suddenly began quivering. Velchaninov was

in absolute terror; this unexpected tone must be cut short at all costs.

"That's enough, Pavel Pavlovitch, please," he muttered, flushing and irritably impatient. "And why," he screamed suddenly, "why do you fasten upon a man when he is nervous and ill, when he is almost delirious, and drag him into this darkness . . . when it's . . . when it's—nothing but delusion, mirage, and falsity, and shameful, and unnatural, and—exaggerated—and that's what's worst, that's what's most shameful—that it is so exaggerated! And it's all nonsense; we are both vicious, underground, loathsome people. . . . And if you like I'll prove that you don't like me at all, but hate me with all your might, and that you're lying, though you don't know it; you insisted on taking me there, not with the absurd object of testing your future bride (what an idea!); you saw me yesterday and felt *vindictive*, and took me there to show me and say to me, 'See what a prize! She will be mine; do your worst now!' You challenged me, perhaps you didn't know it yourself; that's how it was, for that's what you were feeling . . . and without hating me you couldn't have challenged me like that; and so you hate me!"

He rushed about the room as he shouted this. What harassed and mortified him most of all was the humiliating consciousness that he was demeaning himself so far to Pavel Pavlovitch.

"I wanted to be reconciled with you, Alexey Ivanovitch!" the other articulated suddenly, in a rapid whisper, and his chin began twitching again.

Velchaninov was overcome by furious rage, as though no one had ever insulted him so much.

"I tell you again," he yelled, "that you're fastening upon a man who's nervous and ill . . . that you're fastening upon him to extort something monstrous from him in delirium! We . . . we are men of different worlds, understand that, and . . . and . . . between us lies a grave!" he added in a furious whisper, and suddenly realized what he had done. . . .

"And how do you know"—Pavel Pavlovitch's face was suddenly pale and distorted—"how do you know what that little grave here means . . . for me!" he cried, stepping up to Velchaninov with a ridiculous but horrible gesture, pressed his fist against his heart. "I know that little grave here, and we both stand at the side of that little grave, but on my side there is more than on yours, more . . ." he whispered as though in delirium, still thumping at his heart with his fist, "more, more, more . . ."

Suddenly an extraordinarily loud ring at the door brought both of them to their senses. The bell rang so violently that it seemed as though some one had vowed to break it at the first pull.

"People don't ring like that to see me," said Velchaninov in perplexity.

"Nor to see me either," Pavel Pavlovitch whispered timidly, recovering himself too, and at once turning into the old Pavel Pavlovitch again.

Velchaninov scowled and went to open the door.

"M. Velchaninov, if I'm not mistaken?" they heard in a ringing, youthful, and exceptionally self-confident voice in the passage.

"What is it?"

"I have trustworthy information," continued the ringing voice, "that a certain Trusotsky is with you at this moment. I must see him instantly."

It would certainly have pleased Velchaninov at that moment to have given the self-confident young gentleman a vigorous kick and to have sent him flying out on the stairs; but he thought a moment, moved aside and let him in.

"Here is M. Trusotsky; come in. . . ."

Chapter 14

Sashenka and Nadenka

There walked into the room a very young man, of about nineteen, perhaps even less—to judge from the youthfulness of his handsome, self-confident, upturned face. He was fairly well dressed, or at any rate his clothes looked well on him; in height he was a little above the average; the black hair that hung in thick locks about his head, and the big, bold, dark eyes were particularly conspicuous in his face. Except that his nose was rather broad and turned up, he was a handsome fellow. He walked in solemnly.

"I believe I have the opportunity of conversing with M.

Trusotsky," he pronounced in a measured tone, emphasizing with peculiar relish the word "opportunity"—giving him to understand thereby that he did not consider it either an "honour" or a "pleasure" to converse with M. Trusotsky.

Velchaninov began to grasp the position; something seemed to be dawning on Pavel Pavlovitch too. There was a look of uneasiness in his face; but he stood his ground.

"Not having the honour of your acquaintance," he answered majestically, "I imagine that you cannot have business of any sort with me."

"You had better hear me first and then give your opinion," the young man admonished him self-confidently, and, taking out a tortoiseshell lorgnette hanging on a cord, he examined through it the bottle of champagne standing on the table. When he had calmly completed his scrutiny of the bottle, he folded up the lorgnette and turned to Pavel Pavlovitch again.

"Alexandr Lobov."

"What do you mean by Alexandr Lobov?"

"That's me. Haven't you heard of me?"

"No."

"How should you, though? I've come on important business that chiefly concerns you. Allow me to sit down; I'm tired."

"Sit down," Velchaninov urged him; but the young man succeeded in sitting down before being invited to do so.

In spite of the increasing pain in his chest Velchaninov was interested in this impudent youth. In his pretty, childlike and rosy face, he fancied a remote resemblance to Nadya.

"You sit down too," the lad suggested to Pavel Pavlovitch, motioning him with a careless nod of the head to a seat opposite.

"Don't trouble; I'll stand."

"You'll be tired. You needn't go away, M. Velchaninov, if you like to stay."

"I've nowhere to go; I'm at home."

"As you please. I must confess I should prefer you to be present while I have an explanation with this gentleman. Nadyezhda Fedosyevna gave me rather a flattering account of you."

"Bah! When had she time to do that?"

"Why, just now after you left; I've just come from there, too. I've something to tell you, M. Trusotsky." He turned round to Pavel Pavlovitch, who was standing. "We —that is, Nadyezhda Fedosyevna and I," he went on, letting his words drop one by one as he lolled carelessly in the arm-chair; "we've cared for each other for ever so long, and have given each other our promise. You are in our way now; I've come to suggest that you should clear out. Will it suit you to act on my suggestion?"

Pavel Pavlovitch positively reeled; he turned pale, but a diabolical smile came on to his lips at once.

"No, it won't suit me at all," he rapped out laconically.

"You don't say so!" The young man turned round in the arm-chair and crossed one leg over the other.

"I don't know who it is I'm speaking to," added Pavel Pavlovitch. "I believe, indeed, that there's no object in continuing our conversation."

Uttering this, he too thought fit to sit down.

"I told you you would be tired," the youth observed casually. "I told you just now that my name is Alexandr Lobov, and that Nadyezhda and I are pledged to one another; consequently you can't say, as you did just now, that you don't know who it is you have to deal with; you can't imagine, either, that I have nothing more to say to you; putting myself aside, it concerns Nadyezhda Fedosyevna, whom you persist in pestering so insolently. And that alone is sufficient reason for an explanation."

All this he let drop, word by word, through his closed lips, with the air of a coxcomb who did not deign to articulate his words; he even drew out his lorgnette again and turned it upon something while he was talking.

"Excuse me, young man!" Pavel Pavlovitch exclaimed irritably; but the young man instantly snubbed him.

"At any other time I should certainly forbid your calling me 'young man,' but now you will admit that my youth is my chief advantage over you, and that you would have been jolly glad, this morning, for instance, when you presented your bracelet, to be a tiny bit younger."

"Ah, you sprat!" murmured Velchaninov.

"In any case, sir," Pavel Pavlovitch corrected himself with dignity, "I do not consider the reasons you have advanced—most unseemly and dubious reasons—sufficient to continue discussing them. I see that this is all a foolish and childish business. To-morrow I'll make inquiries of my highly respected friend, Fedosey Semyonovitch; and now I beg you to retire."

"Do you see the sort of man he is?" the youth cried at once, unable to sustain his previous tone, and turning hotly to Velchaninov. "It's not enough for him that they've put out their tongues at him to-day and kicked him out—he'll go to-morrow to tell tales of us to the old man! Won't you prove by that, you obstinate man, that you want to take the girl by force, that you want to buy her of people in their dotage who in our barbarous state of society retain authority over her? I should have thought it would have been enough for you that she's shown you how she despises you; why, she gave you back your indecent present to-day, your bracelet. What more do you want?"

"No one has returned me a bracelet, and it's utterly out of the question!" Pavel Pavlovitch said, startled.

"Out of the question? Do you mean to say M. Velchaninov has not given it you?"

"Damnation take you!" thought Velchaninov. "Nadyezdha Fedosyevna did commission me," he said, frowning, "to give you this case, Pavel Pavlovitch. I refused to take it, but she begged me . . . here it is . . . I'm annoyed. . . ."

He took out the case and, much embarrassed, laid it before Pavel Pavlovitch, who was struck dumb.

"Why didn't you give it to him before?" said the young gentleman, addressing Velchaninov severely.

"As you see, I hadn't managed to do so yet," the latter replied, frowning.

"That's queer."

"Wha-a-at?"

"You must admit it's queer, anyway. Though I am ready to allow there may be a misunderstanding."

Velchaninov felt a great inclination to get up at once and pull the saucy urchin's ears, but he could not refrain from bursting out laughing in his face; the boy promptly laughed too. It was very different with Pavel Pavlovitch; if Velchaninov could have observed the terrible look he turned upon him when Velchaninov was laughing at Lobov, he would have realized that at that instant the man was passing through a momentous crisis. . . . But though Velchaninov did not see that glance, he felt that he must stand by Pavel Pavlovitch.

"Listen, M. Lobov," he began in a friendly tone; "without entering into discussion of other reasons upon which I don't care to touch, I would only point out to you that, in paying his addresses to Nadyezhda Fedosyevna, Pavel Pavlovitch can in any case boast of certain qualifications: in the first place, the fact that everything about him is known to that estimable family; in the second place, his excellent and highly respectable position; finally, his fortune, and consequently he must naturally be surprised at the sight of a rival like you—a man, perhaps, of great merit, but so exceedingly young that he can hardly take you for a serious suitor . . . and so he is justified in asking you to retire."

"What do you mean by 'exceedingly young'? I was nineteen last month. By law I could have been married long ago. That's all I can say."

"But what father could bring himself to give you his daughter now—even if you were to be a millionaire in the future or some benefactor of mankind? At nineteen a man cannot even answer for himself, and you are ready to take the responsibility of another person's future, that is, the future of another child like yourself! Why, do you think it's quite honourable? I have ventured to speak frankly to you because you appealed to me just now as an intermediary between you and Pavel Pavlovitch."

"Ah, to be sure, his name's Pavel Pavlovitch!" observed the boy; "how is it I kept fancying that he was Vassily Petrovitch? Well," he went on, addressing Velchaninov, "you haven't surprised me in the least; I knew you were all like that! It's odd, though, that they talked of you as a man rather new in a way. But that's all nonsense, though; far from there being anything dishonourable on my part, as you so freely expressed it, it's the very opposite, as I hope to make you see: to begin with, we've pledged our word to each other, and, what's more, I've promised her, before two witnesses, that if she ever falls in love with some one else, or simply regrets having married me and wants to separate, I will at once give her a formal declaration of my infidelity—and so will support her petition for divorce. What's more, in case I should later on go back upon my word and refuse to give her that declaration, I will give her as security on our wedding-day an I O U for a hundred thousand roubles, so that if I should be perverse about the declaration she can at once change my I O U and me into the bargain! In that way everything will be secured and I shouldn't be risking anybody's future. That's the first point."

"I bet that fellow—What's-his-name?—Predposylov invented that for you!" cried Velchaninov.

"He, he, he!" chuckled Pavel Pavlovitch viciously.

"What's that gentleman sniggering about? You guessed right, it was Predposylov's idea; and you must admit it was a shrewd one. The absurd law is completely paralyzed by it. Of course, I intend to love her for ever, and she laughs tremendously; at the same time it's ingenious, and you must admit that it's honourable, and that it's not every man who would consent to do it."

"To my thinking, so far from being honourable, it's positively disgusting."

The young man shrugged his shoulders.

"Again you don't surprise me," he observed, after a brief silence. "I have given up being surprised at that sort of thing long ago. Predposylov would tell you flatly that your lack of comprehension of the most natural things is due to the corruption of your most ordinary feelings and ideas by a long life spent idly and absurdly. But possibly we don't understand one another; they spoke well of you anyway . . . you're fifty, I suppose, aren't you?"

"Kindly keep to the point."

"Excuse my indiscretion and don't be annoyed; I didn't mean anything. I will continue: I'm by no means a future millionaire, as you expressed it (and what an idea!); I have nothing but what I stand up in, but I have complete confidence in my future. I shan't be a hero or a benefactor of mankind either, but I shall keep myself and my wife. Of course, I've nothing now; I was brought up in their house, you see, from childhood. . . ."

"How was that?"

"Well, you see, I'm the son of a distant relation of Zahlebinin's wife, and when all my people died and left me at eight years old, the old man took me in and afterwards sent me to the high school. He's really a good-natured man, if you care to know. . . ."

"I know that."

"Yes; a bit antiquated in his ideas, but kind-hearted.

It's a long time now, of course, since I was under his guardianship; I want to earn my own living, and to owe no one anything."

"How long have you been independent?" Velchaninov inquired.

"Why, four months."

"Oh, well, one can understand it then: you've been friends from childhood! Well, have you a situation, then?"

"Yes, a private situation, in a notary's office, for twenty-five roubles a month. Of course, only for the time, but when I made my offer I hadn't even that. I was serving on the railway then for ten roubles a month, but only for the time."

"Do you mean to say you've made an offer of marriage?"

"Yes, a formal offer, and ever so long ago—over three weeks."

"Well, and what happened?"

"The old man laughed awfully at first, and then was awfully angry, and locked her up upstairs. But Nadya held out heroically. But that was all because he was a bit crusty with me before, for throwing up the berth in his department which he had got me into four months ago, before I went to the railway. He's a capital old chap, I tell you again, simple and jolly at home, but you can't fancy what he's like as soon as he's in his office! He's like a Jove enthroned! I naturally let him know that I was not attracted by his manners there, but the chief trouble was through the head clerk's assistant: that gentleman took it into his head that I had been 'rude' to him, and all that I said to him was that he was undeveloped. I threw them all up, and now I'm at a notary's."

"And did you get much in the department?"

"Oh, I was not on the regular staff! The old man used to give me an allowance too; I tell you he's a good sort, but we shan't give in, all the same. Of course, twenty-five roubles is not enough to support a wife, but I hope soon to have a share in the management of Count Zavileysky's neglected estates, and then to rise to three thousand straight off, or else I shall become a lawyer. People are always going to law nowadays. . . . Bah! What a clap of thunder! There'll be a storm; it's a good thing I managed to get here before it; I came on foot, I ran almost all the way."

"But, excuse me, if so, when did you manage to talk things over with Nadyezhda Fedosyevna, especially if they refuse you admittance?"

"Why, one can talk over the fence! Did you notice that red-haired girl?" he laughed. "She's very active on our side, and Marie Nikititchna too; ah, she's a serpent, that Marie Nikititchna! . . . Why do you wince? Are you afraid of the thunder?"

"No, I'm unwell, very unwell. . . ."

Velchaninov, in positive agony from the pain in his chest, got up and tried to walk about the room.

"Oh, then, of course, I'm in your way. . . . Don't be uneasy, I'm just going!"

And the youth jumped up from his seat.

"You're not in the way; it's no matter," said Velchaninov courteously.

"How can it be no matter? 'When Kobylnikov had a stomach-ache' . . . do you remember in Shtchedrin? Are you fond of Shtchedrin?"

"Yes."

"So am I. Well, Vassily . . . oh, hang it, Pavel Pavlovitch, let's finish!" He turned, almost laughing, to Pavel Pavlovitch. "I will once more for your comprehension formulate the question: do you consent to make a formal withdrawal of all pretensions in regard to Nadyezhda Fedosyevna to the old people to-morrow, in my presence?"

"I certainly do not." Pavel Pavlovitch, too, got up from his seat with an impatient and exasperated air. "And I beg you once more to spare me . . . for all this is childish and silly."

"You had better look out." The youth held up a warning finger with a supercilious smile. "Don't make a mistake in your calculations! Do you know what such a mistake leads to? I warn you that in nine months' time, when you have had all your expense and trouble, and you come back here, you'll be forced to give up Nadyezhda Fedosyevna, or if you don't give her up it will be the worse for you; that's what will be the end of it! I must warn you that you're like the dog in the manger—excuse me, it's only a comparison—getting nothing yourself and preventing others. From motives of humanity I tell you again: reflect upon it, force yourself for once in your life to reflect rationally."

"I beg you to spare me your sermonizing!" cried Pavel Pavlovitch furiously; "and as for your nasty insinuations, I shall take measures to-morrow, severe measures!"

"Nasty insinuations? What do you mean by that? You're nasty yourself, if that's what you've got in your head. However, I agree to wait till to-morrow, but if . . . Ah, thunder again! Good-bye; very glad to make your acquaintance"—he nodded to Velchaninov and ran off, apparently in haste to get back before the storm and not to get caught in the rain.

Chapter 15

The Account Is Settled

"You see? You see?" Pavel Pavlovitch skipped up to Velchaninov as soon as the youth had departed.

"Yes; you've no luck!" said Velchaninov carelessly.

He would not have said those words had he not been tortured and exasperated by the pain in his chest, which was growing more and more acute.

"It was because you felt for me, you didn't give me back the bracelet, wasn't it?"

"I hadn't time. . . ."

"You felt for me from your heart, like a true friend?"

"Oh yes, I felt for you," said Velchaninov, in exasperation.

He told him briefly, however, how the bracelet had been returned to him, and how Nadyezhda Fedosyevna had almost forced him to assist in returning it. . . .

"You understand that nothing else would have induced me to take it; I've had unpleasantness enough apart from that!"

"You were fascinated and took it?" sniggered Pavel Pavlovitch.

"That's stupid on your part; however, I must excuse you. You saw for yourself just now that I'm not the leading person, that there are others in this affair."

"At the same time you were fascinated."

Pavel Pavlovitch sat down and filled up his glass.

"Do you imagine I'd give way to that wretched boy? I'll make mincemeat of him, so there! I'll go over tomorrow and polish him off. We'll smoke out that spirit from the nursery."

He emptied his glass almost at a gulp and filled it again; he began, in fact, to behave in an unusually free and easy way.

"Ah, Nadenka and Sashenka, the sweet little darlings, he-he-he!"

He was beside himself with anger. There came another louder clap of thunder, followed by a blinding flash of lightning, and the rain began streaming in bucketfuls. Pavel Pavlovitch got up and closed the open window.

"He asked you whether you were afraid of the thunder, he-he. Velchaninov afraid of thunder! Kobylnikov—what was it—Kobylnikov . . . and what about being fifty too —eh? Do you remember?" Pavel Pavlovitch sneered diabolically.

"You've established yourself here, it seems!" observed Velchaninov, hardly able to articulate the words for the pain in his chest. "I'll lie down, you can do what you like."

"Why, you couldn't turn a dog out in weather like this!" Pavel Pavlovitch retorted in an aggrieved tone, seeming almost pleased, however, at having an excuse for feeling aggrieved.

"All right, sit down, drink . . . stay the night, if you like!" muttered Velchaninov. He stretched himself on the sofa and uttered a faint groan.

"Stay the night? And you won't be afraid?"

"What of?" said Velchaninov, suddenly raising his head.

"Oh, nothing. Last time you were so frightened, or was it my fancy?"

"You're stupid!" Velchaninov could not help saying. He turned his head to the wall angrily.

"All right," responded Pavel Pavlovitch.

The sick man fell asleep suddenly, a minute after lying down. The unnatural strain upon him that day in the shattered state of his health had brought on a sudden crisis, and he was as weak as a child. But the pain asserted itself again and got the upper hand of sleep and weariness; an hour later he woke up and painfully got up from the sofa. The storm had subsided; the room was full of tobacco smoke, on the table stood an empty bottle, and Pavel Pavlovitch was asleep on another sofa. He was lying on his back, with his head on the sofa cushion, fully dressed and with his boots on. His lorgnette had slipped out of his pocket and was hanging down almost to the floor. His hat was lying on the ground beside it. Velchaninov looked at him morosely and did not attempt to wake him. Writhing with pain and pacing about the room, for he could no longer bear to lie down, he moaned and brooded over his agonies.

He was afraid of that pain in his chest, and not without reason. He had been liable to these attacks for a very long time, but they had only occurred at intervals of a year or two. He knew that they came from the liver. At first a dull, not acute, but irritating feeling of oppression was, as it were, concentrated at some point in the chest, under the shoulder-blade or higher up. Continually increasing, sometimes for ten hours at a stretch, the pain at last would reach such a pitch, the oppression would become so insupportable, that the sufferer began to have visions of dying. On his last attack, a year before, he was, when the pain ceased after ten hours of suffering, so weak that he could scarcely move his hands as he lay in bed, and the doctor had allowed him to take nothing for the whole day but a few teaspoonfuls of weak tea and of bread soaked in broth, like a tiny baby. The attacks were brought on by different things, but never occurred except when his nerves were out of order. It was strange, too, how the attack passed off; sometimes it was possible to arrest it at the very beginning, during the first half-hour, by simple compresses, and it would pass away completely at once; sometimes, as on his last attack, nothing was of any use, and the pain only subsided after numerous and continually recurring paroxysms of vomiting. The doctor confessed afterwards that he believed it to be a case of poisoning. It was a long time to wait till morning, and he didn't want to send for the doctor at night; besides, he didn't like doctors. At last he could not control himself and began moaning aloud. His groans waked Pavel Pavlovitch; he sat up on the sofa, and for some time listened with alarm and bewilderment, watching Velchaninov, who was almost running backwards and forwards through the two rooms. The bottle of champagne had had a great effect upon him, evidently more than usual, and it was some time before he could collect himself. At last he grasped the position and rushed to Velchaninov, who mumbled something in reply to him.

"It's the liver, I know it!" cried Pavel Pavlovitch, becoming extremely animated all at once. "Pyotr Kuzmitch Polosuhin used to suffer just the same from liver. You ought to have compresses. Pyotr Kuzmitch always had compresses. . . . One may die of it! Shall I run for Mavra?"

"No need, no need!" Velchaninov waved him off irritably. "I want nothing."

But Pavel Pavlovitch, goodness knows why, seemed beside himself, as though it were a question of saving his own son. Without heeding Velchaninov's protests, he insisted on the necessity of compresses and also of two or three cups of weak tea to be drunk on the spot, "and not simply hot, but boiling!" He ran to Mavra, without waiting for permission, with her laid a fire in the kitchen, which always stood empty, and blew up the samovar; at the same time he succeeded in getting the sick man to bed, took off his clothes, wrapped him up in a quilt, and within twenty minutes had prepared tea and compresses.

"This is a hot plate, scalding hot!" he said, almost ecstatically, applying the heated plate, wrapped up in a napkin, on Velchaninov's aching chest. "There are no other compresses, and plates, I swear on my honour, will be even better: they were laid on Pyotr Kuzmitch, I saw it with my own eyes, and did it with my own hands. One may die of it, you know. Drink your tea, swallow it; never mind about scalding yourself; life is too precious . . . for one to be squeamish."

He quite flustered Mavra, who was half asleep; the plates were changed every three or four minutes. After the third plate and the second cup of tea, swallowed at a gulp, Velchaninov felt a sudden relief.

"If once they've shifted the pain, thank God, it's a good sign!" cried Pavel Pavlovitch, and he ran joyfully to fetch a fresh plate and a fresh cup of tea.

"If only we can ease the pain. If only we can keep it under!" he kept repeating.

Half an hour later the pain was much less, but the sick man was so exhausted that in spite of Pavel Pavlovitch's entreaties he refused to "put up with just one more nice little plate." He was so weak that everything was dark before his eyes.

"Sleep, sleep," he repeated in a faint voice.

"To be sure," Pavel Pavlovitch assented.

"You'll stay the night. . . . What time is it?"

"It's nearly two o'clock, it's a quarter to."

"You'll stay the night."

"I will, I will."

A minute later the sick man called Pavel Pavlovitch again.

"You, you," he muttered, when the latter had run up and was bending over him; "you are better than I am! I understand it all, all. . . . Thank you."

"Sleep, sleep," whispered Pavel Pavlovitch, and he hastened on tiptoe to his sofa.

As he fell asleep the invalid heard Pavel Pavlovitch noiselessly making up a bed for himself and taking off his clothes. Finally, putting out the candle, and almost holding his breath for fear of waking the patient, he stretched himself on his sofa.

There is no doubt that Velchaninov did sleep and that he fell asleep very soon after the candle was put out; he remembered this clearly afterwards. But all the time he was asleep, up to the very moment that he woke up, he dreamed that he was not asleep, and that in spite of his exhaustion he could not get to sleep. At last he began to dream that he was in a sort of waking delirium, and that he could not drive away the phantoms that crowded about him, although he was fully conscious that it was only delirium and not reality. The phantoms were all familiar figures; his room seemed to be full of people; and the door into the passage stood open; people were coming in in crowds and thronging the stairs. At the table, which was set in the middle of the room, there was sitting one man—exactly as in the similar dream he had had a month before. Just as in that dream, this man sat with his elbows on the table and would not speak; but this time he was wearing a round hat with crape on it. "What! could it have been Pavel Pavlovitch that time too?" Velchaninov thought, but, glancing at the face of the silent man, he convinced himself that it was some one quite different. "Why has he got crape on?" Velchaninov wondered. The noise, the talking and the shouting of the people crowding round the table, was awful. These people seemed to be even more intensely exasperated against Velchaninov than in the previous dream; they shook their fists at him, and shouted something to him with all their might, but what it was exactly he could not make out. "But it's delirium, of course, I know it's delirium!" he thought; "I know I couldn't get to sleep and that I've got up now, because it made me too wretched to go on lying down. . . ." But the shouts, the people, their gestures were so lifelike, so real, that sometimes he was seized by doubt: "Can this be really delirium? Good heavens! What do these people want of me? But . . . if it were not an hallucination, would it be possible that such a clamour should not have waked Pavel Pavlovitch all this time? There he is asleep on the sofa!" At last something suddenly happened again, just as in that other dream; all of them made a rush for the stairs and they were closely packed in the doorway, for there was another crowd forcing its way into the room. These people were bringing something in with them, something big and heavy; he could hear how heavily the steps of those carrying it sounded on the stairs and how hurriedly their panting voices called to one another. All the people in the room shouted: "They're bringing it, they're bringing it"—all eyes were flashing and fixed on Velchaninov; all of them pointed towards the stairs, menacing and triumphant. Feeling no further doubt that it was reality and not hallucination, he stood on tiptoe so as to peep over the people's heads and find out as soon as possible what they were bringing up the stairs. His heart was beating, beating, beating, and suddenly, exactly as in that first dream, he heard three violent rings at the bell. And again it was so distinct, so real, so unmistakable a ring at the bell, that it could not be only a dream. . . .

But he did not rush to the door as he had done on awaking then. What idea guided his first movement and whether he had any idea at the moment it is impossible to say, but some one seemed to prompt him what he must do: he leapt out of bed and, with his hands stretched out before him as though to defend himself and ward off an attack, rushed straight towards the place where Pavel Pavlovitch was asleep. His hands instantly came into contact with other hands, stretched out above him, and he clutched them tight; so, some one already stood bending over him. The curtains were drawn, but it was not quite dark, for a faint light came from the other room where there were no such curtains. Suddenly, with an acute pain, something cut the palm and fingers of his left hand, and he instantly realized that he had clutched the blade of a knife or razor and was grasping it tight in his hand. . . . And at the same moment something fell heavily on the floor with a thud.

Velchaninov was perhaps three times as strong as Pavel Pavlovitch, yet the struggle between them lasted a long while, fully three minutes. He soon got him down on the floor and bent his arms back behind him, but for some reason he felt he must tie his hands behind him. Holding the murderer with his wounded left hand, he began with his right fumbling for the cord of the window curtain and for a long time could not find it, but at last got hold of it and tore it from the window. He wondered himself afterwards at the immense effort required to do this. During those three minutes neither of them uttered a word; nothing was audible but their heavy breathing and the muffled sounds of their struggling. Having at last twisted Pavel Pavlovitch's arms behind him and tied them together, Velchaninov left him on the floor, got up, drew the curtain from the window and pulled up the blind. It was already light in the deserted street. Opening the window, he stood for some moments drawing in deep breaths of fresh air. It was a little past four. Shutting the window, he went hurriedly to the cupboard, took out a clean towel and bound it tightly round his left hand to stop the bleeding. At his feet an open razor was lying on the carpet; he picked it up, shut it, put it in the razor-case, which had been left forgotten since the morning on the little table beside Pavel Pavlovitch's sofa, and locked it up in his bureau. And, only when he had done all that, he went up to Pavel Pavlovitch and began to examine him.

Meantime, the latter had with an effort got up from the floor, and seated himself in an arm-chair. He had nothing on but his shirt, not even his boots. The back and the sleeves of his shirt were soaked with blood; but the blood was not his own, it came from Velchaninov's wounded hand. Of course it was Pavel Pavlovitch, but any one meeting him by chance might almost have failed to recognize him at the minute, so changed was his whole appearance. He was sitting awkwardly upright in the arm-chair, owing to his hands being tied behind his back, his face looked distorted, exhausted and greenish, and he quivered all over from time to time. He looked at Velchaninov fixedly, but with lustreless, unseeing eyes. All at once he smiled vacantly, and, nodding towards a bottle of water that stood on the table, he said in a meek half-whisper—

"Water, I should like some water."

Velchaninov filled a glass and began holding it for him to drink. Pavel Pavlovitch bent down greedily to the water; after three gulps he raised his head and looked intently into the face of Velchaninov, who was standing beside him with the glass in his hand, but without uttering a word he fell to drinking again. When he had finished he sighed deeply. Velchaninov took his pillow, seized his outer garments and went into the other room, locking Pavel Pavlovitch into the first room.

The pain had passed off completely, but he was conscious of extreme weakness again after the momentary effort in which he had displayed an unaccountable strength. He tried to reflect upon what had happened, but his thoughts were hardly coherent, the shock had been too great. Sometimes there was a dimness before his eyes lasting for ten minutes or so, then he would start, wake up, recollect everything, remember his smarting hand bound up in a blood-stained towel, and would fall to thinking greedily, feverishly. He came to one distinct conclusion—that is, that Pavel Pavlovitch certainly had meant to cut his throat, but that perhaps only a quarter of an hour before had not known that he would do it. The razor-case had perhaps merely caught his eye the evening before, and, without arousing any thought of it at the time, had remained in his memory. (The razors were always locked up in the bureau, and only the morning before, Velchaninov had taken them out to shave round his moustache and whiskers, as he sometimes did.)

"If he had long been intending to murder me he would have got a knife or pistol ready; he would not have reckoned on my razor, which he had never seen till yesterday evening," was one reflection he made among others.

It struck six o'clock at last; Velchaninov roused himself, dressed, and went in to Pavel Pavlovitch. Opening the door, he could not understand why he had locked Pavel Pavlovitch in, instead of turning him out of the house. To his surprise, the criminal was fully dressed; most likely he had found some way of untying his hands. He was sitting in the arm-chair, but got up at once when Velchaninov went in. His hat was already in his hand. His uneasy eyes seemed in haste to say—

"Don't begin talking; it's no use beginning; there's no need to talk."

"Go," said Velchaninov. "Take your bracelet," he added, calling after him.

Pavel Pavlovitch turned back from the door, took the case with the bracelet from the table, put it in his pocket and went out on the stairs. Velchaninov stood at the door to lock it behind him. Their eyes met for the last time; Pavel Pavlovitch stopped suddenly, for five seconds the two looked into each other's eyes—as though hesitating; finally Velchaninov waved his hand faintly.

"Well, go!" he said in a low voice, and locked the door.

Chapter 16
Analysis

A feeling of immense, extraordinary relief took possession of him; something was over, was settled; an awful weight of depression had vanished and was dissipated for ever. So it seemed to him. It had lasted for five weeks. He raised his hand, looked at the towel soaked with blood and muttered to himself: "Yes, now everything is absolutely at an end!" And all that morning, for the first time in three weeks, he scarcely thought of Liza—as though that blood from his cut fingers could "settle his account" even with that misery.

He recognized clearly that he had escaped a terrible danger. "These people," he thought, "just these people who don't know a minute beforehand whether they'll murder a man or not—as soon as they take a knife in their trembling hands and feel the hot spurt of blood on their fingers don't stick at cutting your throat, but cut off your head, 'clean off,' as convicts express it. That is so."

He could not remain at home and went out into the street, feeling convinced that he must do something, or something would happen to him at once; he walked about the streets and waited. He had an intense longing to meet some one, to talk to some one, even to a stranger, and it was only that which led him at last to think of a doctor and of the necessity of binding up his hand properly. The doctor, an old acquaintance of his, examined the wound, and inquired with interest how it could have happened.

Velchaninov laughed and was on the point of telling him all about it, but restrained himself. The doctor was obliged to feel his pulse and, hearing of his attack the night before, persuaded him to take some soothing medicine he had at hand. He was reassuring about the cuts: "They could have no particularly disagreeable results." Velchaninov laughed and began to assure him that they had already had the most agreeable results. An almost irresistible desire to tell the whole story came over him twice again during that day, on one occasion to a total stranger with whom he entered into conversation at a tea-shop. He had never been able to endure entering into conversation with strangers in public places before.

He went into a shop to buy a newspaper; he went to his tailor's and ordered a suit. The idea of visiting the Pogoryeltsevs was still distasteful to him, and he did not think of them, and indeed he could not have gone to their villa: he kept expecting something here in the town. He dined with enjoyment, he talked to the waiter and to his fellow-diners, and drank half a bottle of wine. The possibility of the return of his illness of the day before did not occur to him; he was convinced that the illness had passed off completely at the moment when, after falling asleep so exhausted, he had, an hour and a half later, sprung out of bed and thrown his assailant on the floor with such strength. Towards evening he began to feel giddy, and at moments was overcome by something like the delirium he had had in his sleep. It was dusk when he returned home, and he was almost afraid of his room when he went into it. It seemed dreadful and uncanny in his flat. He walked up and down it several times, and even went into his kitchen, where he had scarcely ever been before. "Here they were heating plates yesterday," he thought. He locked the door securely and lighted the candles earlier than usual. As he locked the door he remembered, half an hour before, passing the porter's lodge, he had called Mavra and asked her whether Pavel Pavlovitch had come in his absence, as though he could possibly have come.

After locking himself in carefully, he opened the bureau, took out the razor-case and opened the razor to look at it again. On the white bone handle there were still faint traces of blood. He put the razor back in the case and locked it up in the bureau again. He felt sleepy; he felt that he must go to bed at once—or "he would not be fit for to-morrow." He pictured the next day for some reason as a momentous and "decisive" day.

But the same thoughts that had haunted him all day in the street kept incessantly and persistently crowding and jostling in his sick brain, and he kept thinking, thinking, thinking, and for a long time could not get to sleep. . . .

"If it is settled that he tried to murder me *accidentally*," he went on pondering, "had the idea ever entered his head before, if only as a dream in a vindictive moment?"

He decided that question strangely—that "Pavel Pavlovitch did want to kill him, but the thought of the murder had never entered his head." In short: "Pavel Pavlovitch wanted to kill him, but didn't know he wanted to kill him. It's senseless, but that's the truth," thought Velchaninov. "It was not to get a post and it was not on Bagautov's account he came here, though he did try to get a post here, and did run to see Bagautov and was furious when he died; he thought no more of him than a chip. He came here on my account and he came here with Liza . . .

"And did I expect that he . . . would murder me?" He decided that he did, that he had expected it from the moment when he saw him in the carriage following Bagautov's funeral. "I began, as it were, to expect something . . . but, of course, not that; but, of course, not that he would murder me! . . .

"And can it be that all that was true?" he exclaimed again, suddenly raising his head from the pillow and opening his eyes. "All that that . . . madman told me yesterday about his love for me, when his chin quivered and he thumped himself on the breast with his fist?

"It was the absolute truth," he decided, still pondering and analyzing, "that Quasimodo from T—— was quite sufficiently stupid and noble to fall in love with the lover of his wife, about whom he noticed nothing suspicious in twenty years! He had been thinking of me with respect, cherishing my memory and brooding over my utterances for nine years. Good heavens! and I had no notion of it! He could not have been lying yesterday! But did he love me yesterday when he declared his feeling and said 'Let us settle our account'? Yes, it was from hatred that he loved me; that's the strongest of all loves . . .

"Of course it may have happened, of course it must have happened that I made a tremendous impression on him at T——. Tremendous and 'gratifying' is just what it was, and it's just with a Schiller like that, in the outer form of a Quasimodo, that such a thing could happen! He magnified me a hundredfold because I impressed him too much in his philosophic solitude. . . . It would be interesting to know by what I impressed him. Perhaps by my clean gloves and my knowing how to put them on. Quasimodos are fond of all that is aesthetic. Ough! aren't they fond of it! A glove is often quite enough for a noble heart, and especially one of these 'eternal husbands.' The rest they supply themselves a thousand times, and are ready to fight for you, to satisfy your slightest wish. What an opinion he had of my powers of fascination! Perhaps it was just my powers of fascination that made the most impression on him. And his cry then, 'If that one, too . . . whom can one trust!' After that cry one may well become a wild beast! . . .

"H'm! He comes here 'to embrace me and to weep,' as he expressed it in the most abject way—that is, he came here to murder me and thought he came 'to embrace me and to weep.' . . . He brought Liza too. But, who knows? if I had wept with him, perhaps, really, he would have forgiven me, for he had a terrible longing to forgive me! . . . At the first shock all that was changed into drunken antics and caricature, and into loathsome, womanish whining over his wrongs. (Those horns! those horns he made on his forehead!) He came drunk on purpose to speak out, though he was playing the fool; if he had not been drunk, even he could not have done it. . . . And how he liked playing the fool, didn't he like it! Ough! wasn't he pleased, too, when he made me kiss him! Only he didn't know then whether he would end by embracing me or murdering me. Of course, it's turned out that the best thing was to do both. A most natural solution! Yes indeed, nature dislikes monstrosities and destroys them with natural solutions. The most monstrous monster is the monster with noble feelings; I know that by personal experience, Pavel Pavlovitch! Nature is not a tender mother, but a stepmother to the monster. Nature gives birth to the deformed, but instead of pitying him she punishes him, and with good reason. Even decent people have to pay for embraces and tears of forgiveness nowadays, to say nothing of men like you and me, Pavel Pavlovitch!

"Yes, he was stupid enough to take me to see his future

bride. Good heavens! His future bride! Only a Quasimodo like that could have conceived the notion of 'rising again to a new life' by means of the innocence of Mademoiselle Zahlebinin! But it was not your fault, Pavel Pavlovitch, it was not your fault: you're a monster, so everything about you is bound to be monstrous, your dreams and your hopes. But, though he was a monster, he had doubts of his dream, and that was why he needed the high sanction of Velchaninov whom he so revered. He wanted Velchaninov to approve, he wanted him to reassure him that the dream was not a dream, but something real. He took me there from a devout respect for me and faith in the nobility of my feelings, believing, perhaps, that there, under a bush, we should embrace and shed tears near all that youthful innocence. Yes! That 'eternal husband' was obliged, sooner or later, to punish himself for everything, and to punish himself he snatched up the razor—by accident, it is true, still he did snatch it up! 'And yet he stuck him with a knife, and yet he ended by stabbing him in the presence of the Governor.' And, by the way, had he any idea of that sort in his mind when he told me that anecdote about the best man? And was there really anything that night when he got out of bed and stood in the middle of the room? H'm! . . . No, he stood there then *as a joke*. He got up for other reasons, and when he saw that I was frightened of him he did not answer me for ten minutes because he was very much pleased that I was frightened of him. . . . It was at that moment, perhaps, when he stood there in the dark, that some idea of this sort first dawned upon him. . . .

"Yet if I had not forgotten that razor on the table yesterday—maybe nothing would have happened. Is that so? Is that so? To be sure he had been avoiding me before—why, he had not been to see me for a fortnight; he had been hiding from me to *spare* me! Of course, he picked out Bagautov first, not me! Why, he rushed to heat plates for me in the night, thinking to create a diversion—from the knife to pity and tenderness! . . . He wanted to save himself and me, too—with his hot plates! . . ."

And for a long time the sick brain of this "man of the world" went on working in this way, going round and round in a circle, till he grew calmer. He woke up next morning with the same headache, but with a quite *new* and quite unexpected terror in his heart.

This new terror came from the positive conviction, which suddenly grew strong within him, that he, Velchaninov (a man of the world), would end it all that day by going of his own free will to Pavel Pavlovitch. Why? What for? He had no idea and, with repugnance, refused to know; all that he knew was that, for some reason, he would go to him.

This madness, however—he could give it no other name—did, as it developed, take a rational form and fasten upon a fairly legitimate pretext: he had even, the day before, been haunted by the idea that Pavel Pavlovitch would go back to his lodging and hang himself, like the clerk about whom Marya Sysoevna had told him. This notion of the day before had passed by degrees into an unreasoning but persistent conviction. "Why should the fool hang himself?" he kept protesting to himself every half-minute. He remembered Liza's words . . . "Yet in his place, perhaps, I should hang myself" . . . he reflected once.

It ended by his turning towards Pavel Pavlovitch instead of going to dinner. "I shall simply inquire of Marya Sysoevna," he decided. But before he had come out into the street he stopped short in the gateway. "Can it be, can it be?" he cried, turning crimson with shame. "Can it be that I'm crawling there, to 'embrace and shed tears'? That senseless abjectness was all that was needed to complete the ignominy!"

But from that "senseless abjectness" he was saved by the providence that watches over all decent and well-bred people. He had no sooner stepped into the street when he stumbled upon Alexandr Lobov. The young man was in breathless haste and excitement.

"I was coming to see you! What do you think of our friend Pavel Pavlovitch, now?"

"He's hanged himself!" Velchaninov muttered wildly.

"Who's hanged himself? What for?" cried Lobov, with wide-open eyes.

"Never mind . . . I didn't mean anything; go on."

"Tfoo! damn it all! what funny ideas you have, though. He's not hanged himself at all (why should he hang himself?). On the contrary—he's gone away. I've only just put him into the train and seen him off. Tfoo! how he drinks, I tell you! We drank three bottles, Predposylov with us—but how he drinks, how he drinks! He was singing songs in the train. He remembered you, blew kisses, sent you his greetings. But he is a scoundrel, don't you think so?"

The young man certainly was a little tipsy; his flushed face, his shining eyes and faltering tongue betrayed it unmistakably.

Velchaninov laughed loudly.

"So in the end they finished up with Brüderschaft! Haha! They embraced and shed tears! Ah, you Schilleresque poets!"

"Don't call me names, please. Do you know he's given it all up over *there?* He was there yesterday, and he's been there to-day. He sneaked horribly. They locked Nadya up—she's sitting in a room upstairs. There were tears and lamentations, but we stood firm! But how he does drink, I say, doesn't he drink! And, I say, isn't he *mauvais ton*, at least not *mauvais ton* exactly, what shall I call it? . . . He kept talking of you, but there's no comparison between you! You're a gentleman anyway, and really did move in decent society at one time and have only been forced to come down now through poverty or something. . . . Goodness knows what, I couldn't quite understand him."

"Ah, so he spoke to you of me in those terms?"

"He did, he did; don't be angry. To be a good citizen is better than being in aristocratic society. I say that because in Russia nowadays one doesn't know whom to respect. You'll agree that it's a serious malady of the age, when people don't know whom to respect, isn't it?"

"It is, it is; what did he say?"

"He? Who? Ah, to be sure! Why did he keep saying 'Velchaninov fifty, but a rake,' why *but* a rake and not *and* a rake; he laughed and repeated it a thousand times over. He got into the train, sang a song and burst out crying—it was simply revolting, pitiful, in fact—from drunkenness. Oh! I don't like fools! He fell to throwing money to the beggars for the peace of the soul of Lizaveta—his wife, is that?"

"His daughter."

"What's the matter with your hand?"

"I cut it."

"Never mind, it will get better. Damn him, you know, it's a good thing he's gone, but I bet anything that he'll get married directly he arrives—he will—won't he?"

FYODOR DOSTOEVSKY

"Why, but you want to get married, too, don't you?"

"Me? That's a different matter. What a man you are, really! If you are fifty, he must be sixty: you must look at it logically, my dear sir! And do you know I used, long ago, to be a pure Slavophil by conviction, but now we look for dawn from the West. . . . But, good-bye; I'm glad I met you without going in; I won't come in, don't ask me, I've no time to spare! . . ."

And he was just running off.

"Oh, by the way," he cried, turning back; "why, he sent me to you with a letter! Here is the letter. Why didn't you come to see him off?"

Velchaninov returned home and opened the envelope addressed to him.

There was not one line from Pavel Pavlovitch in it, but there was a different letter. Velchaninov recognized the handwriting. It was an old letter, written on paper yellow with age, with ink that had changed colour. It had been written to him ten years before, two months after he had left T—— and returned to Petersburg. But the letter had never reached him; he had received a different one instead of it; this was clear from the contents of this old yellow letter. In this letter Natalya Vassilyevna took leave of him for ever, and confessed that she loved some one else, just as in the letter he had actually received; but she also did not conceal from him that she was going to have a child. On the contrary, to comfort him, she held out hopes that she might find a possibility of handing over the future child to him, declared henceforth that they had other duties—in short, there was little logic, but the object was clear: that he should no longer trouble her with his love. She even sanctioned his coming to T—— in a year's time to have a look at the child. God knows why she changed her mind and sent the other letter instead.

Velchaninov was pale as he read it, but he pictured to himself Pavel Pavlovitch finding that letter and reading it for the first time, before the opened ebony box inlaid with mother-of-pearl which was an heirloom in the family.

"He too, must have turned pale as a corpse," he thought, catching a glimpse of his own face in the looking-glass. "He must have read it and closed his eyes, and opened them again hoping that the letter would have changed into plain white paper. . . . Most likely he had done that a second time and a third! . . ."

Chapter 17

The Eternal Husband

Almost exactly two years had passed since the incidents we have described. We meet Velchaninov again on a beautiful summer day, in the train on one of our newly opened railways. He was going to Odessa for his own pleasure, to see one of his friends, and also with a view to something else of an agreeable nature. He hoped through that friend to arrange a meeting with an extremely interesting woman whose acquaintance he had long been eager to make. Without going into details we will confine ourselves to observing that he had become entirely transformed, or rather reformed, during those two years. Of his old hypochondria scarcely a trace remained. Of the various "reminiscences" and anxiety—the result of illness which had beset him two years before in Petersburg at the time of his unsuccessful lawsuit—nothing remained but a certain secret shame at the consciousness of his faint-heartedness. What partly made up for it was the conviction that it would never happen again, and that no one would ever know of it. It was true that at that time he had given up all society, had even begun to be slovenly in his dress, had crept away out of sight of every one—and that, of course, must have been noticed by all. But he so readily acknowledged his transgressions, and at the same time with such a self-confident air of new life and vigour, that "every one" immediately forgave his momentary falling away; in fact, those whom he had given up greeting were the first to recognize him and hold out their hands, and without any tiresome questions—just as though he had been absent on his own personal affairs, which were no business of theirs, and had only just come back from a distance. The cause of all these salutary changes for the better was, of course, the winning of his lawsuit. Velchaninov gained in all sixty thousand roubles—no great sum, of course, but of extreme importance to him; to begin with, he felt himself on firm

ground again, and so he felt satisfied at heart; he knew
for certain now that he would not, "like a fool," squander
this money, as he had squandered his first two fortunes,
and that he had enough for his whole life. "However the
social edifice may totter, whatever trumpet call they're
sounding," he thought sometimes, as he watched and
heard all the marvellous and incredible things that were
being done around him and all over Russia; "whatever
shape people and ideas may take, I shall always have just
such a delicate, dainty dinner as I am sitting down to now,
and so I'm ready to face anything." This voluptuous, comfortable thought by degrees gained complete possession
of him and produced a transformation in his physical, to
say nothing of his moral, nature. He looked quite a different man from the "sluggard" whom we have described
two years before and to whom such unseemly incidents
had befallen—he looked cheerful, serene and dignified.
Even the ill-humoured wrinkles that had begun to appear
under his eyes and on his forehead had almost been
smoothed away; the very tint of his face had changed,
his skin was whiter and ruddier.

At the moment he was sitting comfortably in a first-
class carriage and a charming idea was suggesting itself
to his mind. The next station was a junction and there
was a new branch line going off to the right. He asked himself, "How would it be to give up the direct way for the
moment and turn off to the right?" There, only two stations away, he could visit another lady of his acquaintance who had only just returned from abroad, and was
now living in a provincial isolation, very tedious for her,
but favourable for him; and so it would be possible to
spend his time no less agreeably than at Odessa, especially
as he would not miss his visit there either. But he was still
hesitating and could not quite make up his mind; he was
waiting for something to decide him. Meanwhile, the station was approaching and that something was not far off.

At this station the train stopped forty minutes, and the
passengers had the chance of having dinner. At the entrance to the dining-room for the passengers of the first
and second class there was, as there usually is, a crowd
of impatient and hurried people, and as is also usual, perhaps, a scandalous scene took place. A lady from a sec-
ond-class carriage, who was remarkably pretty but somewhat too gorgeously dressed for travelling, was dragging

after her an Uhlan, a very young and handsome officer, who was trying to tear himself out of her hands. The youthful officer was extremely drunk, and the lady, to all appearance some elder relative, would not let him go, probably apprehending that he would make a dash for the refreshment bar. Meanwhile, in the crush, the Uhlan was jostled by a young merchant who was also disgracefully intoxicated. He had been hanging about the station for the last two days, drinking and scattering his money among the companions who surrounded him, without succeeding in getting into the train to continue his journey. A scuffle followed; the officer shouted; the merchant swore; the lady was in despair, and, trying to draw the Uhlan away from the conflict, kept exclaiming in an imploring voice, "Mitenka! Mitenka!" This seemed to strike the young merchant as too scandalous; every one laughed, indeed, but the merchant was more offended than ever at the outrage, as he conceived it, on propriety.

"Oh, I say: Mitenka!" he pronounced reproachfully, mimicking the shrill voice of the lady. "And not ashamed before folks!"

He went staggering up to the lady, who had rushed to the first chair and succeeded in making the Uhlan sit down beside her, stared at them both contemptuously and drawled in a sing-song voice—

"You're a trollop, you are, dragging your tail in the dirt!"

The lady uttered a shriek and looked about her piteously for some means of escape. She was both ashamed and frightened, and, to put the finishing touch, the officer sprang up from the chair and, with a yell, made a dash at the merchant, but, slipping, fell back into the chair with a flop. The laughter grew louder around them, and no one dreamed of helping her; but Velchaninov came to the rescue; he seized the merchant by the collar and, turning him round, thrust him five paces away from the frightened lady. And with that the scene ended; the merchant was overwhelmed by the shock and by Velchaninov's impressive figure; his companions led him away. The dignified countenance of the elegantly dressed gentleman produced a strong effect on the jeering crowd: the laughter subsided. The lady flushed and, almost in tears, was overflowing with expressions of gratitude. The Uhlan mumbled: "Fanks, fanks!" and made as though to hold out his hand to Velchaninov, but instead of doing so suddenly took it into his head to recline at full length with his feet on the chairs.

"Mitenka!" the lady moaned reproachfully, clasping her hands in horror.

Velchaninov was pleased with the adventure and with the whole situation. The lady attracted him; she was evidently a wealthy provincial, gorgeously but tastelessly dressed, and with rather ridiculous manners—in fact, she combined all the characteristics that guarantee success to a Petersburg gallant with designs on the fair sex. A conversation sprang up; the lady bitterly complained of her husband, who "had disappeared as soon as he had got out of the carriage and so was the cause of it all, for whenever he is wanted he runs off somewhere."

"Naturally," the Uhlan muttered.

"Ah, Mitenka!" She clasped her hands again.

"Well, the husband will catch it," thought Velchaninov.

"What is his name? I will go and look for him," he suggested.

"Pal Palitch," responded the Uhlan.

"Your husband's name is Pavel Pavlovitch?" Velchaninov asked, with curiosity, and suddenly a familiar bald head was thrust between him and the lady. In a flash he had a vision of the Zahlebinins' garden, the innocent games and a tiresome bald head being incessantly thrust between him and Nadyezhda Fedosyevna.

"Here you are at last!" cried his wife hysterically.

It was Pavel Pavlovitch himself; he gazed in wonder and alarm at Velchaninov, as panic-stricken at the sight of him as though he had been a ghost. His stupefaction was such that he evidently could not for some minutes take in what his offended spouse was explaining in a rapid and irritable flow of words. At last, with a start, he grasped all the horror of his position: his own guilt, and Mitenka's behaviour, "and that this monsieur" (this was how the lady for some reason described Velchaninov) "has been a saviour and guardian angel to us, while you—you are always out of the way when you are wanted. . . ."

Velchaninov suddenly burst out laughing.

"Why, we are friends, we've been friends since childhood!" he exclaimed to the astonished lady. Putting his right arm with patronizing familiarity round the shoulders of Pavel Pavlovitch, who smiled a pale smile, "Hasn't he talked to you of Velchaninov?"

"No, he never has," the lady responded, somewhat disconcerted.

"You might introduce me to your wife, you faithless friend!"

"Lipotchka . . . it really is M. Velchaninov," Pavel Pavlovitch was beginning, but he broke off abashed.

His wife turned crimson and flashed an angry look at him, probably for the "Lipotchka."

"And, only fancy, he never let me know he was married, and never invited me to the wedding, but you, Olimpiada . . ."

"Semyonovna," Pavel Pavlovitch prompted.

"Semyonovna," the Uhlan, who had dropped asleep, echoed suddenly.

"You must forgive him, Olimpiada Semyonovna, for my sake, in honour of our meeting . . . he's a good husband."

And Velchaninov gave Pavel Pavlovitch a friendly slap on the shoulder.

"I was . . . I was only away for a minute, my love," Pavel Pavlovitch was beginning to say.

"And left your wife to be insulted," Lipotchka put in at once. "When you're wanted there's no finding you, when you're not wanted you're always at hand . . ."

"Where you're not wanted, where you're not wanted . . . where you're not wanted . . ." the Uhlan chimed in.

Lipotchka was almost breathless with excitement; she knew it was not seemly before Velchaninov, and flushed but could not restrain herself.

"Where you shouldn't be you are too attentive, too attentive!" she burst out.

"Under the bed . . . he looks for a lover under the bed—where he shouldn't . . . where he shouldn't . . ." muttered Mitenka, suddenly growing extremely excited.

But there was no doing anything with Mitenka by now. It all ended pleasantly, however, and they got upon quite friendly terms. Pavel Pavlovitch was sent to fetch coffee and soup. Olimpiada Semyonovna explained to Velchaninov that they were on their way from O——, where her husband had a post in the service, to spend two months at their country place, that it was not far off, only thirty miles from the station, that they had a lovely house and garden there, that they always had the house full of visitors, that they had neighbours too, and if Alexey Ivanovitch would be so good as to come and stay with them "in their rustic solitude" she would welcome him "as their guardian angel," for she could not recall without horror what would have happened, if . . . and so on, and so on —in fact, he was "her guardian angel. . . ."

"And saviour, and saviour," the Uhlan insisted, with heat.

Velchaninov thanked her politely, and replied that he was always at her service, that he was an absolutely idle man with no duties of any sort, and that Olimpiada Semyonovna's invitation was most flattering. He followed this at once with sprightly conversation, successfully introducing two or three compliments. Lipotchka blushed with pleasure, and as soon as Pavel Pavlovitch returned she told him enthusiastically that Alexey Ivanovitch had been so kind as to accept her invitation to spend a whole month with them in the country, and had promised to come in a week. Pavel Pavlovitch smiled in mute despair. Olimpiada Semyonovna shrugged her shoulders at him, and turned her eyes up to the ceiling. At last they got up; again a gush of gratitude, again the "guardian angel," again "Mitenka," and Pavel Pavlovitch at last escorted his wife and the Uhlan to their compartment. Velchaninov lighted a cigar and began pacing to and fro on the balcony in front of the station; he knew that Pavel Pavlovitch would run out again at once to talk to him till the bell rang. And so it happened. Pavel Pavlovitch promptly appeared before him with an uneasy expression in his face and whole figure. Velchaninov laughed, took him by the elbow in a friendly way, led him to the nearest bench, sat down himself, and made him sit down beside him. He remained silent; he wanted Pavel Pavlovitch to be the first to speak.

"So you are coming to us?" faltered the latter, going straight to the point.

"I knew that would be it! You haven't changed in the least!" laughed Velchaninov. "Why, do you mean to say" —he slapped him again on the shoulder—"do you mean to say you could seriously imagine for a moment that I could actually come and stay with you, and for a whole month too—ha-ha?"

Pavel Pavlovitch was all of a twitter.

"So you—are not coming!" he cried, not in the least disguising his relief.

"I'm not coming, I'm not coming!" Velchaninov laughed complacently.

He could not have said himself, however, why he felt so particularly amused, but he was more and more amused as time went on.

"Do you really . . . do you really mean it?"

And saying this, Pavel Pavlovitch actually jumped up from his seat in a flutter of suspense.

"Yes, I've told you already that I'm not coming, you queer fellow."

"If that's so, what am I to say to Olimpiada Semyonovna a week hence, when she will be expecting you and you don't come?"

"What a difficulty! Tell her I've broken my leg or something of that sort."

"She won't believe it," Pavel Pavlovitch drawled plaintively.

"And you'll catch it?" Velchaninov went on laughing. "But I observe, my poor friend, that you tremble before your delightful wife—don't you?"

Pavel Pavlovitch tried to smile, but it did not come off. That Velchaninov had refused to visit them was a good thing, of course, but that he should be over-familiar to him about his wife was disagreeable. Pavel Pavlovitch winced; Velchaninov noticed it. Meanwhile the second bell rang; they heard a shrill voice from the train anxiously calling Pavel Pavlovitch. The latter moved, fidgeted in his chair, but did not rise at the first summons, evidently expecting something more from Velchaninov, no doubt another assurance that he would not come and stay with them.

"What was your wife's maiden name?" Velchaninov inquired, as though unaware of Pavel Pavlovitch's anxiety.

"She is our priest's daughter," replied the latter in uneasy trepidation, listening and looking towards the train.

"Ah, I understand, you married her for her beauty." Pavel Pavlovitch winced again.

"And who's this Mitenka with you?"

"Oh, he's a distant relation of ours—that is, of mine; the son of my deceased cousin. His name's Golubtchikov, he was degraded for disorderly behaviour in the army, but now he has been promoted again and we have been getting his equipment. . . . He's an unfortunate young man. . . ."

"To be sure, the regular thing; the party's complete," thought Velchaninov.

"Pavel Pavlovitch!" the call came again from the train, and by now with a marked tone of irritation in the voice.

"Pal Palitch!" they heard in another thick voice.

Pavel Pavlovitch fidgeted and moved restlessly again, but Velchaninov took him by the elbow and detained him.

"How would you like me to go this minute and tell your wife how you tried to cut my throat?"

"What, what!" Pavel Pavlovitch was terribly alarmed. "God forbid!"

"Pavel Pavlovitch! Pavel Pavlovitch!" voices were heard calling again.

"Well, be off now!" said Velchaninov, letting him go at last, and still laughing genially.

"So you won't come?" Pavel Pavlovitch whispered for the last time, almost in despair, and even put his hands before him with the palms together in his old style.

"Why, I swear I won't come! Run, there'll be trouble, you know."

And with a flourish he held out his hand to him—and was startled at the result: Pavel Pavlovitch did not take his hand, he even drew his own hand back.

The third bell rang.

In one instant something strange happened to both of them: both seemed transformed. Something, as it were, quivered and burst out in Velchaninov, who had been laughing only just before. He clutched Pavel Pavlovitch by the shoulder and held him in a tight and furious grip.

"If I—I hold out this hand to you," showing the palm of his left hand, where a big scar from the cut was still distinct, "you certainly might take it!" he whispered, with pale and trembling lips.

Pavel Pavlovitch, too, turned pale, and his lips trembled too; a convulsive quiver ran over his face.

"And Liza?" he murmured in a rapid whisper, and suddenly his lips, his cheeks and his chin began to twitch and tears gushed from his eyes.

Velchaninov stood before him stupefied.

"Pavel Pavlovitch! Pavel Pavlovitch!" they heard a

scream from the train as though some one were being murdered—and suddenly the whistle sounded.

Pavel Pavlovitch roused himself, flung up his hands and ran full speed to the train; the train was already in motion, but he managed to hang on somehow, and went flying to his compartment. Velchaninov remained at the station and only in the evening set off on his original route in another train. He did not turn off to the right to see his fair friend—he felt too much out of humour. And how he regretted it afterwards!

A Gentle Creature

A Fantastic Story

TRANSLATED BY DAVID MAGARSHACK

SHORT PREFACE BY THE AUTHOR

I HOPE MY readers will forgive me if, instead of my "Diary" in its usual form, I am giving them only a story this time. I am afraid my only excuse is that I have been really working on this story for the better part of a month. I should, in any event, like to ask my readers for their indulgence.

Now a few words about the story itself. I have given it the subtitle of "A Fantastic Story," though I myself regard it as eminently realistic. But there is indeed a subcurrent of fantasy in it, particularly in the very form of the story, which I think it necessary to explain before starting on the story proper.

The point is that it is neither fiction nor biography. Imagine a husband whose wife had committed suicide a few hours before by throwing herself out of a window and whose dead body is lying on the table. His mind is in a state of confusion, and he has not as yet had time to collect his thoughts. He keeps pacing the room, trying to find some reason for what has happened, "to gather his thoughts to a point." He is, besides, an inveterate hypochondriac, one of those men who talk to themselves. So there he is, talking to himself, telling the whole story, trying to *explain* it to himself. Notwithstanding the apparent consistency of his speech, he contradicts himself several times, both in the logic of his arguments and his feelings. He is justifying himself, accusing her, indulging in explanations that have no possible bearing on the case: you have here a certain crudity of mind and heart as well as genuine deep feeling. Little by little he really does *explain* the whole thing to himself and "gathers his thoughts to a point." A succession of memories which he recalls does at last lead him inevitably to *the truth*, and truth inevitably elevates his mind and heart. Towards the end even the tone of the story changes as compared with the general untidiness of its beginning. Truth dawns upon the unhappy man in a form that is both clear and definite, at least so far as he himself is concerned.

That is the theme. No doubt, the telling of the story, interrupted by all sorts of digressions and interludes, takes up a few hours, and it is told in a rather rambling way: sometimes he is speaking to himself, sometimes he is addressing an invisible listener, a sort of a judge. And, as a matter of fact, this is how it actually happens in real life. If a stenographer could have overheard him and taken down his words in shorthand, the result might have been a little rougher, a little less finished than the way I am telling it; but the psychological sequence (so at least it seems to me) would have remained pretty much the same. It is this suggestion of a stenographer taking everything down in shorthand (after which I should have edited it) that I consider the fantastic element in this story. But this sort of thing, or something very like it, has been done several times in works of fiction. Victor Hugo, for instance, uses almost the identical method in his masterpiece *The Last Day of a Man Condemned to Death*. And though he does not actually pretend to employ a stenographer, he has recourse to an even greater improbability by assuming that a man sentenced to death is able (and has the time) to keep a diary not only on his last day, but also during his last hour and, literally, his last minute. But had he not adopted this fanciful way of telling the story, his novel—one of the most realistic and most truthful he ever wrote—would not have existed.

Chapter 1

I. WHO WAS I AND WHO WAS SHE

. . . Well, while she is still here everything is all right: I go up and have a look at her every minute. But they will take her away tomorrow and—how can I stay here alone? She is now in the sitting-room, on a table. Two card tables put together side by side. They will bring the coffin tomorrow. A white coffin. White gros-de-Naples. However that's not what. . . . I keep on walking and walking. Trying to explain the whole thing to myself. It's six hours now that I've been trying to explain it to myself, but I just can't gather my thoughts to a point. Can't do it. Can't do it. The trouble is I'm always walking, walking,

walking. . . . Now, that's how it was. I'll simply tell it just as it happened. In the right order. (Order!) Ladies and gentlemen, I do not pretend to be a literary chap, as I expect you can see for yourselves, but never mind. I'll tell it just as I understand it. That's the horrible part of it—I understand everything!

You see, if you must know, I mean, if I'm to tell you everything from the very beginning. I first met her because she used to come to me to pawn things. She wanted the money to pay for an advertisement in *The Voice*. Trying to get herself a job as governess. No objection to living in the country, or giving lessons to children at their homes, and so on and so forth. That's how it began. At the time I didn't of course think her any different from anyone else. She used to come to me like the rest, and so on. But later I began to notice the difference. She was such a slender girl, very thin, fair, of medium height, always a little awkward with me, as though embarrassed. (I cannot help thinking that she must have been the same with all strangers, and to her of course I was not different from anyone else, considered as a man, I mean, and not as a pawnbroker.) The minute she got her money, she'd turn round and go away. And all without uttering a word. Others usually started arguing, begging, haggling, to get more money. But not this one. Took what she was given. . . . I'm afraid I'm getting a little muddled. . . . Yes, it was the things she brought which first of all attracted my attention. Silver gilt ear-rings, a cheap medallion—there wasn't anything I'd give more than sixpence for. She knew herself, of course, that they were only worth threepence, but I could see that to her they were priceless. As a matter of fact, it was all that was left her by her mother and father. I got to know about it later. Only once did I permit myself to smile at her things. For, you see, I never permit myself anything of the kind. In my dealings with the public my manners are always those of a gentleman: a few words, polite and stern. "Stern, stern, stern." But one day she actually brought me the remnants (I mean, literally) of an old hareskin coat, and I couldn't refrain from making a rather mild joke about it. Dear me, how she flushed! Her eyes were large, blue, wistful, but—how they blazed! She never said a word, though. Took her "remnants" and went out. It was then that for the first time I noticed her *specially*, and I thought something of the sort about her, that is, something of a special sort. Yes. There's something else I remember. Another impression. I mean, if you really want to know, it was really the most important impression which summed up everything, namely, that she was awfully young. So young that I could have sworn she wasn't a day older than fourteen. Actually, however, she was fifteen years and nine months, to be exact. However, that wasn't what I wanted to say. That wasn't the total impression. The next day she came again. I found out later that she had been to Dobronravov and Mozer with that precious fur coat of hers, but they don't accept anything but gold, so they wouldn't even talk to her. I, on the other hand, had once accepted a cameo from her (a really cheap one it was, too), and, having thought it over, was afterwards surprised at myself. For, you see, I don't accept anything but gold and silver, either, and yet I took the cameo from her. That was the second time I had thought about her. I remember it very well.

This time, that is, from Mozer, she brought me an amber cigar holder. Not a bad thing, something for a connoisseur, but again hardly worth anything to me, for we only deal in gold articles. As she came to me the day after her *rebellion*, I received her sternly. Sternness with me means dryness. However, as I was handing her the two roubles, I couldn't resist saying to her with a certain note of exasperation in my voice, "I'm only doing it *for you*, for Mozer would never have accepted such a thing from you." I put a special emphasis on the words *for you*. Invested them quite deliberately with *a certain meaning*. I was furious. She flushed crimson again at the *for you*, but swallowed the insult, didn't fling the money back at me. Took it like a lamb. That's what poverty does for you! But, Lord, how she blushed! I realised that I had hurt her feelings. But when she went out, I suddenly asked myself, Is this triumph over her really worth two roubles? Dear, oh dear! I remember I asked myself that very question twice: "Is it worth it? Is it worth it?" And, laughing, decided that it was. Felt very jolly that time. But it wasn't a bad feeling: I did it deliberately, intentionally. I wanted to put her to the test. I wanted to do that because suddenly certain plans with regard to her began stirring in my mind. That was my *third* special thought about her.

. . . Well, it was from that time that it all started. I, naturally, took immediate steps to find out what could be found out about her in an indirect way, and I waited for her next visit with particular impatience. For I had a premonition that she would come soon. When she did come, I entered into a very amiable conversation with her, doing my utmost to be as civil to her as possible. I have had quite a good education, you see, and my manners are irreproachable. Well, it was then that I realised that she was good and gentle. Good and gentle creatures do not offer a very stiff resistance, not for long, anyway, and though they may not open their hearts to you altogether, they don't know how to steer clear of a conversation: they reply in monosyllables, but they do reply, and the further they get drawn into it, the more talkative they become, so long, that is, as you don't get tired of it yourself, so long as you want to make the most of your opportunity. I need hardly tell you that she did not explain anything to me at the time. It was afterwards that I found out about *The Voice* and everything else. She was just then advertising wildly, first, of course, in a rather high and mighty fashion, "A governess, ready to take a situation in the country, please reply about conditions of employment by post," but later it was, "Willing to accept anything, to give lessons, to be a companion, to look after the household, to act as a nurse to a sick lady, plain sewing," and so on and so forth. The usual thing. All this of course was put in for publication at different times and in different versions, but in the end when things got really desperate, it was even "without salary, in return for board." But nothing doing. She could not find herself a job! It was then that I made up my mind to put her to the test for the last time. I suddenly picked up the last issue of *The Voice* and showed her an advertisement: "A young lady, orphan, looking for situation as governess to young children, preferably with an elderly widower. Willing to help with household duties."

"You see, this advertisement appeared this morning and I'm ready to bet you anything she'll have her job before the evening. That's the way to advertise."

Again she flushed. Again her eyes blazed. She turned round and went out at once. That pleased me very much. However, at that time I was already sure of everything and had no longer any fear. No one you see, would take her cigar holders. And, besides, she had no more cigar holders to pawn. Well, I was right. Two days later she called again, looking very pale and agitated. I realised that she must have had some trouble at home, and so it was. I'll explain presently what the trouble was. At the moment I just want to mention how I suddenly impressed her and how I rose in her estimation. It was a sort of scheme I suddenly conceived. You see, as a matter of fact she brought this icon (had made up her mind at last to bring it!) . . . . Now, listen. Please, listen. It was just then that everything began. I'm afraid I've been a bit muddled till now. . . . You see, I'm trying to recall all this—every detail—every little thing. I'm trying all the time to gather my thoughts to a point, but—but somehow I can't do it, and all these little details count. All these little details are frightfully important. . . .

An icon of the Virgin. The Virgin with the Babe. A family icon, an ancient one, the embossed metal of silver gilt—worth—well, shall we say, six roubles at most. I could see that the icon was precious to her. She was pawning it, you see, without removing the embossed metal.

"Why don't you take off the metal setting and take the icon back with you?" I said. "For, after all, it's an icon, and it's hardly what you might call the done thing to pawn an icon, is it?"

"Why not? Aren't you allowed to take it?"

"Oh yes, I can take it all right, but don't you think you may perhaps yourself. . . ."

"All right, take it off, if you like."

"Well, I'll tell you what," I said, thinking it over. "I shan't take it off, but I'll put it here together with the other icons in the icon case under the lamp (I always had a lamp burning above the icons, ever since the day I first opened my pawnshop), and I'll give you ten roubles for it."

"I don't want ten. Five will be quite enough for me. I'll most certainly redeem it."

"Are you sure you won't take ten? The icon is worth it, you know," I said, noticing that her eyes flashed again.

She made no answer. I went into the other room and came back with five roubles for her.

"Don't despise anyone," I said. "I was once in such straits myself, perhaps even in worse straits, and if you see me now engaged in this sort of business, it's—I mean, after what I've been through——"

"You don't mean you're revenging yourself on society, do you? Is that it?" she interrupted suddenly, with rather a caustic smile, which was quite innocent, though (I mean it was a "general" sort of smile, for at that time she made no distinction whatever between me and anyone else, so that she had said it almost without offence).

"Aha!" thought I. "So that's the sort of person you are! Showing your claws, my pretty one! I shouldn't wonder if you are not a member of one of the new movements!"

"You see," I said at once, half jokingly, half mysteriously, "I—I am part of that Power which still doeth good, though scheming ill. . . ."

She shot a glance at me, a glance that betrayed a great deal of interest, though, I suppose, there was quite a lot of childish curiosity in it, too.

"Wait—what kind of an idea is that? Where is it from? I believe I've heard it somewhere. . . ."

"Don't rack your brains. It's in these words that Mephistopheles introduces himself to Faust. You've read *Faust*, haven't you?"

"No, I mean, not really. . . ."

"You mean you haven't read it at all, don't you? You ought to read it. However, I can see that sardonic smile on your lips again. Please don't imagine I've so little good taste as to wish to disguise my part as pawnbroker by introducing myself to you as a sort of Mephistopheles. Once a pawnbroker, always a pawnbroker. I know."

"You're so strange. . . . I never dreamt of saying anything of the kind to you."

What she really meant to say was, "I never expected you to be an educated man." But she didn't say it, though I knew she thought it. I had pleased her enormously.

"You see," I observed, "one can do good in any profession. I'm not of course referring to myself. I'm quite ready to admit that I do nothing but evil, yet——"

"Of course one can do good in any business," she said, with a quick but keen glance at me. "Yes, in any business," she suddenly added.

Oh, I remember it all! I remember all those moments! And I'd like to add here that when these young people, these dear young people, want to say something clever

and profound, they betray it suddenly and rather too
openly and naïvely by a look on their faces—"See? I'm
saying something clever and profound to you!" And not
out of vanity, either, like people of my age. You could see
how she herself valued it so enormously, believed in it, esteemed it so highly, and was dead certain that you too
esteemed it as highly as she did. Oh, how important sincerity is! It is their sincerity that assures them their victory. And in her this was so delightful!

Yes, I remember it all. I've forgotten nothing. As soon
as she was gone, I made up my mind. The same day I
went out to make my last inquiries and found out all the
latest details about her present circumstances. I knew
every detail of her past from Lukerya, who was their
maid at the time and who had been in my pay for some
time. These details were so terrible that I don't know how
she could have laughed as she did the other day, or have
been so curious about the words of Mephistopheles when
she herself was in such a dreadful position. But—youth!
Yes, that is just what I thought about her at the time
with pride and joy. For there is magnanimity there too:
though I may be standing on the very brink of a precipice,
Goethe's grand words still shed a radiance! Youth is always magnanimous, though only a little bit, though
wrong-headedly. I mean, it's about her I'm thinking—
about her alone. And, above all, even at that time I already regarded her as *mine*, and not for one moment did
I doubt my own power. It's one of the most voluptuous
thoughts in the world, you know. Not to be in doubt, I
mean.

But what's the matter with me? If I go on like this I
shall never be able to gather everything to a point. Quick,
quick—oh God, that's not it at all.

II. A PROPOSAL OF MARRIAGE

The "details" I found out about her I can explain in a
few words. Her father and mother were dead. They had
died three years before I met her, and she had been left
with her disreputable aunts, though "disreputable" is
hardly the right word for them. One aunt was a widow,
a mother of a large family—six children, all close to one
another in age. Her other aunt was an old maid, as bad
as they make 'em. Both were bad. Her father had been

a civil servant. A clerk in a Government office, a non-hereditary nobleman. In short, everything was in my favour. I appeared as though from a higher world. After all, I'm a retired first lieutenant of a famous regiment, a nobleman by birth, independent, etc. As for my pawnshop and money-lending business, the aunts could only have looked upon it with respect. She had been slaving for her aunts for three years, but in spite of that she seemed to have found time to pass her school exams somewhere, passed them by hook or by crook, passed them for all her daily drudgery. And that after all meant something, if only as showing her desire to achieve something higher and nobler! Why, what did I want to get married for? However, to blazes with me! I'll discuss that later. Besides, that isn't the point really. . . . Anyway, she taught her aunt's children, made their underclothing for them, and in the end not only made their underclothing for them, but scrubbed the floors as well, and that with her weak chest, too. Why, not to put too fine a point on it, they even beat her, begrudged her every bite of bread she ate. And they ended up by intending to sell her. Damn 'em! I'll leave out the sordid details. She told me all about it afterwards. A whole year the fat shopkeeper next door had been watching it all. Not an ordinary shopkeeper, either. Owned two grocery shops. He had already driven two wives into their graves, and as he was not looking for a third one, he cast his eyes on her. "A quiet one," he thought, "brought up in poverty, and I am marrying her for the sake of my motherless children." And he had children all right. So he opened up negotiations with her aunts. Asked for the girl's hand in marriage. He was fifty. Of course, she was horrified. It was then she began coming to me to get money to pay for the advertisements in *The Voice*. At last she began imploring her aunts to give her a little time to think it over. Just a little time. They gave her a little time, only a very little time, not a minute more. Made her life a hell on earth. "We don't know how to fill our own bellies without an extra mouth to feed!" I knew all about it, and after her visit in the morning that day made up my mind finally. That evening the shopkeeper came to see them. Brought her a pound of sweets from his shop worth a shilling. While she was entertaining him, I called Lukerya out of the kitchen and told her to go and whisper to her that I was waiting for her at the gate and wanted to see her on a very urgent matter. I felt very pleased with myself. As a matter of fact, I was tremendously pleased with myself all that day.

It was at the gates, and in the presence of Lukerya, that I told her, thunderstruck as she was at having been sent for by me, that I should be happy and honoured if she . . . Further, I begged her not to be surprised at the manner of my proposal, nor that I was proposing to her in the street. "I'm a blunt man," I said, "and it's unnecessary for me to tell you that I know all about your circumstances." And I was not lying. I am a blunt man. Anyway, what does it matter? I spoke to her not only decently, that is to say, showing that I was a man of education, but also with originality, and that's what matters. Well, is there any harm in admitting it? I want to judge myself, and I am judging myself. I must speak *pro* and *contra,* and I do. I always remembered it with pleasure afterwards, though it may have been silly. I told her frankly at the time, without the slightest embarrassment, that, in the first place, I was not particularly talented or particularly clever and, perhaps, not even particularly good. I told her that I was a pretty cheap egoist (I remember that expression: I had thought of it on the way and was rather pleased with it), and that it was indeed very likely that I possessed a number of other highly unpleasant qualities. I told her all that with a special sort of pride—we all know how one talks of such things. Mind you, I had enough good sense not to speak of my virtues after having so nobly enlarged on my bad qualities. I did not say, "But to make up for that I possess this or that or the other virtue." I saw that for the time being she was terribly frightened. But I didn't tone anything down, either. On the contrary, seeing how frightened she was, I deliberately painted everything in blacker colours. I told her bluntly that she would not have to worry about food, but as for fine clothes, theatres and balls, she couldn't count on that. Not at first, at all events. Later on when I had attained my object—possibly. This stern tone most decidedly appealed to me. I added, though, and that casually too, that if I was engaged in that sort of business, that is, kept my pawnshop, it was because of a certain object I had in mind, because, that is, there was a certain circumstance. . . . But, surely, I had a right to talk like that, for I really had such an object in mind, there really was such a circumstance. One moment, ladies and gentlemen, one moment, please: I always hated this moneylending business, I hated it all my life, and, as a matter of fact, though I admit it's absurd to talk about oneself in such mysterious phrases, I *was* "revenging myself on society." Indeed, I was! So that her gibe that morning about "revenging myself" was unfair. I mean, if I had told her straight, "Yes, I am revenging myself on society," and she had burst out laughing as she nearly did that morning, the whole thing would indeed have appeared rather ridiculous. But by the use of an indirect hint, by a mysterious phrase, one can, it seems, bias the imagination in one's favour. Besides, at that time I was no longer afraid of anything. For I knew very well that the fat shopkeeper at any rate was more hateful to her than I, and that when I made my proposal to her at the gate I would appear as a deliverer to her. I knew that. Oh, a man knows a dirty trick when he sees one! But was it a dirty trick? How is one to pass judgment on a man? Didn't I really love her even then?

Wait a bit. At that time of course I never said anything about conferring a favour upon her. On the contrary. Oh, quite on the contrary! "It is you," I said, "who are conferring a favour on me, and not I on *you!*" So that, as you see, I even put it into words. I couldn't restrain myself, and I daresay it must have sounded rather silly, for I noticed a fleeting expression of dismay on her face. But on the whole I most certainly got the better of it. Wait, though. If we must recall all this sordid business, then let me recall that last bit of beastliness too. As I stood there, the thought that was stirring in my mind was, "You are tall, well-built, educated and—and after all, without boasting about it, not bad-looking, either." That's what kept recurring to my mind at the time. Well, anyway. She of course said *yes* to me right away, at the gate. But—but perhaps it is only fair to add that out there, at the gate, she thought a very long time before she said *yes*. She pondered so long that I could not refrain from asking, "Well, what do you say?" And I even put the question to her with a certain air of gallantry, "Well, what do you say, madam?"

"Please wait. Let me think."

And her sweet little face looked so serious, so serious, that even then I might have read it! But I felt hurt.

"Why," I thought, "is she really choosing between me and that shopkeeper?" Oh, I did not understand then! I did not understand anything. No, I didn't understand anything then! I didn't understand till today! I remember Lukerya ran after me as I was going away, stopped me in the street, and said, speaking very fast, "God will reward you, sir, for marrying our dear young lady. Only please don't tell her that, sir. She's proud!"

Proud, is she? "Well," I thought, "I like them proud." Proud women are particularly good when—well, when you're no longer in doubt about your power over them. Eh? Oh, base, blundering man! Oh, how pleased I was! Do you know, while she was standing there by the gate, pondering whether to say *yes* to me, and I was wondering why she was taking such a long time over it, do you know that she may have even had some such thought as this: "If it means unhappiness for me either way, then why not choose the worst? Why not choose the fat shopkeeper and have done with it? For he would be quite sure to beat me to death in one of his drunken fits!" Eh? What do you think? Might not such a thought have occurred to her at the time?

No, I don't understand it even now. I don't understand anything even now! I've just said that the thought might have occurred to her: why not choose the worst of the two evils, that is, the shopkeeper? But which was worst for her at that moment? The shopkeeper or I? A shopkeeper or a pawnbroker who quotes Goethe? That's the question. What question? Why, don't you see even that? The answer is lying on the table, and you say, It's a question! But—to hell with me! I'm of no consequence. . . . Besides, what does it matter to me now whether I am or whether I am not of consequence? That, I am afraid, is something I cannot possibly tell. I had better go to bed. My head aches. . . .

III. THE NOBLEST OF MEN—BUT I DON'T BELIEVE IT MYSELF

I couldn't sleep. And how could I with that pulse throbbing in my head? I want to get at the bottom of it. At the bottom of all that filth. Oh, the filth! Oh, what filth I had dragged her out of then! Surely, she ought to have realised that! She ought to have appreciated my action. Other thoughts, too, pleased me at the time. For instance, that I was forty-one and she was only sixteen. That fascinated me—that feeling of inequality. Yes, it's delightful, very delightful!

Now, for example, I wanted to have our wedding *à l'anglaise*, that is, a quiet wedding, just the two of us and, of course, the two witnesses, one of whom would be Lukerya, and then straight to the train, say to Moscow (I had, incidentally, some business there), staying at an hotel for a fortnight or so. But she was against it. She would not hear of it. And so I was forced to pay visits to her aunts and to present my respects to them as the relations from whom I was taking her. Yes, I gave in, and the proper respect was paid to the aunts. I even made a present to the creatures of one hundred roubles each, and promised them more, without of course telling her anything about it, so as not to distress her by the meanness of the whole situation. Her aunts at once became as smooth as silk. There was also some argument about her trousseau: she had nothing in the world, literally nothing, but then she didn't want anything. I succeeded, however, in persuading her that it was not right and proper for a bride not to have anything at all, and I got her the trousseau. For who else was there to do anything for her? Well, anyway, to hell with me! Still, I did convey certain of my ideas to her then, so that she should at all events know. I was perhaps a thought too hasty about it. The important thing was that from the very start, however much she tried to restrain herself, she did her best to show her affection for me. Met me whenever I came to visit them in the evening with protestations of delight. Told me in that chatter of hers (her sweet chatter of innocence) about the days of her childhood, her babyhood, her old home, her mother and father. But I never hesitated for a moment and poured cold water upon all her raptures. That was essentially what my idea amounted to. To her transports I replied with silence. Benevolent silence, no doubt, but all the same she soon realised that we were different and that I was an enigma. And it was the enigma that was my trump card! For to create this enigma, for the sake of it, I perpetrated all this folly! Sternness above all! And it was with sternness that I led her into my house. To put the whole thing in a nutshell, though I was eminently pleased at the time, I created a whole system. Oh, it came naturally enough, without the slightest effort on my part. Besides, it couldn't have been otherwise. I had to create that system owing to one unavoidable circumstance—why indeed should I be slandering myself! The system was perfect. A real system. No, listen! If you want to pass judgment on a man, you must first know all the facts about him. Listen.

Now, how shall I begin? For the whole thing is very complicated. Whenever you start justifying yourself, things become complicated. You see, young people as a rule despise money, so I at once made a special point of money. I laid particular stress on money. And I did it with such consummate skill that she grew more and more silent. She would open her large eyes, listen to me, look at me, and fall silent. You see, young people are generous. I mean, young people who are good are generous and impulsive. But they have little tolerance. If anything doesn't turn out the way they like, they immediately begin to despise you. And I liked her to take a broad, a tolerant view of things. I wanted to instil the idea of tolerance into her mind. I wanted her to accept that idea with all her heart and soul. That was my plan, wasn't it? Let me give you a trivial example. How do you think I should have explained this money-lending business of mine to a girl of such a character? Naturally, I did not speak of it directly, for if I did it would have appeared that I was apologising to her for my pawnshop. Well, in the end I did it as it were through pride. I spoke almost without words. And I am an old hand at speaking without words. I have spent all my life speaking without words. I have lived through whole tragedies without uttering a word. Oh, I too had been unhappy! I was cast out by the whole world, cast out and forgotten, and no one, no one knows it! And all of a sudden this sixteen-year-old girl collected a whole dossier of the most detailed information about me from all sorts of scoundrels, and she thought she knew everything, while the innermost mystery remained buried in the breast of this man! I went on being silent. Yes, I went on being silent especially, especially with her—until yesterday. Why was I silent? Well, because I am a proud man. I meant her to find out for herself, without my help, and not from the tales told by all sorts of scoundrels. I wanted her to discover *by herself* this man and understand him! When I took her to my house, I expected the fullest possible respect from her. I wanted her to stand in homage before me because of my sufferings. And I deserved it. Oh, I was always proud. I always wanted all or nothing. And it is just because I never compromise where my own happiness is concerned, just because I wanted everything, that I was forced to act as I did that time. "Find out for yourself," I as much as told her, "and learn to appreciate me!" For you must admit that if I had started explaining everything to her myself, if I had prompted her, if I had humbled myself before her, if I had begged her to respect me, it would have been the same as if I had begged her for charity. . . . However—however, why am I talking about this? It's so silly! Silly, silly, silly! I explained to her in a few words, without beating about the bush, brutally (I stress the brutality of it!), that nothing in the world was more delightful than the generosity of youth, but—it wasn't worth a farthing. Why not? Because it costs them nothing. Because it is merely the result of their inexperience. Because all that, as it were, is nothing but "the first impressions of life." But, I said, "let's see the sort of people you'll be if you have to work hard for a living. Cheap generosity is always easy, even to give one's life—yes, even that is easy, because it is merely the result of high spirits, of a superabundance of energy, of a passionate desire for beauty! Oh, no! You try a different kind of generosity, the really heroic kind, the difficult, calm, silent kind, without glitter, with odium, the kind that demands great sacrifices, the kind that doesn't bring you a scrap of fame or glory, in which you—a man of shining virtue—are exhibited before the whole world as a blackguard, while you are really the most honest man of them all! Well, try that, my dear girl. Just try it. Try and see what sort of a hero you'll prove yourself to be! But no, ma'am! I can see that you don't want that sort of heroism, while I—well—I have done nothing in my life but bear that cross!" At first she argued. Good Lord, how she argued! Then she began lapsing into silence. Wouldn't say a word. Only opened her eyes as she listened to me, opened them wide, those big, big eyes of hers, those observant eyes of hers. And—and, in addition, I suddenly saw a smile on her face, a mistrustful, silent, evil smile. Well, it was with that smile that I brought her into my house. It was true, of course, that she had nowhere else to go. . . .

IV. PLANS, PLANS, PLANS. . . .

Which of us began it first?

Why, neither. It all began of itself from the very start. I have said that I brought her to my house with sternness. However, from the very beginning I made things easy for her. I took pains to explain to her while we were still engaged that she would have to help me with taking the pledges and paying out money. Well, at the time she said nothing (mark that, please!). And, moreover, she actually began helping me in my business with great enthusiasm. Mind you, my flat, my furniture, everything in fact, remained as before. My flat consists of two rooms, one large reception room with the pawnshop partitioned off, and the second room, also large, was our own room, our sitting-room and bedroom. My furniture is rather poor; even her aunts had better furniture. My icon case with the lamp is in the reception room where the pawnshop is. In my own room I have a book-case with a few books and a small trunk. I always keep the keys of the trunk. Then there is, of course, the bed, tables, chairs. I told her before we were married that I'd let her have one rouble a day for our board, that is, for food for herself, me, and Lukerya, whom I had enticed away from her aunt. One rouble a day and no more. "I must have thirty thousand in three years," I said, "and there is no other way of saving it up." She raised no objections to that, but I myself increased her daily allowance by thirty copecks. The same thing with the theatre. I told her before our marriage that she needn't expect to be taken to the theatre. However, I decided to take her to a play once a month. And decently, too. To the stalls. We went together. We went three times, as a matter of fact. Saw *The Chase After Happiness* and *Singing Birds,* I think. (Oh, to hell with it!) We went there in silence and we came back in silence. Why, oh why, did we from the very beginning make no attempt to speak to each other? At first there were no quarrels, but just silence. In those days, I remember, she always used to watch me furtively. As soon as I noticed that, I became more silent than ever. It is true, it was I who made a point of keeping silent and not she. On her part there were one or two outbursts of affection when she would rush to embrace me. But as these outbursts were quite obviously morbid and hysterical, and as what I wanted was secure happiness, with respect from her, I received them coldly. And I was quite right: we always had a quarrel the day after such an outburst.

But perhaps I am being a little unfair: there were no real quarrels, only silence and—and more and more insolent looks from her. "Rebellion and independence"— that's what it was. Only she wasn't very good at it. Yes, that gentle face was getting more and more insolent. Believe it or not, I was becoming loathsome to her. Oh yes, I know what I am talking about. I observed it carefully. You see, the fact that those outbursts of hers were the result of strained nerves was quite undeniable. Why else should she, after emerging from that squalor and destitution, after scrubbing floors, begin sniffing at our poverty? As a matter of fact, there was no question of poverty at all. It was just economy. I never stinted myself in what was necessary. In linen, for instance, and cleanliness. I've always been of the opinion that cleanliness in husbands attracts a wife. Still, it was not poverty she found fault with so much as with my so-called meanness in economising. "There's some purpose behind it," she seemed to say. "Wants to show off his strength of character." She herself quite suddenly refused to go to the theatre. And that scornful smile of hers was to be seen more and more often on her face. And I grew more and more silent. More and more silent.

I wasn't going to justify myself, was I? You see, it was the pawnshop that was the chief source of trouble between us. Mind you, I knew that a woman, and particularly a girl of sixteen, simply must submit to her husband. Women have no originality. That—that is axiomatic. Yes, I regard it as axiomatic even now. Even now! Never mind what's lying there in the sitting-room. Truth is truth, and John Stuart Mill himself can do nothing about it! And a woman who loves—oh, a woman who loves—will worship even vice, the crimes even of the man she loves. He would himself never invent such justifications for his crimes as she will find for them. That is generous, but it is not original. It is the lack of originality that has been the ruin of women. And what, I repeat, are you pointing at the table in the sitting-room for? Is that original? Is what's lying there on the table original? Aha!

Listen. I was quite certain of her love then. After all,

she did fling herself on my neck even at that time. That proves that she loved or, at all events, wanted to love. Yes, that's what it was: she wanted to love, she did her best to love. And the point is that there were no crimes there for which she might have had to find a justification. You say, a pawnbroker. And every one else says the same. But what if I am a pawnbroker? I mean, there must have been some reasons for one of the most generous of men to have become a pawnbroker. You see, there are ideas —I mean, if one were to put some ideas into words, say them out loud, they would sound very silly. Why, I'd be ashamed of doing it myself. And why? For no reason at all. Just because we are all rotters and can't bear the truth. At all events, I know of no other reason. I said just now —"one of the most generous of men." It may sound ridiculous, and yet that is how it was. It is the truth. It's the truth and nothing but the truth. Yes, *I had a right* to want to make myself secure at the time. *I had a right* to open the pawnshop. You have rejected me, you—the people, I mean—have cast me out with contemptuous silence. For my passionate desire to love you, you have repaid me with a wrong from the consequences of which I shall suffer all my life. Now I have the right to erect a wall against you, to save up the thirty thousand roubles and spend the rest of my life somewhere in the Crimea, on the south coast, among the mountains and vineyards, on my own estate bought with the thirty thousand, and—above all—far away from you all, with malice against none, with the woman I love at my side, with a family, if God will send me one, and—and "being an help to them that dwell in the country round about." Well, of course, it doesn't matter if I'm saying this to myself now, but at the time what could have been more stupid than making a long story to her about it. That was the reason for my proud silence. That was why we sat together in silence. For what could she have made of it all? She was only sixteen, a girl in her teens—what could she have made of my justifications and sufferings? What I had to deal with was a straitlaced, uncompromising attitude, ignorance of life, the cheap convictions of youth, the utter blindness of "a noble soul," and, above all, the pawnshop. Good God, the pawnshop! The pawnshop! (And was I a villain in the pawnshop? Did she not see how I treated people? Did I ever take more than was my due?) Oh, how awful truth is in the world! That exquisite creature, that gentle creature, that heavenly creature was a tyrant, she was the pitiless tyrant and torturer of my soul! I must say it. I shouldn't be fair to myself if I didn't. Do you think I did not love her? Who can honestly say I didn't love her? Don't you see? That was the irony of it, the terrible irony of fate and nature! We are accursed. The life of people (and mine, in particular) is accursed. For I can see now that I must have made some mistake. That something went wrong somewhere. Everything was so clear. My plan was as clear as daylight. "Stern—proud—is in need of no moral consolations from anyone—suffers in silence." And that was true. I was not lying. I was not lying. "She will see herself later on that it was generosity on my part, though now she cannot see it. And when she does realise it one day she will appreciate me ten times as much, and she will fall in the dust at my feet, her hands folded in supplication." That was my plan. But there was something I forgot or failed to see. There was something I mismanaged badly. But enough, enough! Whose forgiveness am I to ask now? What is done is done. Be brave, man, and proud! It is not your fault! . . .

Well, why should I not tell the truth? Why should I be afraid to face the truth squarely? It was *her* fault, *her* fault. . . .

V. THE GENTLE CREATURE REBELS

Our quarrels began as a result of her sudden decision to issue loans for any amount she pleased. On two occasions she presumed to start an argument with me on this very subject. I told her I could not allow it. And then the captain's widow turned up.

The old woman brought a locket. A present from her late husband. The usual thing—a keepsake. I gave her thirty roubles. She started wailing plaintively, asking me to be sure not to lose the thing. I naturally told her not to worry: it would be safe. Well, anyway, five days later she came again to exchange it for a bracelet that was not worth eight roubles. I, quite naturally, refused. But I suppose she must have read something in my wife's eyes, for she came back later when I was out, and my wife exchanged the medallion for her bracelet.

Having learnt about it the same day, I spoke to her

gently, but firmly and sensibly. She was sitting on the bed, her eyes fixed on the floor, tapping with the toe of her right boot on the carpet (a habit of hers); an ugly smile played on her lips. Then, without raising my voice, I told her quietly that the money was *mine*, and that I had a right to look on life with *my own* eyes, and—and that when I had asked her to become my wife I had concealed nothing from her.

All of a sudden she jumped up, all of a sudden she began shaking all over, and all of a sudden—what do you think—she stamped her foot at me. She was a wild beast. She was in a rage. A wild beast in a rage. I was petrified with amazement. I had never expected her to behave like that. But never for a moment did I lose control of myself. Never by a movement did I betray my astonishment. Again, in the same quiet voice, I told her straight that from now on I would not allow her to meddle in my affairs. She laughed in my face and walked out of the flat.

Now, you see, the point is that she had no right to walk out of the flat. She was to go nowhere without me—that was our understanding before our marriage. She came back in the evening. I never said a word.

Next day too she went out in the morning; the day after again. I closed my pawnshop and went to see her aunts. I had broken off all relations with them after our wedding: I did not want them to call on us, and we did not call on them. But it seemed she had not been there. They listened to me with great interest, and then laughed in my face. "Serves you right!" they said. I expected them to laugh at me. Anyway, I at once bribed the younger aunt, the old maid, with a hundred roubles, giving her twenty-five in advance. Two days later she came to see me. "An army officer is mixed up in this," she said. "A lieutenant by the name of Yefimovich. A former regimental colleague of yours." I was very much astonished. That Yefimovich had done me more harm than anyone in the regiment, and about a month ago, lacking all sense of shame, he had come to my pawnshop once or twice on the pretext of pawning something, and, I remember, begun laughing with my wife. I went up to him at once and told him not to dare to show his face in my house again in view of what our relations had been. But I had no idea that there was anything between him and my wife. I simply thought that it was just his confounded cheek. But now the aunt informed me that she had already made an appointment to meet him, and that the moving spirit behind the whole affair was a former acquaintance of theirs, Julia Semyonovna, a widow and a colonel's wife, to boot. "It is her your wife goes to see," the aunt told me.

I shall be brief about this affair. Altogether it cost me about three hundred roubles, but in a couple of days everything was arranged. I was to be in an adjoining room, behind closed doors, and overhear the first *rendez-vous* between my wife and Yefimovich. In expectation of this, on the day before, there occurred between us a brief, but for me significant, scene.

She came back late in the afternoon, sat down on the bed, and looked at me sardonically, tapping the carpet with her foot. As I looked at her, the idea suddenly flashed through my head that for the whole of the last month, or rather the last fortnight, she had not been acting in character, or one ought perhaps to say, she was acting out of character. I saw before me a creature of a violent, aggressive nature; I don't want to say shameless, but disreputable, one that seemed to be looking for trouble. Yes. Asking for it. Her gentleness, however, seemed to be in her way. When such a woman gives way to violence, however she may overdo things, she cannot conceal the fact that she is behaving against her better nature, that she is egging herself on, that she is quite unable to overcome her own feelings of shame and her own outraged sense of decency. It is because of this that such women sometimes behave so outrageously that you can hardly believe your eyes. A woman accustomed to a life of immorality will, on the contrary, always try to tone everything down; she will make everything a hundred times more disgusting, but all under the pretence of decorum and decency, a pretence that in itself is a sort of claim to superiority over you.

"Is it true that you were turned out of the regiment because you were afraid to fight a duel?" she asked suddenly, without rhyme or reason, and her eyes flashed.

"It's quite true. Following a decision of my fellow-officers, I was asked to leave the regiment, though as a matter of fact I had sent in my resignation before that."

"They expelled you for being a coward, didn't they?"

"Yes, they sentenced me as a coward. But I refused to fight this duel not because I was a coward, but because I would not submit to their tyrannical decision and send a challenge to someone when I did not consider myself to be insulted. You ought to know," I could not resist the temptation to proceed, "that to take action against such tyranny in spite of all the consequences it might entail meant showing more pluck than fighting any kind of duel."

I am afraid I could not restrain myself. By the last phrase I tried, as it were, to justify myself. And that's what she was waiting for. She wanted this new proof of my humiliation. She laughed maliciously.

"And is it true that for three years afterwards you wandered about the streets of Petersburg like a tramp, begging for coppers and sleeping under billiard-tables?"

"Yes, it's quite true. I slept in the markets and in Vyazemsky's dosshouse. Quite true. There was a lot of disgrace and degradation in my life after my expulsion from the regiment. But not moral degradation. For even at the time I was the first to hate my own actions. It was only a degradation of my will and mind, and was only caused by the desperateness of my position. But all that is over now. . . ."

"Oh, now you're a man of importance—a financier!"

A hint at my pawnshop, you see. But by then I had already succeeded in taking a firm hold of myself. I saw that what she wanted most was explanations that would be humiliating to me, and—and I did not give them. Besides, just then the doorbell rang and I went out into the large room to attend to a client. Afterwards, an hour later, when she suddenly put on her things to go out, she stopped in front of me and said:

"You didn't tell me anything about it before we were married, did you?"

I made no answer, and she went away.

So next day I was standing in that room behind the closed doors, listening to hear how my fate was being decided. I had a gun in my pocket. She had dressed up for the occasion, and she was sitting at the table while Yefimovich played the fool before her. And what do you think? The result was—I say it to my credit—the result turned out to be just as I had anticipated, though at the time I might not have realised that I did expect it. I don't know whether I am expressing myself clearly.

This is what happened. I listened for a whole hour, and

for a whole hour I was present at a battle of wits between a woman, a most honourable and high-principled woman, and a man about town with no principles, a dissolute and dull creature with a cringing, grovelling soul. And how, thought I, lost in amazement, how does this innocent, this gentle, this reserved woman, know it all? The most witty author of a comedy of manners could not have devised this scene of ridicule, most innocent laughter, and sacred contempt of virtue for vice. And how scintillating were her words and sly digs! What wit in her quick repartees! What withering truth in her condemnation! And, at the same time, what almost girlish artlessness! She laughed in his face at his protestations of love, at his gestures, at his proposals. Having arrived with his mind made up to take her crudely by storm and without expecting to meet with any serious opposition, the bubble of his conceit was suddenly pricked. At first I might have thought that she was flirting with him. "The flirtation of a witty, though vicious, creature to enhance her own value." But no. I was mistaken. Truth shone forth like the sun, and there was no room left for doubt in my mind. She, who had so little experience of the world, could have made up her mind to keep the appointment only out of hatred for me, an impulsive and insincere hatred, but as soon as matters came to a head her eyes were opened at once. It was simply the case of a woman who was trying her hardest to humiliate me, but having made up her mind to stoop so low, she could not bear the horrible disgrace of it. And how indeed could Yefimovich, or any other society rake, hope to seduce a woman like her, a woman so pure and innocent, a woman who had such an unquenchable faith in her ideals? On the contrary, he merely aroused laughter. The whole truth rose up from her soul, and her indignation evoked sarcasm from her heart. I repeat, in the end the damn fool looked utterly dumbfounded. He sat there frowning, hardly replying to her, so that I was even beginning to fear that he might go so far as to insult her out of a mean desire for revenge. And I repeat again: to my credit be it said that I listened to the scene almost without surprise. It was as though I had come across something I had known all my life. It was as though I had gone there on purpose to meet it. I went there without believing anything against her, without making any accusations against her, though I did have a gun in my pocket.

That is the truth! And how could I have imagined her to be different? Why else did I marry her? Oh, it's true enough I knew perfectly well at the time how she hated me, but I was also convinced that she was guiltless. I brought the scene to a sudden close by opening the door. Yefimovich jumped to his feet. I took her by the hand and asked her to leave the house with me. Yefimovich recovered himself and burst into loud peals of laughter.

"Oh," he said, "I've certainly nothing against the sacred right of holy matrimony. Take her away! Take her away! And, you know," he shouted after me, "though a decent man would think twice before fighting a duel with you, I feel that out of respect for your lady I ought to tell you that I'm at your service if, that is, you'd care to run the risk——"

"Do you hear?" I said, stopping her for a second on the threshold.

Then not another word all the way home. I led her by the arm, and she offered no resistance. On the contrary, she was too bewildered, too much taken by surprise by all that had happened. But that only lasted till we got home. Once at home, she sat down and stared at me. She was very pale, and though when she sat down there might have been a sardonic smile on her lips, she regarded me a moment later with a solemn and grim challenge in her eyes, and I believe that at first she was quite convinced that I would kill her with the gun. But I took it silently out of my pocket and laid it on the table. She looked at me and the gun. (Note that she knew all about the gun. I had acquired it and kept it always loaded ever since I had opened my pawnshop. For when I opened my pawnshop I made up my mind that I would not keep huge dogs or employ a strong manservant as Mozer does, for instance. My cook opens the door to my clients. But people in my profession cannot afford to dispense with the means of self-defence in case of need, and I kept a loaded revolver. During the first days of our marriage, she took a great interest in that gun. She asked all sorts of questions about it, and I explained to her its mechanism and how it worked. I even persuaded her one day to fire at a target. Note that, too, please.) Taking no notice of her frightened look, I half undressed myself and lay down on the bed. I felt terribly exhausted: it was about eleven o'clock. She remained sitting in the same place, without moving, for

about an hour. Then she extinguished the candle and lay
down, also without undressing, on the sofa by the wall.
For the first time she did not come to bed with me. Note
that, too, please. . . .

VI. A TERRIBLE REMINISCENCE

Now about this terrible reminiscence. . . .

I woke in the morning at about eight o'clock, I think,
and it was already quite light in the room. I woke all at
once, with all my mental faculties wide awake, and suddenly opened my eyes. She was standing by the window
with the gun in her hand. She did not see that I was awake
and that I was looking at her. Suddenly I saw that she
began moving slowly towards me with the gun in her
hand. I quickly closed my eyes and pretended to be fast
asleep.

She went up to the bed and stood over me. I heard
everything. The silence in the room was so deep that I
could hear it. All at once I became conscious of one spas-
modic movement, and I opened my eyes suddenly, irresistibly, against my will. She was looking straight at me.
Straight into my eyes. And the gun was already near my
temple. Our eyes met. But we looked at each other for
no more than a second. With a great effort I closed my
eyes again, and in that instant I resolved with all the
strength I possessed not to make another movement, not
to open my eyes, whatever happened.

And it does happen of course that a man who is fast
asleep suddenly opens his eyes, raises his head just for a
second, and looks round the room, then a moment later
quite unconsciously replaces his head on the pillow and
falls asleep without remembering anything. When, after
meeting her glance and feeling the gun at my temple, I
suddenly shut my eyes and did not stir, she certainly could
have assumed that I was really asleep and that I had seen
nothing, particularly as it is scarcely conceivable that,
having seen what I had seen, I should at *such* a moment
have closed my eyes again.

Yes, it was inconceivable. And yet she could have
guessed the truth all the same. It was that thought that
flashed through my mind suddenly, at one and the same
instant, and—three cheers for the lightning speed of
human thought! If that was so (I felt), if she guessed the

truth and knew that I was not asleep, then I had crushed her already by my readiness to accept death, and now her hand might falter. Her former determination might be shattered against a new startling impression. It is said that people standing on a great height seem to be irresistibly drawn into the abyss. I suppose many suicides and murders have been committed only because the gun was already in the hand of the murderer or self-destroyer. Here, too, is a yawning chasm. Here, too, is a declivity, a slope at an angle of forty-five degrees, on which it is impossible not to slip, and something seems to force you irresistibly to pull the trigger. But the knowledge that I had seen everything, that I knew everything, and that I was waiting for death at her hands in silence, could have checked her on that slope.

The silence continued, and suddenly I felt the cold touch of steel at my temple, at my hair. You will ask me, did I have any hope of escape? I will answer you—and God knows I am speaking the truth—none at all, not an atom of hope, except perhaps one chance in a hundred. Why, then, did I accept death? Well, let me ask you in turn: of what use was life to me after a gun had been levelled against me by a human being I adored? Besides, I realise with the whole force of my being that at that very moment a struggle was going on between us, a life and death struggle, a duel in which I—the coward of the day before who had been expelled by his fellow-officers for cowardice—was engaged. I knew it, and she knew it too, if she had guessed the truth and knew that I was not asleep.

Perhaps nothing of the sort really happened. Perhaps I never had those thoughts at the time. But all that must have taken place even without conscious thought, yet I have done nothing but think of it every moment of my life since.

But (you will ask again) why did I not save her from so heinous a crime? Oh, I've asked myself the same question a thousand times since, every time when, with a cold shiver down my back, I have called that moment to mind. But my soul was then sunk in black despair: I was in mortal peril, I myself was on the very brink of total extinction, so how could I have saved anyone? And, besides, what makes you think that I wanted to save anyone at that moment? How can one tell what I was feeling then?

But all the time my mind was in a turmoil. The seconds passed. There was a dead silence. She still stood over me. Then all of a sudden I gave a start as hope returned to me. I opened my eyes quickly. She was no longer in the room. I got out of bed: I had conquered and she was conquered for ever.

I went out to have my tea. Tea was as a rule served in the other room, and she herself poured it out. I sat down at the table without uttering a word and took a glass of tea from her. About five minutes later I glanced at her. She was dreadfully pale, paler even than the night before, and she looked at me. And suddenly—suddenly—seeing that I was looking at her, she smiled palely with her pale lips, with a timid question in her eyes. "So she is still uncertain, she is still asking herself: does he or doesn't he know? did he or didn't he see?" I averted my eyes with a look of indifference.

After tea I locked up the shop, went to the market and bought an iron bedstead and a screen. On returning home, I had the bed put in the front room and the screen round it. That bed was for *her*. But I never said a word to her. She understood without words. The bed made her realise that "I saw everything and knew everything," and that there could be no more any doubt about that.

That night I left the gun on the table as usual. She crept silently into her new bed at night: our marriage was dissolved. "She was conquered but not forgiven." During the night she became delirious and in the morning she was in a high fever. She was in bed for six weeks.

Chapter 2

I. A DREAM OF PRIDE

Lukerya has just told me that she will not remain with me and that she will leave immediately after the funeral of her mistress. I knelt and prayed for five minutes. I wanted to pray for an hour, but all the time I kept thinking, thinking—and all such aching thoughts, and my head aches—what's the use of praying?—it's a sin! It is strange too that I should not be able to sleep. When one is unhappy, especially when one is very unhappy, one always feels like sleeping after the first violent outbursts of grief. Men condemned to death, I'm told, sleep very soundly indeed on the last night. And so it ought to be. It is only natural. Or they would not have been able to endure it. I lay down on the sofa, but I could not fall asleep.

. . . She was ill for six weeks, and we looked after her day and night, Lukerya and I and the trained nurse I had engaged from the hospital. I did not care how much money it cost me. On the contrary, I liked spending money on her. I called in Dr. Schroeder, and I paid him ten roubles for a visit. When she regained consciousness, I stopped going into her room unless it was absolutely necessary. However, why am I describing all this? When she got up at last, she sat down quietly and silently in my room at the special table I had also bought for her at the time. Yes, it is quite true: neither of us spoke at all. I mean, later on we did begin talking to each other, but just the usual things. Of course, I spoke as little as possible on purpose; but she, too, I could see very well, was glad not to have to say an unnecessary word. I thought that quite natural on her part. "She is too shaken and too subdued," I thought to myself, "and she must of course be given time to forget and to get used to things." And so it was that we were silent. But every minute I was preparing myself for the future. I could not help thinking that she was doing the same, and I found it extremely diverting to try and guess what she was thinking of just then.

One more thing I will say: no one, of course, oh, no one in the world, knew of the agonies I suffered during her illness. I kept my worries to myself and did not even let Lukerya see how troubled I was. I couldn't imagine, I couldn't even admit to myself, the possibility that she might die before learning the truth, the whole truth. But when she was out of danger and began to regain her health, I recovered my composure, I remember, very quickly and completely. And that was not all. I made up my mind *to put off our future* for as long a time as possible and for the time being to leave things as they were. Yes, just then something strange and peculiar happened to me (I don't know how else to describe it): I had triumphed, and the consciousness of that was quite sufficient for me. And so the whole winter passed. Oh, I was pleased as I had never been pleased in my life, and that all through the winter.

You see, there had been a most terrible event in my life which until then, that is to say, until the disastrous incident with my wife, weighed heavily upon my mind every day and every hour of the day: the loss of my reputation and my forced retirement from the army. To put it in a nutshell: I had been the victim of a most abominable injustice. It is true that my fellow-officers never liked me for my difficult character, and perhaps even for my absurd character, my ridiculous character, though it often happens that what you regard as great, what is dear to you, what you esteem most highly, strikes your friends for some unaccountable reason as extremely funny. Oh, I was never liked at school. People never liked me. Never at any time. Even Lukerya finds it impossible to like me. While, however, the incident in the regiment undoubtedly arose out of this general unpopularity of mine, its direct cause was quite certainly due to an accident. I am saying this because I don't think there can be anything more aggravating and intolerable than to be ruined by an accident which might or might not have happened, by a fortuitous concatenation of circumstances which might have passed away like a cloud. For a man of education nothing can be more humiliating.

Now what had happened was this:

During an interval at the play I went out to the bar which was crowded with people, including a large number of army officers. While I was there, the hussar officer A—v came in suddenly and began talking in a loud voice to two other hussar officers. He was telling them about Captain Bezumtsev of our regiment who (so he said) had just created a disturbance, and who (he added) "seems to be drunk." The subject was soon dropped. Besides, the whole story was a mistake, for Captain Bezumtsev was not drunk at all, and the disturbance was not really a disturbance, either. The hussars began talking about something else, and that was the end of it. But next day the story reached our regiment, and of course the fact that I was the only officer of our regiment in the bar at once became the subject of general talk. It was remarked that when the hussar A—v had spoken so insolently about Captain Bezumtsev, I had not gone over to him immediately and stopped him by rapping him on the knuckles. But why on earth should I have done that? If he had a bone to pick with Bezumtsev, it was their own personal affair and no business of mine. The officers of my regiment meanwhile decided that it was not a personal affair at all but concerned the whole regiment. And since I was the only officer of our regiment present, I had by my failure to take action shown both to the officers and the civilians in the bar that there were officers in the regiment who did not care a damn for their honour or for the honour of their regiment. I could not agree with such an interpretation. I was given to understand that I could still put everything right, late though it was, if I demanded a formal explanation from A—v. This I did not choose to do. In fact, I resented the whole thing most violently. I would not compromise with my pride, and refused to have anything to do with their suggestion. I then at once resigned my commission. That is the whole story. I left the regiment a proud, but a broken man. Both my will and my mind had suffered a bad shock. As it happened, my sister's husband in Moscow just then squandered our small family fortune, including my own part in it (a tiny part, it is true), and I was left without a penny in the world. I could have got myself some civilian job, but I didn't. After my splendid uniform, I wasn't going to become some railway official. And so—if it had to be shame, then let it be shame; if it had to be disgrace, then let it be disgrace; if it had to be degradation, then let it be degradation—the worse the better! That was my choice. Then followed three years of terrible deprivation and horror, and even Vyazemsky's dosshouse. A year and a half ago my godmother, a wealthy old lady, died in Moscow and among other bequests she quite unexpectedly left me three thousand roubles in her will. I thought things over and there and then decided what I was going to do with myself. I made up my mind that I would become a pawnbroker and ask no favours from anyone. First I must get money, then a home of my own, and then a new life far away from the memories of the past. That was my plan. Nevertheless, my sombre past and a reputation ruined for ever were a constant source of mental anguish to me. The memory of it haunted me every day, every minute. And then I got married. Whether by chance or not—I don't know. But when I brought her into my home, I thought I was bringing a friend, and it was a friend I needed most of all. But a friend had to be taken in hand, licked into shape, and—yes—even mastered. And how could I possibly explain it all at once to a six-teen-year-old girl, and one, besides, who was prejudiced against me? For instance, could I have convinced her that I was not a coward without the accidental assistance of the dreadful incident with the gun? Could I have convinced her that I had been falsely accused of cowardice in the regiment? But that dreadful incident came just in the nick of time. Having passed the test of the gun, I avenged the whole of my horrible past. And though no one knew about it, *she* knew, and that meant everything to me because she herself was everything to me. All the hopes of a bright future that I cherished in my dreams! She was the only person I had hoped to make my true friend in life, and I had no need of anyone else. And now she knew everything. At least she knew that she had been too hasty in joining the camp of my enemies. That thought filled me with delight. In her eyes I could no longer be a blackguard, but at most perhaps a queer fellow; and even that, after all that had happened, was not at all displeasing to me. Queerness is not a vice in a man; on the contrary, it often exercises a powerful attraction on a woman's imagination. In fact, I deliberately postponed the final explanation. What had happened was for the moment quite sufficient for my peace of mind. It contained too many exciting scenes and a lot of material for my dreams. You see, the whole trouble is that I am a dreamer: I was quite satisfied to have enough material for my dreams. As for her, she, I thought, could *wait*.

So the whole winter passed in a sort of expectation of something. I liked to steal a glance at her now and again when she sat at her little table. She was busy with her work, her sewing, and sometimes in the evening she would read books taken from my book-case. The choice of books in the book-case should also have spoken in my favour. She hardly ever went out. Every day after dinner, before dusk, I used to take her out for a walk. We took our constitutional, and not entirely in silence as before. At least, I did my best to pretend that we were not silent and that we were talking amicably together. But, as I have already said, we both saw to it that our talks were not

not too long. I did it on purpose, and as for her, I thought, it was important "to give her time." It is, I admit, strange that not once till the end of the winter did it occur to me that while I liked looking at her stealthily, I had never during all those winter months caught her looking at me! I ascribed it to her shyness. And indeed her whole appearance did convey a picture of such gentleness, such utter exhaustion after her illness. No, thought I, don't interfere with her. Better wait and—"she will come to you all of a sudden and of her own free will. . . ."

The thought filled me with intense delight. I will add one more thing: sometimes I would, as though on purpose, so inflame my own mind that I'd in fact succeed in working myself up into a mental and emotional rage against her. And it went on like that for some time. But my hatred of her could never ripen or strike roots in my heart. And, besides, I couldn't help feeling myself that it was only a sort of game I was playing. Why, even when I had dissolved our marriage by buying the bed and the screen, I could never for one moment look upon her as a criminal. And not because I took too light a view of her crime, but because I had the sense to forgive her completely, from the very first day, even before I purchased the bed. That, I confess, was a little odd on my part, for where morals are concerned I am very strict. On the contrary, in my eyes she was so thoroughly subdued, so thoroughly humiliated, so thoroughly crushed that I could not help feeling horribly sorry for her sometimes, though, for all that, the idea of her humiliation was at times certainly very pleasing to me. What pleased me was the idea of our inequality. . . .

That winter I happened to be responsible for a few acts of real kindness. I remitted two debts and I advanced money to one poor woman without a pledge. And I never breathed a word about it to my wife. Nor did I do it at all so that she should learn about it. But the woman herself came to thank me, and almost on her knees. In that way it became public property. I could not help thinking that she had learnt about the woman with real pleasure.

But spring was close at hand. It was mid-April. We took out our double windows, and bright shafts of sunlight began lighting up our rooms. But the scales still covered my eyes and blinded my reason. Oh, those fatal, those dreadful scales! How did it all happen that the scales suddenly fell from my eyes and that I suddenly saw and understood everything? Was it chance? Did the appointed day come at last? Was it a ray of sunshine that suddenly kindled a thought or a surmise in my dull brain? No. It was neither a thought nor a surmise. It was a chord that had been mute a long time and that now came to life and began vibrating suddenly, flooding my darkened mind with light and showing up my devilish pride. I felt as though I had leapt to my feet. It all happened with such incredible suddenness. It happened towards evening, at about five o'clock, after dinner. . . .

II. THE SCALES SUDDENLY FALL

Just two words before I go on. Already a month ago I noticed a strange wistfulness about her. She was not only silent. She was also wistful. Of that, too, I became aware all of a sudden. She was sitting and sewing something at the time, her head bent over her work, and she did not see that I was looking at her. It suddenly struck me how thin she looked, how haggard, her face so pale, her lips so white, and this together with her wistfulness came as a great shock to me. I had already before heard her little dry cough, especially at night. I got up at once and went out to see Schroeder without saying anything about it to her.

Schroeder came next day. She was very much surprised, her eyes wandering from Schroeder to me and back again.

"But I'm quite all right," she said with a sort of vague smile.

Schroeder did not examine her very carefully (those doctors are sometimes so maddeningly off-hand), but told me in the other room that she was suffering from the after-effects of her illness and that it would not be a bad idea to take her to the sea-side in the spring or, if that were impossible, to take a country cottage for the summer. He did not say anything, in fact, except that there was a weakness or something of the sort. When Schroeder had gone she suddenly said to me, looking very gravely at me:

"I'm quite all right. Indeed, I am!"

But as she said it she suddenly blushed, from shame, no doubt. Yes, it was quite obviously shame. Oh, now I understand it! She was ashamed, you see, that I was still *her husband*, that I was taking care of her as though I were her real husband still. But at the time I did not realise it, and I ascribed her smile to her humility. (Oh, those scales!)

And so, a month later, at five o'clock in the afternoon, on a bright, sunny day in April, I was sitting in the pawn-shop, making up my accounts. All of a sudden I heard how, sitting at the table in our room, at her work, she began softly, ever so softly—to sing. This new incident made an overwhelming impression on me. To this day I can't explain it. Till then I had hardly ever heard her sing, at all events not since the first days of our married life when we were still able to have some fun together, practising target shooting with my gun. At that time her voice was still strong and clear, though hardly true, but very pleasant and healthy. But now the song sounded so feeble. Oh, I don't mean it was a plaintive tune (it was some love song), but it sounded as though her voice were cracked, broken, as though her dear little voice could not manage it, as though the song itself were sick. She sang in an undertone, and suddenly her voice, rising on a high note, broke. Such a poor little voice, and it broke off so miserably. She cleared her throat and started singing something again in a very soft and hardly audible voice. . . .

You may laugh at my agitation, but no one will ever understand the reason for it. No. I wasn't sorry for her yet. Not yet. It was something quite different. To begin with, during the first few minutes at any rate I suddenly felt bewildered and terribly surprised. It was a horrible, strange sort of surprise, painful and almost vindictive. "She is singing, and—while I am in the house! *She hasn't forgotten about me, has she?*"

Thunderstruck, I sat there for some time without stirring from my place. Then I suddenly got up, took my hat, and went out, as though acting on impulse. At least I don't know why or where I was going. Lukerya was helping me on with my coat.

"She is singing?" I asked Lukerya, involuntarily.

Lukerya did not seem to know what I was talking about, and she went on staring at me incomprehensibly. But of course I was rather incomprehensible.

"Is it the first time you've heard her sing?"

"No, sir," said Lukerya, "she sometimes sings when you are out."

I remember everything. I went down the stairs, went out into the street and walked along at random. I walked to the corner, and started looking vaguely ahead of me. All sorts of people passed by me, knocked against me, but I was not aware of anything. I hailed a cab and told the driver to take me to the Police Bridge. I haven't the faintest idea why. Then suddenly I changed my mind and gave him a twenty-copeck piece.

"Sorry to have troubled you," I said, laughing stupidly at him, but my heart was suddenly filled with a strange ecstasy.

I went back home, quickening my pace as I walked along. The poor, cracked broken note was again ringing in my heart. My breath failed me. Yes, the scales were falling, falling from my eyes! If she had started singing while I was in the house, it could only mean that she had forgotten all about me. That's what was so terribly clear. I realised it in my heart, but my soul was aglow with ecstasy and it proved stronger than my fear.

Oh, the irony of fate! Had there been anything else in my soul the whole winter, could there have been anything else but this feeling of ecstasy? But where had I been myself all the winter? Had I been there with my soul? I ran up the stairs in a great hurry, and I don't remember whether I was apprehensive or not when I went in. All I remember is that the floor seemed to be swaying and that I felt as though I were floating on a river. I entered the room. She was sitting in her usual place, with her head bent over her sewing, but she was no longer singing. She threw a rapid and casual glance at me. It was hardly a glance really. Just the usual indifferent sign of recognition one gives when someone comes into the room.

I went up straight to her and sat down beside her. Close to her, like one demented. She looked at me quickly, as though she were afraid of me. I took her hand, and I don't remember what I said to her, or rather what I meant to say to her, for I couldn't even speak properly. My voice shook and did not obey me. Nor did I know what to say. All I did was to gasp for breath.

"Let's talk—you know—say something!" I suddenly stammered out something utterly idiotic.

Oh, how could I think of anything sensible to say at that moment? She started again and, as she looked at my face, she drew back from me in horror, but almost immediately a look of *stern surprise* came into her eyes. Yes, surprise and *stern*. She looked at me with wide-open eyes. That sternness, that stern surprise seemed all at once to deal me a stunning blow. "So it's love you still want? Love?" that look of surprise asked me, though she herself never uttered a word. But I read it all. I read it all. My world came crashing about my ears and I just collapsed at her feet. Yes, I fell down at her feet. She jumped up quickly, but I seized her hands and held her back with all the force at my command.

And I fully understood my despair. Oh, I understood it all right! But, you see, ecstasy was blazing so fiercely in my heart that I feared I should die. I kissed her feet rapturously, in a transport of happiness. Yes, in a transport of happiness. Boundless, infinite happiness. And I did it though I realised full well all the hopelessness of my despair. I wept, I tried to say something, but could not speak. Her surprise and terror suddenly gave way to a sort of worried thought, a thought of great urgency, and she looked at me strangely, wildly even. She wanted to understand something without a moment's delay, and—she smiled. She was ashamed that I was kissing her feet, horribly ashamed, and she kept drawing them away from me. But I immediately kissed the spot where her foot had rested. She saw it and began suddenly laughing from embarrassment (you know the feeling when one starts laughing from embarrassment). She became hysterical—I saw it coming—her hands were trembling. But I paid no attention to it. I went on murmuring that I loved her, that I wouldn't get up. "Let me kiss your dress. Let me worship you like this all my life!" I don't know, I don't remember, but suddenly she broke into sobs and trembled all over. She had a terrible fit of hysterics. I had frightened her.

I picked her up in my arms and carried her to the bed. When her attack was over, she sat up in bed and, looking terribly distressed, she seized me by the hands and begged me to calm myself. "Come, don't torment yourself! There, there. Be calm, please!" and once more she burst into tears.

All that evening I remained at her side. I kept telling her that I'd take her to Boulogne to bathe in the sea— now, at once, in a fortnight—that she had such a cracked little voice—I had heard it that afternoon—that I would give up my pawnshop—sell it to Dobronravov—that we should start life afresh. But, above all, Boulogne, Boulogne! She listened to me, but she was still afraid. It was not that, however, that worried me at the time. What worried me was that I felt more and more irresistibly drawn to fling myself at her feet again, to kiss again and again the ground on which her feet rested, and to pray to her, and "I shall ask nothing, nothing more of you," I kept repeating every minute. "Don't answer me. Don't take any notice of me at all. Only let me look at you from a corner. Make me your slave, your lapdog!" She wept.

"And I thought you'd let me alone," she said suddenly, the words escaping her involuntarily, so much so that quite possibly she herself was not aware of what she said. And yet. . . . Oh, that was the most important, the most fateful sentence she uttered that evening, and one that was only too easy for me to understand, and it stabbed my heart as though with a knife. It explained everything to me. Everything! But while she was beside me, while she was before my eyes, I was full of hope, and I was terribly happy. Oh, I exhausted her completely that evening, and I realised it, but I kept thinking that any moment I might succeed in changing it all. At length, towards night, she was utterly worn out, and I persuaded her to go to sleep. She fell asleep at once, and slept soundly. I expected her to be delirious, and she was a little. I kept getting up every minute in the night, and went softly in my slippers to have a look at her. I wrung my hands over her, as I looked at that sick creature in that poor little bed, the iron bedstead I had bought her for three roubles. I knelt down, but I did not dare to kiss her feet while she was asleep (and without her permission!). I knelt to pray, but jumped to my feet almost at once. Lukerya was keeping an eye on me, and kept coming in out of the kitchen. I went out to her and told her to go to bed. I told her that tomorrow everything would be "quite different."

And I believed it. Blindly, madly, frighteningly. Oh, my heart overflowed with rapture! I was only waiting for the next day. No, I did not believe in any trouble, in spite of the symptoms. I had not come to my senses yet, though the scales had fallen from my eyes. And for a long, long time I did not come to my senses. Oh, not till today, till this very day! And how could I have expected to come to my senses then? Wasn't she still alive then? Wasn't she still before me and I before her? "Tomorrow she'll wake

up, and I'll tell her all this, and she will see it all." That
was what I kept saying to myself then. It was so clear
and simple, and hence my ecstasy. The main thing was the
trip to Boulogne. For some reason I kept thinking that
Boulogne was everything. That there was something final
about Boulogne. "To Boulogne! To Boulogne!" I waited
frantically for the morning.

III. I UNDERSTAND IT TOO WELL

And all that was only a few days ago. Five days—only
five days ago. Last Tuesday! Oh, if there had been a little
more time! If only she had waited a little longer, I would
have dispersed this terrible cloud of darkness. And was
she not absolutely calm and composed? The very next
day she listened to me with a smile, though no doubt she
did look a little embarrassed. Yes, that above all. Her
embarrassment, I mean. All the time, all during those
five days, I could not help noticing that she was either
embarrassed or ashamed. And frightened, too. Very
frightened. I don't want to argue about it. I would be mad
to deny it. She *was* frightened, but after all that was natural enough. How could she help being frightened? For
hadn't we been strangers to one another for such a long
time? Hadn't we become so terribly estranged from
each other? And now suddenly, like a bolt from the blue,
all this. . . . But I paid no attention to her fear. A new
life shone like a bright star before me! It is true, it is absolutely true: I made a mistake. Perhaps many mistakes.
As soon as we woke next morning (it was on Wednesday)
I at once made a mistake. I at once began to treat her as
my friend. I was too much in a hurry. Much too much in
a hurry. But I simply had to confess everything to her.
Yes, my confession was absolutely necessary. Even
more than a confession! I did not conceal from her what
I had been concealing from myself all my life. I told her
frankly that all during the winter I had never for a moment doubted that she loved me. I explained to her that
my money-lending business was nothing but a symptom
of my loss of willpower. It was nothing but a mental aberration. A personal idea of self-castigation and self-exalta-
tion. I explained to her that I *was* a coward in the bar of
the theatre that evening. I couldn't help it. It has something to do with my character, my oversensitiveness. I

was thrown into a panic by the surroundings. It was the fact that it took place in a theatre bar that unnerved me. What had made me so nervous was—how could I walk up to the hussar officer? How could I do it without cutting a ridiculous figure? What I was afraid of was not the duel but that I might make a fool of myself. Later, of course, I would not admit it. And I tormented myself and everybody else. I had tormented her for it, too. In fact, I only married her so as to be able to torment her for it. In general, I spoke for the most part as though I were in a fever. She kept clasping my hands, begging me to stop. "You're exaggerating. . . . You're tormenting yourself!" And again she was weeping. Again she was on the point of becoming hysterical. She kept asking me all the time not to say anything about it. Not to think of it at all.

I disregarded her entreaties, or almost disregarded them. Spring! Boulogne! There was the sun there! There was our new sun there! I could speak of nothing else. I shut up the pawnshop. I transferred my business to Dobronravov. On the spur of the moment I even proposed to her to distribute all my money among the poor. All but the original three thousand roubles I had received from my godmother. That money would pay for our trip to Boulogne, and when we came back, we'd start a new life. A life of honest work. So it was decided, for she did not contradict me. She said nothing. She only smiled. And it seemed that she smiled more out of consideration for me, so as not to disappoint me. I realised, of course, that I was worrying her. Do not imagine I was such a fool or such an egoist as not to see it. I saw everything. Everything to the last detail. I saw and I knew everything more than anyone. All my despair was laid bare.

I told her everything about myself and about her. And about Lukerya. I told her that I had wept. . . . Oh, I, too, changed the subject. I did not want to remind her of certain things. And once or twice she looked quite cheerful. Yes, I remember that. I remember it distinctly! Why do you say I looked at her and saw nothing? If only *this* had not happened, everything would have been different. Why, didn't she tell me that amusing story about Gil Blas and the Archbishop of Granada herself the day before yesterday? We were discussing books. She was telling me about the books she had been reading that winter, and it was then that she told me about that scene from *Gil Blas*. And she laughed, too! Yes, she laughed, and, good Lord, what a sweet, childish laughter it was! Just as she used to laugh at the time of our engagement (A moment! Only a fleeting moment!). How glad I was! How happy! I was terribly struck by it, by the story of the Archbishop, I mean. She could then find so much happiness and peace of mind as to be able to enjoy a literary masterpiece. What else could it mean but that she was beginning to regain her self-composure completely, that she was already beginning to believe that I would *let her alone*. "I thought you'd *let me alone!*" that was what she had said on Tuesday, wasn't it? Oh, the thought of a ten-year-old girl! And she did believe that everything would really remain *as it was*. She believed that she'd always be sitting at her table and I at mine, and that the two of us would go on like that till we were old. All of a sudden I come up to her as her husband, and a husband wants love! Oh, how blind I was! Oh, what a frightful misunderstanding!

Another mistake I made was to have looked at her with such rapture. I should have controlled myself. For my transports only frightened her. But did I not control myself? Did I kiss her feet again? No. Never for a moment did I betray the fact that—well—that I was her husband. Oh, that thought never entered my head. All I did was to worship her. But it was quite obviously impossible for me to have been silent all the time. I had to say something. I suddenly told her that I enjoyed talking to her. I said that I thought her incomparably—yes, incomparably—better educated and mentally developed than I was. She blushed crimson and looked very embarrassed. She said I was exaggerating. Then—fool that I was!—I could not restrain myself and I told her with what delight I had listened to her battle of wits with that awful swine! How overjoyed I had been when I realised, as I stood behind the door, how much hatred there lay hidden in all her replies to that unspeakable cad. How pleased I had been with all her clever repartees, her brilliant sallies, combined with such child-like artlessness. She seemed to start, she murmured something about my exaggerating again, and all of a sudden her face darkened, she buried it in her hands, and broke into sobs. . . . Here I was unable to restrain myself any longer. I went down on my knees before her again, I began kissing her feet again, and again, as on Tuesday, it all ended in hysterics. . . . That was yesterday evening, and in the morning. . . .

In the morning? Why, you madman, it was this morning, only a few hours ago, only a few hours ago!

Listen and try to understand. When we met at the tea-table a few hours ago (after last night's fit of hysterics), she surprised me by her calmness. Yes, she was absolutely self-composed. And all night I had been trembling with fear because of what happened yesterday. And quite suddenly she herself came up to me and, folding her hands, began telling me (only a few hours ago, only a few hours ago!) that she was guilty, that she was fully aware of it, that her guilt had been torturing her all the winter, that it was torturing her even now, that she appreciated my generosity very much, that "I will be a true and faithful wife to you," that "I will always respect you. . . ." Then I leapt to my feet like a madman and embraced her. I kissed her. I kissed her face. I kissed her on her lips like a husband for the first time after a long separation. And why, why did I go out after that? Only for a couple of hours! Our passports for abroad! . . . Oh, God, why didn't I come back five minutes earlier? Only five minutes earlier. And that crowd at our gates. Those eyes staring at me! Oh, God!

Lukerya says (Oh, I shall never let Lukerya go now! She knows everything. She's been with us all the winter, and she'll be able to tell me everything!), Lukerya says that when I had gone out of the house, and only about twenty minutes before I came back, she suddenly went into our room where her mistress was at the time, intending to ask her something (I forget what), and she noticed that her icon (the same icon of the Holy Virgin) had been taken out of the case and was standing before her on the table, as though her mistress had only a moment ago been saying her prayers before it. "What's the matter, madam?" "Nothing, Lukerya, you can go." Then she said, "Wait a minute, Lukerya," and she went up to her and kissed her. "Are you happy, madam?" Lukerya asked. "Yes, thank you, Lukerya, I am happy." "Master ought to have asked your pardon a long time ago, madam. Thank God, you've made it up now." "All right, Lukerya," she said. "You can go now, Lukerya." And she smiled so—so strangely. So strangely that ten minutes later Lukerya went back to have a look at her.

"She was standing by the wall, sir," Lukerya told me, "close to the window. Leaning with her arm against the wall, she was, and her head pressed against her arm. Standing like that she was, sir, and thinking. And so deep in thought was she that she did not hear me open the door of the other room. She didn't see me standing there and watching her. Then I saw her smile, sir. She was standing by the wall near the window, thinking and smiling. I looked at her, turned round quietly and went back to my kitchen. Preoccupied with my own thoughts I was, sir. Only suddenly I heard the window open. I went back at once, meaning to tell her that it was very fresh outside and that she might catch her death of cold if she wasn't careful, and, Lord, sir, I saw she had climbed up on to the windowsill, standing there drawn up to her full height she was, in the open window, with her back to me, clasping the icon in her hands. I called out to her 'Madam! Madam!' and she must have heard me, sir, for she made a movement as if to turn round, but she didn't. Took a step forward, she did, then pressed the icon to her bosom and—threw herself out of the window!"

All I remember is that when I went into the yard, she was still warm. The horror of it was that all the time I felt those eyes staring at me. At first they shouted, then they suddenly fell silent, and all at once the crowd parted to let me through, and—there she lay with the icon. I dimly remember going up to her silently and looking at her a long time. All of them crowded round me and began saying something to me. Lukerya was there too, but I did not see her. I only remember the workman. He kept shouting at me, "A handful of blood poured out of her mouth! A handful of blood! A handful!" and pointing to the blood on a stone. I believe I touched the blood with my finger, smeared my finger, and looked at my finger (I remember that), while he kept shouting at me, "A handful! A handful!"

"What the hell is a handful?" I yelled at him with all my might (so I'm told) and, raising my hands, rushed at him.

Oh, the whole thing is mad! Mad! An awful misunderstanding! It's improbable! Impossible!

IV. I WAS ONLY FIVE MINUTES TOO LATE

And isn't it? Isn't it? Is it probable? Can one really say that it was possible? Why did this woman die? What made her do it?

Oh, believe me, I understand. I understand everything! But why she died is still a mystery. Was she afraid of my love? Did she really ask herself seriously whether to accept it or not? And was the question too much for her and did she prefer to die? I know. I know. It's no use my racking my brains. She had promised me too much. Given me too many promises. And she was afraid that she would not be able to keep them. That's clear. There are a number of other facts which are simply dreadful. For there is still the unanswered question—why did she die? That question keeps hammering at my brain. I would have *let her alone*, if she had wanted me to *let her alone*. But, she did not believe it. No, she didn't. And that was the real trouble. No, no! It's a lie! It wasn't that at all. It was simply that she had to be honest with me. She knew that to me "to love" meant "to love entirely," and not as she would have loved the shopkeeper. And, being too chaste and too pure, she did not want to deceive me with a love that would have satisfied the shopkeeper. Did not want to deceive me with a love that was only half a love, or a quarter of a love. Too honest. That's the trouble. I wanted to instil tolerance into her—remember? A curious idea.

Another terribly interesting question is whether she respected me or not. I don't know whether in her heart she despised me or not. I don't believe she did. It certainly is very strange. Why didn't it ever occur to me all the winter that she despised me? I was absolutely convinced she didn't until that moment when she looked at me with *stern surprise*. Yes, *stern*. It was then that I knew at once that she did despise me. I knew it irrevocably. For ever! Oh, let her, let her despise me all her life, so long as she was alive—so long as she was alive! Only a few hours ago she was still walking about. She was still talking. I can't for the life of me understand why she should have thrown herself out of the window. And how was I to have suspected it even five minutes before she did it? I've asked Lukerya to come in. I shall never part with Lukerya now.

No, I shall never part with her. Not for anything in the world!

Oh, I daresay we could have still found some way of patching things up. The trouble was we got so terribly estranged from one another during the winter. But couldn't we have grown used to one another again? Why, why couldn't we have come together again? I am generous, and so was she—that was one point we had in common! A few more words, two more days—no more—and she would have understood everything.

What is so awful is that the whole thing was just an accident—an ordinary, horrible, senseless accident! An accident that would never have happened if I hadn't been late. I was five minutes too late. Only five minutes! Had I come five minutes earlier, that impulse which drove her to commit suicide would have passed away like a cloud. And it would never again have occurred to her to do anything so horrible. And it would have all ended by her understanding everything. And now again empty rooms. Again I'm alone in the whole world. I can hear the pendulum ticking away. What does it care? There's nothing it can be sorry for. I've no one left in the world—that's the horror of it!

I keep walking, walking. Always walking. I know. I know. You need not prompt me. You think it's damned funny that I should be complaining about an accident. About being five minutes too late. An accident? But it's as plain as a pikestaff. Just think: why didn't she leave a note behind, just a few words to say, "Don't blame anyone for my death," as people always do? Is it likely that it should never have occurred to her that Lukerya might get into trouble with the police over her? "She was alone with her mistress," people might have said, "and she could have pushed her out of the window." She might at any rate have been dragged off to the police, blameless though she was, but for the fact that from the yard and from the windows of the next-door house four men had seen her stand with the icon in her hands and jump out of the window. But that too was an accident. I mean, that she should have been seen by some people who just happened to be about at the time. No, the whole thing was not premeditated. It was just an impulse. An unaccountable impulse. A sudden impulse. A momentary aberration. What does the fact that she had been praying in front of the icon prove? It certainly doesn't show that she had been saying her prayers before committing suicide. The whole impulse probably lasted only about ten minutes. Her decision to do away with herself must have been taken when she was standing by the wall, her head pressed against her arm, and smiled. An idea flashed through her mind, set it in a whirl, and—she could not resist it.

Whatever you may say, the whole thing is quite obviously a misunderstanding. I am not as bad as all that: she could have lived with me. And what if the whole thing was caused by anaemia? Simply by anaemia. By exhaustion. Utter exhaustion of all her vital energies. She got so terribly exhausted last winter. Yes. That's what it is.

I was too late! ! !

How thin she looks in her coffin! How sharp her little nose has grown! Her eyelashes lie as straight as arrows. And nothing was crushed in her fall. Not a bone was broken. Just that "handful of blood." A dessert-spoonful, I suppose. Internal haemorrhage. A strange thought: what if it were possible to keep her here and not to bury her! For if they take her away. . . . But no! I shan't let them! I'm damned if I'll let them! Oh Lord, I mustn't talk like that. Of course she'll have to be taken away. I know that. I am not mad. I'm not raving. As a matter of fact, I don't think I've ever been as clear-headed as I am now. But I can't—I just can't get used to the idea that once more there will be no one in the house, once more two rooms, and once more I shall be here by myself with the pledges. It's mad! Mad! That's where real madness lies. I had tortured her till she could stand it no longer. Yes, that's what it was.

What do I care for your laws now? What are your customs to me? Your morals, your life, your State, your faith? Let your judges judge me. Let me be brought before your courts, before your public courts, and I will declare that I do not recognise anything. The judge will order me to hold my peace. "Silence, officer!" he'll shout. And I'll shout back at him, "What power do you possess to exact obedience from me? Why did dark insensibility destroy what was dearer to me than anything else in the world? What do I care for your laws now? I shall live my own life!" Oh, nothing makes any difference to me now!

She is blind, blind! She is dead. She cannot hear me. Oh, you don't know what a paradise I should have built for you! Paradise was in my soul, and I would have planted it all round you! What does it matter if you did not love me? What does that matter? Everything would have been as it was. I should have *let you alone*. You would have talked to me only as a friend, and we should have laughed and been happy together. We should have gazed joyfully into each other's eyes. And so we should have lived. And even if you had fallen in love with another man, it wouldn't have mattered a bit. It wouldn't have made any difference to me. Fall in love if you wish! You'd have walked with him and laughed, and I'd have watched you from the other side of the street. . . . Oh, I don't care what would have happened, if only she would open her eyes just once! Just for one moment. For one moment only. She would have looked at me as she did a few hours ago when she stood before me and swore to be a faithful wife to me. Oh, I'm sure she would have understood everything at a glance!

Insensibility. Oh, nature! People are alone in the world. That's what is so dreadful. "Is there a living man on the plain?" cries the Russian legendary hero. I, too, echo the same cry, but no one answers. They say the sun brings life to the universe. The sun will rise and—look at it. Isn't it dead? Everything is dead. Dead men are everywhere. There are only people in the world, and all around them is silence—that's what the earth is! "Men love one another!"—who said that? Whose commandment is it? The pendulum is ticking away unfeelingly, dismally. Two o'clock in the morning. Her dear little boots stand by her little bed, as though waiting for her. . . . No, seriously, when they take her away tomorrow, what's to become of me?

The Dream of a
Ridiculous Man

A Fantastic Story

TRANSLATED BY DAVID MAGARSHACK

I AM A ridiculous man. They call me a madman now. That would be a distinct rise in my social position were it not that they still regard me as being as ridiculous as ever. But that does not make me angry any more. They are all dear to me now even while they laugh at me—yes, even then they are for some reason particularly dear to me. I shouldn't have minded laughing with them—not at myself, of course, but because I love them—had I not felt so sad as I looked at them. I feel sad because they do not know the truth, whereas I know it. Oh, how hard it is to be the only man to know the truth! But they won't understand that. No, they will not understand.

And yet in the past I used to be terribly distressed at appearing to be ridiculous. No, not appearing to be, but being. I've always cut a ridiculous figure. I suppose I must have known it from the day I was born. At any rate, I've known for certain that I was ridiculous ever since I was seven years old. Afterwards I went to school, then to the university, and—well—the more I learned, the more conscious did I become of the fact that I was ridiculous. So that for me my years of hard work at the university seem in the end to have existed for the sole purpose of demonstrating and proving to me, the more deeply engrossed I became in my studies, that I was an utterly absurd person. And as during my studies, so all my life. Every year the same consciousness that I was ridiculous in every way strengthened and intensified in my mind. They always laughed at me. But not one of them knew or suspected that if there were one man on earth who knew better than anyone else that he was ridiculous, that man was I. And this—I mean, the fact that they did not know it—was the bitterest pill for me to swallow. But there I was myself at fault. I was always so proud that I never wanted to confess it to anyone. No, I wouldn't do that for anything in the world. As the years passed, this pride increased in me so that I do believe that if ever I had by chance confessed it to any one I should have blown my brains out the same evening. Oh, how I suffered in the days of my youth from the thought that I might not myself resist the impulse to confess it to my schoolfellows. But ever since I became a man I grew for some unknown reason a little more composed in my mind, though I was more and more conscious of that awful characteristic of mine. Yes, most decidedly for some unknown reason, for to this day I have not been able to find out why that was so. Perhaps it was because I was becoming terribly disheartened owing to one circumstance which was beyond my power to control, namely, the conviction which was gaining upon me that nothing in the whole world *made any difference.* I had long felt it dawning upon me, but I was fully convinced of it only last year, and that, too, all of a sudden, as it were. I suddenly felt that it made *no* difference to me whether the world existed or whether nothing existed anywhere at all. I began to be acutely conscious that *nothing existed in my own lifetime.* At first I couldn't help feeling that at any rate in the past many things had existed; but later on I came to the conclusion that there had not been anything even in the past, but that for some reason it had merely seemed to have been. Little by little I became convinced that there would be nothing in the future, either. It was then that I suddenly ceased to be angry with people and almost stopped noticing them. This indeed disclosed itself in the smallest trifles. For instance, I would knock against people while walking in the street. And not because I was lost in thought—I had nothing to think about—I had stopped thinking about anything at that time: it made no difference to me. Not that I had found an answer to all the questions. Oh, I had not settled a single question, and there were thousands of them! But *it made no difference to me,* and all the questions disappeared.

And, well, it was only after that that I learnt the truth. I learnt the truth last November, on the third of November, to be precise, and every moment since then has been imprinted indelibly on my mind. It happened on a dismal evening, as dismal an evening as could be imagined. I was returning home at about eleven o'clock and I remember thinking all the time that there could not be a more dismal evening. Even the weather was foul. It had been pouring all day, and the rain too was the coldest and most dismal rain that ever was, a sort of menacing rain—I remember that—a rain with a distinct animosity towards people. But about eleven o'clock it had stopped suddenly, and a horrible dampness descended upon everything, and it became much damper and colder than when it had been raining. And a sort of steam was rising from everything, from every cobble in the street, and from every side-street if you peered closely into it from the street as far as the eye could reach. I could not help feeling that if the gaslight had been extinguished everywhere, everything would have seemed much more cheerful, and that the gaslight oppressed the heart so much just because it shed a light upon it all. I had had scarcely any dinner that day. I had been spending the whole evening with an engineer who had two more friends visiting him. I never opened my mouth, and I expect I must have got on their nerves. They were discussing some highly controversial subject, and suddenly got very excited over it. But it really did not make any difference to them. I could see that. I knew that their excitement was not genuine. So I suddenly blurted it out. "My dear fellows," I said, "you don't really care a damn about it, do you?" They were not in the least offended, but they all burst out laughing at me. That was because I had said it without meaning to rebuke them, but simply because it made no difference to me. Well, they realised that it made no difference to me, and they felt happy.

When I was thinking about the gaslight in the streets, I looked up at the sky. The sky was awfully dark, but I could clearly distinguish the torn wisps of cloud and between them fathomless dark patches. All of a sudden I became aware of a little star in one of those patches and I began looking at it intently. That was because the little star gave me an idea: I made up my mind to kill myself that night. I had made up my mind to kill myself already two months before and, poor as I am, I bought myself an excellent revolver and loaded it the same day. But two months had elapsed and it was still lying in the drawer. I was so utterly indifferent to everything that I was anxious to wait for the moment when I would not be so indifferent and then kill myself. Why—I don't know. And so every night during these two months I thought of shooting myself as I was going home. I was only waiting for the right moment. And now the little star gave me an idea, and I made up my mind then and there that it should *most certainly* be that night. But why the little star gave me the idea—I don't know.

And just as I was looking at the sky, this little girl suddenly grasped me by the elbow. The street was already deserted and there was scarcely a soul to be seen. In the distance a cabman was fast asleep on his box. The girl was about eight years old. She had a kerchief on her head, and she wore only an old, shabby little dress. She was soaked to the skin, but what stuck in my memory was her little torn wet boots. I still remember them. They caught my eye especially. She suddenly began tugging at my elbow and calling me. She was not crying, but saying something in a loud, jerky sort of voice, something that did not make sense, for she was trembling all over and her teeth were chattering from cold. She seemed to be terrified of something and she was crying desperately, "Mummy! Mummy!" I turned round to look at her, but did not utter a word and went on walking. But she ran after me and kept tugging at my clothes, and there was a sound in her voice which in very frightened children signifies despair. I know that sound. Though her words sounded as if they were choking her, I realised that her mother must be dying somewhere very near, or that something similar was happening to her, and that she had run out to call someone, to find someone who would help her mother. But I did not go with her; on the contrary, something made me drive her away. At first I told her to go and find a policeman. But she suddenly clasped her hands and, whimpering and gasping for breath, kept running at my side and would not leave me. It was then that I stamped my foot and shouted at her. She just cried, "Sir! Sir! . . ." and then she left me suddenly and rushed headlong across the road: another man appeared there and she evidently rushed from me to him.

I climbed to the fifth floor. I live apart from my landlord. We all have separate rooms as in an hotel. My room is very small and poor. My window is a semicircular skylight. I have a sofa covered with American cloth, a table with books on it, two chairs and a comfortable armchair, a very old armchair indeed, but low-seated and with a high back serving as a head-rest. I sat down in the armchair, lighted the candle, and began thinking. Next door in the other room behind the partition, the usual bedlam was going on. It had been going on since the day before yesterday. A retired army captain lived there, and he had visitors—six merry gentlemen who drank vodka and played faro with an old pack of cards. Last night they had a fight and I know that two of them were for a long time pulling each other about by the hair. The landlady wanted to complain, but she is dreadfully afraid of the captain. We had only one more lodger in our rooms, a thin little lady, the wife of an army officer, on a visit to Petersburg with her three little children who had all been taken ill since their arrival at our house. She and her children were simply terrified of the captain and they lay shivering and crossing themselves all night long, and the youngest child had a sort of nervous attack from fright. This captain (I know that for a fact) sometimes stops people on Nevsky Avenue and asks them for a few coppers, telling them he is very poor. He can't get a job in the Civil Service, but the strange thing is (and that's why I am telling you this) that the captain had never once during the month he had been living with us made me feel in the least irritated. From the very first, of course, I would not have anything to do with him, and he himself was bored with me the very first time we met. But however big a noise they raised behind their partition and however many of them there were in the captain's room, it makes no difference to me. I sit up all night and, I assure you, I don't hear them at all—so completely do I forget about them. You see, I stay awake all night till daybreak, and that has been going on for a whole year now. I sit up all night in the armchair at the table—doing nothing. I read books only in the daytime. At night I sit like that without even thinking about anything in particular: some thoughts wander in and out of my mind, and I let them come and go as they please. In the night the candle burns out completely.

I sat down at the table, took the gun out of the drawer, and put it down in front of me. I remember asking myself as I put it down, "Is it to be then?" and I replied with complete certainty, "It is!" That is to say, I was going to shoot myself. I knew I should shoot myself that night for certain. What I did not know was how much longer I should go on sitting at the table till I shot myself. And I should of course have shot myself, had it not been for the little girl.

II

You see, though nothing made any difference to me, I could feel pain, for instance, couldn't I? If anyone had struck me, I should have felt pain. The same was true so far as my moral perceptions were concerned. If anything happened to arouse my pity, I should have felt pity, just as I used to do at the time when things did make a difference to me. So I had felt pity that night: I should most decidedly have helped a child. Why then did I not help the little girl? Because of a thought that had occurred to me at the time: when she was pulling at me and calling me, a question suddenly arose in my mind and I could not settle it. It was an idle question, but it made me angry. What made me angry was the conclusion I drew from the reflection that if I had really decided to do away with myself that night, everything in the world should have been more indifferent to me than ever. Why then should I have suddenly felt that I was not indifferent and be sorry for the little girl? I remember that I was very sorry for her, so much so that I felt a strange pang which was quite incomprehensible in my position. I'm afraid I am unable better to convey that fleeting sensation of mine, but it persisted with me at home when I was sitting at the table, and I was very much irritated. I had not been so irritated for a long time past. One train of thought followed another. It was clear to me that so long as I was still a human being and not a meaningless cipher, and till I became a cipher, I was alive, and consequently able to suffer, be angry, and feel shame at my actions. Very well. But if, on the other hand, I were going to kill myself in, say, two hours, what did that little girl matter to me and what did I care for shame or anything else in the world? I was going to turn into a cipher, into an absolute cipher. And surely the realisation that I should soon cease to exist *altogether,* and hence everything would cease to exist, ought to have had some slight effect on my feeling of pity for the little girl or on my feeling of shame after so mean an action. Why after all did I stamp and shout so fiercely at the little girl? I did it because I thought that not only did I feel no pity, but that it wouldn't matter now if I were guilty of the most inhuman baseness, since in another two hours everything would become extinct. Do you believe me when I tell you that that was the only reason why I shouted like that? I am almost convinced of it now. It seemed clear to me that life and the world in some way or other depended on me now. It might almost be said that the world seemed to be created for me alone. If I were to shoot myself, the world would cease to exist—for me at any rate. To say nothing of the possibility that nothing would in fact exist for anyone after me and the whole world would dissolve as soon as my consciousness became extinct, would disappear in a twinkling like a phantom, like some integral part of my consciousness, and vanish without leaving a trace behind, for all this world and all these people exist perhaps only in my consciousness.

I remember that as I sat and meditated, I began to examine all these questions which thronged in my mind one after another from quite a different angle, and thought of something quite new. For instance, the strange notion occurred to me that if I had lived before on the moon or on Mars and had committed there the most shameful and dishonourable action that can be imagined, and had been so disgraced and dishonoured there as can be imagined and experienced only occasionally in a dream, a nightmare, and if, finding myself afterwards on earth, I had retained the memory of what I had done on the other planet, and moreover knew that I should never in any circumstances go back there—if that were to have happened, should I or should I not have felt, as I looked from the earth upon the moon, that *it made no difference* to me? Should I or should I not have felt ashamed of that action? The questions were idle and useless, for the gun was already lying before me and there was not a shadow of doubt in my mind that *it* was going to take place for certain, but they excited and maddened me. It seemed to me that I could not die now without having settled something first. The little girl, in fact, had saved me, for by these questions I put off my own execution.

Meanwhile things had grown more quiet in the captain's room: they had finished their card game and were getting ready to turn in for the night, and now were only grumbling and swearing at each other in a halfhearted sort of way. It was at that moment that I suddenly fell asleep in my armchair at the table, a thing that had never happened to me before.

I fell asleep without being aware of it at all. Dreams, as we all know, are very curious things: certain incidents in them are presented with quite uncanny vividness, each detail executed with the finishing touch of a jeweller, while others you leap across as though entirely unaware of, for instance, space and time. Dreams seem to be induced not by reason but by desire, not by the head but by the heart, and yet what clever tricks my reason has sometimes played on me in dreams! And furthermore what incomprehensible things happen to it in a dream. My brother, for instance, died five years ago. I sometimes dream about him: he takes a keen interest in my affairs, we are both very interested, and yet I know very well all through my dream that my brother is dead and buried. How is it that I am not surprised that, though dead, he is here beside me, doing his best to help me? Why does my reason accept all this without the slightest hesitation? But enough. Let me tell you about my dream. Yes, I dreamed that dream that night. My dream of the third of November. They are making fun of me now by saying that it was only a dream. But what does it matter whether it was a dream or not, so long as that dream revealed the Truth to me? For once you have recognised the truth and seen it, you know it is the one and only truth and that there can be no other, whether you are asleep or awake. But never mind. Let it be a dream, but remember that I had intended to cut short by suicide the life that means so much to us, and that my dream—my dream—oh, it revealed to me a new, grand, regenerated, strong life!

Listen.

III

I have said that I fell asleep imperceptibly and even while I seemed to be revolving the same thoughts again in my mind. Suddenly I dreamed that I picked up the gun and, sitting in my armchair, pointed it straight at my heart—at my heart, and not at my head. For I had firmly resolved to shoot myself through the head, through the right temple, to be precise. Having aimed the gun at my breast, I paused for a second or two, and suddenly my candle, the table and the wall began moving and swaying before me. I fired quickly.

In a dream you sometimes fall from a great height, or you are being murdered or beaten, but you never feel any pain unless you really manage somehow or other to hurt yourself in bed, when you feel pain and almost always wake up from it. So it was in my dream: I did not feel any pain, but it seemed as though with my shot everything within me was shaken and everything was suddenly extinguished, and a terrible darkness descended all around me. I seemed to have become blind and dumb. I was lying on something hard, stretched out full length on my back. I saw nothing and could not make the slightest movement. All round me people were walking and shouting. The captain was yelling in his deep bass voice, the landlady was screaming and—suddenly another hiatus, and I was being carried in a closed coffin. I could feel the coffin swaying and I was thinking about it, and for the first time the idea flashed through my mind that I was dead, dead as a doornail, that I knew it, that there was not the least doubt about it, that I could neither see nor move, and yet I could feel and reason. But I was soon reconciled to that and, as usually happens in dreams, I accepted the facts without questioning them.

And now I was buried in the earth. They all went away, and I was left alone, entirely alone. I did not move. Whenever before I imagined how I should be buried in a grave, there was only one sensation I actually associated with the grave, namely, that of damp and cold. And so it was now. I felt that I was very cold, especially in the tips of my toes, but I felt nothing else.

I lay in my grave and, strange to say, I did not expect anything, accepting the idea that a dead man had nothing to expect as an incontestable fact. But it was damp. I don't know how long a time passed, whether an hour, or several days, or many days. But suddenly a drop of water, which had seeped through the lid of the coffin, fell on my closed left eye. It was followed by another drop a minute later, then after another minute by another drop, and so on. One drop every minute. All at once deep indignation blazed up in my heart, and I suddenly felt a twinge of physical pain in it. "That's my wound," I thought. "It's the shot I fired. There's a bullet there. . . ." And drop after drop still kept falling every minute on my closed eyelid. And suddenly I called (not with my voice, for I was motionless, but with the whole of my being) upon Him who was responsible for all that was happening to me:

"Whoever Thou art, and if anything more rational exists than what is happening here, let it, I pray Thee, come to pass here too. But if Thou art revenging Thyself for my senseless act of self-destruction by the infamy and absurdity of life after death, then know that no torture that may be inflicted upon me can ever equal the contempt which I shall go on feeling in silence, though my martyrdom last for aeons upon aeons!"

I made this appeal and was silent. The dead silence went on for almost a minute, and one more drop fell on my closed eyelid, but I knew, I knew and believed infinitely and unshakably that everything would without a doubt change immediately. And then my grave was opened. I don't know, that is, whether it was opened or dug open, but I was seized by some dark and unknown being and we found ourselves in space. I suddenly regained my sight. It was a pitch-black night. Never, never had there been such darkness! We were flying through space at a terrific speed and we had already left the earth behind us. I did not question the being who was carrying me. I was proud and waited. I was telling myself that I was not afraid, and I was filled with admiration at the thought that I was not afraid. I cannot remember how long we were flying, nor can I give you an idea of the time; it all happened as it always does happen in dreams when you leap over space and time and the laws of nature and reason, and only pause at the points which are especially dear to your heart. All I remember is that I suddenly beheld a little star in the darkness.

"Is that Sirius?" I asked, feeling suddenly unable to restrain myself, for I had made up my mind not to ask any questions.

"No," answered the being who was carrying me, "that is the same star you saw between the clouds when you were coming home."

I knew that its face bore some resemblance to a human face. It is a strange fact but I did not like that being, and I even felt an intense aversion for it. I had expected complete non-existence and that was why I had shot myself through the heart. And yet there I was in the hands of a being, not human of course, but which *was*, which existed. "So there is life beyond the grave!" I thought with the curious irrelevance of a dream, but at heart I remained essentially unchanged. "If I must *be* again," I thought, "and live again at someone's unalterable behest, I won't be defeated and humiliated!"

"You know I'm afraid of you and that's why you despise me," I said suddenly to my companion, unable to refrain from the humiliating remark with its implied admission, and feeling my own humiliation in my heart like the sharp prick of a needle.

He did not answer me, but I suddenly felt that I was not despised, that no one was laughing at me, that no one was even pitying me, and that our journey had a purpose, an unknown and mysterious purpose that concerned only me. Fear was steadily growing in my heart. Something was communicated to me from my silent companion—mutely but agonisingly—and it seemed to permeate my whole being. We were speeding through dark and unknown regions of space. I had long since lost sight of the constellations familiar to me. I knew that there were stars in the heavenly spaces whose light took thousands of millions of years to reach the earth. Possibly we were already flying through those spaces. I expected something in the terrible anguish that wrung my heart. And suddenly a strangely familiar and incredibly nostalgic feeling shook me to the very core: I suddenly caught sight of our sun! I knew that it could not possibly be *our* sun that gave birth to our earth, and that we were millions of miles away from our sun, but for some unknown reason I recognised with every fibre of my being that it was precisely the same sun as ours, its exact copy and twin. A sweet, nostalgic feeling filled my heart with rapture: the old familiar power of the same light which had given me life stirred an echo in my heart and revived it, and I felt the same life stirring within me for the first time since I had been in the grave.

"But if it is the sun, if it's exactly the same sun as ours," I cried, "then where is the earth?"

And my companion pointed to a little star twinkling in the darkness with an emerald light. We were making straight for it.

"But are such repetitions possible in the universe? Can that be nature's law? And if that is an earth there, is it the same earth as ours? Just the same poor, unhappy, but dear, dear earth, and beloved for ever and ever? Arousing like our earth the same poignant love for herself even in the most ungrateful of her children?" I kept crying, deeply moved by an uncontrollable, rapturous love for the dear old earth I had left behind.

The face of the poor little girl I had treated so badly flashed through my mind.

"You shall see it all," answered my companion, and a strange sadness sounded in his voice.

But we were rapidly approaching the planet. It was growing before my eyes. I could already distinguish the ocean, the outlines of Europe, and suddenly a strange feeling of some great and sacred jealousy blazed up in my heart.

"How is such a repetition possible and why? I love, I can only love the earth I've left behind, stained with my blood when, ungrateful wretch that I am, I extinguished my life by shooting myself through the heart. But never, never have I ceased to love that earth, and even on the night I parted from it I loved it perhaps more poignantly than ever. Is there suffering on this new earth? On our earth we can truly love only with suffering and through suffering! We know not how to love otherwise. We know no other love. I want suffering in order to love. I want and thirst this very minute to kiss, with tears streaming down my cheeks, the one and only earth I have left behind. I don't want, I won't accept life on any other! . . ."

But my companion had already left me. Suddenly, and without as it were being aware of it myself, I stood on this other earth in the bright light of a sunny day, fair and beautiful as paradise. I believe I was standing on one of the islands which on our earth form the Greek archipelago, or somewhere on the coast of the mainland close to this archipelago. Oh, everything was just as it is with us, except that everything seemed to be bathed in the radiance of some public festival and of some great and holy triumph attained at last. The gentle emerald sea softly lapped the shore and kissed it with manifest, visible, almost conscious love. Tall, beautiful trees stood in all the glory of their green luxuriant foliage, and their innumerable leaves (I am sure of that) welcomed me with their soft, tender rustle, and seemed to utter sweet words of love. The lush grass blazed with bright and fragrant flowers. Birds were flying in flocks through the air and, without being afraid of me, alighted on my shoulders and

hands and joyfully beat against me with their sweet fluttering wings. And at last I saw and came to know the
people of this blessed earth. They came to me themselves.
They surrounded me. They kissed me. Children of the
sun, children of their sun—oh, how beautiful they were!
Never on our earth had I beheld such beauty in man.
Only perhaps in our children during the very first years
of their life could one have found a remote, though faint,
reflection of this beauty. The eyes of these happy people
shone with a bright lustre. Their faces were radiant with
understanding and a serenity of mind that had reached
its greatest fulfilment. Those faces were joyous; in the
words and voices of these people there was a child-like
gladness. Oh, at the first glance at their faces I at once
understood all, all! It was an earth unstained by the
Fall, inhabited by people who had not sinned and who
lived in the same paradise as that in which, according to
the legends of mankind, our first parents lived before they
sinned, with the only difference that all the earth here was
everywhere the same paradise. These people, laughing
happily, thronged round me and overwhelmed me with
their caresses; they took me home with them, and each
of them was anxious to set my mind at peace. Oh, they
asked me no questions, but seemed to know everything
already (that was the impression I got), and they longed
to remove every trace of suffering from my face as soon
as possible.

IV

Well, you see, again let me repeat: All right, let us assume it was only a dream! But the sensation of the love
of those innocent and beautiful people has remained with
me for ever, and I can feel that their love is even now
flowing out to me from over there. I have seen them myself. I have known them thoroughly and been convinced.
I loved them and I suffered for them afterwards. Oh, I
knew at once even all the time that there were many
things about them I should never be able to understand.
To me, a modern Russian progressive and a despicable
citizen of Petersburg, it seemed inexplicable that, knowing so much, they knew nothing of our science, for instance. But I soon realised that their knowledge was derived from, and fostered by emotions other than those

to which we were accustomed on earth, and that their aspirations, too, were quite different. They desired nothing. They were at peace with themselves. They did not strive to gain knowledge of life as we strive to understand it because their lives were full. But their knowledge was higher and deeper than the knowledge we derive from our science; for our science seeks to explain what life is and strives to understand it in order to teach others how to live, while they knew how to live without science. I understood that, but I couldn't understand their knowledge. They pointed out their trees to me, and I could not understand the intense love with which they looked on them; it was as though they were talking with beings like themselves. And, you know, I don't think I am exaggerating in saying that they talked with them! Yes, they had discovered their language, and I am sure the trees understood them. They looked upon all nature like that—the animals which lived peaceably with them and did not attack them, but loved them, conquered by their love for them. They pointed out the stars to me and talked to me about them in a way that I could not understand, but I am certain that in some curious way they communed with the stars in the heavens, not only in thought, but in some actual, living way. Oh, these people were not concerned whether I understood them or not; they loved me without it. But I too knew that they would never be able to understand me, and for that reason I hardly ever spoke to them about our earth. I merely kissed the earth on which they lived in their presence, and worshipped them without any words. And they saw that and let me worship them without being ashamed that I was worshipping them, for they themselves loved much. They did not suffer for me when, weeping, I sometimes kissed their feet, for in their hearts they were joyfully aware of the strong affection with which they would return my love. At times I asked myself in amazement how they had managed never to offend a person like me and not once arouse in a person like me a feeling of jealousy and envy. Many times I asked myself how I—a braggart and a liar—could refrain from telling them all I knew of science and philosophy, of which of course they had no idea? How it had never occurred to me to impress them with my store of learning, or impart my learning to them out of the love I bore them?

They were playful and high-spirited like children. They wandered about their beautiful woods and groves, they sang their beautiful songs, they lived on simple food—the fruits of their trees, the honey from their woods, and the milk of the animals that loved them. To obtain their food and clothes, they did not work very hard or long. They knew love and they begot children, but I never noticed in them those outbursts of *cruel* sensuality which overtake almost everybody on our earth, whether man or woman, and are the only source of almost every sin of our human race. They rejoiced in their new-born children as new sharers in their bliss. There were no quarrels or jealousy among them, and they did not even know what the words meant. Their children were the children of them all, for they were all one family. There was scarcely any illness among them, though there was death; but their old people died peacefully, as though falling asleep, surrounded by the people who took leave of them, blessing them and smiling at them, and themselves receiving with bright smiles the farewell wishes of their friends. I never saw grief or tears on those occasions. What I did see was love that seemed to reach the point of rapture, but it was a gentle, self-sufficient, and contemplative rapture. There was reason to believe that they communicated with the departed after death, and that their earthly union was not cut short by death. They found it almost impossible to understand me when I questioned them about life eternal, but apparently they were so convinced of it in their minds that for them it was no question at all. They had no places of worship, but they had a certain awareness of a constant, uninterrupted, and living union with the Universe at large. They had no specific religions, but instead they had a certain knowledge that when their earthly joy had reached the limits imposed upon it by nature, they—both the living and the dead—would reach a state of still closer communion with the Universe at large. They looked forward to that moment with joy, but without haste and without pining for it, as though already possessing it in the vague stirrings of their hearts, which they communicated to each other.

In the evening, before going to sleep, they were fond of gathering together and singing in melodious and harmonious choirs. In their songs they expressed all the sensations the parting day had given them. They praised it and bade it farewell. They praised nature, the earth, the sea, and the woods. They were also fond of composing songs about one another, and they praised each other like children. Their songs were very simple, but they sprang straight from the heart and they touched the heart. And not only in their songs alone, but they seemed to spend all their lives in perpetual praise of one another. It seemed to be a universal and all-embracing love for each other. Some of their songs were solemn and ecstatic, and I was scarcely able to understand them at all. While understanding the words, I could never entirely fathom their meaning. It remained somehow beyond the grasp of my reason, and yet it sank unconsciously deeper and deeper into my heart. I often told them that I had had a presentiment of it years ago and that all that joy and glory had been perceived by me while I was still on our earth as a nostalgic yearning, bordering at times on unendurably poignant sorrow; that I had had a presentiment of them all and of their glory in the dreams of my heart and in the reveries of my soul; that often on our earth I could not look at the setting sun without tears. . . . That there always was a sharp pang of anguish in my hatred of the men of our earth; why could I not hate them without loving them too? why could I not forgive them? And in my love for them, too, there was a sharp pang of anguish: why could I not love them without hating them? They listened to me, and I could tell that they did not know what I was talking about. But I was not sorry to have spoken to them of it, for I knew that they appreciated how much and how anxiously I yearned for those I had forsaken. Oh yes, when they looked at me with their dear eyes full of love, when I realised that in their presence my heart, too, became as innocent and truthful as theirs, I did not regret my inability to understand them, either. The sensation of the fullness of life left me breathless, and I worshipped them in silence.

Oh, everyone laughs in my face now and everyone assures me that I could not possibly have seen and felt anything so definite, but was merely conscious of a sensation that arose in my own feverish heart, and that I invented all those details myself when I woke up. And when I told them that they were probably right, good Lord, what mirth that admission of mine caused and how they laughed at me! Why, of course, I was overpowered by the

mere sensation of that dream and it alone survived in my
sorely wounded heart. But none the less the real shapes
and forms of my dream, that is, those I actually saw at the
very time of my dream, were filled with such harmony
and were so enchanting and beautiful, and so intensely
true, that on awakening I was indeed unable to clothe
them in our feeble words so that they were bound as it
were to become blurred in my mind; so is it any wonder
that perhaps unconsciously I was myself afterwards driven
to make up the details which I could not help distorting,
particularly in view of my passionate desire to convey
some of them at least as quickly as I could. But that does
not mean that I have no right to believe that it all did
happen. As a matter of fact, it was quite possibly a thousand times better, brighter, and more joyful than I describe it. What if it was only a dream? All that couldn't
possibly not have been. And do you know, I think I'll tell
you a secret: perhaps it was no dream at all! For what
happened afterwards was so awful, so horribly true, that
it couldn't possibly have been a mere coinage of my brain
seen in a dream. Granted that my heart was responsible
for my dream, but could my heart alone have been responsible for the awful truth of what happened to me
afterwards? Surely my paltry heart and my vacillating
and trivial mind could not have risen to such a revelation
of truth! Oh, judge for yourselves: I have been concealing it all the time, but now I will tell you the whole truth.
The fact is, I—corrupted them all!

V

Yes, yes, it ended in my corrupting them all! How it
could have happened I do not know, but I remember it
clearly. The dream encompassed thousands of years and
left in me only a vague sensation of the whole. I only
know that the cause of the Fall was I. Like a horrible
trichina, like the germ of the plague infecting whole king-
doms, so did I infect with myself all that happy earth that
knew no sin before me. They learnt to lie, and they grew
to appreciate the beauty of a lie. Oh, perhaps, it all began
innocently, with a jest, with a desire to show off, with
amorous play, and perhaps indeed only with a germ, but
this germ made its way into their hearts and they liked it.
The voluptuousness was soon born, voluptuousness begot

jealousy, and jealousy—cruelty. . . . Oh, I don't know, I can't remember, but soon, very soon the first blood was shed; they were shocked and horrified, and they began to separate and to shun one another. They formed alliances, but it was one against another. Recriminations began, reproaches. They came to know shame, and they made shame into a virtue. The conception of honour was born, and every alliance raised its own standard. They began torturing animals, and the animals ran away from them into the forests and became their enemies. A struggle began for separation, for isolation, for personality, for mine and thine. They began talking in different languages. They came to know sorrow, and they loved sorrow. They thirsted for suffering, and they said that Truth could only be attained through suffering. It was then that science made its appearance among them. When they became wicked, they began talking of brotherhood and humanity and understood the meaning of those ideas. When they became guilty of crimes, they invented justice, and drew up whole codes of law, and to ensure the carrying out of their laws they erected a guillotine. They only vaguely remembered what they had lost, and they would not believe that they ever were happy and innocent. They even laughed at the possibility of their former happiness and called it a dream. They could not even imagine it in any definite shape or form, but the strange and wonderful thing was that though they had lost faith in their former state of happiness and called it a fairy-tale, they longed so much to be happy and innocent once more that, like children, they succumbed to the desire of their hearts, glorified this desire, built temples, and began offering up prayers to their own idea, their own "desire," and at the same time firmly believed that it could not be realised and brought about, though they still worshipped it and adored it with tears. And yet if they could have in one way or another returned to the state of happy innocence they had lost, and if someone had shown it to them again and had asked them whether they desired to go back to it, they would certainly have refused. The answer they gave me was, "What if we are dishonest, cruel, and unjust? We *know* it and we are sorry for it, and we torment ourselves for it, and inflict pain upon ourselves, and punish ourselves more perhaps than the merciful Judge who will judge us and whose name we do not know. But we have science and with its aid we shall again discover truth, though we shall accept it only when we perceive it with our reason. Knowledge is higher than feeling, and the consciousness of life is higher than life. Science will give us wisdom. Wisdom will reveal to us the laws. And the knowledge of the laws of happiness is higher than happiness." That is what they said to me, and having uttered those words, each of them began to love himself better than anyone else, and indeed they could not do otherwise. Every one of them became so jealous of his own personality that he strove with might and main to belittle and humble it in others; and therein he saw the whole purpose of his life. Slavery made its appearance, even voluntary slavery: the weak eagerly submitted themselves to the will of the strong on condition that the strong helped them to oppress those who were weaker than themselves. Saints made their appearance, saints who came to these people with tears and told them of their pride, of their loss of proportion and harmony, of their loss of shame. They were laughed to scorn and stoned to death. Their sacred blood was spilt on the threshold of the temples. But then men arose who began to wonder how they could all be united again, so that everybody should, without ceasing to love himself best of all, not interfere with everybody else and so that all of them should live together in a society which would at least seem to be founded on mutual understanding. Whole wars were fought over this idea. All the combatants at one and the same time firmly believed that science, wisdom, and the instinct of self-preservation would in the end force mankind to unite into a harmonious and intelligent society, and therefore, to hasten matters, the "very wise" did their best to exterminate as rapidly as possible the "not so wise" who did not understand their idea, so as to prevent them from interfering with its triumph. But the instinct of self-preservation began to weaken rapidly. Proud and voluptuous men appeared who frankly demanded all or nothing. In order to obtain everything they did not hesitate to resort to violence, and if it failed —to suicide. Religions were founded to propagate the cult of non-existence and self-destruction for the sake of the everlasting peace in nothingness. At last these people grew weary of their senseless labours and suffering appeared on their faces, and these people proclaimed that suffering was beauty, for in suffering alone was there thought. They glorified suffering in their songs. I walked among them, wringing my hands and weeping over them, but I loved them perhaps more than before when there was no sign of suffering in their faces and when they were innocent and—oh, so beautiful! I loved the earth they had polluted even more than when it had been a paradise, and only because sorrow had made its appearance on it. Alas, I always loved sorrow and affliction, but only for myself, only for myself; for them I wept now, for I pitied them. I stretched out my hands to them, accusing, cursing, and despising myself. I told them that I alone was responsible for it all—I alone; that it was I who had brought them corruption, contamination, and lies! I implored them to crucify me, and I taught them how to make the cross. I could not kill myself; I had not the courage to do it; but I longed to receive martyrdom at their hands. I thirsted for martyrdom, I yearned for my blood to be shed to the last drop in torment and suffering. But they only laughed at me, and in the end they began looking upon me as a madman. They justified me. They said that they had got what they themselves wanted and that what was now could not have been otherwise. At last they told me that I was becoming dangerous to them and that they would lock me up in a lunatic asylum if I did not hold my peace. Then sorrow entered my soul with such force that my heart was wrung and I felt as though I were dying, and then—well, then I awoke.

It was morning, that is, the sun had not risen yet, but it was about six o'clock. When I came to, I found myself in the same armchair, my candle had burnt out, in the captain's room they were asleep, and silence, so rare in our house, reigned around. The first thing I did was to jump up in great amazement. Nothing like this had ever happened to me before, not even so far as the most trivial details were concerned. Never, for instance, had I fallen asleep like this in my armchair. Then, suddenly, as I was standing and coming to myself, I caught sight of my gun lying there ready and loaded. But I pushed it away from me at once! Oh, how I longed for life, life! I lifted up my hands and called upon eternal Truth—no, not called upon it, but wept. Rapture, infinite and boundless rapture intoxicated me. Yes, life and—preaching! I made up my mind to preach from that very moment and, of course, to go on preaching all my life. I am going to preach, I want to preach. What? Why, truth. For I have beheld truth, I have beheld it with mine own eyes, I have beheld it in all its glory!

And since then I have been preaching. Moreover, I love all who laugh at me more than all the rest. Why that is so, I don't know and I cannot explain, but let it be so. They say that even now I often get muddled and confused and that if I am getting muddled and confused now, what will be later on? It is perfectly true. I do get muddled and confused and it is quite possible that I shall be getting worse later. And, of course, I shall get muddled several times before I find out how to preach, that is, what words to use and what deeds to perform, for that is all very difficult! All this is even now as clear to me as daylight, but, pray, tell me who does not get muddled and confused? And yet all follow the same path, at least all strive to achieve the same thing, from the philosopher to the lowest criminal, only by different roads. It is an old truth, but this is what is new: I cannot even get very much muddled and confused. For I have beheld the Truth. I have beheld it and I know that people can be happy and beautiful without losing their ability to live on earth. I will not and I cannot believe that evil is the normal condition among men. And yet they all laugh at this faith of mine. But how can I help believing it? I have beheld it—the Truth—it is not as though I had invented it with my mind: I have beheld it, I have beheld it, and the *living image* of it has filled my soul for ever. I have beheld it in all its glory and I cannot believe that it cannot exist among men. So how can I grow muddled and confused? I shall of course lose my way and I'm afraid that now and again I may speak with words that are not my own, but not for long: the living image of what I beheld will always be with me and it will always correct me and lead me back on to the right path. Oh, I'm in fine fettle, and I am of good cheer. I will go on and on for a thousand years, if need be. Do you know, at first I did not mean to tell you that I corrupted them, but that was a mistake—there you have my first mistake! But Truth whispered to me that I was *lying*, and so preserved me and set me on the right path. But I'm afraid I do not know how to establish a heaven on earth, for I do not know how to put it into words. After my dream I lost the knack of putting things into words. At least, onto the most necessary and most important words. But never mind, I shall go on and I shall keep on talking, for I have indeed beheld it with my own eyes, though I cannot describe what I saw. It is this the scoffers do not understand. "He had a dream," they say, "a vision, a hallucination!" Oh dear, is this all they have to say? Do they really think that is very clever? And how proud they are! A dream! What is a dream? And what about our life? Is that not a dream too? I will say more: even—yes, even if this never comes to pass, even if there never is a heaven on earth (that, at any rate, I can see very well!), even then I shall go on preaching. And really how simple it all is: in one day, *in one hour,* everything could be arranged at once! The main thing is to love your neighbour as yourself—that is the main thing, and that is everything, for nothing else matters. Once you do that, you will discover at once how everything can be arranged. And yet it is an old truth, a truth that has been told over and over again, but in spite of that it finds no place among men! "The consciousness of life is higher than life, the knowledge of happiness is higher than happiness"—that is what we have to fight against! And I shall, I shall fight against it! If only we all wanted it, everything could be arranged immediately.

And—I did find that little girl. . . . And I shall go on! I shall go on!

Chronology

1821   Born October 30 to Mikhail Andreyevich, head physician at Mariinsky Hospital, Moscow, and Mariya Fyodorovna, daughter of a merchant family.

1838   Dostoevsky enters School of Military Engineering, St. Petersburg; he is described as a pensive, solitary student, prone to fits of depression.

1839   Dostoevsky's father killed by his peasants, profoundly affecting Fyodor.

1843   Passes his final examinations.

1844   Resigns his Commission in the army; starts writing seriously. Finishes *Poor Folk* in November.

1845   *Poor Folk* is much praised. Dostoyevsky enters literary society. Work on *The Double* and "Mr. Prokharchin."

1847   Writes for St. Petersburg *Gazette*. Between 1847 and 1848 writes "The Landlady," "White Nights," "A Faint Heart," "A Christmas Tree Party and a Wedding," "The Jealous Husband."

1849   Works on unfinished novel, *Netochka Nezvanova*. Joins a group of socialist thinkers, is arrested. Sentenced to death; a sentence which is altered to four years penal servitude, the announcement being made after Dostoevsky had been led out, with twenty others, to face a firing squad.

1850   Arrives at the prison at Omsk.

1854   Dostoevsky is released. Is forced to enroll as a private in the Seventh Line Battalion at Semi-palatinsk. Through friendship with Baron Vrangel meets his future wife.

1855   Promoted to non-commissioned officer.

1857   Marries the now widowed Mariya Dmitriyevna Isayeva.

1858   Writes *The Village of Stepanchikovo,* "Uncle's Dream."

1859   Returns to St. Petersburg after ten years' exile.

1860   *The House of the Dead, The Insulted and Injured.* Becomes Editor of *Time,* a literary journal.

1862   Goes abroad for the first time.

1863   "Winter Notes on Summer Impressions." Mariya Dmitriyevna seriously ill. Dostoevsky again travels abroad, and forms a liaison with Appollinariya Prokofyevna Suslova.

1864   His wife dies in April, and his elder brother, Mikhail Mikhailovich, dies in July. Dostoevsky works on *Notes from the Underground.*

1865   Lonely, in despair, still writing, Dostoevsky leaves Russia to escape his debts, and goes to Wiesbaden. Gambles and loses. Writes *Crime and Punishment.*

1866   Writes *The Gambler; Crime and Punishment* is published.

1867   Marries Anna Grigoryevna Snitkina, the stenographer to whom he dictated *The Gambler.* They settle in Dresden.

1868   A daughter, Sofiya, born, but dies five months later. Works on *The Idiot.* They move to Italy.

1869   A daughter, Lyubov, born in Dresden. The family in great poverty.

1870   Franco-Prussian War. Dostoevsky longs for Russia; works on *The Devils. The Eternal Husband.*

1871   Dostoevsky stops gambling. A son, Fyodor, born in July in St. Petersburg.

1873   Becomes editor of *The Citizen*, but resigns in 1874.

1874   *A Raw Youth*. At Ems for a cure for emphysema, winters in Staraya Russa.

1875   A son, Aleksey, born. At Ems again for a cure.

1876–77   *The Diary of a Writer*, published in installments in *The Citizen*. "A Gentle Creature, "The Dream of a Ridiculous Man."

1878   Works on *The Brothers Karamazov*. His second son dies.

1880   *The Brothers Karamazov* finished. Dostoevsky returns to Moscow to speak at an unveiling of a monument to Pushkin, and is wildly acclaimed. Returns to Staraya Russa. Works on January installment of *The Diary of a Writer*.

1881   January 28: Dostoevsky dies.